A MAN'S DUTY...
A WOMAN'S PASSION...

THE EDGE OF HONOR
CUTS BOTH WAYS.

"Anyone who loves compelling stories, appealing characters and fast-paced action will find *The Edge of Honor* keeping him on the edge of his seat."

—*Stars and Stripes*

"The rare book that addresses the complexities of war at the front and also at home. Brian and Maddy are rich, flawed characters, and the supporting cast is equally believable. The author captures the Vietnam period and its confusion perfectly. Particularly interesting is the culture depicted on board the *Hood*."

—*Baltimore Sun*

"Absorbing . . . Suspenseful . . . Crammed with authentic details of sea and shore life . . . Deutermann makes the missile technology completely interesting. The settings and characters are believable, and his readers will appreciate the candor and honesty with which he tells his powerful story."

—*New Smyrna Beach,* FL *Observer*

"A powerful human wartime thriller with a steady flow of action, both military and human. One of the best plots to come our way in years, with strong military flavor and a very dramatic old-fashioned romance."

—*Macon Beacon,* MS

**St. Martin's Paperbacks Titles
by P. T. Deutermann**

SCORPION IN THE SEA
THE EDGE OF HONOR

THE EDGE OF HONOR

P.T. DEUTERMANN

ST. MARTIN'S PAPERBACKS

This is a work of fiction. Characters, military organizations, ships, and places in this novel are either the product of the author's imagination, or, if real, or based on real entities, are used fictitiously without any intent to describe their actual conduct or character. Insofar as this book addresses military issues, policies, and history, the work represents the views of the author alone and does not necessarily represent the policies and views of the United States Department of Defense.

THE EDGE OF HONOR

Copyright © 1994 by P. T. Deutermann.

Official Privilege excerpt copyright © 1995 by P. T. Deutermann.

Library of Congress Catalog Card Number: 94-2670

ISBN: 0-312-95396-8

Printed in the United States of America

St. Martin's Press hardcover edition published 1994
St. Martin's Paperbacks edition/May 1995

10 9 8 7 6 5 4 3 2 1

This book is dedicated to the thousands of
men and women of the United States Navy
who served honorably during the Vietnam War.

Acknowledgments

I wish to thank George Witte, Carol Edwards, and Sally Richardson at St. Martin's Press for their extensive help with this book, and also my wife, Susan, for her sustaining confidence in this story.

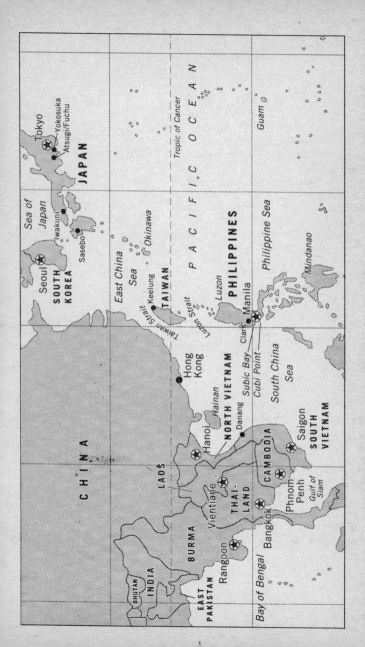

1

San Diego, California, September 1969

Brian Holcomb stood naked at the darkened bedroom window, staring out at the park across the street. The pale bark of the gray eucalyptus trees was daubed in orange from the glow of the new sodium-vapor lights along Balboa Park Drive. At least something around here had a glow on; he sure as hell did not. Maddy, his wife, spoke to him from the bed.

"Brian, it's all right. Brian, come back to bed."

"It's not all right. Nothing's all right. It's deployment day, and I'm going away for seven months, and you're miserable, and I can't even—"

"Brian, please. It's our last time to be together. Please, let's not fight. I'm sorry I'm being such a bitch about the deployment. But come back to bed."

Brian sighed and turned around. The sight of Maddy in the soft light of the bedroom, that mass of blond hair, her lovely face, her glorious breasts bared above the sheet, was still enough to take his breath away, even after almost four years of marriage. So then why the hell on this, their last night, morning, whatever, together, couldn't he perform?

As if reading his thought, Maddy patted the bed next to her.

"Come on, Brian. I hate it when you're right there but not right here beside me. We should have just cuddled, like we agreed. We both know this is a lousy time for sex. Please?"

He walked back over to his side of the bed. She was right—as usual. He sat down on the edge of the bed and she slid across, folding her arms around him, her hair enveloping the side of his face. Her skin was warm against his back.

1

"Hey?" she whispered. "We'll get through this; everyone else seems to manage. This isn't the first ship that has to go to WESTPAC. I've got my job, and the rest of the wives—"

"Whom you don't like very much."

"I do like them. It's more a question of not having very much in common with them, Brian. I work, most of them don't, and we have no—"

"Yeah."

He felt her stiffen slightly, and the blade of anger from the night before slipped between them again. They had gone out to dinner at Mr. A's, an expensive restaurant overlooking the San Diego skyline, whose tall windows gave a cockpit-level view of the jetliners as they swooped down into Lindbergh Field below. Brian had thought of going out to dinner as an activity, something to do that would eat up three or four hours of the "last night." As Maddy had fretted more and more about the ship's departure, everything they did had acquired the adjective *last*: the last supper, the last night, the last morning—the last everything, because it was now deployment day.

He had made the mistake of mentioning children again, and the last evening had gone right off the last tracks. And now, in just a few short hours, he would get up, shower, button and zip into his whites, and as Lt. Brian Holcomb, USN, Weapons officer in USS *John Bell Hood,* go down to the ship at the Thirty-second Street Naval Station and sail away to the Vietnam War for the next seven months.

And Maddy, his beautiful young wife of three-point-something years, was not taking it too well. The ship's schedule had not helped. The thirty days prior to deployment were called POM: Preparation for Overseas Movement. Perversely, as far as families were concerned, the closer a ship got to deployment day, the more time it demanded of its officers. The POM preparations were seemingly endless as the avalanche of supplies, repair parts, new people, the latest tactical manuals, and a flurry of final grooming and repairs on the ship's weapons and operations systems all conspired to produce twelve-hour workdays at precisely the time that the wives tended

2

to become clinging vines, desperately anxious for every moment of contact. Brian's nights at home during the last thirty days had been punctuated by dramatic mood swings on Maddy's part, from loving wife who poured on the affection to shrill harridan who railed against the deployment, the Vietnam War, and his Navy career in general.

The hell of it was that he was excited to be going. He was beginning a prime assignment aboard a modern guided-missile ship, and they were bound for the Red Crown station up in the Gulf of Tonkin, to the heart of the carrier-air-war action on the one ship that controlled the skies over the Gulf. Damn it, he shouldn't have to feel guilty about that. And more than that, this assignment was a make-or-break tour of duty: His promotion to lieutenant commander depended on his doing very well in this ship. Maddy was not helping. As a matter of fact, Maddy was on the verge of doing some damage. On the other hand, he fully recognized that she was acting this way only because he was going away.

He turned to her then, putting his arms around her, breathing in her sweet, familiar fragrance, his face pressed against her throat as she hugged him. He knew that all the noise was not aimed at him, but at what was coming for her—the empty apartment, the empty bed, long-delayed letters in place of a touch in the night. He would be in the thick of fleet operations in the Gulf of Tonkin and she would face the same empty routine day after day. His heart ached, not for the first time, at the thought of being away from her for seven long months. At moments like this, even he was willing to think of the Navy as the goddamned Navy, lately her favorite expression. And then there was that enormously sensitive nerve about children upon which he had just touched. He wanted kids; she did, too, but she had set what he felt was an impossible condition: "We'll have a family only when you're going to be home to help." A successful career in the seagoing Navy did not necessarily lend itself to that proposition. They had both finally realized that the whole subject of starting a family was becoming a dangerous minefield, a complication that neither of them needed, especially just now. He sighed again.

"What time is it?" he asked, his voice muffled in her hair.

"It's not time yet," she whispered, hugging him tighter, pulling his face down to her breasts. He felt the familiar stirring of desire and wondered whether it was worth another try. She leaned down, violet eyes huge in the semidarkness, and kissed him deeply. He decided that it was.

Maddy lay back in the rumpled bed, the sheets pulled up to her chin, her hands clenched, and listened to the sounds of Brian in the shower. Her breathing had returned to normal, although she was definitely not going to play any tennis today. After the debacle of dinner at Mr. A's, a fitful night talking about everything but the deployment, and finally an aborted attempt at lovemaking, Brian's second wind had come on like a gale, with a violence and passion that had caught her by surprise and then swept her up despite the gloom and doom of deployment day. Afterward, she wondered fleetingly how much of that passion had been anger and how much love. She knew she had been making life difficult, and even if their almost frantic lovemaking had managed to dissolve her depression for even a little while, she sensed his underlying frustration. She had to keep telling herself, he's not doing this on purpose; he's not leaving me. It's just the ship.

Deployment day—sounds like Judgment Day. Seven months. If everything went well, seven months; otherwise, longer. She clenched her fists and squeezed her thighs together until it hurt. They had been through half a deployment to the Mediterranean when he was in *Decatur,* and then two glorious years ashore at the Monterey Naval Postgraduate School. Then came the revelation that his fitness reports from *Decatur* had been not quite up to par and that he would have to retour as a department head, this time in a bigger ship. He must have told her a hundred times, the detailers were doing him a favor, sending him to a deploying ship to enhance his chances for promotion. She knew all the whys and wherefores by heart, and it still didn't help. Seven months, two hundred and ten days, more or less. More, probably. And if Brian's career advanced and the war continued, there would be even longer, more dangerous missions. Ostensibly, she could fill up her days with her job at the bank, but seeing the civilians there was already making the imminent separation more painful—their comparatively stable lives offered a stark contrast to her peculiar status as a Navy wife whose husband was deployed. One of her cohorts in the bank had made an ironic comment about the benefits of getting an occasional minidivorce, courtesy of the USN, but Maddy failed to see the humor.

And she knew the secret reason, even if Brian did not appreciate it. She harbored a deep fear of being alone. She had never and would never tell Brian, but that was one of the reasons she had said yes when this engaging young naval officer had come barging into her life as she was finishing college and asked her to marry him. With her graduation approaching, she had looked into the future and seen that she would soon have to resume a life alone, without roommates, her school crowd, and the artificially hectic schedule of senior year. She had almost jumped into his arms when Brian had finally popped the question. He was good-looking, fun, intelligent, and established in his Navy career, and she hadn't hesitated. Oh, he had told her about the deployments, the prospects for separation, but in the first blush of love, romance, and the exciting discovery of how good they were for each other in bed, the very word *deployment* had had no meaning. And even the three months when Brian had gone to the Med had been broken up when she flew over to meet the ship in Naples for a five-day holiday.

But seven months—seven months was the better part of a year, and the Gulf of Tonkin was not the Med. Vietnam was an ugly, bloody, and increasingly futile war, and the nightly television news was much too full of body bags and casualty statistics to leave room for any starry-eyed notions of glory. She nearly wept at the possibility of losing Brian, at the thought of losing her love and the specter of being left really alone. She squeezed that thought right out of her mind, but the fear remained.

Brian came out of the bathroom, a white towel wrapped around his waist, his hair standing up in all directions as if he had touched a live wire. He paused in the doorway, his body silhouetted against the bathroom light. She could barely see his face. But he was looking at her, and after a long moment, he came over to the bed, sitting carefully on the edge to keep from getting the sheets wet. She tried to sit up, but her body betrayed her. He smiled at her disability.

"Well, Mrs. Holcomb, the day we've all been waiting for has finally arrived," he said with a smile. A sad smile, she thought. "Are you going to change your mind and see us off?"

"I . . . I really don't want to do that, Brian," she replied. "I don't think I could stand to see that big gray thing go down the harbor right now. We've been through—"

"Right. Well, it's six-thirty. If I go now, I can beat the traffic. I'll call Jack Folsom, hitch a ride in with him. He can swing by here easily enough."

"Brian, I'm sorry. I know—"

"Hey, don't sweat it. I understand. You should have done what Angela Benedetti does on deployment day: She leaves town for a week with the kids and comes back after the ship is long gone."

"Yes, I should have. Except I have this little job they expect me to show up for."

"And no kids."

She felt herself shrinking into the covers, even as his expression changed when he realized what he had said.

"Maddy, I'm sorry. I didn't mean that the way it sounded."

"So what did you mean, Brian?" she asked in a small voice.

"I only meant that, well, if you had kids, you wouldn't be alone when the ship left. The family would still be here. I know it's not the same, but—"

"Brian."

"What?"

"All we're doing is picking at each other. I hate the fact that you're leaving, and I understand that you're not

6

doing this to hurt me or to leave me alone. I'm angry with *it*, not you. I think the best thing now is to get it done: We should both get dressed and go. The sooner you leave, the sooner you'll be back, okay? I don't know how else to put it, and anything we say now is going to hurt. Please."

He nodded and got up to find his uniform. Maddy rolled over in the bed, only the top of her head showing above the covers. He dressed rapidly, made a phone call to confirm that he had a ride, and then gathered up his wallet and his rings. But no keys—today his keys stayed home. He came back into the bedroom and walked briskly over to the bed. He bent down and kissed the top of her head.

"I love you, Maddy."

"I love you, too, Brian," she said in a muffled voice.

And then he was gone, the front door shutting quietly. Only then did she begin to cry in earnest.

2

USS *JOHN BELL HOOD*
The approaches to Subic Bay, Luzon, the Philippines

Three weeks later, the mountains of central Luzon cut a sawtooth pattern of purple darkness against the eastern horizon as the guided-missile frigate *John Bell Hood* nosed her way into Subic Bay from the South China Sea. The waters of the bay were perfectly flat, a broad turquoise mirror across which the ship cut an expanding, silent wedge of wake lines. A scent of tropical greenery hung over the flat calm of the bay, interlaced with the pungent stink of burning charcoal from several huts perched on pilings along the beach. Fluttering candle pots twinkled on the water, marking the end of drift nets along the edges of the channel. Mahogany-skinned Filipino fishermen squatted impassively in their *banca* boats, their faces in shadow under large straw hats, watching the eight-thousand-ton warship slide silently by.

Brian Holcomb stood in the very eyes of the ship, alongside the ship's outsized chief boatswain, BMC Louis Jesus María Martinez. Brian, whose Weapons Department was responsible for all topside spaces, had decided earlier to take a turn about the weather decks when sea detail had been called, to see that his department was ready to enter port. The chief, alerted immediately by his omnipresent crew of deckhands, had intercepted his department head halfway down the port side, looming out of the shadows of the boat decks with a mug of black coffee in each hand and a rumbling "Morning, boss." Brian was still getting used to the sheer size of the boatswain, whose massive bulk and obsidian-eyed Apache features set him apart from the other chief petty officers. It was commonly thought that his two middle names reflected his mother's first words on seeing her baby, more than any expression of religious piety.

Of the four divisions in his Weapons Department, Brian held a natural affinity for First, or Deck, Division, having been a Deck Division officer in his first ship almost seven years ago. He had taken an instant liking to Chief Martinez and often found himself seeking out the chief boatswain when he would take a break from his departmental paperwork. At sea or in port, Chief Martinez could usually be found topside, prowling the decks where First Division was responsible for the preservation and maintenance of all deck gear, topside decks and bulkheads, boats, and all of the underway replenishment equipment. Salt air and salt water mounted a continuous chemical attack on all things metal, and Brian knew firsthand that First Division was hard pressed to keep the ship from rusting away beneath their feet. And because First Division was where a man landed if he could not cut it in one of the other divisions aboard ship, the chief boatswain was equally hard-pressed to keep his ragged band of deck apes, as the men in First Division were called, on the job.

Now Brian accepted a mug of coffee and the two began a walking tour, heading aft down the port side, passing the twin three-inch gun mount, the helicopter flight deck, and then dropping down a steep ladder to the fantail to check on the layout of the mooring lines, which were faked out in elliptical figure eights near the base of the five-inch gun mount. They turned and headed forward, going up the starboard side, climbing back up to the flight deck, walking underneath the starboard side three-incher, past the boat decks, through the forward weather breaks, and out onto the sheer expanse of the forecastle deck, where the steel ramp of the missile house rose out of the deck to point at the twin-armed guided-missile launcher. Then they moved forward through the small crowd of line handlers, stepping carefully across the clean sweep of slick gray steel to the anchor windlass and the capstan, from which bulky ribbons of black anchor chain stretched to the hawse pipes, to stand in the forwardmost point of the steeply overhanging bow. The sound of the cutwater below rose in a clean hiss on the morning air.

Everywhere along the way, Brian noted that the chief had something to say to the small knots of Deck Division personnel as they laid out mooring lines, clamped down the salt-covered decks with swabs and steaming buckets of fresh hot water, polished the brass turnbuckles on the lifelines, and coiled up heaving lines in preparation for going alongside the pier. To Brian, the chief's instructions sounded like a continuous rumble of grunts and growls interspersed with nicknames like "Sloopy," "Injun," and "Cooter." Several men were apparently related, all being called "dickhead." While impressed with all the activity, he was also aware that it seemed to peak as the mammoth chief approached and then to subside in his generous wake, with the subsidence accompanied by sly smirks and an aura of insolence among the deck ratings. He mentioned this to the chief as they approached the breaks.

"Ain't like it usta be, boss," said the chief, shaking his head. "Guys'n Deck Division, they usta take some pride in gettin' up before everybody else, gettin' the decks clamped down and the brightwork shinin'. They usta go down to the mess decks and dump on 'em puffy-eyed twidgets standin' in the mess line. Usta was, nobody got up earlier'n a bosun mate 'cept the night baker, and that pogue been up all night, anyways. These little shits, they's all sneakin' around doin' small-shit crime, fuckin' off when they supposed to be workin', doin' dope onna weather decks at night, sleepin' on watch on after lookout, breakin' inta guys lockers'n stealin' each others' wallets'n stuff. We got a coupla good guys in this gang, but now it's mostly a lotta assholes Navy used to jist shitcan. Ask me, it's all that long-hair shit goin' on on the outside, that fuckin' noise they call music, all that hippie faggot protest shit, guys burnin' their draft cards'n stuff. Ever since that Tet thing last year in Nam, country's gone to shit.''

Brian nodded. "I've noticed that some of the enlisted in this ship are—I don't know—kind of hostile," he said. "Even the younger petty officers seem to be sporting a bad attitude, especially toward officers. I'm talking about E-Fives, and even some E-Sixes. You guys in the chiefs' locker seeing the same thing?"

The chief stopped as they approached the forecastle breaks, a tunnel-like space leading from the main deck to the foredeck of the ship.

"Yes'n no, Mr. Holcomb. Any white hat knows he gives a *chief* some lip, it's gonna grow on him—you know what I'm sayin'? They gonna have a little accident, trip over a knee-knocker, maybe bump into a stanchion. But this here crew, I dunno. I hear some stories—main-hole snipes doin' dope on watch, somma the first class doin' a little loan-sharkin' and card-sharkin', some kinda drug gang that's movin' all the shit on board—I dunno if it's just the *J. B. Hood* or it's the whole damn Navy."

Brian slammed the heavy steel door behind them as they stepped out onto the forecastle.

"I'm just not used to seeing this stuff in the destroyer force," he said.

"Yeah, well, the *Hood,* she's bigger'n a tin can but smaller'n a cruiser. We got, what, almost five hunnert—some guys here. If ten percent're serious assholes, that's fifty serious assholes, see?"

As they walked forward up the forecastle, the ship swung around the northwest side of Grande Island. Brian smiled mentally but kept his face impassive. The chief's words reminded him of the game the Navy played with Congress on the *Hood* class of ship. *Hood* was officially classified as a guided-missile frigate, or DLG. After the Korean War, Congress, in one of its periodic antimilitary moods, declared that it would not authorize any more large ships such as cruisers or battleships, on the grounds that the Navy wanted only big ships to carry around admirals and their staffs. The Navy had obligingly requested no more cruisers, choosing instead to produce an entire class of eight-thousand-ton guided-missile "frigates," a classification normally given to a much smaller ship.

As *Hood* steadied up in the turn, they could see a small forest of black lattice masts of other Seventh Fleet warships etched against the metallic bulk of the *godowns* behind the piers. A blue-white blaze of sodium-vapor lights lining the piers became visible through the trees of Grande Island, where shattered Japanese coastal guns lay rusting on the humid margins of the jungle. Ahead on the port bow, two Navy harbor tugs lingered off to one side of the ship's track, emitting intermittent puffs of diesel exhaust punctuated by a swirl of green water under their broad sterns and the whoosh of the air clutch as they maintained position out of the way of the approaching ship. On one tug, the figure of the harbor pilot was visible, standing casually out on a pilothouse fender, waiting to come alongside and board.

"Well, there she is, Weps boss, number one *ichiban* liberty port in the whole fuckin' world," said the chief.

"If half the stories are true, it must be something indeed," replied Brian.

"Somethin' don't half cut it," replied the chief. "Yer a LANTFLEET sailor. No offense, sir, but there ain't nothing' on the LANTFLEET side like Subic. Wasn't fer ports like Subic and Olongapoo and Kaohsiung, us PACFLEET guys wouldn't even come to this here war in Nam. Here in Olongapoo, you kin do anythin', buy anythin', and sell anythin' you want, and I mean *anythin'*. There, you smell it, boss?"

Brian nodded silently as the amalgamated odors of jungle rot, fuel oil, diesel exhaust, old hemp, creosoted pilings, cheap perfume, and raw sewage rolled out, over-powering the pristine dawn air.

"Yea-a-ah-h!" The chief sniffed, and finished off his coffee. "Shame we ain't gonna stay in for liberty this time."

"BSF, Chief. Brief stop for fuel and the Task Force Seventy-seven briefings. Then back under way at eighteen hundred and up to the Gulf to relieve *Long Beach*. But I understand we come back here after the first line period."

"Sure as hell hope so," said the chief fervently. Then he turned around and roared to the forecastle crew at large, "Hey, dickhead, we're outa goddamn coffee up here!"

Two sailors in ratty-looking dungarees sprang forward from the capstan to retrieve their empty mugs.

"Seem to know their names," observed Brian as one of the men trotted aft to find coffee.

"Yeah, well, they all been dickheads one time or another or they wouldn't be deck apes, so they jump. Safer that way."

"Roger that," said Brian. He had almost jumped himself.

The chief lumbered aft to supervise bringing the tug alongside, and Brian walked back out of the way to the base of the missile launcher to observe the workings of the forecastle crew. He glanced up at the windows of the bridge two levels above the forecastle, but the green-tinted outward sloping windows spreading across the front of the superstructure revealed nothing but reflections of the pier lights ahead.

At twenty-eight, Brian Holcomb was a tall, spare man with an unruly shock of corn-straw hair and blue eyes in an unlined boyish face. His youthful features had long been a secret source of insecurity in a Navy culture where craggy, weather-beaten features seemed to command more respect than blue eyes and a ready smile. Deceived by his boyish looks, officers who were his contemporaries in age and experience would often dismiss him, only to be surprised later to find out that he had almost seven years commissioned service in the

Navy and was in the promotion zone for lieutenant commander.

As he watched First Division get ready to come alongside, he reflected on the past few months that had brought him to his first WESTPAC deployment and a critical juncture in his career, a department head tour in a frontline guided-missile ship headed for Vietnam operations. He had reported aboard in San Diego six weeks ago, as *John Bell Hood* was completing final preparations for return to the western Pacific after a brief seven months back in home port. As a senior lieutenant relieving a lieutenant commander, it was clearly expected that he would be on the next promotion list in December. But the words of his detailer still echoed in his mind: "Your first department head tour fitness reports were not as good as they should have been; we're going to have to retour you in a second department head job. You apparently pissed somebody off. You are promotable, but just barely; if we didn't have this war going, you'd have a problem. So, you'd better ring a bell in *Hood*. And given the timing, with the lieutenant commander promotion board meeting in November, it would be helpful if they'd write you a special fitness report before the board convenes." He would really have to impress his new captain to get a special. Make or break time, hotshot.

The news that he had not done well in his previous department head billet had come as a surprise. His skipper in *Decatur* had given no indication that he was anything but pleased with Brian's performance as Weapons officer. In retrospect, though, Brian thought he knew what the problem had been. He had reported aboard from the Navy's new Destroyer School up in Newport, where they trained up-and-comers to take on any of the three line department head jobs in the tin-can Navy—Weapons, Operations, or Engineering. He had hit *Decatur* as maybe a little too cocky, a little bit too much of the know-it-all. Brian knew he was smarter than the average bear; his top standing in all the Navy schools, starting with the Naval Academy, demonstrated that. He had spent his first year in an elderly destroyer that had been decommissioned, and then had two and a half years

13

in a more modern destroyer, all of which gave him more sea time than the average lieutenant. But he also realized now that he still had a lot to learn about how to handle himself in a professional culture where there were many officers whose value was not measured in class rank alone.

The tugboat came alongside smoothly, snubbing up under the overhang of the bow long enough to let the pilot climb through the lifelines, and then eased herself out a bit so that the deck crew could make her up alongside. The pilot was met by Ens. Jack Folsom, the ship's first lieutenant, who escorted him aft on his way up to the bridge. The piers at Subic were so crowded with ships that traditional destroyer-force ship handling was not really safe. Tugs were used to push a ship as big as *Hood* sideways into her berth with a minimum of fuss. The tugs were made doubly necessary by this "frigate's" glass jaw, a huge, bulbous sonar dome right at the foot of the bow, which meant that razzle-dazzle, "drive up to the pier and back her down hard" ship handling was out of the question.

Brian glanced back up at the bridge and saw a cluster of khaki moving out onto the port bridge wing. The captain and the Operations officer, Lieutenant Commander Austin, were standing in the conning position along the bull rail. Brian recalled with some warmth the friendly welcome-aboard extended by Capt. Warren L. Huntington on Brian's first day. In contrast, Austin had been noticeably cooler. As the senior department head, Austin was Brian's designated sponsor. He had made it clear at the outset that while he, Austin, was an old hand in WESTPAC, Brian was going to be playing catch-up ball in *Hood*. Brian was well aware that the four department heads competed for ranking in the fitness-report system. One of them would win the coveted 1 of 4 ranking; somebody else would have to be 4 of 4. Brian also knew that he had better place in the top half of that ladder or he could forget lieutenant commander. As the new guy, and a novice at Seventh Fleet operations to boot, he knew he faced an uphill battle.

The tugboat drowned out his thoughts with a loud *blat*

of its horn, answered by another horn from the tug made up back aft. The ship was making bare steerageway now as the pilot brought her close in to her designated berth at the bulkhead pier. Brian could see Filipino line handlers waiting on the pier and men standing out on deck on the destroyers already moored to the pier, watching as the newest ship to join the Seventh Fleet was brought alongside. There was a sudden blaze of bronze tropical light as the sun surmounted the eastern mountaintops. He realized that he was already perspiring freely in the damp tropical heat.

The destroyers at the pier looked well used, with running rust and a weather-beaten look to their paint jobs. The older ships, some dating back to World War II, clearly showed their ribs through the thinning hull plating. The long line periods of escorting the heavy carriers on Yankee Station, or conducting night-and-day firing missions on the shore-bombardment gun line off South Vietnam, beat both men and ships down. Brian was suddenly acutely aware of how clean and new *John Bell Hood* must look to these salty veterans. He glanced at his watch. The briefing team was due onboard at 0730, and he was designated to greet them and take them up to the wardroom. He started aft toward the quarterdeck as the first heaving lines snaked over the side to the pier.

Professionally, Brian had jumped at the orders to be Weapons officer in *John Bell Hood*. *Hood* was one of the ships that operated the Red Crown station up in the Gulf of Tonkin. With her powerful three-dimensional air-search radars that could see over two hundred miles, long-range surface-to-air missile systems, and large helicopter flight decks, *Hood* would serve as the air-control nerve center for all the air operations over the Gulf, including the surveillance flights, the combat air patrols, the strike flights of Navy carrier bombers into the North. The Red Crown station also coordinated search-and-rescue operations whenever Navy, Marine, and Air Force pilots bolted out over the Gulf with their Phantoms, Prowlers, or Voodoos in flames, looking for a safe place to eject.

For Brian Holcomb, whose sea service up to this

juncture had been in conventional gun destroyers of the Atlantic Fleet, this was a dramatically new and exciting world. Professionally, he was also stepping up to the Seventh Fleet, which, after years of conflict in Vietnam, was the premier operational fleet in the Navy. While Atlantic Fleet ships conducted rote-step exercises in the politically sensitive waters of NATO Europe, the Seventh Fleet did it for real in Vietnam. The first team, as anyone with Seventh Fleet experience would proudly point out. All the rest of the Navy was training and drills. Out there, in WESTPAC, it was the real thing, man. Brian knew that any officer coming from the Atlantic side would have to prove himself to the old WESTPAC hands, learning a whole new operational jargon in the process. When he reached the flight deck, he stopped to watch the big ship come alongside.

3

"Attention on deck!"

The officers stood up from their chairs as first the captain and then the executive officer entered to take their seats at the head of the senior table. Capt. Warren L. Huntington was a distinguished-looking officer, with silver gray hair, a pleasant, fatherly face and demeanor, and a trim figure on a five-foot-ten-inch frame. To Brian, the captain looked like a captain should: dignified without being stuffy. Huntington projected quiet authority but was engaging in his approach to people, soft-spoken and yet able to command immediate attention. Brian thought the only discordant note in the captain's otherwise-immaculate persona was that his uniforms looked to be slightly too large for him. The exec, Comdr. David Mains, was the captain's exact opposite in appearance and personality: a beefy, round-faced ex–football player type, whose rough-and-ready personality, edged occasionally with a hint of steel, made a perfect foil to the avuncular style of the captain.

16

The captain greeted and shook hands with the senior briefer, an aviator commander from the air station across the bay at Cubi Point, and his briefing team of one lieutenant and one chief petty officer. Everyone then took his seat except the captain. There were two tables in the dining area of the wardroom, one designated as the senior table, which seated the captain, exec, the four department heads, and some of the senior lieutenants. The rest of the ship's officers were seated at the larger junior table. Standing against the bulkhead on either side of the wardroom were several chief petty officers and, conspicuous in their dungarees among all the khaki, the six enlisted air controllers.

As the junior line department head, Brian sat midway down the senior table, following the exec, the Operations officer, Lieutenant Commander Austin, and the chief engineer, Lt. Comdr. Vincent Benedetti. Lt. Raiford Hatcher, the Supply officer and the ship's only black officer, sat next to Brian. The captain cleared his throat.

"Gentlemen," he began, "Commander Wingott is here from the CTF Seventy-seven detachment at Cubi Point. He's going to give us a quick briefing on what's going on up in the Gulf these days. I know we've all been studiously reading our message traffic on the way over from EASTPAC and that we've had briefings up the gumpstump back in Pearl. But now we've formally chopped to COMSEVENTHFLEET and CTF Seventy-seven, so now comes the straight skinny. Commander."

Commander Wingott had a ruddy face that bore the marks of recent scars or burns. He wore the pristine, well-pressed khakis of a staff officer, with no little daubs of gray paint or the oil stains typical of ship's company uniforms. He also displayed an extensive set of ribbons under his aviator wings, including a Silver Star and a Purple Heart, and a pair of mirrored glasses was suspended from the button of his right shirt pocket. Brian noticed that he walked with a slight limp over to a briefing easel set up behind the senior table.

"Gents, welcome to WESTPAC and Task Force Seventy-seven, the first team. The *J. B. Hood* is, of course, no stranger to TF Seventy-seven, and you have a first-class reputation as Red Crown. I believe I see some of the same faces here as when I outbriefed you all seven months ago. On behalf of Commander Task Force Seventy-seven, we're glad to have you back. Things have heated up here since you left in January."

He turned to the briefing easel and flipped down the first page, then proceeded to give them an update on what ships were where in the Tonkin Gulf attack-carrier formations. He reviewed the mission of the Red Crown station, which was to act as the focal point for air-control and air-defense operations for the entire Gulf area, with secondary missions of providing the air-navigation reference point for any U.S. military aircraft operating over northern Vietnam, as well as being the seagoing base for two search-and-rescue helicopters.

Brian listened carefully. Because he was a department head, Brian was designated an evaluator in the ship's watch bill. As evaluator, he was going to be the senior officer in tactical control of the ship's operations when he was on watch. The evaluator was the captain's direct representative on watch in Combat. All of the module watch supervisors in Combat reported to him for direction. If the ship was subjected to a surprise attack, he would have the authority to launch missiles and fire the ship's guns at an attacker without having to wait for the captain's permission. Brian was under no illusions that he would be qualified technically on day one as evaluator, but he also understood that his main job was to ensure that the highly trained watch standers in Combat did their job, namely, to launch the ship's defensive systems in the critical seconds between detection of a raid and impact. He also knew that, by the end of their first forty-five day stint, or line period, on the PIRAZ station, he would be expected to know a great deal more.

The commander emphasized the importance of the ship's mission in terms of the fact that every pilot and aircrewman who flew the Gulf of Tonkin depended on Red Crown.

"You guys come up on the air as Red Crown, you speak with complete authority for air control, traffic control, missile defense, and search-and-rescue. You guys have done all this before, but I want to stress to you that where you're going, there are no more drills and exercises. From here on out, it's all for real, gents.''

The commander paused for effect before going on. "I understand you've had your full-scale briefings from CINCPACFLEET back in Pearl. What we have to give you today is current dope. Lieutenant Henson over there has a detailed brief with the current overlays for the CIC folks, the buffer zones for Red China and Hainan Island, and the daily flight plans from the carriers. RMC Batterton, next to him, needs to meet with the Comm Center people, and I need to discuss a few things with the CO and XO. Other than that, I'm done, unless there are any more general questions.''

Before a general question-and-answer session could get going, the captain intervened by rising from his chair.

"Commander Wingott, thank you. I'm sure there are lots of questions, but we're limited on time here. The engineers have to get on with refueling, and the Supply folks need to get on the beach to chase some parts and top off the consumables. We'll have the full Weps and Ops teams assembled in CIC in ten minutes for the lieutenant's briefing. Our Radioman Chief Furman there will escort your RMC to Radio. Gents, let's get rolling. Commander, let's go up to my cabin, shall we?''

The captain and the executive officer left the wardroom with Commander Wingott in tow. Lieutenant Commander Austin turned to Brian and Benedetti, the engineer, as the other officers milled around, refilling coffee mugs.

"Vince, this briefing in CIC requires all three of us; it's primarily for SWICs and the evaluators.''

"Goddamnit, I gotta refuel, Ops,'' complained Benedetti. Brian studied the deck while the two lieutenant commanders argued. He was a department head but not yet a lieutenant commander.

"Then I recommend you get the refueling evolution started and come to CIC, Vince. You've spent minimal time in CIC during the workup and—''

"Don't gimme that shit, Austin,'' interrupted Benedetti. "You got all those precious twidgets working for you in your squeaky-clean, air-conditioned CIC. I got a bunch of dope-smoking, give-a-shit no-loads to contend with in the holes. We're lucky this boat got this far, with the people I've got in my main spaces. I'm the chief engineer first and an evaluator second, and since I don't want to see a fuel spill, that means I personally oversee the refueling. You listen real good and then *you* can brief me on the first turnover. See ya."

Brian watched as the engineer, a rumpled, balding figure whose uniform smelled perpetually of fuel oil, stomped out of the wardroom, followed by his main propulsion assistant and the Boilers Division officer. Austin shook his head.

"You and I will both pay a price for that attitude, I'm afraid," he said, picking up his hat. "The three of us are supposed to be in three watch sections, six on, twelve off. But what really happens is that the engineer is so weak in the combat systems area that if anything happens, either you or I get called up to Combat. Or the captain takes him off the watch bill when things go wrong down below. As Vince well knows. Come on."

They left the wardroom and began to climb the steep interior ladders to CIC.

"What's the special brief Commander Wingott's giving the CO and XO?" Brian asked as he followed Austin up the ladder.

"Probably special rules of engagement stuff, the 'Personal—For Commanding Officers' message file from CTF Seventy-seven and COMSEVENTHFLEET, any unwritten personnel policies regarding drug abuse, liberty incidents, or any other problem-related policies like that," said Austin over his shoulder. "Be patient. After a while, the word always trickles down to the evaluators."

Brian knew all about being patient. He was one of those rare birds, a native of Washington, D.C. His father had been a professional mechanical engineer in the Navy Department's Bureau of Ships, and his mother was also a civil servant, a chemist who worked for the Department of the Interior. His parents had met during the Great Depression at a scientific symposium in Washington, then married in 1937. Brian had come along in 1939, a few months before war broke out in Europe. The Holcomb family had lived in the Chevy Chase area for as long as Brian could remember, on a quiet side street off Military Road. No brothers or sisters followed, a fact that Brian came to regret in late childhood, without really knowing why. He had attended the local Catholic elementary school up on the boundary between Maryland and the District, in deference to his mother's Catholic upbringing. It was a choice his father supported because it was the best school around; William Falwell Holcomb took no interest in organized religion.

Brian had been imbued early on with the importance of academic achievement by the attitude of his technically educated parents, aided and abetted by the occasional application of a ruler to the back of his hands by Sister Paul Marie. He was less of a brilliant academic superstar than he was a patient, hardworking slogger, and by the time he hit high school, he was gravitating closer and closer to the top of his class each year. He became a junior varsity and then a varsity trackman, excelling in long-distance endurance running. He was popular with his classmates, both boys and girls, and well liked for his easygoing and sincerely friendly way with people.

His parents assumed, and therefore so did he, that he would follow in their footsteps in one of the hard sciences or engineering disciplines when he went off to college, although it was an open secret in the family that money for college would be hard to come by. But one weekend, his father had taken him down to Annapolis to see the Naval Academy, having found out that Navy Department civilians could also apply for Academy appointments. Brian had been dutifully impressed, but he did not become really infected with the Academy bug until another side trip with his father, this to the Naval Weapons Station in Dahlgren, Virginia, where he sat enthralled one afternoon as he watched the test-firing of sixteen-inch naval guns. Two years later, on a hot and steamy July day in Annapolis, he found himself being sworn in by the Naval Academy superintendent in the expansive brick courtyard of Bancroft Hall, along with about a thousand other new plebes.

His parents were both delighted and very proud. Not only was it an achievement to be selected, appointed, examined, and then accepted but it was also a free education, leading to a bachelor's degree in naval and marine engineering. The entire cost to his parents had been the three-hundred-dollar admission fee, which paid for his initial issue of midshipman uniforms. After a summer of physical training, rifle pits, drill fields, sailing, and small-boat seamanship, Brian was delighted with Annapolis—until plebe year descended with a roar as the remaining three thousand upperclassmen returned to the Yard.

Plebe year had changed Brian in ways he was still discovering, years later. The Naval Academy's plebe year was designed to teach some harsh lessons about personal accountability, strict adherence to the truth and the facts of a situation, and the concepts of loyalty to a classmate and his class. It was an entire year of the plebes against the entire world, and the front gates along Maryland Avenue offered exit for anyone who could not or would not conform. Brian, who up to this point had been a bright, happy-go-lucky, "get through life with a minimum of fuss" young man and accustomed to success, suddenly had to work very hard to stay even with the demands of plebe year. The first-year hazing, amplified by an intensely difficult academic curriculum, had shaken his confidence in himself and his choice of a college. His remaining three years were spent showing himself more than anyone else that he could cut the mustard and maybe even succeed. He had been determined to show these people that they not only wouldn't get to him but that maybe he was going to get to them, even as nearly a third of his entering class had dropped by the wayside by the end of the second year. Brian studied hard and aimed at high grades after he realized that the seniors wearing stripes were also the seniors who wore the stars of academic achievement on their shirt collars. He graduated in the top 10 percent of his class, intensely proud that he had beaten the system, grown up physically and mentally, and attained a certain veneer of toughness and purpose not necessarily characteristic of a brand-new college graduate. In later years, he would sheepishly admit that the system had taken the defeat gracefully.

By the time he had reached *Hood,* those same values instilled with such thoroughness at the Academy had produced a seasoned lieutenant who still tended to take things seriously, to assume that everyone else did, too, and that the people he worked for and with had the same sense of dedication to duty that he did. But the assignment to *Hood,* accompanied by his detailer's warnings about where his career stood, had raised the first real doubts Brian had experienced professionally. He was still not quite sure why his CO in *Decatur* had dinged him, but was beginning to think that he might have more to learn about the real nature of people than he had managed to learn so far. Up to this point, he had assumed that you did your job and did it well and that's all it took to get to the top. And if others couldn't cut it—why, they fell by the wayside, just as they had at Annapolis. Except by 1969, letting people fall by the wayside was no longer, if it ever had been, a viable option in the real fleet, beset as it was with declining enlistments and declining support in American society for the traditional values of the armed forces, as the unpopularity of the Vietnam War ensured that military people were no longer unquestioningly admired. Fleet commanding officers seemed to expect that successful officers would be able to make even the indifferent sailors produce, and Brian was beginning to realize that he had been slow to pick up on this expectation. He recognized that his assignment to *Hood* was going to be a test of sorts, to see whether he could cope with the changing circumstances of being a fleet officer as well as he had coped with the academic rigors of the Academy and various Navy schools.

And then there was Maddy. The memory of their dismal parting was now locked up in a psychological black box somewhere in the magazines of his heart, secure, but to be opened with great care. The exec in *Decatur* had given him a gentle warning about the career damage a discontented wife could do, especially if she looked like Maddy. What to do about Maddy? Sounded like one of the new hippie folk songs. He loved her dearly, but as lieutenant commander approached, he was beginning to wonder whether they were headed for one of those "career or wife" choices—a choice he feared that Maddy might make for him.

Now Brian and Austin climbed the two levels to the 03 level and went into the CIC through the front vestibule between the CIC and the expansive pilothouse. Brian had been standing watches as evaluator in CIC for several weeks during the ship's workup in home waters and transit to WESTPAC, but he was still getting used to its size and complexity. Combat, as it was called, extended the full sixty-foot width of the ship and almost eighty feet back from the bridge. Combat was divided into functional areas called modules, where command and control functions were concentrated around their respective computer complexes. There were modules for surface operations, weapons control, electronic warfare, antisubmarine warfare, air detection and tracking, and the central command station, display and decision. The modules were interconnected on a local-area computer network called the naval tactical data system, which linked the ship's sensors and weapons systems in a large computer complex one deck below CIC. The system also communicated with other similarly equipped ships over a radio data link, like several spiders with connecting webs, all poised off the coast of Vietnam.

The CIC, normally kept darkened to enhance the scopes, was brighter than usual. The blue-filtered overhead fluorescents were on, bathing the entire room in blue light to provide maximum contrast to the amber-colored radarscopes on the consoles. Brian noticed that the lighting did interesting things to people's faces. Austin, with his long, thin face, prominently bridged nose, hooded eyes, and heavy-lidded, haughty expression, looked like a vampire prince from a thirties movie. Brian could now see why Austin's nickname was "the Count." Brian smiled as he recalled hearing a sly remark in the wardroom that the word *count* could have one vowel or two, depending on whether or not Austin was present.

Austin went directly to the display and decision module, or D and D. He wasted no time with formalities. The entire CIC team, some sixty officers, chiefs, and enlisted men, was assembled in and around the display and decision module. Austin stood with his back to the central command console.

"Gentlemen, please be quiet and pay attention. This is Lieutenant Henson from the CTF Seventy-seven staff detachment at Cubi. He has the preturnover package. Warrant Officer Barry, Lieutenant Henson has the PIRAZ overlays and the buffer-zone patches for the NTDS op program. I want them installed today and used for all future training sessions, which, by the way, commence at ten hundred today with watch section one."

There were some groans and moans among the crowd.

"We gonna be able to go over to the Exchange?" asked a voice from the back.

"That's negative. The only people going ashore are Supply types, and only for urgently required repair parts. We get underway at eighteen hundred. This is not, I repeat, not a liberty visit. That comes after the first line period. I'm having Warrant Officer Barry bring up Link Eleven with the ships in the Gulf this morning, with us radio-silent in receive mode. The XO intends that we'll do a standard *Hood* turnover, which means we're going to be in the link, with the Gulf picture fully soaked in, from the time we leave Subic. We're not coming up there like some East Coast makee-learn and taking three days to turn over with *Long Beach*. We'll do the turnover in about three hours, or as long as it takes to do the cross-deck transfers with the helos. And that means we start the watches and we practice internally for the next two days. This should not be news, people."

Austin's announcement was met by a stony silence from the CIC team. The officers stared down at their shoes, the chiefs smoked cigarettes and looked bored, and the enlisted men exchanged expressions of resignation, disinterest, or open hostility. What a happy crew, thought Brian. The ship's announcing system, called universally the 1MC, blared out the news that the smoking lamp was out throughout the ship while taking on fuel.

There was a quiet shuffle as cigarettes were squashed out in the butt cans all over Combat.

"Okay," Austin continued. "Lieutenant Henson has some general stuff for all hands, and then he needs to sit down individually with the AICs, the track supes, and AC net operators."

"And your GLO," said Henson, speaking for the first time. He was a short, spindly officer with glasses, who looked to Brian like an intelligence officer.

"The gunnery liaison officer? What's that about?" asked Austin, frowning.

"Commander Wingott is briefing your CO right now, Commander. Once that's done, we can talk about it some more. I'll see the GLO last."

"Well, well, well," mused Austin. "All right, let's get to it."

The crowd began to break up into their functional groups, migrating back to their modules. Austin turned to Brian.

"Lieutenant Holcomb, I recommend you listen in to each of the briefings that Lieutenant Henson is going to give. You won't necessarily understand all of it, but this is the good stuff, and it's better information than we received at Pearl Harbor."

"Okay," said Brian. He resented Austin's constant supercilious references to his new-guy status. But he also recognized that, compared with Austin, he *was* ignorant. There was a lot of insider knowledge in the Red Crown game.

Two hours later, the exec pushed through the door, looking for Austin. Brian watched from his seat on a stool next to the air controllers' consoles as Commander Mains spoke urgently to the Operations officer. He saw Austin's face register surprise.

"You've got to be kidding! NGFS? With *Hood*!"

"You got it, sunshine," said the exec. "And I'll bet you haven't drilled on that since San Clemente."

"Yes, sir. Unfortunately, you're right." Austin turned to find Brian. "Lieutenant Holcomb, front and center, please."

"Hiya, Brian," said the exec with a grin. He often

seemed to be deliberately trying to offset Austin's imperious formality. The exec had come from *Hood*'s sister ship, USS *Sterrett*, where he had been the Operations officer. He appeared to be more than happy to stick a pin in Austin's balloon on a regular basis, especially when it came to who knew more about WESTPAC operations. Brian realized that the exec enjoyed playing off Austin's instinctive "I'm right and you're wrong" stance with his equally strong desire to please his superior officers.

"XO here tells me we're going to do some shore bombardment," Austin said. "Which, I must say, is a real departure for a Red Crown ship. I assume you and your people remember how to do naval gunfire support?"

"Morning, XO. Yes, Mr. Austin, I remember how to do NGFS. If your plotters can plot and your naviguessers can navigate, and your radio talkers can radio-talk, my gunners can shoot."

The exec's eyes twinkled. He was obviously of the school that thought competition among the department heads was healthy as long as it did not begin to hurt the ship.

"Brian, that's great," he said. "I suggest you get your chief gunner's mate, the gunnery officer, and your director officer up here in about twenty minutes. Count, you round up your surface module NGFS people. Brian, apparently we're going to divert on our way up to Red Crown to join a Sea Dragon task unit for a surface shoot above the DMZ. They need one more five-inch fifty-four gun, and that's us."

Brian felt a surge of interest. A fire mission against North Vietnamese targets. And, unlike operations in the South, the Communists often shot back. Suddenly, the war business seemed very real; his apprehensions about his career were pushed into the background.

"Aye, XO, I'll get 'em right up here."

4

RD1 Jack Rockheart came out of the chow line with a trayful of Navy-standard heavy lunch. He was nearly six feet tall, heavyset in the chest and shoulders, with a large head and face, slicked-down black hair, wide-set dark brown eyes under heavy black brows, and a hooked nose. His face was framed in a full, neatly trimmed black beard. Rockheart walked deliberately, as if aware he needed more space than most men, and maintained an alert, aggressive expression. His uniform was immaculate, with sharp creases pressed into his short-sleeved chambray shirt, a custom-tailored patch containing the three chevrons of a petty officer first class on his sleeves, and clean, trim-fitting dungarees above his highly polished shoes. A master-at-arms badge gleamed on his left shirt pocket, indicating that he was one of the six deputies on the ship's master-at-arms force, in addition to being a radarman.

He spied two other radarmen at a table on the crowded mess decks and joined them, stepping over the steel swing-out chair with his tray and settling carefully into his seat. The air in the mess decks felt unusually humid and smelled of fried chicken. There was a hum of general excitement at being in Subic and finally on the way to the Gulf. Rockheart greeted the other two radarmen with a nod.

"Yo, Rocky," responded Radarman Second Class Bartley, a tall, thin redhead whose freckled face was almost obscured by his gray plastic navy-issue eyeglasses. The other man at the table, Radarman Third Class McKinnon, simply grunted as he concentrated on a piece of chicken. McKinnon was a beefy individual with an oversized belly, and he was already eyeing the chow line to see when he might go back for seconds. Rockheart suddenly realized he was not very hungry; he had not been paying attention when the messmen filled his tray.

"I hear the Cunt is going to start the Red Crown watches as soon as we leave Subic," said Bartley, talking around a mouthful of mashed potatoes.

"Yup," replied Rockheart. "Trying to show the Old Man that he cares."

"Only thing that fuck cares about is his next fitness report."

"Well, that's what we all work for, isn't it?" said Rockheart with a cynical grin. "Get those evals, make rate, all that extra money, do your twenty years, retire, and then sit back and relax in a trailer in Florida."

"Jesus," said Bartley. "I grew up in a trailer in South Florida. I hate fucking Florida."

The new Weapons officer, Lieutenant Holcomb, came walking through the mess decks on his way back to the Weapons office. Bartley eyed him surreptitiously.

"You talk to the evaluators. What's the new guy like?" he asked Rockheart after Brian had passed by.

"Like any other department head—sweating the load, trying not to fuck up," replied Rocky, picking at his food.

"I heard he's from LANTFLEET; doesn't know shit about WESTPAC."

Rockheart shrugged and said, "He's a lieutenant in a lieutenant commander's billet, you know? Doesn't know NTDS, doesn't know PIRAZ, so sweat pumps on max. But so far, he's not acting like that prick Austin."

Bartley nodded and went back to his lunch. As a rule, Rockheart didn't pay too much attention to officers, other than to identify the ones who were going to give him a hard time or who were otherwise jerks about salutes and saying sir. He had observed Brian standing his break-in watches as evaluator in Combat. He had quickly realized that Brian knew next to nothing about the PIRAZ business and thus would be dependent on the junior watch officers and the senior radarmen to keep him out of trouble until he learned the ropes in *Hood*'s state-of-the-art CIC. From the enlisted perspective, how Brian handled the awkward situation of being the senior officer on watch while still not knowing everything there was to know about Combat would be a good measure of the man. The smart ones simply asked until they got everything down; the pricks tried to fake it. Austin was a notorious prick, but from what Rocky could tell, Brian looked as if he was playing new guy for as long as he could, which to Rockheart was eminently sensible—the CO and the XO would have to wait a while before jumping in his shit.

"They gonna let us go over, hit the PX?" asked Bartley.

"I don't think so," replied Rockheart. He suddenly decided he did not want fried chicken and began to pick suspiciously at his dessert, a sodden lump of what was supposed to be apple pie. McKinnon began to eye Rockheart's chicken.

"That's a bummer," complained Bartley. "I need to get some shit; my old lady is all hot to trot for WESTPAC goodies."

"You gonna eat that chicken?" inquired McKinnon, looking up over the bones on his tray.

"Have at it, Mac," said Rockheart. "Shit's too greasy for me. Besides, I have to watch my figure; the birds don't go for any lardass."

McKinnon just grunted and speared Rockheart's chicken onto his own tray.

"I don't give a rat's ass what women go for," he said, his mouth working ponderously. "I want some gash, I go buy it. They don't like my big gut, that's too fuckin' bad. Actually, most of 'em don't bitch much—it keeps their heads warm."

Rockheart grinned. He was a handsome man in a rough-cut, frontiersman fashion. His spotless uniforms and correct military bearing classified him among the officers as a squared-away, highly professional career enlisted man who was bucking for a chief petty officer's hat. He was the only radarman first class who was not one of the air-intercept controllers in CIC, having chosen to specialize in surface operations.

McKinnon finished off Rockheart's chicken, looked over his shoulder at the dwindling chow line, and pushed away from the table to get another load. A very tall black petty officer first class appeared at the table, carrying an empty tray. He wore a leather tool belt filled with electrician's tools around his narrow waist. He acknowledged Rockheart with a bare nod of his shiny bald head, swept the mess decks with his eyes for an instant, and then asked, "Rocky, my man, you got that twenny you owe me?"

"Sure do, Bullet," replied Rockheart, craning his neck to look Bullet in the face. "Wallet's in my locker, though—where can I find you?"

Bullet, nicknamed for the conical shape of his bald head, appeared to think for a moment.

"I be back in the electrical shop in a li'l bit. Be seein' you there."

"You got it."

Bullet moved on, striding toward the scullery with what appeared to be great dignity but what was really an effort to avoid hitting his head on the maze of pipes and cables bundled against the overhead.

Bartley finished his lunch and got up from the table, followed by Rockheart. They took their trays back to the steaming scullery, where trays and silverware were turned in through a window counter to a pair of red-faced, heavily perspiring mess cooks. The mess cooks scraped the trays, banged food scraps into large garbage cans under the counter, and flung the silverware into a deep sink filled with very hot water. The trays were then tossed onto a conveyor belt that led to the scullery machine itself. Despite the fans and the exhaust vents, it was over one hundred degrees in the scullery; the men worked fast to get the job done.

Rockheart reversed course after depositing his tray, walking back toward the forward end of the mess decks, nodding hello to some of his buddies at their tables. Forward of the mess decks he went down Broadway, the central passageway containing the barbershop, the personnel and disbursing offices, the post office, and the ship's store, with its eternal line. Past the post office, Broadway narrowed down and then ended in a T-junction, intersecting an athwartships passageway. The blank white bulkhead taking up the forward side of the junction was the after bulkhead of the missile magazine. Rockheart turned right, walked twenty feet, and then made a left into a narrower passageway that continued forward toward the bow. After stepping through two hatches, he stopped at a doorway labeled FORWARD CREW'S HEAD. He looked up and down the passageway before stepping through the door into the humid, astringent atmosphere of the head. There were six urinals, eight toilet stalls, and six shower stalls crammed into a compartment that was barely twenty feet by twenty-five. The smell of pine-oil disinfectant mixed with salt water misting up from the urinals easily overwhelmed the efforts of the two exhaust fans in the overhead.

He walked across the herringbone-patterned stainless-steel deck to the urinal farthest from the door and went through the motions while examining the row of toilet stalls behind him to see whether anyone else was in the head. They all appeared to be empty, which made sense. At this hour, most of the crew was grabbing a nooner before turn-to went again at 1300. The only sounds in the head came from the constantly flushing urinals and the vent fans laboring against the noxious atmosphere. Making one last visual sweep of the compartment, he stepped up on his toes and reached into one of the large cableways that ran through the overhead of the compartment. Feeling among the bulky armored cables and smaller wires, his fingers closed on a bundle of soft plastic-covered blocks, each the size of a school eraser. He grabbed one and swiftly inserted it into his Jockey shorts, then zipped up. The feel of the plastic against his genitals was erotic, like a girl's panties. He concentrated on something else immediately, such as the prospect of getting caught. The block gave him enough of a bulge without adding complications.

He left the head and retraced his steps through the passageways, passing back through the mess decks. He had to make his way all the way to the electrical shop, which was on the second deck, underneath the fantail. There he would meet Bullet, who would give him three hundred dollars for the single block of powdered Mexican hashish. Bullet would then break the block down into small individual tokes and sell them through his network to customers throughout the ship.

Rocky smiled as he walked aft. He was going to be a rich man before he finished his tour in *John Bell Hood*. Hell, he was already a rich man, especially by Navy pay standards. As the main supplier, Rocky had been dealing dope in the ship for nearly two years, courtesy of another first class radarman by the name of Rackman, who had decided to get out of the seagoing dope business when he made chief and transferred off the ship to shore duty in San Diego.

Radarman First Class Rackman had been the leading petty officer in OI Division when Rocky reported aboard as a fresh-caught E-6, and Rackman had taken Rocky under his wing after the first month and made him something of a protégé. They had been buddies for nearly a year, going out on liberty together and often double-dating. Rocky realized later that the fact they had been close friends for so long without the smallest hint of Rackman's other profession spoke very highly of Rackman's security system. The revelation had come when Rocky and Rackman had been out on the beach one night to celebrate Rackman's promotion to chief petty officer. They had brought along a couple of beach-bar debutantes, one of whom had produced some grass and started passing the stuff around. Rocky, a reformed smoker, had declined until Rackman pulled him aside and told him that he had something very important to talk to him about, but only if Rocky would first do a joint with him.

Intrigued, Rocky had tried the marijuana. He coughed a lot but found it to be a pleasant-enough buzz if you could get by the awful smell. Then Rackman had revealed his shipboard avocation and offered to let Rocky take over the business. Rackman would show him the ropes for a month or so before he transferred off and would then become Rocky's main supplier ashore. Rocky, flying low on the effects of several beers and the joint, had begun laughing hysterically, until Rackman described the profit structure, the secure nature of the distribution system aboard ship, and revealed that he had squirreled away over $150,000 in tax-free money during the three years he had been in business in *Hood*. Rocky had stopped laughing. Rackman had told him to think it over, and Rocky had.

Rocky was thirty-three, unmarried, had twelve years in on his twenty, and would be eligible for the chief's exam in two more years. He had been born and raised in Seattle, the second son of a career fireman whose attachment to rye whiskey had killed him in a car wreck one night as he drove home from his neighborhood bar. His mother had carried on, helped out financially by the generosity of her husband's fellow firefighters, raising three large boys in a small house on the north side of the city. Rocky had gone into the Navy after high school, as there had been no possibility of going to college, given the financial situation at home. His older brother, John, had become a fireman. His younger brother, Timmie, had drifted into the growing ranks of professional hippies, war protestors, and dropouts populating greater Seattle toward the end of the sixties.

Being a high school graduate, Rocky had qualified for radar A-school after boot camp. He had no idea what a radarman was when he signed up, but he had been told that you stood your watches in cool air-conditioned spaces, sitting in chairs instead of standing on your feet all day, and that there was proficiency pay for those who made rate, all of which seemed to him to beat hell out of being a boiler tender or a deck ape. He had progressed through a series of seagoing billets to E-6, or petty officer first class, by being good at his job and exceptionally accommodating when it came to pleasing officers and chiefs. To Rocky, the Navy was an extremely simple and even generous proposition: They clearly told you the rules, they trained you exhaustively in your rating, they encouraged you and even helped you to make rate, they gave you a change of scenery every three years or so, and they let you out after twenty years, with a paycheck for life. From what Rocky could see, the only way you could screw it all up was to piss off an officer or a chief.

Being a survivor at heart and an extremely practical man, Rocky had made it a point not only to get along with officers and chiefs but to become something of an expert at it. He took special pains to turn himself out in immaculate uniforms, paying for custom-fitted shirts and trousers. He kept his shoes shined, his hair cut, his demeanor sincere, and his performance of duty scrupulously professional. When he realized that not very many of his enlisted peers had figured out the system, he knew he was onto a good thing. He was treated with respect by his superiors and also by the other sailors, even the give-a-shit brigade, because as long as Rocky played the game, the rest of them could goof off, serve their time, and get out. Even after all these years, Rocky thought of it all as a big con, but, having adapted beautifully to the system, he was completely secure in the Navy. He was unconcerned about his future, which the Navy would take care of, and casually ignorant about what was happening in the outside world.

He was by no means a saint; you could not get to E-6 in the Navy or any of the services without being able to play the enlisted game as well as he played the officer's game. As a divisional leading petty officer, he could read through a junior enlisted man's scam in a flash and knew by heart the standard liturgy of enlisted excuses, the "my car, it," "my kids, they," "my wife, she" stories by which the white hats worked the system for a little slack. He had worked his own share of scams and deals over the years, but always within the system and always under the protection of the chiefs. As far as the officers were concerned, Rocky was comfortably in the groove, a solid citizen aboard ship, a dependable petty officer who never gave anybody any trouble. He was, in every sense of the term, a certified lifer.

When the sixties, with the Kennedy assassinations, the civil rights upheavals and killings, the burgeoning Vietnam War protest movements, the advent of rock and roll, free love, and the drug culture, began to roll over America like a wave train of social tsunamis, Rocky had done what most military career people did: ignored it all. He had been content to go to sea, go on deployments, and serve his time on twenty. But by 1967, when Rackman first made his pitch, even Rocky's secure little world in the Navy had begun to wobble just a little bit. He had set up a bachelor pad over in Ocean Beach when he made E-6, and it wasn't long before all the antiwar, antimilitary, antigovernment, and antiestablishment noise began to get in his face. And then there was the money angle: With Johnson's Great Society programs and the Vietnam War inflating the economy, budget-capped Navy pay began to lose its historically secure buying power. Even Rocky, who was no economist, had become acutely aware that the twice-monthly paycheck was covering less and less ground, and he paid attention when he heard the chiefs grumbling as they began to realize how little that pension check was going to cover when they hit their twenty. Rocky had never looked that far ahead, being satisfied to nod agreeably when the older hands talked about hitting that magic twenty-year gate, rolling out, and living on their retired pay. As life began to turn on its ear out there in the world, Rocky had begun to nurture some doubts as to the system's intentions and ability to take care of him, which lent Rackman's proposition an immediate appeal, especially the money.

But it had been more difficult to deal with the ethical and moral complications. He had been raised in a family that put a high value on having a solid job, turning in solid performance in return for solid benefits and security, and doing something with the flavor of public service to it. After twelve years in the Navy, Rocky was no longer bemused by any maudlin concepts of patriotism, but he also knew full well that going into the drug business would be a major insult to a value system that had served him well so far.

Like most of his other career decisions, though, it came down to a matter of practicality. He had long since adopted the typical enlisted view of drugs on board ship: As long as people were discreet, doing an occasional joint or pipe of hash to take the edge off all the boredom, then there was nothing seriously wrong with it, other than the penalties for getting caught. His attitude was reinforced by the seemingly casual attitude held by the command in *Hood*, which, unlike his last ship, did not operate a high-profile anti-drug-use program. A couple of the chiefs were known to kick some ass if somebody was flagrant about what he was doing, but the key seemed to be discretion. As Rackman had put it, the command did not seem to be after him personally or his operation, and he had given Rocky the impression that the Old Man actually did not believe there were drugs in his ship. Just to be sure, though, Rackman took great pains not to attract attention to himself by flashing a lot of money or living visibly beyond his means, and the operation ran itself.

But for Rocky, it was a girl named Lucy who opened his eyes to what was happening in America. He had met Lucy at one of those all-weekend beach parties that bloomed out on Ocean Beach when the coastal weather cooperated. He had been soaking up rays and nursing a six-pack with three other first class petty officers from the ship when this vision had come ambling down the beach: long, stringy beach blond hair, clingy bathing suit, legs up to h'yar, as the song went, enormous eyes, and a lopsided, lazy smile on her face that told every man who stared that she could read his mind and was not offended. Rocky had held up a cold beer and she had put the rudder over and joined him on his beach blanket.

Lucy came from a well-to-do middle-class family in San Mateo who thought she was productively enrolled as an English major at UCSD. At the end of her first semester in Southern California, Lucy had aligned her orbit with the appropriate celestial spheres and declared her personal emancipation from all recognized conventions, especially those of the people who were paying her tuition. She focused single-mindedly on the task of expanding the horizons of her personal experience, adopting the rule that one should rule absolutely nothing out of the spectrum of personal experience, including this thoroughly square sailor with the pleasant manner and the dynamite black beard.

Over the next few weeks that the ship was in port, Rocky became something of a project for her as she turned him on and tuned him in to the dizzying kaleidoscope of Southern California freedom, which included the uninhibited questioning of all existing value systems, decrying the Vietnam War, despising LBJ, embracing a host of ill-defined isms, indulging in mind-expanding substances, and screwing his brains out anytime he was in the mood and sometimes when he wasn't. Rocky was mostly in it for the great sex, but he could not help but be affected by the views of Lucy and her friends. Collectively, they showed him that there was not only a whole new world out there but that it was altogether different from his world, and, even more disturbing, they actively disliked what he did for a living and even what he was. And there were lots of them, as even a cursory glance at the television revealed.

When Lucy finally slipped down the ecliptic in search of new galaxies and experiences, Rocky was a changed man. Lucy's breathtaking interpretations of what it meant to be a child of the sixties had shattered his complacent notions about the value of conformity, playing by the rules, and unquestioning cooperation with the system. By even his own admission, his successful career as an enlisted man in the Navy had been vividly exposed as a pawn's game. While he had not bought into the whole scene, especially all the isms, and while he often wondered who was paying the rent for all these free spirits, if these were the people he was in the Navy to protect and defend and *they* thought that drugs were just one part of the process of personal enlightenment, not in themselves evil and wrong, then maybe Rackman's deal wasn't such a bad thing. Somebody would supply the ship: Why not him, especially when the whole deal was being handed to him on a silver platter? He had experienced a sudden ambition to do better, much better, than continuing with his complacent drift toward the holy grail of twenty. Rackman's offer suddenly looked tailor-made.

Rackman had explained that being the main man required intelligence, a great deal of acting ability, and effective cover—the very reasons, he said, he had picked Rocky. Rocky was obviously intelligent enough to get to first class in a highly technical rating, and it was equally obvious that he was a consummate actor: All the officers thought Rocky was a model petty officer. Plus, Rocky had damn-near-perfect cover: He was a member of the master-at-arms force, which would give him an inside look at any program the command put in motion to quash drug use aboard the ship.

Rackman had explained that the distribution system was already in place. Rocky would deal with only one man, a black electrician's mate first class who went by the name of Bullet. It was well known among the crew that Bullet was the acknowledged, if unofficial, leader of the younger, more radicalized blacks in *Hood*. Bullet ran a network he called his "associates." A doper interested in scoring a little relaxation would strike up a casual conversation with one of the associates about his needs and desires and the associate would speculate on where something might be found after a certain time had passed. The doper would then speculate about where a small wad of cash might be found and would then go off to wait a while before going exploring. Rackman did not know and didn't want to know precisely who Bullet's associates were, other than to assume that all them were black. His righteous brothers, Bullet called them, just like the hit rock band. Rocky could see that Bullet's use of ancient racial fears as a tactic against infiltration or potential snitches was brilliant, especially since almost all of his customers were white.

Continuing aft, Rocky smiled again at his sweet deal. Crewmen passing him in the passageway saw the smile and figured Rocky was thinking about his many women.

5

San Diego

"Tizzy, this is crazy!" Maddy Holcomb held on to what was left of her hairdo with her left hand while gripping the door-side armrest with her right. Tizzy Hudson just laughed and steered the convertible down the ramp from Highway 5 to the Rosecrans exit at a speed that had Maddy pressing her right foot into the floorboards.

"Maddy, relax, for crying out loud," said Tizzy, turning onto Rosecrans with only passing deference to the stop sign at the bottom of the ramp. "Just because MCRD's a meat market doesn't mean you have to take one home with you. It's perfectly okay just to go and watch. It's even funny."

"But we're married, Tizzy. *Tiz-zy!*" Maddy squeaked as Tizzy cut off a bus trying to pull away from the curb.

"So're half the women there, honey buns," shouted Tizzy over the wind. "I've been a good little nun for a whole month, and now I need to get out and rock and roll, just a little bit. MCRD's perfect; you can find whatever you need there—a little or a lot. Like I said earlier, lots of people go there just to enjoy the show. Especially the Marines. Or better yet, the Marine aviators. They're so full of themselves, it's kind of fun to pretend to take them seriously, like they were humans or something. You know, 'Oooh, you fly a *Phantom*! How totally *groo-o-o-vy*!' Then watch them squint their eyes trying to look like John Wayne while they light up a cigarette and say something really clever like 'Yup.' "

Maddy laughed nervously and shook her head as Tizzy sped up Rosecrans toward the base known throughout San Diego as MCRD, shorthand for the Marine Corps Recruit Depot. Her right hand fingered her bare ring finger as she thought about what Tizzy had said. It was well after dark on a Thursday night, but the overcast San Diego sky reflected enough of the city lights to dilute any sense of nighttime. Tizzy had picked Maddy up at her Balboa apartment to go to a seven o'clock movie, after which they had put down a Big Mac attack. While stuffing debris into the white bag, Tizzy had proposed they go check out the scene at the MCRD Officers' Club. Initially, Maddy had had some reservations. She tended to distance herself from knowing much about the Navy scene in San Diego, much to her husband's annoyance. But even she had heard MCRD O-Club stories and was aware that Thursday night offered one of the city's hotter body exchanges. She was also mildly apprehensive about Tizzy Hudson. She suspected Tizzy might have more on her mind than just spectator sports. It was rumored among the wardroom wives that the Hudsons' high-flying, swinging sixties lifestyle was centered on what the wives delicately called an "open relationship." Tizzy's instructions to take off her rings hadn't helped.

Maddy gave up on her hair, clasped her hands in her lap, and closed her eyes, as much an attempt to relax as to ignore Tizzy's outrageous driving. The ship had been gone how long? Four weeks, two days, twelve hours, seven minutes—but who's counting? Only six months to go. What's half a year between friends? As she listened to Tizzy's hilarious description of several standard MCRD opening lines, she realized that Tizzy knew more about that scene than any proper Navy wife should.

Tizzy Hudson was a tall, dark-haired, vivacious woman whose appearance inevitably inspired the adjective *cute*. She seemed to be irreverent about wardroom protocol in general and the intricate network of Navy wives' social functions in particular. Maddy had been attracted to her from their first meeting at Brian's hail-and-farewell party. They had become even closer friends now that the ship was gone, if only because Tizzy displayed no inhibitions about saying what many of the wives so obviously felt. Like Maddy, Tizzy had a day job, while most of the other wardroom wives stayed at home raising children. The two of them generally declined invitations to join the coffee klatches, shopping trips, and playground gatherings that united the wives.

Maddy's quiet sigh was snatched away by the wind. Her life had gone into limbo with Brian's departure to WESTPAC. She woke up each morning with an oppressive amalgam of sadness, self-pity, rejection, and even despair puddled in her stomach like a lump of yesterday's oatmeal—the "poor me's," as the captain's wife, Mrs. Huntington, described it, feelings we endure but do not enunciate, especially in letters to the ship, girls. Or, as Tizzy was wont to put it, "Deployments really suck." Maddy experienced the familiar flash of guilt for being so self-centered about the separation, realizing that her own anger and sense of abandonment implied that Brian felt none of these things as he chased around some godforsaken place everyone called the Gulf on his oversized "frigate." And all because of this tragically absurd war in Vietnam. Like most Navy wives, Maddy despised the disheveled, screeching antiwar protestors who were paraded nightly on the television news by supercilious anchormen. But as the deployment dragged on, she sometimes found herself wishing they would prevail. At least now, President Nixon was talking about ending it.

She tugged on her skirt as Tizzy swung the white convertible into the bright lights of the MCRD main gate area. She noted that Tizzy didn't bother and that the Marine guard very definitely did not keep his eyes in the boat as they drove through. Tizzy, who was almost five ten, wore a very short bright yellow one-piece summer dress that complimented her trim figure nicely, even if it did not leave her many secrets when she sat down. Maddy realized now that Tizzy must have had MCRD on her mind right from the start. She, on the other hand, had not had time to change after work. She wore a straight white above-the-knee skirt with a cream-colored sleeveless blouse and a short-sleeved white linen jacket over her shoulders. She was always surprised at how cool San Diego could get at night.

Maddy Holcomb had an arresting face, with finely arched eyebrows over large violet-blue eyes. Her upper lip described a perfect red bow; her lower lip was prominent and pendulous, giving her mouth a slightly breathless look. Her dense blond hair was cut in a long pageboy that framed her face and fell around her shoulders in a shimmering mantle. With her face in repose, she had a direct gaze that bordered on a stare, an expression accentuated by a slightly down-curving nose and a tendency, because of her height, to tilt her face slightly to one side to look up at people. Where Tizzy was the tall, slim, athletic, and outgoing California girl, Maddy was barely five six in low heels and presented an image of curves and soft roundness, accentuated by wide shoulders and the graceful poise of her Atlanta upbringing. She had lost a good deal of her southern accent and Georgia idiom after four years at school in Boston, although she could turn it on if the situation warranted.

Maddy's real first name was Madison, in deference to

the southern tradition of a daughter taking her mother's maiden name as a given name. With a mental smile, she recalled a remark Brian had made once, comparing Maddy with Tizzy, after it had become evident they were going to be friends. Tizzy, he had said, was eminently streetable, a tall bundle of fun and flash, the perfect partner for a night on the town, especially in Southern California. Maddy, on the other hand, had the kind of looks that men wanted to get off the street and into the bedroom before some other man saw her and wanted to fight.

"Here we are, boys and girls," announced Tizzy, whisking the car into a parking place with a scrunch of complaining gravel. She shut off the engine, twisted the rearview mirror toward her, and began to fix her own hair.

Maddy let out a breath and looked around. The MCRD Officers' Club was a low, sprawling Spanish hacienda-style building complete with red tiled roof and rose-colored stucco walls. The club was surrounded by groves of palm and eucalyptus trees interlaced with gravel walkways. The manicured lawns and lush shrubbery bespoke Mexican gardeners and generous irrigation. The grounds and the walkways were illuminated by faux gaslights placed strategically near the trees. The distinctive smell of eucalyptus blended with the tang of salt air from the nearby harbor. She could hear the whining rush of jet engines from the San Diego airport, which adjoined MCRD on the harbor side. She noticed that the parking lot was full and that a steady stream of young people filed into the O-Club's main entrance, the men and women arriving separately but already giving one another the once-over. The sounds of a rock band thumped through the gardens surrounding the club. There were even a few couples strolling around the gravel pathways in the gardens. Maddy felt torn: She was definitely up for a night out but uncomfortable at coming to a singles watering hole.

"This place looks jammed," she said, brushing out her own hair and appraising her day-old makeup in a compact mirror. The flickering yellow lights made the assessment difficult. "If we get separated, what time do you want to meet back here?"

"Separated? Separated?" asked Tizzy, giving Maddy a speculative look from under her own busy hairbrush. "The southern belle thinking of maybe scoring a little Marine action tonight?"

"Oh, Tizzy, don't be ridiculous. Really. I just meant . . ."

"Yeah, yeah, I know. Well, look—it's ten-thirty. Let's say midnight back here at the car. After midnight, they're all so drunk, they, uh . . ."

It was Maddy's turn to cock her head to one side. "Yes, Tizzy? Something you want to tell me?" To remove any implied criticism, she half-smiled when she said it. But she was a bit curious.

Tizzy grinned and looked down, smoothing her dress over her legs. "Well, not exactly," she said. "Although if something fun came up, er, along—I mean, I might not be opposed to going somewhere to party a little bit. Just for a while. You know."

"Tizzy, maybe we shouldn't be doing this," said Maddy, her expression suddenly serious. "We don't really belong here, and I've got to get home at a reasonable hour. So do you—we have jobs, remember?"

Tizzy made a face. "Oh, Maddy, ease up. I just want to go in and have a glass of wine and dance a little—it's so crowded in there, you can just let yourself go, dance with whomever turns up; everyone's anonymous. You'll see. Pretend for a little while that you're not some old married hag stuck in an empty apartment for the next half a year. MCRD's always got a great band. You want to, you can just sit and watch, although I'll bet you don't. Anyway, if we do get split up, I *promise* I'll meet you back here at the car around midnight and I *promise* to get you home. It's not like your husband's going to call and check up on you or anything."

"Okay, but I'm serious about the witching hour."

Tizzy rolled her eyes. "Yes, dear."

They left the car and joined the stream at the main entrance, small groups of two or three women and a similar number of young officers, each group trying to

44

eye the action without seeming to do so. The noise from the band and the exuberant crowd within washed over them as Maddy and Tizzy stepped through the front doors. The entrance portico led to a large hallway, rest rooms, and offices to the right and a large combination dance floor and main bar to the left. The hallway was crowded with people milling about or going to and from the rest rooms, and groups of men were standing along the wall, talking, smoking cigarettes, and holding drinks. Maddy noticed that the standees were not being at all discreet about appraising the women, making comments, whistling, or expressing feigned horror at the talent coming through the front door. The entrance to the bar itself was packed with people looking for tables, partners, or both. They had to wait in line for several minutes before they could get near the doorway leading to the dance floor. When the standees finally noticed them, they actually drew some cheers as they moved up to the doorway. Maddy flushed; Tizzy smiled and winked. Two large Marines immediately put down their drinks, detached themselves from the standees, and swooped down, taking Maddy and Tizzy by the hand without a word. They pushed through the crowd at the doorway, which parted according to the unwritten rule that people with partners had priority over those who were still window-shopping.

Maddy lost Tizzy as soon as they reached the dance floor, and after shouting something about Bob in her ear, her Marine launched into a frenetic dance routine that exactly matched the tempo of the bombastic noise coming from the bandstand. Maddy gave it her best shot, but her experience with dancing to rock-and-roll music was limited. Brian liked the soft and slow stuff, but this music, with its overwhelming bass beat, jangling electric guitars, and incomprehensible lyrics, was definitely of the hard-and-fast variety. And it was nonstop; once a set began, the band segued into each new number while the final crashing chords of the last song were still buzzing in the speakers.

The room was larger than she'd thought, but with over two hundred people packed inside, it was hot and smoky despite the air conditioning. Silvery planet lights hung from the ceiling and threw moving spots of light all over the room and the dancers. Small bar tables lined the perimeter of the floor, and these, too, were packed with people. Maddy was amazed at the number of good-looking women out on the dance floor, all in their twenties or early thirties, with expensive clothes and hairstyles, and every one of them dancing with surprising intensity. Here and there, waitresses made their way gingerly through the gyrating crowd, writing shouted orders on tiny pads of paper before escaping to the service lines at the bar. Within minutes, they would start back into the crowd, where eagle-eyed customers would wave five- and ten-dollar bills at them until the trays emptied. The crowd on the dance floor was so thick that people consumed their drinks without ever leaving the floor.

Maddy's partner managed to secure two rounds of drinks this way, and Maddy found herself drinking scotch on the rocks on the first round and gin and tonic on the second, while the music and the dancing went on non-stop. She had no idea of how long she had been dancing and she downed the drinks quickly, wondering whether she could get off the dance floor for a minute to shuck the linen jacket. Handing her empty glass to a passing waitress, she shook the lapels at Bob to signify that she was dying of the heat. Bob grinned and shouted, "Take it off!" She laughed, slipped the jacket off, and continued to dance with it in her left hand. As the drinks took effect, the jacket became something of a prop, which she let fly around her hips, and she closed her eyes and concentrated on the insistent beat, no longer quite so worried about looking ridiculous, moving her body in time with the music as she got into the whole scene and tried now to keep up with the insistent pumping movements of her partners.

Partners? Opening her eyes, she found that she was now dancing with two men, both in front of her and both as close as they could get to her without running into each other. She sensed there were other men behind her, but she couldn't tell in the dim light whether they had other partners or whether she had become the local center of attraction. When a pair of strong hands settled on her hips from behind, she knew the answer and began looking for a way out, but they were too close, big men, looking strangely alike with their buzz haircuts, sport shirts worn outside of their trousers, and direct, leering eyes. When she turned to see whether there was an opening, they turned with her. She could feel hands touching her and heard their taunting voices, "Do it, baby. Shake that thing, mama. C'mon, c'mon," mimicking the refrain from the rock group as they moved closer and then withdrew as the music grew even louder. Someone pressed another drink into her hands. It tasted like fruit juice of some kind, and she downed it in one motion, desperately thirsty, still wanting out of the small knot of men around her but also beginning to feel the sexual energy flowing from the dense pack of human bodies, the pounding music, and, despite herself, responding, moving more provocatively, looking back at the men, letting them press closer, aware that there were other groups like hers on the floor with one or even two women in the center of a ring of anonymous men. Now she understood why Tizzy wanted to come here. She lost track of time, working herself into a dreamy state of rhythmic exertion, letting the music and crowd and the noise carry her along, letting the anonymous males into her space, forgetting about the Navy and the deployment and the wardroom wives and her job and the fact that Brian had disappeared into the sunset for the next half a year.

When the music finally stopped, the room seemed to decompress, the crowd breaking up with a collective sigh and starting to mill around, and most of the male dance partners disappearing to the bar. She looked around for Tizzy, but it was hopeless. Bob said to stay right there, that he was going for some more drinks, but she thought that it was probably time to get the hell out of there. Embarrassed and a little tipsy, she pushed through the crowd, fanning her face with the jacket and walking unsteadily from the heat and the drinks. She was perspiring and starting to feel uncomfortable with what had been going on out there on the dance floor. What on earth had gotten into her to act like that? She looked at her watch, looked again, and saw that it was well past midnight.

Sobered, she hurried past the crowd of drunks milling around the front door and headed for the parking lot beyond, her shoes scrunching on the gravel walks in quick time, some bawdy comments following her from the club steps. She peered again at her watch. Damn, no doubt about it. And she had been the one pinging on Tizzy! Her carping words about the witching hour echoed in her ears and the sinking feeling in her stomach was confirmed when she could not find the white convertible. As if hoping to make it reappear, she walked slowly over to the empty spot, looked around the now-half-empty lot, dropped her purse onto the gravel, and said, "Shit!" in a loud voice. Then she heard a scuffling noise behind her. She started to turn but was seized from behind by two strong arms and literally pulled up off her feet and up against a large male body that stank in equal proportions of beer, sweat, and cigarette smoke. She struggled, but he was immense and he had her arms pinned along her sides, inside of his own arms, and his hands were fumbling with the sides of her skirt. She tried to yell for help, but his arms were squeezing the breath out of her. All she could manage was a series of small yelps. She tried kicking back at him, but he was much too strong. She realized with growing horror that she could feel his erection pushing against the small of her back. He was talking to her in a low, slurred voice: "Gotcha, baby. Come to papa now. You been wigglin' yer pretty ass at me all fuckin' night, and now, yeah, now—there, yer gonna love it, baby. Stop yer kickin' now. Just lemme— yer gonna—"

He was dragging her backward toward the bushes lining the edge of the parking lot, her struggles doing no good, her stockinged heels barely touching the ground. She realized her shoes were gone and that he now had her dress pulled all the way up over her hips, the night air suddenly, shockingly cold on her thighs. He was fumbling with his own pants as he dragged her toward the shadows. Her eyes filled with tears as she realized that she had absolutely no leverage, no way to get away from him, no—

"Problem here, miss?" said a man's voice from behind them. "Why don't you put her down there, Marine."

Her assailant stopped in his tracks and turned his head, lurching sideways, and relaxing his grip for an instant. The movement landed her back on her feet and she dropped straight through his arms, sprawling on her bottom. She bounced back up to her hands and knees, then, rising, spun around to face him, backing away rapidly, yanking her skirt down. She could see the figure of another man behind the Marine, but his face was in shadow.

"Help me, please, help me," she cried. "He was—he was—"

"He's going to go back to his buddies, aren't you, Marine? Going to go eighty-six for the night. Had a little too much beer, right, Marine?" The man's voice was flat, emotionless, but somehow menacing.

The big Marine was fumbling with the front of his pants. Maddy could see that he was weaving unsteadily, trying to keep her in sight while looking at the other man. She backed away a few more steps, laboring to get control of her breathing and her runaway, pounding heart.

"Who the fuck're you?" grumbled the Marine. "Wasn't gonna hurt her or anything. I was only gonna fuck her, for Chrissakes. You saw her. Askin' for it, man. Who the fuck're you, anyway?"

"I don't know you, Marine," said the man in a quiet voice, stepping into the lamplight for the first time. "But you know me. I'm Autrey."

The big Marine straightened up and stopped weaving for a moment. "Autrey? You're fuckin' Autrey?" He put his massive paws in front of his chest as if to push something away. "I don't want no fuckin' trouble, man. Not with you. Not over some twist. Shit. I'm gone." He staggered off toward the club, missing the gravel walkway, colliding with the hedge before floundering back toward the club building like a bear crashing through brambles.

Maddy bent forward and started to gasp. Suddenly, she could not get her breath. The man who called himself Autrey came over to her swiftly.

"Give me your jacket," he ordered.

She just looked up at him blankly, still trying desperately to get a breath. Then he reached toward her and started to take her jacket. She froze, then tried to back away, starting to panic again.

"Hold still," he said. "I'm going to take your jacket. You're hyperventilating. I'm just taking your jacket. Hold still. You're okay." He took the jacket and bunched it into a makeshift sack. "There, now put your face into it, breathe slower. That's right, little breaths, smaller than that, in, out. Good, steady it up. Now blow into the jacket. You got it. You got it, into the jacket, easy now, slow it down."

Slowly, she regained her breath as he stood in front of her, talking quietly, not touching her, coaching her with his voice. When she was finally able to lift her face, he nodded and then led her over to a car, a large four-door Chevrolet Impala. He opened the right-front door and steered her into sitting down sideways in the car's doorway, her feet barely touching the ground. She slumped over, her face almost on her knees, her arms wrapped around her middle as she tried to control her shaking. She felt him standing nearby, his hand on her shoulder now. Suddenly, she experienced a wave of nausea. She looked up.

"I think I—I'm going—"

He lifted her out of the car doorway in one smooth motion and trotted her over to the bushes, where she was immediately very sick. He stood to one side and held her shoulders until she was still, then gently walked her back to the car. She heard the crackle of a cigarette pack and then the distinctive click of a Zippo lighter. She smelled the pungent aroma of tobacco and realized he was holding a cigarette in front of her face.

"I don't—I don't smoke," she said in a choked voice.

"Take one drag," he said. "It'll kill the nausea. Go ahead." He put the cigarette to her lips, and she hesitated, inhaled once in a shallow puff, followed by a little cough. "Deeper," he ordered. "Inhale it." She did, then exhaled slowly, trying not to cough. He took the cigarette away. He was right. The waves of nausea reaching for

50

her throat seemed to subside back into her stomach almost at once. She looked up, but Autrey was a dozen feet away, retrieving her shoes and purse. He walked back and dropped them on the floor on the passenger side.

"I think maybe you need a lift home, miss."

She looked up at him. His face seemed foreign, almost Spanish, yet different from the typical San Diego Latino. He wore his hair in an uneven, spiky-looking flattop and was dressed casually in chinos and a loose-fitting long-sleeved white shirt. His face was narrow and angular, with a prominent nose, heavy eyebrows, dark, even black, eyes, and thin lips. He was tall, perhaps six feet, with exceptionally wide shoulders, not big and beefy like the Marine, but rangy. He appeared to be on the verge of smiling, but she could not be sure in the semidarkness.

"Uh, Maddy. Maddy Holcomb. And thank you, Mr. . . . Autrey? Thank you very much. I—"

"Yeah. Well, you're very welcome. That didn't look exactly like friendly persuasion. Do you have a car out here?"

She shook her head. "No. My ride left, I guess. I don't know. Can I—can I get a taxi somewhere?"

"There're pay phones up at the club. But you may have a problem getting a cab. They don't like to come to MCRD on Thursday nights—too many drunks. They fight, get sick, don't pay. You know." He smiled at her. "Well, maybe you don't know. I think maybe you're new to this scene."

He was smoking the remains of the cigarette and took a final drag before flipping it into the parking lot in a shower of sparks. "I can give you a lift if you don't live too far away. I've gotta get in early tomorrow."

"Thank you, but I can't just—I mean, I don't know you."

The man nodded slowly, looking politely over her head. She suddenly felt like an idiot. This man had rescued her from certain rape, and she was going to tell him that she couldn't accept a ride from a stranger? She shook her head impatiently.

"Let me try that again. Yes, I would very much appreciate a ride. And forgive me for—"

"No sweat," he said, definitely smiling now. Smiling made his face go crooked. He had very white and even teeth. "And I would kick my girlfriend's pretty tail feathers around the block if she ever accepted a ride from a perfect stranger—that's if I had a girlfriend. But you don't want a ride from that crew," he said, pointing with his chin to the rowdy bunch exchanging military noises at the club's entrance.

She nodded again and swung her legs into the car. He closed the door and went around to the driver's side. She pulled her skirt down out of habit, although it occurred to her that he had already seen a great deal more than just a few inches of thigh. She flushed and stared straight ahead as he started the car and backed out. He drove out of the parking lot slowly and deliberately, and she wondered for a moment whether maybe he had been drinking, too. She looked around at the darkened base. She could always ask him to let her out at the main gate. But then she realized that the only smell of liquor in the car was coming from her.

"So," he said as the car cruised down toward the main gate. "You'll have to give me directions."

"We . . . uh, I . . . live in the Florentine Apartments. Do you know where the entrance to the Balboa Zoo is?"

"Sure."

"Well, the Florentine is on the other side of that park area across from the entrance to the Balboa Zoo."

"Got it."

"That's not too far out of your way, I hope. I really appreciate this, Mr. Autrey."

"Just Autrey. Like in the cowboy, Gene Autry—but with an *e*."

He slipped through the main gate and turned right on Rosecrans, heading inland toward the Highway 80 freeway. He drove right at the speed limit, keeping in the right-hand lane. Cars zoomed past them on the left. The cool night air suddenly felt very good. Her nausea was almost gone.

"That's your name, Gene Autrey?" she asked, looking over at him. She thought she saw his face twitch. He was a strange-looking man, but he seemed to be nice enough.

He sat slouched against the door on his side of the seat, one hand on the wheel, the other cocked up on the open window. His face looked deeply tanned, but then she realized that it wasn't a tan. His nose was hooked in two clear segments. He was smiling a little now; she was sure of it. He knows I'm looking at him. His cheekbones were pronounced, casting small shadows on his face in the flashes of light from the freeway streetlights. His short black hair stuck out in all directions over the collar of his shirt. He had long, muscled hands, and his forearms were smooth, with no visible hair.

"Not quite. Autrey is my first name. My full name is Autrey Catches Crows. I'm an Indian, Maddy Holcomb."

"Oh," she said, not knowing what else to say. She had never met an American Indian, but that explained the exotic face and dark skin. He pushed the big Chevy up the ramp onto the freeway and headed east through the twinkling lights of Mission Valley. She looked straight ahead. The feel of the drunk Marine's hands on her body made her shiver. He caught the movement.

"Cold? I can turn on the heat."

"No, that's all right. I was just—well, never mind."

"I've got to ask, Maddy Holcomb."

"Ask what, Mr. Autrey?" Mr. Autrey? Or should she say Mr. Catches Crows?

"Just Autrey'll do it, Maddy Holcomb. What I've got to ask is the famous question: What was a nice girl like you doing in a place like MCRD?"

She laughed despite herself. She relaxed further when he made the correct exit onto Route 163 and headed up the hill through the sudden darkness of the Balboa Park canyons.

"Seemed like a good idea at the time," she quipped, trying to keep it light. "Actually, it was Tizzy's idea. Tizzy's another one of the—of my friends." She had almost said "wardroom wives." "We went to a movie, and then Tizzy decided she wanted to go check out MCRD. I'd never been, and so, well, there we were. We were supposed to meet back at the car at midnight, but—"

"Tizzy got lucky, and you got left. So what did you think?"

"I've heard it called a meat market. I think it's a meat market."

"But you didn't care much for being the meat, did you?" he asked. His tone of voice sounded neutral, not accusing, just making a casual observation.

"No," she said in a soft voice. "Although for a while there, out on the dance floor, with all those people, it was kind of good just to let go. But afterward . . . well, it was a mistake to go there. That man, that awful man—"

He nodded slowly in the darkness. Out of the corner of her eyes, she could see the high chain-link fences shining in the darkness along the zoo grounds on either side of the parkway.

"That awful man is a Marine second lieutenant on temporary duty with a special training platoon. He'll be shipping out, probably next week. Most of that crew in there tonight's on the way over to the Nam."

"How do you—are you a Marine?"

"Nope. I'm a civilian. I'm an instructor at MCRD."

She nodded in the darkness. Then she remembered.

"You said your name, and that . . . man backed off. Your name was enough to scare him off. What do you, uh, instruct?"

"Oh, it's no big deal. I'm in the Physical Training Department. You know, PT? 'Gimme a hundred push-ups' sort of thing. We instructors have unlimited power to discipline people by ordering up exercise. Nobody wants to be on the bad side of the PT instructors."

Maddy had the feeling that he was not telling her the entire truth about what he did, but then the sign for Balboa Park flashed overhead and he took the next exit, circling around in a tight turn to come out a block away from the park. Behind them in the distance, a cluster of office buildings marked the edge of the hills descending down to the harbor. The red neon sign for Mr. A's was just visible on one of the buildings.

"You don't look or sound like a PT instructor," she said.

"That so? What's a typical PT instructor look like?"

"Well, all the ones I've ever seen look like middle-aged football players, great big bodies, no necks, you know."

He nodded once. "True strength doesn't always require a huge body," he said.

She thought about that as he waited for the light along Park and then made the left toward her apartment building. She remembered with what ease he had lifted her out of the car when she was sick and the way the Marine had scuttled away at just the mention of his name.

"I guess I saw a demonstration of that tonight, didn't I?"

He laughed. "Aw, shucks, ma'am. It warn't nothin'."

She smiled in the darkness.

"That's better," he observed as he pulled up in front of the building. "I'd offer to take you to a bar for a drink, but I figure you're ready for a hot shower to wash this evening away."

"You are exactly right," she said, looking down at her knees. Then she looked over at him. "But I do thank you. I was in real trouble out there."

His face grew serious. "Yeah, that's probably so. I'm glad I was there."

"Not as glad as I am."

They sat there for a moment. He had left the car's engine running. He did not look directly at her, but seemed to be staring past her. She sensed he was about to say something else, perhaps ask to see her again, a complication that she didn't need or want after the experience of MCRD.

"Well," she said again, "thank you very much. I'll get out now."

He nodded. "I'll wait till you get inside."

"Thank you, Mr. Autrey. Good night."

As she got out of the car, she thought she heard him say, "It's Autrey, just Autrey."

She let herself into the lighted lobby and saw the car pull away. She took the elevator to the fifth floor, then unlocked her apartment door and headed directly for the bathroom, turning lights on as she went. After using the bathroom, she went into the bedroom and shucked all of her clothes onto the floor and walked naked back out into the kitchen to the liquor cabinet. She kept her mind blank as she fumbled for a glass and Brian's bottle of Courvoisier, trying to ignore the trembling in her hands as she poured a hefty measure. Returning to the bathroom, she turned on the shower full force and stepped in, perching the glass of cognac on the rim of the tub. She shampooed her hair, a chore that she normally limited to twice a week. But after MCRD, she knew she smelled of smoke, alcohol, and sweat—and, admit it, girl, fear. She scrubbed her body vigorously, trying to erase the feel of the Marine's hands and body. Her mind shied sideways as the word *rape* surfaced. Thank God that man Autrey had come along. She scrubbed harder.

Once clean, her skin almost red, she tripped the shower valve and put in the tub stopper, allowing the tub to fill. She stood in the tub, toweling her hair, while the water rose around her feet. Wrapping her hair in the towel, she sat down in the tub, settling slowly into the tumbling water with a loud sigh. She reached for the cognac and took a sip. When the water was deep enough, she raised her knees and slid her upper body completely under the water, her left arm holding the glass in the air as she waited for the hot water to wash away the last traces of a horrible evening.

Surfacing, she took another sip of cognac, welcoming the familiar steadying warmth in her stomach. That goddamn Tizzy Hudson. Had to go to MCRD. But then a voice in her mind intruded: It wasn't Tizzy Hudson who got to going out there on the dance floor in the middle of a crowd of drunk Marines. Nobody made you slug down three glasses of booze in an hour, and nobody kept you from getting out to the car by midnight. Face it, child, you turned it loose out there. What had that animal said? You been shaking your ass at me all night . . . well, that wasn't true—she had never seen him. But she had been shaking it, and from long experience, she knew exactly the effect she was having on those men, the ones dancing with and near her, and the others, staring from the tables clustered around the dance floor. You're still a tease, aren't you? Your Boston ways coming out even after three and a half years of marriage.

The problems had begun when she elected to major in business after her freshman year. For all her feigned indifference, the condescending smiles from all those bright northern boys in the business school had at first intimidated and then infuriated her. She could still remember the mocking asides about the southern belle studying men's work and the patronizing questions about how did one make really good southern biscuits. It wasn't that she was not making good grades, she simply was not fitting in. She had tried to affect the offhand, understated dress and casual intellectual attitudes of the northern girls but had not been able to carry it off; too many years of Atlanta training got in the way. She had become increasingly depressed, until she was rescued by her roommate, Julia, an extremely plain-looking young woman with a flair for economics.

Julia had set her straight: "You've got the brains, Maddy; you simply need to differentiate your markets. The business school is a man's world, so first you have to deal with the men, then you can deal with the business school. With your looks, the secret is simple: Tantalize the bastards. Turn on that southern charm, never appear in class without a lot of attention to makeup, perfume, and flattering skirts, move into their personal space, touch their arms and hands when you talk to them until they're a bunch of quivering wrecks, and then bat your pretty blues at them with a soft 'Bye, darlin, and thanks.' And do precisely the opposite to the professors: Sit up front, pay studious attention, and let your hair fall over one side of your face and stare directly into their faces when they're lecturing. But don't *do* anything, no leg-crossing peep show, no asking questions, and never speak directly to them until they first speak to you. Then be shy, be unsure if you should even be taking the great man's time. The straight ones will want you to come around for after-hours conferences and the fairies will want to know how you manage that hair. You've got this dynamite aura of bedroom presence, Maddy, so flaunt it with the boys and withhold it from the men, and you'll go through this so-called man's world here like a hot knife through butter."

When she had stopped laughing, Maddy had seen the sense of it. Hell, this was no different from the way southern women kept southern manhood in perpetual thrall. Every girl from a good family in Atlanta practiced those rules every day. Her momma would have approved, had Maddy been willing to give her the satisfaction of knowing.

She had graduated from the business college with distinction, having decimated the sexual psyches of half the business-management class and doing some serious damage to two or three professorial egos. But that was all in the past, or supposed to be. She was married now, and that's not how married women, especially southern married women, were supposed to act. And yet here she was, pulling the same old game at the Marine Officers' Club, for God's sake. She sighed again. This wasn't where things were supposed to be after three and a half years of marriage. Brian in WESTPAC and his devoted wife letting her hair down and her skirts up at the local meat market, and nearly getting raped in the process. Momma would definitely not approve of this kind of behavior; in fact, Momma would have pitched a proper fit.

She leaned back in the water, sliding down until the towel just touched it. She examined her body, shimmering just beneath the surface. Still too short, she thought, but all the basic equipment seemed to be in order. She had full, round breasts, which Brian, ever the sailor, had immediately christened port and starboard. Port was a little bigger than starboard, a source of endless fascination to her husband. She could still wear waist-size 26 jeans, but she would never have a flat tummy, and only her frequent tennis workouts kept her from developing what she would consider thunder thighs. But all in all, she knew she was very sexy and that men usually stopped what they were doing when she came by in a flattering skirt. A lot of good that did her, with her husband over there in some Gulf place. She closed her eyes and let the water do its work.

Three and a half years—or, to be more precise, three years with, a half year without during the *Decatur* deployment and his training schools enroute to *Hood,* keeping score like any good Navy wife. She had met Brian on a Newport weekend during her senior year at college. He was attending a Navy school, and she was part of a mixed-doubles group partying at the Old Viking Hotel in downtown Newport. Her date, an MBA student at the business school, had decided to impress her by drinking himself stupid. She had noticed the young naval officer with the boyish face giving her the eye, and he had moved in from the dance floor, whisking her off into the crowd as the pride of Harvard passed out in a sloppy heap on the table.

She had just pinched off a steamy relationship with her business-ethics professor after he started talking about breaking up his marriage, so she was subconsciously ready for something different. But Brian, with his aggressive enthusiasm about a Navy career, unassuming ways, and infectious smile, had simply ambushed her. Used to dealing with men on a strictly manipulative basis, she had few defenses against a handsome young man who was genuinely delighted to be in her company, impressed but not threatened by her academic achievements, and lots of fun in the bargain. He thoroughly turned her head. They had dated for three months, mostly in Newport, where he had a bachelor pad out near Easton's Beach, and only occasionally up in Boston for the obligatory dose of culture. Then he had left Newport for a ship in Norfolk, giving her her first taste of the gone dimensions of Navy life. But the pain of separation had been masked by the excitement of upcoming graduation, the end of school, and dreamy, passionate letters that preceded hurried weekends in New York City, which was budgetarily halfway between Norfolk and Boston. The weekends had started out being touring safaris around the city, but they had increasingly become love-soaked forty-eights in a succession of darkened hotel rooms.

Brian was the first man she had been with who seemed to assume that they should take love to its natural conclusion and get married. He was completely different from the young men of Boston, most of whom affected a pseudointellectual indifference to getting involved, because careers, you understand, had to be attended to first. When Brian started talking marriage, Maddy found herself thrilled, although she had had to think about it, because up to now, men had been, generally speaking, means to various ends. Given the events of her late childhood, getting married took on an increased significance. Her marriage was definitely not going to turn out like her parents'.

But Brian, with his genuine affection for her and his sincere belief in the natural course of love, prevailed, and they were married in a simple ceremony at the Navy chapel in Norfolk, with the wardroom officers of *Decatur* in splendid crossed-sword attendance. Getting married in the Navy chapel had neatly sidestepped the logistics problem of who put on the wedding, and the captain had happily consented to give her away. Her mother had come, of course, as always the eternal gracious southern lady, the disapproval in her eyes glittering dangerously above the perpetual smile with which she continued to plow through life. Mother, dearest Mother—Mrs. Frances Madison McNair, the poor thing, abandoned by her awful husband, the banker. Just like that. Can you just imagine? Maddy could just imagine. I had to go all the way to goddamned Boston to get away from Mother and the cloying social webs of Atlanta, yes, ma'am, GA.

She would have given just about anything for her father to have been there. But her father, the banker, had left them one day in the same brisk style with which he had made his fortune in Atlanta after the war, which was with grace, beaming good humor, and politely disarming efficiency. Two weeks into her sophomore year at the Marshall Academy in Buckhead, her father had announced brightly at breakfast one Saturday morning that he was leaving his two gracious southern ladies to get on with the rest of his life. Their big house on Randolph Street was bought and paid for, he declared, and there was a trust fund in the bank for the proper keeping of his wife and the household, and another one for Maddy's college education, provided that she went to school well north of the Mason-Dixon line. With her mother sitting in stunned silence for the one and only time in Maddy's living memory, her father had come around the table, kissed each of them on the forehead, paused for a moment in the doorway to survey the wreckage, and walked out of their lives and Atlanta forever.

For Maddy McNair, the next three years at home had been an unsettling time of complicated stories, carefully choreographed social adjustments, a graceful withdrawal from the Driving Club (even though her mother was a Madison, Father had been the member) and other face-saving gestures aimed at defining their changed status in proper Atlanta society, and the opening of a deep chasm of antagonism between mother and daughter. Maddy remembered those years as serial images, each framed in a halo of sepia-colored insubstantiality, scene after scene of role-playing propelled by an increasingly urgent longing for the day when she, too, could make a grand announcement and leave her mother. Maddy now understood that most daughters and mothers were bound to battle, but in her heart she still blamed her mother for driving her father away at a time when her own adolescent devotion to him was in full flower.

When it had come time for her to choose a college, the conditions of her trust fund and the association of the name Massachusetts with everything antithetical to the South led her directly to Boston. The daughter of a banker at least in spirit, if no longer in fact, she had elected to take a degree in financial management. Graduation with honors had made possible the management intern position she now held with the giant California financial conglomerate, Bank of America. Who would expect her to be on deck at eight-thirty tomorrow—correction, today—Miss Priss, bright-eyed and bushy-tailed, for the morning staff meeting. She groaned and pulled the plug with her toe.

She got out of the tub, dried off, and slipped into her nightgown. She dried her hair with an electric blower, brushed her teeth, tipped the rest of the cognac into the sink, and went back through the apartment, turning off lights and checking the locks. Slipping into the queen-sized bed with a sigh, Maddy turned off the bedside lamp, automatically hugging the second pillow.

Brian, she thought, where the hell are you? As she tried to squeeze out of her mind the memory of the foregoing hours, she felt more and more like an ass. Getting married had not been a trivial proposition for her, especially given what she had been through when her father decamped. Brian had been so different from the boys she had known in Atlanta and in college up north. His love for her seemed to be pretty uncomplicated, and he was direct, fun, interested in life, serious about his career for the right reasons, and determined to do a good job at whatever he tackled, including marriage. But the fitness reports from *Decatur* had been a real surprise, and the scope of his new job in *Hood* another one. The combination of those two things, the upcoming promotion board and her own distress at the length of the deployment, had not helped matters between them.

She stared up in the darkness, watching but not seeing the reflections of passing car headlights as they rippled across the ceiling. In retrospect, she also realized that she had not been sufficiently sensitive to how much he wanted children. She could not really put her finger on why she was hesitating, but the more he pushed, the more she had been resisting. She sensed that it was psychological and related to what had happened in her own family, but she had shied away from really trying to figure it out, hiding instead behind her stubborn streak when Brian pushed the issue. And now what? How in the hell do we resolve some of these things by mail?

There had been no real mail since the ship left Pearl Harbor, only a couple of gushy Hawaiian postcards. The painful awkwardness of deployment day still weighed on her mind. She should have gone. She had been the only wardroom wife less one not on the pier, a fact that was conspicuously not mentioned at the "wake" held on the evening of deployment day by the captain's wife. She should have done what Angela Benedetti had, even if the thought of going home to Momma was untenable. The silence in the apartment brought to mind the image of the anguish on Brian's face when he'd left, and her own when he had gone out the door. She cared deeply for him, and somehow she had managed to make him feel guilty about going off to do what successful naval officers did: go to sea.

She had written three long, emotional letters after the ship left, trying to express how she really felt, how she wasn't mad at him for the separation, how it was the goddamned Navy and its interminable deployments, but she had torn up each of them after the captain's wife had explained the rules about mail to those wives facing their first WESTPAC deployment. With a minimum of four weeks between dispatch of a letter and receipt of a reply, there were some things that were too sensitive to deal with in letters. There were too many opportunities for inflicting unintentional hurt and for totally missed communications. Beyond that, the mail pipeline itself was fragile: Letters went from San Diego to the Fleet Post Office in San Francisco, then by military cargo planes to Clark Air Force Base in the Philippines, and then by truck to Cubi Point in Subic Bay, and from Cubi by carrier cargo plane to the carrier on Yankee Station in the Gulf, and from the carrier to the ships by the daily logistics helicopter.

"Everybody tries his best," Mrs. Huntington had said. "But there's a war on, you know, and letters do get lost. If you want to pour your heart out, do it on one of these cassette tapes. Hold on to it for a couple of days and then listen to it before you mail it. Ask yourself, what's he supposed to do with this? It's okay to tell him you miss him, that you're lonely, that life's a drag while he's gone. But won't wander into Indian territory: Don't lay down ultimatums, don't berate the Navy, and don't talk about other men. Don't say things that require a reaction, because with that much dead time, the reaction will be meaningless. They're at sea in a war zone; they've got enough to worry about without your piling it on."

She had gone home to think, then realized that, in tearing up her first letters, she had guaranteed that Brian would not get any mail from her in Pearl or even Subic. She had hurriedly written what the other wives called a weekly report letter, filled with trivial news about her job, the car, the wives' social activities, a letter deliberately devoid of real feelings. Only in closing had she said that she loved him and missed him terribly.

The captain's wife had also explained that wives could not blame the Navy for the deployment without attacking their husbands' careers. Your husbands can't do anything about the Navy and its deployments except leave it. If you constantly complain about the Navy, you implicitly, and perhaps unintentionally, pose the question of their having to choose between you and the Navy. Don't pose that choice unless you can stand *all* the possible answers.

But during that first week after the ship had left, she had almost convinced herself that this was the issue. Brian was gone for the next half a year, and she was already miserable. As much as she tried to repress the preceding hours, the earthy side of her personality that had shown its grinning face earlier in the evening only heightened her fear about being left alone. If tonight's any indication, what kind of a basket case am I going to be seven months from now? Even as she asked herself this question, she realized that the one person who could answer it was beyond the asking, vanished down the black hole of a WESTPAC deployment. Her husband was now a disembodied voice, diminished to a piece of paper in her mailbox, if every element of the Navy mail system worked right.

6

Subic Bay

Chief Wesley Jackson stood just inside the forward end of the mess decks, leaning against a bulkhead with his arms folded, as the crew began to file in for the evening meal. "The Sheriff," as *Hood*'s chief master-at-arms was known, was a well-built forty-four-year-old black man who had been a chief gunner's mate before converting to the master-at-arms rating three years before joining *Hood*. At nearly six feet tall, with a gleaming head, round face, and piercing black eyes, he presented a no-nonsense, even stern, demeanor, befitting a man who had spent many years on deck with five-inch guns and rough-cut gunner's mates.

Wesley Jackson came from Chicago and had developed many of the tough traits for which his hometown was famous. He had been distracted from the streets through the intervention of the local police Boys Club, and all through his adolescent years he'd yearned to become a cop. His father had never really been in the family picture, and his mother had simply carried on the business of raising Wesley and six more brothers and sisters. When the money got tight, Jackson had dropped out of high school to find a job, which doomed his chances for the police force. When he turned eighteen, his former mentor in the Boys Club had steered him to the military. His first choice was the Marines, but the Marine recruiter had been on a road trip, and the Navy chief holding down the office that day had seen his chance. Wesley never looked back, but he had still harbored the desire to be a cop during all those years as a gunner's mate. When the Navy-wide call had been issued for volunteers to become professional MAAs, Wesley Jackson had answered. In the intervening years, he had finished his high school GED and even achieved a year's worth of college credits during his only shore-duty tour.

Jackson was unmarried and sometimes regretted that fact, especially on those emotional days when ships came home from a long deployment. Nothing was quite so lonely as a ship on homecoming day about an hour after the married men had left with their families. The Jackson family had been raised on an ethic of hard work, high personal standards, and a strong sense of duty. Two of his brothers had joined the Army and a third worked for Cook County, Illinois. His three sisters had married young and were still married. But when Jackson realized that the ways of the Navy were incompatible with what he knew would be his strong sense of duty to a wife and children, he had chosen to stick with the Navy. His sisters and brothers had produced a crowd of kids, to whom he was Uncle Wesley, so there were plenty of nephews and nieces back home should he want to be around children, and Navy towns were always full of women.

In his reincarnation as an MAA, Jackson tended to take everything pretty seriously. His tailored khaki uniforms and spit-shined shoes made it clear that he believed in setting military uniform grooming standards by personal example. Because of his baldness, he looked older than he was, but he was well spoken, reserved, and watchful, and he was one of only two chief petty officers in the ship who had some college time.

As the ship's chief master-at-arms, Jackson was responsible for enforcing regulations and maintaining good order and discipline. He supervised the MAA force, which consisted of six first class petty officers who served as masters-at-arms within their duty sections in port, in addition to their regular divisional duties. The MAA force was analogous to a part-time police force in the ship. The first class MAAs were distinguished from the rest of the crew by silver badges worn on the left breast pocket of their chambray shirts. If there was an altercation or other disruption to the day's routine, the bridge would pass the word for the duty MAA to lay down to the compartment involved. If the problem was large enough, the call would go out for all MAAs not actually on watch to visit the scene of the problem.

Jackson wore a gold MAA badge in recognition of the fact that he performed his duties as a full-time job. He worked directly for the executive officer on the so-called executive staff, along with the chief hospital corpsman, the doc, and his assistant, the baby doc, as well as the chief yeoman and chief personnelman. Jackson maintained a small office on Broadway, the *Hood*'s central passageway, which contained a desk, two chairs, two file cabinets, and a bulky evidence safe. Most of his time was spent supervising the pursuit of petty crimes, such as wallets being stolen, locker break-ins, fistfights, curfew violations, insubordination to senior petty officers—shirking, in short, the typical problems encountered in any military organization that spent the bulk of its time training and maintaining.

Jackson surveyed the mess decks as the men came off the chow line and settled at the tables. He was always fascinated by how they grouped: the blacks sitting separate from the whites, the engineers from the deck apes, the nonrated men from the petty officers. The younger black sailors especially interested him. For the past three years, the Navy had been making a significant and apparently sincere effort to expose and expunge racism throughout the fleet by using a variety of human-relations and leadership and management programs, of which Jackson had been a willing supporter. He was well aware that, as a result of the civil rights turmoil throughout the country, the races were deeply polarized in the Navy's ships. Black men, especially the young nonrated black men in the crew, tended to stick together, practicing a kind of reverse segregation now that race relations were increasingly becoming a big deal. Young blacks in the Navy reflected all of the hostility and anger that characterized black-white relations in America at large, driven as much by the watershed civil rights movement as by the growing recognition that young black men were filling a disproportionate share of the body bags coming back from Vietnam. Black militancy was barely being kept in check by the restraints of military discipline, as evidenced by racial disturbances aboard several ships. Older black petty officers and chiefs, who had learned to accommodate the system, were as suspicious of the younger blacks as were their white counterparts, because they felt that the young hotheads were going to screw things up for everybody, which, in turn, further isolated the young blacks.

White crew members were indignant at all the noise about race and angry about having to undergo mandatory racial-sensitivity training, what they called "hug 'em and love 'em" sessions. But some were beginning to realize their discomfiture with the process stemmed in part from the fact that racism had long been institutionalized in the Navy. Jackson remembered one counselor's remark during a racial-sensitivity session back in Dago: A white man sees six white sailors congregating on the fantail; they're shooting the shit; six black men congregating on the fantail are undoubtedly planning a race riot. He also remembered the muttered, "Well, yeah!" reactions that had floated around the mostly white classroom. But he was becoming bitterly disappointed with many of the younger blacks, whose resentments blinded them to the opportunities being offered in the service. To his disgust, many of them used reverse segregation as some kind of statement, as if to say, Now that you want us to be part of you, up yours.

He knew that when the hotheads congregated, the name of Chief Wesley Jackson was firmly enshrined on the Uncle Tom list, along with the ship's black Supply officer, Raiford Hatcher, and three other chief petty officers. He tended to respond to their contempt for him by exacting even stricter standards of discipline, military appearance, and military courtesy from them than he ever applied to junior white people. But in truth, any individuals or groups in the ship that exhibited a defiant stance attracted Jackson's undivided attention.

He looked at his watch. Sea detail would go down in forty-five minutes. Stifling a yawn, he decided to head back to the chiefs' mess to have supper. This looked like a perfectly normal night on the mess decks. Even though they were in Subic, he wasn't expecting any trouble, since the crew was not going to be going over on liberty. The ship was scheduled to sail in two hours for the Gulf. He clenched his mouth into a flat line. The less time spent alongside the pier in places like Subic, the fewer problems for the Sheriff. He was ready to get her up to the Gulf, back out to sea, where ships and sailors belonged, by God.

7

The Gulf of Tonkin

The console chairs in Combat trembled to the vibrations of *Hood*'s twin screws driving her along at twenty-seven knots. Brian Holcomb stood behind the weapons control console, dressed out for general quarters with a steel helmet over his intercom headphone, an inflatable life jacket strapped around his hips, a long-sleeve khaki shirt, and his trouser legs tucked into his socks. Combat was dark, hot, and humid, with the full GQ team present and every station and console manned up. Over his shoulder, he could see the captain in his high-backed chair and Austin standing behind the central command console. To his left, in the surface module, the gunnery officer and the CIC officer leaned over the surface plotting table as the gunfire support team set up the target coordinates and coaxed the computers below onto a smooth track.

Brian sensed the tension in Combat as *Hood* plunged along in formation with two other destroyers on her first real combat mission. They had steamed out of Subic two days ago and had begun standing Red Crown watches as they drove across the South China Sea at seventeen knots. Normally, they would have made a straight shot northwest up to the PIRAZ station to relieve the nuclear cruiser *Long Beach* on station. Instead, they had diverted to the west to rendezvous with a task unit consisting of the guided-missile destroyer *Berkeley* and the all-gun destroyer *Hull. Berkeley* was carrying a Destroyer Division commander, and *Hood* chopped to his tactical command for the operation.

Brian had studied up on the Sea Dragon operations for the past two nights while standing his training watches as evaluator in Combat. The CTF 77 periodically sent groups of destroyers up off the North Vietnamese coast to conduct shore-bombardment operations against concentrations of the North Vietnamese army whenever they gathered within naval gunfire range above the so-called demilitarized zone (DMZ) between North and South Vietnam. The ships would typically rendezvous in darkness well offshore, form a column, and then race in at twenty-seven knots, usually just at sunrise, turn parallel to the target area along the coast, and open fire with their long-range five-inch guns at preplanned targets that lay within eight to ten miles of the coast. The attacks were not necessarily as accurate as sending in carrier bombers, but there was the decided advantage of not having to risk airplanes or pilots flying into heavily defended troop concentrations. The destroyers would usually fire two hundred rounds each and then turn out to sea before the North Vietnamese coastal-defense artillery batteries could find the range and hit back. During his prebrief, Austin had made it clear that *Hood,* a PIRAZ-capable ship packed full of sensitive electronics systems, would normally never be risked in this kind of operation. The two destroyers carried five guns between them, but only three of these were operational, due to equipment problems on both ships. CTF 77 had decided to send *Hood,* with her one gun, to augment the task unit.

The mission put Brian and his Weapons Department directly in the spotlight. He had met with his gunnery team the night before down in Main Battery Plot, the gunfire computer room two decks below the waterline. The gunnery officer, Ens. John McCarthy, and the first lieutenant, Ens. Jack Folsom, had been joined by the chief gunner's mate, Max Carpenter, and the gunfire control chief, Marty VanHorn, in the cramped quarters of the gun system computer room. It was the first time that Brian had met with the gunnery team for anything but an exercise.

"Okay, guys," he began. "This is a little out of the ordinary for *Hood,* but we do carry that five-inch fifty-four back aft, and the bosses wanted us to go kill a Commie for Mommy."

"Suits the shit outta me," said VanHorn, a leathery individual who wore his hair in a waxed flattop and who was reportedly a genius at repairing the ship's MK 68 gunfire control system.

"How many rounds?" asked Chief Carpenter.

"They want a hundred and fifty from us," answered Ensign McCarthy. John McCarthy was known as "Pretty Boy" in keeping with the Navy's tradition of sometimes bestowing nicknames that were precisely inappropriate. McCarthy personified the word *homely,* if not downright coyote ugly, but Brian had found him to be a reliable officer who did a conscientious job with a minimum of noise.

Ensign Folsom, the first lieutenant, and technically Chief Martinez's boss, had come aboard the same week as Brian. He had been an offensive tackle on the Penn State football team. He was almost as big as the chief, and between the two of them, Brian expected little trouble out of First Division. Folsom whistled at the number of rounds required.

"That gun good for a hundred fifty rounds without busting something?" Brian asked McCarthy.

"I actually kinda doubt it," intervened Chief Carpenter. "You know how it is, boss," he said. "We fire that thing maybe six, ten times a year, twenty rounds a pop, for exercises. This here ship, the action's in CIC with the Red Crown stuff. These five-inch fifty-fours, you gotta shoot 'em all the time if you want 'em to stay up. And even then, they break. Look at *Berkeley* and *Hull:* They do nothing but shoot, and they got only three outta five guns up and running."

Brian had stared hard at the chief. He did not like what he was hearing. This was going to be the ship's first mission in WESTPAC, and it was going to be a Weapons Department show. The chief's frank admission that the gun might not be up to shooting a continuous stream of 150 rounds without having a mechanical failure was disturbing, but even more disturbing was the realization that the chief was probably right. Chief Carpenter had begun to squirm a little under Brian's look. Ensign McCarthy was staring hard at the deck. Chief VanHorn came to their rescue.

"Mr. Holcomb, you come from the tin-can Navy. You know that's straight skinny. We're all the time asking to shoot Mount Fifty-one and even the three-inchers. But

Mr. Austin, he doesn't wanta hear that shit. The Ops chiefs have told us that Austin's convinced the shock from the gun raises hell with his electronic systems, like the forty radar or the NTDS. You've felt it—that gun bein' all the way back on the fantail *does* put a whip in *Hood*'s tailbone. So he talks to the Old Man, and the Old Man, he puts us off. For *Hood*, PIRAZ is where it's at, not gun shoots."

"Is the gun system fully operational, Chief?" asked Brian, his voice taking on a formal note. VanHorn got the picture.

"Yes, sir. We did op checks and safety checks, and she's ready to go."

"Well?"

VanHorn hesitated, measuring his words. "Well, Mr. Holcomb, after the first twenty or thirty rounds, I can't guarantee she'll stay on the line. Them damn things are temperamental. Everybody knows that."

Brian straightened on his stool. "Well, gents, I'm temperamental myself. I owned three five-inch fifty-fours on my previous ship as Weps boss, and my guns worked. Five rounds or fifty. And if we East Coast LANTFLEET pussies can manage it, I expect you grizzled WESTPAC veterans to manage it—in your sleep. If that son of a bitch stops firing back there, I better see assholes and elbows flying into that gun pit to get her going again. Understand? And keep in mind, this isn't San Clemente Island we're shooting at—these guys shoot back, and if I were them, I'd shoot at the first ship whose gun stops working. Now. Mr. McCarthy, let's run through the prefire brief."

Brian reviewed the prefire in his mind as he watched the formation take shape on the radarscope. The shimmering green outline of the North Vietnamese coast filled the northwestern sector of the radar screen as the bright pip in the center representing *Hood* merged into the column of three—*Hood* in the middle, *Berkeley* astern at one thousand yards, and *Hull* in the van one thousand yards ahead of *Hood*. He wondered again whether he had set the gunnery crew up for an accident with his little tirade. The five-inch fifty-fours were notorious for electrical and hydraulic failures. His crew had been only telling the truth about the likelihood of such a failure from lack of regular firing, and he would have to rectify that with the captain once this mission was over. It was also true that the five-inch gun was sometimes capable of doing shock damage to the big air search radars, such as the three-dimensional SPS-48, or the two-dimensional SPS-40. But he was damned if he was going to begin his tour as Weapons officer listening to excuses about the guns or any other Weapons Department system. He looked over at the captain, who was watching the plotting team set up in the surface module. The exec, who had come in from the bridge wearing a flak jacket, steel helmet, and binoculars hanging from his neck, saw Brian looking and gave him a broad wink and a grin, as if to say, Go get 'em tiger.

"Plot set!" announced Lt. Gerry Beasely over the intercom. Beasely was the ship's CIC officer in charge at the naval gunfire support plotting table. "Computer checks SAT. Mount Fifty-one in automatic, rounds loaded to the transfer trays, able-able common set for surface burst at sixty feet."

"Very well," responded Brian. He looked over at Beasely, standing in the surface module ten feet away. Beasely, wearing a sound-powered phone headset, nodded back at him. So far so good. They felt the ship swing into station in the line of ships and steady up on a northeasterly heading. Brian could visualize the gun mount on the fantail, the long gray barrel trained out over the lifelines to the north, rock-steady as the ship rolled gently in the seaway, the train warning bell ringing under the back of the mount to keep people from getting near a firing gun mount.

Not that that's likely, thought Brian. The ship's at general quarters. There better not be anybody walking around on deck.

"Weapons Control, Director One."

Brian closed his intercom key. "Control."

"Mount Fifty-one looking good. Stable track in train and elevation. Pecker's up about forty degrees."

"Elevation angle is forty-two degrees, range nineteen

73

thousand, seven hundred yards," announced Chief VanHorn from gun plot.

"How's the solution, Chief?" asked Brian.

"Smooth as a baby's ass, Control."

At that moment, the encrypted task unit maneuvering radio circuit in D and D crackled into life with a tone burst.

"Impulse, this is Magnavox. Stand by to commence firing in three-zero seconds. Report if not, I say again, if not ready, over?"

The captain swiveled around to look at Brian, as did Austin and the exec. Brian gave a thumbs-up and the captain turned back around in his chair. Neither of the other two ships came up on the circuit. The exec headed back out onto the bridge, which was his station when the captain was in CIC.

"Control, Director One, I can see *Berkeley* trained out. I can't see *Hull*—she's in my blind zone."

"Control, aye." Brian wished he was topside in the boxy gun director atop the helicopter hangar back aft. In *Decatur*, he would have been out on the windswept bridge, where he could physically see his guns. He felt uncomfortable and less in control running things from inside the CIC. His mouth went dry as he wondered how the gun would perform.

"Impulse, this is Magnavox. Commence firing. Commence firing."

"Batteries released," declared the captain.

Brian keyed his intercom: "Batteries released, commence firing!"

The gun answered with a muffled, thumping *boom,* then a dreadful pause that caused Brian to hold his breath, and then a steady progression of *boom, thump, boom, thump* as the recoil shook the ship along her length. Brian could hear the dull thuds of the other ships firing between the concussions of Mount Fifty-one interspersed with muffled "Yeahs!" and "Go, Mount Fifty-one!" from the other module crews. He keyed the mike again.

"Director One, Control, be alert for any signs of counterbattery. Remember your procedures."

"Director One, aye!" Folsom sounded excited, his voice pitching high. Brian could hear the sounds of the forty-knot wind whistling through Folsom's mike, and the boom turned into a loud bang in his headset when Folsom keyed his mike. Brian yearned to be outside where he could see. Suddenly, he heard a commotion as a chorus of groans swept through Combat. At first, he did not understand, then he did. He felt the change in the ship's motion. *Hood* was slowing down, her bows beginning to mush into the seas instead of pounding them flat.

"Control, Director One, I can't see shit! Snipes are making black smoke from number-one stack. Damn!" shouted Folsom, coughing into his mike.

"Get down inside the director and button up, Director One."

"Director One, aye," replied Folsom, still coughing. Mount Fifty-one continued to boom in reassuring cadence. The captain was bent over the squawk box, talking urgently to the chief engineer down in Main Engineering Control four decks below. Then the radio circuit came up again.

"Tango Four, this is Magnavox. Cease making smoke! I say again, cease making smoke, over?"

The captain nodded to Austin, who rogered for the order over the maneuvering net.

"Control, Plot, what the fuck's going on? We're getting power fluctuations down here."

"Plot, Director One, Control, hang on, something's gone wrong in the main spaces. Sounds like a boiler problem."

"Control, Director One, *Berkeley*'s gonna run up our ass in a minute. Aw shit, now number-two stack's making smoke. Now I really can't see, Control!"

Brian's mind whirled. The ship was losing propulsion power and slowing down in the middle of twenty-seven-knot formation, with the tail end destroyer coming up from behind, close enough for her guns to be clearly audible through the CIC bulkheads over the sound of *Hood*'s own gun. The captain and the Ops officer were both shouting at once, and then came the dreaded sound of a general electrical power failure, with all the lights going dim and then out and the vent fans on the consoles winding down in a pathetic spiral of diminishing sound. Mount Fifty-one stopped firing as the weapons control systems lost electrical power, and everyone in CIC seemed to be shouting at the same time to turn off equipment. He saw Gerry Beasely take off his headset and throw it down on the deck plates cursing furiously.

Brian reached down and switched his intercom set from the electrical intercom to the sound-powered control circuit.

"Director One, Control."

Silence. The shouting of orders in CIC got louder and then diminished. Without power, the sixty men in Combat were next to useless.

"Director One, Control!"

"Control, this is Plot. We're up on the JC and JP circuits. I'll get him for you."

"Control, this is Director One on JC."

"Yeah, Jack, okay. What's happening out there?" Brian felt *Hood* beginning to wallow from side to side as she lost speed. The sound of another ship's five-inchers was much louder now, a steady double *blam* sound clearly audible throughout the CIC.

"Control, Director One, *Berkeley*'s hauled out and coming by on our port side, still firing. I can't see a fucking thing astern but black smoke—we must look like we're on fire or something. It looks like a refinery fire behind us."

Brian thought fast, reviewing procedures for a power failure. He knew the ship's emergency generators would be lighting off in a moment.

"All stations, Control, it looks like the snipes lost the load, both ends, and we're going DIW. Strip down all power loads so we don't overload the emergency diesels. Plot, we got a hot gun back there? Gimme a bore report."

"Plot, aye, yes, sir, we technically have a hot gun— fifty-six rounds in less than two minutes. Hang on." There was a long moment of silence, then the chief's voice returned. "Mount reports bore's clear, so no problem."

Brian acknowledged and reported the bore clear to the captain, who gave him a distracted thumbs-up acknowledgment as he listened to the chief engineer on the squawk box. Benedetti's voice rose hysterically out of the box from Main Control. He was almost drowned out by the sounds of engineers yelling and the sound of steam or compressed air escaping in the background.

Brian took a deep breath and wiped his face with his hand. With the air-conditioning systems gone, the temperature in Combat was already rising. Fifty-six rounds. Not too shabby, as they said out here in the Seventh Fleet. But also not 150. He wondered fleetingly whether the power failure had saved him from the embarrassment of a gun failure. We'll never know, said a voice in his head. He felt relieved and guilty simultaneously.

The CIC watch standers were grabbing for loose gear as the ship began to roll more heavily. The only light came from battery-operated battle lanterns positioned around the bulkheads. Console operators were fastening their seat belts and talking quietly. The sounds of *Berkeley*'s guns moved forward and away from them as she raced past outside at twenty-seven knots, rocking *Hood* with her wake moments later. With CIC hot, dark, and blind, the captain left D and D to go out to the bridge. Brian was wiping his mouth with the back of his hand when he heard a rapid-fire *thump-thump* from somewhere aft. Every man in CIC heard it at the same time. Not a one of them had ever heard that sound before and yet every man knew instantly what it was.

"Whoa, Control, Plot this is Director One! Counterbattery! Counterbattery!" shrilled Ensign Folsom over the sound-powered phones. "Port side, astern of us, three hundred yards! Right on the edge of the smoke."

Having been a gunnery officer, Brian knew the drill: Direct Plot to switch control of the gun mount to the director officer. The mount would be slaved electrically to the director's movements, so when the director officer pointed his optics at the gun flashes on the beach, assuming he could see where the shooter was, the gun's barrel would be pointed where the optics were looking. He was keying down his mike when he remembered that, without power, none of this would work. The ship was helpless, unable to shoot back until power was restored.

"Well, you might as well sit back and enjoy it, Director One. Ain't shit we can do about it now," drawled Chief VanHorn from down in Plot.

"We need to turn this hog around and get back in our own smoke screen," shouted Folsom.

"COUNTERBATTERY, COUNTERBATTERY," announced the 1MC, as if no one knew that the ship was under fire. "ALL HANDS TOPSIDE. TAKE COVER, ON THE DOUBLE!"

The voice on the 1MC sounded to Brian like that of the exec. He doubted anyone topside needed to be told to take cover. *Hood* was really beginning to roll now. With almost no "way" on the ship, she was turning across the wind and the seas. Brian felt utterly useless, but technically he could not leave his station. He could no longer hear the other destroyers' guns. The noise level in Combat was down to next to nothing; the men looked anxiously at one another and waited to see what would happen next. Brian knew that the ship had two emergency generators, but from the sound of things down in Main Control, it did not appear likely that the engineers had things sorted out yet. His thoughts were interrupted by a sound like a giant sheet of canvas being ripped in two above the ship, followed by two more thumps that were clearly a lot closer than the first two.

"Control, Director One, those were pretty fucking close!"

"At least they're going off in the water, Director One," said the calm voice of the chief. "They go to frag, you sightseers are in for some interesting shit."

"Easy for you to say, Chief. You're below the waterline."

Brian broke in. "Keep your head down, Jack. I'm sure the snipes are busting their asses to get some steam up. They can hear those things in the main holes, too, you know."

"Director One, aye."

Across the room in D and D, Austin was conferring anxiously on a sound-powered phone with the computer center one deck below as the electronics technicians assessed the damage from the power drop. The ship's complex radars and computers were very sensitive to power fluctuations. A clean power drop usually did little damage, but a lingering voltage ramp-down like this one often burned out vital electronic components. Brian wedged himself in between the engagement controller and the fire control systems coordinator consoles to keep upright as the ship rolled deeply. They must be almost dead in the water. The two chiefs sitting the consoles looked up at him and shook their heads.

"Fucking snipes," growled Chief Iverson, the senior missiles radar chief. He was worried about his SPS-48 radar. If the 48 had been damaged, their whole PIRAZ capability was endangered.

The sound of ripping canvas came again and everyone tensed, trying to shrink into their seats without anyone seeing. There was a second of deathly silence, followed by a single thump. As everyone began to exhale, there was a loud bang from the port side, followed by a very loud rattle of what sounded like hail all along the port-side bulkheads of CIC. A fluorescent light fixture exploded in a dusty popping noise over the aisle leading to the ASW module, and a radarman third class named Festerman, standing by the tracking table, grabbed his left hand.

"Fuck me!" he howled, staring at his hand as blood welled up through his fingers and dripped all over the dead-reckoning tracer table. Several men got up at once to help Festerman, who continued to stand there in shock, staring at his bloody hand.

"Director One, you catch any of that?" Brian asked. His throat clenched as he realized that the enemy's shrapnel had penetrated the CIC.

"Looks like we finally got the paint chipped out on the director, Control, but we're all okay. You should see the spray pattern that one made. This isn't little stuff they're shooting."

The surface module team quickly bandaged up the radarman's hand as Austin, his face pale, reported one injury in CIC and possible equipment damage from shrapnel. The ship was rolling steadily now, making it difficult to stand up. Brian felt like the proverbial fish in a barrel, standing in a darkened and useless CIC while the bad guys fired heavy artillery at them. He decided to go to the bridge. He passed over the headset to Chief Iverson.

"I'm going out to the bridge, Chief. You have control."

"Aye, sir. Keep your head down."

Brian opened the front door to CIC, stepped into the small vestibule by the navigator's chart room, and then stepped through another door out into a blaze of morning sunlight. He blinked against the glare and saw the captain and the exec standing over on the port bridge wing, binoculars to their faces, the captain now wearing his steel helmet and flak jacket. The lookouts were clustered in the pilothouse with the rest of the bridge team, with everyone trying to stand on the starboard side without seeming to do so. About a mile off the port bow, he could see that both *Berkeley* and *Hull* were turning around. They were steaming across the glinting gray sea in a loose column at high speed, pointed to pass between *Hood* and the shooters on the beach. Both ships were streaming copious amounts of black smoke from their stacks. As he watched, *Berkeley* swung her forward gun mount to face the shore and opened a brisk fire. *Hull* joined her a moment later with two guns.

Brian started over to join the captain and the exec on the bridge wing, when the tearing sound of two more incoming shells stopped him in his tracks. This time, he got to watch as one burst underwater off the port bow, creating a bright green ribbon of bubbles underwater before punching up a dirty spout of water and smoke eighty feet into the air. He was looking for the second splash when a giant swung a hammer down on the pilothouse roof with an earsplitting clang, followed seconds later by another waterspout burst one hundred yards off the ship's starboard side. Light bulbs, acoustic tiles, a radio speaker, and a cloud of dust rained out of the overhead while the men on the bridge team grabbed their helmets against flying debris. Brian, still standing in the doorway, realized that the shell had ricocheted off the deck of the signal bridge above before whining off to the starboard side. He found himself, covered in dust and paint chips, staring at the captain and the exec through a cloud of cordite smoke blowing back across the pilothouse from the blast to starboard. The captain said something to the exec and then hurried across the pilothouse to his chair, where he mashed down the squawk-box key and called the engineers. The debris littering the deck of the pilothouse began to slither around as the ship rolled again. The exec came into the pilothouse and gave Brian a bleak smile.

"Welcome to WESTPAC, Mr. Holcomb. Bet they don't do this shit over there in NATO, do they?"

"No, sir, they do not."

The exec came closer. "Have you left your GQ station for a reason, Brian, or were you just getting a little nervous back there in the CIC?" He deliberately spoke in a soft voice so the enlisted men could not hear.

Brian felt his face flush. "Uh, yes, sir, I came out to . . . uh—"

"Yeah, okay. You're not used to doing everything from Combat. But maybe you better go back in there. We get power back, the Old Man's gonna want to shoot at least some token rounds before we slink away from this fiasco, okay?"

"Yes, sir. Right away."

"Attaboy."

Brian, his face still red, waited for the ship to steady after a deep roll, then headed back into Combat as the smoke screen from the two destroyers blotted out the sunlight in the port-side bridge windows. The booming of the *Hull*'s guns followed him through the vestibule doorway. He almost collided with Austin as soon as he reentered Combat. *Berkeley,* for some reason, had stopped firing.

"Snipes say they'll have a boiler back on the line in two minutes," Austin said. "I'll need a status report on the combat systems ASAP, especially the forty-eight radar."

Brian nodded and went to the weapons control module. As he grabbed for a stanchion to steady himself through another deep roll, Chief Iverson swiveled around in his console chair.

"Good news, Mr. Holcomb. The radar guys say they had the system off-line for the gun shoot—they were worried about shock and vibration. So it should be okay for the power drop."

"Very good news, Chief. What about the missile systems and the MK Sixty-eight?"

"No status till they get the juice back, boss. Apparently, that'll be comin' up most skosh."

As if in answer to Iverson, the sound of the ventilation systems spooling up throughout the ship filled the unnatural quiet of CIC. Overhead, the fluorescent light fixtures buzzed on in concert with the twittering of digital alarms from the consoles. Austin came back into CIC as the rumble of propellers shook the ship.

"All right, everybody, get your systems back on the line and get me reports of any electronics casualties. Surface, D and D, when you get a radar, give us a course directly away from the coast."

"Surface, aye, and we need one-four-zero to go directly away."

"Evaluator, aye. Pass that recommendation out to the bridge."

The ship's head was already swinging around to the southeast when two more rounds came overhead, falling long now that the ship was hidden behind the destroyers' smoke screen. For some reason, Brian found the sounds of incoming fire to be less threatening now that the ship had mobility and combat systems power back up. The chief was tugging his sleeve.

"We get the gun system back up, we ought to set up on the beach and scatter some rounds up and down the coast."

"But we don't have a target."

"Yes, sir, I know that. But those tin cans couldn't really see anything, either—once they shifted from their point targets inland, they were just setting up on a band a thousand yards wide along the coast and hopin' the shooters were in there somewheres. I mean, what the hell, it would make everybody feel good. . . ."

The destroyers had swept by and were now somewhere astern of them, but on the other side of the massive pall of black smoke they had laid down. *Hood*'s gun mount was on the fantail, so she could fire and still drive away from the coast. Brian grinned at him.

"Okay, Chief, get it set up. I'll see if Austin wants to play."

He walked over to D and D from the weapons control module. Austin was talking to the captain on a sound-powered phone handset. The ship was steadying on a southeasterly heading and gathering speed. Brian waited for an opportunity to break in, then made his pitch. Austin relayed it to the captain, paused, nodded his head, and hung up the phone.

"Captain says no: We don't have a surface-search radar up and we can't see the two destroyers through the smoke. We don't want to hit one of our own ships accidentally."

"Okay, makes sense," acknowledged Brian. "I should have thought of that." They were interrupted by the maneuvering circuit.

"Tango Four, this is Magnavox. Request advise when you have power restored and if you have a medical officer on board, over?"

Austin tapped CWO Garuda Barry on the shoulder. Barry was sitting at the ship's weapons coordinator console, called SWIC. Barry switched over to radio communications and selected the maneuvering circuit.

"Magnavox, this is Tango Four. Propulsion power restored. I am clearing to the southeast. And affirmative on the medical officer, over."

"Tango Four, this is Magnavox. Request you come alongside Tango Three as soon as we are out of gun range of the coast for transfer of medical assist team to Tango Three. Recommend boat transfer, as Tango Three does not have a helo deck. Twelve-plus casualties, over?"

"This is Tango Four, roger out," transmitted Barry.

"Holy shit, they musta got clobbered good," said one of the air controllers sitting to Barry's right. Brian now knew why *Berkeley* had stopped firing. The word spread throughout CIC as Austin grabbed for the captain's line again to report the message. Realizing that a boat transfer was a Weapons Department function, Brian walked quickly back to weapons control and took Chief Iverson's headset.

"Director One, this is Control. Jack, we're gonna do a boat transfer with *Berkeley*. She apparently took a round and has several casualties."

"Are we done shooting, sir?"

"Yeah. As soon as we're out of range of the beach, we'll set condition Yoke. The bridge will be passing the word in a minute to assemble the docs and the boat crew. Pass the phones to your director operator and get on it."

"Aye, aye, sir. Plot, get word to Chief Martinez."

Brian handed the headset back to Chief Iverson.

"Chief, I'm going down to the boat decks. You assume weapons control and get Mr. Austin a status of the systems as soon as all stations report in."

He left CIC as the 1MC made the announcement to secure from general quarters and prepare for a boat transfer with *Berkeley*. Thirty minutes later, it was Brian, not Jack Folsom, who was bundled up in a bulky orange kapok life jacket and jammed in with *Hood*'s medical officer, the chief hospital corpsman and the junior hospital corpsman, three metal cases of medical supplies, and the three-man boat crew. Brian found himself squinting through salt spray as they approached the starboard quarter of the guided-missile destroyer *Berkeley* in *Hood*'s twenty-six-foot motor whaleboat. The seas were choppy and the heavily loaded boat was shipping a lot of water. Brian, used to the frigid Atlantic, was surprised at the warm Pacific. The medical officer hung on to the side of the pitching whaleboat. He was apparently no seaman, based on the greenish hue of his face. Brian looked away as the doctor fed the fishies.

Ordinarily, the ship's first lieutenant would have been the boat officer, but at the last minute, the captain had summoned Folsom to the wardroom to help with the after-action incident report. The exec had directed Brian to make the run as boat officer. The steel sides of *Berkeley* loomed above them as they closed in under her starboard quarter. From a hundred yards out, Brian had been unable to see any visible signs of damage to the destroyer. As the whaleboat closed in, however, he noticed the telltale smudge marks of heavy smoke around the deckhouse hatch leading out to the DDG's starboard-side quarterdeck area. Forward of the hatch at about head height, he could see a dinner plate–sized black hole in the bulkhead. There were several fire hoses leading into the blackened hatchway and one of the exhaust vents still billowed dirty steam. Some of the men clustered around the deckhouse wore oxygen-breathing apparatus, or OBAs. As the boat drew closer, he could see soggy mounds of burned insulation piled on either side of the hatch.

A crew of deck seamen waited at the top of the steel pipe ladder toward which the coxswain pointed *Hood*'s whaleboat. It took about three minutes to get the boat stabilized alongside, then the doctor and his team of corpsmen clambered up the ladder, followed by Brian. On deck, the docs were greeted by a gray-faced lieutenant commander whose khaki uniform was spotted with dark brown stains. Without a word, he grabbed the pasty-faced doctor and pointed him forward up the main deck toward the wardroom. The two corpsmen followed as the boatswain mates pitched lines down into the boat to begin hauling up the medical supplies. Brian realized that he was in the way and stepped aside. He spoke to a frightened-looking ensign who was watching at the lifeline.

"So what happened here, mister?"

The ensign, whose pale face Brian realized was streaked with tears, appeared not to have heard him. A chief standing a few feet away on the fantail glared at Holcomb, so Brian walked over to the other side of the quarterdeck, where the stink of smoke, burned insulation, and, sickeningly, cooked meat was suddenly very strong. Brian noticed that the paint on the barrel of the *Berkeley*'s after five-inch fifty-four gun on the next deck up was burned black and still smoldering from the heat of the fire mission. He had to pick his way through a pile of empty brass powder casings that were clanging back and forth into the lifelines as the ship rolled. Several dazed-looking men stood around on the fantail.

A lieutenant sitting on the deck by the base of the missile launcher looked over at Brian. His khakis were in ruins, soaked by salt water and bloodstains, and the edges of his face were blackened by smoke. He put his head back in his hands and stared down at the deck. Brian spoke to the chief, who continued to glare at him.

"I'm the Weapons officer in *Hood,* Chief. What happened here?"

The chief cleared his throat and spat over the side. His eyes were red and his khaki uniform soaked with sweat and fire-fighting water. His face had the telltale marks of an OBA mask imprinted on his skin. He spoke in a flat tone, quivering with suppressed anger.

"When the fuckin' *Hood* went DIW, we had to turn around and come back down our track to lay down a smoke screen. Gave the goddamned NVA a second chance to get the range. After we went by you, we started a turn out to make another firing run and the fuckers put a one-hundred-thirty-millimeter into Repair three, back there by the post office. We had a full damage-control party, Repair Three, stationed in that passageway. Round went off in the middle of 'em. We got nine dead and three more cut to shit up in the wardroom.''

"Jesus Christ!"

"Yeah, Jesus Christ. We were doing okay until your fuckin' snipes went and dropped the load." He stared hard at Brian and then seemed to wilt, realizing that he was out of line. He took a deep breath and started to apologize, but Brian cut him off. The people in *Berkeley* had every right to be pissed off.

"Christ, I'm sorry, Chief. We sure as hell didn't do it on purpose, and we got hit, too. But not like this." Brian felt his face flush as he mentally compared Festerman's cut hand with the death and destruction in *Berkeley.* The chief nodded silently. Then the lieutenant sitting on deck looked up at him again.

"You from the *Hood*?"

"That's right. I'm very sor—"

"Fuck your very sorry. You go on up there to the wardroom, take a look at what happens when a ship can't keep her plant on the line in a gunfight. Go on, get your ass up there. Take a look at what you sonsabitches did."

Brian started to reply but then became aware that everyone on the fantail was now staring at him. The only sounds came from the whistle of the wind through the lifelines, the chug of *Hood*'s whaleboat engine, and the clanging and banging of the shell casings rolling around the fantail.

"Go on, mister. If you don't know where it is, just follow the trail."

Brian was torn: *Hood*'s motor whaleboat was no longer alongside, but it was pretty clear from their faces that he needed to get off the fantail. Reluctantly, he turned and walked forward up the main deck. Several exhausted-looking men stumbled by in their GQ gear, ignoring him. *Berkeley* was laid out much like his last ship, *Decatur*, so he knew where the wardroom was. He also knew that in a destroyer, the officers' wardroom mess doubled as the principal medical battle-dressing station, since a destroyer's sick bay was only a tiny one-room compartment. "Follow the trail," the lieutenant had said, and indeed there was a slick red path of blood glistening on the gray nonskid and leading up the starboard side to the forward athwartships passageway. Pausing before the open hatch, he took a deep breath and tried to fill the growing pit in his stomach. He stepped in through the hatch and then turned right into the narrow passageway leading up to the wardroom. Two men slumped against the bulkhead at the other end of the passageway looked at him and then back down at the deck. The linoleum tiles in the passageway felt greasy under his seaboots.

The door to the wardroom was closed, but he could hear the sounds of frantic activity on the other side. There was a round four-inch-wide glass porthole in the wardroom door. Brian peered through the glass and felt his stomach grab. Blood was everywhere—on the ceiling, on every bulkhead, covering every chair and piece of furniture in the wardroom. On what was normally the dining room table for fourteen officers were the bodies of three almost-naked men who were literally cut to pieces. The man nearest the door had no legs beneath his knees. An arterial wound in his upper chest pumped bright red blood in huge spurts onto the overhead, where it dripped back down all over the table in a ghastly crimson rain. The man laid out beyond him had the top of his head missing and Brian could see glistening gray membranes bulging out of the broken skull. The third man was still, a fist-sized hole punched through his abdomen, his skin as white as marble except where blood from the first man had spattered him. *Hood*'s doctor and both corpsmen, together with *Berkeley*'s two corpsmen were drenched in blood as they tried to stop the arterial fountain. Brian stared in growing shock until the glass porthole was suddenly spattered with blood, causing him to jerk his face back. Blood was seeping out from under the door, pooling under his boots. His feet windmilling, he backed away from the door and then bolted from the passageway with a small cry, ran out past the two startled sailors to the port side, and vomited over the weather breaks bull rail. When his stomach stopped its spasms, he straightened up and took several deep breaths, wondering why it was dark, until he realized that his eyes were clenched shut. As he turned around, he saw that there were several black rubber body bags stacked inside the breaks enclosure to his right. A chief petty officer was standing among the body bags, his breathing apparatus dangling down from his waist, a red firefighter's helmet in his hands.

"Who're you, Lieutenant?" he asked.

"I came with the . . . uh, the boat crew. We brought the doctor." He was embarrassed that he could not bring himself to say *Hood*'s name. The chief just nodded silently and resumed his vigil in the breaks, his hands turning the red helmet over and over as he looked down at the sodden body bags. Brian wiped his face off with his handkerchief, took a deep breath, walked back through the passageway to the starboard side, and then headed back aft to the quarterdeck, his stomach still churning over the charnel-house scene in the wardroom. He saw *Hood*'s boat crew looking at him from their pitching boat fifty yards away. He gave the coxswain a curt hand signal to come back alongside. By the time he got back to the pipe ladder, the boat was bobbing and bumping alongside. Ignoring the hostile stares of the *Berkeley* people on the fantail and not waiting for the boat to make up, he dropped down the ladder and into the boat.

"Shove off, Coxswain. Back to the ship. Now!" he ordered. The crew jumped to it after seeing his face, and the whaleboat roared off in a cloud of exhaust toward the gray bulk of *Hood*, waiting a half mile away. Brian sat stiffly in the bow, staring at nothing, oblivious to the soaking spray.

8

Brian stepped out of the motor whaleboat and through the lifelines as the boat was hoisted up to the railing on *Hood*'s 01 level. The chief boatswain stood at the railing.

"Bumpy ride, boss?" Martinez asked, eyeing Brian's pale face as he climbed over the lifelines.

"Bad scene over there, Boats. I'll tell you about it later."

He shed his kapok life jacket and headed for the wardroom. He needed some coffee to wash out the foul taste in his mouth. He jumped sideways when a blast of 1,200-psi steam thundered out of the forward stack for ten seconds before subsiding in a wet hiss of white spray. Snipes must be setting safeties on the boilers, he thought. When he arrived in the wardroom, he found several of the CIC officers, chiefs, and senior petty officers gathered around the junior table working on charts and traces from the plotting table in Combat. He headed straight for the coffeepot, trying to conceal his trembling hands, but Jack Folsom jumped out of his chair to intercept him.

"Captain's having a meeting of department heads up in his cabin. They said for you to join them as soon as you got back. Uh, you don't look so good, Mr. Holcomb."

"After what I saw over in *Berkeley*, I don't feel so very good, Jack," he replied, mixing a heavy dose of sugar into the ink black coffee. The rest of the men in the wardroom went silent. Brian stirred his coffee for a few seconds and then described the scene in *Berkeley*. When he was finished, no one said anything for a moment, then everyone began talking at once. Brian left them to it and headed for the captain's cabin.

He stopped by his stateroom, located two doors away from the captain's cabin. Brian and the Operations officer had adjoining staterooms with a shared bathroom. He smiled grimly at the word *stateroom*: The rooms were eight feet by seven, each equipped with a double bunk bed, washbasin, and two desks built into the bulkheads. Although each room was equipped for two officers, the luxury came from not having a roommate. Only the captain, executive officer, and the three line department heads had their own rooms; everyone else shared. He took a couple of minutes to wash his face, rinse out his mouth, and put on a clean uniform shirt and then made a halfhearted attempt to brush his unruly hair.

Trying to quell the vision of hell he'd just witnessed, Brian looked wildly around the stateroom and found his wife's picture on the cubbyhole desk. Maddy. The mass of blond hair framing that exquisitely posed smile. He felt a sudden urge to open his desk and get the other pictures, Maddy on the beach, both of them at Tahoe or on the weekend to San Francisco, scenes of normalcy that might help erase the horrifying red-on-gray images from his mind. He wondered where she was, what she was doing at this moment. There would be no mail until they were on station at Red Crown. He would get a letter off to her tonight, tell her what had happened, what he had seen in *Berkeley*. On second thought, maybe not. That kind of stuff scared the wives witless. But he had to tell somebody, not so much about what he had seen but how he had reacted, the revulsion, the fear, getting sick over the side. Naval officers were supposed to be made of sterner stuff than that. But I can tell Maddy—I think. He took a deep breath. Time to go see the captain.

He left his stateroom and walked forward into the narrow passageway between the staff office and the captain's pantry. He knocked once on the captain's door and stepped in. The captain's cabin consisted of a living room and a separate bedroom and bathroom. The living room, approximately twenty feet by twenty, doubled as the captain's personal office and reception room. The room was carpeted and furnished with a couch, two upholstered chairs, and a round dining table. A row of portholes stretched across the front bulkhead, which overlooked the forecastle. The pilothouse stood directly above. The exec, Austin, and Benedetti sat at the captain's dining room table, the captain in his desk chair, his back to the desk, while he listened on a sound-powered phone handset. The cabin felt cool, and the captain was wearing a tan civilian sweater over his khakis, his usual at-sea rig. The Captain said, "Very well," and hung up the phone.

"The Da Nang helos are inbound to us right now. We're to stand by *Berkeley* to provide a helo deck for casualty transfers. Brian, please sit down. What's the situation over there?"

Brian took the fourth seat at the round table. "Sir, there were about a dozen men involved. From what I saw, they're all either dead or about to be dead."

"Jesus Christ!" exclaimed the exec. "*All* of 'em?"

"Yes, sir. I saw seven or eight body bags out on deck, and in the wardroom—" He swallowed hard as the gory images returned. "In the wardroom, it was . . . it was just blood . . . blood everywhere. One guy was partially decapitated; another guy had no legs. And the third guy was—he was—"

"Okay, Brian," said the captain. "We get the picture. Their CO told me that they took a one-hundred-thirty-millimeter round right in the middle of a damage-control team. I can believe the casualties. How much damage is there?"

"Sir, it hit in Repair Three, back by the post office and the after athwartships passageway. I didn't go in, but the fires are apparently out. You can't see anything from the weather decks except smoke. I would guess that the Mount Fifty-two handling room is out of commission. The people I saw were exhausted." And none too friendly, he thought to himself. The 1MC burst into life.

"FLIGHT QUARTERS, FLIGHT QUARTERS. ALL HANDS MAN YOUR FLIGHT-QUARTERS STA-

TIONS TO RECEIVE TWO CH-FORTY-SIXES FROM DA NANG. NOW, FLIGHT QUARTERS.''

"Count," said the captain, "go to Combat and conduct whatever boat transfers are necessary to get their casualties over here and into the helos. Use one of our P-boats if we have to; I don't want to drag this out, and the whaleboat can't carry that many, uh, people. Coordinate on the secure net with *Berkeley*. Move the ship into two hundred yards. Call me if there's a problem."

"Aye, Captain," said Austin, rising from the table. He gave Brian a significant look before leaving the cabin. With Austin's departure, Vince Benedetti ended up sitting by himself on one side of the round table. The engineer looked exhausted. His uniform was still wrinkled and smudged with sweat stains and his face was drawn. He stared down at the tabletop. Brian wondered what had been going on before he arrived; he had a sense that it had not been a pleasant conversation. The exec seemed to be waiting for the captain to take the lead, which he did.

"Okay, gentlemen. Brian, to bring you up to speed: We've sent out our after-action report. We had to explain what happened to the engineering plant and why we went DIW in the middle of a fire mission. It would have been embarrassing enough if we'd been the only ones to take fire, but the *Berkeley* casualties make the whole incident very serious. There are those who are going to blame us for the fact that *Berkeley* took that hit, since the destroyers were basically home free until they had to reverse course to lay down a smoke screen. The exec feels that the only thing going for us politically is that there are bound to be questions as to why a PIRAZ ship was put on the Sea Dragon gun line in the first place. My guess—or rather, my hope—is that our bosses will not want to answer that question, so they'll play down the incident. You're the only *Hood* officer who's been on board *Berkeley*. Are they mad at us?"

"Yes, sir, they are, or at least the junior people are. I didn't see the exec or the CO."

"I can well imagine." Brian thought he saw Benedetti flinch, but the engineer continued to stare down at the deck, as if this conversation did not apply to him.

The captain continued. "Although they could have been hit at any time during that kind of mission, we were the obvious target, with all that smoke and being dead in the water. *Berkeley* was just unlucky enough to have to retrace her track. You read the Sea Dragon op order: It was pretty clear about never retracing your track, because the NVA is usually set up on where you've just been. *Berkeley* should have veered in toward the coast when she came about. But I guess that's hindsight."

"That's probably not something we should say in a message, Captain," observed the exec.

"I quite agree, XO. But I think it's something that the squad dog will comment on, which might get us off the hot seat. The important thing now is that we do this helo evolution and then get up to Red Crown station. The systems have all come back on the line, thank God. Brian, your gun mount did well. Fifty-six rounds. That's a record for Mount Fifty-one."

Brian was embarrassed to be praised when his brother department head was indisputably up to his neck in deep trouble. He was not sure that this was the moment, but he plunged ahead.

"To tell the truth, I was worried about the mount, Captain," he admitted. "My guys didn't think it would do the hundred and fifty rounds without a breakdown. I'd like to ask that we shoot it more often once we get on Red Crown station. The chiefs think a couple of daily rounds might up its reliability."

Benedetti flashed Brian a brief but grateful look before fixing his eyes on the deck again. Brian could just as well have pocketed the captain's compliment and distanced himself from the trouble Benedetti faced. The captain was nodding.

"What that will probably do is break it, Brian. But I agree. Give me a plan for a daily or at least a weekly test-firing, although you'll find that, with helo ops, it will be hard to schedule. And we'll both have to put up with a lot of grief from the Count."

"I'll help with that problem," said the exec.

"Okay. Brian, that's all I have for you right now."

"Aye, aye, sir," said Brian, standing. Benedetti

seemed to shrink as Brian picked up his cap and left the cabin. He exhaled heavily when he got back to his stateroom, then shivered at the thought of being in the chief engineer's shoes just now. While using the head, he heard a knock on the stateroom door. He zipped up and answered.

"Come in."

Chief Boatswain Martinez stepped through the stateroom door, his huge bulk seeming to fill the stateroom.

"Boss, the chiefs were wonderin' how bad the *Berkeley* got zapped; there's all kindsa rumors goin' around."

Brian described the *Berkeley*'s damage and casualties. Martinez shook his head.

"Hope those fuckers aren't in Subic when we get there. They're gonna have a hate-on for the *J. B. Hood* for sure."

"They're already pretty pissed, Chief. I thought I was going to get to walk the plank over there. I don't think anybody in that repair party survived the hit. Most of them are in bags, and the three I saw . . . well, you wouldn't believe it."

"Yeah, I would. I was in the riverboats in country for a year. I seen some shit there, make you puke."

"I did puke."

"Oh. Yeah, well, I puked sometimes myself. Nothin' to be ashamed of. We ride around out here in these ships, three squares, a hot flop, and clean Skivvies and we don't have no idea of the shit's goin' on in country."

"Now we do. Now I do, anyway. Shook my young ass up, Bosun's Mate, and that's no lie."

"Yes, sir. I hear you. Mr. Austin, he says we need to launch the P-boat to bring the body bags over. I better get down to the boat decks; it's a little choppy out there for a P-boat."

"Yeah, but we have to use it. Captain wants to make the transfer as quickly as possible for the sake of the people in *Berkeley*."

"Yes, sir, I hear that."

"Chief?" Brian's voice was tight and his eyes suddenly felt wet. "They're going to have to use a fire hose to wash down the wardroom in the *Berkeley*."

Martinez looked at him for a minute and then down at the deck. "Yeah," he said. "People jist don't know." He looked back up at Brian. "It's gonna be okay, Lieutenant. We jist gotta get this boat transfer done, and then we'll get back to Red Crown, where we belong. The *Hood,* she shouldn'ta been doin' this shit."

"We're a goddamned warship," Brian protested. "We've got a five-inch gun. Why shouldn't we be doing this? We're supposed to be able to do any combat mission—"

"Yes, sir, but we got some things goin' on here. We get some time, we gotta talk."

Brian stared at him. Things? "You mean drugs, don't you? Let me guess, some snipes were high and that's why we dropped the load."

"That's what I'm hearin'. But it ain't jist snipes who're into the dope. We got it in Weapons Department, and so do the Ops people."

"Well, we need to kick some ass and shitcan some dopers, then."

The chief studied the deck, twisting his CPO hat around and around in his massive paws. "There's more to it than that, boss," he said. "Look, I gotta git back to the boat decks."

"Okay, but I want to know what's going on. Every ship in the Navy has a drug problem of some kind, but we're not supposed to pussyfoot around with it."

"Yes, sir."

"OK, Chief. But later, hear?"

"You got it, boss."

9

After two hours of observing the Red Crown watch setup in Combat, Brian went down to the wardroom to get some decent coffee. The ship was headed north into the Gulf, its somber casualty-transfer duty completed just before sundown. Two Marine CH-46 helicopters had clattered out of the afternoon sky from Da Nang to remove *Berkeley*'s dead. The captain had ordered a ten-man honor guard mustered on the flight deck when the bodies had begun to arrive by boat. Brian, watching from the after gun director platform, had needed to turn away from the sight of the lumpy rubber bags lined up in still rows on the edge of the flight deck, watched over by the file of *Hood* sailors, looking awkward in dress whites, leggings, and guard belts.

As he stepped into the wardroom vestibule's passageway, he felt a humid current of night air streaming in through the darken-ship curtains to the boiler room below. Someone had locked back the starboard-side hatch leading out to the weather breaks. The pungent smell of the sea air was a pleasant contrast to the air-conditioned cigarette smoke of Combat.

He entered the wardroom in red-lighted semidarkness. The evening movie had finished an hour ago, leaving residual smells of popcorn and cigarette smoke. In another hour, the midwatch people would stagger in for a cup of soup and a sandwich before taking the midnight-to-four watches throughout the ship. The wardroom was kept red-lighted at night to preserve the deck watch standers' night vision. He peered into the stainless-steel coffeepots and found one empty and the other busily making asphalt. He rinsed out the empty one and fired up the coffeemaker, only then discovering that he was not alone.

The chief engineer slumped in an upholstered chair in

the far corner of the wardroom, his legs straight out before him, his oil-stained khaki trousers hiked up over steel-toed safety shoes, and a battered *J. B. Hood* ball cap shoved to the back of his head. He had deep shadows under his eyes and a pallor of exhaustion on his face. He saw Brian looking at him.

"What're you looking at, Holcomb?" he asked in a tired voice. "Come to get your licks in, too?"

Brian banged the steel coffeepot onto the heating element. "I don't rate that, Mr. Benedetti."

"Yeah? You got to walk outta there today. You didn't have to stay there and explain how come we lost the load in the middle of a live fire mission. It wasn't your department that caused the tin cans to turn around, run back through a red zone, and get clobbered. You didn't—ah, fuck it. . . ."

Brian walked over to the corner of the wardroom and sat down on the couch across from the engineer. He looked at Benedetti.

"Well, that's all true," he said. "But I'm not part of some crowd in the colosseum holding out a thumbs-down, either. I may be just a lieutenant and you're a lieutenant commander, but I'm a department head in this ship just like you are. I'm a shipmate, Mr. Benedetti, not your enemy."

The engineer looked at him for a long moment, rubbed his eyes, and then nodded his head.

"Yeah. Shit. I apologize, Holcomb—Brian. I put you in the same category as Austin, and you're right, you don't rate that. And call me Vince, for Chrissakes. You makin' coffee?"

"It's just started."

Benedetti slumped farther into the chair and continued to rub his face with his hands. "What a way to start a fucking cruise." He sighed. "WESTPAC is supposed to be fun."

They sat there in the semidarkness. Brian suddenly realized that he, too, was very tired. Vivid memories of standing in Combat, listening to enemy artillery shells exploding in the water and raining steel fragments against the ship's side, the palpable anguish in *Berkeley,* and the carmine horrors of *Berkeley*'s battle-dressing station flooded his mind. Fun?

"I've heard some scuttlebutt," Brian said.

"Yeah, like?"

"That we lost the load because some guy was high on dope. I'm sure you're sick of rehashing this, but . . ."

Benedetti stopped rubbing his face and peered at Brian through his fingers. For an instant, Brian saw a flare of what looked like alarm in the engineer's eyes, but then it was gone, replaced by a look of resignation.

"Well, Brian, I'll tell you what. Officially, that's kinda hard to say. Especially in the good ole *J. B. Hood*. We were doing twenty-seven knots, which is max load for two-boiler ops. You know we got four main holes—fire room, engine room, fire room, engine room. Two propeller shafts, one from each engine room. Just like a tin can, only bigger. We were split out, each shaft being driven by its own boiler–engine room set. We lost One A boiler forward because number-one automatic-combustion-control air compressor tripped off the line in One Fire Room. Nobody knows why. It just tripped off. Compressors do that. Main Control called for number two ACC compressor to be cross-countered to supply both fire rooms. Should've been no big deal. Open two valves in Two Fire Room and you're cross-connected. But the BT Two in Two Fire Room got the valves wrong. He opened one valve in the cross-connect bank. The other valve he opened was the ACC system bleed-down valve. Net result was that *all* the control air bled to the bilges, so then we lost Two B boiler about a minute later."

"Couldn't they have taken the boilers in hand?" asked Brian, remembering his Destroyer School engineering course.

Benedetti snorted. "At twenty-seven knots? You gotta be kidding. The only two guys in the ship who can operate a twelve-hundred-psi plant in manual at that speed are the BT chiefs, and they would have had to be on the console, hands-on, the moment it happened. Besides, it shouldn't have been necessary. One ACC compressor can supply both fire rooms, no sweat. Long as you get the air to the ACC systems and not to the fucking bilges."

"This was an E-Five? A petty officer?"

"Yeah. BT Two Dwyer Gallagher. You know him?"

"Hell, I still don't know everybody in my own department."

"Yeah. Well, he's one of my B Division badasses. Red hair, red beard, red face, red motorcycle, and perpetual red ass. My senior BT chief, Tony Fontana, was down in Two Firehouse when it all went down. He got to the lower level about a minute after they pulled fires on Two B and everything went hot and dark. Said he found Gallagher with a shit-eating grin on his face, lookin' at a feed pump. Said Gallagher was stoned out of his gourd. Shined his flashlight in the fat fuck's face. Pupils big as pennies. Said he yelled at him but that Gallagher just sat down on a bale of rags and giggled like a fucking girl. He's lucky Fontana didn't kill him right then and there. I probably would have."

"You tell the captain this?"

"I told the XO. You gotta understand something here. The Old Man, all these guys are like his kids, see? His *kids* don't get high, fuck up the works. They 'make mistakes,' just like children. You tell him something like this, he just shakes his head, gives you that patient, 'you're letting me down' smile, and says, 'Vince, Vince, you've got it wrong. Must have. These men are good men. They work hard under hellish conditions in those fire rooms. Hundred-ten-degree heat down there when we're in the tropics. Six on, six off, weeks on end. They get bone-tired. They make mistakes. We all make mistakes.' "

Benedetti sighed and rubbed his eyes again. "Makes you feel like you're some kinda shitheel, and the hell of it, he doesn't mean it that way. It's just that he's a nice old man, still living in the old Navy, whatever the hell that is. Believes the best of everybody. You'll find out the first time one of your stars fucks up. He'll give you a fatherly lecture and you'll crawl outta that cabin ashamed of yourself for picking on his *kids*."

"He won't admit that the ship has a drug problem? Hell, every ship in the fleet has a drug problem. What's he scared of?"

"Scared? Naw, I don't think he lacks for courage—he used to be in the bomb squad, you know, the EOD guys, when he was a white hat. Still carries his 'instruments' around with him; showed us all one night how you take apart an unexploded bomb. Scared me just to listen to him. That's where he got that Navy Cross—something to do with a bomb on a ship. No, it's more a question of righteousness. If it ever penetrated that a lot of his *kids* were doin' marijuana or hashish on board, off watch, on watch, hell, at GQ, I think he'd just wail and melt down like that witch in *The Wizard of Oz*."

"The XO. Tell me the XO knows the score, right?"

"The XO? Hell yes. He nails the bastards whenever he can, but it's all done off the books. Gets some of the bigger guys in the chiefs' mess to have little 'talks' with any doper he catches or even suspects. Tries to terrorize the little shits into knocking it off. Your chief bosun is part of that scene. Terrorize me, I had to go 'talk' to Martinez back in after steering. But they don't go to captain's mast."

"Why the hell not?"

"Because—and I don't know this; I just think this is how it is—the Old Man just won't hear it. I think what happens is that the XO is shielding him from this shit. Says he's the best CO we're ever going to see on a ship like this. And he's right. Usually these PIRAZ ships get up-and-coming crown princes—you know, guys on their way to flag rank. I don't know how Captain Huntington got *Hood*, except everybody in the Navy seems to like the guy. You'll never meet a kinder, nicer four-striper in the Navy. Everybody knows he'll never make admiral—he's too old. So this is it; this is his big command. And I gotta admit, Huntington'll do anything for his people: go up against the Bureau, get the orders they want, give 'em special leave—you name it. There are people in this ship who worship the Old Man. I think the XO is trying to make sure nothing happens to spoil it for him."

"But what's he doing to his ship?"

Benedetti gave him a weary smile. "Ah, well. You got a lookee-see at that today, didn't you? What do they say in country—*Sin loi*? Sorry about that, USS *Berkeley*. I gotta tell you, I don't want to be in port with *Berkeley* for a while."

"That's what Chief Martinez said. But isn't *Hood* going to get some static over what happened today?"

"I don't think so. You heard the Old Man. I think the basic decision to send a PIRAZ ship to the gun line is going to be questioned. That aviator admiral on Yankee Station is gonna have to put a lid on that, which means he can't then jump in *Hood*'s shit. The chain of command in this war has elevated second-guessing the front-line troops to an art form."

Benedetti leaned back in his chair. Brian got up to check on the coffee. He returned with two mugs and handed Benedetti one before sitting down. The engineer sipped his coffee noisily for a minute before continuing.

"There's another reason why we have to go easy on the drugs bit. It's the Bureau of Personnel's little catch-twenty-two."

"I don't think I want to hear this."

"You don't, but you should. The no-replacements catch. See, you bring a guy up on charges of drug use aboard ship, CO finds him guilty at mast, you gotta discharge his ass. Nothing wrong with that, is there? Let the dopers get back to the streets, drop acid, do speed, go find Alice in the Sky with Diamonds, and sing protest songs with the rest of the longhaired, creeping Jesus, hippy freaks. 'Cept for one little 'oh by the fucking way': You don't get a replacement for that guy you just discharged. Oh, one day you will, maybe six, seven months from now. But for right now, you drum a BT Two or an RD Three or an FT Two out the main gates, you're one down on the watch bill, pal, which, if you haven't noticed, is already port and starboard, six on, six off. They call it an unplanned loss. Now, you know every ship in PACFLEET is undermanned. In some rates, like boiler tender, we're at like sixty percent. All of which the XO makes perfectly clear to you when you're ready to hang one of these dopers."

Brian nodded his head. "I remember having to send guys from *Decatur* to the PACFLEET. You think *Hood* is undermanned, you ought to see the LANTFLEET ships.

Some of the LANTFLEET ships don't have enough people even to get under way.''

"Yeah, I know, but LANTFLEET doesn't do shit 'cept go to NATO cocktail parties and play booga-booga with Russian subs. Even with the involuntary transfers out here, there're still not enough guys to go around. So, you shitcan a guy, you'll feel it on the watch bill pretty quick.''

Brian nodded. His division officers had briefed him on the manning situation on his first day. There were plenty of deck seamen, but when it came to fire-control technicians, guided-missile repair techs, and even gunner's mates, *Hood* was averaging only 70 to 75 percent of complement. A drug hit would hurt Weapons Department just about as hard as it would Engineering.

"Chief Martinez implied drugs were not confined to the Engineering Department,'' he said.

Benedetti laughed—an unpleasant sound. " 'Implied,' did he? You better Hong Kong fucking believe that, shipmate. Your deck, missiles, and sonar gangs are as dirty as my M, B, and Auxiliary divisions. The gunner's mates, for some reason, won't tolerate it. They're all gung ho, go around acting like Marines. Weight lifters, short hair, no beards. You've seen 'em. Good shit. Chief VanHorn's the good guy behind that. Chief Jackson, the Sheriff, he used to be a gunner's mate. But otherwise, take a tour topside between taps and midnight, see what it smells like out there on the weather decks.''

"Good guy? You make it sound like we have a good guys and bad guys crew, some kind of us-against-them situation here.''

Benedetti laughed again. "I don't believe you said that. Where you been, for Chrissakes? This is the LANTFLEET Navy talking? Man, I gotta get me some orders to LANTFLEET, I can see that. Must be nice out there in never-never land.''

Brian frowned in sudden embarrassment. Was he being that naïve? Had this drug shit been going on in *Decatur* during his first department head tour? Was his ignorance about what was going on below decks somehow behind those not-so-good fitness reports? Benedetti was watching him.

"Hey, man," Benedetti said gently, "you gotta wise up. These days, there're three kindsa people in every ship. There's the doper, usually an E-Five or below enlisted type, any division you want to name, does his job but also does his dope and doesn't see anything wrong with it. Knows he can get his ass kicked if he gets caught, but that's just cops-and-robbers shit—same as being in high school. But he doesn't see anything *wrong* with going up on deck at night and smoking a joint from time to time. Takes the edge off, you know? Relieves the boredom, the fatigue. Like you and me having a couple of shooters over at the club after a long day at the pier."

"Except he's intoxicated aboard ship," interrupted Brian. "Anything happens, a fire, a steam leak, you've got a doper responding to it."

"Bingo. But, see, that's lifer talk, you're thinking about the ship. Thinking about the ship, that comes with seniority, with experience, after you've seen a thing or two, *and* after you make a commitment to a Navy career. Then the ship becomes important. To the dopers, they're just doing time in the Navy—beats doing time in the mud and the blood in country, right? They don't give a rat's ass about the ship. That's for us khaki to worry about."

Benedetti sat back, sipped some more coffee, fished in his shirt pocket for a cigarette, and lighted up, blowing a cloud of smoke at the overhead.

"Then there're the good guys, officers, CPOs, most, not all, of the first class POs. Comes to dope on the ship, the good guys're hell on wheels. Get a whiff of marijuana smoke, they round up the nearest master-at-arms and go chase it down, see if they can catch the little fuck. You met Chief Jackson, the Sheriff? He's a fanatic about it, looks for dopers in every fan room. Stays up nights and patrols the decks, pops up like fuckin' Houdini in unexpected places, trying to catch 'em."

"What happens when he does?"

"He arranges a visitation from Jesus."

"What!"

Benedetti grinned. "Yeah, Louis Jesus María Martinez—your chief boats." Benedetti chuckled. "First, he lays Injun shit on 'em. You know, steps outta nowhere when the guy's alone in a passageway, shoots him the evil eye, or gets somebody else to get the asshole on the phone, then talks scary to him. Tells him he's got bad medicine, that the chicken guts and the bones say the guy's gonna have bad luck real soon. Then the guy usually does have some bad luck: He falls down a ladder, trips into a bulkhead, bangs his face up somehow, breaks an arm, you know.''

"But that's . . . well, illegal."

"So's doin' dope on one of Her Majesty's ships of war, Brian. And if you don't have the option of taking the guy to mast and putting his useless ass on the beach with the rest of those fucked-up civilians out there, you gotta do something, right?"

"You said there were three kinds of people."

"Yeah. The third kind's the one that pisses me off, and we got some of those up and down the chain of command. The third kind just sorta goes along. I think his highness, the Count of Monte Austin, is one. These are the guys who say, Look, probably thirty to forty percent of the enlisted people are doing marijuana or hashish on an occasional basis. There are officers in the wardroom who would do it, except they're smart enough to see the consequences. Now, these people were doing it before they came into the Navy and they're going to resume doing it when they're out of the Navy. They don't see that it's a big deal. Most of them are doing it off watch, after hours. Okay, it's illegal, it's risky if some bad shit goes down, and it'd be better for everybody if they didn't. But if we hassle 'em, bust 'em, throw 'em out, all we do is screw ourselves, because we run out of crew pretty quick. Plus, we give the ship a bad rep by revealing publicly that we have a big drug problem, when we know it's no bigger or smaller than any other ship in the Navy. We do that, we fuck over our Old Man, who's one of the last of the good guys. And we maybe fuck over our own careers, 'cause you throw enough people out, your gear stops working, ship doesn't look so hot.

"So . . . we do the smart thing—look the other way. Judiciously, now. Some guy gets blatant, you kick his ass. But a smart guy knows who his dopers are and makes sure they're not put in a position to do any real damage, see? Besides, most of what we do out here is command and control, like the Red Crown stuff—it's all radarscopes and computers and radios. It's not actually *combat;* it's just stuff the twidgets do up in CIC."

"Except for today," interjected Brian. "That turned into combat."

"The laissez-faire guys'd say today was a fluke. The brass would *never* put one of these PIRAZ ships on the gun line. And I'll bet they never do it again, either."

"Because of what happened to *Berkeley*?"

"Hell no. You're missing the point. This is political. It's because of that round that went off and put some scrap metal through the CIC bulkhead, or the one that bounced off the pilothouse overhead. If we'd taken a real hit that blew up Combat, or the computer rooms, or the forty-eight radar, or the TACAN, you realize what would happen? For starters, the *Long Beach* couldn't go off-line. She'd have to stay up there in the Gulf until they got another ship out here that was PIRAZ-capable. Remember, we only have five of these hummers in the whole PACFLEET. That's two in WESTPAC to keep the Red Crown station manned up—one ship on station, the other resting up—and one in the yards at home. Then there're two more working up on the West Coast to come back over here and relieve the two that're deployed out here. Navy can't afford for *anything* to happen to one of these babies. So the go-along guys figure, if all we do is CIC work, what's it matter if some of the little dears step out on deck after a midwatch for a quick toke?"

Benedetti rolled his eyes and took a deep drag on his cigarette. "Be *sophisticated* about it, they say. *Manage* it. There's no point to this cops-and-robbers shit, because you only screw yourself if you succeed in catching your bad guy. You just cause all sorts of problems. And you know how much our superiors on the staffs *love* problems."

Brian exhaled explosively. He stood up, unable just to sit there anymore.

"But that's total bullshit," he began.

"Yeah, buddy," agreed Benedetti.

Brian shook his head. "The PIRAZ station is only forty, fifty miles off the North Vietnamese coast. If the North Vietnamese or the Red Chinese ever decided to attack the ships in the Gulf, their MiGs could be on top in what—three minutes? And they supposedly have antiship missiles, those Styx missiles the Soviets gave them. And they have missile boats. Shit, that close to the beach, anything could happen."

"Yeah," Benedetti said with a gleam in his eye. "But is any of that shit likely? We've had ships out here in the Gulf since '64, and since the original Tonkin Gulf incident, it's never happened, has it? Everybody knows this war is a political war. Shit's all managed in Washington and Moscow and Peking and Hanoi. Tit for fucking tat. Commies pulled the Tet offensive, we restarted the bombing in the North. The slopes make nice in Paris, we suspend the bombing in the North. Now ole Tricky Dicky announces he's gonna wind this thing up. If that's so, what're we *doin'* here? Is this a real war? It sure as shit is for the pilots who have to go north and do the bombing and get shot down or shot up. Their war is for fucking real. For tin cans like *Berkeley* who get to run the gun line all the time in range of the coastal guns, *their* war is real. But the *Hood,* man? Shit, we do PIRAZ. We do Red Crown. We're a TACAN out in the Gulf, a voice on the radio keeping all the support aircraft from running into one another. We provide a deck for the SAR helos when the guys who do the real war get their asses in a sling. So, a little reefer here, a pinch of hash in your Mixture Seventy-nine there, no big deal, see? This isn't the fifties, I Like Ike, okay? Ike was square, man. These days, you gotta be cool, be with it, be hip, man, be smart. Drug problem in the Navy? You go along, keep your head down and your eyes in the boat, draw your combat pay, get 'combat operations' fitness reports, and you move right along. Leave the drug problem to the NIS guys."

Brian was silent for a moment. "You almost make it sound pretty reasonable," he said.

"Yeah, well, you and me, we know it's a crock. 'Cause eventually, some bad shit is gonna come howling out of the night and, like you said, we'll have a space cadet on the console and we'll get our asses waxed. The dopers and the good guys, I can see where they're coming from. White hats and black hats. But the go-along, go-easy fuckers, they're lower than whale shit in my book.''

He paused, taking a long drag on his cigarette. "There's another angle to this, though. You're a department head now, in a lieutenant commander's billet on a big-deal missile ship. The system expects you to be savvy about all this by now, see? Which means you gotta make a decision on how *you're* gonna play it.''

"That's not hard.''

"Oh, is that so? Lemme see. I'm guessing you're in the same boat, careerwise, as I'm in. You're being re-toured in a second department head tour because the first one wasn't all that terrific. Now, you tell me: Can you afford to be a caped crusader with that lieutenant commander promotion board coming up? You gonna do a drug sweep, go piss-test your whole department tomorrow? You remember the old Navy staff rule, don't you? Maybe you don't—you've never been a staff puke. It goes like this: Don't go asking a question if you can't stand *all* the possible answers.''

Brian was again silent. Benedetti finished his coffee and stubbed out his cigarette in the saucer. "Actually, you don't wanta answer that question. It's too easy to say what you're going to do, Brian,'' he said, getting up. "But the first time you walk in on the one guy who can always fix the missile launcher, the primo star who keeps it up and running, and he's got a red face and big dopey eyes and there's reefer stink in the compartment—that's when you're gonna have to decide who you are and where you stand. It's tougher than it sounds.''

"After what I saw in *Berkeley*'s wardroom today, it's not tough at all.''

Benedetti stretched. "I hear you. But I think the first time you run into it, you're gonna call the XO and Chief Jesus and not the CO and the chief master-at-arms. You gotta admit, at least your bosun's mate, he gives you satisfaction. CO's gonna give you a little pep talk.'' He looked at his watch, shook it, and looked at it again. "Tomorrow's turnover day,'' he said. "We become Red

Crown for real. Or actually, you and Austin become Red Crown."

"How's that?"

"After today's fiasco, the Old Man took me off the CIC watch bill, so you and Austin are going to do the evaluator job six on, six off for the next forty-five days. I get to spend my time in the holes holding shit together." He eyed Brian speculatively. "Welcome aboard, shipmate."

"It's a real pleasure to be here, sir," said Brian, repeating the old formula and digesting the news that he and Austin would be on port and starboard watches for perhaps the rest of the cruise, "I think."

Benedetti laughed, slid his mug into the pantry window, and left. Brian sat in the silent wardroom with his cold coffee, thinking about what Benedetti had told him. He looked around the wardroom. The furnishings were much fancier than those in his last ship—upholstered armchairs and a couch and even some end tables with real lamps. The overhead was tiled in acoustic panels, giving a softer look to the room than the expanded metal usually found in destroyers. The walls were white. The only patch of white in the *Berkeley*'s wardroom had been the bone white pallor of the bodies on the table. He shivered as the image intruded. He sat back and closed his eyes.

His first sight of what war really looks like and he had puked like a seasick recruit. And the look on the exec's face: What are you doing out here on the bridge, Mr. Holcomb? Did a little death scrabbling on the outside bulkheads unnerve you? Admit it, you were scared. Okay, but anyone who wouldn't be scared when that shit starts is a fool. Yeah, but you're not supposed to show it, Mr. Senior Lieutenant. No puking in front of the troops. He suddenly wondered whether Benedetti's frustration with his job had more to do with the drug scene and how he was being forced to play it by the go-along-to-get-along people than with the normal travail of being chief engineer.

He thought again about Maddy. They would get their first logistics helo tomorrow after the turnover. He wondered whether he would get a letter. He had sent cards from Pearl and a letter from Subic. Mail from the States took almost three weeks to get out to the ships. He relived the unreasonable feeling of guilt that settled in his guts whenever he went off to sea, a feeling amplified by the tormenting notion that perhaps the important things in life were passing him by, real life, with a family, kids, maybe. But in their many rounds on the subject before the deployment, Maddy had been adamant, in that sweet but steely voice she came up with sometimes: no kids until Daddy was going to be ashore for more than two weeks at a pop.

He knew that his tour in *Hood* would cap off the longest stint of sea duty in a typical career. The first eight to nine years for a surface ship officer were traditionally spent on sea duty, or in schools preparing for sea duty. Maddy had had a brief taste of Navy life when they were married three months into his tour in *Decatur*. Two months after their wedding, the ship had gone to the Mediterranean for a six-month deployment, abbreviated for Brian when orders for postgraduate school came. But the months of separation had taken a toll on their young marriage. If the tour in *Decatur* had not been followed by two years in Monterey at the Navy Postgraduate school, he might have lost her. Brian knew Maddy feared abandonment more than anything else. Now he was deployed again, this time for seven months. If they could only get by this hump, and if he made lieutenant commander, he would go ashore for a two- to three-year shore-duty tour before coming back to sea as an exec in a destroyer—assuming Maddy would wait. Her first letter would reveal a lot.

He heard the stewards stirring in the wardroom pantry and looked at his watch. Almost time for midrats. Austin wanted him in Combat by 0500 to help with the turnover evolution. He got up, pushed his mug into the pantry window, and headed up to his stateroom.

10

Chief Jackson peered down into the shiny hatch coaming of Number Two Fire Room. A stainless-steel ladder went straight down for four rungs, then bent to the left at an angle, disappearing into the jungle of machinery and steam lines on the upper level of the after fire room. A small hurricane of air from the ship's interior rushed by his head into the fire room. Jackson had a secret fear of heights, and the vertiginous view from the top of the ladder, accentuated by that awkward bend, gave him pause. He took a deep breath and climbed over the coaming, turned around, and went down the ladder backward. He knew that the snipes prided themselves on going down the other way, facing into the fire room, the ladder rungs at their heels. He had also seen one BT carried out of this very fire room with his leg broken backward from a fall on the ladder, so he chose the "twidget style," as the snipes called it. A twidget was anybody who wasn't an engineer, and therefore, according to the snipes, not a real man.

He was already perspiring by the time he reached the upper level of the fire room. The nominal temperature on the upper level was 110 degrees, despite the efforts of the eighteen-inch-diameter exhaust vents roaring in the overhead of the space. The ladder landed on a steel-grid catwalk that extended between the two main propulsion steam boilers and gave access to main feed pumps and other auxiliary machinery arranged around the boilers. The upper level was unmanned, as the control consoles, the firing alley, and the relatively cooler air was down on the lower level, closer to the bilges. The lighting in the space shined yellow due to the steam-tight shields on the bulbs; the space stank of fuel oil, hot salt water, steam, and old asbestos lagging. Jackson's objective was the tool crib and BT2 Gallagher, who was rumored to be hiding out there. He walked across the catwalk to the next ladder, careful not to touch any hot metal, and, turning around once again, went down the ladder to the lower level.

This ladder gave onto the firing alley, a space about ten feet wide between the burner fronts of the two boilers. It was called the firing alley because the burners that supplied fuel oil to the two 1,200-psi steam boilers were loaded and serviced from this area. At the other end of the alley was the control console, where a boiler tender first class leaned nonchalantly on a battered three-legged stool and watched his dials. Two other men in oil-stained dungarees sat sweating on the step up from the alley to the console platform, directly under an air-supply vent. Because the supply vents terminated on the lower level, the temperature here was a slightly more humane 100 degrees. The machinery noise was terrific as the muted roar of the firebox in the one boiler on the line combined with the turbine whines from main feed pumps, fuel-oil service pumps, the combustion-control compressor, the air vents, all of it amplified by being confined in the steel compartment of the fire room, which was beneath the waterline. The three engineers wore spring-clip hearing protectors, and Jackson wished he had plugged his ears before he'd come down here. After his many years around the guns, he could not afford much more hearing loss.

The engineers, all white, looked at him with blank expressions as he walked over to the console flat. If there was any division in the ship that was a hard-core bastion of racist whites, it was B Division.

"I'm looking for BT Two Gallagher," Jackson shouted to the first class. The first class pushed one earplug aside and asked him to say it again. Jackson complied, louder this time, sensitive to the fact that they were playing with him. The first class looked over at his two watch mates and then back at Jackson.

"Haven't seen him," he shouted back.

Jackson thought for a minute. His sources had been pretty sure that this is where Gallagher was hiding out. The chief engineer had reputedly told Gallagher that he would go get his .45 and shoot him if he laid eyes on him, and Gallagher had apparently decided that the smart thing to do was to lie low for a week in case Mr. Benedetti meant it. The chief boiler tender, incensed over what Gallagher had done, had put in a special request chit to the exec asking to get Gallagher transferred over to *Berkeley,* which Jackson thought was a capital idea. Let them shoot him.

"Where's the tool crib?" Jackson shouted back.

"It's over there, behind two Able boiler. But it's locked up; chief's got the key."

"That's okay. You," he said, pointing to one of the sitting men, "you show me where it is."

The BT1 suddenly looked worried. "I think maybe you better call—"

Jackson walked right up close to the BT1. "Don't give me any shit, BT One," he said. Funny, the man could hear him *now.* "If I say so, you'll cut the lock on the tool crib and empty it out for inspection. Right, BT One?" He turned back to the other man. "Now, you—let's go."

The BT1 scowled and reached for the phone. The younger petty officer got up as slowly as he could without being clearly insubordinate and led Jackson around to the back of 2A boiler, where he pointed to the tool crib, a wire cage ten by ten feet, constructed against the forward bulkhead of the fire room and lined with shelves for spare parts, rags, lubricants, and tools. The light fixture on top of the tool crib was not working. No supply vents cooled this area behind 2A boiler, so the heat was stupefying. The engineer spat into the bilges and then sidled away, leaving Jackson standing in the two-foot space between the forward bulkhead of the fire room and the hot steel air casing of the boiler.

Although the tool crib was dark, Jackson thought he could see someone in there. As he approached it, he noticed that the door, chain link on a steel frame, was not locked. He opened the door and found Gallagher asleep on a bale of rags. He nudged the petty officer with his foot and woke him up. Gallagher sat up with a start, and when he saw khaki in the dim light behind the boiler, his face grimaced in fear. Jackson had an idea why, and it had nothing to do with Mr. Benedetti.

"On your feet, Gallagher. I want to talk to you."

Gallagher got up slowly, rubbing his face. He was dressed in a ragged, oil-soaked pair of dungarees, which the main-space engineers called their bilge diving suit. He stank, and Jackson wondered how long he had been holed up there. There was a dirty mess-decks tray lying in the small wash sink inside the tool crib, and an oil-smeared plastic water jug in the corner. All the comforts of home. Jackson looked over his shoulder to make sure the other man had left, then stepped back so Gallagher could come out of the tool crib.

Gallagher was a short, squat, heavily muscled young man of about twenty-five; he had perpetual grease and oil stains on his hands, lower arms, neck, and face, and red hair everywhere.

"You know who I am?" Jackson asked. It was somewhat quieter behind the boiler, so he did not have to shout. He wiped his face.

"Yeah. You're the Sheriff."

"That's right, Gallagher. And you're the guy who got high on marijuana, dropped the load, put us dead in the water, and killed ten guys over in *Berkeley*."

Gallagher frowned and stared down at the deck plates. Hot black bilgewater sloshed around beneath the stainless-steel plates. His lips were working, but he said nothing.

"So now that you're famous," Jackson pressed, "what I want to know is, where'd you get the dope?"

Gallagher shook his head but still said nothing. Then he looked up. "I don't gotta say nothin'," he said. "Those're my rights."

Jackson leaned forward, getting in the shorter man's face. He bared some teeth and hardened his voice.

"This isn't mast, shithead. This is just a friendly little discussion. See, I'm the first guy's gonna talk to you, but the way I hear it, the second guy's gonna want to dance first, talk later. You catch my drift?"

Jackson saw the flash of fear in Gallagher's eyes. He knew what was coming. Gallagher shook his head again, looking from side to side as if to escape. Then he seemed to wilt.

"Okay," he said. "I brung it with me. I don't sell it or nothin'; just a toke now'n then."

"At general quarters."

"Okay, so I fucked up. Nobody told me about no GQ. I was in my tree, the bell rang . . ."

"So you were spaced-out when you got down here for GQ."

"Maybe. A little."

Jackson stared down at the man, willing him to look up from the deck, but Gallagher kept his face down.

"So where's your stuff?"

"I deep-sixed it after . . . after . . . you know. I don't got no more, honest."

"Why do I not believe you, hunh? You know what? I heard the chief BT had a brain-fart. He's offering to transfer your sorry ass over to the *Berkeley,* along with a letter telling them who you are and what you are and what you did two days ago. I mean, hell, it ought to beat living in the tool crib, right? Even if it'd be sort of a short tour, you know?"

Gallagher looked confused and then afraid as he thought it through. The crew of *Berkeley* would put him *in* a boiler and throw the torch in after him. Jackson watched him weigh the possibilities and then saw a cunning look come into his eyes.

"You're just fucking around with me," he mumbled.

"Am I? Want to see the chit? XO's got it, and I'll tell you what—he's thinkin' about it. They would see that justice was done, and there'd be no shit on our hands, see?"

This was a logic that Gallagher could indeed understand.

"So what's the deal?"

"Deal? What deal?"

Gallagher looked from side to side as if to see whether there was anyone else around. "C'mon, Chief," he said. "I'm in enough shit already. What do you want?"

"I want the guy or guys you'll have to go see to replenish your little treasure, that's what I want."

Gallagher stepped back away from Jackson and glanced back into the tool crib, as if he wanted to get back under his rock. Jackson heard some bells ringing around in front of the boiler and heard the pitch of the forced draft-blower turbines rise as the ship increased speed for some reason. Gallagher's face streamed with sweat, and Jackson's as he waited, his own khaki shirt glued to his back in the heat. Gallagher looked around again, sighed, and then gave a little nod.

"Okay, okay. I sure as shit don't want no transfer to the fuckin' *Berkeley*. You wanna know who moves product in this boat, you go see the ni—you go see your soul brothers."

Jackson glared at him. "Meaning exactly what by that?"

Gallagher stared back, an impudent look spreading on his face, but did not answer him. Jackson wanted to hit him.

"You saying the drug ring is black?"

"Don't know nothin' about no ring. Didn't say nothin' about no ring, did I? Did I? Look, those fuckers find out I even talked to you, they're—"

"Lemme tell you something, Gallagher: You've got bigger and sooner problems than that," Jackson interrupted.

Gallagher's eyes widened. "Jesus Christ, c'mon, Sheriff, I gave ya somethin', didn't I? You ain't gonna let—"

Jackson straightened up. "You didn't give me diddly-shit, Gallagher. You're still calling black people niggers, so why am I not surprised you'd say you're getting your dope from 'em, hunh? See you, Gallagher. And you better get a bigger lock on that door. The bosun'll bite through that one and call it practice."

He left Gallagher standing by the tool crib and climbed up out of the fire room. He shivered in the almost-cold air of the main passageway and walked forward to his small office on Broadway, where he kept some clean spare shirts. He thought about what Gallagher had said. Supposing Gallagher was telling the truth, which would be a rare event, that blacks had the drug concession. That complicated matters—a lot. Any investigation targeted specifically against blacks would trigger an instantaneous hue and cry about oppression and persecution from the hotheads on the ship's Human Relations Council, even if Jackson was leading the charge.

One other doper had claimed the same thing—that he got his marijuana from one of the blacks, hinting that they had the lock on selling dope on the ship. If it was true, Jackson knew that it was likely to be a small group of younger blacks who were disaffected from the rest of the crew, including most of the other blacks. Having a seat on the ship's Human Relations Council, he knew the stats: *Hood* had about three dozen black men in the crew, with a fair mixture of nonrated men, petty officers and chiefs, and one officer, the Supply officer, Raiford Hatcher. He knew that most of them were upstanding citizens, sincerely interested in getting ahead and making something of themselves just like anyone else. But there was one group of about eight men who were clearly and openly hostile to whites and, for that matter, to the Filipinos and Hispanics who made up the rest of the minority mix in the ship. Chief Martinez called them equal-opportunity racists: They seemed to hate everybody. Since one of Jackson's responsibilities was to keep an eye out for racial flash points, he had been watching them. If these guys were involved in the drug business, it would add a whole new dimension to a problem that he had thought was primarily racial.

He reached his office, unlocked the door, and closed it behind him. He shucked the wet shirt and toweled off his face and arms. Jackson did not approve of the exec's off-the-books, gun-deck justice system, although the thought of Martinez closing in on Gallagher provided a certain satisfaction. Jackson wanted to do it right: conduct a regular investigation, a Navy *regulation* investigation, penetrate the ring, turn some snitches, find the main man, catch his ass, and blow up the whole thing with courts-martial and brig time. He knew he would have to find an ally in the wardroom if he was ever going to pull this off, preferably one of the department heads, because it would take a department head to run interference with the XO. Martinez said that the new guy, Holcomb, was a straight arrow. Maybe he would try that route, get something going. If they could pull it off, they could bring it up as a package to the XO, and then maybe they'd do it right. There was a loud knock on his door and then Chief Martinez stepped into his office.

"He there?" growled the boatswain.

"Gallagher? Yeah, he's there. And scared shitless, too. He knows you're on the prowl. But guess what—he gave me some news."

"No shit. He name somebody?"

"Not exactly, but he said that if you want a little taste, you have to go see one of the brothers." Jackson slipped on a clean shirt, transferred the insignia and his badge, and began to button up.

Martinez was silent, his ugly round face twisted in thought. "I wouldn'ta figured that," he said finally. "Guess I got too many buddies who're black."

"Well, it wouldn't be news on the outside, least that's what they told us in MAA school. And I can guess which bunch it is, if it's true. But what I'm trying to figure out is who, among the blacks in *Hood,* would be the main man. I mean, yeah, we've got racists on both sides of the street, but a kingpin drug dealer? I can't put a face on that."

"One of them new guys, that black-power bunch."

Jackson rolled up the wet shirt and threw it onto his cluttered desk. Martinez cracked his knuckles, making a sound like a bundle of firewood being run over by a tire.

"That guy Bullet, the electrician, he's a leader," Martinez mused. "Every time the hotheads get to running their mouth, he's one of the guys who can put a lid on it. He don't talk much, but the young bloods are always lookin' to see what he thinks."

"EM One Wilson?"

"Yeah."

"I'll take a look at his record, but I don't have anything on him one way or the other. If he's a big man on campus with the radical bunch, he's keeping real quite about it."

"Yeah. Doesn't want to attract no attention, maybe. Might be worth a lookee-see."

Jackson was straightening out his shirt. He paused to look at Martinez. "Yeah, okay. I see what you mean."

11

"Red Crown, this is Wager on Air Force Green."

Brian lifted the red radiotelephone handset from its
mounting, keyed the switch, waited for the squeak of
the encryption tone burst, and replied, *"Wager, Red
Crown, over."*

*"And this is Wager. Going off-station for three hours
to happy hour; ETA back on station nineteen-thirty."*

"Red Crown, roger, out."

Brian replaced the handset and raised his eyebrows at
Garuda Barry, who acknowledged the message from
Wager. The Wager Bird, as it was known on PIRAZ, was
an Air Force Boeing 707. It flew several thousand miles
from Guam to the Gulf every day of the year and then
orbited over the Gulf at 45,000 feet to provide UHF
radio-relay service for all the American air forces—Navy,
Air Force, and Marines—operating over North Vietnam.
Brian looked at his watch. Austin should be up to relieve
him in an hour or so. The time had flown on this his
first watch as evaluator on the PIRAZ station. He was
thoroughly fascinated.

Combat had settled out after the flurry of the morning
turnover, with its helicopter transfers of PIRAZ station
files, computer tapes, message air plans for each of the
four carriers now in WESTPAC, and the watch station
pass-down-the-line logs. Officers and senior enlisted from
Long Beach's CIC had transferred over to *Hood* to
brief their counterparts in *Hood*'s CIC formally on the
peculiarities of radar and communications conditions in
the Gulf, the latest enemy air-activity profiles, and the
electronic-warfare environment. They brought radar
video and audio tapes of the most recent air strikes and
files of other intelligence matters. When *Long Beach*
returned in a month and a half, all of it, updated by
Hood, would be transferred back.

Informally, the word came on which of the carriers had the most aggressive fighter pilots, what were the best bribes to keep the daily logistics helo happy to ensure a steady flow of replacements and mail, and what kinds of mistakes were likely to provoke the current admiral on Yankee Station into sending hate mail. At a predesignated time, *Long Beach* had turned off her TACAN beacon and *Hood* had turned on hers.

The TACAN was one of the PIRAZ ship's main reasons for being: Since the PIRAZ ship remained within a five-mile geographically fixed station in the Gulf of Tonkin, any U.S. or Allied aircraft operating over or around North Vietnam and the Gulf could switch to the Red Crown TACAN frequency and get an instant positional fix. And if the aircraft's TACAN was not working, he could switch to the Red Crown control frequency, transmit a specified transponder code, and the PIRAZ ship's powerful air-search radar would find him, fix his position, and give him a steer to his home base.

"We're baby-sitters," Austin had said. "They get into trouble, they know we're here. They navigate all over this part of Southeast Asia using our TACAN, and they know there's an SAR helo if they have to ditch. There's some evidence that the Communists use it, too."

"I had no idea there were so many aircraft operating out here," Brian had observed, staring at the amber scope with its intricate and glittering digital symbology.

"Nobody does. But when the bombing campaign is active, there can be as many as a hundred aircraft up over North Vietnam or the Gulf, night and day. That's what all those people back in the detection and tracking module do. It's Red Crown's job to sort them out and especially to ensure that a MiG doesn't slip in with a gaggle of aircraft returning to the carrier, say, after a night strike."

"Do you think they'd actually try that?"

"No, because I think the carriers are politically off limits. But ask me if they *could* do it, and I'd have to say yes, or at least they could try. That's what PIRAZ really stands for: positive identification radar advisory zone. We positively identify every aircraft within two hundred

119

miles. And that's why we're stationed out here in the Gulf between the main North Vietnamese airfields and our carriers to the south. We're the gatekeepers."

Brian stood behind the ship's weapons coordinator console. The SWIC controlled everything that happened in Combat by means of keyboard actions and intercom commands. All of the module supervisors reported to the SWIC: detection and tracking, known as the Cave because it was totally darkened to enhance radarscope contrast, weapons control, surface operations, computer control, antisubmarine control, electronic warfare, and the PIRAZ air controllers. The SWIC could communicate with all of the modules and could access any one of the ship's thirty-six radio-communications links. He usually had the intercom circuit in one half of his headset and a radio channel in the other ear. The SWIC was a prestigious qualification. It took at least a year to qualify an officer on the SWIC console, and very few officers in the ship could manage the intricate mix of hand-eye coordination in executing computer commands and the concentration required to interpret the symbology while the intercom whispered in one ear and a radio circuit squawked in the other.

Because Brian was new to the PIRAZ station, Austin had assigned Chief Warrant Officer Barry, the ship's computer officer, and the most qualified SWIC to stand watches with Brian. After only a few hours, Brian had come to appreciate Austin's choice. The word *garuda* meant "dragon" in pidgin Chinese, and Barry was the technical dragon of CIC. An ex-enlisted radarman who had come up through the ranks to chief petty officer and who then had been commissioned as a technical specialist, Barry knew more about *Hood*'s CIC and supporting combat systems than any other officer or chief in the ship, and he was fiercely proud of his technical knowledge. Barry was thirty-five but looked forty-five; he was a short, rotund man with prematurely gray hair, a round face, steel-rimmed glasses, shaky hands, and a cigarette permanently embedded in his mouth. He had spent his entire career in the Pacific Fleet and his speech was full of WESTPAC slang, acronyms, and pidgin Chinese and Japanese expressions. He had taught himself computer programming and he could restore the NTDS operations program in a flurry of button smashing. He could diagnose an intermittent electrical fault in one of the systems, track it down to a precise pin on a connector, and then repair it quicker than most of the techs. He had given Brian a tour of the symbology on his scope with the patience of someone who knew he would have to do it again several times.

"That's a quick an' dirty," Garuda had said after a twenty-minute point-and-explain drill on the scope for his fledging evaluator. "And that's a 'quiet' scope, 'cause there isn't a strike going in. When there's a strike, it goes times three."

"Right. Got it all. Piece a cake. I'm qualified to do SWIC now," Brian had replied, rolling his eyes. Garuda had grinned.

"Trick is," he had said, "you study one kind of symbol each watch and concentrate on what it does through the watch. After about a month, you'll be able to read this display like a book. And the other trick is, if you try to learn it, you'll be ahead of most people who never even try. Then they'll think you're an expert."

From his station at a desk in D and D, Brian could see directly into the surface module, where the surface watch officer and his three radarmen stood their watch, keeping track of all surface contacts within twenty miles of the ship. They used the SPS-10 surface-search radar and plotted contacts on a glass-topped plotting table, feeding information out to the officer of the deck on the bridge. To the right of surface was the weapons control module, containing two user consoles and the guided-missile system launch-control panels. To his left was the entrance to the Cave, the module in which radarmen converted raw video detected by the ship's two air-search radars into computer symbology on eight input consoles. The consoles looked like large gray desks with slant tops and round televisions mounted flush into each slant top. Directly to the right of the SWIC console were the two primary air-controller consoles. One air controller directed a pair of Phantom jets on a continuous barrier station off the coast of North Vietnam. The other controller was the PIRAZ controller, who issued advisory control instructions to the dozens of support aircraft operating over the Gulf. Taking Garuda's advice, Brian dedicated his first watch to learning the names of everything he could see from his chair.

Garuda pushed his headset back off his ears for a moment. "Wager Bird goes off-station, everything quiets down a bunch," he said. "Those staffies down on Yankee Station do love their secure-voice radio."

"No Wager, no secure voice?"

"Not with the faraway bosses. The Gulf has one secure-voice circuit—Air Force Green. Because it's secure, Air Force Green has become the virtual command circuit for the Gulf—the admiral, who's the anti–air warfare commander down the carrier, the PIRAZ ship, the Air Force air control center on Monkey Mountain at Da Nang, and the North and South SAR ships—we're all up on Green."

Garuda moved the electronic pointer around the scope. "The carriers are about a hundred and twenty miles away on Yankee Station—right here. Da Nang is a hundred and forty-five miles, in the land smear, here. The South SAR destroyer station is around sixty miles, there, and North SAR is also about sixty miles away, up off of Haiphong harbor, there. So Green has to be relayed, and that's what the Wager Bird does. From forty-five thousand feet, most of Southeast Asia is in his line-of-sight range."

"Seems like an expensive way to talk, having a whole seven-oh-seven dedicated to just one radio circuit."

"Yes, sir, but it's real nice when trouble starts to be able to call that bird farm and get some fighters up without having to go through a buncha voice codes on a clear HF circuit."

"What happens when Wager goes home?"

"We have no secure voice with the carriers between about midnight and dawn. We just hope the bad guys stay in their boxes between those hours."

"If they don't?"

"We'd be on our own, Mr. Holcomb. But I been out here on PIRAZ since 1966. We've never seen a MiG come feet-wet yet. They know we'd smack their asses, they get within range of our missiles. And we got the barrier combat air patrol, that's BARCAP in CIC talk. Two Phantom jets on-station twenty-four hours a day, just itchin' to bag a MiG. Those guys wanta come out over the Gulf and mix it up, let's do it to it.''

"I copy that," chimed in the BARCAP controller from the other side of the SWIC console.

Brian nodded. He was still getting used to the unique status of the ship's full-time air controllers. *Hood* had five fully qualified air-intercept controllers, or AICs. An AIC's job was to take Navy fighters under close control on his radarscope and direct them via UHF radio circuit to a tactical position in space from which they could lock onto an enemy aircraft with their own missile systems and bring it down.

Brian recognized that the AICs in *Hood* were an elite group. The bonds of trust between the controllers and their fighter pilots had risen to almost mystical levels of human interaction and dependence. The controller sat in front of a radarscope that displayed an area of 250 miles in diameter in three dimensions—direction, distance, and altitude. Because the tactical geometry of a fighter engagement was basically an exercise in spherical trigonometry, where the enemy started out somewhere on the edge of a sphere whose diameter could be a hundred miles, the fighter pilot was obliged to follow almost blindly the controller's directions on heading, course, speed, altitude, and turns as the controller contracted the sphere on his radarscope to put the enemy aircraft in his fighter's gun sights. Depending on what kind of missile was going to be used, the controller strove to put his fighters behind and below, or head-to-head, with the enemy aircraft. The crucial difference was that the controller could see and the pilot could not, right up until the final seconds when his target appeared magically right in front of him, allowing the radar-intercept officer in the backseat of the Phantom to take over, lock on, and make the kill.

That the controllers were enlisted and the pilots all officers made the bond even more special, because the pilots unequivocally put their lives in the hands of their controller. AIC training was intense and continuous, and the controllers had to requalify at school or through live control once every three months. They were certified by the FAA and they kept logbooks recording their licenses, training, and recertifications just like their civilian brethren. They were intensely proud of their skills and they were uniformly aggressive in their desire to bag a MiG, which perfectly reflected the aggressive spirit of fighter pilots throughout the Navy. Bonds of confidence developed over time to the point where pilots would ask for controllers by name if they thought a tough tactical problem was shaping up.

Brian discovered that the AICs, imitating pilots, had all acquired nicknames and deliberately laid-back speech patterns on the radio. There was a great deal of slang in use, much of which was inspired by the recent CB radio craze sweeping the States. Eavesdropping on one of the AIC circuits, Brian noted that both pilots and controllers had adopted a carefully contrived degree of radio cool, behind which lay the very real tensions of life-and-death maneuvers at forty thousand feet and six hundred miles per hour. If an actual intercept situation developed, however, Brian observed that the slang and the CB nonsense disappeared in an instant, to be replaced by the razor-sharp commands of standardized fighter-control procedures.

Garuda had explained that there were not enough AICs to go around in the Navy, so they were often cross-decked to a ship going out to PIRAZ, did a seven-month cruise, came back to the States for a month or so, and then cross-decked to another PIRAZ-bound ship. Many of them adopted the mannerisms of hired gunslingers, which, in effect, was exactly what they were. They tended to be taciturn about their craft and carried themselves with a staged indifference to their surroundings until they manned up an AIC scope.

Beyond the mechanics of their craft, the AICs held special status in the crew. They were paid more than other E-6s and typically had no other duties except air control. They seemed to adjust their own watches to accommodate their individual physical abilities to focus on the screen, wandering in and out of CIC at will. Garuda had pointed out another fact: Because the AICs sat at the right hand of the SWIC in D and D and were thus privy to the conversations among the ship's senior officers, they were the source of the best gossip on the crew's grapevine.

The AIC on watch was nicknamed HooDoo. HooDoo, whose real name was Alonzo Jones, was a tall, very thin black man with an arresting face: deeply hooded and intense eyes, sharply hooked nose, thin lips, and a predatory, almost-cruel expression. He was purportedly into African spiritualism, voodoo, and other occult interests. He had an astonishingly deep voice, which he used to great effect when controlling. Many of the blacks in the ship were more than a little unsettled by HooDoo, who combined the expected aloofness of an AIC with an occasional incantation often enough to put the more superstitious off their feed.

"SWIC, I'm gonna tank these BARCAP in about eleven mikes," HooDoo announced.

"SWIC, aye, and Red Crown controller, where's the basketball?"

"Basketball is two-four-zero for eighty miles," replied the PIRAZ controller. The PIRAZ controller kept everybody from running into one another; as such, he was an advisory controller, not a close-control fighter-directing controller, and therefore something of a lesser being.

"What's a basketball?" asked Brian. He was little tired of having to ask the "What's a" question every time Garuda did something, but Garuda's patience appeared to be endless.

"Basketball is a Marine C-One twenty-four cargo plane configured as an air-to-air tanker. He orbits northeast of Da Nang and refuels any Gulf aircraft that needs gas. We run the BARCAP off-station to refuel at least once during each mission. That way, they keep minimum combat package in case we have to vector them for a bogey."

Brian shook his head. Three more questions had popped up with Garuda's explanation, but he decided to give it a rest. He just nodded and wandered over to surface to get some coffee. And he had thought missile school was hard. But he was impressed with how quickly *Hood*'s Combat crew had settled into their PIRAZ station routine. Each of the modules appeared to be humming along, the watch standers doing their thing against a backdrop of radio-circuit chatter, the clicking of buttons on the consoles, and the steady rush of cooling air from the sixteen consoles.

Radarman First Class Rockheart was in charge of surface in Brian's watch section. He greeted Brian with a sincere "Afternoon, sir" and filled the evaluator's cup with fresh coffee. Brian was impressed with Rockheart's appearance and military bearing. Rockheart was obviously CPO material.

"All quiet on the surface front?" he asked. Surface was the one module he thought he understood. The familiar plotting tables and the SPS-10 surface-search radar were common to just about every Navy ship.

"Yes, sir," replied Rockheart. "No surface contacts, although this blip right here might be a log helo on the way up from Yankee Station." He pointed to an intermittent surface contact out at around forty miles.

"You surface guys doing air search with the ten?"

"No, sir, but the helos fly pretty low, maybe one or two thousand feet, so's not to attract attention from the other side's air-search radars. They could be MiG bait before we could get a CAP into it. And at that low altitude, the ten can see 'em."

"That would be pretty unusual, wouldn't it, RD One? As I understand it, the MiGs stay feet-dry as long as Red Crown is out here."

"Yes, sir, but there's a hole in the protection envelope for part of the helo's trip. Lemme show you on the NTDS scope."

They walked over to the surface console. Rockheart had the operator switch the display to the 150-mile range and suppress all symbols except surface ships. "See, we're here in the center; that forty-mile circle is our missile envelope. There's the south SAR station; there's nobody there now, but you can visualize the forty-mile circle around him. You can see there's a hole between the two of us where there's no missile coverage. For about fifty miles of their run, the logistics helo has no one covering him except the CAP."

"But MiGs would still have to come out over the Gulf to get at them."

"Yes, sir, and the BARCAP would be on 'em like a snake on a rat, but probably not until *after* they'd bagged the helo. Last year a couple of MiGs came out of the Vinh airfield—that's right here, due west—and shot down a Jolly Green Giant SAR helo that was orbiting twenty miles offshore during a strike." He switched the range scale down to sixty miles and pointed to a hook of land visible on the western edges of the radarscope. "The MiGs were loitering in the radar shadow of the mountains south of their base. None of the Gulf tracks got a look at 'em until they popped up feet-wet—that means over water—and zapped the helo, then zipped back into the mountains before anybody could react. That's why the log helo guys keep it on the deck when they come up here."

"I'll be damned. They could do the same thing to us if we weren't looking. We're only what—forty, fifty miles offshore right now?"

"Yes, sir, Mr. Holcomb, but, begging your pardon, sir, that's what your air side's for. MiGs show up, the AICs sic the BARCAP on 'em. If that doesn't work, your weapons module guys take 'em with our Terriers. The MiGs would be in range in about two seconds after they came feet-wet."

Holcomb nodded. "Assuming everything works. And assuming we or one of the surveillance tracks detects them before they get to the coast. Because if the first time we saw them was when they came over the beach, they could be in our face in around a hundred and eighty seconds. The BARCAP would have to be right overhead the MiGs' coast-out point to be of any use, and the Commies know where the BARCAP is just as well as we do."

"Yes, sir, I suppose. But Mr. Austin says they'd never try it on one of our ships 'cause there'd be a political shit storm. Bagging a helo's a different deal from hitting a ship. And, besides, Mr. Hudson says a straight-in shot like that is lunch meat for our Terriers."

"Assuming that they work."

Rockheart grinned. "Well, yes, sir. That there's a whole nother question. But I assume they'd work. And you own the Terriers, sir."

Brian laughed. Touché. Rockheart was tactfully pointing out that the Weapons officer had better not be saying that his Terrier surface-to-air missile systems might not work. But both men knew the truth, as anyone who had been in Combat during Terrier missile exercises could attest: The complex Terrier missile-guidance systems and their fire-control radars were notorious for tripping off the line at critical moments. Just like Benedetti's control air compressor, Brian mused.

"You just gotta have faith, RD One," he said, and returned to D and D, where Garuda confirmed that a log helo was inbound.

"We'll have the bridge call flight quarters when he's thirty minutes out," he announced. "That's usually how long it takes to get the flight-deck crew and the firefighters on deck and to get Radio to patch the land-launch circuit correctly out to PriFly. That usually takes about five tries."

"Roger that," replied Brian, unconsciously imitating the AIC's slang. A log helo might mean some mail was inbound. It had been nearly a month since they left San Diego. Mail call, Brian thought. Sugar report, in Navy slang. Everyone longed for mail call. But for the first time, he wondered what might be coming in the mail—Dear Brian or Dear John.

"Evaluator, SWIC, calling flight away quarters now."

Evaluator. That's me, Brian thought. "Evaluator, aye," he replied.

12

San Diego

The Sunday a week following her experience at MCRD, Maddy attended her second wardroom wives' get-together at the captain's house on the island of Coronado. She really liked Coronado, the part natural isthmus, part man-made island that extended across the front of San Diego harbor. Although Coronado was approachable from downtown San Diego only by a ferry ride, it was not strictly an island, attached as it was by a long strip of empty beach to the South Bay shore area down near the Mexican border. There were two major Navy installations on Coronado, the Amphibious Base on the south end and the North Island Naval Air Station on the north end. Sandwiched in between was some of the most exclusive real estate in San Diego, with its golf courses, prime beach, the palatial Hotel del Coronado, and the residential areas themselves, laid out on spacious avenues, beautifully landscaped, and containing some very expensive homes along the Pacific Ocean side. Like many Navy people, the Huntingtons had bought a modest rambler on Coronado back in the early fifties and hung on to it as a potential retirement residence. The house was now worth far more than they could ever afford to pay for it today, even on full captain's pay.

Maddy drove off the ferry onto First Street, then turned onto Orange Avenue. Consulting a piece of notepaper with the directions, she made her way to the Huntingtons' house. She recognized several other wardroom cars parked along the palm-lined street, especially Tizzy Hudson's convertible. She almost blushed again when she remembered the phone call from Tizzy Friday at work.

"And where exactly was Cinderella at midnight? The world wants to know." Tizzy had laughed.

Maddy had bobbed and weaved verbally, but finally told Tizzy of what had happened in the parking lot.

"Oh shit, I should have stayed. I should have come and found you. That's why everyone goes in twos and threes—those guys can get fairly elemental. I'm sorry. But what about this Gene Autry guy—is he good-looking?"

"He's an Indian, or part Indian. And I think it's just Autrey."

"O-ooo-oh. We got past the name stage, did we? How delicious. Does he have one of those big Indian noses? Is he fierce-looking?"

"Tizzy, the man saved me from being—you know. It was after midnight in a dark parking lot. He gave me a ride to the apartment, let me out the door, and left. I was too busy being sick to my stomach to notice too many personal details, okay? It's not like we made arrangements to meet again."

"Too bad. He sounds pretty interesting. And you were very lucky he came along. You going Sunday night?"

"Oh God, I forgot. I guess there's no way around it, is there?"

"No way that wouldn't attract attention. That's why she set it up for Sunday. No real excuse for not coming, even for us working girls, but no one will stay late except the ass-kissers."

"Mrs. Huntington didn't strike me as the type that would have much time for ass-kissing."

"You're right; she's sorta tough, but actually very nice. I think she'd let the 'extremely serious wives' stay just because she has a generous nature. You like her, don't you?"

"I guess," Maddy had said. "I'm just not used to this whole organized female scene."

"They call it a support system, whatever that means." Tizzy had laughed. "For the wives who need it, I suppose it's a good thing. Mrs. Huntington has been around; she's good people. She doesn't approve of me, but she treats me like a grown-up, anyway. I'll see you there, and I *will* want to know more about Mr. Autrey."

Maddy parked the car and walked up the shrub-lined

walk. She was dressed in a knee-length pleated skirt, a short-sleeved silk blouse, open at the throat, with a bright scarf, and low heels. She had not yet quite figured out the dress code for the wives' functions, so she tended to overdress, forgetting that she was no longer on the East Coast. As she waited for the door to open, she plumped her hair, wondering whether she ought to cut it. No one wore long hair out here.

The door opened; Mrs. Huntington was smiling at her.

"Maddy, come in. I'm so glad you could make it. We don't see enough of you career girls. You found it okay? Good. Come in, come in."

The captain's wife was dressed in slacks and a sleeveless blouse and wore red sandals. Her hair was silver throughout and cut short. She maintained a trim figure for a woman in her late fifties, and Maddy could see that she must have been something as a bride. Her face was tanned and lined after nearly thirty years of traipsing around the Navy, and some of her husband's commanding presence had worn off on his wife. A consummate hostess, self-assured and at ease in any company, she was old enough to be motherly toward all the wardroom wives, even the exec's. Maddy felt more than a little in awe of her.

Mrs. Huntington took Maddy through the living room area and out onto a trellis-covered lanai, which in the fall evening air was delightfully cool. The rest of the wives had scattered around the lanai, sitting on lawn chairs and some kitchen furniture that had been moved outside. Trays of canapes filled the tables and several bottles of wine stuck out of an ice-filled cooler. A second cooler contained soft drinks. Tizzy Hudson waved and patted an empty chair next to her. Mrs. Huntington went back inside to get the door again and Maddy joined Tizzy gratefully. She said hi to some of the other wives, many of whose names she did not know. She recognized Angela Benedetti and, of course, Cynthia Hatcher, the Supply officer's wife, who sat rather stiffly next to the executive officer's wife, Barbara Mains. Tizzy passed her a glass of wine and made small talk until the nearest of the women sitting next to them got up to see someone else.

"Okay, kid, give—what'd you think of MCRD?"

Maddy looked around, not sure what to reveal. "I think it's no place for a proper married lady," she began. "But I have to admit, I got into it for a while. I think it was the crowd—it's so packed in there that you're sort of dancing with everyone but not with anyone in particular." She looked around again. "Should we be talking about this? I mean, here?"

Tizzy laughed out loud, drawing a few curious looks. But most of them were used to Tizzy and her devil-may-care outlook.

"For heaven's sake, Maddy, relax already. This is 1969. These people can't tell you what you can and can't do."

"Yes, but I think it might hurt Brian's career if the captain's wife wrote to the captain that Mrs. Holcomb was hitting the bars."

Tizzy rolled her eyes and moved closer. "Well, yes, it might," she said, lowering her voice. "So you're right: You don't tell them. Honestly, some of these girls are regular busybodies. Nothing better to do, I guess. But when they ask me where I've been or why I didn't come for bridge, or tea, or lunch, I just give 'em a little of my Dizzy Tizzy routine, and my business stays my business. Look, you're still new to this Navy stuff. You can't let the wives' organization get ahold of your life, or you'll have no life."

"But the rest of them seem happy to be part of the wives' deal."

"It depends—some of them are afraid not to. Figure their husbands' careers depend on having a good little wife who takes the wives' group seriously, gets close to the CO's and the XO's wives, that sort of stuff. And some of them literally have nothing else, no jobs or other interests, so they just sort of naturally gravitate to a group."

She refilled their wineglasses from a bottle she had appropriated for the two of them. "And there are wives who need the group—women who are literally afraid of being alone in their empty apartments or houses, or who need constant reassurance that everything's okay with the ship and the guys. Hey, look, I'm not knocking it, okay? I've just got other fish to fry, a full-time job that I like and the freedom to do what I want with my own time.''

Maddy nodded, feeling a little better. But she could relate to the dread of being alone.

"So tell me more about this Autrey guy who rescued you from the Marine monster.''

Maddy covered her embarrassment with a laugh. "You tell me where you were when I came out to the parking lot at quarter to one?''

It was Tizzy's turn to laugh. "At quarter to one, Maddy? You didn't show up at midnight, and I was, uh, otherwise engaged, shall we say. Don't you just love this California wine? I've never had a bad one, have you? And have you tried that dip? It's absolutely—''

"Okay, okay, I give up. Spare me the routine, Tizzy.''

Tizzy's eyes sparkled at her over a cracker and cheese. "Autrey," she said, trying not to drip cracker crumbs. Maddy saw that the captain's wife had returned to the lanai, but she was not within hearing distance. Nevertheless, she, too, lowered her voice.

"Autrey. Autrey in the dark. Tall, black hair, dark eyes, Indian face. He didn't look all that big, but the guy who grabbed me literally ran away when Autrey told him his name, so there's something . . . but that's all I know. Oh, and he said he was a civilian PT instructor at MCRD, and he had a Chevy. And he smokes.''

"Groovy. You have to admit, he made an impression.''

"He saved my careless tail is what he did, and, yes, that did make an impression. And the way the Marine took off, that made an impression. But I'm not sure I was told the whole deal there.''

"So . . . you going to see him again?''

"*Tizzy!*" Maddy forgot to lower her voice, and Mrs. Huntington glanced over at them. Tizzy started laughing, trying to hide it behind her hand. Maddy hoped that Mrs. Huntington would think Tizzy was telling dirty jokes. The phone rang inside the house and Mrs. Huntington got up and went inside.

"I was just kidding," Tizzy said when she stopped giggling.

"I should hope so. It's bad enough I went to MCRD in the first place."

"Oh, BS," Tizzy said. "So you let off a little steam, ground the old horns down an inch or two, so what? Admit it, you did have some fun out there on that dance floor. I sure as hell did."

"I just don't want you to do anything to screw up Brian on this ship," Maddy said. "He's got to do well here to make lieutenant commander."

"Well, Fox is probably going to get out after the *Hood*," Tizzy said. "We're both pretty tired of the going away and the lousy pay. I'm going to support us while he goes to a good business school for an MBA, and then he's going to get out there and make some real money. The Navy is just hopeless. I don't know how these other gals live."

Maddy nodded. At the moment, she wouldn't mind if Brian did the same thing, but so far, Brian seemed pretty serious about the Navy, and especially about getting to command his own ship one day. And the *Hood* tour would determine his future, at least the way he talked about it. She wondered how he was doing with all that. Mrs. Huntington came back out on to the lanai. From the expression on her face, it was apparent there was news, and the lanai fell silent in just a few seconds as the Navy wives' antennae detected trouble.

"Oh shit, what's this?" muttered Tizzy.

"Girls, I've just had a call from the flotilla staff duty officer. The *Hood* was involved in a shooting incident somewhere off North Vietnam. There apparently was some trouble with the engineering plant and the ship took a couple of near misses of gunfire from the shore, but only one man, a radarman in CIC, was slightly injured. There was another ship involved—he didn't give me her name—that had several casualties, but not *Hood*. They're apparently all safe and the ship is on her way to the Red Crown station."

There was a twittering of female voices as the rest of the wives gathered around Mrs. Huntington to press for details. Tizzy stared down at the flagstone patio.

"We forget, don't we? Our guys are off to war."

Maddy was still getting over the sudden chill that had flooded her belly. The most exciting thing that had happened on Brian's last deployment was a near collision during a night training exercise in the Mediterranean, between an aircraft carrier and one of the ships in the screen, whatever a screen was. At least Brian had found that to be very exciting. But now her husband was on a ship that was being shot at? By the North Vietnamese? This wasn't how Brian had described the Red Crown station at all. It was supposed to be all CIC work, directing aircraft over the Gulf of Tonkin and spending endless hours staring at radar screens. She got up abruptly, leaving Tizzy to her wine, and joined the small crowd around Mrs. Huntington. When she could break in, she asked a question.

"Mrs. Huntington, what were they doing that they were close enough to North Vietnam to get shot at? I thought this Red Crown thing was out in the middle of the Gulf."

Mrs. Huntington nodded at her. "Yes, I asked the same question. He told me they were diverted to join a Sea Dragon operation—that's where the ships go up off the coast of North Vietnam and do shore bombardment. He said it was really unusual for a PIRAZ ship to do that, but *Hood* has a long-range gun, so off they went, I guess. But he assured me they were on their way to the Red Crown station and that all was well, Maddy."

Maddy listened to some more questions, then drifted back to where Tizzy was opening another bottle of wine.

"Doesn't that sort of thing bother you?" Maddy asked.

"Fox has told me a hundred times—he wanted to go to WESTPAC because that was where the action was. Sounds like they saw some action. Fox'll be higher than a kite if he got to shoot those guns. We'll find out more in the letters."

"Ugh, that's three weeks," groaned Maddy. She was amazed at Tizzy's indifference and wondered how much of her aplomb was real. She had not liked the expression on Mrs. Huntington's face one bit, and that was before she had heard the news. Tizzy handed her a fresh glass of wine.

"I hope she serves dinner pretty soon, or I'm gonna get loopy," Tizzy said.

"That's looped," Maddy replied.

"Whatever. So, you going back to MCRD with me next Thursday?"

"No, thank you; one rape scene's enough for me. I think I'm going to play more tennis and start going to more wives' functions."

"You'll be bored right out of your skin, sweetie. Right out of your ever-lovin' skin."

"Maybe. But frankly, I don't want to be the cause of Brian's not getting a clear shot at lieutenant commander. God, I hate this deployment."

"If he makes lieutenant commander, you're going to see some more of them."

Maddy was silent for a minute. "I suppose that's true, too. But Brian was up front with me when we got married: This is what he does, what he is. I happen to love him, Tizzy—he was the first honest-to-God straight arrow I ever ran into. So whatever my feelings are about the Navy, I owe it to him not to do any damage."

Tizzy gave her a speculative look over the top of her wineglass.

"There are other alternatives, you know," she said finally.

"Yes, I do," Maddy replied. "And maybe we'll come to that. But if we do, we'll have to do it together. Just like you and Fox have, right?"

Tizzy smiled and saluted her with her wineglass.

13

"Evaluator, SWIC. Log helo's on final, under visual flight-deck control."

"Okay, Garuda. Where's our SAR helo?"

"Big Mother Fifty-three is orbiting at one-five-zero for ten miles. He'll have to stay out there till we get this log helo off the deck."

"They care if I go out to the bridgewing and watch?"

Garuda shook his head. "Evaluator can go out to the bridge anytime he wants. Although—"

"Yeah?"

"If something went wrong during land-launch ops, the Old Man might wonder why you weren't in here taking charge. . . ."

"Good point. SWIC, the evaluator has decided to stick around," Brian announced, remembering the exec's look when he had appeared on the bridge during the Sea Dragon shooting. "It's just that I'm having a little trouble getting used to running everything from CIC."

"Yes, sir, I copy that, especially when you're comin' from the small-boy force. But the fact is, every system related to command and control in this ship terminates here in Combat. We could land that helo using one of the air controllers and the gun-director radar if we wanted to; it's just aviator ops safety rules that we use the first lieutenant back on the flight deck to actually bring him in. You know how those flyboys are—gotta have a guy waving paddles at 'em when they land; they need a cheering section, I think."

Brian grinned. Garuda fired up another cigarette, highlighted a track on his scope, and switched over to intercom to lambaste a miscreant in the Cave for sloppy tracking, all in one motion. Radarman First Class Rockheart stuck his head in from surface; he wore a sound-powered phone headset.

"Mr. Holcomb? Helo control says there's a four-striper on this helo. I passed it out to the bridge. He's also got some mail."

"Evaluator, aye. I'll call the captain."

Brian picked up the black sound-powered phone handset that the junior officers called the bat phone. It was wired directly to the captain's cabin one deck below. He pushed a buzzer switch, heard a clunking sound and then the captain's voice.

"Captain."

"Evaluator, sir. The helo controller says there's a four-striper—er, a Navy captain—embarked in this log helo."

"Is that right? Well, I guess I'm not entirely surprised. Have the JOOD go down and meet him and escort him to my cabin."

"Aye, aye, sir." Brian hung up and passed the captain's orders out to the OOD on the bridge via the 21MC intercom system, otherwise known as the bitch box. Garuda lifted an eyebrow at him.

"What?"

"Better also call the XO on that one."

"Right you are, Garuda." He dialed the exec's number on the ship's regular telephone system. "I'll get the hang of this yet," he said to no one in particular.

"XO."

"Yes, sir, evaluator in Combat. This log helo's got a four-striper on board. Captain's having him brought to his cabin."

"Shit. Do we know who he is?"

"Uh, no, sir. I can—"

"Na-ah, forget it. I'm gonna bet it's the ACOS for Ops from the Carrier Group staff."

"Then this is not necessarily a friendly visit?" asked Brian. He was aware that both Garuda and the AIC were now listening hard.

"If it was friendly, we'd have known he was coming. JOOD gonna go get him?"

"On the way now."

"Roger that. This helo bring any mail?"

"Yes, sir, flight deck said he had mail."

"Well, it's not a total loss. I'll go intercept our visitor."

Brian hung up. Rockheart was speaking to him from across the module again.

"Log helo is on deck, chocks and chains. Helo control says this guy's gonna shut down and stay on deck till his passenger's ready to go back."

"Evaluator, aye. Garuda, is that gonna be a problem for our SAR bird?"

"No, sir, they like to get Mother off the deck. They'll rattle around out there till this guy's gone."

"Roger that. This will probably be a short visit."

Garuda twisted fully around in his chair and looked expectantly at Brian, who shrugged.

"XO thinks it's some Ops guy from the staff," he offered.

The captain's line buzzed. Brian grabbed it quickly. Garuda turned back to his console.

"Evaluator, sir."

"Alert Mr. Austin and Mr. Benedetti to be ready to come to my cabin right away. You tell XO that we have a visitor?"

"Yes, sir. He's going to intercept our guest on the way up to your cabin."

"Very good. We may need you down here, as well, Brian."

"Aye, aye, sir." Brian hung up and sat down in the evaluator's armchair. Garuda punched buttons on his console for a few minutes, made two calls to the input world, and lighted another cigarette from the butt he was smoking. The AIC had resumed his murmurings to the BARCAP pilots, fifty miles away at 42,000 feet. His scope was filled with the spidery traces of computer-generated air-intercept geometry lines.

ACOS Ops, Brian thought. The assistant chief of staff for Operations on the Carrier Group commander's staff. Not a flunky. A full captain, USN, making an unannounced visit. It had to be about the Sea Dragon debacle. Benedetti had predicted that there would be some heat and that it would probably be private heat. This guy sounded like heat.

"This on the Sea Dragon screwup, you think?" Garuda was turned around in his chair again, one eye on Brian, the other on the clutter of symbology on his scope. Rockheart came in from surface to begin writing the new daily call signs on the vertical status boards.

"Most likely. Mr. Benedetti figured we were going to catch some shit over it, especially in view of the *Berkeley* casualties. But he also said that the staff wouldn't be able to get too vocal with their criticism, because it was their idea to send a PIRAZ ship to the gun line in the first place."

"Yeah, that computes. And the engineer's right: This here's a very special capability. Stupid friggin' thing to do, expose Red Crown's relief to shore batteries."

"Didn't care for all that racket outside, hunh, Garuda?"

"No, sir, I did not." Garuda grinned. "You're lookin' at a serious twidget here; I'm too old for that John Wayne shit."

"Guy's on the *Berkeley* didn't much like it, either. Especially the dead ones. And they're blaming us."

Garuda's grin vanished. He punched some more buttons, updating tracks on the display. He appeared to be thinking about a reply. Brian was amazed at how quickly the warrant officer's stubby fingers flew over the console keyboard.

"They'd really be pissed, they knew why we lost the load," said Garuda finally.

Brian hitched his chair closer to Garuda's. "I've already heard some scuttlebutt about that, some snipe doing a little reefer during GQ," he said softly.

"Yes, sir, that's what I'm hearing." Garuda lowered his voice, too, conscious of the AIC sitting four feet away and Rockheart working the status board on the back side of D and D. "I hear a coupla the chiefs are going to have a little powwow with this guy."

"Powwow—as in my chief boats?"

"Yes, sir, most likely. Word is that the snipe, that Gallagher guy, hasn't come outta the holes for the past day. Some of the other snipes're bringing him chow and he's sleepin' in the tool crib in Two Firehouse—with one eye open."

"Probably the sensible thing to do." Brian paused,

wondering how much he should reveal to the warrant. What the hell, he thought, if this guy isn't regular Navy, who is? He plunged on.

"But I'm wondering if this is the right way to handle a doper. Engineer told me the BT chief caught this gomer obviously spaced-out. Why not charge his ass, bring him to mast, and let the Old Man handle it, regulation Navy?"

Garuda looked around Combat for a moment before answering. He took a deep drag on his cigarette and blew a cloud of blue smoke into the overhead. He lowered his voice even more, his tone urgent.

" 'Cause that ain't how it goes here in the *J. B. Hood*, Mr. Holcomb. We ever catch the kingpin, the head doper, guy *sellin'* this shit, him we'd bring up, regulation style, hopefully before Chief Louie JM feeds him to the propellers. He'd get a court-martial, probably a general court, with hard time at Leavenworth. But for usin'? You can't do that and still keep this here Red Crown deal runnin'."

"But wouldn't we be better off with the druggies gone? *Berkeley* might have been, from the looks of it."

Garuda shook his head emphatically. "You'd end up shitcanning a third of the crew, if not more. And some a these guys'd like nothing better; they want out—outta the Nav and outta these deployments. Be more'n happy to get caught with a little dope, get an admin discharge or a 'less than honorable' or even a general-discharge ticket. They don't give a shit about what kinda discharge they get. They've got no idea how that can hurt 'em later on. They just want out. I mean, you look around—mosta these guys are nineteen, twenty years old. To them, anyone's been in the Navy for more than one hitch is automatically a lifer. I think the XO's got it right; lower-decks justice is the way to go. Let that monster Injun crack some ribs."

Garuda straightened up and turned back to his console, fingers flying again as he growled at the track supe over the intercom. Brian sat back in his own chair and examined the faces surrounding him in Combat. The two dozen positions in his sight were indeed manned by mostly very young men. His last XO had described it as going to sea with this year's high school class. The user consoles, such as the air control, weapons control, and the SWIC, were all manned either by senior petty officers or chiefs—lifers, as the junior enlisted called them. The input consoles were manned exclusively by first-term enlistees, nineteen to twenty-one year olds, most of whom had enlisted in the Navy to avoid the televised horrors of Army life in country. Can't blame 'em for that, thought Brian. But he wished to hell that they'd left their damn drug habits on the beach. The bat phone buzzed again.

"Evaluator, sir."

"Brian, turn the watch over to Mr. Barry and come down here, please."

"Aye, aye, sir." He replaced the handset, his stomach tightening, and waited for Garuda to end his telephone conversation with computer control. After a minute, Garuda hung up and shook his head.

"Goddamn guys don't mind the store. This op program's beginning to deteriorate, they've got a control panel with three system alarms showin', and *I* have to call *them*. We're gonna hold a little extra instruction when I get off watch."

"Well, hang in there, because I have to join the séance in the captain's cabin. You are hereby promoted to evaluator."

"Oh shit, oh dear," declared Barry. "Better thee than me-e, as the Quakers say."

"I hear that," replied Brian, looking for his cap.

"Mr. Holcomb?" Garuda stood up, pushed his intercom headset down onto his shoulders, and stepped closer.

"Yeah?"

"Remember the white-hat rule."

"Which one?"

"Don't volunteer."

Brian gave Barry a long look. Don't volunteer. If asked a question, you say, Yes, sir, no sir, but no more than that, sir. But you don't volunteer information. Brian felt a spike of annoyance.

"My style is to tell it like it is, Garuda."

"Yes, sir, I roger that. Nobody expects an officer to lie. But if he don't ask, you don't gotta say."

"What are you really telling me?"

"Try not to hurt the ship, Mr. Holcomb. Don't say somethin' for free that's gonna hurt the command or the Old Man less you gotta."

"I'll try not to, Garuda." Brian found his cap, put it on, and left Combat through the front door. He walked across the chart room's vestibule and headed down the ladder, the chill of apprehension spreading in his stomach. This would be his first loyalty test in his new command, and he was undecided on how to play it. He knew the *Hood* way wasn't the right way to deal with the drug problem. But the practical consequences of prosecuting the dopers were serious: The ship could never stand the hemorrhage of people that would ensue. And besides, the captain apparently did not believe there even was a drug problem. He stepped into the athwartships passageway on the next level down and headed for the captain's cabin.

There was also the question of his upcoming fitness report. Because he had been on board for less than ninety days, the captain was not obligated to write one. But Brian had made the exec aware that he needed a good ticket from *Hood,* even if it was for a short reporting period, to bolster his chances for promotion. It would be the only fitness report in his record that could overcome the not-so-good reports from his last ship. Not so good because he hadn't paid enough attention to lining up with the system, maybe. The whole point of retouring in a department head job, going on deployment, suffering through another separation from his unhappy wife was to achieve lieutenant commander and a shot at an exec's job. He had a feeling that, up to now, he'd still been the new guy. Whatever happened in the next few minutes, he would no longer be the new guy.

As he raised a fist to knock on the captain's door, it opened and Lieutenant Commanders Austin and Benedetti stepped through. Austin paused for just an instant, as if to say something, but he settled for giving Brian a look, then passed by. Benedetti had his head down and gave no indication that he had even seen Brian, who then stepped into the captain's cabin.

The captain and the exec leaned forward in the room's two upholstered chairs. The staff officer sat at the dining room table, a small black notebook spread out before him. The captain pointed to the sofa, which put Brian between the two ship's officers and facing the dining room table, his back to the hazy afternoon sunlight coming through the portholes.

The staff captain wrote something in the notebook. He was a tall, thin officer with a narrow, pinched face. Steel-rimmed glasses with prominent bifocal lenses accentuated his no-nonsense expression. Captain Huntington waited for the staff officer to finish his notes, then made introductions.

"Bill, this is Brian Holcomb, our new Weapons officer. He was in Combat at the time of the incident. Brian, this is Capt. Bill Walsh, from the CarGru staff."

Brian got up to shake hands with Captain Walsh, then returned to the couch. The exec appeared to be studying the carpet, his face neutral. The captain continued.

"Brian, Captain Walsh wants to ask a few questions about the incident yesterday. This is just a debriefing, if you will; nothing formal, like an investigation. Okay?"

Brian nodded. "Yes, sir." The captain did not appear to be on edge or trying to warn him in any fashion. Captain Walsh looked down at his notes and then back up at Brian, fixing him with a businesslike stare. Heat, Brian thought. Definitely heat.

"Mr. Holcomb, what was your station during the Sea Dragon incident?" Walsh's voice was surprisingly high; he sounded more like a clerk than a captain, USN.

"Sir, I was at my GQ station in Combat, which is weapons control. I stand physically between the FCSC and the EC."

"I am an old steam engineer, Mr. Holcomb. Haven't spent a lot of time in CIC, and certainly not in an NTDS CIC like you have here. Could you explain what these FCSC and EC people actually do?"

"Yes, sir. The names correspond to console positions in the NTDS system. FCSC assigns missile and gunfire-control radars to potential air targets when directed by the SWIC; that's ship's weapons coordinator, SWIC.

Once a fire-control radar channel is locked on and tracking a radar target and the captain wants to shoot a missile, FCSC tells the engagement controller, that's EC, to load the launcher with two surface-to-air missiles. Once the birds are on the rail, the EC assigns the launcher to whichever fire-control channel has the target locked up in track. The main computers watch the tactical geometry as it shapes up, and when the target enters the lethal envelope, it tells the EC to shoot. The EC then fires the missiles."

"And your job?"

"Well, sir, if the NTDS system is in automatic, I don't really have a direct console role. All the engagement commands come from SWIC via the computer network and appear as symbology orders on FCSC's screen. Nobody actually has to *say* anything. The FCSC and the EC acknowledge and execute the orders by button actions, which are echoed back to the SWIC so he knows they're doing what he told them to do. I'm there because I'm the Weapons officer. I'd get into it if something went wrong."

"Like what, exactly?"

"Well, like if one of them performed an incorrect button action, or if there was a computer fault in missile plot, or one of the radars drops track at a critical instant . . . I know the missile systems well enough to order corrective actions."

"What kinds of people sit these consoles?"

"FCSC has a chief; EC will have either a second chief or one of the first class petty officers from the guided-missile division."

"And you know these fire control and launch systems better than these people do?" The staff captain's voice held an audible note of skepticism.

The exec looked up as if to interject something, but Brian spoke first. "That's a fair question, sir. They know their individual *equipments* much better than I do, but I know the whole *system* better than most of the troops. The FTM chief knows his fire-control radars, and the GMM chief knows his launcher and the birds better than I will ever know them. But I've been trained to know the missile system as an integral part of the ship's overall *combat* system. It's more a matter of being one step back from the action, sir. There's a hell of a lot of pressure when you're stepping down through a launch sequence against a target that's coming in at you at two thousand feet per second. Of course, the guys on the console know lots more than I do about how the systems are wired up and where to go to fix things, but if something goes wrong, they may not see the operational fix to the problem as fast as I will, because I'm not concentrating on button actions and I've had more training in that role than they have. That's the main reason I stand there during a shoot."

"I see. So it's not like a destroyer, where the gun boss stands out on the bridge with the CO and orders up each step of the engagement process."

"No, sir, not at all. We're more like overseers, watching the computer systems do their thing. And if we want, we can put the system in full auto, designate an air contact as hostile, and tell the system to take him. The master computers will assign the fire-control radar, load the launcher, assign it, and shoot it."

"I find that a scary concept, Lieutenant. But it must take some time to learn all this."

"I was a Weapons officer in my last ship, and I was sent to the Navy's guided-missile school en route to this ship. That was three months of concentrated study. What I'm learning now is the ship's entire combat system, of which the missile system is one part. I'm not there yet, but I will be." Brian though he detected the ghost of a smile on the exec's face. Captain Huntington nodded approvingly.

"No doubt," said Walsh. "And on the day in question, nothing went wrong with the weapons systems?"

"No, sir. We had the gun in shore-bombardment mode, which means that it was under the control of the gun system computer in Main Battery Plot down below, which is a separate system from the missile system. The people in the surface module established the navigation track and an initial gun-target line and sent that down to plot. The gun system computer checks were held and then the gun was assigned to the computer for the shoot. It was standard NGFS, sir.''

Walsh nodded and made a note in his book.

"And what happened when *Hood* lost the load?'' Walsh looked up from his notebook at Brian.

"Well, sir, we all heard the blowers winding down and the guys in Combat began shutting down their gear as the power failed. It's kind of an unmistakable sound.''

"Oh? Do you lose the load that often?''

Brian sensed a trap. "No, sir, it's just a sound anyone who's been around steamships recognizes.''

Captain Walsh frowned. Brian wondered whether he had struck a nerve. "As an engineer,'' Walsh said, "that comment should hurt my feelings. But yes, I guess it is an unmistakable sound. Now, the entire gun system failed when the power went out?''

Brian didn't like the connotation of the word *failed*. "Well, not really, sir. We stopped firing when the gun system lost electrical power. The gun system didn't really fail, per se.'' After answering, Brian felt a moment of hesitation. His answer sounded a bit sea lawyer–ish. But Captain Walsh was nodding again, as if accepting the point. He looked down at his notebook for a moment before resuming his questions.

"Do you know why the power was lost, why the ship lost the load at such a critical moment, Mr. Holcomb?'' Captain Walsh stared at him again, the size of his eyes exaggerated when seen through the thick lenses of his eyeglasses.

Brian was taken aback by the question. This is where we've been going with all these questions. He sensed that Captain Huntington was watching him carefully, but he kept his eyes on Walsh's face.

"Uh, no, sir, I don't, not exactly. I heard—''

"Yes, what exactly have you heard, Mr. Holcomb?'' Walsh interrupted, leaning forward.

Don't volunteer, Brian thought. But he just had. Decision time, smart guy. He made up his mind.

"Well, sir, I heard that the boiler casualty was caused by loss of ACC air. That the on-line ACC compressor tripped off when we were at twenty-seven knots and that they couldn't hold it.''

"Do you know why they couldn't hold it, Mr. Holcomb? Why they did not cross-connect the ACC air from one fire room to the other? The captain says you're a Destroyer School graduate, so you've been instructed on steam plants; you know the ACC system can be cross-connected, right?"

"Yes, sir. But the answer is no, I don't know why they didn't get it cross-connected."

"You've heard nothing about an engineer being high on marijuana as the cause, Mr. Holcomb?"

Brian tried to hold his face still, but it was difficult. Where the hell did that come from? Had Benedetti admitted the real cause of the incident? Am I being set up by this guy, or worse, by the captain and the exec? Can't be.

"No, sir," he said, his mouth dry. "That's the first I've heard anyone say anything like that."

"You look surprised at what I just said, Mr. Holcomb."

"Yes, sir, I am. That's a pretty serious accusation. . . . Sir."

"Indeed it is, Mr. Holcomb." Captain Walsh leaned back in his chair and closed his notebook. "You see, we had a report from one of the *America*'s log helo crews on the day of the incident, after the Marine choppers had come up to remove *Berkeley*'s casualties. This man claimed that someone on *Hood*'s flight-deck crew told him that one of the BTs was spaced-out and turned the wrong valve when they tried to cross-connect the ACC air. We all recognize how suspect such rumors are, of course, but the admiral told me to pull the string. Captain Huntington here assured me that a BT made a mistake but that drugs were not involved. And you've heard nothing about anybody being drugged up at GQ, correct?"

"Yes, sir. I mean, no, sir, nothing like that."

"So. I guess that's all I need from you, Mr. Holcomb. Thank you for your cooperation."

"Thank you, Brian," said the captain, indicating that he could go. The exec gave him a brief smile and a nod as he left the captain's cabin.

He stopped outside the captain's door and exhaled

audibly. Then he walked to his stateroom to use the head before going back up to Combat. He washed his face in the stainless-steel sink in his room, toweled off, and then looked at himself in the mirror. Well, well, well, he thought. First lie's the toughest one. I guess you've decided how you're going to play this game, Mr. Holcomb, sir. Well shit, what else could I do? Blurt out that, yes indeedy, simply everybody knows that BT2 Gallagher was flying high, that the ship is loaded with dopers, and that somebody really ought to look into things here in the good ship *Hood*? After all, he didn't know for a *fact* that any drugs were involved; he was like everybody else, going on scuttlebutt. Uuh-huh. And where'd you get *your* law degree?

He shook his head as if to dislodge the mocking voice. As he left his stateroom and headed back up the ladder to Combat, he recalled the discussion with Benedetti the night before. I guess this makes me one of the good guys, he thought. Or at least one of the guys, whispered his conscience. Well, I may have retreated on the notion of going after the dopers the regulation way, but I will *not* look aside when *I* find it. He'd have to have that talk with the bosun, old Louie Jesus, and his division officers. I guess for now, I'll do it the *Hood* way. There really was no other choice.

Austin and Benedetti were up in Combat when Brian came through the door. Garuda was standing next to the SWIC console, his intercom wires draped over his shoulder as he did a button-smashing drill on the adjacent computer control panel. As Brian walked over to the evaluator's table, Benedetti looked at him expectantly and Austin raised his eyebrows.

"Well?" he said. Garuda tried to look as if he was not listening. The rest of the people in Combat all appeared to be very busy.

"Well," said Brian, joining the two lieutenant commanders at the evaluator table, "he had a bunch of questions about my GQ station, but what he really wanted to know was what I'd heard or knew about the cause of our dropping the load."

"And?" said Austin.

"And," he said, looking at Benedetti, "I told him that I'd heard it was an ACC air failure."

"He ask you anything else?" said Benedetti, stepping closer and lowering his voice.

"Yeah, he asked if I'd heard anything about one of the snipes being high on dope when it happened. I told him no."

Austin looked down at the deck and smiled, nodding slowly. Benedetti did not move. "He say where he got that?"

"He told me that a helo crewman from the *America*'s log helo had heard it from somebody on our flight-deck crew. Did he ask you two the same question?"

Austin nodded. "It came up, but we both drew a blank. Vince here even got indignant, didn't you, snipe?"

But Benedetti was not in a joking mood. He gave Brian a straight look and said, "Appreciate it, shipmate."

Austin laughed. "Now isn't that touching. Now I suppose the XO's gorilla squad is going to engineer an accident of some kind for poor Gallagher. Let's see, what will it be this time? I think we're overdue for a hand injury—yes, a problem with a hatch coaming."

"I suppose you'd give the little fuck a commendation, tell him to keep up the good work," growled Benedetti.

Austin looked down his nose at the engineer, with an aloof expression, and shook his head.

"All this goon-squad stuff, this cops and robbers, good guys and bad guys—what purpose is it serving? Do you think you're deterring this riffraff"—he swiveled his face around Combat to indicate the enlisted men—"from doing their stupid drugs with all this hugger-mugger? No way, gentlemen, no way. Let me give you some advice, Mr. Holcomb. You find out who's clean and who's dirty, and you make sure the dirties aren't in a position to put *your* career on the block."

"Easy for you to say, Austin," snorted the engineer. "Your watch stations are full of senior petty officers, chiefs, and officers. Any swingin' dick in my main holes can bring the plant down, and all of your fancy twidget stuff with it."

Austin arched his eyebrows. "Well, Vince, I can't help

it if you picked engineering as the horse to ride, eh? Should have stuck with a white-collar specialty like Ops or Weapons, or Supply. Supply's really good for staying detached.'' He made a show of looking at his watch. "I've got to get down below for dinner so I can relieve Mr. Holcomb here." Austin gathered his notebook and cap and left Combat. Garuda looked back over his shoulder.

"You got it, Mr. Holcomb? No changes since you left, 'cept I had to reload the op program.''

"Yeah, Garuda, I got it." He looked at Benedetti, who was staring down at the deck plates.

"Is that the end of it, then?''

"Yeah,'' replied the engineer. "No tellin' what this guy's saying to the CO and XO, but the staffies won't pursue the drug angle—especially when they don't *want* to pursue it. I'm sure the admiral and this staff guy know full well that it's probably true, but they also know what can and can't be done about it. He's probably down there saying something brilliant, like 'Don't let this happen again.' Shit. How many days is it?''

"Days?''

"Yeah, days. They used to keep a count on the status board, up here—yeah, there it is. See?'' He pointed to one of the Plexiglas boards at the back of D and D, where a box had been drawn in yellow grease pencil and the number 179 inscribed in it. "That's days till we get back to Dago. Actually, it's a hundred and seventy-eight days and a wake-up. But who's counting, huh? Anyway, you made the right call down there. And there's some truth in what Austin said—you gotta know who's dirty and who's not.''

"Ask the chiefs?''

"Right. In Weapons Department, it's your bosun and Chief VanHorn. And see the Sheriff. You definitely need to talk to Jackson. He's black, but he's tough as fuckin' nails on this subject. I'm not sure about some of your other twidget chiefs. But Fox Hudson and Jack Folsom, they're switched in. And Garuda here.''

Brian nodded, taking it all aboard. He looked around the darkened modules of Combat, at all the young faces bent over consoles, their skin tinted with amber scope light. His face must have shown his frustration, because Benedetti gave him a rueful smile.

"Yeah, it's a bitch, ain't it? You come on here expecting to have to work your ass off learning all this technical stuff but assuming your people are your people. But that's not how it is, shipmate. The bad guys, they know who they are, and they know who the good guys are, too. You gonna get through this tour in one piece, you're gonna have to play at every level. I gotta split."

Benedetti left Combat. Brian looked at his watch. He had forty-five minutes before Austin came back up and relieved him for the evening meal. Garuda was discussing the scheduling of tanking the BARCAP with HooDoo. Brian could see Rockheart talking on his sound-powered phones to the flight deck. The captain's phone buzzed.

"Evaluator, sir."

"Tell the flight deck Captain Walsh is on his way back, Brian."

"Aye, aye, sir." He hung up and passed the word over to surface. Garuda followed that up with instructions to land *Hood*'s own SAR helo once the logistics bird was clear of the flight deck.

"Fucking musical helos here, Garuda," Brian observed.

"Yes, sir, you're gonna come to hate fling-wings before we get done out here. Every time any other helo comes up here or anytime we want to get the Clementine bird outta the hangar for some flight ops, we gotta get Big Mother airborne and out of the way. For every hour of flight time on combat SAR station, they'll fly ten hours doing musical helos. I hate helos. Everybody hates helos."

Brian found a single letter on his desk when he got down to his stateroom, a letter on tissue-weight yellow stationery smelling faintly of perfume, with Maddy's graceful handwriting on the envelope. He pitched his ball cap onto his rack, sat down at his desk, and ripped it open. Three pages, mostly mundane news, but the closing lines were what he was looking for: "Love you and miss you very much." No hate and discontent about the deployment. No dark hints of serious talks to come. A good letter. Not a great letter, but a good letter. Certainly no hint of a Dear John.

He wondered now as he put it down why he had even felt he might get a Dear John. How had the good years at Monterey, all the fabulous times, suddenly been eclipsed in a few short weeks by his return to sea duty? He remembered the conversations: "I've got orders to a great ship, a guided missile ship, a big mother—eight thousand tons, one of the brand new PIRAZ ships. They call her a frigate, but she's as big as a World War Two cruiser. Weapons officer. Wonderful! We're going to deploy in six weeks for seven months." Silence. "Well, okay, that's not such great news for a wife who has to stay behind while the guy goes off to play Navy. But you've got this great offer from Bank of America, a management intern slot with great pay, the wardroom wives' group—they're bound to be good people on a front-line ship like this—and then we're back for the balance of my tour."

More silence. And for the six weeks leading up to deployment day, no direct attacks: just this sad silence, exacerbated by his long days on the ship, the pressures of taking over a new department, learning all the new systems, twenty-four-hour duty days every fourth day, the macabre mechanics of the predeployment updating of wills, powers of attorney, briefings on survivor benefits.

He realized now that he had left San Diego subconsciously harboring some grave reservations, a fear almost, of what changes his wife might have been going through in those frantic final weeks before deployment. In their outings with Fox and Tizzy Hudson, Brian had often wondered about the Hudsons' entirely relaxed attitude toward the upcoming deployment. Both of them seemed to be almost looking forward to the deployment, as if it would provide an interlude for them to resume temporarily their single ways. That was not Brian's idea of a marriage, but he was uncertain if Maddy shared his opinion of the Hudsons. But now that the pressure cooker was over, the ship finally on her way, and the days counting off toward homecoming, maybe she had leveled off. He read the letter again, especially the last paragraph. Yeah. It was going to be okay. He would write her back tonight, tell her about Sea Dragon. He wasn't sure whether or not to tell her about the drug problems. He'd have to think about that.

14

Rocky arranged to run into Bullet up on the boat decks just after sunset. Several other small clumps of men were either inhaling some fresh air or smoking a last cigarette topside before going below, so the sight of two first class lounging by the lifelines, shooting the shit, was unremarkable. Even so, both first class had taken the effort to make their encounter look entirely casual.

Everyone in the crew was still trading rumors about the Sea Dragon op and what had happened to *Berkeley*.

"You believe that asshole Gallagher?" muttered Rocky.

"Boy, a dumb ass, what he is." Bullet looked off into the dark and took a final drag on his cigarette. The brief red glow momentarily illuminated his dark-skinned features, which had begun to dissolve in the darkness. He adjusted the heavy electrician's tool belt around his waist; Bullet was never without his tools, in case GQ went down and he had to scramble to his repair party GQ station.

"Fucking snipes," Rocky said. "It's stunts like that bring the gorillas out. Jackson is going around like he's ready to arrest the whole crew. We don't need this kind of heat."

"You wanna see heat, go catch Louie Jesus. Way I be hearin' it, that snipe is holed up in Two Firehouse 'cause LJM say he gonna fuck him up."

"He can be my guest. I heard that the admiral sent some four-striper up here to check out the whole deal;

word is that they heard there was dope involved. Guy was in with the Old Man for an hour and a half. Next thing you know, there'll be some kind of fucking investigation.''

Bullet nodded slowly, pitching the butt out over the side with a flick of his long fingers. Then he turned to look at Rocky.

"You gotta be cool, Rockheart. This Old Man, he ain't gonna do nothin' 'bout no dope. Be steppin' in his own shit, he do that. B'sides, he don't believe in no dope, anyways. Uuh-huh. What we gotta be lookin' out for's them chiefs, Jackson and Martinez. One a my 'sociates, he hear Jackson sayin' he tired of bustin' no-count dopers, he wantin' to find the main man, shut the whole fuckin' thing down. Thass what we gotta be watchin' out for, not no admiral's staff man.''

"What do you think Jackson actually knows?''

Bullet was silent for a minute. Rocky often wondered about Bullet. Each had enough on the other to bring him down, so there was a nice balance there, what the wise guys called a lock. But there was always the question of what Bullet would do if he was caught and then offered a deal to finger Rocky. Rocky had been around him long enough to know that Bullet played the dumb street black when he talked to whites, but Rocky had seen the books lining Bullet's rack and heard him speak to other blacks in an entirely different dialect, one that revealed education and intelligence. Rocky kept his own counsel. The first class were not friends.

"I doan know what he know. You see the man more'n me. He doan act like he's onto my game, but there ain't no way a-tellin'. He do a lot of sneakin' around, plays the Dick Tracy bit, but maybe he just crazy.''

Rocky stroked his beard before replying. "If Jackson really wants to dig, he's going to start at the bottom and work his way up the chain by making deals with anyone he catches, just like the narcs. What's to keep the customers from fingering one of your guys?''

Bullet grinned, a flash of white teeth in the darkness. "Way it is, my fish is all white boys. We let them white boys know, somethin' go down and they go runnin' they mouth, buncha the brothers gonna be on they honky asses, bloods gonna come around, fuck 'em up. They's s'posed to say they brought the shit with 'em, thass all. Ain't no way to prove different."

"I suppose that oughta do it."

"Better'n that," Bullet continued. "This XO, he doan wanna know *nothin'* about no organization. Shit like that gets out, command's gonna look bad. Uuh-huh. He just send fuckin' King Kong around, kick some ass and take some names when somebody fucks up. S'why Gallagher hidin' out in the tool crib? Man ain't gonna take no chances, go runnin' his mouth when he hidin' out and they's nobody askin'."

"Yeah, well, I know that's the way it's been," Rocky said, looking around the darkened boat deck to make sure no one had moved near enough to overhear them. "But I'm not so sure now. For instance, I hear this new Weapons officer's making noises like he wants to get into it. Like he thinks there ought to be a full-scale investigation of what's going down, mast cases, the whole bit."

"Thass somethin' you *know,* or somethin' you been hearin'?"

Rocky shrugged. "I saw the chief engineer and Cunt Austin up in Combat after they had to go see this four-striper from the staff. Then they called for Holcomb. The other two looked like they were sweating bullets over what the new guy might be saying in the Old Man's cabin. I heard Austin say he hoped to shit that Holcomb wasn't going to queer the deal. That's why I thought there might be something new going down."

"Shee-it, you just guessin'."

"Yeah, shit, it's just scuttlebutt. The officers talk up in Combat; I hear some things."

"Bet you do, you bein' Mr. A-J-Squared Away an' all," Bullet said, tapping Rocky's MAA badge with his fingernail.

Rocky grinned. "Yeah, well, you gotta admit, it isn't bad cover. Jackson tells me shit in the MAA office, I gotta work real hard to keep a straight face."

"Awright, then. Way I see it, we cool."

"And you think Gallagher's going to keep his mouth shut?"

"Shee-it. That Injun ain't lookin' for that dumb ass for no conversation, man. How's he gonna talk, Injun's steel-toe boot in his mouth? I gotta boogie. Be cool."

Rocky laughed as Bullet sauntered away into the shadows. He looked around again and found himself alone on the boat decks. The night sky was moonless and overcast and only the occasional slap of a wave along the ship's side indicated that they were even under way. The atmosphere remained hot and muggy, the smell of stale air, dirty laundry, cigarette smoke, and steam machinery brought topside by the exhaust vents overpowering the salt-air smell of the sea.

He had watched with a good many of the crew when the helo came for the *Berkeley*'s body bags. Fuckin' shame, the ship getting hit like that. He had heard the scuttlebutt about the crew in *Berkeley* blaming the crew in *Hood* for the whole thing, but that was just bullshit. Hell, that round had *Berkeley*'s name on it, that was all. This shit with Gallagher had nothing to do with nothing. Guy was dumb enough to do dope at GQ, he, Rocky, wouldn't mind if that bosun busted him up in little pieces. Rocky suddenly wished again for a cigarette, which surprised him. But he had to make sure his own backfield was still clear. He walked over toward the port side to the hatch leading below. Time to talk to Garlic.

15

Commissaryman First Class Wolcezjarski, nicknamed "Garlic," surveyed his kingdom from the doorway to the mess decks' office. He was a very fat man whose huge paunch billowed out from under his apron strings in a doughy mass that clearly proclaimed his cook's rating. He wore soiled white cotton trousers, a white T-shirt, and a stained white apron. The front of his T-shirt was sweat-soaked, revealing a coiled mass of black hair on his large belly. His thinning gray hair lay in flat, sweaty strands on his large head. He had tiny ears and a flushed, heavily larded face with multiple chins, and his close-set dark gray eyes, framed in fat rolls, completed a piggish expression of contemptuous suspicion, accentuated by a cigarette butt dangling perpetually from the right side of his mouth. The rest of him, the huge forearms, massive shoulders, and pawlike hands, revealed that Garlic was also a very powerful man.

Garlic was forty-two, a permanent petty officer first class who would never make chief. He had acquired his nickname from his propensity to put garlic into very nearly everything he cooked. When he had first reported aboard, he had made a small reputation for improving the desperately bland cooking of the chief commissaryman he replaced. But when garlic began to show up in the morning's scrambled eggs and hash browns, in the freshly baked bread, on the toast, and in almost every entrée item served for lunch and supper, a muttering chorus of complaints had begun. Garlic-flavored ice cream from the ship's ice cream machine precipitated a full-scale revolt, causing the exec to have a word with Lieutenant Hatcher, the Supply officer, who told Wolcezjarski to eighty-six the garlic, at least until the noise died down. Mr. Hatcher happened to enjoy garlic in his food, so there had been no hint of a real ass-chewing. But the nickname stuck, mostly because it was easier to pronounce Garlic than Wolcezjarski.

Garlic scowled at two mess cooks who were completing the sweep-down after the noon meal. His glower produced a perceptible increase in broom movement. Garlic was both the senior cook in *John Bell Hood* and also the mess decks master-at-arms. This latter role meant he was king of the twenty-one mess cooks, all junior enlisted men, required to spend their first ninety days in the ship doing the Navy's version of KP. Mess cooks lived in fear of Garlic because he had the power to keep them on past their normal ninety-day tours if they did not perform to his expectations, and it was made clear to each of them that Garlic was a man who enjoyed this power. Under the outward guise of high standards of cleanliness and sanitation, Garlic made their lives miserable in a variety of ways, and there were a few mess cooks who were now going on four months.

While the officers and the chiefs had separate messes in the wardroom and the chiefs' quarters, respectively, the rest of the crew, from the first class on down, ate on the mess decks. The largest open compartment in the ship, the mess decks seated up to seventy-two men at closely spaced four-man tables. The chow line, on the port side, was a combination stainless-steel serving bar and steam line that separated the mess decks from the galley proper. At one end of the chow line were the twenty-five-gallon coffee urns from which everyone in the ship could draw coffee twenty-four hours a day. In addition to serving four meals a day to 300 men, the mess decks doubled as a training area during the day between meal hours, served as the crew's movie theater after the evening meal, and was a place for the night owls to congregate after taps to write letters or just hang out. The fact that the entire enlisted crew gathered there at least three times a day made the mess decks the focal point for the daily supply of rumors generated in the ship. It was a standing joke in the wardroom that any really good rumor had to originate with the port butter-cutter on the mess decks. If that was the source, it had to be true.

Since the space was in use for all but the wee hours of the morning, the mess cooks had a continuous cleaning job on their hands, and it was Garlic's job to crack the whip. After every meal, the tables had to be cleaned with hot soapy water and the tiled deck swept, swabbed, and then buffed up with a floor polisher. The executive officer conducted a formal inspection of the galley and mess decks every day. If they were not spotless, he would share his thinking with Mr. Hatcher, who in turn would generously share the experience with Garlic. This was a hassle Garlic did not need, and thus the mess cooks were subject to a great deal of encouragement and exhortation.

"Bronson! Refoe!" Garlic yelled. "Do that area again, only this time get all that shit out from under them tables! You can't buff fuckin' tiles with dry cereal on the fuckin' deck, you fuckin' idiots. Goddamnit, you want permanent assignment to mess-crankin'? Hanh?''

Rocky walked into the mess decks from the main after passageway as the two mess cooks scrambled to retrace their sweeping paths, banging the push brooms noisily against the support columns of the steel tables to show their sincerity. Garlic shook his head in disgust at their total lack of energy, initiative, and professionalism.

"Them sonsabitches are gonna be mess-crankin' until we get back to fuckin' Dago, they keep fuckin' off like this," he grumbled to Rockheart, who had stopped to fill his coffee mug.

"Sounds fair to me," Rocky replied, eyeing the coffee suspiciously. He thought he had seen a lump.

Garlic grinned. "Fuck fair; I may keep 'em here, anyway." He swept his eyes around the mess decks to make sure there were no ears nearby. "So," he said, lowering his voice even though the mess cooks had moved their sweeping effort to the other side of the mess decks, "you all set for the first hump?"

Rocky nodded, stirring sugar into the coffee with a wooden stir stick while he took his own look around the space before examining the coffee again. Not only a lump but a moving lump. A large bald man known to everyone in the ship as Poppa Steiner ambled through the space and headed into the galley. Steiner, an elderly commissaryman, was a Pennsylvania Dutchman with a strong accent. He was the night baker, who, as the name implied, stayed up most of the night making bread, rolls, and pies for the following day. He would then sleep for most of the day, resurrecting himself around midafternoon to do it all again. Rocky snapped the stir stick in two.

"Got plenty of product and no lack of demand," he said. "We ought to do all right this cruise."

"That's what I wanta hear. Between you dealin' and me sharkin', we'll make all that bread rise a coupla times."

Rocky looked around again before replying. There was no one but the mess cooks on the mess decks and the galley was empty except for Steiner, who had begun to rattle pans.

"I'm a little worried about some of the snipes," Rocky said. "Some of those bozos don't use much sense as to when they blow their weed," he added, throwing the stir stick's pieces into a large GI can at the end of the chow line.

"If they had a fuckin' brain, they wouldn't be snipes in the first place—or doin' dope. You say somethin' to Bullet?"

"Yeah, but he isn't going to get any closer to 'em than he has to. It isn't like he can go playing career counselor to the customers, you know? Calls 'em fish." Rocky shook his head. "It's just that it would be so fuckin' easy if they just were a little more discreet."

"Discreet, my ass. There's a reason they call it dope, remember?"

Rocky grinned. Garlic fulfilled the role of banker. Rocky and Bullet invested their individual cash hoards with Garlic, who was the ship's loan shark. Garlic loaned cash to the ship's liberty hounds, gamblers, and cardplayers at straight six-for-five interest, payable on the next payday. Paydays came every two weeks, so if there was a problem, Garlic had time to work on it, which was a facet of life he enjoyed as much as he enjoyed tormenting the mess cooks. But he rarely had real trouble; his regulars knew better than to mess with him, and besides, they needed his services.

Everyone knew that the loan-sharking aboard ship was, of course, illegal, but in the pantheon of shipboard crime nowhere near as dangerous or odious as drug dealing. Every ship had at least one loan shark, who usually operated with the tacit permission of the chiefs. The chiefs let him ride because sometimes even chiefs needed some spare cash, the difference being that the chiefs did not pay interest, in return for letting the loan shark operate. The connection between the loan shark and any drug money going around the ship was not generally known.

"You resupply in Subic?" Garlic asked.

"No. I'm pretty well stocked, and there was no liberty, anyway. Be too dangerous to put a chit in to go see the people I have to see. First port visit, I'll go see some *mamasans* out in Olongapo, refill my stash. It's no big deal.''

" 'No biggee in the PI,' " intoned Garlic in a singsong parody of Filipino pidgin.

Rocky looked around again. "Yeah, but that fucking Chief Jackson, he's starting to take the drug scene here personally.''

"Shit, Jackson suspects everybody," Garlic said. "Guy's a fuckin' paranoid. Black guy tryin' to be a white guy. I keep waitin' to see him with a magnifying glass and one a them funny hats. But I'll tell ya who is startin' to be a problem, and that's that fuckin' Martinez. After this Gallagher shit, I heard he put the word out that he's gonna start kickin' some serious ass, and I don't mean just a fall down a ladder. He gets close to our organization, we might have to do somethin' about that.''

Rocky snorted. "Oh yeah? *We?* You got a Marine battalion in your pocket or something? Just what the fuck you suggest we do about a guy who chases trucks and bites their back tires off for fun, hunh? That fucking Injun goes on the warpath after guys like Gallagher, that's not *my* fuckin' problem; that's their nightmare, shipmate.''

Garlic shook his head impatiently. "Yer not thinkin','' he said. "Other commands, guy gets caught, gets wrote up, gets busted, restricted, whatever, he'd say he brought the shit with him. On here, guy gets terrorized 'cause the fuckin' Injun comes around to lift his hair, he might say who he really got the shit from, you readin' me? That starts to be your fuckin' problem, right there.''

Rocky stared hard at the fat man. "If that monster ever figures out where most of your bank comes from," he said, "it's gonna be your problem, too, so don't go getting all holy on me, Mr. Rockefeller.''

Garlic returned the hard look. "Only way he'll find that out is if you or Bullet tell him, and I figger he'll be tearin' your arms off right about then, so I ain't exactly worried about it. Ain't nobody made no connections between the bank and the dope, so if he's on the rag about dope, he ain't gonna come after me.''

They both stared at the deck for a minute as they considered the potential wrinkles. Each realized that

Rockheart and Bullet had the same lock on Garlic that they had on each other, so finger-pointing was a waste of time. Finally, Garlic pulled out a dirty handkerchief and blew his nose.

"Shit," he grumbled. "This fuckin' AC gives me a cold every time I come out to WESTPAC. Look, this is all bullshit. Everybody knows Jackson is a fuckin' nut. Stays up all night, sneakin' around like some kinda hound dog; nobody takes him seriously. What the fuck you gettin' all spooked for?"

Rocky sampled the coffee and made a face. He checked out the two mess cooks and then waited while a couple of snipes walked by on their way to one of the main holes before replying.

"It's not really Jackson. It's the combination of Jackson and Godzilla. What it might mean is that the command is thinking about coming down on the dope scene. Like I've seen Jackson talking to the new department head, Holcomb. Martinez works for Holcomb, and they've been buddy-buddy lately. And Holcomb's East Coast Navy; I hear he's making noises about tightening up on guys who get caught with dope. Originally, I thought the new guy was okay, but now . . ."

Garlic shook his head. "That ain't what I'm hearin'. This Old Man don't believe there is any such thing as drugs. And even if he did, this is his last cruise; he don't want to make no waves. He ain't gonna start no fuckin' doper purge right at the beginnin' of a cruise. No way. Make the ship look bad, make him look bad. Get ahold of yerself. Forget about the khaki in this boat—they all just want to get by, just like the rest of us. And the WESTPAC guys'll straighten out the new guy."

"Man, I hope you're right. Look, I gotta roll."

Garlic cuffed him on the shoulder; Rocky tried not to stagger. Garlic was grinning again.

"Hang in there, Rocky baby," he said. "We got the whole cruise to get through. Just think about how rich we're gonna be, we get back. And don't sweat Jackson; he's black: He ain't gonna be lookin' at the brothers to be runnin' the system. We gotta, we can always offer up some dumb bastard once in a while, throw the fuckers a bone, give Jackson a drug bust and Louie Jesus somebody to squash. Feed the animals, man, they don't go eatin' on the keepers.''

16

Rocky climbed down the ladder from the main deck passageway to the second deck level, being careful to lower the scuttle over his head as he went down. As duty master-at-arms, he was conducting his after-chow tour of the sounding-and-security route, a function that involved checking the compartments and hatches in the bowels of the ship to ensure they had been properly secured for the night. It was perfect cover for his real mission, which was to add to his cash stash in the starboard shaft-alley pump room down on the third deck. The first ladder led down into a small vestibule compartment, barely big enough for two men to stand side by side next to the hatch in the deck that led to the shaft alley itself. The vestibule was lighted with a steam-tight incandescent fixture, but there was nothing in it except electrical junction boxes, a fire-main branch rising from the pump room below, and the hatch to the shaft alley.

Rocky stepped off the ladder at the bottom, turned around, leaned down, and spun the actuating wheel on the scuttle leading to the shaft-alley pump room. The round steel scuttle popped open with a faint hiss of air smelling of salt water and ozone. Reaching down through the hole, he found the light switch for the shaft alley and snapped it on, revealing a second stainless-steel ladder leading to a long, narrow compartment twelve feet below. The outboard bulkhead of the compartment was the ship's hull, curving inward at the bottom and lined with steel racks in which lengths of angle iron and steel pipes were stored in a jumble of metal. Directly below the ladder was a cage that ran the full length of the compartment; within the cage was the starboard propeller shaft, a thirty-inch-diameter horizontal column of steel rotating silently on its pedestal line-shaft bearings mounted at the forward and after ends of the compartment. The shaft had been painted with red barber-pole stripes so that anyone coming near it could see if it was rolling or not.

Rocky let himself down the final ladder, once again tripping the scuttle closed over his head before descending. He had every right to be in here if somebody was to question it, because he was required to inspect the space for possible flooding as part of his MAA tour. He climbed down the final rungs of the ladder and stepped out onto a small bridge over the line-shaft cage. Walking across the bridge, he dropped down onto the deck plates of the pump room, where number-four fire pump, a four-hundred-pound centrifugal pump driven by a sixty-horsepower electric motor, was mounted on the deck. The fire pump was also running, emitting a low roar from elderly bearings, supplying 125-psi seawater pressure to the ship's damage-control fire mains. Its cooling seals dripped a steady trickle of salt water down into the bilges, and one of Rocky's responsibilities as MAA was to see whether the sounding-and-security watchman had pumped the bilges down in the past two hours. Rocky knelt down on the deck plates and inspected the bilge area, shining his flashlight into the maze of steel pockets created by the confluence of the inward-curving ship's hull and the support structures for the fire pump and the shaft bearings. There appeared to be a normal water level in the bilge. He then checked to make sure the eductor pump was running. The eductor was nothing more than a four-inch vacuum pipe that took a constant suction on the bilges to keep the water from rising and shorting out the fire pump's motor.

He snapped off the flashlight, looked up to make sure that the hatch was still closed, and walked over to an electrical junction box on the after bulkhead. The box had no cables coming to or from it, and a steel plate on the door was marked SPARE—NO TERMINATIONS. He inspected the top of the box with his finger to feel for the strip of Scotch tape across the crack. It was intact. Then he undid eight steel butterfly nuts and swung back the panel's door, ripping the tape in the process. The box was three feet high, two feet across, and five inches in depth, with a heavy rubber gasket on its four edges to keep connections dry if the space ever flooded out. Flattened inside was a plastic bag filled with rags.

Rocky pulled out the bag and fished in his pocket, extracting a tight roll of greenbacks. He found a loose rag in the bag, wrapped the roll in it, tied the corners in a knot, and stuffed it back into the bag. He hefted the bag. Not too bad, for the first line period. There was probably eight to ten thousand dollars hidden among the bundles of rags. He folded up the bag, pressed it back into the box, closed and secured the cover, stripped an inch of Scotch tape off his belt, and put it over the crack on the top. By the end of the cruise, he expected to have six times that amount secreted in the junction box. Tax-free, untraceable green cash money.

He checked around the pump room one more time to make sure he hadn't missed anything. When he thought about where he was actually standing, well below the waterline, within about ten feet of the keel, it always gave him an eerie feeling. The shaft alley was hot and humid from the heat of the fire room next door and the loose water in the bilges, and there was that huge propeller shaft rolling silently through it in its wire cage. Despite the heat, he shivered. He checked the box again, then began the climb back to the second deck, dogging down hatches and securing lights on the way up. His shirt was damp with perspiration by the time he lifted his head through the hatch into the second deck passageway. As he was dogging down the final hatch, he noticed that one of the Deck Division's prime weirdos, Seaman Coltrane, was loitering in the passageway about ten feet away. Coltrane saw Rocky and grinned at him. Rocky scowled back at Coltrane, who promptly scampered down the passageway. Rocky completed dogging down the hatch, nodding to Ensign Folsom as he walked by. Radarman First Class Rockheart, the ever-conscientious MAA, making his duly appointed rounds.

17

Brian sat bolt upright in his rack as the ship's announcing system blared out an urgent call:

"SAR! SAR! SAR! SET THE HELO DETAIL FOR EMERGENCY LAUNCH OF BIG MOTHER FIVE-THREE. I SAY AGAIN, SAR! SAR! SAR! SET THE HELO DETAIL FOR EMERGENCY LAUNCH OF BIG MOTHER FIVE-THREE. ALL HANDS NOT IN-VOLVED IN FLIGHT OPERATIONS STAND CLEAR OF THE FLIGHT-DECK AREA."

Brian snapped on his bunk light and looked at his watch. It was 2240. He had gone to bed at 2030 in attempt to get some sleep before taking the midwatch in his six on, six off rotation with Austin in Combat. He shook his head, trying to clear the cobwebs, as the 1MC repeated the whole announcement. He had been dreaming about Maddy. He felt the ship lean into the beginning of a turn, the hull trembling as she came up in speed. He could not remember whether he had a role in the launch of the SAR helo. Jack Folsom, the first lieutenant, would already be on his way back to the flight deck to act as the landing signals officer. Brian remembered the drill: Each night the search-and-rescue (SAR) helo was preflighted and then tied down on the flight deck. Depending on the state of readiness required, the helo crew, two pilots and two crewmen, might be anywhere from asleep in the aircraft to belowdecks in their bunks. A regular launch took up to forty-five minutes to walk through all the inspections and preflight procedures. An emergency daytime launch could get off in less than five minutes; at night, it took a few minutes more.

He looked at his watch again, trying to focus on the radium dial, and decided to get up and go see what this was about. The ship lurched again as she bent into another turn, the deck thrumming now as the sixteen-foot-diameter propellers bit in. He pulled on his khaki trousers and shirt and slipped into a pair of black Wellington-style seaboots, grabbed a foul-weather jacket and his red-lens flashlight, and headed up to Combat.

As he came through the door, he found a scene of barely controlled pandemonium. Austin was hunched over the SWIC console on one side, with the captain on the other. Fox Hudson was sitting SWIC. There were three air controllers standing around the AIC consoles in various states of uniform. He heard a radio circuit chattering in the overhead; it sounded like an air-control circuit. There was a general cross fire of comments and conversation going on at the watch stations and consoles in Combat. Hudson was talking on Air Force Green to the staff down on Yankee Station, giving them a situation report. The surface watch team was busily rigging phones for the helo-control circuit and setting up a SAR box on the plotter. In D and D, the officers were concentrating on the SWIC scope, which had been scaled down to cover a sixty-mile area to the immediate west.

"What's the deal?" Brian asked one of the AICs, RD1 Monty Montana, who, like himself, had come up to Combat when the word was passed for night SAR.

"Air Force F-Four got shot up on a photoflash run over the Red River Valley. Recce bird, camera pod, no ordnance. They're trying to make it out over the Gulf so we can get 'em. Say they're on fire. That's him on the scope there, 'bout fifty miles northwest, just comin' feet-wet."

At that moment, Austin noticed that Holcomb was in Combat.

"Mr. Holcomb," he said, "you're supposed to be getting your beauty rest so you can relieve me promptly at twenty-three-forty-five."

"One MC woke me up; I decided to come see what's happening."

"I think we can manage, thank you. You'll have to get used to leaving emergencies up to the evaluator on watch."

The captain turned around and nodded. In the garish scope light, Brian noticed that he looked much older, with dark circles under his eyes and the lines in his face accentuated by the harsh scope light. Brian saw that the captain had pulled on a pair of khaki trousers and an aviator's leather flight jacket but not a shirt. He had bedroom slippers on instead of shoes or boots.

"Brian," he said, "Count's right; it's not like a destroyer where everybody turns out when there's a fire bell in the night. But if you want to watch, you ought to go back to director one. A night launch is quite an evolution."

"Aye, aye, sir, I think I will. Didn't mean to intrude."

"Oh, no, no, I didn't mean that at all," replied the captain. "It's just that if both my principal evaluators jump out of bed every time something happens at night, I'll have two zombies up here. Short of GQ, you let the other guy do it if you're off watch. But now that you're up, go back and take a look."

"Aye, aye, sir." Brian left Combat. As he dropped down two ladders to the wardroom level, the 1MC came on again.

"AIRCRAFT TYPE IS AIR FORCE FOX FOUR; TWO SOULS ON BOARD; BEARING IS TWO-NINER-TWO DEGREES MAGNETIC; RANGE, FIVE-SEVEN MILES, DESCENDING, INBOUND TO RED CROWN. EJECTION IS IMMINENT. FLIGHT DECK IS PREPARING FOR EMERGENCY LAUNCH OF BIG MOTHER FIVE-THREE. THE CLEMENTINE HELO WILL NOT, I REPEAT, NOT LAUNCH. LAUNCH WINDS WILL BE THREE-TWO-ZERO RELATIVE AT THREE-ZERO KNOTS. PITCH AND ROLL IS ZERO-ZERO. ALTIMETER IS TWO-NINER-DECIMAL-NINER-FIVE." Brian realized that the helo pilots were getting their launch brief via the 1MC rather than taking the time to come to Combat.

He let himself out onto the weather deck through the port breaks passageway hatch. He stopped immediately upon stepping out on deck as the hatch closed behind him with a bang in the stiff breeze. For a moment, he was totally blind. He could hear the rush of the sea along the ship's sides and the whistle of the wind through the lifelines, but he could see nothing. He stood there, waiting for his eyes to develop some peripheral vision. Then he remembered his red flashlight, swore, pulled it out, and illuminated the deck walkway leading back to the after end of the ship. He had emerged on the same level as the flight deck but would have to climb two levels up to reach the gallery on top of the helo hangar overlooking the flight deck. He headed aft along the port side, walking through the midship replenishment station and the boat decks. As he made his way farther aft, he began to see the red glow of the flight-deck lights looming in the darkness and hear the sounds of the big SH-3 helicopter's jet engines turning up. When he reached the port-side three-inch gun, he turned and began climbing a long vertical ladder that led to the top of the helo hangar. The wind rose in velocity as if trying to strip him off the flimsy aluminum ladder, which rattled with vibrations coming from the propellers.

Letting himself through the safety chains hung across the top of the ladder, he walked aft across the roof of the hangar and found himself with a bird's-eye view of the flight deck below. With a start, he realized that he was also almost face-to-face with the whirling disk of the SH-3's rotor blades below and in front of him. Standing in the port-quarter corner of the lifelines surrounding the top of the hangar was Jack Folsom, his arms outstretched like a Christos, with red-colored light wands in each hand. Next to Folsom was a huge dark figure who had to be the chief boatswain. Folsom looked like a spaceman in the glow of the flight-deck lights. He had on a cranial helmet and full-face shield similar to the ones being worn by the helo crew, which protected his face and ears from the clattering roar of the helicopter below. The helmet headset also contained the LSO communications, a sound-powered phone circuit in one ear and the land-launch radio circuit in the other. Brian found himself holding his own fingers in his ears as he watched, his face buffeted by the wind coming over the bow and the occasional hot vortex of jet exhaust whipping up off the flight deck. Folsom and the chief were not aware of his presence in the darkness behind them as they concentrated on the launch.

On the flight deck below, fire-fighting crews crouched behind their hoses and foam nozzles on either side of the hangar, prepared for the worst. They were dressed out in steel helmets, heavy asbestos gauntlets, and goggles. Right at the front of the port-side crew was the hot-suit man, dressed in an asbestos suit coated with highly reflective aluminum and carrying an access ax. If the helo caught fire on deck, it was his job to rush into the fireball and hack his way into the cockpit to rescue the pilots.

Brian waited while the helicopter turned up at full rpm, chained down to the deck with tie-downs and chocks in place, as the pilots completed an abbreviated prelaunch checklist. The aircraft's navigation lights glowed along its fuselage and the bank of red lights shining down on the flight deck from the top of the hangar were reflected in the helo's windshield like the multiple red facets on the eyes of some giant insect. An aircrewman crouched under each wheel mount; each wore a cranial set and held on to the chains that secured the wheels, his dungarees whipping in the down blast from the rotors.

Brian felt the ship steady up on the flight course, which was designed to put a thirty-knot wind diagonally over the flight deck from port to starboard, into which the helicopter could lift without forward motion. Folsom suddenly dropped his arms and the red wands in his hands went out. He squatted down and reached into a bag at his feet, pulled out two new wands, turned them on, revealing dim green lights, stood up, and again extended his arms. On the flight deck, the helicopter's fuselage rotating red beacon came on and the pitch of the blades began to change. Folsom, looking down over the railing, pointed the wands at the aircrewmen and made a sweeping motion by swinging his arms back and forth across each other. The aircrewmen, watching for the signal, unsnapped the chains and kicked the chocks away from the wheels. They scampered out from under the blades, keeping low, their arms full of tie-down chains, paused for an instant to show the chains to the pilots, and then ducked under the partially closed hangar door in front of the helo. Folsom confirmed that they were clear, straightened his arms out again, and slowly lifted them up to a *V*. In response, the big white helicopter lifted off the deck and hovered momentarily about ten feet over the deck, close enough that through the windshield Brian could see the pilot's legs working the controls. Then the helo dipped to port and swooped across the port-side lifelines and buzzed away into the darkness, leaving behind a sudden silence and the stink of burned kerosene.

Brian took his fingers out of his ears. Folsom and the chief saw him at about the same moment and Folsom pulled the cranial off his head. Brian realized he could see perfectly well now that his eyes were night-adapted, aided by the red flight-deck spotlights. A small crowd of dark figures had appeared on the flight deck below. The fire crews remained on-station, relaxing into dark lumps amidst their fire-fighting gear.

"Sight-seein', boss?" asked the chief.

"Yeah, Boats. One MC woke me up, so I thought I'd come watch. What happens next?"

Folsom answered, "Well, the controller in Combat will run Big Mother down the bearing of the guy in trouble and try to position the helo in the area where they punch out."

"I heard the guy was on fire when I stopped through Combat," Brian said.

Folsom was about to reply when there was a chorus of shouts from the flight deck below. Brian looked down and saw several arms pointing into the black sky to the west. Brian lifted his head in time to see a flickering glow up in the overcast that progressed in color from dark red through orange, its deadly significance emphasized by the absence of any sound other than that of the wind created by the ship's own motion across the sea. The glowing cloud dimmed for an instant and then changed from orange to bright yellow before being extinguished in a flash of light that looked like heat lightning, followed moments later by a muffled thump.

"He ain't flyin' no more," observed the chief.

"I just hope they had time to punch out," said Folsom. He shook his head as if to acknowledge the low probability of the aircrew having had time to eject.

"Shit," Brian said.

Folsom was staring down at the deck. He shook his head again. "Well," he said, "we'll be up here a while. They'll keep that helo out looking until they're bingo fuel. Sometimes one of 'em gets out. I've heard some real survival stories up here in the Gulf."

"Bingo—meaning?"

"Bingo state means you have enough fuel to get back to the bird farm and land. When a guy's bingo, he's gotta beat feet for home plate."

"I guess I'd better go get some coffee," said Brian, glancing at his wristwatch. "It's almost time for my next watch."

"Catch you on the phones, Mr. Holcomb."

Brian made his way down to the wardroom to get a cup of soup and half a cheese sandwich, standard fare for midnight rations, or midrats, as it was called. The midnight-to-four watch was supposed to be relieved by 2345, which meant that the oncoming watch stander usually got up at 2300, held reveille on his face, stumbled down to the mess decks or the wardroom for something to eat and a cup of coffee, and then went to his watch station. Enlisted turnovers took about a minute; for the evaluator in Combat, the process could take as long as an hour, depending upon what was going on.

Brian returned to Combat by 2330, and Austin spent the next twenty minutes handing over the watch as he reviewed what tracks were up over the Gulf, what enemy indications were active, what the carrier-flight cycles for the night entailed, the plan of the day for the next day, and the captain's night orders. Since there were no strikes planned for the next twenty-four hours, the turnover was routine. Garuda Barry conducted the same turnover with Fox Hudson. The final part of the brief concerned the helo search for survivors from the Air Force reconnaissance F-4.

"Big Mother Five-three is out there in the area of the probable splash point," said Austin, pointing down to the SWIC's screen. "Although they reported seeing nothing of any size come down. There's been no beeper, and nothing on the Guard frequency to indicate a survivor.

But they'll conduct a directed search for another two hours or so, then they'll have to come in."

"I saw the fireball, or rather, its reflection."

"Yes, well. Sometimes they get lucky. But usually what we find is some burned insulation, an oil slick, and a helmet filled with brains the next day. The helmets float, you see."

"Wonderful."

"Yes. You've heard the old saying, The aviators don't earn any more money than the rest of the Navy with all that flight pay; they just earn it sooner. Any questions?"

"Who's directing the search?"

"We've got one of the AICs directing; he's using the surface console over there."

"Will we launch the Clementine helo?"

"No. We would if we had had indications of an ejection or survivors—a beeper, flares, a call on Guard—something besides a fireball. For a long search, the SH-Three is the bird of choice—they can set it down in the water if they have to, and they carry a bigger crew. And if they picked someone up while we had the Clem bird rolled out on deck, we'd have a clobbered deck until we could launch Clem. Sometimes getting a guy back to the ship quickly makes a big difference. So, no—Clem stays in the barn."

"Got it."

"This is Mr. Austin. Mr. Holcomb is the evaluator in Combat," Austin announced.

"This is Mr. Holcomb, I have the evaluator watch," announced Brian. There was a chorus of "Aye, aye, sir," and, at a few minutes before midnight, Austin and Fox Hudson left Combat. They would be back at 0630 to resume the watch. Garuda fired up his first cigarette of the midwatch and reached for the large brown jar of aspirin tablets kept in a rack above the SWIC console.

"Headache already?" Brian asked, lowering himself into the evaluator's chair.

"Yes, sir, midwatches always give me a pain." Garuda popped two pills in his mouth and chewed them audibly.

"Jesus. You chew that shit?"

"Yes, sir. Then I wash it down with coffee and a

smoke. Mouth tastes so bad after that, it keeps me awake for the first half of the mid; after that, it's downhill.''

"I'm gonna stay awake just thinking about that. Where's that helo now?''

"Recommend you go over to surface and let them brief you on the search plan and everything. They're operating on the twenty-mile scale, and I have to keep the two-hundred-and-fifty-mile scale here at SWIC. I collapse my picture, it takes me a while to get it back. The ole air side–surface side problem, remember?''

"Right. I forgot.'' Brian walked over to surface, where Radarman First Class Rockheart had assumed the surface supervisor's watch. Rocky walked him through the mechanics of the search pattern, an expanding square search around the most likely point of entry for the aircraft wreckage. Brian was impressed by Rocky's calm professionalism; Rockheart had a good reputation in the eyes of the wardroom officers.

"It doesn't help that this guy went in at midnight,'' Rockheart was saying. "If it was daylight, there'd be more aircraft out here looking, but at night, and with no indications they got out before it went bang, well . . .''

"Yeah. So they'll do this square search until their fuel gets low, and that'll be it?''

"They'll come in for fuel and crew rest, then they'll probably go back out at first light. We'll hang around the area for the next few days—we're still on the edge of our PIRAZ box, so it doesn't cost us anything to hang around and keep an eye out.''

"And there were no last-minute transmissions before the guy blew up?''

"No, sir,'' said the AIC. "Monty had him on Guard, steering him to Red Crown. Last thing the guy said was, 'Descending out of angels three-five.' He was already on fire then. The BARCAP came down on the deck for forty minutes after the guy went in, but they didn't see anything and then they were bingo.''

Brian watched the little blob of video drive around the computer-generated lines on the scope for a few minutes and then returned to D and D. The captain called up for a status, but there was little to report.

Combat quieted down. Most of the surveillance and special-flight aircraft had gone home for the night, back to their bases in Vietnam, the Philippines, Guam, or Thailand. The status board said that one of the two carriers at Yankee Station was in stand-down mode for twenty-four hours to let the crew rest. The other was flying minimum sorties for missions such as the BARCAP station to the west of *Hood*'s station. The weather messages told the tale: There had been heavy fog for the past week over the North, especially in the target-rich Red River Valley. The carrier strikes were suspended until the next front swept out of China and blew away the fog.

Brian sat at the evaluator table, leafing through the huge stack of messages that had come in since he had left Combat at 1800. Combat's daily mail. His mind wandered off to the letter he had written Maddy a few hours before. He had told her about the Sea Dragon operation and what had happened to *Berkeley,* omitting the gory parts. He had also decided to tell her about the staff captain's visit and his own suspicions that there was a fairly significant drug problem in the ship. He had closed with almost a page of encouragement for the home front, noting that by the time she got this letter there would be less than six months to go before the ship got back. Pushing it a little, he thought, but what the hell—sounds better than seven months.

He continued to sort through the stack of messages, discarding most of them but keeping any that bore on the PIRAZ operations. Message air plans, logistics reports, admin traffic, Navy policy messages, fleet schedules, intelligence summaries, and the countless reports flowing out from the MACV headquarters down in Saigon accumulated at the rate of six hundred separate messages every day. Each of the evaluators had to sort the stack continuously during his watch to keep up with it.

"Feel like a goddamn message clerk," Brian grumbled.

"Yes, sir, there's a ton a that shit. And wait till they get the strikes going again—it doubles."

Brian groaned. He was having trouble keeping his eyes open, and several of the messages blurred as he thumbed through them. Then there was a commotion over in surface.

"Evaluator, Surface," came a voice over the bitch box. "Five-three reports a tracer!"

"All *right*!" exclaimed Garuda. He switched over to an air-control circuit to call the airborne early-warning E-2 aircraft to relay the news to the carrier. Brian went over to surface to stand behind the controller, who was talking urgently to the SAR helicopter pilot.

"What's a tracer?" he asked. "Where was it?"

Rockheart pointed to a glowing symbol near the helicopter's video. "Right there, Mr. Holcomb. The pilots carry a thirty-eight with tracer bullets. On a night SAR, they're supposed to shoot 'em off when a helo gets close enough to see them. Mother says he's on a flare-out now to hover in the area and see if they get another one."

"Second tracer! They have a guy—they have a guy in sight!" shouted the controller. "Five-three on final to datum, swimmer on the wire!"

Brian went back over to D and D and buzzed the captain to report that Big Mother 53 had a possible survivor and was preparing to lower a swimmer down to pick him up.

"Call the exec, and make sure there's a medical team back there on the flight deck when Five-three lands," ordered the captain. "You inform CTF Seventy-seven yet?"

"No, sir, I was waiting to make sure they pick the guy up and give us an initial condition report before I called CTF Seventy-seven."

"Okay, but then tell 'em right away."

"Aye, aye, sir." Brian hung up. Garuda was grinning sheepishly.

"What?"

"I reported the tracer to the E-Two on UHF secure; they'll have told the staff on the carrier. I didn't realize—"

"Yeah, that's okay. I just didn't want to get bombarded with questions before I had at least one or two answers."

"I'll ask the next time. I forgot who was the evaluator."

"Well, hell, Garuda, I didn't tell you not to. It's no big deal." The bitch box's red light came on.

"Evaluator, Surface, Big Mother Five-three reports one soul recovered and they are RTB."

"Evaluator, aye. Garuda," he said, "what's—"

"RTB means returning to base, or in aviator-speak, returning to boat. They're on their way back. You better call the XO."

"Oh shit, yes. I forgot." Brian got on the phone as Garuda called out to the bridge to get the ship back on flight course and speed.

Twenty minutes later, Ensign Folsom came into Combat from the bridge. He was still dressed out in his flight-deck gear, with a green jersey pulled over his khaki shirt and two Navy flashlights jammed in his pockets. He wore a CO_2 life jacket in a pouch strapped to his waist and he was carrying his cranial helmet. Coming in from the darkness of the bridge, he blinked his eyes rapidly in the relatively bright lights of CIC. The lower part of his face was red from the winds across the deck and the rotor downwash. He walked over to where Brian was standing.

"Got one back!"

"Yeah, you did. The CO's really pleased, not to mention the CTF Seventy-seven people. They've passed the word to the Air Force. Guy able to tell what happened?"

"Sort of, but Jesus, you should've seen him." Folsom shook his head as if trying to dislodge the memory. Garuda was turned around in his chair, and the surface module watch standers were gathered in the doorway to D and D, listening hard.

"What, was he badly injured?"

"Well, from what the baby doc says, no. But apparently you punch out of an F-Four at altitude, there's shit that comes with the territory—his eyes, for instance. His eyes were like fucking baseballs. I mean he looked like some kinda space alien. Something to do with the sudden pressure drop. And his ears were bleeding, the rest of his face looked like raw hamburger, and his ankles looked like softballs puffing up through his poopy suit. When they brought him out of Big Mother on a stretcher, I almost puked. Bad shit." He shook his head again.

"And did he say what happened to the other guy—was this the pilot or the backseater?"

"Guys in the helo said this was the RIO, the back-seater. He said the pilot command ejected him, that the bird was on fire both sides, and that it blew up a few seconds later. He said it happened too fast for the pilot to have made it out. Guy saved his RIO's ass but bought the farm."

"Damn. They take the guy to sick bay?"

"Yes, sir. They'll keep him there with the medical officer overnight and then take him off on the log helo tomorrow, I guess. They better not let anybody see him with those eyes, though. Guys'll be having nightmares. You should've heard the chief boats when he saw him—started talking Indian shit."

"I'm guessing it's sort of like explosive decompression," said Brian. "His eyes should be normal by morning. We have to be grateful for getting one back at least. Garuda, we have to do some Op reps or anything?"

"No, sir, I've made the reports by voice. The CTF Seventy-seven people will send out the Op reps. What we gotta do now is secure from flight quarters." The other people standing around D and D began to drift away to retell the story.

"Right." Brian keyed the bitch box's key down and called the bridge, telling the OOD to secure from flight quarters. He looked at his watch; it was 0230. For his first midwatch on Red Crown, time was moving right along. For the first time in days, he felt enthusiastic and energized.

By the following morning, however, the reality of being up since midnight began to intrude. At 0930, Brian found his eyelids drooping as he plowed through the backlog of departmental paperwork. He decided it was time to get out on deck for some fresh air. Maybe have his little talk with Louie Jesus. What a name. He called down to the Weapons office and told the yeoman to find the chief boatswain. Five minutes later, Chief Martinez tapped on the stateroom door; it sounded like he was using a two-by-four. He stuck his head in and Brian grabbed his ball cap and took the chief by the wardroom to get coffee. They went out onto the weather decks, through the breaks, and up on to the forecastle, shifting the hot paper coffee cups from hand to hand.

It was a typical day in the Gulf. The sky was overcast and hazy, a mass of warm, humid air suspended over a flat, glare-filled sea. The horizon was indistinguishable except where the dark underside of a rainsquall marked the demarcation between sea and sky. *Hood* was barely moving, maintaining station in the PIRAZ box and conserving fuel. There were none of the usual sea sounds, or even a hint of a breeze. Patches of dried sea salt sparkled at the base of the missile launcher.

Three sweating crews of deckhands were chipping paint and chasing rust spots on the forecastle. A boatswain's mate second class by the name of Strickland was supervising the work in the style of boatswain's mates everywhere: leaning against the side of the missile launcher, positioned so he could watch all three gangs, one foot hooked over a sound-powered phone box, the beginnings of a pendulous beer belly hanging over his belt, along with a holster for his fid and knife, a dirty china mug of black coffee in his hand, and his ball cap pulled down over his eyes against the glare.

They walked forward, across the gray expanse of steel, heading for the point of the bow. Brian glanced back up at the bridge, but the green-tinted windows were bright with glare and revealed nothing. Brian realized that for the rest of the crew not directly involved in the PIRAZ operations, the forty-five-day line periods must be exceedingly boring. He mentioned this to the chief.

"Well, yeah, it is and no, it ain't," replied the chief. "We get a lot of time to do this kinda chippin' and paintin', which is good, 'cause we don't got enough guys to cover all the topside spaces, a ship this size. I got gangs workin' up here, and midships on the boats and the davits, and we do some trainin' for unreps and stuff like that. And then there's helo ops, sometimes night 'n day, like last night. First Division guys are on the fire-fighting team, and we gotta man up the motor whaleboat every time they set flight quarters. Trick is to keep 'em busy and workin', then they ain't got time to bitch so much."

Brian nodded. "We get all wrapped up in Combat doing the Red Crown thing," he said. "It's like being in another world. And being on port and starboard, I'm pretty much reduced to watch-standing and sleeping. Weapons Department must think I'm the missing man."

"Well, it ain't like bein' in Dago, but this is WESTPAC. Mostly everybody stands watch, eats, and sleeps. The routine shit can wait."

Coltrane and Hooper came walking by, carrying large buckets of nonskid sand from a storeroom to the boatswain locker. Brian shook his head as they passed. He remembered the first time he had seen these two, on a tour of the First Division area conducted by Jack Folsom and the chief a few days after he had reported aboard. While they had been talking, a curious pair of sailors had emerged from the forecastle hatch, tugging and heaving a paint-stained ten-foot-long aluminum punt up the steep ladder. At the bow of the punt had been an extremely short, scrawny black-haired man of about twenty-two, with a hatchet-shaped face, a birdlike pointed nose, slightly bulging eyes, and a gap where two of his upper front teeth should have been. He had been issuing a steady stream of directions and orders in a broad Brooklyn accent to the other man, who was struggling with the heavier end of the punt.

Brian had stared in wonder at the scrofulous second sailor. He had been dressed in what looked like a selection from the engineers' ragbag, and even the rags were disheveled. He wore baggy, torn, and paint-stained dungarees, a shirt three times too big for him, and sported a round red face right out of the comics, complete with slightly crossed eyes, a large nose, protruding ears, and a vacant smiling expression under a mop of strawberry blond hair that stuck out in all directions as he nodded agreeably in time with the smaller man's stream of orders. Brian had thought he looked like an animated scarecrow as the two made their way past them, hauling the punt aft to the fantail area through the weather breaks.

"What in the world was that?" Brian had asked.

The chief laughed as Jack Folsom explained. "That's *Hood*'s dynamic duo," he said. "The side cleaners—Coltrane and Hooper. The little one's Jimmy Hooper; he thinks he's a wise guy. The village idiot is Seaman

Apprentice Hulanny Coltrane, who's the product of a cosmic joke gone wrong at the Navy Recruiting Command."

Folsom went on to explain that Coltrane had been inducted at a recruiting station in northeastern Tennessee as a joke by the chief in charge at one of the rural stations, then sent on to Memphis to see what would happen. Through a series of mistakes that only a bureaucracy could cobble together, Coltrane had made it all the way to the boot camp in San Diego, where a horrified master chief had spent a day burning up the phones into the Recruiting Command trying to undo it. While he was shouting at Washington, however, Coltrane and four hundred or so of his contemporaries had been dutifully sworn into the U.S. Navy out on the parade field, making the master chief's protestations moot.

It would not have been quite so bad if only Coltrane could speak, but, in fact, he could not. He apparently could read, at least a little, and amiably followed everyone's orders at boot camp, to the point where even the other boots would dispatch him on amusing errands. But when spoken to, he could respond only with a series of sounds that made no sense whatsoever, a fact that had been collectively covered up by every chief at the Recruit Training Center. Coltrane had slowly became a covert project, wherein the chiefs decided to see whether they could actually get him through boot camp and out to a ship without anyone finding out.

"His actual name is Coaltrain," Folsom said. "Absent a father, his mother apparently named him after the most prominent feature of their lives, the coal trains that went through their trailer patch. Guy at the recruiting station heard Coaltrain and automatically put down Coltrane, like the jazzman. XO did a little checking after he came aboard last year, once he came down off the overhead. Jesus Christ, was that an interesting day. I saw this creature on the quarterdeck and just knew he was going to become one of mine. Talk about your basic deck-force Cro-Magnon. But the word the XO got back was that, yes, the Navy had fucked up egregiously, but there was no way to undo it without embarrassing a whole lot of people. So we were stuck with him."

"Fact is," said the chief, "he's perfect for side cleanin'. It's a shit job, down there in that punt on the waterline with all them overboard discharges from the shitters and all that oil an' stuff."

"And he gives nobody trouble," Folsom added. "You figure, a deck ape that can't talk can't give anybody any lip, either. It's just that he couldn't really function very well by himself in the division. He wanders off. Shit, we'd find him wandering all over the ship. Guys'd call us on the phone, tell us to come get our dummy. Still does it. He needed a keeper."

"Enter Hooper, I suppose," Brian said.

"Oh, yes indeedy, enter Hooper. Came aboard in the same batch as Coltrane. Like I said, he thinks he's a wise guy doing a sabbatical in the Navy. Tells all these incredible stories about Guido the Gutter and Manny the Mouth, you know, goombah stuff. Perfect little con man and artful dodger, always on the make for some angle or another, has shirking down to an art form. Total pain in the ass, and headed for an admin discharge."

"Until we stuck him with Coltrane on side cleanin'," continued the chief. "See, in port, cause a what they gotta do, side cleaners don't stand duty, so they get liberty every night. It's a shitty job, but it comes with this really good deal. Hooper went right for it, until we told him he had to take care of Coltrane, make sure he got fed and cleaned himself up, keep him from wandering away, and work the sides with him."

"Hooper fight the program?" asked Brian.

Folsom chuckled. "Yeah, he objected, but then we sent him on a tour of the fire rooms as a possible alternative, and he decided Coltrane and side cleaning was better."

"So now he bosses poor Coltrane around, who loves it, I guess, and the two of them keep the sides cleaned. Wow."

"When Hooper ain't gettin' 'em into some kind bullshit scam or another," the chief said. "Coltrane, he goes adrift from time to time, anytime Hooper ain't with him. But he's okay, you know, harmless. Not like that fuckin' Hooper. Especially when he gets inta the firewater on the beach."

Brian now watched the side cleaners disappear down the forecastle hatch, shaking his head at the sight. Martinez nodded his massive head up and down amiably, as if to say that even Coltrane and Hooper had a place. They stood in silence for a few minutes, absorbing the horizon, the chief waiting to see what it was his department head wanted to talk about.

"Chief," Brian said finally.

"Yeah, boss?"

"You said a while ago we needed to talk—about this drug stuff. I had a little talk with the chief engineer, and I have to tell you, I'm really not too comfortable with . . . well, with the way we handle drug problems in this ship."

The chief looked down at the deck but kept silent, giving Brian time to frame what he wanted to say.

"I guess what I mean is, I understand all the departments have the problem, that the dopers aren't confined to Engineering. I also understand what happens if we bust each and every guy we find using or carrying or otherwise dirty—that we run out of bodies pretty quick."

"Yes, sir."

"But . . . well, I guess it's what we're doing to 'em when we do catch 'em. And I've heard that you play a big part in that. Like what happened to that guy Gallagher—his hand being broken."

"That was an accident, way I heard it," said the chief. Brian looked sideways at the chief's impassive face, wondering how far he was going to get with this. Then he looked around. The nearest people were fifty feet away. He decided to let it all hang out.

"Well, Chief, way *I* heard it, Gallagher hid out in Two Fire room until the engineer finally threw him out of there, and *then* he had his accident. And the way I hear that it goes down is that a certain large CPO, namely you, with maybe some help from the Sheriff and a couple of other CPOs, get the nod from the XO to administer some fairly direct justice to any shitbird who gets cocky about using drugs."

The chief remained silent, his black eyes seemingly fixed on the horizon. Brian had to turn his head up to see the chief's face. A lone seagull glided by, headed aft to search the wake for treasures from the garbage chute.

"Now, I'm not asking you to confirm or deny any of this. And please believe me when I say I can see the justice of it, especially when our hands are somewhat tied by the system. I think a guy who uses drugs aboard ship, or booze for that matter, puts all of his shipmates in danger, not to mention the ship. I'd hate to think of what might happen if the North Vietnamese ever tried us on and some people up in Combat were spaced-out when they came at us. But that's not what's bugging me."

The chief said nothing. Brian, still wondering whether he was making a mistake, continued anyway.

"My problem is twofold: First, when we catch a guy doing the crime, and we aren't handling the case regulation Navy. We, or you, kick his ass instead, and by doing so, we put ourselves in jeopardy. I mean, we both know it's illegal for an officer or a CPO to beat up someone junior to him. In other words, we're getting down on the level of the bad guy by answering a crime with a crime."

The chief nodded slowly, still not looking at Brian. An air-driven needle gun began to rattle and buzz behind them.

"The second problem I have with it is that I'm not sure we keep the guy from doing dope again, because all we've done is to reinforce what he already knew: You get caught, you're gonna pay for it. Now I'll admit, this guy, this snipe, Gallagher, was pretty blatant about it. The ship's at GQ, and he's flyin' in the purple haze. So now he's had his little 'accident.' Is he going to stop doing dope? It seems to me that he's gonna be a lot more careful about when and where he smokes his next joint. And maybe from now on, it'll only be after the midwatch, when he's got six hours of rack time before his next watch. But if that's true, the next time GQ goes, say, maybe when the guy's off watch, we can still get Gallagher the space cadet again when the action goes down. You see what I'm saying?"

"Yes, sir."

"So, you want to know, what's my fix. Well, my fix is you bring 'em to captain's mast, throw the book at 'em, and give them a BCD or one of these new 'other than honorable' discharges, and then you throw the bastards out. Yes, it might get shorthanded around here, but at least then you *know* that the guys who're left aren't gonna show up drugged on duty when you call away GQ in the middle of the night.''

The chief stared down at his boots for a moment. He finished his coffee, crumpled the paper cup into a tight little ball, and pitched it over the side. He turned to put his back to the lifelines and looked sideways and down at Brian.

"No you don't, Mr. Holcomb."

"Don't what, Chief?"

"You don't know nothin' about the guys you ain't caught yet, 'cept'n you ain't caught 'em yet. This engineer, this Gallagher wipe? I'll tell you what I *know* about his young ass: I know he knows, we catch him again, he's gonna get his back broke. He's gonna have trainin' wheels for legs and go around in fuckin' diapers the resta his life. The only hard thing 'neath his belt he'll ever know about'll be the fuckin' wheelchair they roll his ass around in, sittin' in a pile his own shit. I see Gallagher every fuckin' day. Go outta my way to see him, I hafta. I look at him, he gets reminded. An' the guy who Gallagher buys from, or usta buy from, he goes around to see his old customer, Gallagher, and Gallagher, he gets this white-eye sorta look about him, says, 'No more, man, no thank you very fuckin' much. See, I done got me some religion.' That's what I *know* about Gallagher, 'cause we had this little talk, me'n him. An' I ain't worried about doin' crime, 'cause the dopers, they started it, see? They don't do no dope, I don't hafta stomp their nuts.''

"So you're telling me that everybody who's been caught and, uh, talked to is now a born-again Christian?''

The chief grinned. "I don't know about no Christians, boss. Me, I'm just a three-quarter-breed Injun, remember? A Christian was something my people staked out over an anthill with a little honey in their eyes and ears.'' He grinned again, as if momentarily relishing a memory. "But these guys I talk to, they believe. Me, Jackson, and, yeah, some a the other guys in the goat locker, we make sure they believe. Your way, well, it just won't work, not in this ship. 'Cause a two things.''

"But my way gets rid of the dopers, gets 'em off the ship."

"And then we jist get some more. Yeah, it takes a little while, but then the Bureau, they send replacements, and you jist end up with more dopers, only now you don't *know* who they are. You gotta find the little fucks all over again. Look, these fuckin' kids nowadays, they do dope like you'n me did cigarettes and beer after school, we wuz growin' up. I mean, what kid *likes* ta smoke, huh? And beer, beer don't taste no good till you get a taste for the alky in it. You and me, we did it 'cause it wasn't legal, 'cause it was ba-a-a-d, an all the teachers and your momma and poppa said it was ba-a-a-d. Nowadays, beer and cigarettes, that's pussy stuff. That's what the fuckin' girls do, when they ain't paradin' their little asses in them miniskirts and then gettin' all pissed-off, some guy sees their Skivvies. Guys, nowadays, they go get some dope. Whadda they know: Guy's onna TV sayin' it's no different from cigarettes or booze, the longhair rock'n'roll millionaires doin' it onstage, the college kids all doin' it, it's all jist some chemical shit, so why not do it? See, it jist cops and robbers; they don't see nothin' bad in it." He stared over at two men who had stopped working, precipitating instant industry.

"That's the first thing. So our way, we find out who the dopers are and we squeeze 'em a little. They keep it up, we squeeze 'em some more, only harder. Shit, I tell 'em, I let 'em hear me sayin' it, guy can fall over the side real easy, he ain't careful, an' it's a bitch to swim with broke arms. They get the fuckin' message. Our way, we know what's what and who's who. And we hafta do it this way, 'cause a the second thing."

"Which is?"

"Which is, this command ain't gonna let you bring a buncha guys up to mast and run up a buncha admin discharges. Makes the ship look bad, makes the command look bad."

"Yeah, I know, and we end up standing watches port and report."

"Yeah, but that ain't it; the main bang is that the word gets around, *Hood*'s got a real bad drug problem, they'll

187

yank this CO offa here, send in some hotshot whose sweat pumps are runnin' on max, and life in the ole *Hood-maru* turns to shit.''

Brian thought about that for a moment. "Okay, I can see that, but it seems to me like we're betting on the come here, big time. Long as nothing happens, no big deal in the middle of the night, no sneak attack, no local Pearl Harbors, we might pull it off, keep a lid on it. Seems to me the captain ought to be thinking about the chances he's taking.''

The chief shook his head. "I ain't gonna argue that, Mr. Holcomb. Yer talkin' the way it oughta be done, regular Navy, like the regs say. But me, the resta the chiefs, we been goin' to sea long enough to know that you take the captains as they come. You gotta make do with what you get, and we got an Old Man now who don't bust chops, who don't dump on the crew with a buncha mickey mouse. Hell, he's an old guy, served in Korea, okay? Wears a Navy Cross for saving a ship when he deep-sixed some kinda bomb or somethin'. Way I hear it, he don't even *believe* this dope shit's really goin' on. Yeah, maybe he don't wanna know; maybe he's got other reasons. But that's what we got. And we got an XO who wants maybe to do it the right way, maybe not, but you know how it is, it ain't his ship. So we all do the best we can. You think you can go in, siddown with this Old Man, make him see what's goin' on, shit, you go do it. Chiefs'd love it.''

"You think that would do some good, Chief?"

"No, sir.''

"Terrific.''

It was Brian's turn to stare silently over the lifelines. He felt that the chief's logic was simplistic but probably realistic. The subtleties of what was legal and illegal and all the theories on what constituted professional good order and discipline were irrelevant to the likes of Chief Martinez. Brian understood that military discipline ultimately depended on the willingness of subordinates, from admirals to seamen recruits, to be disciplined in the first place. The drug culture disavowed that notion.

And yet, he still didn't buy it entirely. He tried another

tack. "If your way works so well, how come we had an incident like the other day, when one shithead, this guy—what's his name—Gallagher brought the whole ship dead in the water?"

"That's what's really bad about the dope, Mr. Holcomb. Unless you got some kinda antidope program goin', the only way you usually catch these assholes is when they fuck up somethin' really important. And there's another thing: We chiefs got this kinda code here—you don't go really stompin' in a guy's shit for dope less'n you catch his ass usin' or carryin'. I mean, suspicion don't cut it, see? Hell, we'd hafta kick all their asses, we did it on suspicion. The chief BT, and Mr. Ames, too, he's the B divvo, they kinda thought Gallagher was dirty. But nobody could catch his ass till he fucked up public like. Now, everybody gets the message, see? You go fuckin' up big time like that, somethin' bad's gonna happen. Not no admin discharge, not some piece a paper, but somethin' bad, like a bad broke hand. Even the wardroom knows. Now, maybe some guys thinkin' about buyin' a little reefer, maybe now they thinkin' they better not."

Brian finished his own coffee and pitched the paper cup over the side. He wasn't sure where to go from here. He wanted the chief's respect and did not want to sound like some kind of liberal do-gooder or by-the-book pussy. He also wanted to be part of the 'good guy' element in the ship, to be on the inside, since there was obviously an insiders' operation going on here with respect to the dopers. The chiefs could not get away with their vigilante system unless they were protected and even encouraged by at least the executive officer, if not by the captain himself. But he sensed the flaw in the *Hood*'s system. They ought not to be just sitting around, waiting for a drug user to show himself; they ought to be in hot pursuit of the whole druggie organization—there had to be one.

"I hear you, Chief," he said finally. "I can't quarrel with the right and wrong of it, and I like the thought of the dopers getting their asses kicked. I just guess I'm not used to gun-deck justice taking the place of the regulation Navy way of doing things. Maybe it's the difference between PACFLEET and LANTFLEET."

"I'll bet you had jist's much drugs in the LANT-FLEET's we got out here in WESTPAC, boss. Way I see it, regulation Navy, that's the way to go. Long as it works. Us bosun mates, we do our unreps, we handle ammunition, drive the boats, clean the heads 'n compartments, chip paint, and tie the fuckin' knots regulation Navy, every day. But this here drug shit, the regulation Navy way ain't doin' us no good. This drug shit, it's underground shit. Takes underground medicine to git aholt of it. Tell you what, you don't want to know about it, that's okay. You don't gotta know about it."

Brian laughed. "No way, Chief, I want to be a player in this ship. I'm not going to sit on the sidelines, pretend there isn't a problem. I just have this feeling that this isn't the right way to go, no matter how logical it sounds and how satisfying it is to see guys like Gallagher with a big hand. The *Hood* way leaves us all exposed to what the druggies do. We ought to be beating the bushes, uncovering the distributors, finding the kingpin, and breaking up the druggie organization. I guess I'm going to have to think about it some more."

"Yes, sir, I hear that. Officers're supposed to think. But like I said, you can always let the chiefs take care a this shit. That's kinda our job, you know what I'm sayin'?"

Martinez stood up to his full height, put his hands together, and cracked his knuckles. The movement made his huge shoulders and biceps swell and the buttons on his shirt strain. The nearest clump of deckhands looked nervous and chipped harder. Martinez grinned down at Brian. "They didn't make me a bosun chief 'cause I pass the tests real good, you know what I mean?"

Brian grinned back. "They made you chief because they were afraid not to, in all probability."

"Yes, sir, boss, so well, that's gotta be part of my job, right? Officers won't go wrong, you let the chiefs handle the potheads. Tell you what, you wanta go diggin', and you go findin' out who's the kingpin, who's the guy bringin' all this shit aboard, who's makin' the money, there's some chiefs'd like to know what you find out, okay? Talk to Jackson, I think he's thinkin' the same way's you are. But then, you better get the fucker offa here real quick like.''

''Why's that?''

'' 'Cause I find him first, I'll jist naturally hafta kill his ass. Now, I don't mind doin' that, but you betcher ass there'd be a buncha paperwork, they go findin' some guy in the main engine reduction gears fuckin' up the monkey mates' lube oil.''

''Got the picture, Chief.''

18

San Diego

Maddy slipped a TV dinner into the oven and headed for the bathroom, where she stripped off her tennis outfit and took a quick shower. She ached all over, the result of a challenge set with this innocent-looking little old lady who had run her all over the court for an hour and a half. Maddy was an avid tennis player. She tried for a daily match at the public courts in the park across the street. Today, she had encountered a genuine ringer. She wasn't strong enough to beat a male player of better-than-average expertise, but she could usually hold her own and often defeat other women players. Not this afternoon, though. Damn woman had simply stood there waving that dinky racket like a flyswatter and putting every shot right on the line or in a corner. Six–love, straight games. Yuk. Back to the backboard.

The tennis game had come on top of her first day in the Accounting Department at Bank of America. As a management intern, she was being cycled through all the departments at the San Diego headquarters, and there was, of course, no avoiding Accounting in a bank. But the Accounting manager was sixty-one and fancied himself a ladies' man. He had bad teeth, bad breath, a cheap hairpiece, a potbelly, and an incredibly good opinion of himself. She had spent a good part of the afternoon fending off not-so-subtle passes. She foresaw that she was going to have to pitch a little fit sometime in the next few days to put a stop to it. Stupid damn man.

But the job was too good a deal to just stomp out. They paid eight hundred dollars a month, which was precisely ten dollars a month more than Brian made in his Navy base pay. By wardroom standards, the Holcombs were very nearly rich.

As she rubbed the bar of soap on her skin, she thought of Brian. They often took showers together, and the soaping ritual had often led to better things, much better things. She remembered the first time they had tried to make love in the shower. It had ended in a major deflation of romantic egos, rescued only when they caught sight of one another in the bathroom mirror and laughed themselves to tears. She suddenly realized that life was just no fun without him. Oh, there was plenty of human interaction, the people at work, the wardroom wives, men she occasionally flirted with at the office, but the intimacy of that secret sense of being ridiculous together that they shared, that's what was missing.

She sighed and got out of the shower, dried off, slipped into her bathrobe, and went into the kitchen to retrieve the atomic dinner. She took it into the living room on a tray. The living room was already dark, even though it was only six o'clock. The rose quartz streetlights bathed the park across the street. Winter cometh, but not like in Boston, she thought, as she drew the curtains. She turned on some lights and the television and went to fetch a glass of wine. She was watching the evening news and absently eating mystery meat in salt gravy when the phone rang.

"Yes? Hello?"

"Maddy Holcomb?"

Oh my God, she thought, it's *him*. It had been three weeks since her memorable trip to MCRD, and yet she recognized the voice instantly.

"Maddy Holcomb?"

"Uh, yes?"

"This is Autrey. From MCRD of the evil memory. Do you remember me?"

She swallowed. "Uh, well, yes, of course, Mr. Autrey. How could I not remember you, I mean, you—"

"Autrey, just Autrey. Yes, well. I was calling—I was calling to see if you might have dinner with me. There, said it."

Oh Lord, I was afraid of this. Now what? You tell him you're married and that dinner is out of the question, that's what.

"I'm afraid I've already had dinner, Mr. Autrey."

"Please, just Autrey. Mr. makes me edgy and other people look around for the cowboy."

Maddy laughed nervously.

"And I didn't mean tonight, of course. I meant . . . well, how about Friday? At the Grant Grill. It's a really fancy restaurant, and they're famous for prime rib. I'll even wear a coat and tie. And shoes, if you insist."

Maddy laughed again. "Mr. Autrey," she began.

"Autrey, just Autrey."

"Okay, Just Autrey. I really think I should just say thank you again for all you've done. I shouldn't have been down there at MCRD in the first place, and I don't ever plan to go back. And I think—"

"But you owe me."

"I beg your pardon?"

"Well, I guess you don't really. But I was thinking, I did save you from great harm, and I would really like it if you would just have dinner with me. I want to see you again when you're not scared to death and polluting the azaleas."

"Autrey—"

"Yeah, I know. I'm pressing an unfair advantage. But that's how bad I want to see you."

"Well, yes, you are pressing an unfair advantage. I mean, how—"

"That's because we're sneaky."

"What?"

"We Indians. We're known for being a sneaky bunch. Maybe if I just said please. Please? Just dinner? The lighting's subdued, so you won't be embarrassed."

"Embarrassed? By what?"

"When someone yells, 'Hey, handsome,' I don't usually turn around, you know?"

"Well, my goodness, Mr.—I mean, Autrey—you're hardly ugly."

"I know. That was a play for sympathy and a compliment. I told you, we're sneaky. I'm trying everything."

"Yes, you certainly are." She was weakening. The man was amusing. And she did sort of owe him, certainly more than a hasty thank-you over her shoulder as she bolted from his car. The only way she could kill the whole deal immediately was to admit to him that she was married. And even though he might already know that, as long as she did not admit it, her being at MCRD wasn't quite so embarrassing, so maybe . . . Wow, you're really working at this, girl.

"Autrey, okay. Dinner. Friday. Where is this Grant Grill?"

"I can pick you up. . . ."

She sighed quietly and waited.

"Right. You want to be in your own car. See, we're sneaky, but we're also a little dense sometimes. The Grant Grill—it's in the U.S. Grant Hotel, downtown, on Third and Broadway. Main door's on Broadway. Go in the main entrance, walk down the lobby, turn right. How's about seven?"

"Make it seven-thirty. I play tennis every day after work."

"Right. Damn. I'm so glad you said yes. I've been thinking about you for three weeks now. And it took that long to get up the courage to call you, Maddy Holcomb."

Maddy smiled into the handset. "Enough. I'll see you Friday, Autrey."

"Yeah, great. That's really great. Well, good night."

"Good night."

She hung up the phone and sat down on the couch. Her heart was actually pounding just a little. What the hell was she doing? Going out on a *date*? It's not a date. Really, it's not. The man had saved her from a rapist and now was asking, asking nicely, for the favor of her having dinner with him. That's all. Not to go back to his apartment, see the etchings, or to go to a party, or anything else. And would you listen to him: He was as scared and nervous as a farm boy, for crying out loud.

Three weeks to get up his courage to call her. The phone rang again. She grabbed at it.

"Yes?"

"Maddy, Tizzy here."

"Oh, Tizzy."

"Yeah, oh, Tizzy. Sorry to disappoint. Just calling to see if you wanted to double up on Friday?"

Maddy drew a mental blank. Friday?

"You know, the wives' outing thing to the Del Mar racetrack? It's almost an hour's drive up there, and there's no point in both of us driving, and I can't stand the thought of going with Suzanne Kirschning, which right now is my other possibility."

Maddy swallowed hard. "Uh, Tizzy, I think I'm going to take a pass on racetrack night. That's not really my scene, and I've got something else to do that night."

"Oh yeah? Who is he? What's he look like?"

"Tizzy, for cryin' out loud. It's nothing like that."

"But you're not going to tell me, are you, sweetie pie?"

Maddy felt an edge of irritation. "I didn't think I was required to, Tizzy."

"O-ooo-oh! A hit, a palpable hit! Now I know it's a guy. Look, honey, this is Aunt Tizzy you're talking to, okay? You know that Tizzy doesn't give two hoots if you're stepping out. Matter of fact, I think it's the only way to present a sane wife when the *Hood* gang gets back. And you know I don't give a damn what the rest of the wives think, either, mostly 'cause the Hudsons are getting out. You've got a little different situation there, so you need to learn some things. Like about the cover-story business. Now, what's the cover?"

"Tizzy, I don't need a cover story. I've got something else to do Friday night, and I do believe that's all I have to tell those women."

Tizzy sighed audibly. " 'Ah do b'leeve.' Listen to you, Maddy. No, listen to me. You are absolutely right. You don't have to check in and check out with the rest of the wives. But life when the ship is deployed is so much simpler if you tell them *something*—anything. Hell, you work in a bank. Your office has a do of some kind that

195

you have to go to. You tell the wives that it's something you *have* to do. A command performance—Navy wives can relate to that, okay? But, Maddy, be cool. Call Mrs. Huntington, tell her you won't be coming along, and give her the story—that story or some other story. That way, when the kitties begin to scratch around in the litter, the captain's wife can stop it with some authority. It's as easy as that, honey.''

Maddy was nodding into the phone. ''Yes, Momma Tizzy. That does makes sense. I just didn't feel that I had to report to someone, you know? I mean, there's nothing wrong with the wardroom wives and all, but I—''

''Hey, kiddo, you don't have to tell me. God knows what they think of me, but I simply don't give a damn, my deah, as Mr. Rhett supposedly said.''

''Tizzy? That's not even close to a southern accent. Really, now!''

''I know, I know. But the sentiment is accurate. Gotta run, find another ride. Probably Suzanne, after all. Aarrgh. Say hi to Mr. Autrey. Bye now.''

Mr. Autrey! Tizzy hung up before Maddy could think of something to say. Damn that woman for seeing right through her. Am I that transparent? She made a mental note to call Mrs. Huntington, turned the TV back up, and finished her dinner. The national news followed the familiar nightly sequence, scenes of young men dying in the mud of Vietnam, followed by scenes of old men talking around a table of white linen and crystal decanters in Paris, followed by scenes of rabid-looking college students protesting in some city or another, all orchestrated by a smug-looking anchorman huffing and puffing about how the protests proved how awful the American government and its military were.

Autrey. She was going to go out to dinner with Autrey. Okay, but just once. She was married and she was not going to travel down the heedless trail being blazed by the likes of Tizzy Hudson. In her mind, the Hudsons' so-called open lifestyle was nothing more than evidence of a very superficial commitment, two selfish people who wanted to be married when it was convenient and single when they got hot pants. Maddy knew that she loved her husband. Love wasn't the problem, damnit; it was all this damned separation. She loved her husband and he wasn't here, and wouldn't be here for another half a year. So what was Autrey? A diversion. Something to do on a Friday night besides listen to the same old "My car, it," "My baby, she" talk among the rest of the wardroom wives. Just this once, darlin', her inner voice warned. Damn sure better be just this once. The man was both attracted and attractive, and he was totally different from Brian. She was used to men being attracted; God had made her that way. But the contrast between her loving, gentle, patriotic, straight-arrow husband who was a zillion miles away and this exotic-looking man with dark eyes whose name made grown Marines scuttle into the bushes and who was right here, well, that was a flame, and dinner with Autrey was the act of a moth.

In her mind, she knew she was in control, but she was pretty sure—not positive, but pretty sure—that there were some depths in her psyche that she had never really plumbed. Long as you know what you're doing, Maddy. Of course I do. I've been manipulating men since I went to college. Just make damn sure this one isn't manipulating you and that all this is as harmless as you're making it. Oh, hell's feathers, it's just dinner. This is 1969, for God's sake.

19

Brian found that the next two weeks passed quickly as the ship settled into the routine of the PIRAZ station. With Benedetti off the watch bill in Combat, Brian's days and nights tended to blur together, with his consciousness of the time of day determined by the relentless demands of the six hours on, six hours off watch schedule. Austin had done him a favor by giving him Garuda Barry as his right-hand man, but he had also given him the tougher of the two watch rotations. The night rotation was a killer.

Austin stood from 1745 until almost midnight, after which he could go to sleep until 0545, during his natural sleep time. Brian, on the other hand, stood watch from noon until nearly 1800. After dinner, he had to meet with his departmental officers to catch up on their day. He would tend to paperwork until about 2100 and then grab a few hours of sleep before rising groggily at 2300 to prepare for the watch from midnight to six in the morning. Mindful of the special fitness report, Brian had figured he had to cover fully the watches and his department head job. Relieved for breakfast, he would then force himself to attend to the daily routine of his department straight through the morning until it was time to take the watch again at noon.

After a few days of getting only two to three hours of sleep a day, he began to bump into things, and the exec had taken him aside.

"Look, Brian, you can't keep this up. As long as Vince is off the evaluator watch bill, you come off the midwatch in the morning, eat breakfast, do *not* drink coffee, and hit your tree until ten-thirty. Get up, clean up, attend to Weapons Department business for half an hour, and then get lunch and take your afternoon watch. Same deal at night. You get chow and then hit your tree, early, like by nineteen hundred, and you sleep until twenty-three hundred."

"Yes, sir, but what about the day-to-day stuff? There's a hell of a lot of paperwork, maintenance supervision, training, and all the people problems to attend to."

"You delegate. With the exception of Fox Hudson, all your other officers and CPOs are in three sections, four on, eight off. So they do it. They can come see you in Combat when you're on watch and there's nothing much going on. Just use your judgment."

"Yes, sir." He hesitated, then asked, "How long will this six-and-six stuff last, XO?"

"I'm going to talk to the CO this week about putting Vince back on. But, as you know, we've still got probs down there."

And well he did know. There had been two more instances of losing the load, one of which had done some damage to one of the missile fire–control radars. The radar could not now be used until the logistics system flew in a repair part. One of the ship's two freshwater evaporators had gone down as well, putting the whole crew on water rationing until a brine-pump motor could be overhauled down on the carrier. Brian had seen almost nothing of the chief engineer, who apparently spent most of his waking hours down in the main holes trying to keep a lid on things.

Brian was getting used to the routine of the Red Crown station, though, and learning daily more and more about the intricate combat systems. The bombing campaign against the North was being prosecuted at low levels in deference to resumption of the peace talks in Paris. The carrier operations against North Vietnam focused on reconnaissance missions, with strikes coming only as direct response to missile batteries and concentrations of triple-A that fired on the recce birds, rather than as sustained attacks against military and infrastructure targets throughout North Vietnam. The rest of the two carriers' strike aircraft were busy in South Vietnam, where units of the North Vietnamese main-force armies were gathering along the perimeter of Marine positions in the DMZ.

While the midnight-to-six watches were relatively dead, the afternoon watches were just the opposite. The fall weather patterns clobbered the North with fog and mists, which usually did not burn off until early afternoon, leaving a short window every day for the reconnaissance runs. Brian had learned the composition of the recce runs, which normally consisted of one or two specially equipped reconnaissance aircraft. The recce birds were escorted by sections of fighter-bombers called Iron Hand, whose mission was to roll in on any sites that tried to bring down the low-flying, unarmed recce birds. The Iron Hands were supplemented by the Wild Weasels, also Phantoms, which were configured as electronic jammers and anti-SAM radar strike aircraft. The Weasels would actively provoke the North Vietnamese missile gunners into turning on their radars by flying directly at known or suspected missile sites. When the Communists obliged, the Weasels would release Shrike antiradiation missiles, which would fly straight down the tracking beams to obliterate the SAM position. Offshore, there would usually be one or two Navy A-6 Intruders, specially configured as jammers against the enemy search radars, to prevent the air-defense system from initiating the deadly sequence of search, acquisition, and handoff of American planes to the SAM radars. Two Jolly Green Giant SAR helos would lift off out of Da Nang to the southwest and position themselves under the missile envelope of the south SAR ship in case an in-country rescue was called. The BARCAP F-4s would be augmented from two aircraft to four on the off chance that the Communists would send up some MiGs to make a run on the recce birds.

Brian realized that the marshaling of all these air assets out over the Gulf clearly telegraphed a warning to the Communists that something was coming, but that suited CTF 77 just fine. The more missile sites, radars, triple-A positions and associated infrastructure taken out during the "peaceful" recce runs meant that much less opposition when and if full-scale bombing resumed.

Hood's Combat truly came alive whenever there were air operations into the North. All the AICs came up to watch over the shoulders of the two on-duty controllers assigned to do the strike-following function. Strike following meant keeping track of what went in over the beach and what came out, ensuring that all the good guys did come out and that none of the bad guys tried to blend in with the returning flights. The SAR helos would be launched, Big Mother and Clementine together, and positioned along the preplanned exit corridors. *Hood* would close in to the western edges of her station box, primarily to move her missile envelope over more of the area where the action would take place.

The typical recce run took about forty minutes to launch, rendezvous, and form up and about five minutes to execute once the recce birds made their run in over the coast. In the two weeks since first assuming station, *Hood* had participated in sixteen recce runs, during which two recce aircraft had been brought down over

North Vietnam and two more had been hit but had made it out over the Gulf to the capable hands of Big Mother 53.

Completion of the recce run usually brought a flurry of helo ops as the log helo from the carrier arrived in the late afternoon, usually just about the time that the Big Mother and Clementine birds needed to get back aboard for fuel, causing a helo traffic jam and hours of deck time for the flight-deck crew and the firefighters. Garuda had been right: Brian came to hate helos.

The Admiral had also run a surprise Alfa-strike feint one night, which had shown Brian the true complexity of the Red Crown air-control function. The carriers had recovered a recce run at sundown and *Hood* had finally put all the helos to bed or sent them off to their home carrier. Austin had relieved Brian at 1745 and told him to come back up to CIC at around 2000. Brian had seen the captain and the Ops officer discussing a top-secret message earlier in the afternoon, but Austin declined to elaborate.

After dinner and a meeting with off-watch Weapons Department officers, Brian had climbed wearily back to CIC. This was his designated sleep time, so he found himself thinking this had better be worth it. Coming into CIC, he found almost the full general quarters team crowding around the consoles in D and D. The captain and the exec were watching over Fox Hudson's shoulder at the SWIC console, and the senior air controllers were manning both air-control consoles. Garuda. Barry was nursing a cup of coffee and a cigarette over in weapons control, where the FCSC console had been commandeered by yet another air controller. Brian gravitated to Garuda.

"So what's going down, Garuda?"

"CTF Seventy-seven is gonna run a feint, remind the Commies that there's more than recce birds out here in the Gulf."

"What exactly is a feint?"

"They activate both bird farms down on Yankee station instead of just one, and they launch about thirty, forty fighter-bombers, A-Sixes, F-Fours, the Jolly Greens SAR helos from Da Nang, a full suite of support tracks, and generally create an aluminum overcast over the Gulf with all kinds of electronic and radio noise. See these tracks down here, coming off the carriers? Each one of those symbols represents two aircraft."

Brian could see literally dozens of tracks clustered around the link symbols representing the carriers, which were 120 miles away. The tracks were clustered in a confused swarm that slowly sorted itself out into formations that began to head north and west, toward North Vietnam. Garuda pointed out some other tracks that appeared to be orbiting off the coast of Hainan Island, a Red Chinese stronghold that formed the outer margins of the Gulf of Tonkin.

"These guys here are the special tracks—like Navy P-Threes called DeepSea. They're filled with ELINT gear. When an Alfa-strike heads in, the North Vietnamese usually light off all their radars, SAM, search, gunfire control—the works. The DeepSea guys tape it all and take cross-bearings. That's how we know where the SAM and triple-A sites are, for when our guys go in for real."

"So there's more than a game of chicken going on here," said Brian.

"Yes, sir, lots more. The aviators, they need to practice this shit, because making a full-blown strike is complicated enough even before the enemy takes defensive action. Plus, being aviators, they forget everything they've ever learned after a day or so on the carrier."

Brian grinned. "And what's our role?"

"We have two roles: The first is PIRAZ. We make sure that the same number of airplanes come out as went in. If we're short, we'll need to execute a rescue. If we're over, it means some MiGs are trying to tag along with the formations as they go back to the bird farms. Especially at night."

"Jesus. Have they ever done that?"

"Nope, but the Japanese did it during World War Two. And lemme tell you, the last thing you need in the landing pattern is an enemy fighter-bomber when everybody's low on fuel and trying to get back aboard the boat at night. Fuck things up pretty good, one ever got through. But that's our job. They use to call it Tomcat; now it's PIRAZ."

"And the second thing?"

"The second thing is strike-flight following. The fighter-bombers go in country, go feet-dry, they're under control of the strike leader, usually a CAG or squadron commander who hangs back and directs his guys into the targets. Or, if it's a really big gaggle, like this one's gonna be, the E-Two does it. He's right here, out in the middle of the Gulf where he can look in country with his radar. Our controllers set up their scopes so they can track individual strike cells—those're small groups of bombers—in over the beach and back out again. Our guys listen but don't talk on the strike circuits. A pilot gets hit, or gets disoriented, or anything else goes wrong, Red Crown has him under positive track and can come up on the air and give him a vector to get out of trouble, or a vector to get to his target. Sorta a mother hen function, to help the E-Two controllers."

"I had no idea that carrier attacks were so controlled."

"Yeah, you see the movies, you think it's just Helldivers rolling in out of the clouds. But it's complex as hell, and you see, we've got three controllers set up to work. Tonight, we'll just watch, maybe exchange tracks with the E-Two. But when it's for real, it's sweat-pump city up here."

Brian watched with Garuda as the screen filled with bright amber symbols representing three dozen attack aircraft now sixty miles out from Red Crown station and headed toward the North Vietnamese coast. Even though it was a feint and the attackers would sheer off at the last minute, he felt a thrill of excitement watching the strike form up into three distinct columns of aircraft, with another dozen support and cover aircraft assembling along the coast. The electronic warfare module kept up a steady stream of reports as the Communist radars came on the air and the air-defense networks were activated ashore.

Over in D and D, Austin stood behind the SWIC chair, fielding reports and forwarding them to the admiral's battle staff via the Air Force Green net. The captain and the exec watched intently. Around Combat, every watch stander was focused on his scope, the hum of operational data interchange flowing from console to console and module to module. Fox Hudson's hands were a blur as his fingers flew over the keyboards while he switched back and forth from intercom to air control to the strike circuit, correlating what he was hearing on the airborne circuits to what his radars were painting on the SWIC scope. As the cluster of symbols swarmed invisibly and silently overhead at thirty thousand feet, Brian wondered whether he would ever achieve that degree of proficiency in the system. Then the bitch box spoke.

"Evaluator, Special Tracker: I have video in the Dong Ha Mountains, two-eight-five for sixty-seven miles. Possible bandits. Initiating special tracks."

"*Awright!* MiGs!" exclaimed Garuda as a buzz of excitement swept through D and D and especially among the AICs. The feint had provoked the launch of air-defense MiGs.

"Now what happens?" asked Brian.

"The strike birds will all go in, right up to the turnaway line. Behind them, probably these guys right here, are some MiGCAP, six F-Eight Crusaders, three sections of two each. Gunman-wingman pairs. When the strike birds turn outbound, the MiGCAP will go supersonic, fly through them and see if they can kill a Commie for Mommy."

"Where are the MiGs?"

Garuda pointed to three triangular symbols that were larger than the rest of the symbology. The three appeared to be loitering inland and were difficult to distinguish in the smear of video clutter representing the rugged mountains that ran north-south along the coast of North Vietnam. As they watched, bright white lines suddenly shot out from a small group at the back of the attack wave to attach themselves to the MiG symbols.

"Yeah, there's the assignment. The E-Two's paired the MiGCAP up with the MiGs. The lines show which CAP's been paired against which bogey. The controllers on the E-Two have begun the engagement. The E-Two's computers'll have 'em go supersonic in about thirty seconds. The bad guys' controllers won't see 'em because there's that crowd of attack birds out in front of 'em. When the feint groups turn back out, those F-Eights'll be on them MiGs like snakes. Look, see the speed leaders?''

Brian could indeed see that the MiGCAP symbols now had arrowlike lines projecting from them, lines that grew in length as the F-8s went into a shallow dive and ignited afterburner, building up to velocities of 1200 miles per hour, and hurtling toward the back of the attack formation. As the strike group's symbols began to diverge in a turn-away maneuver, the MiGCAP symbols speared through the dissolving formations and flashed down from altitude to catch the unwary MiGs ahead and beneath them, perfect targets for their missiles. The AICs were out of their chairs with excitement, itching to get into it but disciplined enough to keep their hands off their keyboards as the airborne controllers in the E-2 pressed home the attack.

Brian held his breath as the symbols converged over the mountains, trying to visualize the Crusaders and MiGs dogfighting down the mountain valleys, missiles blasting into the night in supersonic pursuit of glinting gray shapes maneuvering frantically to evade the bolts of death stabbing out for them in the darkness.

"Splash! Splash!" yelled one of the controllers, his voice high with excitement. Brian watched the symbols pause, seemingly suspended in the area of the dogfight. The rest of the strike was forming back up into orderly outbound corridors, pointed back toward the carriers, seemingly oblivious to the dogfight going on behind them. There were more splash calls and then a moment of silent tension as the controllers counted heads. First section out, then the second section. Silence, excruciating seconds.

"There!" HooDoo pointed on the FCSC scope, his finger tapping the scope to indicate the video of the third section. "South. They went the long way. The MiGCAP is feet-wet!"

There was jubilation in D and D. The MiGCAP had bagged two, perhaps three MiGs and come out clean.

"Oughta hear these bad boys," said HooDoo, laughing and pressing his earphones to his ears. "Jubilation T. Cornpone goin' on up there."

"Fuckin'-a good deal," said Garuda, taking a tremendous drag on his cigarette before dropping it into a butt kit. "We haven't had a MiG kill in a coon's age. The flyboys'll be doin' barrel rolls all the way back to the bird farm. Who were those guys, HooDoo?"

"They's Black Eagles, off the *America*. Talkin' some shit, now." HooDoo was actually smiling, even though slightly disappointed that the E-2 had controlled the kills instead of the Red Crown controllers. But getting to watch it on 3-D radar was almost as good.

The PIRAZ controllers remained poised over their screens, physically counting heads with a grease pencil, toting up the symbols to make sure that the numbers tallied. Brian noticed that the crowd was beginning to thin out in Combat. Austin made some concluding reports on Green and then Wager reported going off-station for his nightly "happy hour" with the KC-135 tanker. Brian realized that the captain had swiveled around in his large armchair and was speaking to him.

"Well, Brian, what'd you think of an Alfa-strike?"

"Quite a show, Cap'n. And MiGs for dessert."

"Yes, that was an unusual dividend. The MiGs don't usually show their noses until after the carrier formations are on their way out. That was a pretty good MiG trap. Sometimes it goes the other way, though."

"How's that, sir?"

"Sometimes the MiGs come up and orbit on top of some recently emplaced SAM sites that we didn't know about. Our CAP goes blasting in after them; the MiGs run like hell and drag our guys over a missile battery, which can be a very nasty surprise."

"How did the E-Two know that wasn't what was going on tonight, sir?"

"He didn't. But it's kind of an unwritten Gulf rule out here, Brian. You see MiGs, you go for them. You can be sure any *Hood* controller is going to vector for bogey the instant he thinks he has a valid target. That's the way they're all taught: The other side shows his face, you draw and shoot." The captain climbed down out of his chair and winced, clutching at his side. Brian saw the exec start toward him and then stop as the captain straightened out. The captain saw Brian's expression.

"Old bones, Brian, just old bones. XO, I guess I'll secure. Count, you let me know if there's any residual activity. Sometimes after they lose a MiG, they put up a couple more and come out to the coast, like a kid who gets brave after the bully's gone home. Keep us in the western sector of the box. Night, all."

As the captain left Combat, Brian asked Garuda what that was all about.

"Cap'n's dyin' to bag his own MiG with our Terrier missiles. Only one Red Crown's actually shot down a MiG before."

"Wouldn't they'd have to really come feet-wet for us to actually reach them?"

"It's real close. You know the envelope better'n me, but theoretically we can shoot forty miles. So if we was to hang around forty miles offshore and one of 'em got careless and came feet-wet, even, say, five miles, they'd be in the envelope."

"Not really. That would be a very doubtful shot, Garuda. Guy would have to remain inbound to make the geometry work."

Garuda shook his head. "Guy would just have to be there for this Old Man to take a shot." He looked at his watch. "Tree time; I'll see you 'round the midwatch."

"Roger that, Garuda."

The MiGs did not come out to play that night or the next. The captain had ordered *Hood* to resume normal box position, abandoning his perch on the western edge. But on the third night after the feint, at 0230, Garuda was over at the coffeepot getting a refill when the duty AIC, HooDoo, leaned over his scope, made an adjustment, looked hard, and then said the magic word softly.

"Bandits."

Garuda slopped coffee on the deck plates getting back to his chair, and the word flashed around Combat like lightning. Garuda switched the range scale down to sixty miles and studied the faint smudges of video shimmering under the two unknown symbols HooDoo had put in the system.

"Where are the BARCAP?" asked Brian, assuming that the F-4s would be used if the MiGs presented a reasonable target.

"They be tankin'; they on a basketball, two-three-five for eighty-five miles. They off-station. 'S why these boys came up, most like. BARCAP's outta position."

Brian examined the scope and saw the faint trace of *Hood*'s missile circle reaching just over the beach to the west. The unknowns' video was barely ten miles beyond the circle.

"Surface, SWIC. How much room we got in the box to go west?"

"Wait one," responded Rockheart. "Seven miles, SWIC."

Garuda turned to Brian. "Recommend tell the bridge to turn west, come up to fifteen knots, and close the western boundary. Then call the Old Man, tell him we got MiGs up."

Brian nodded, set the maneuver in motion via the bitch box, and then informed the captain of their contacts and that he had turned the ship to close the beach.

"Good move. I'll be right up. Get the Count and the exec up there."

Brian hung up and made the calls, a little disappointed that the captain's immediate reaction was to get the first team up into D and D. On reflection, though, it made sense. He was still a makee-learn.

"What're they doing?" he asked.

Garuda adjusted his scope. "Orbiting, just west of Vinh military airfield. Altitude's unreliable from the forty-eight, which means they're low, keeping down in the mountains for radar cover. Bet the fuckers know the BARCAP's off-station, too."

"Should we assign a missile director to them?"

"Negatory. That would tip 'em off. Old Man, he's gonna want to see if they'll come east, see if they've forgotten about us while they fixate on the BARCAP."

"Shouldn't we break off the BARCAP and get 'em back?"

"Negative. They've just started fueling; they'd come back below minimum combat package, no good for anything. HooDoo's not even telling them what we got, 'cause they'd come back on their own, most likely."

The captain came through the door, followed by Austin.

"Okay, Garuda, lemme have it," he said. Austin stepped in front of Brian to look at the scope. Brian suddenly felt superfluous as Garuda briefed the captain and answered Austin's rapid-fire questions. When he was finished, the captain turned to Brian.

"Tell the bridge to bring her up to twenty knots, then get your Weapons people ready. Count here will take evaluator. Maybe we can get a shot at one of these guys. You told CTF Seventy-seven yet?"

Garuda answered for him. "The unknowns went out over the link, and they've called in over the HF net asking us to confirm validity. I told him affirmative, we had skin, that we were watching and waiting for the BARCAP to finish tanking. I'm keeping the symbology at unknown for now. We'll need to change that to hostile before we engage them."

The captain nodded and climbed into his chair. He was dressed in khaki trousers, slippers, and a green foul-weather jacket over his undershirt. Once again, Brian noted that he looked a hundred years old in the harsh lights of CIC. Austin was fully dressed and did not appear to have been roused from a sound sleep.

"This is Mr. Austin, I have the evaluator watch," Austin declared peremptorily.

There was a chorus of "Aye, aye, sir" throughout Combat, and Brian retreated to the weapons module as the exec came into Combat. Chief VanHorn had the FCSC watch, and a first class petty officer named Carter was sitting in the engagement controller position. Van-Horn was aware of the MiGs and also of the fact that the ship had turned west at twenty knots.

"Old Man wants a shot." It was not a question, and Brian, who had moved over to the weapons module, nodded in confirmation.

"Apparently so, but these guys are way out of the envelope."

"These Terriers been known to go fifty miles, if the conditions are right," observed VanHorn. He looked up at Brian with an amused expression.

"You know as well as I do, Chief, that the kill probability goes to shit beyond thirty, thirty-five miles. We'd be throwing one away, we try to take a crossing, low-altitude jet at eighty thousand yards."

"Bet he takes the shot," muttered VanHorn.

"You just better hope your one director holds up," replied Brian. "What's the system status, anyway?"

VanHorn became all business. He punched out some codes on the keyboard and a display came up showing that the missile fire–control system was in two-minute standby, with one director available and the launcher unassigned and empty. The second missile director was still down for parts after the last power transients. Courtesy of the Engineering Department, Brian thought unkindly. The ship trembled as the engineers brought the main engines up to twenty knots. Brian computed that they would reach the western edge of their station in twenty minutes at that speed. He stared down at the scope, watching the unknown symbols. He could no longer see video underneath the symbols.

Austin was making a radio report to the CTF 77 staff down on Yankee Station. With Wager gone for the night, the unencrypted high-frequency circuit had to be used, so there was a great deal of code-making. Everyone had been taught that Soviet HF intercept stations all over the east coast of Asia were listening constantly and that they could flash a warning to the North Vietnamese if *Hood* revealed that she was tracking two of their MiGs.

The exec came over. "Your systems up and ready, Brian?"

"Yes, sir, although it's *system,* not systems. We're down to one missile director. But the launcher reports ready, and I've got a wing-and-fin crew standing by in the magazine."

"Hate to only have one director," said the exec. "Goddamn Spook-Fifty-fives are unreliable enough when they're working. At least with two, you've got a chance of completing a shot."

Brian nodded in agreement. As a graduate of the Navy's Guided Missile school, he knew that the A/N-SPQ-55B missile fire–control radars, called Spook-55s, were highly complex systems. Contained in two turrets mounted on barbettes above the CIC, they looked like giant gray searchlights. Within each director mount were three radars bore-sighted concentrically on a common axis. One emitted a narrow cone of energy called the acquisition beam. The second emitted a very high-energy beam barely the thickness of a pencil lead, called the tracking beam. The third broadcast a wide cone of energy called continuous wave illumination. The Spook-55s were the eyes and claws of the *Hood*'s missile system.

Brian knew the launch sequence by heart. When a designation was ordered by SWIC, digital data from the SPS-48 air-search radar would be streamed to the directors, which swiveled around to the appropriate bearing and elevation so that the acquisition beam could pick up the designated target, often at ranges of one hundred miles or more. Once the acquisition beam saw the target, the director moved to center the target in its tracking circuits so that the second tracking beam could see it. Once the pencil beam got on target, the target's return was captured by computer-tracking circuits. At this point, it was considered "locked up," and the Spook tracked it automatically under control of the missile fire–control computers. A target, such as a jet aircraft, could twist and turn and do all sorts of evasive maneuvers, but it could rarely defeat the tracking algorithms working at near light speed in the computers.

If the target closed in within the ship's forty-mile missile envelope, the command to fire could be given. The launcher crew down in the missile magazine would slap wings and fins onto the body of a Terrier missile and report ready to the engagement controller in Combat via keyboards. The EC would press the load button and the launcher would lock its arms to the front face of the missile ramp structure on the forecastle as the magazine doors swung open. The missile would then slide up on rails within the ramp and out onto the launcher rails. The doors would close and the launcher would be assigned to the control of the tracking director, turning to point in the same direction as the Spook, and the final beam, the illumination beam, would be activated. The launcher would continue to point in the general direction of the target, and a three-second pulse of warm-up power would be applied to the missile, after which it would be fired.

The Terrier would be kicked off the rail by a solid-rocket booster. Once the eight-second boost phase was completed, propelling the Terrier to a velocity twice the speed of sound, the missile's seeker head would be uncaged and energized by its onboard computers and the seeker would begin looking for energy being reflected off the target from that third continuous wave illumination beam. Once it detected the reflected energy, the missile would home in on the target and typically fly right through it at about five times the speed of sound. But as everyone knew, every element of the system—the computers, the three radars, the launcher, the missile's seeker head—had to work perfectly for any of it to work.

"We try a shot out there on the edge of the envelope, we're gonna waste a bird," Brian said again.

The exec overheard and shot him a warning look. "We could always get lucky," he said.

Brian shook his head. "No, sir, not unless the target is coming right at us at a great rate of knots. The Terrier has no energy left for anything but a head-on shot at that range. It can't do pursuit out there."

The exec drew closer, put his hand on Brian's shoulder, and turned him away from the FCSC console. He spoke softly. "Brian, I suggest you talk to the captain about doctrine sometime when there aren't MiGs up. But otherwise, let me give you some advice—he says shoot, you shoot it."

Brian was taken aback. "Of course, XO. The captain gives an order, we carry it out. But—"

"Yeah, I hear you. And I'm not saying you're necessarily wrong. But remember my advice. This kind of an engagement, there won't be a lot of time to discuss it. His MiG gets away 'cause the Weps boss wanted to talk about it instead of shoot it, life'll get unpleasant. Follow me?"

"Yes, sir. Clear as a bell."

"Now don't get all huffy. This is still his ship, remember. If the geometry is out of envelope, report it. He says shoot it, pull the damn trigger."

"Aye, aye, sir."

The exec went back over to the SWIC console. Brian stared down unseeing at the FCSC picture, his face flushed, while Chief VanHorn tried to pretend he had not overheard the exec's counseling session. They're wrong, Brian thought. They're going to shoot a missile at a target that's basically out of range. Anybody who looks at the reconstruction will be able to see it. He tried to focus, to see where the MiG symbols were. The exec was talking to the captain, who looked over briefly in Brian's direction.

"Give me a bearing and range," Brian ordered, his voice curt.

The chief worked some buttons. "Unknowns are bearing two-seven-six degrees true, range ninety-six thousand, five hundred eighty-five yards, crossing. Forty-eight miles."

The MiGs appeared to be keeping just out of range, as if they knew the critical distance to the *Hood*'s station. Except that the ship was closing them. If nothing else changed and the MiGs maintained their current orbit, the ship would close in to forty-one miles. He overheard CTF 77 ask for the time remaining to tank the BARCAP. Austin looked over at HooDoo, who said fifteen minutes. Austin looked at the captain, who nodded.

"Alfa Whiskey, this is Red Crown. ETC is two-zero mikes."

Brian mentally shook his head. The air controller had said fifteen minutes. Austin had reported twenty. Why? Because, he realized, that carrier admiral obviously wants his Phantoms to go after the MiGs, and the captain wants a shot at them with his missiles, that's why.

"Brian?" The captain had swung his chair around.

"Sir?"

"If they come in range, this has to go quick. We won't have the luxury of establishing track for a couple of minutes to make sure we have a smooth firing solution like we usually do in a missile exercise. The moment we bring the Spook Fifty-five on the air, those guys're gonna head for the deck and get the hell out of Dodge. So if I give you the take order, the moment you get a track light, assign the launcher and fire at once. Understand?"

The captain's tone of voice did not seem to encourage a dialogue. "Yes, sir. Understood." Brian glanced over at the exec, but the exec looked away.

Feeling cornered, Brian studied the FSCS scope and the panel of system status lights on its side. The panel for system one was dark. The panel for system two showed the system to be waiting in standby, its three radars warmed up and ready to go into radiate, but not transmitting. The director itself was still centerlined.

"What's the track number of the nearest MiG?"

"Track two-one-three-two is here; two-one-four-seven is—here."

"Give me trial geometry, track two-one-three-two," he said.

Chief VanHorn pushed some buttons and a spidery grid of lines appeared on the scope, indicating lines of probability for an intercept with the nearest MiG if the missile was to be fired right now. On the upper-right-hand block of a data readout panel, a "Pk Low" alert was flashing. The computer was telling the FCSC operator that the probability of a killing intercept was too low to warrant launch.

"What's his range?"

"Range is eighty-four thousand, seven hundred fifty yards."

A little over forty-two miles. Brian checked his watch. Ten more minutes to the western boundary of the PIRAZ box. As long as the MiG kept going north, up the coast, the range would be in the low Pk band. Brian looked again at the exec, who looked back this time and gave a barely imperceptible shake of his head.

VanHorn turned his head and spoke in a low voice. "Mr. Holcomb. Recommend we go to dummy load on system two."

"Can't they detect that?"

"The Russians could. I don't know if these guys can.

But it'll give us instantaneous response to a take order; otherwise, we wait two minutes. Recommend ask the Old Man for permission."

Brian thought about it. The system was in a two-minute standby to radiate mode. The chief was right. If they wanted an instantaneous reaction, they should bring up the radar transmitters and radiate them into an electronic box called a dummy load, which acted like an antenna but did not put a full-powered signal out on the air. The Intel people felt that specialized ELINT ships could detect a missile radar in dummy load, but it was not known whether the North Vietnamese had this capability. Brian requested permission to do it. The captain thought about it for a moment, then told him to go ahead, before turning around to talk to SWIC.

"What're they doing now, Garuda?" asked the captain.

"One's orbiting the airfield, low and slow. The other guy is headed north, up along the coast, but not like he's trying to get somewhere. He's the closest, Captain. Forty . . . uh . . . forty-two and a skosh miles. He's dipping in and out of the hills along the coast, giving us intermittent video."

"Brian, how's the geometry look?" asked the captain over his shoulder.

Brian took a deep breath before answering. VanHorn punched up new geometry to refresh the data. The alert still flashed.

"It's a no go, Captain," Brian said, his throat dry. There was an instant of silence in D and D. "The geometry indicates a crossing shot at max range; there's no Pk to speak of."

The Captain swiveled back around in his chair, a displeased look on his face. Brian could see that this had not been the expected right answer. The exec was studying the deck plates. Austin shot him a pained look. The silence in D and D persisted. Chief VanHorn refreshed the data once more, with the same results. And then the MiG began a turn, a slow, lazy turn to the east, toward the *Hood*. HooDoo was the first to catch it.

"Bogey turning," he announced. "Bogey turning *inbound*."

This report galvanized D and D. The officers clustered around the SWIC scope, watching intently. The MiG's turn continued, still low and slow, its course and speed leader pointing progressively clockwise, until it was obvious that he was turning all the way around, not toward *Hood* but back toward his base. But his turn had consumed about five miles in lateral distance, bringing him within the missile envelope.

"Now what's the range?" asked the captain.

"Range is thirty-seven, thirty-seven and a quarter miles."

"What's his CPA?"

Garuda executed a function code. "Closest point of approach will be thirty-six and a half, sir."

"Change 'em from unknowns to hostiles."

"Unknowns to hostiles, aye."

The captain turned around to Brian.

"You ready to do some business?"

Brian thought quickly. Thirty-six miles, crossing target, still a very low probability. He looked over at Van-Horn, who nodded vigorously. Before Brian could answer, the captain saw the chief's gesture and swiveled the chair around again, took a deep breath, and said, "Okay, SWIC, this is the captain. Take track two-one-three-two, birds."

Instantly an alert from SWIC flashed on the FCSC console screen and a buzzer sounded, indicating a take order. Chief VanHorn punched two buttons, brought the Spook 55 to radiate, and accepted the designation. Everyone in Combat could hear the big director slew around overhead. Austin warned the bridge to check that the forecastle was clear. The excitement level rose in Combat.

"Track light, two-one-three-two," declared VanHorn. "Loading the launcher. Launcher is loaded. Assigning the launcher. Launcher assigned. Energizing CWI. CWI is on the air." He flipped up the plastic cover over the firing key and glanced at Holcomb.

"Shoot," Brian said.

"Shoot, aye." The chief closed the key and a Terrier missile thundered off the forecastle outside. "Birds away!"

"Bogey going buster!" shouted Garuda. He manipulated his trackball to stay on the target, which had accelerated the moment *Hood*'s CWI beams had been detected.

"Reloading the launcher," announced VanHorn. It was standard procedure to reload at once, even if another shot did not look likely.

"Alfa Whiskey calling on HF, sir," said a console operator in the cave. "Wants us to verify two-one-three-two as hostile, wants us to verify birds engagement, two-one-three-two."

"Tell him affirmative, engaging, birds, track two-one-three-two," replied Austin.

The captain and exec stared over Garuda's shoulder at the MiG symbol, which was visibly accelerating across the screen, as if trying to merge with the video smear that was the cover of the mountains. On the FCSC scope, a digital clock was ticking down seconds to intercept. Fox Hudson burst through the back door to Combat, roused out of his sleep three decks below by the noise of the missile launch.

"Range?" asked Brian quietly, already knowing the answer.

"Range is forty-one miles. And opening."

"No way," Brian muttered. "No way. That puppy's home free."

"Track unstable," announced VanHorn. He switched over to intercom and snapped out a quick question, nodded, and glanced up at Brian. "Bogey's in the weeds."

Brian nodded. The track radar was having trouble distinguishing the MiG from the backdrop of the mountains. Hopeless. They waited another five seconds. The track light on FCSC console was intermittent.

"Mark time to intercept," VanHorn announced finally into the silence in D and D. "No video in the gate. No intercept. Energizing destruct signal. Destruct confirmed. Evaluate miss. Evaluate target out of envelope and opening."

Everyone exhaled. Fox Hudson, standing at Brian's elbow, asked what was going on. "What the hell," he said. "You can't get an intercept out there." His uniform was disheveled, as if he had been sleeping in it.

"Cool it," replied Brian, mindful of the captain ten feet away.

"Call your bogey," ordered the captain.

"Bogey tracks are stationary. No video. Prob'ly landed or are in the pattern at Vinh, sir," replied Garuda.

"Bogey's gone," pronounced HooDoo. "Done gone."

"Well, what the hell, XO," said the captain with a sigh, rubbing his jaw. "It was worth a shot. Even if Weps is going to give me an 'I told you so.' "

"Might still have been a hit, Captain," interjected Austin. "The forty-eight video went down at intercept time. That bird may have smacked him as he was on final at Vinh."

"We still should have seen video in the gate, right, Weps?"

Brian nodded. The missile radar held the target locked in a notchlike presentation on the scopes down below. A hit was usually indicated when the video that was the missile flashed through the gate and merged with the video that was the target.

"Yes, sir. On the face of it, we missed. But the track was unstable—the gate may have already slipped off and locked up the hillside."

"So it's a possible?"

Brian frowned. Yes, it was possible. Not likely, but it was possible. "Remotely possible, yes, sir. But if the target was evading, the Terrier had almost no kinetic energy left to chase him."

"Shit, I'll take a possible; sounds a hell of a lot better than a miss, right, XO? Count, tell Alfa Whiskey we have a possible kill."

"Aye, aye, sir." He turned to Garuda. "SWIC record the latitude/longitude of the computed intercept point. Maybe we can get a recce run in that area, see if there's a downed aircraft on the outskirts of that airfield."

"Unload the launcher, Chief," Brian ordered.

"Unloading the launcher."

* * *

The following morning after breakfast, Brian was talking to his departmental officers at morning quarters when the exec walked over.

"Need to talk at you soon as you're finished here," he said.

"I think we're done, XO. Jack, get the fo'c'sle cleaned up today; we need to get that booster burn mark off the paint."

The officers dispersed to their divisions and Brian joined the exec on one side of the midships area. There was enough of a sea breeze to require a handhold on their ball caps. The exec handed Brian a one page-message.

"This just came in."

Brian scanned it and whistled. "Personal For from CTF Seventy-seven; looks like the admiral is not happy with us."

"That's putting it mildly. Captain needs you to draft a technical defense of our missile firing last night. He'll put the right political twist on it, but he wants the technical stuff from you."

Brian reread the message. The admiral was taking issue with the use of Terrier missiles at what appeared to be an excessive range and inconsistent tactical geometry. He was also unhappy with the idea of shooting at MiGs that were not doing anything overtly hostile.

"Tough to defend, XO. The missile systems are programmed to ignore crossing targets—by definition, if he's flying by, he's not a threat. This guy was barely brushing up against the envelope. Basically, it was a wasted shot."

"Wrong answer, bucko. See, there's a political dimension to this. These aviator admirals want MiG kills to be the exclusive province of carrier aviation. Nobody gets to be an ace when a surface ship bags a MiG. As you can see there, he thinks we should have tanked the BARCAP to minimum package, brought 'em back, and gone after the MiGs with CAP."

Brian nodded. He had heard senior officers talking about the tension between the surface Navy and the aviator Navy. The carrier admirals took pains to point out at every opportunity that the surface ships assigned to the Gulf were subordinate to the mission of the carriers, an assertion that had the merit of being true. Despite the harrumphing and ahems of the surface Navy, the basic role of the PIRAZ ship was to protect the carriers.

"Yes, sir, I'll try to think of something. Although if there's anyone down there on the staff who's been to missile school or had G-ship experience, it won't wash."

"We'll worry about that problem when and if it arises. Draft a reply; bring it to me. I'll take it up the line. And we need it this morning. I know you're beat from the midwatch—give it thirty minutes and bring it to me. Then you can hit your tree."

"Aye, aye, sir."

Brian went down to the wardroom for coffee. He usually drank no coffee at breakfast so that he could sleep. His eyes were burning from having been up since 2315 the previous night. He knew that his brain was not at its highest level of acuity, which made the problem of responding to the message doubly hard. He reread the Personal For as he waited for the steward to bring out some fresh coffee. Garuda Barry was sitting over in one corner, reading his own stack of message traffic. He looked up inquisitively at Brian.

"Get a Dear John?"

Brian laughed even as a corner of his mind tilted at the thought. "No, this is a Personal For from CTF Seventy-seven."

"Oh, hate mail." Garuda went back to his message stack, silently acknowledging that his right to pry ended at Personal For messages. Brian got a cup of coffee and walked over to Garuda's corner of the wardroom. He could not technically let Garuda see the message, but he did want advice. He sat down on the couch opposite Garuda and waited for a few seconds until Garuda looked back up at him.

"Garuda, I've been given this, uh, task to do. XO wants me to draft a reply to this Personal For."

"Yes, sir?"

"And, my problem is that basically, CTF Seventy-seven says we shouldn't have fired that missile last night. The XO says he wants me to write a 'technical defense' of what we did. Now, you're pretty checked out on the whole NTDS system, including the weapons side, right?"

Garuda nodded, sat back, and fished for a cigarette. He took a little longer than usual, as if mustering his thoughts. He lighted up, producing a cloud of blue smoke that he had to wave away from his face. He squinted through the smoke but said nothing, inviting Brian to continue.

"Well, my problem is that, technically, the shot we took last night is indefensible. The target was never really in the envelope because it was either crossing or outbound during the entire engagement. And now I'm not sure what the hell to say."

"You keep on with that, Mr. Holcomb, that'll be two wrong answers."

"Two?"

"Yes, sir. Like last night, when you said it was a no go, that was the first wrong answer. Old Man didn't want to hear that."

"So I gathered; everybody looked at me like I'd farted in church."

Garuda grinned, then got serious. "The way out is the fact that, technically, he went from unknown to hostile. When he made that turn to the east and pointed his nose at us, I redesignated him hostile, remember? Second, he came feet-wet in the process of that turn. You know and I know he was probably just turning around to go back to his base at Vinh, but, technically, when he pointed at us and came feet-wet, he was our meat. So we can claim rules of engagement as the reason why we fired, and because he was probably a MiG of some kind, based on his loiter speed, we had every right to engage earlier rather than later."

"Yeah, but that makes it sound like he steadied up and headed in at us. We both know that the speed-leader arrow on the scope never stopped turning."

"Yeah, but Alfa Whiskey probably does *not* know that, and can't know it unless he asks for reconstruction or an NTDS data extract on that time period. That would take weeks."

Brian sighed in exasperation. "I see what you're saying. But, goddamnit, it's not true. That MiG never did present a threat. And, if I understand it, the MiGs have

221

never presented a threat to the ships out here—they've defended their airspace against our attacks, but only when our planes come in over the beach at them.''

Garuda raised his eyebrows. ''With all due respect, Mr. Holcomb, I thought what you wanted was the right answer, something to put in your message.''

Brian studied the carpet. He knew that Garuda was absolutely right. What was needed here was a right answer. He was dead tired and tried unsuccessfully to suppress a yawn.

''Mr. Holcomb, can I give you some advice? I'm just a warrant officer, and you're a department head, but I got about ten years of PACFLEET time on you. Way I see it, you shouldn't be wastin' a whole lot of time on this. Lay it out like I just told you, add some stuff about the target being engageable based on the geometry at the time of the decision to shoot, and that only after we had birds-away did the geometry change, probably when the MiG's ESM systems detected the illuminator beam. That's it. No more, no less. Then let the XO and the captain wordsmith it and put some political paint on it.''

''Even if I don't believe it?''

Garuda paused to take a final huge drag on his cigarette and stub it out in the ashtray. He rubbed his chin as he thought about his answer.

''Lemme put it this way: The *Hood* ain't like a destroyer. Most ships aren't in the big game that we're in. It's a big show, see, this whole Red Crown deal, Attack Carrier Task Force Seventy-seven, the Gulf. It's the biggest show in the Navy, and lotsa people're lookin' for time on the stage, okay? What you've got there is part of the old aviator–surface guy contest, the brown shoes versus the black shoes. We black shoes don't want to ever let the aviators catch us fuckin' up, because that gives 'em points to say that they always gotta be in charge, 'cause they got the biggest ship out there, the carrier, see? You gonna be an evaluator on the Red Crown station, you gotta be conscious of that contest, all the fuckin' time, 'cause that staff down there is always gonna be second-guessin' everything we do up here, just like CINCPAC, back in Pearl there, is second-guessin' everything that carrier admiral does, and Tricky Dicky and the Joint Chiefs are second-guessin' old CINCPAC.''

"You make it sound like this is all just one big game.''

"Well, it ain't a game when we do strike following or when we delouse a gaggle of F-Fours on their way back to the bird farm, or when some guy jumps out of a jet at thirty thousand feet 'cause it happens to be blowing up. But the politics, that's always there, sitting in the background of everything we do out here. You just gotta keep this question in mind: Is what I'm about to do or say gonna make us look bad? If you think it might, you ask the captain if we oughta do it. And if we do fuck up, you look for a way to make it look like less of a fuckup, or maybe even no fuckup at all, 'cause those staff guys are always lookin'. Like that captain who flew up here, unannounced, you remember, to snoop around about the Sea Dragon deal.''

Brian looked at him for a moment. He had enough time in the Navy to know that all of this was not really news. The ship is your family. You look after your family.

"Okay, I hear that. And I don't argue it except for one thing: If we continually cover our mistakes, we'll start to believe our own bullshit. When real trouble comes, we're gonna hurt somebody.''

Garuda shrugged. "Yeah, well, we do the best we can, Mr. Holcomb. That's all I can tell you. We do the best we can with what we have. I've been on here for going on two years, and that's the right answer.''

Brian nodded. "Okay, you're right. And thanks, Garuda. I appreciate the input—and the help.''

Brian went topside to his stateroom and drafted the reply to the message, printing it out on a yellow legal pad, using the arguments put forward by Garuda. Then he headed out to find the exec. One of the radarmen said that the XO was in Combat, so Brian climbed up one more level. The exec was not in Combat, as it turned out, but Brian had an inspiration; he asked Austin to read the Personal For and then his draft reply.

"I've seen the Personal For," muttered Austin. "The RMC makes sure I see everything going through Radio unless the CO or the XO specifically says no. Now, let's see what you've got here.''

He scanned Brian's draft reply, nodding slowly as he read through it. Brian stifled another yawn. He was rapidly losing his morning sleep window. He would either have to get some more coffee or climb into his tree pretty quick.

"Not bad, not bad," Austin said. "Change this word to *urgency;* otherwise, I think you've got it right. I'll even chop it." He initialed the draft and, lowering his voice, said, "I think maybe you're starting to get the picture here."

"Well, this isn't especially true, but it sounds plausible."

"Precisely." Austin eyed Brian for a moment over the message draft. "You resent having to do this, don't you?"

"In a way. That shot was a waste."

Austin handed him back the message draft. "Mechanically, you may be correct. But consider this: What the captain did last night was, at one level of abstraction, an exercise in independent command authority. In his best command judgment, which he and he alone is paid to exercise in this ship, it was necessary to fire a missile at an enemy aircraft. He didn't call down to CTF Seventy-seven and ask permission; he just did it. That Personal For is the admiral's way of expressing his resentment of the captain's exercise of independent command authority. You do acknowledge the captain's authority?"

"Of course. But—"

"Let me finish. Part of what he was doing—because I admit he wanted to bag a MiG; we all do—but part of what he was doing was to assert his authority to make a decision to fire a missile. That staff down there on the carrier wants us to ask permission before we do *anything*. We ever get into a real mess up here, we won't have time to go ask Mommy if we can go potty. We'll just do it and hope to hell all that expensive gear of yours and mine works and that nobody's smoking dope in the missile magazine. You may disapprove on technical grounds, but the captain's assertion of independent tactical authority from time to time might be vital to our survival up here someday, especially if it's *you* in the hot seat when it goes down. That help your attitude about writing this message?''

Brian considered Austin's argument, which certainly sounded better than Garuda's. He suddenly felt very much more like a lieutenant talking to a lieutenant commander than one department head to another. He felt a wave of dismay at how much he had to learn.

"I guess it does," he answered. He exhaled. "This WESTPAC Navy is very different from what I'm used to.''

"I'll tell you a little secret, Mr. Holcomb. Consider it a freebie: Politically, there's no difference whatsoever. You're just having to face up to it for the first time, because you're now an evaluator and a department head in a PIRAZ ship. Now you better find the exec.''

Brian used the ship's phone to dial the exec's stateroom number and found him in. He went down and aft to get to the exec's stateroom and handed in the message draft. The exec asked him to sit down while he read it. He nodded when he was finished.

"Good. That should do it. And I see you got the Count's chop. That was smart. Anytime you get a sensitive or important message to do, you run it by Ops. He knows the ins and outs of WESTPAC politics cold.''

"Yes, sir. We talked. I was kind of surprised at the political dimension of all this. I guess I'm still feeling my way around. In *Decatur,* any message I wrote as Weps was just a message.''

"Well, maybe, but I suspect that either your exec or the CO put the required spin on it. Personal For messages require some care, since they go directly to the flag officer or CO involved. Count explain what's behind this one?''

"Yes, sir, he did," Brian replied, stifling another yawn. "I hadn't thought of what we did last night in terms of some kind of statement. All I saw was the fact that we weren't gonna hit that MiG.''

"But you saw how excited your guys were this morning—that they got to shoot a missile at a real target. It also put the MiGs on notice. Watch your socialist ass when *Hood*'s out there: trigger-happy bunch of Yankee running dogs. And, hell, we don't know for a fact that we didn't get him—the track beam was wandering all over the place at the end, but it's the illuminator that counts, not the track beam, once the bird's in flight. As long as the bird's seeker head could see energy being reflected from the target, that missile would chase his ass. I mean, hell, *I* know it's not likely, but it is possible. Or in his haste to get away from our bird, he may have hit the side of a mountain. Who knows. We'll see if the recce guys can get some BDA."

"Yes, sir. I guess I'm still in the new-guy mode."

"Yeah, well, WESTPAC is different. But you're catching on. Right. I'm sorry I had to cut into your tree time. Go grab some shut-eye before your next watch."

Brian left the XO's cabin and headed for his own stateroom. If there were no more pop-ups, he could snatch an hour and half before he had to get ready for the next watch. "You're catching on," the XO had said. Well, that's a medium good sign. When he reached his stateroom, he flopped directly down on his rack and drifted off to sleep, wondering what Maddy was doing.

20

San Diego

Maddy arrived at the U. S. Grant Hotel at 7:45. It was one of San Diego's older hotels, so there was no inside parking. She drove around the block a couple of times before finding a spot on Broadway. She parked, shut off the engine, and pulled the mirror sideways to check out the war paint and run the brush through her hair once more. She wore a one-piece sleeveless black velvet number, modestly cut in the front and knee-length, with a slim silver belt around her waist. Over the dress, she wore an almost transparent cream-colored short-sleeved jacket, accented with a silver pendant at her throat. Medium heels, a patent-leather black clutch purse, and shiny dark stockings completed the outfit. And once again, no rings. She felt badly about that. Taking off the rings was an act of deception. She remembered making that same comment to Tizzy on their way to MCRD, and Tizzy's surprising reply: "We're married women, honey; our whole life is an act of deception."

She had made her excuses to Mrs. Huntington the day after Tizzy's phone call, and the captain's wife had said she appreciated the call. There had been no hint of a question, only a courteous regret that Maddy's job did not allow her to join in more of the wives' activities.

"It's not the activities themselves that are important," Mrs. Huntington had said. "It's the fact that we're all in this deployment boat together, and when life closes in, as it will, dear, the group's a good resource. And, of course, it becomes vital if something happens to the ship."

"Happens to the ship?"

"Well, they are in a war zone, aren't they? What *Hood* does is pretty safe, considering, but there are always the other things—collisions, fires, groundings, the standard perils of the sea, you know. That's why we have the telephone tree and the calling lists and why the Navy calls me to get information or news, good or bad, to all of you. But enjoy your cocktail party, and watch out for all those bankers."

Bankers. If she only knew. She took a deep breath and got out of the car. The hotel's main entrance was across the street. She put a couple of dimes in the parking meter, just in case. There was little traffic at this, the dinner hour, so she jaywalked as fast as heels would allow, aware of the doorman's undisguised stare as she approached the entrance. He tipped his hat and said good evening in a Spanish accent as he opened one of the large glass doors. In the main entrance, down the lobby, and turn right, he'd said. She followed the directions, turned right, and saw a pair of oak bat-wing doors ahead, with a maître d' standing almost at attention behind them. A brass sign next to the doors proclaimed GRANT GRILL in large block letters.

Two businessmen checking in at the reception desk

straight ahead had turned around to look at her as she headed for the Grill, giving her the urge to check her zippers. But they probably weren't looking at her zippers. The maître d' opened the bat-wing doors for her and asked if she was Miss Holcomb. She almost corrected him on the Miss but nodded instead, and he bowed graciously and said, "Right this way, Miss Holcomb." The room was about sixty feet square, with high ceilings and subdued lighting, rich red carpeting, a great deal of oak paneling, and brass accoutrements. About half the tables were filled, and they were spaced for privacy, each equipped with a single silver candlestick, a heavy white linen tablecloth, and real silverware. The waiters, all appearing to be about sixty years of age, were dressed in tuxedos and bow ties.

The maître d', who looked even older than the waiters, threaded his way through the ornate tables, going slowly to show her off to the rest of the diners, well aware that beautiful women were always good for business in a restaurant. Autrey was standing at the side of a corner table, and she found herself staring as she followed the maître d'. Autrey was dressed completely in white— white slacks, a white linen sport jacket, off-white ruffled-front shirt, and, in place of a conventional cloth tie, he wore an intricate silver-and-turquoise string tie. Dark tooled leather boots completed his ensemble. With his prominent nose, exotic features, bronze skin, and black eyes, Maddy thought the whole effect was that of a Spanish grandee. As she drew near, she realized that he was much taller than she remembered. Maybe the boots. He was looking at her with frank admiration. He inclined his head in a small bow as she reached the table and the maître d' pulled back a chair.

"Maddy Holcomb," he said.

"Just Autrey, I believe."

He smiled then, and his face seemed momentarily younger, even boyish. She wondered again as she sat down why the Marine had fled at the mention of his name. Brian had a boyish face. Where the hell did that come from? she wondered. The maître d' brought menus and a wine list, then withdrew. Autrey was looking at her, taking all of her in but trying not to be too obvious about it. A jarring image of what she must have looked like in the MCRD parking lot intruded, and she felt herself sitting up straighter and breathing just a bit faster. She also felt the faintest warmth of a flush at her throat as she remembered her exposure that night. This man was—interesting; she shied away from the other word that had come to mind.

She was wondering what to say when a waiter appeared with a silver tray and two champagne flutes. The champagne, however, had a reddish tinge.

"A kir royale, madam," intoned the waiter, seeing her confusion. "Champagne traced with a touch of chambord."

He placed the drinks on the table and left without a word. Autrey raised his glass to her and she picked hers up.

"This is to say thank you for joining me tonight," he said. "I was afraid you would change your mind."

She smiled, lowered her eyes, and sampled the champagne. She said nothing, wanting to see what he would do. Her mind was racing on two levels; the one that asked herself what the hell she was up to; the other, that old familiar other, happily mobilizing forces to begin the games she had played so well in Boston, the tantalizing games. To her surprise, he seemed content to keep silent as well, savoring his drink. He let the silence build until she finally felt compelled to break it. First point to Autrey.

"This is a lovely dining room," she said.

"Yes," he said. "Old-style. Not very in these days. No rock music, no psychedelic lighting, and all the food is fattening or bad for you."

"Do you come here often?"

"No. Only when I want to feel like I'm surrounded by the best." He paused for a fraction of a second, to include her in that category. "They do it well here. May I order for you?"

She almost said no, to maintain some semblance of distance, independence. But then she acquiesced.

"If you'd like."

"Okay. How about cold medallions of abalone in their special Grant dressing and then prime rib, medium rare. Maybe crêpes suzette for dessert?"

"Sounds divine." She liked her beef medium, not medium rare, and thought abalone was overrated, although she'd never had it cold. Crêpes suzette was fine. She wouldn't tell him. Can't spoil it. Don't want him to do everything right. Although the kir royale was new, and sinfully delicious. She was not aware that she had finished her glass, but the waiter appeared from nowhere to collect the glasses.

"The rest of the champagne with the first course, please," Autrey said. She could not place his accent. At times, it was Southern California, which was to say, no accent at all, in her book. At other times, there was a faint southwestern twang, a hint of Arizona cowboy. She realized that she had been matching his control of his accent, precise when he was precise, then slipping into Georgia southron when the cowboy crept into view. He was watching her again; once again, she felt the tiniest tingle in her stomach.

The waiter materialized again and Autrey placed the order. The waiter was a stout man with enormous dignity and a fantastic gray pompadour. Maddy knew at once there would be no breathless "Hi, I'm Jon" chanting of the house specials for the night, and she was amused when the waiter looked entirely to Autrey for the order. Shades of Boston, she thought. And rather pleasant. She was still uncomfortable with the brash informality and immediate first-name intimacy of Southern California. Both her Atlanta upbringing and her college days automatically bridled at the implied presumption. A question occurred as the waiter glided away.

"So, Just Autrey," she said. "Tell me why that Marine turned tail when he heard your name in the parking lot. I have to believe it had very little to do with push-ups."

For a moment, Autrey studied his hands, which rested on the table in front of him. Her eyes were automatically drawn to them. She saw that he had long, sinewy fingers and that he veins on the back of his hands were pronounced. Good hands, she thought. Good for what, girl?

The waiter returned with their champagne. Autrey waited to speak until the waiter was gone.

"I am the only civilian on the training staff at MCRD," he began. "And the only American Indian. I train Marine second lieutenants—those are the brand-new officers—who are going to lead the recon platoons in country. Before they get to me, they receive a lot of specialized training in the whole recon business. The recon guys in the Marines are like the SEALS in the Navy. Special forces. Behind-the-lines stuff."

"And your contribution?"

"I train them to be predators."

"Predators?"

"Over and above basic woodcraft—you know, how to survive, make fires, get clean water, take animal prey, improvise tools and weapons, that kind of stuff—I run what you might call a finishing school. I teach them how to be aware of humans when they're in the bush behind enemy lines. I teach them how to track other humans, and how to avoid being tracked, and how to deal with someone who is tracking them."

"Now that sounds a little scary."

"Well, yes. But I think that was your question, Maddy Holcomb."

She nodded slowly in understanding. A finishing school for human hunters. Autrey steepled his fingers and stared right at her for a second before continuing. For just that second, she realized that he had a predator's eyes, a straight stare with perfect parallax: Anywhere you were, he was looking right at you.

"If you assume the instructor knows his stuff, then the only other problem in training anyone is motivating him to learn. I use fear. We put them in the field and leave them alone for a few days to practice woodcraft, and then I begin to stalk them, terrorize them even. Fear sharpens their senses. When they've learned to sharpen all their senses, to *feel* their environment like the animals do, then I teach them what to do and how to do it."

"But you would have to keep them afraid, wouldn't you, for that to work?"

He smiled broadly, his teeth white and even, making his face more than a little feral, she thought.

"Yes, exactly. I'm Autrey, the man who scares them in the night. That's why the drunk took off. Now, I have to tell you, we also do a little Hollywood in this business."

"Hollywood?"

"Yeah, like making movies. Fantasy. The strongest fear of the unseen, unknown, is the fear produced by your own imagination. So the staff sets my act up by manipulating their imagination. One instructor accidentally mentions my name and the staff sergeant next to him gets the shivers. Gets a scared look on his face, tells him to be quiet. The meat pick up on it, ask questions. What's this Autrey stuff? Who is this guy? Why are the gunnies afraid of him—if the gunnies are afraid, maybe I should be afraid. And the gunny says, Best believe it, podner. They never even see me until about the third night that I've been doing the number on 'em—you know, sticks breaking in the woods, animal sounds, things rearranged in the campsite in the morning. That way, when they do, they pay attention."

"The 'meat'?"

"The new trainees. As in fresh meat."

"Lovely. And this is the U.S. Marine Corps you're talking about? As in from the Halls of Montezuma?" Maddy had heard a zillion Marine jokes from Brian and his Navy friends. Autrey was imputing a level of sophistication to the Marines that did not seem possible.

Autrey gave her an amused look.

"In the field of small-unit combat tactics," he said, "the U.S. Marine Corps has developed some of the most sophisticated training systems in the world. They also produce some of the world's most lethal shock troops. Despite all the Marine jokes, I've come to believe the Marine Corps knows precisely what it's doing in this business. Don't let all the hoorah and short hair fool you."

"You'll have to excuse me," she replied softly. "My experience with Marines has been less than, er, sophisticated."

"I apologize for them," he said, his expression suddenly serious. He seemed ready to qualify his apology, but he said no more as the waiter approached with the first course. It had not escaped her that his speech had lost a lot of its foot-shuffling, aw shucks dialect.

To her surprise, the abalone, sliced transparently thin and interlaced with a lobster-based sauce, was exquisite, especially when accompanied by the last of the cold champagne. The prime rib was pink all the way across, a feat she had never managed to achieve in her attempts with supermarket standing ribs.

"This is perfect," she exclaimed as the waiter poured them each a glass of seven-year-old Mondavi cabernet. "And so is this," she said, sampling the wine. The waiter nodded agreeably, as if the compliment was only his due.

After the champagne, she knew she would have to pace herself with the dinner wine or they'd be carrying her out of there—or he would. He was smiling again, enjoying her pleasure. Their eyes met over the wine for an instant, and she had to work to look away. Her body was whispering to her that it was more than the champagne and the wine, while her totally logical mind bravely fought off the notion. Out of nowhere, she remembered that Kingston Trio song with the bawdy refrain "Have some Madeira, m'dear"—and smiled despite herself. When he asked what she was smiling about, she could only shake her head and giggle. She missed this game.

She asked for some coffee after the crêpes, welcoming the caffeine. A kir royale, champagne, red wine, and the liqueurs in the dessert added up to more alcohol than she had had in a coon's age. She felt deliciously relaxed but also somewhat on guard. Her mind wandered, and she tried to remember the old country expression, something was nice, but likker was quicker. She couldn't for the life of her remember the first line. She suddenly hoped that this wasn't all a big come-on, a standard seduction, with the inevitable invitation to go to his apartment and see the record collection or something. Or something, yeah. Oh, shut up. You get back in your box. Yeah, right, in your box, in your box.

"Mercy," she said out loud, taking a deep breath to banish the whispering thoughts in her head. "I think I need some more coffee."

"Can do," he replied, signaling the waiter.

After a second round of coffee, he reached into his jacket and produced two tickets.

"Do you like jazz?"

"Well, some kinds of jazz. I don't think much of the New Orleans stuff—it all sounds the same after fifteen minutes."

"No, this is the real thing; the Ramsey Lewis Trio is playing at the Bali Hai, on Shelter Island. These get us a table on the lanai at ten o'clock."

She glanced reflexively at her watch; it was 9:30.

"I said dinner, Autrey," she said, hearing the weakness in her objection even as she voiced it.

"After a dinner like this, jazz is the perfect digestive. We can go in my car; I'll bring you back here when the show's over and you can get your car. You're not ready to drive anywhere, are you?"

He was entirely correct. "And you are?"

"Oh yeah. Besides, the harbor's downhill from here. Makes it easier."

They went in his car, memories of the first time she had been in it lurking in the shadows of the backseat. She rolled down the window on her side to dispel some of the alcohol. The cool night air was refreshing, and she closed her eyes, trying to determine when they reached the harbor area by the smell of the harbor and salt water. He woke her when he had parked in the restaurant's gardenlike parking lot, lighted by flaming patio torches and mantled in swaying palm trees. The looming figure of a fake Easter Island monolith startled her as she woke up, and he laughed at her. He came around the front of the car and had the door opened before she realized how far her skirt had hiked up on the ride over. She tried to fix things as she turned to get out of the car, but she ended up showing a lot of snow down south, as the girls used to say in Atlanta. Oh, well, she thought, getting out as he took her hand, that's why girls wear skirts and guys still open car doors, right?

Inside, the lanai was crowded with as many tiny tables as could fit within the fire code; the stage was equally small, but the trio, actually a quartet this evening, took up very little room for the size of the jazz they produced. The waitress seemed put out when they ordered coffee instead of drinks, but Autrey gave her a five-dollar tip, which seemed to solve things. They sat perforce fairly close together, but not touching, and listened to the casual skill of the group as they drove through the intricate rhythms of "Take Five" and other jazz classics. During the break, they ordered more coffee and people-watched.

Maddy withdrew to the powder room halfway through the break and did a little repair work on her makeup, although everything was pretty much in order. She stepped back from the mirror over the sink counter, smoothed down the front of her dress, and did a quick appraising turn. An older, heavyset woman standing three mirrors away watched.

"Honey, if that package don't get it, your man must be dead," she commented as she smeared on some orange lipstick.

"This is just for looks tonight," Maddy replied casually, brushing her hair.

"Well, damn, if that's just for looks, I'd hate to see you decked out for action; rest of us plain Janes all have to go home."

Maddy flashed her a quick smile as she put away her things and left the bathroom. Autrey watched her as she picked her way through the closely spaced tables, along with every other male on the lanai, and rose to seat her just as the musicians came back on stage. As she sat down, their eyes met again, and this time, she took a few seconds longer to look away. They listened to the soft patter of introduction coming from the stage as she examined her feelings. Even though the booze was wearing off and the coffee taking its effect, she measured the attraction and found it undiminished. Over the next half hour, the nightclub, the stage, and even the musicians faded to the periphery of her attention and she let herself become totally aware of him as he sat there in the dark, about one foot away, apparently lost in the intricate music. She watched him without looking, willing him to pay attention while staring absently into the middle distance, wondering what it would be like just to tap a man like this on the arm, look directly into his eyes, and say, "Let's go," knowing he would stand up without a word, ignoring protests from the people sitting nearby, and take her hand to lead her out of there. In her college days, before Brian, she had done that to a besotted business professor who had taken her to a nightclub, and they had made love three minutes later in the front seat of his car in a frenzied coupling, saved from being caught in the crowded parking lot by the condensation on the car's windows. Listening now to the subtle chords and tantalizing beat of the jazz, she was feeling the same warmth, the same thigh-squeezing flush of awareness and desire coursing through her veins as she sat next to this man who had done nothing more overt than look at her. She wondered whether he knew it, this man who taught other men to hunt humans, to be aware of their surroundings, like the animals; she wondered whether he could feel her heat, her sexual vibrations interleaving delicately with the bass guitar's as she sat perfectly still, her legs crossed demurely, her left arm on the table, her right in her lap, not daring to stir as much as a finger lest she disturb this exquisite sense of being right on the edge. . . .

The trio slid seamlessly into a more lively number and the mood vanished like a mirage; she heard herself let out a sigh. Mighty hunter indeed, she thought. All you had to do was put one finger on the back of my hand just then and I would have closed this place *and* the Ramsey Lewis Trio down. The second set ended and, as she clapped enthusiastically with the crowd, the evening ended, as well. She smiled at Autrey and thanked him for the dinner and the show, then said she had better be getting back to the car. His face lighted up with that boyish smile and he took her out to the Chevy. They had to wait for some traffic on the causeway street, lined with yacht brokerages, but then made quick time back to the Grant Hotel. She showed him where her car was parked and he pulled into the spot in front and went around again to open the door. Her exit this time was more demure, but he looked anyway, a smile in his eyes. He walked over to the driver's side of her car and waited while she unlocked it, looking up and down the street to make sure there were no cars coming. She opened the door and then turned to face him, the door partway between them.

"Autrey, that was a lovely evening. And I thank you again for bailing me out the other night." Standing in front of him, she had to look up. He was close to her, but not too close. His face was solemn now.

"You were lucky, that's all," he said. She thought he was talking about MCRD. But then he continued. "Back there at the Bali Hai. You were lucky."

She felt herself almost stop breathing. Had he, did he—

"I think you know what I'm talking about," he was saying. "I can even prove it. I'll bet you can't pass the count test."

"Prove it? Count test?" Her voice sounded weak, even to her own ears.

"Yeah, the count test. Let's hear you count to ten. Out loud. C'mon."

She was baffled. If he'd asked her to close her eyes—

"C'mon," he said gently, smiling now. "Count to ten. Out loud."

"Autrey—"

"Out loud. One, two, three—you know how it goes."

She sighed impatiently and started to count. "One, two, three—"

He looked directly into her eyes but did not move closer, as she had expected. Then, holding her eyes with his, he reached forward with his right hand around the edge of the door, his index finger extended, and, barely touching her, drew his fingernail slowly across the fabric of her dress, across her belly, just below the belt, from left to right. She heard her voice quaver as he did it and she stopped counting, her voice gone, her eyes locked on his.

"See?" he said softly, withdrawing his hand and straightening up. "In case you thought I wasn't listening." He stepped back and smiled at her again. "I will call you again, Maddy Holcomb. Now, get in before we get hit by a car."

Still looking at him, she swallowed and slid into the front seat. He made sure she was clear, then pushed the door shut. He bent down. She rolled down the window.

"I will call you again, Maddy Holcomb."

"Yes," she said, in spite of herself, a thin line of fire tingling just below her belt. "Yes."

As she drove home to the apartment, that yes reverberated in her mind and elsewhere. The answer is no, you dummy, no. Okay, you had a little relapse, went back to your Boston days and the mating game. Fine. But, no, you will not be seeing any more of Mr. whatever the hell his name is. You know nothing about him, and we wouldn't exactly introduce him to Brian, now, would we? It's not like this is a social or professional friendship, or even an acquaintance. There is no basis whatsoever for your seeing this man. Then why can I still feel that fingertip? Because you're just horny, that's all. You know nothing about this man except what he has chosen to tell you. Yes, but . . . in another sense, I know everything I need to know.

Gnawing a fingernail on her left hand, she had to drive around to the side of the building to find a parking spot. She got out, locked the car, and headed for the front entrance. It was a beautiful night and the orange lights across the street made the park look like a carnival about to open. Stepping through the glass doors to the lighted lobby, she remembered that she had not checked the mail earlier. Opening her mailbox, she found two bills and a single crumpled airmail letter. In place of a stamp, the word *Free* was scrawled. From Brian, of course. A wave of embarrassment swept over her as she held the letter, which had been here the whole time she was out on her—what, date? Well done, girl. Great job of keeping the home fires burning.

Upstairs, she turned on the living room lights, locked her front door behind her, shucked her jacket, and flopped down on the couch to read his letter. It was several pages, describing the first weeks since leaving Subic, including the business about the shooting incident. There were a few paragraphs on his worries about drugs in the ship. She sat up. Drugs? Surely not on a ship at sea? The so-called drug culture, that was something that went on back here. Hippies, Lucy in the Sky with Diamonds, Timothy Leary. Roaches, lids, acid, freaks, speed, mushrooms. What the hell did all that garbage have to do with the Navy? Oh, Brian, don't be crusading again. But then he closed with an entire page about the number of days left till they came home and how the next tour would be ashore for two, maybe even three years. He loved her and missed her and thought about her every night.

Shit! She threw the letter on the coffee table and slumped back, her head resting on the back of the couch and her eyes closed. She tried to picture Brian sitting in that little stateroom, scribbling away on a letter to her, contrasting that with the sinful taste of a kir royale at the Grant Grill. Enough, that's enough. Mr. Autrey calls again, you tell him firmly but politely that it was delightful but it is over. Done with. Finito. Kaput. He'd saved her from her own stupidity and she'd had dinner with him. Enough. Damn it, Brian, if you were only here. Oh, right, this is Brian's fault? She groaned out loud. Goddamn navy. Goddamned deployments.

21

WESTPAC; Red Crown Station

Halfway through the sixth week of *Hood*'s first line period, everything changed. The radio messenger had interrupted the after-dinner movie in the wardroom with a high-precedence top-secret message for the captain. The captain had read it, stopped the movie, and then picked up the bat phone to Combat and instructed Austin to have the exec and all department heads meet with him in his cabin. Ten minutes later, a bleary-eyed Brian joined the exec, Benedetti, Austin, and Raiford Hatcher in the captain's cabin.

Brian had enjoyed only an hour of sleep and was having trouble waking up. With Vince Benedetti still off the evaluator watch bill, Brian had been operating on a desperately tiring schedule, catching an average of three hours of sleep after dinner, and a midmorning nap of an hour or so against six hours of watch in the afternoon and six more hours from midnight to dawn. The exec had talked the captain into putting Benedetti back on the watch bill for one three-day period, which allowed the other two department heads to go into a comparatively easy six on, twelve off schedule. But then one of Benedetti's stars had run a boiler into a serious low-water casualty, so the chief engineer had been once more remanded into the main spaces. Austin, who managed five and half hours every night and a nap in the afternoon, all coincident with his body's natural sleep cycle, was doing much better. Brian remembered those three days wistfully; now he was desperate for some coffee as the captain began his briefing. His eyes felt as if they were full of sand.

The United States, the captain announced, was going to resume full-scale air strikes against the North in order to relieve the pressure being put on Marine bases at the western end of the so-called demilitarized zone, between North and South Vietnam. The captain summarized the message.

"They initially plan a seventy-two hour campaign of Alfa-strikes, beginning tomorrow night at eighteen hundred. Targets are mostly in the southern half of North Vietnam; we're after NVA troop concentrations and their staging areas. Both carriers will be on the line, which means we'll have surge strike ops, with one cycle every ninety minutes for three days and nights."

The exec whistled. "Surge ops? They'll barely have time to manage the traffic control at that rate."

Austin nodded. "The outbound waves will meet the incoming strike about halfway back to the carriers," he said. "We're going to need all the AICs up there, probably three on, three off."

The exec eyed Brian's drooping eyelids. "Captain, I'd like to propose that Vince come back on the evaluator watch bill—tonight, if possible, so that Brian can get a full night's sleep. Once this starts, we'll need to be short-cycling the evaluators, too."

The captain paused and then nodded. "Can you take

the midnight-to-six tonight, Vince? I know this is short notice, but—''

''Yes, sir. Can do. I'll go up at twenty-three hundred so Count can give me a good long turnover.''

''Okay, good. Brian, you're new to continuous Alfa-strikes. What we usually have to do is have two evaluators available to Combat when surge operations are in progress. One guy officially has the watch and oversees the strike-following function. The other guy is on call for an SAR or any other significant problem that pops up. It's up to the guy on watch to make the call as to when he needs help. With three of you, one's on watch, the guy who just came off watch is in the bag, and the third guy is on call. The exec and I will spell each other as necessary. It's exhausting when they do this, but it's also rather exciting.''

''Yes, sir. And they'll do this for three days?''

''Right. After three days, the flight-deck crews on the carrier are worn out, and then at least one of the carriers has to go off-line to replenish bombs and fuel. Seventy-two hours of surge ops is about the max they can do with both carriers; after that, they'll go to straight cyclic ops. That's where one carrier is on the line making strikes for sixteen to twenty-four hours and then the other one steps up while the first one rests and refuels.''

Brian thought about it for a moment, forcing his dragging brain to concentrate. ''But if they go directly into cyclic ops after these three days, it means nothing changes for us, Captain.''

''Right on, Weps. As long as even one carrier is putting bombers over the beach, we're expected to be up and running at max. Although typically, they do the cyclic ops for, say, eighteen hours, then break for six to eight hours. We'll just have to wait and see what they do.''

Brian wondered how long *Hood* could keep that up, or how long he could keep that up. As if reading his thoughts, the exec grinned and said, ''As long as they want; see, from their point of view, we've got it easy. We just do our thing sitting at NTDS consoles in an air-conditioned CIC. Those guys climb into airplanes and fly into North Vietnam to drop bombs, get shot at, maybe get shot down, get taken prisoner, or, if they're lucky, make it out to the Gulf or into Laos for an SAR pickup. Compared to what the flyboys are going to do for the next seventy-two hours, Red Crown is just a spectator sport."

Brian nodded slowly in comprehension. His sleep-deprived brain recognized that this was a big deal, but it kept returning to the imminent prospect of an entire night in the rack. He listened with half an ear as the exec ran through some changes to the daily routine in the ship and adjustments to the CIC watch bill. Raiford Hatcher confirmed that his supply Department and the mess decks could go into a constant serve mode for the many Operations and Weapons people who would be standing odd or extra hours of watch. The captain wrapped it up.

"Now, this is all still very much close-hold. We especially have to make sure nobody in the Cave or any of the other modules runs his mouth on an open radio circuit about the impending strikes. So—Count, brief your principals that we're going into high-intensity ops soon, but warn them to keep their mouths shut. The troops will figure it out by around midmorning tomorrow, so they'll have to be reminded not to yap about it. Let's do a prebrief at around, say, sixteen hundred tomorrow so as to let everyone get as much rest as possible. Because once this starts, it goes like hell."

Brian had a thought and groaned out loud, then caught himself, embarrassed. The other officers looked at him.

"Helos," he said. "What happens to the daily helo dance? We don't still—"

The exec and Austin laughed out loud; even the captain smiled.

"Never fear, Weppo, you still get to play ringmaster for your beloved helos, only now you get continuous flight-deck operations for SAR birds. Big Mother and Clementine will alternate on-station every time a strike goes in—on top of everything else. And you haven't lived until one of the fling wings breaks down on deck while the other guy is still out there."

"I hate helos," grumbled Brian. His face was so glum that the others laughed even harder. Everyone hated helos.

The meeting broke up and Brian headed back to his stateroom while Austin and the exec went back topside to Combat. He flopped down in his rack, fully dressed, in anticipation of having to get back up in an hour, then remembered that Benedetti was going to take his mid. He got back up, stripped, and took a Hollywood shower, standing in the rain locker for a full five minutes instead of the get wet, turn off the water, soap up, turn on the water, get rinsed, and get out regulation Navy shower. He put on clean Skivvies, set his alarm for 0630, and was asleep in one minute. He awoke with a start at 1030 the next morning, having slept through reveille, breakfast, his alarm, and most of the morning. He felt better than he had in weeks. He shaved, dressed, and headed down to the wardroom. As he came out of his stateroom, he discovered that someone had taped a DO NOT DISTURB sign on his door.

At 1600, nearly the entire wardroom, minus only the bridge watch standers, was assembled in D and D. Brian and Garuda had the watch. There were already indications on the screens that something was up, with extra support aircraft beginning to fill the eastern sectors of the Gulf. There had been six recce runs made since midnight, which Brian felt had surely given the game away.

The captain replayed his briefing for the principals, which included the three evaluators, the SWICs, all the AICs, the senior helo pilots, and the LSO, Jack Folsom, as well as the module supervisors from each watch section. Brian found it interesting that the bridge watch standers were not included, but then he remembered that, on a scale of 250 miles, the movements of the ship itself were not particularly important. *Hood* would probably remain in her box for the duration of the strikes.

Austin briefed the message air plans, and the status-board supervisors busied themselves posting all the call signs and identification codes from the various carrier squadrons that would be involved. The senior helo pilot reviewed the endurance rules for continuous SAR operations, generally trying to put the best face he could on the circus that would be played out on *Hood*'s flight deck over the next three days. Everyone mentally rolled his eyes at the thought of seventy-two hours of nearly continuous helo ops; Chief Martinez's fire-fighting crews would camp out in the flight-deck catwalks for the next three days and nights.

Brian went down to the evening meal, but then, not feeling sleepy after getting an entire night's sleep, went back to Combat to watch. He wasn't the only one with the same idea. D and D was crowded with khaki, as most of the principals had come up to take a look at their deployment's first Alfa-strikes. The captain sat in his chair, with the exec standing beside him. They were watching the action on SWIC's screen, which was a blur of amber, with a stream of tracks going to and from the carriers down on Yankee Station, and the heavenly host, as the support tracks were called, filling the skies over the Gulf with electronic-warfare jammers and listeners, Navy tactical radio-relay aircraft, SAR birds and their escorts, the Iron Hands, the ubiquitous E-2, who was controlling the strikes, and the Wager Bird, whose KC-135 tanker now came to him during the course of the strikes.

Brian could not get close enough to the SWIC scope to see details, so he went into the surface module, where, as he expected, the surface guys had their NTDS console tuned into the air show going on to their west. Because he was an evaluator, they made room for him at the console, even asking him who was who in the myriad of symbols streaming across the scope. It gave him a small surge of pride to be able to identify which symbols were the bombers, which the escorting Iron Hands, and to point out the crazy, taunting tracks of the Wild Weasels trying to stir up SAM sites. He watched for an hour as one wave tracked out of North Vietnam, to be overflown by the next wave coming in. The radio speakers in Combat were alive with crackling reports of targets engaged, SAM sites neutralized, and the yelled warnings among the strike aircraft of SAMs punching up into the night sky. The exec wandered into surface and nudged Brian on the arm.

"Just can't stay away, huh?" he said to Brian.

"No, sir. It's quite a show."

"Well, it's going to be here for another three days and nights. I recommend you go hit your tree; you're making the Count nervous."

Brian looked surprised. "Why is that, sir?"

"Well, he wants to make sure you get back here on time to relieve him. And remember, it will take more than fifteen minutes to turn this show over. You should be up here by twenty-three hundred at the latest."

"Aye, aye, sir. And thanks for getting Vince back into the game. I think I was at the end of my rope."

"Yeah, well, you will be again if you don't get your tree time while you can."

"Yes, sir." Brian hesitated, pointing at the screen with his chin. "All this doing any good?"

The exec shrugged. "Yeah, I suspect it is. They're going after troop concentrations, vehicle parks, ammo and fuel dumps, all the things the NVA needs to sustain its operations in the DMZ and farther south. Their logistics system is primitive, which makes it hard to find worthwhile targets most of the time. When they do stack it up or park it somewhere, yeah, this sort of surge does a lot of damage."

"Don't they do anything about it? Like send up their MiGs?"

"Not usually. I mean, look at the scope. Half that shit is attack birds; the other half is support and CAP—BARCAP, MiGCAP, SARCAP, Iron Hand—basically, a whole gruncha fighters tooling around praying that a MiG will show its Communist face. No, we won't see MiGs until the dust settles. Even the MiGs that usually come up around Hanoi are going to stay in their bunkers. Now, you quit spectatin' and lay below."

Brian grinned and left Combat.

To a passing outside observer, the ship did nothing for the next three days but push along at a sedate five knots, boring endless holes in the sullen waters of the Tonkin Gulf, cranking up speed and turning into the wind every ninety minutes to recover and launch the next SAR helo. The bridge watch standers fought boredom and sunburn and the engineers sweated in 110-degree heat in their steel jungle of steam lines and roaring machinery. While some of the deck apes continued their relentless pursuit of running rust, the bulk of the Deck Division spent their time dressed out in fire-fighting gear, hunkering down in sweaty lumps along the 01 level aft, by the sides of the helo hangar, around their hoses and foam generators, rising to their stations about every ninety minutes as Big Mother, the log helo, or Clementine exchanged places on the deck.

Throughout the rest of the ship, the mess cooks toiled through four meals a day, while the yeomen and disbursing clerks and the personnelmen pursued their paperwork. Only the occasional distant thunder of jet engines or multiple contrails across the sky gave any indication to the rest of the crew as to what was going on. For about half of them, there was simply nothing going on. The ship was just killing time before the Subic port visit.

For Brian and the other half of the crew, the next three days and nights passed in a blur of scope symbology and radio transmissions as hundreds of Navy sorties screamed over the long coastline of North Vietnam, raining 750-pound general-purpose bombs, napalm, and cluster-bomb units on truck-staging areas, tank parks, ammo dumps, and artillery concentrations across the countryside. Some of the attack aircraft skimmed along the numerous canals and inland waterways, dropping five-hundred-pound bombs configured as mines into them to interdict nocturnal barge traffic. The military airfield at Vinh and three other southern bases were struck and their runways cratered from end to end. No MiGs were found.

The grueling tempo of the bombing campaign began to take its toll by the third day as the air controllers started to lose their edge and require relief more frequently and the trackers in the Cave began to screw up the correlation of radar video to symbols. The pilots turned querulous as their own fatigue began to poison their physiological effectiveness. On the morning of the third day, after having done no SARs in the previous thirty hours, *Hood* scrambled to conduct three. They were all in daylight and all successful. But that afternoon, two outbound A-6 bombers collided in midair twenty miles west of the Red

Crown station as they executed a low-altitude join-up for the trip back to the carrier. Both plunged into the sea before anyone got out, a fact witnessed by a third A-6, which called off the SAR with a chillingly laconic "Ain't no point—nobody walked" report. The captain requested permission to take the ship into the area of the crash site anyway for the few remaining hours of daylight, and CTF 77 concurred.

As the ship nosed through the area of the crashes, the bulk of the crew not on watch came topside into the late-afternoon light to assist in spotting wreckage and any possible survivors. *Hood* steamed slowly through the area, encountering widely scattered patches of shimmering jet fuel and streaks of confetti-sized debris but finding nothing of consequence. Brian, who had the evaluator watch, did not bother to call Vince Benedetti, as this was not officially an SAR operation. He kept the duty SAR helo in its designated offshore holding area to be ready for any new SAR, one where there might be better prospects for recovering someone alive. The fate of the men in the two A-6s was a foregone conclusion, as nothing bigger than a dollar bill was sighted in the area. At sundown, the captain called it off and headed back to his station in the Gulf. Most of the crew drifted back inside, uninterested in the spectacularly glowing sunset unfolding behind them. Brian had to write a message report on the incident, but the controller who had watched it happen could tell him nothing more than "one of 'em fucked up and ran into the other one; guys're tired."

CTF 77 must have agreed with that sentiment, because he suspended the round-the-clock strike ops at 1700 that evening, ordering up the beginning of single-carrier cyclic ops for noon the following day. The break was welcomed in Combat, as many of the augmenting watch standers could get an entire night's sleep for the first time in three days. Brian had relieved Austin at 1800 and was scheduled to be relieved by Benedetti at midnight. An hour after Brian had taken the watch, Austin called him from his stateroom.

"The snipes have apparently managed to contaminate

the boiler feed-water system forward with salt water. Vince has been down there since noon, so I'll be relieving you at midnight. Make sure the wake-up people get the word."

"Can do. Does this mean we're back on port and starboard?"

Austin sighed. "Hopefully not. I'm planning on calling Vince at oh-five-thirty. But we'll see."

"Wonderful."

Brian groaned as he hung up the phone. He dreaded the thought of going back to a watch and watch schedule. He looked around Combat. Compared with the past three days, the place seemed deserted and quiet. Garuda was on with him for the first time in the two days of the staggered watch rotations. They had taken over the watch and now concerned themselves with the business of staying awake. The screen was almost entirely clear, with only the BARCAP idling overhead at forty thousand feet, patrolling their endless sixty-mile racetrack pattern along the coast of North Vietnam. The ship was on the western edge of the Red Crown box, where she had remained for the previous three days to be closer to the SAR helo stations. The only air activity around the carriers to the south was the single tanker launched to refuel the BARCAP. Both of Hood's helos were on deck for the first time in three days, with maintenance crews poring over them. HooDoo, the controller who had most recently caught some sleep, had been elected the duty AIC by the rest of the AICs, and RD1 Rockheart had the surface module. The Cave was quiet; with almost nothing to track, the operators sent ticktacktoe patterns from console to console in order to stay awake. Garuda, who usually spotted new video before any of the kids in the Cave did, let their games slide for the moment.

"Chee-rist, what a breeze, as the parrot said," declared Brian, stirring a cup of coffee. Garuda nodded. They were both glad for the respite.

"I'll bet the bad guys are glad it's over for a while, too. The receiving end of that many sorties must have been medium shitty."

"Noisy, anyway. But they're Commies; they deserve

it. Besides, one a the basketballs said our jungle bunnies had been catchin' a lot of artillery in the DMZ. Fuckers knocked it off about an hour into the Alfa-strikes.''

Brian shook his head. "But the little bastards always seem to manage to come back. It reminds me of clapping my hands over my head to get rid of a cloud of gnats—a moment of silence and then there they are again. I think maybe's there's just too many of 'em.''

Garuda snorted. "Problem is, we're smackin' the shit outta the doggies in the weeds, but the gutless bastards back in Washington won't let us do anything about all them Russian ships full of new tanks, new trucks, ad new SAMs, all parked up in Haiphong Harbor. We go get that shit, they won't any of 'em come back so quick.''

"BARCAP are off-station for happy hour,'' announced HooDoo.

"SWIC, aye,'' intoned Garuda, lighting up in an indignant cloud of blue smoke while Brian stood behind him, staring down at the scope, focusing on the familiar amber hook of the coastline near Vinh airfield to the west. The two symbols that represented the BARCAP drifted to the southeast, headed for their rendezvous with the airborne tanker. Brian studied the eerily clear picture of the North Vietnamese coastal mountains being produced by the digital air-search radar. If the atmospheric conditions were just right, the big SPS-48 radar would give as good a surface picture as the SPS-10. After a moment of silence, he saw what appeared to be a tiny piece of the land echo move. He blinked his eyes for a moment and waited for the 48 radar's sweep to come back around the scope. He saw it again.

"Hey, is that moving?'' he asked Garuda, touching the screen with his right index finger. Garuda stopped in midinhale and positioned the cursor on the speck of video. The next sweep came around and the video had moved to the right, out from under the cursor, heading north along the coast. HooDoo, overhearing Brian's question, had expanded his scope picture to focus into the land smear. He saw it about the same time Garuda confirmed the motion and slapped an unknown track symbol on it.

"Where those BARCAP?" asked Garuda.

"They off-station. Like I jes reported. They right at minimum combat package."

"What the hell, we can move the tanker. See if we can get 'em back; let's see if we can bag this guy."

"This a MiG?" asked Brian, already knowing the answer. A couple of the guys near the doorway of the Cave straightened up at the sound of the word *MiG*.

"It ain't one of ours, that's for damn sure. Good eye on seein' that sumbitch. HooDoo, take it in special track so you're ready for engagement."

"I roger that," HooDoo replied. "But them BARCAP, they aren't gonna be no good. They below minimum package; cain't engage nobody, Mr. SWIC. You know the rules."

"Yeah. Shit. And this guy is ten miles, naw, fifteen outta range for our missiles. Shit, I hate this, just watching these bastards. They know, they fuckin' *know* when the BARCAP go off-station! Shit!"

"Maybe someday we ought to fuck around," Brian said. "You know, tank the BARCAP before they assume station, then let 'em wander off when it's about the right time. MiG comes up, jump his ass."

"Damn right. We should do just that."

"Evaluator, D and T, Alfa Whiskey wants us to confirm the unknown track in the system."

Garuda responded. "Tell 'em we have video and a good skin paint, but the BARCAP are famished. And you guys in the Cave, get hot, down the games, and start looking at your fucking scopes. The evaluator shouldn't be the first guy to see a fucking MiG."

"D and T, aye."

Brian and Garuda stared down at the scope in frustration. The unknown was making a steady course up the north coast. The data readouts said he was at fifteen thousand feet, heading 340, speed 350, composition unknown. HooDoo bent over his scope, tracking the unknown with all the concentration of a spider on its web.

"You call the Old Man?" asked Garuda, adjusting his cursor.

"Christ, no, I forgot." Brian was reaching for the

captain's phone when an emergency late-detect alert came buzzing in from the Cave onto the SWIC's scope.

"Son of a bitch, lookit that!" Garuda exclaimed, rising halfway out of his chair.

To the southwest, at a range of about seventy miles and with speed leaders pointing in their direction, were three distinct pieces of video. In the time it took Brian to digest the fact that something bad was happening, the NTDS computers automatically slapped late-detect symbols on the new video, classifying them as unknowns. Garuda just about simultaneously changed the unknowns to hostiles and sent an engagement order to FCSC. Suddenly, consoles were buzzing all over Combat. The sound of the missile-director amplidynes spinning up one deck above Combat filled the forward end of Combat, and then the rumbling began as the Spook 55s snapped around to pierce the night with the acquisition beams.

"What's the range?" asked Brian.

"Sixty and inbound. Those sonsofbitches. I can't believe they're doing this shit! Hey, Mr. Holcomb—you ever call the Old Man?"

"Fuck me, no, I didn't." As he reached for the phone again, he asked Garuda, "Shouldn't we be going to GQ?"

"Negatory—doctrine says we defend from Condition Three. But I'm gonna shoot these suckers soon as either one a those systems gets a track."

"SWIC, D and T, Alfa Whiskey—"

"Yeah, yeah, I know—tell 'em affirmative, we have skin paint, three bogies, late detect, taking with birds!"

Rockheart in surface heard the take order and grabbed the bitch box's switch to alert the bridge to clear the forecastle. Brian buzzed the captain's cabin, but no one answered. Shit. It was movie time. He'd be in the wardroom. He fumbled for the wardroom switch and held it down. As he heard someone pick up the phone, the word blared out on the 1MC.

"ALL HANDS, CLEAR THE FO'C'SLE FOR MISSILE LAUNCH. I SAY AGAIN, ALL HANDS STAND CLEAR OF THE FO'C'SLE FOR MISSILE LAUNCH!"

"SWIC, FCSC. System One tracking! System Two tracking. Loading the launcher and energizing CWI!"

Brian felt like a bystander in the middle of a bad traffic accident as the missile fire–control system stepped through its countdown. Three targets, two directors. Not enough time to get them all, not nearly enough.

"Range is fifty miles, inbound!"

"Wardroom. XO. What the hell's going on up there?" Brian could hear the grinding noise overhead as the directors went into their tracking mode.

"SWIC, FCSC. CWI to radiate. Launch countdown initiated."

"SWIC, D and T! That other gomer's turned inbound. The track to the north, now bearing three-three-five, range seventy-two, and inbound! We have a raid!"

Garuda punched out another engage order to the missile systems and promptly received a system-busy alert back. Brian thought fast. Two directors against *four* targets. They were in trouble.

"Uh, XO, we have, uh, we have three bogies inbound from the southwest, range now just under fifty miles, preparing to take with birds. And there's another guy—this guy's to the north; he's still out at seventy miles; he's turned inbound. Should I sound GQ?"

Instead of an answer, Brian heard the sound of the phone being dropped on the table in the wardroom two decks below. Now what the fuck do I do? he thought.

"SWIC, D and T, bogies turning, bogies turning. Range holding at forty-five miles."

"Fuckers!" yelled Garuda, spitting his cigarette butt onto his chair.

"SWIC, AIC—I've got the BARCAP coming back. These fuckers stay feet-wet, maybe we can nail one."

Garuda reluctantly punched out a break-engage order on the southern bogies. FCSC promptly redesignated to the northern bogey, which was still inbound. The exec came bursting through the door to Combat just as one of the missile directors rumbled ninety degrees to the right on its barbette, hunting the new target with its acquisition beam. The three blips of video to the southwest merged into one and began accelerating into the interior of North Vietnam just as the BARCAP disengaged from the tanker.

"What the hell's going on up here?" shouted the exec. Austin came into Combat right behind him, buttoning his shirt.

"SWIC, D and T, north bogey is turning outbound. I say again, outbound. All bogeys outbound at this time."

"SWIC, FCSC. The geometry is cold. Breaking engagement."

"Brian, goddamnit, what's going on? Brian?"

Brian didn't know where to begin. It had all happened so fast. He looked at the exec. All he could manage was an "Uh, sir—"

Thirty minutes later, Brian sat in the captain's cabin with the exec, Austin, the captain, and Garuda Barry. The captain looked as if he had been awakened from a winter's hibernation. His silver hair was tousled and his eyes were not quite focused. He was wearing a bathrobe over his Skivvies. Brian noticed for the first time how thin and bony the captain's knees and legs were.

The exec, on the other hand, was visibly angry. Brian realized that the captain apparently was going to sit in his chair and let the exec handle the debrief. Brian still held his partially crumpled coffee cup as he explained what had happened, how they had become fixated on the one target as it floated up the coast, well out of range, and how the other three had popped onto the screens from the southwest, closing at high speed.

"Garuda locked 'em up, or at least two out of three, right away, as soon as we could get the directors on the air."

"Why wasn't the captain called when the first MiG came up?" The exec's voice was taut. Brian took a deep breath.

"That was my fault, sir. When the first bandit showed up, we got into a discussion of whether or not to bring back the BARCAP, but HooDoo said they didn't have enough fuel to make a run on him. That's when Garuda reminded me to call the captain, and I was reaching for the phone when the second bunch appeared on the scope."

"And?"

"Well, at that point, Garuda had the system in auto

and I was concentrating on the engagement as it was shaping up. Garuda reminded me again to call you, which is when I pushed the button to the captain's cabin. Then I realized he was probably in the wardroom, since it was movie time. As I pushed the button for the wardroom, the other bandit, the bandit to the north, was reported turning inbound, and I was trying to decide whether or not to call GQ, since we seemed to have a full-scale air raid on our hands and only two directors to deal with four targets."

The exec exhaled audibly, visibly trying to control himself. The captain continued to sit in his chair, his face neutral, as if bemused by all the sudden excitement in his cabin. Brian found the captain's detachment unsettling, but he was waiting to see where the exec was going with this. Austin had his usual disapproving look on his face, but he, too, appeared to be waiting to see which way the exec was headed with his interrogation. Brian stared down at the tabletop and tried not to crumple the paper cup any more. The exec got up and began to pace around the table.

"Okay," he said. "Okay. You realize that this was totally unsat. But what we need right now is light, not heat. Let me see if I have the sequence right. First, you guys detected a single bogey, headed north."

"Yes, sir."

"Actually," interrupted Garuda, "it was Mr. Holcomb who detected it. He saw the video first on my scope, and then the rest of us got on it."

Brian felt a small wave of gratitude for Garuda's input.

Austin sighed. "Sounds like the Cave was asleep; detection and tracking is not the evaluator's job."

The exec acknowledged the comment. "Right. Okay," he said. "That's very interesting. You got the first guy, then got into a discussion of what to do about it. He was well out of missile range, and the BARCAP were out of position, on their way to be tanked. Now, Brian, you understand that right then and there the CO should have been called?"

"Yes, sir," said Brian and Garuda together.

"Okay. But you didn't. And when you were about to,

three new bogeys showed up out of nowhere, and suddenly you were in a world of shit, three hostiles inbound from the beach, and only two directors. Right?''

"Yes, sir."

"And Garuda took engagement action, which was entirely correct, and again reminded you to call the CO, and you did but pressed the wrong button."

"Well, I hit the CO's cabin button. When there was no answer, I hit the wardroom button. Then you picked up, sir."

He wondered briefly why the exec had answered the bat phone in the wardroom—the captain never missed the evening movie. If he had not been in the wardroom, why hadn't he picked up in his cabin when Brian first buzzed? The exec sat back down.

"Okay. That's the first thing we can fix. Count, I want the bat phone's call system rigged so that all three phones—the one on the bridge, in the captain's cabin, and in the wardroom—sound anytime either the bridge or Combat pushes any one of those buttons."

"Aye, aye, sir." Austin made a note in his notebook.

"Now, Brian, I hate to say this, but I think you clutched up a little when everything started to happen simultaneously. Do you agree?"

Brian stared down at the table. Clutched up: the old Naval Academy expression for freezing under stress. An extremely serious failure for a line officer. But there was no real getting around it. His brain had failed open, as the engineers liked to say. He had frozen.

"Yes, sir, I guess I did."

Austin looked away, a disdainful expression on his face. The captain even looked a little embarrassed, as if something scatological had come up at dinner, but said nothing. The exec pressed on.

"Okay, that's the second fix required, only this one is procedural. Brian's problem here was that he was trying to absorb the tactical situation while also trying to find the captain. I think we need a panic signal."

"How about three buzzes, one, two, three—means Captain to Combat, right now. Or we can pass the word on the One MC. We have a One MC mike right there in D and D," offered Austin.

"Yes, I think so. Something like that. Something that means, I don't have time to talk about it, but please get up here most skosh. I like the OneMC option. Okay. Now, the third thing: You and Garuda had a discussion on whether or not to call general quarters. By our doctrine, we're set up to fight the ship from Condition Three, which is our normal watch condition when we're out here on Red Crown station. I'm kind of interested, Brian: Why did going to GQ even come up?"

Brian hesitated for a moment. The exec was clearly in charge here, but he seemed to have converted his anger to intense professional interest.

"Well," he began, "I do know the doctrine, and I know we can defend from Condition Three—in fact, we engaged the missile systems right away, as soon as we saw the three pop-ups."

"You mean Garuda engaged them, don't you?" asked Austin.

Brian bristled at the cheap shot. "Well, I thought that was our doctrine, too—command by negation. If the combat system is doing the right thing, the evaluator stays silent. Or am I mistaken?"

Austin shrugged but said nothing.

"GQ?" prompted the exec.

"What raised the GQ question in my mind was the fact that we had more targets than directors—four to two, to be precise. From the geometry, it looked to me like at least one, if not two MiGs had a chance to get into their weapons release point." He looked around the table. The exec and Austin were listening closely. Austin was slowly shaking his head back and forth, like one student trying to show the teacher that another student was coming up with the wrong answer. The captain seemed to be only mildly interested. What was the matter with him?

"Well," Brian continued, "I thought GQ would button the ship up, put the first-team guys on the consoles, and have the damage-control parties at their stations when and if we got hit."

The exec sighed. "Okay," he said. "I hear you. But in reality, at those ranges, you're talking sixty to ninety seconds from start to finish. If you had sounded GQ and

256

some of the bad guys had burned through our missile defenses, what you'd really get would be the whole crew running through the ship trying to get to their GQ stations at about the time the surviving bad guys went bombs-away on us. You'd have the entire crew in motion, the GQ team pouring into Combat, yelling questions, trying to take over the consoles, distracting the guys already sitting the consoles, at the precise instant when max concentration was required. And instead of having the ship buttoned up, you'd have damn near every door and hatch open as four hundred people tried to get to their GQ stations.''

He leaned back in his chair and raised his eyebrows at Brian. Austin had a triumphant smile on his face.

"See, Brian," the exec continued, "you've said this yourself: We're in a tough tactical position here. By attack jet–aircraft standards, we're about one hundred twenty to one hundred eighty seconds from their coast-out point, especially if they can build up velocity out of sight of our radars in those coastal canyons. Now, if we had a prior indication that a raid was shaping up, yes, of course, we'd go to GQ.''

"Like perhaps when that first MiG came up and started drifting north,'' offered Austin in an "I told you so'' voice.

"Well, no,'' said the exec, in a tone that indicated he was tired of Austin's sniping from the sidelines. "The MiGs have never come feet-wet before, and we've never even considered going to GQ for just one MiG—even when we shot at one.''

"Well, they surely came feet-wet tonight,'' mused the captain, speaking for the first time. "Maybe CTF Seventy-seven will have to change his procedures. Four enemy aircraft making what was obviously a coordinated feint-and-attack maneuver, right when the BARCAP were out of position for routine refueling. I wonder if they're practicing for something.''

"Mr. Holcomb had an idea about that earlier,'' offered Garuda. "He said we ought to do a fakeout on 'em, like hide a tanker in with the BARCAP, make like they were going off-station, then double back on 'em if they show their faces.''

The exec nodded enthusiastically. "I like that. Count, let's write something up on that," he said. "I suspect we've all gotten into a rut about taking the CAP off-station. They were off-station when we took that shot at 'em, weren't they?"

"Yes, sir." Austin made a second note, frowning.

"Captain, if I may suggest," said the exec, leaning forward. "Maybe we ought to exercise getting to GQ once in a while. If the North Vietnamese are getting ready to try us on with an air attack, we should maybe tighten up the reflex a little."

"When was the last time we called GQ for a drill?"

"No notice? I mean, not as a scheduled GQ? I can't remember, exactly—before Subic, anyway."

"Yes. Okay. Maybe you're right."

"And I'd still like to exercise the gun mounts, Captain," Brian interjected. "Admittedly, I didn't think of it tonight, but I could have assigned the gunfire-control radar to one of those bogies."

"Oh, honestly," said Austin. "What good is a five-inch gun against a Mach One air target; that's just a waste of time, and the vibration does more damage than the gun can do good."

"A GQ drill would be a perfect time to do it, XO," said Brian, ignoring Austin.

The captain put a stop to it. "Okay, yes, let's schedule some GQ drills and shoot at least the five-incher. The three-inch guns are the ones that do the most vibration damage. I'm not sure what we're seeing here, whether it's just a reaction to three days of round-the-clock strikes or maybe something a little more sinister. Although, politically, I still can't see them actually attacking the ships out here."

"But they could," said Brian quietly. The others turned to look at him. "They *could* do it."

The captain looked at Brian for a moment. Brian thought he detected a flash of annoyance in the captain's eyes, or was it pain? But then the captain slumped back in his chair and once again seemed to withdraw from the discussion.

The exec pursed his lips and nodded slowly. "Yes, I

suppose they do have the capability to mount an air raid out here in the Gulf. I suppose we need to think about that. But we've got some in-house problems to sort out first. Okay, I think that's enough. This could have turned into a mess tonight, and it's best to review an incident like this right away. The good news is that we've exposed some holes in our procedures and the captain's phone system. Now you two go back on watch and we'll talk some more about this later.''

22

The rest of the watch seemed to drag after the North Vietnamese feint. Brian and Garuda avoided any more discussion of the incident. Brian was still embarrassed by the exec's declaration that he had clutched up. Garuda appeared to be embarrassed by Brian's embarrassment. Thirty minutes after the meeting in the captain's cabin, the exec came up to Combat, without Austin, and summoned the ship's chief electrician, whom he directed to rewire the bat phone's buzzer system.

The chief electrician looked pointedly at his watch. "Tonight, XO? It's almost taps.''

"Tonight, Chief. The electrical gang seems to get plenty of sleep. I want it done now—like before midnight.''

The Chief sighed and left Combat to round up some troops. Electrician mates were not known to be an energetic rating, and the exec seemed to take pleasure in demanding some after-hours work from them. He then told Garuda to take the watch and invited Brian out to the bridge wing.

Even with the low lighting levels in Combat, they were both night-blind for the first few minutes. They felt their way through the dim shapes in the pilothouse to the starboard bridge wing, after the bosun had announced, "XO on the bridge.'' The OOD joined them for a few minutes, glad for any kind of diversion from the tedium of steaming from one end of the Red Crown box to the other, but then he sensed that they wanted some privacy and retreated to the other bridge wing, taking the JOOD with him.

"I'm always amazed at how long it takes to get my night vision back," began the exec. The night air was oppressively warm, without the relief of a breeze usually provided by the ship's own motion. The starboard running light cast a bloom of green light into the misty night air and there was an occasional whiff of stack gas from the forward stack. Brian felt his uniform shirt begin to wilt. He had been spoiled by Combat's air conditioning.

"Brian, I don't want you to think we were ganging up on you down in the cabin tonight," the exec began. "Especially about clutching up when the MiGs came."

Brian let out a long breath. "I felt more superfluous than clutched up, XO. Garuda had the systems doing their thing, and there wasn't anything I could do about the arithmetic—two directors, three, four targets. And when the Old Man didn't answer his phone—"

"Yeah. Well, he wasn't feeling well tonight. I think the doc maybe gave him something, I don't know. But that's why I picked up in the wardroom. And we learned something important tonight about the captain's call circuit."

"Yes, sir."

"I guess what I wanted to say is don't take this as too big a deal. The captain's not really mad. And he's not one to stay mad even when he does get pissed off, so don't sweat that angle."

Brian was not worried about the captain being mad at him. He was more worried about the captain's apparent indifference to the whole incident. Not indifference, exactly; there was something else—*distracted,* maybe that was the word. The exec was still talking.

"Let me tell you that you're doing all right for someone who's brand-new to this combat system and the whole Red Crown business. What we've got to focus on now is what the hell the North Vietnamese are up to, sending MiGs feet-wet."

They talked for several minutes about the implications of the sudden change in the North Vietnamese air tactics and the fact that there would be some high-level interest in what had happened tonight, and probably some interesting message traffic on the subject. Brian had the sense that the exec sincerely was trying to take the sting out of the session in the captain's cabin, especially when he recounted some of the times he had clutched up when he had been an Operations officer. When the conversation dwindled, Brian realized that the fence-mending was over and he was supposed to get back on watch.

"Appreciate the words, XO. I guess I better get back in there. It was a good lesson in the consequences of doing nothing."

The exec laughed. "Consequences? You ever hear the one about the ninety-year-old lady who called the cops, told 'em she'd just pushed her ninety-one-year-old husband of sixty-five years out a second-story window? The cops get there, ask what the hell, both of 'em ninety something, married sixty-five years, why had she done such a thing. She said he'd done gone and got a younger girlfriend, and she figured, if he could fuck, he could probably fly. Hang in there, Brian. Remember, it all counts on twenty."

"Yes, sir." Brian laughed.

Brian returned to Combat and resumed the watch. A disgruntled-looking electrician was working under the evaluator's table on the bat phone's wiring, with a very tall, thin black first class supervising. Garuda was fixing coffee and a cigarette at the same time, the wire on his headset stretched across D and D to the coffeepot.

"All quiet on the western front?"

"Yowsir, boss. No more MiGgies; Wager Bird is off-station and the link is quiet."

"Right. I got it."

"You got it."

Garuda made the appropriate announcement in Combat and came back to his chair and settled in. The electricians left to get some more buzzer relays. Brian sat in his evaluator's chair at the table next to SWIC and rubbed his face. He would normally have had another cup of coffee, but after the evening's events, he was not sleepy. He looked at his watch. Austin would be up in ninety minutes to relieve him.

"Go get absolution out there with the XO?" Garuda asked without looking at him.

"Yeah, sort of. A little damage control after the session in the CO's cabin. But you know, there was something weird about all that."

"In the Old Man's cabin?"

"Yeah. You notice it? Like who was in charge down there? It sure as hell wasn't the captain."

Garuda was silent for a minute. "Well," he said, "you gotta realize, Cap'n Huntington's almost sixty years old. Woke up out of sound sleep with someone telling him his ship nearly got waxed by a gaggle of MiGs. Mess with your mind, too."

Brian glanced over at Garuda, but the warrant was focusing on his scope, his empty scope.

"Tell me about the CO, Garuda."

Garuda finished his cigarette and fired up a replacement.

"Huntington came in back in 1940, right before the big one let go. Saw action in the Pacific mostly, on a cruiser that went down at Savo in '42, then in a tin can with Arleigh Burke's Eager Beavers, then in another tin can that was beat to shit by the kamikazes off Okinawa. That's where he got that Navy Cross."

"Something about a bomb, as I recall."

"Yes, sir. Jap Betty came in low over the bridge and dumped a bomb through the pilothouse and into CIC before impaling itself on the mast. CO was killed, buncha other people tore up pretty good, and everybody knocked flat on their asses on the bridge. This bomb, apparently it was just sitting there in all the wreckage of the CIC, but there was some kinda fuze burning on it. Huntington had been up on Sky One—you know, gun control in the old days—and had actually fallen through the overhead of CIC into Combat. And there was this fuckin' bomb and all these wounded and burned guys just staring at it. So he climbs over all the busted metal and tries to move the bomb. No go—three hundred and fifty pounds. So he pulls out a knife and unscrews the fuze cap. Pulls the fucking thing out, still sputterin' and smokin', and throws it over the side. End of story. Nobody could believe he did that. Got him the Navy Cross.''

"I guess you fall through the roof and practically land on a smoking bomb, you'd have little left to lose in trying to defuse it. But—''

"Fuckin'-a, but. I'm not sure how steady my hands woulda been, pickin' a fuze on a three-hundred-and-fifty-pounder with my bosun knife. A smoking fuze, to boot.''

"After that?''

"Kicked around the tin-can force for a coupla years after Willy Willy Twice, then got out. Went to school, worked in CivPac, didn't like it, came back in when Korea broke, and came up the line in tin cans and cruiser duty. Was XO in the cruiser *St. Paul,* before they put her out a coupla years back, and then got *Hood.* Been here going on two years. Nicest four-striper in the whole world. Super wife—you've met her. She takes care of the wardroom wives like he takes care of us. Really likes people, and they—hell, we—all respond to it.''

Brian studied the SWIC scope absently for a few minutes and then asked the question that had been nagging at the back of his mind.

"Any chance he's sick?''

Garuda gave him a guarded look. "Sick? How do you mean?''

"I mean sick like in a heart condition or something. He just doesn't look all that well. Tonight, he looked almost . . . well, almost drugged. You saw him.''

Garuda shook his head emphatically. "Naw. I don't think so. I think it's just his age and nearly thirty years of kicking around the Nav. Some of those years pretty hard years, considering.''

"Yeah, I guess you're right.'' Brian yawned. "It'll be nice to get off watch and sleep at night for a change,'' he said.

"Chief snipe coming off the watch bill again?''

"I hope not, but if he is, Mr. Austin is welcome to the mids and the afternoons.''

23

Brian eyed the oily black coffee in his cup, felt his stomach lurch, and set it back down on the evaluator table, wedging the cup between a three-ring binder and the night's stack of messages. *Hood* was rolling slowly across a lumpy sea, the result of three days of sloppy weather. It was not enough to make people sick, but sufficient to be uncomfortable and to warrant care with coffee cups. Garuda, who was losing the battle to cut back on cigarettes, squirmed uncomfortably in his SWIC chair. At 0130, Brian was fighting the familiar stay-awake battle. His hopes for the watch bill had been dashed when Benedetti had done one more evaluator watch before being sucked back into the holes. Austin, who had the privilege of being the senior watch officer, had conveniently rigged it so that Brian ended up with the midwatches again. Brian even tried thinking about Maddy, but his eyes kept betraying him. His attempts to rouse up some of their better bedroom encounters kept ending in a longing just to cuddle up on the couch with her in front of a fireplace and going to—

"SWIC, Track Supe, E-Two is RTB!"

"SWIC, aye."

The SWIC screen was almost empty. The BARCAP were on-station, but the heavenly host, and now the duty E-2, had bagged it for the night. The main air-search radars were degraded by fast-moving low clouds scudding through the darkness outside. The land smear of North Vietnam was fuzzy around the edges, partially obscured by the rainsqualls that were expending themselves against the coastal mountains.

Brian looked again at his watch. Four and a half hours to go. He remained standing beside the evaluator's desk, knowing that if he sat down, he'd be asleep in a minute. The rest of the watch standers in Combat were stepping through their own small routines of trying to stay awake: standing-up in front of their chairs, rubbing their eyes, drinking the asphaltlike midwatch coffee, smoking yet another sour cigarette, reading a tech manual, or fooling with their console controls, each trying desperately to keep from tumbling over into his individual sleep trench.

One more week, and then *Long Beach* relieves us. And then a couple of weeks in Subic, followed by a repair-ship availability in Kaohsiung, Taiwan. And then back here. He groaned inwardly at the thought of another seven weeks on-station but quickly replaced that thought with speculation on the Subic visit. From everything he had heard, Subic and Olongapo City were something else. Even discounting as total BS half the stories about Olongapo, the riotous sailor town that crouched on the outskirts of the naval base, he still found it hard to believe what the old WESTPAC hands had been telling him.

"SWIC, AIC, tanker inbound to BARCAP station for happy hour."

"SWIC, aye," said Garuda. After the last MiG incur-sion, CTF 77 had changed the pattern, bringing the airborne tanker to the CAP on their patrol line rather than taking the CAP off-station. Now if something popped, they could theoretically break off the refueling evolution and be on it in a heartbeat. Brian looked over at the scope again and saw the lone symbol representing the tanker moving slowly across the screen toward the amber line of the BARCAP station. An A-6 with wing tanks strapped on instead of bombs. It would make a good practice target—which gave him an idea.

"Garuda, have the AIC call that tanker and tell him we want to do a missile radar tracking drill with him. Let me know when he gives the okay." He spoke softly, not wanting to alert the FCSC, Chief Correy, that he was going to start something.

"SWIC, aye." Garuda gave the instructions to the AIC on intercom. The AIC switched over to the tanker's control freq and obtained the pilot's permission to track him with missile fire–control radars. It was more than a formality: When the tracking beams found the A-6, all sorts of alarms would go off in the cockpit.

"Tanker says do it to it," announced the AIC.

"SWIC, aye. We'll need to go off the link when we do this, Mr. Holcomb. I gotta make him hostile before I can send the engage order. Computer won't engage a friendly air."

"Rog. Go ahead. This won't take long. I just want to see if they're alive down there in missile plot."

"Roger that." Garuda had the track supervisor inform link control down on the carrier that Red Crown was coming off the link for five minutes for "maintenance." Brian studied the tanker's symbol. It was about halfway up the Gulf between the carriers and the BARCAP station, passing in and out of patches of weather. Garuda finished his arrangements and then took control of the tanker's track and turned it into a hostile air. He then sent an engage order to the FCSC, who sat up abruptly, as did the EC.

"The fuck did this come from!" he exclaimed as he punched buttons quickly on his console to accept the designation. The EC moved to load the launcher, but Brian cut him off.

"Tracking drill only," he called. "That's an A-Six tanker. Get on him, Chief."

The directors rumbled on their trunnions overhead and then settled into their fine-search patterns, looking for aluminum skin among the rain clouds some 60 miles away and 25,000 feet up. Director one went into nutation, which was a pattern of motion around the track axis. To a human observer, the big director would appear to be nodding and shaking its head at the same time in tiny increments as the beam went through a statistical search pattern to find its target. In Combat, nutation sounded like a large garage door opener starting and stopping in a rhythmic pattern.

After a minute, it became obvious that neither director was getting on the target. Brian walked over to the weapons module. Chief Correy was talking urgently on his sound-powered phones to missile plot.

"What's the prob, chief?" Brian asked. "That's an A-Six with air-to-air refueling tanks strapped on and broadside to us. Should be a piece of cake for the Spooks."

"Yes, sir, but they can't seem to get a lock."

"So what's the problem?"

"Uh, I'm not getting a whole lot of info just yet, Mr. Holcomb. It's—hang on a second."

Brian waited while the chief listened. Then he heard the chief starting to get angry.

"Goddamn it, Marcowitz, I don't wanna hear that shit. You get on the scope if you have to, but that's bullshit. We shoulda been locked up an hour ago."

Brian watched and waited while the chief listened some more. Something wasn't right here. The systems had been reported fully operational, and this was an easy target. And he had the feeling that the chief was being evasive. He wondered.

"SWIC, FCSC, System Two's tracking. Going IDD. System One's tracking." The chief sat back, relaxing slightly, and looked up at Holcomb expectantly.

"Break track and centerline. We'll do it again," Brian said. "Garuda, prepare to redesignate."

Garuda gave him a thumbs-up and waited for the directors to slew off their target and come back to their centerline position. He punched the buttons and the alarms sounded again at FCSC. The chief accepted the designation, and once again, the directors rumbled out to the bearing. This time, they locked on independently within ten seconds.

"More like it," muttered Brian. "Turn on CWI."

The chief energized illuminator radiation. After a few seconds, the AIC reported that the pilot had missile-radar illumination alarms.

"Down CWI. Break track. Centerline. Go standby."

"CWI down. Breaking track. Ready, standby, sir."

Brian walked back over to D and D ad thought about it. Garuda redesignated the tanker friendly, had the AIC tell the pilot to regard all further alarms, and put *Hood* back into the task force data link. It had sounded like a people problem, not a system problem. The chief was still chewing on someone down in plot but trying to keep Brian from hearing it. He leaned close to the SWIC.

"Garuda, I'm going to take a little unannounced walk down to missile plot," he whispered. "Something's not kosher here. You take the watch, okay?"

Garuda nodded. Brian stood back up and stretched.

"SWIC, I'm gonna make a head call," he announced in a loud voice. "You got it."

"I got it. SWIC, aye."

Brian walked to the ladder at the rear of Combat and headed down below, passing the level of his stateroom to come out on the level of the wardroom, and then descended one more deck to Broadway. As he turned to go forward, he met the chief master-at-arms, who apparently was out on one of his late-night tours.

Brian remembered the first time he had talked to Jackson about the drug problem in the Navy and asked him about the antidrug program in *Hood*. He also remembered his surprise at the Sheriff's answer: The chief had as much as said that there wasn't a drug program in *John Bell Hood*. That thought crossed his mind again when he encountered Jackson in the passageway.

"Sheriff," he said. "Just the guy I need."

Jackson's eyebrows rose. "Yes, sir?"

"I'm making a little unannounced visit to missile plot. I've got a funny feeling there's something going on down there. Care to come along?"

"Yes, sir. My pleasure." Jackson looked as if he meant it. Jackson suspected everyone, all the time.

They walked rapidly forward along Broadway, which at this hour was deserted. All the ship's offices were locked up and the passageway lights were set on red lighting. They went forward to the missile magazine passageway, turned left, and stepped down a ladder to the next deck. There they walked back aft twenty feet to the door of the missile fire–control equipment room, known as missile plot. As they strode through the darkened passageways, Brian had briefed the Sheriff on the sequence of events in Combat and why he suspected something was amiss.

The first thing they both noticed was that the missile plot's hatch door was completely dogged down, its chrome-plated operating handle pushed all the way over to the full dogged position. He paused for a moment and looked at Jackson, who was nodding thoughtfully. Under normal watch-standing conditions, the handle would have been only partially closed. Hatches were only fully dogged down for general quarters or when the people inside wanted some warning that someone might be coming through.

The chief leaned forward and put his ear against the hatch door. At first, he heard nothing and then he heard someone laugh, a high, giggling sound. It was loud enough for Brian to hear it, too. Like a drunk, he thought. Jackson had a gleam in his eye when he straightened up. He looked at Brian and Brian nodded once. The chief squatted down on his haunches, took the handle in both hands, drew a deep breath, and then stood straight up, undogging the hatch in one sudden flowing movement, popping the door open. He stepped into the white lights of plot, followed by Brian.

There were two men in plot. The senior man, FTM2 Marcowitz, was sitting on the deck between the two fire-control radar consoles, a stupid grin on his face and his eyes dilated into large black circles. He giggled again when he saw the two khaki-clad figures appear. The second man, FTM3 Warren, was sitting at the System One console, his headphones still on, the eyes in his black face going round with the shock of seeing the Weapons Department head and the chief master-at-arms standing in the hatch. The burning camel-dung stink of marijuana smoke was everywhere.

"Well, well, suspicions confirmed," Brian declared, glaring at Marcowitz. Jackson walked over to where Marcowitz was sitting and grabbed his shirt, hauling the slender petty officer to his feet and shaking him.

"Morning, asshole," Jackson growled. "Having us a little toke, are we?"

As Brian watched from the hatchway, Marcowitz tried to grin, but his face failed him. "Wow, man. Not me, Chief," he said. "I don't do no dope."

"Yeah, right. I suppose it's Warren here been stinking up the place with weed, huh?"

"I dunno, man. I dunno what'cher talkin' about. Honest, Man."

The chief, still holding Marcowitz up on his tiptoes, his large fist bunched in the man's shirtfront, turned his head towards the junior petty officer, who was sitting mutely at his console. "All right, Warren, what the fuck's going on in here?"

"Honest, Chief, I don't know. I mean—"

"Chief," interrupted Brian, "why don't you take that shithead to your office and write him up. Get the doc to give him a piss test. Let me talk to Warren."

Jackson understood at once. Separate them so that maybe Brian could get the story from Warren. Jackson spun Marcowitz around and frog-marched him out the hatch into the passageway. Brian stared at Warren for a full thirty seconds before speaking.

"Tell FCSC I'm down here in plot and that you need a relief for Marcowitz. Tell him why."

Warren relayed the message to Chief Correy at FCSC. He listened for a moment and then nodded his head. "Plot, aye," he said in a weak voice, then turned to look back up at Brian.

Brian walked over to stand right next to Warren's chair, forcing the young petty officer to crane his neck to look at him.

"Let me lay it out for you, Warren. Either you were both doing dope or it was just Marcowitz. You don't look intoxicated, and he is definitely blown away. So, what's the story?"

Warren, obviously frightened, stared up at him, swallowed, but said nothing.

"You smoking marijuana down here, Warren? Doing dope on watch? In a war zone? You ready for a general court-martial for dereliction of duty? How's ten years breaking rocks in Fort Leavenworth Federal Penitentiary sound to you, Warren? That what you joined the Navy for?"

"No, suh," the man blurted, his eyes close to tears. "I didn't do nothin'. I don't wanta be no fink, Mr. Holcomb. But I didn't do nothin'. You can piss-test me if you want. But I don't do that shit."

"Did you see Marcowitz smoke marijuana?"

"I . . . uh . . . I don't wanta say, Mr. Holcomb. Some a those guys, they'll—"

"They'll what, Warren? You afraid somebody's going to kick your ass if you fink out on Marcowitz?"

"Yes, suh. I heard—I heard you can get thrown over the side, you go blabbin' about guys doing shit. Please, Mr. Holcomb, I didn't do no dope. But don't make me say nothin'."

"Explain to me why the missile radars couldn't get on track the first time but could the second time."

"Uh, it's the weather, sir? The autotrack circuits were climbin' all over the clutter from the rain and shit. We had to take them in manual to get a lock."

"You didn't answer my question. Why it failed the first time and worked the second. Who was primary scope the first time?"

"Uh, he was, suh—Marcowitz."

"And the second time?"

"That was me, suh."

Brian took a deep breath. "Okay. You stay here until Marcowitz's relief shows up. Then you go to Chief Jackson's office. He and the doc'll give you a piss test. You better not come up blue, you understand me? We'll talk about the rest of this later." He turned away as if to leave, then paused. "By the way, where's his stash?"

"Stash? I don't know, Mr. Holcomb. He just had the one—"

Brian smiled grimly as the kid realized what he had just said. "Thank you, Warren. Leave the hatch open until this place smells like humans again, understand?"

"Yes, suh," said Warren in a small voice, looking genuinely frightened now. As he left plot, Brian wondered about the fact that the kid was as frightened of being fingered as a storyteller by the druggie crowd as he was of being caught by the command. It was bad enough that a second class petty officer was using dope on watch; but if the druggies were organized enough to be capable of retribution against witnesses, that was something else again.

As Brian reached the CMAA's office, one of the main-hole snipes was looking over his shoulder at the activity while he filled a steel thermos with coffee from the mess decks urn. Brian gave him a hard look and the man decided he had enough coffee and disappeared. Brian found a rapidly sobering Marcowitz sitting at attention in a straight-backed chair while the chief hospital corpsman watched the Sheriff add a chemical to the contents of a urine-sample bottle. As Brian stopped in the doorway, the doc held the bottle up to the light. The yellow sample turned bright blue.

"Bingo, motherfucker. You're down," said Jackson. Marcowitz stared straight ahead, saying nothing at all.

"Doc," Brian said. "I need you to test FTM Three Warren when he gets relieved. He'll be coming up here in a few minutes."

"Aye, sir. No problem. Got this shitbird dead to rights, don't we?"

"Looks like it to me. Sheriff, I'm going back up to Combat. I presume we see the XO in the morning with the report chits?"

Jackson stepped around Marcowitz and out into the passageway while the doc filled out the test-result report. Jackson motioned for Brian to come with him, pulling the door ajar before answering.

"Yes, sir, although you probably ought to give him a call tonight so's he knows about it before he hears people talking. You know how word gets around."

"Right, I'll take care of it. I gotta tell you, this really pisses me off. We caught this guy in the middle of a drill, but it could just as easily have been for real. You're an ex-gunner's mate. You know what I'm talking about."

"I surely do, Mr. Holcomb." Jackson paused for a moment, choosing his words. "But I'm not sure you're going to get a lot of satisfaction out of the XO on this."

"Meaning precisely what?"

"I think the best thing is for you to see how it goes. Then perhaps we can talk again. Please, sir."

Brian stared at him, but the Sheriff's black face was impassive. He obviously had more to say but wanted to wait.

"Okay, Sheriff. You've piqued my interest, so I'll play along. But this isn't a game for me. Missile techs smoking marijuana on watch could get us all killed out here."

"I couldn't agree more, Mr. Holcomb. I'll get the report chit drawn up right now."

"Okay, Chief. I'll call XO tonight and we'll go see him first thing after quarters."

Brian went back up to Combat and resumed the watch as evaluator. After he received a call from the doc confirming that Warren was clean, he called the exec to report the marijuana incident. The exec listened to the story and then instructed Brian to close-hold the incident until he had had time to brief the CO in the morning.

"I don't think young Warren had anything to do or say about it, XO," Brian concluded. "And his piss test was clean. The other guy is dirty as hell. He's the one we'll want to bust."

"We'll talk about it in the morning, Weps."

Brian hung up and found Garuda swung around in his chair.

"Nothing going on; the BARCAP will be relieved in about thirty minutes. The weather is getting shittier and the crud is clobbering up the radar picture, but nothing seems to be stirring ashore, so I guess the lousy radar doesn't matter too much. What'd XO say about the doper in missile plot?"

Brian just looked at him for a moment. So much for keeping a lid on it. Garuda grinned. "FCSC told me what went down after you were done with your, uh, head call," he offered.

"Yeah, well, what it looks like is the FTM Two was doing a joint and the other kid was keeping his mouth shut. We can mast the FTM Two for doing dope on watch; that's some serious brig time. We can hit the FTM Three for not doing anything about it, but that's a little tenuous, apparently—and probably unfair, too. XO said we'd talk about it in the morning."

"Surprise me if anyone actually goes to mast," said Garuda.

"You gotta be shitting me. I mean, I know we handle simple possession in our own in-house way, but this was blatant: Suppose the MiGs had come out and that little fuck was so stoned he couldn't establish missile track? He could have killed the whole ship."

Garuda fished for a cigarette before replying. His latest attempt to quit smoking had lasted two weeks. "Yes, sir, I hear you," he said, speaking through the familiar blue cloud. "And I may be all wrong here, but I just don't think this Old Man's willing to have real go-to-mast drug busts while we're out here on the line. Now, if we were in Subic and this maggot got caught doing a joint in the BEQ, that'd be different. That'd be an on-base drug incident, not a shipboard drug incident. But, like I said, I could be wrong."

Brian thought about it as Garuda went back to his scope, remembering what the boatswain had told him. Brian looked over into the weapons module and found Chief Correy looking his way. The chief turned back to his console. Fox Hudson had told him that Chief Correy was a go-with-the-flow kind of guy, not one to impose much discipline on his troops. That's part of my problem, Brian thought. It's not good enough to play gun-deck justice with this shit, he thought. We've got to rip these slimeballs out of the crew when we find them, and we have to find the druggie organization. Just like you take a tumor and the lymph nodes out when you find it. I can't have that shit going on down in missile plot. His blood ran cold at the thought of what might have happened if that tracking drill had not been a drill. We'll just see, he thought to himself. We'll just see.

As Brian was finishing breakfast after getting off watch, the exec came into the wardroom. He sat down at the senior table with Brian and Raiford Hatcher and scribbled down his breakfast order. Then he looked over at Brian.

"Captain would like to see you before you hit the bag for your morning nap," he said. "Has a piece of paper for you."

"Aye, sir. Do you know what it's about?"

"I'll let him tell you. But you'll like it, so relax and finish your breakfast."

Brian nodded and drained the last of his milk. He had been about to bring up the missile plot incident, but the exec was busy skimming his morning message traffic, so Brian excused himself and headed topside. He stopped in his cabin to wash his face and comb his hair, debating whether or not to shave, and then said to hell with it and went up and knocked on the captain's door.

"Come in."

"Yes, sir, Cap'n," Brian said as he stepped through the door. "XO said you wanted to see me, sir?"

The captain was sitting at his dining table, dressed in a bathrobe and slippers. He looked better than he had the last time Brian had seen him, which was when? Brian found himself trying to remember. Despite that, the captain's face still seemed gray in the sullen light slatting through the rain-streaked portholes. The captain motioned toward a seat at the table.

"Come in. Sit down. Want some coffee? No, I guess not, huh? You need to recover from the mid."

Brian sat down at the dining table across from the captain, who picked up a manila file folder and passed it over to him. Brian opened it and found a fitness report with his name on it. He looked back up at the captain, startled to find the captain watching him with a look that reminded Brian of the look a hawk gives a rabbit. But then the captain appeared to smile and said, "Go on, read it. It's a special. I'm putting it in before the lieutenant commander board next month."

Brian read it and smiled in spite of himself. This was what he needed. He skimmed the words. Less than ninety days, but doing an outstanding job in combat operations. Lieutenant serving in a lieutenant commander's job. Learning quickly. Department running well. Fully recommended for promotion. This would do it. He put the folder back down on the table.

"Thank you for this, sir. It'll sure help."

"Well, I mean what's in it. You've come up to speed nicely, and we've been through some interesting times, as the Chinese say. Keep up the good work, and I'll look forward to seeing your name on the list a month from now. Now, go get some sleep."

"Yes, sir," said Brian, standing. "Thank you again."

Brian left the cabin and walked aft to his own stateroom and flopped on his rack. He felt a sense of elation and relief. His detailer had told him that a good special fitrep would help a lot to lock in the promotion to lieutenant commander. But a CO was under no obligation to submit one. The fact that Captain Huntington had given him one was a strong signal that he was doing all right. He was back on track professionally and the future was opening back up for him. Taking this assignment was going to pay off in a set of oak leaves on his collar. And the oak leaves opened the door to an XO job, and the XO job made it possible to get a command of his own one day. He flopped down on his rack without turning on the lights in his room. The sound of a driving rain was audible outside, lashing the aluminum sides of the superstructure next to his head. He began to daydream about the day when he would be the Old Man, then remembered that there were some big gates to get through yet. Before drifting off to sleep, he wondered briefly about the strange look on the captain's face.

At 1030, he got his wake-up call from the bridge. His eyes were stiff with sleep and it took a minute to remember why he was in the rack and still dressed. He groaned his way off his bed and proceeded with his morning ablutions. The phone rang as he came back into the room from the shower.

"Weps," he said. His voice sounded like a croak.

"Sir, this is the bridge messenger. XO'd like to see you in his cabin. At your convenience."

"Say what it's about?"

"No, sir."

"Okay."

Brian hung up and began to get dressed. Marcowitz. He'd forgotten about the drug bust. Now he'd find out what the good ship *Hood* did with no-shit, caught-in-the-act dopers. He stopped by the wardroom to grab a paper cup of coffee on his way aft to the exec's cabin. He had to wait in front of the exec's cabin for ten minutes while the exec conferred with the medical officer on the week's sanitation inspection. Finally, the exec called him in.

"Sit down, Brian. Let me reread the Sheriff's incident report one more time."

Brian sat on the couch that doubled as a Hide-A-Bed in the exec's cabin. The exec sat at a desk that was built into a steel chest of drawers. There were four baskets of paperwork scattered around the tops of file cabinets and there was very little desk visible underneath yet another mound of paperwork. The exec read through the three-page report, including the urinalysis reports. Then he pitched the report into his hold basket.

"I'm curious," he said. "What prompted you to go down to missile plot?"

"Combat was dead, and everybody was falling asleep on their feet. We had this perfect tracking opportunity with an A-Six tanker, so I decided to run a missile-radar tracking drill. Should've been a two-minute deal, piece of cake." Brian shook his head. "They couldn't get a lock. And when I couldn't get a straight answer as to why, I decided to go check it out."

"So you suspected maybe somebody was smoking dope? That why you took the Sheriff?"

"No, sir. It was just a coincidence I ran into Jackson. Come to think about it, I really didn't suspect anything, not until I found the hatch dogged down. I figured maybe the senior guy was asleep in a corner and the junior guy had screwed up the evolution and it might be useful to kick ass and take names." He paused for a moment to recollect. "But as soon as we got there, I think maybe Jackson knew. He suspected dope right away."

The exec laughed. "Jackson suspects dope every time someone yawns."

"Was I wrong to go check it out?"

"No. Your instincts told you something was wrong, and pros always listen to their instincts, especially when they involve guided-missile systems. Okay, here's what we're going to do. Warren, as you reported, was clean from the dope angle, although as a petty officer he should not have condoned drug use in the ship and on a weapons system watch station. But you and I know that there's not much he could do about it in a practical sense, especially when it involved a white petty officer senior to him. I'll probably call him in and share my thinking with him in an informal counseling session. Marcowitz is a different problem."

"Yes, sir. I presume we'll take him to mast today and award him a court-martial."

"You presume wrong, at least for now."

"*Sir!?*"

"We'll take him to mast, but not until we're in port at Subic. Nobody has time for a serious mast case like this while we're out here on Red Crown station. Don't worry, it'll keep. It's not like he's going to slip ashore on us. We have this report, the urinalysis, your testimony as to what you found, and Warren's testimony if we need it. We'll be in port in another week. Marcowitz isn't going anywhere."

"Yes, sir. But we may not get Warren to say much. He seemed to be very apprehensive about possible retribution if he talks. Talked like the dopers are organized and have an enforcement squad."

The exec stared at him for a long moment.

"Well," he said finally, "They probably do, or at least they tell people they do. But I don't expect much out of Warren, and we don't really need him, when you get down to it, not for mast. The captain can hang Marcowitz on your say-so and the urinalysis alone. And we have ways to protect Warren. I think you know one of them fairly well."

Martinez. "Yes, sir. But a court-martial, that would require full rules of evidence—then we'd need Warren, right, XO?"

"If and when it gets to that."

Brian was puzzled. Of course it would get to that. Captain's mast could not impose an appropriate sentence for this offense, which deserved some serious brig time. Captain's mast in this case would simply be a formality, a referral of the case up the line to a special or even a general court-martial.

"XO," Brian began, but the exec held up his hand, cutting him off.

"Look, Brian, we'll handle this. I know what you're thinking, that this case automatically goes to court-martial, that we should hold mast today so that the court can be set up by the time we get in. Well, let me just say that there're other ways to handle this deal, and you'll just have to trust me for now till you see how it works out. Believe me, Marcowitz will go down for this. In the meantime, we take Marcowitz off the watch bill and relieve him of his duties."

"You mean he just gets to sit around in the compartment?"

"You trust him to sit the weapons-radar consoles?"

"No, sir, but—"

"But what? He's still an E-Five. I can't send him mess-cooking and I can't transfer him to the deck gang. Until the system takes legal action, all I can do is suspend him, as it were. But consider this: His buddies in the division will initially grin and think he's gotten away with it. But the longer they have to stand extra watches while he sits on his ass in the compartment, the less kindly they're going to feel toward him. By the time we get in port, he's gonna *want* a court-martial."

Brian sat back for a moment. "But sir, this is really unorthodox. I mean, by the regs, we should take him to mast now. That way, he gets a court-martial awarded now, gets a defense counsel lined up, and then he can stew about that for the next two weeks."

"Nope. We're gonna wait. I've already talked to the captain about it, and that's what he wants to do. So that's what we're gonna do. We'll take care of Marcowitz in Subic, okay?"

Brian took a deep breath. Justice and discipline were ultimately the Old Man's call. "Aye, aye, sir."

"Good. And the captain showed you your special fitrep this morning?"

"Yes, sir. I appreciate that."

"Good. All part of fostering the team effort here. See you at lunch."

"Aye, aye, sir."

Brian left the cabin, glanced at his watch, and stepped out into the weather decks passageway that led to the boat decks. He had fifteen minutes before the early sitting for lunch, and then back to Combat for the next six hours. The weather remained foul, with a low overcast blowing a warm light rain through the masts and yellowish confused seas causing the big ship to pitch and roll in an uneven, jerky motion, just enough to keep everyone's stomach on edge.

He stared out at the uneasy waters of the Gulf and thought about what the exec had said. Fostering the team effort. Well, that message was pretty clear. You like your special fitrep? Want to make sure it gets mailed off on the next log helo? Then play ball, sunshine. We know how *we* want to handle this drug case. We send in the fitrep, you become one of *us*. That's fair, isn't it? Captain doesn't have to submit a special fitrep, but he did, which almost certainly means you get promoted. Now, we've got a way *we* want to handle this Marcowitz business, and you're going to go along, right? Shit, even Garuda had known how this would come out. He wondered what would happen now, if Marcowitz was going to have a bad accident between now and going into port.

As he was about to turn to go back inside, Chief Jackson came walking carefully toward him across the boat decks, which were slippery from a combination of rain and assorted oils leaking from the boat winches. Jackson obviously wanted to talk.

"Mr. Holcomb. I understand the exec wanted to see you about Marcowitz?"

"You've got good spies, Sheriff."

Jackson laughed. "Sometimes they're good. Sometimes—" He grimaced.

Brian understood. "Well, you're right," he said. "And the decision is, we do nothing—until Subic, where some kind of legal proceedings will be taken against him."

"No mast?"

"No mast; no nothing, apparently. Until Subic."

Jackson considered this news with a frown, then shook his head.

"They can't just tube it. The whole ship knows the guy got nailed red-handed. He's off the watch bill, and some of my prime suspects are nosing around."

"You think he's bosun meat?"

Jackson shook his head. "No, sir, I don't. Not directly, in the sense that he's going to have an accident. No, I think something will happen in Subic, but what, exactly, I don't know."

Brian was tempted to share his own doubts about what had happened, but then he would have to explain the fitness report.

"Well," he said, "the captain supposedly made the call, and it's his boat, I guess."

Jackson nodded again. "It's the Navy's boat first; then it's his boat. Thing is, Marcowitz is small fry. I mean, what he did was a big deal and everything, but the guys we really need to nail are the guys who're moving this shit, selling it to potheads like Marcowitz."

"You mentioned your prime suspects. I presume you have at least a fair guess as to how the drug deal works here?"

"I've been aboard awhile now. I think there's a small group of the younger blacks involved, but even to mention that idea is a trip wire these days, even if I'm the guy bringing it up. These guys are all group fours."

Brian wiped rain off his forehead. "What the hell are group fours?"

"It's all part of that Project One Hundred Thousand nonsense. You remember, when LBJ directed the Defense Department to accept a hundred thousand mental group fours. These are guys who the recruiters usually turn away because they score at the bottom of all the aptitude tests, not to mention that they're usually social misfits—inner-city gang members, street punks, a lot of them. The idea was to go ahead and take them into the military services, give them an opportunity to escape their 'deprived heritage,' to help LBJ's Great Society."

"I remember that. But I thought it was only the Army."

"I wish. But all of the services got tagged with a quota. And it's been a disaster from the git-go. You figure, in terms of a disciplined ship environment, these guys are total misfits; they're not too bright in the first place, so they basically don't know how to act. They can't pass the tests, so they automatically become deck apes or firemen—permanent junior enlisted snuffies. No smarts, they can't advance. They know they don't belong, and unfortunately, most of them are black, so what we get is an alienated ex-criminal in the crew whose worst suspicions about a racist military are confirmed."

Brian nodded. "So naturally they would gravitate together."

"Right, and that's the bunch I'm watching. Given their background, it's only natural that they'd gravitate to a gang of some kind. I've had two indications that they're into the dope scene, which would figure: That's what they came from. But the guy I'm really after is the kingpin. If I could take him, we'd make a real dent."

"Nailing one guy would make that big a difference?"

"Yes, sir. Right now, probably one guy brings all the dope on board. You nail him, and then everybody has to freelance. The one guy knows how to do it, has some kind of distribution system set up, has security in place. Freelancers wouldn't have time to set that up, so we'd nail more of them. So if we can catch the main man, yes, we'd make a dent."

"Chief Martinez said the same thing—only he wants to make more than a dent."

Jackson smiled and pulled out a handkerchief to wipe the rain off his glasses. "Yeah. I sympathize with his methods more than he knows, even though it's illegal as hell. But what's missing here is the command. We're way outside the system on this ship, and that appears to be command policy. I hope I'm not stepping in shit saying this to you, Mr. Holcomb."

Brian shook his head. "I'm of the same opinion, Chief. But I'm also just a little bit mousetrapped. You know, you go along to get along."

"Oh yes, sir. Trust me, I know that score. It's just . . . it's not that I think the CO and the XO are crooked, or involved in drug dealing, or even condone it. I just think they're holding things together as best they can in the least damaging way they can. The problem is—"

"The problem is, we're all at risk. The other night, up in Combat, four MiGs faked a raid at us. Four MiGs, two directors—they both have to work gangbusters. You get the picture? If we had had Marcowitz—"

"Got it."

"I'm glad I ran into you on the way down to plot, though. I'm not sure we'd even have a promise of action if I had been alone when I found Marcowitz."

"Well, yes, sir," Jackson said, looking briefly at the horizon. "I guess you should know that Mr. Barry gave me a call after you left D and D, which is maybe how you and I managed to meet."

Brian looked at him for a moment. Garuda must have sensed what was going on, too. Maybe he wasn't entirely alone on his little crusade. The topside speakers blared to life as the boatswain mate on the bridge piped mess gear. Brian looked at his watch and then back at Jackson.

"No, I didn't know that. I've got to make early chow. Let's see what happens in Subic, Chief. Then maybe we can work something out."

"You know where to find me, Mr. Holcomb."

Brian nodded and went below.

24

Rocky walked aft along the main deck passageway, past the doors of after officers' country, and underneath the helo deck. Just aft of the helo deck, he went down a ladder to the second deck and continued aft to the warren of engineering spaces under the fantail, which included the machine shop, the electrical shop, the laundry, the after emergency diesel generator room, and the steering machinery rooms. He stopped at the doorway to the laundry and looked in. Two black pressmen were sweating over their work about fifteen feet from the door, the noise of the presses and the dryers drowning out any sounds of Rocky's presence. Rocky lifted the telephone off the hook and dialed the electrical shop, a space no more than twenty-five feet from where he stood. Bullet picked up the phone.

" 'Lectric shop, EM One Wilson speakin', suh."

"It's me. You clear?"

"Um-hmmh."

Rocky hung up and walked around the corner to the electrical shop. The shop was a rectangular compartment, about fifteen feet long and nine wide, arranged against the hull at about the waterline, with a single hatch entry. Rocky swung the dog handle and stepped through the hatch, pushing the handle back down three-quarters of the way to full dogged position. That way, there would be warning if someone came in, but it would not otherwise attract attention. The shop had workbenches running down either side; a large assortment of electrical cable, light fixtures, switches, small motors, bearings, and tools were stashed in the angle-iron and strakes of the hull that ran down both bulkheads.

Bullet was sitting on a stool at the forward end of the shop, smoking a pipe, Eldridge Cleaver's *Soul on Ice* on his lap.

"You heard about that guy Marcowitz?" Rocky asked.

"I heard."

Rocky leaned against one of the workbenches and put his hands in his pockets. "They've taken him off the watch bill, but they haven't done anything else yet. Jackson says that Holcomb wants to write the guy up, take his ass to mast."

"Be a change."

"Sure as shit would. But they haven't done it yet. I'm wondering if that boy's thinkin' about doing some kind of deal."

"Why's that?"

"Because. They take him to mast, the Old Man's gotta give him a special or even a general court. That means heavy-duty investigation, lawyers, and federal time. Big incentive there to give them something."

Bullet took a long, reflective drag on his pipe. Then he shook his head slowly. "He ain't got nothin' to give. Onliest thing that boy knows is, he talked to one a the bloods and got told where he could find some dope. Ain't no money changed hands; ain't no dope changed hands."

"But he can finger your guy. Your guy can finger you."

"Won't happen. They ax my guy, he deny. Shee-it. What proof this skin got that my man did any fuckin' thing?" Bullet looked bored, a man totally unconcerned. His seeming disinterest irritated Rocky.

"Yeah. I can see that," Rocky said. "It just makes me nervous, they start doing something different. And there's something else. Jackson is interested in you."

Bullet looked up. That got your attention, Rocky thought.

"Yeah," Rocky continued. "He has your service record on his desk. Saw it this morning when we changed over duty MAA."

"What that old fool want with my record?"

"He didn't say and I didn't ask. But I'll tell you what: It makes me think Jackson is working the problem, no matter how the CO and the XO have been playing it. And you know he had help the other night: It was Lieutenant Holcomb started that bust."

"So?"

"So, Holcomb's a department head. Up for light commander next month. Something's goin' down. And there's another thing."

"Man, you fulla good shit tonight."

"Yeah, well, what can I tell you—I'm concerned. We get complacent, they nail our asses."

"What's this other thing?"

"The fact that Louie Jesus isn't out on the warpath for Marcowitz. I hear the guys in his division'd like to kick his ass 'cause they're standing his watches. But Geronimo hasn't made a single move on him, hasn't been around to stare at him and do his monster mash."

Bullet put his pipe down and studied his boots. Rocky remained silent, giving him time to think. Finally, Bullet nodded once.

"Maybe you right. Maybe we slow it down for lil while. Lock it up until after Subic."

"Might be a good idea. This could all be nothing, but there's too many things in motion to suit me. I'll try to find out what Jackson is up to, but I have to be real careful about that."

Bullet squinted down at him. "Everybody know you be real careful," he said. "You gonna fill it up, we gits to Subic?"

"Oh yes. But I'm going to keep it light—grass and hash. No snow, no acid till I see what's going down here."

"Yeah. Thass all them skins want, anyways. Ain't got nobody doin' skag or takin' trips, leastwise not yet."

Rocky nodded, another question occurring to him.

"You doin' all right with Garlic?"

"I s'pose," Bullet said. "I gits my money every pay-day, jist like you."

"Yeah, but what I meant is, is he playing it straight with us? I heard some scuttlebutt that he's charging some guys seven for five, not six for five."

Bullet shrugged. "I doan give a shit. My deal was six for five an' a three-way split on the juice. He skimmin', he ain't hurtin' me none. You neither, my man."

"I guess. But here's the thing: If Jackson and company ever tumble to the money angle, they'll start with Garlic, because he's the loan shark. We both need to watch his ass, because he can do us both."

Bullet snorted. "You spookin', man. You gonna be watchin' so many dudes, you gonna go cross-eye."

The hatch handle moved, paused, and then swung up. Rocky headed for the door and Bullet put his pipe back in his mouth and resumed his careless pose by the bench. The hatch opened and a young black fireman electrician came through the door, his arms full of expended light-bulbs. He stopped when he caught sight of an MAA in the shop, looking to Bullet. Rocky turned back to Bullet.

"You talk to that sailor, EM One. Tell him to straighten up or Jackson is going to get on his ass."

"Thanks, man. I be doin' it," said Bullet. Rocky stepped through the hatch and was gone.

The EMFN put the load of dead bulbs in a steel trash barrel and looked over at Bullet.

"I be doin' it? What's with the shuck and jive?" he asked.

Bullet chuckled. "That's how the Man expects all God's darkies to talk. I'm just fulfilling their expecta-tions. Keeps them complacent." He tapped the Cleaver book. "Against the day, brother. Against the day."

25

Chief Jackson locked his office door, yawned, and sat down at the desk, wedging his chair in against the ship's slow roll. There was a mass of paperwork piled on the deck, courtesy of a high-speed turn earlier, after helo detail. Damn stuff wouldn't stay on the desk, so let it sit on the damn deck. He picked up EM One Wilson's service record and flipped through it for page two, the emergency-data card, which would show relatives, next of kin, and place and date of birth. Wilson had been born in Macon, Georgia, and was thirty-five years old. His parents were both still living in Georgia, although no longer in Macon. The blocks for siblings, spouse, and children were empty. The death-gratuity-benefit block at the bottom of the page indicated that it was to be split between a woman named Alice Byron in San Diego and his parents in Georgia. Otherwise, page two was blank.

Page nine had a surprise for him. It listed Wilson's educational profile, which showed that the electrician had graduated from both high school and a two-year college in Macon, with an associate degree in political science. Political science? Jackson lowered the record and thought about that. He looked again at the Armed Services Vocational and Basic Skills profile, which showed high lines in verbal and math. Something didn't compute, starting with the speech Wilson used, which was replete with street slang and almost a Stepin Fetchit dialect. A college graduate?

He went back to the record. Electrician's A-school: class rank three of forty-one. Leadership, management, education, and training course: two of sixteen. Twelve Navy correspondence courses in eight years, all with high marks. No dummy, this guy. He went to the performance-profile page: good marks across the board, except in verbal expression, with a quick rise to E-6. But then, four years back, a plateau in the marks, with some down-checks in military aptitude and loyalty. That would explain the no chief's hat. He flipped through the actual evals. Something had changed, something not specified or directly called out. So these were marks to stop his career: military aptitude and loyalty. Wilson was black, and, in the Navy's secret code, those were the mark categories that took a hit when somebody's racial attitude upset the command, whether he was black or white.

Wilson had been in *Hood* for three and a half years, almost time for orders. Jackson flipped back through the performance evals again and found that the plateau in his performance marks started during a tour at the San Diego Naval Station, where Wilson had been a master-at-arms. Master-at-arms?! Damn. Another surprise. Why hadn't the exec assigned him to *Hood*'s MAA force? He frowned. Something amiss here, and he was now pretty sure it had to do with race relations. He had seen that Wilson had his own circle of exclusively black friends, but, hell, that wasn't unusual. And there had never been the slightest hint of radical activity attributed directly to Bullet. The man kept to himself. Solid achievement up to E-6 in a technical-engineering rating. So why the Sambo dialect?

Looking at his watch, he had an idea. It was 2210, which meant that Fireman Baker, one of his snitches in the IC gang, ought to be back in forward Gyro rewinding the movie reels right about now. Baker usually had the night movie detail. He picked up the phone and dialed the IC room.

"Forward gyro, Baker speakin', sir." Jackson could hear the whirring of the rewind machine in the background.

"Baker, this is Chief Jackson."

"Oh, yeah, Chief, what's up?"

"Baker, I need you to patch my phone into the electrical shop's phone so that when it rings, mine rings, and when they make a call, I get me a ding up here."

"Now, Chief?"

"Yeah, now, chief, and Baker? This is official business, which better not leave the IC room. Do we understand each other?"

"Gotcha covered, Chief. You'll be on in two minutes."

"Okay. Patch me out at twenty-three-thirty."

"You got it, Chief."

Jackson hung up. Six months ago, he had caught Baker and another fireman soaping each other up in the shower together after taps. Rather than turn them in for homosexual activity or, worse, tell their division mates, he had turned them into snitches. All of the ship's interior communications, including the admin telephones, went through the IC room's switchboards. Baker the Twinkie had turned out to be extremely useful.

The telephone dinged once and then again. He waited for a few seconds and then carefully lifted the handset. It was one of the electricians, a white man's voice, calling Main Control. He listened in and hung up when the other two did. Ten minutes later, another ding. Another call, same guy, this time to CIC: Something about the new call circuit—the buzzers still weren't working. Lieutenant Commander Austin's voice and the same white voice in the electrical shop. Did it work now? he asked. No, only two of the three stations were getting the buzzer. Could they test it tonight? No, the Old Man had secured. Try again tomorrow. He hung up when they did.

A half hour later, his phone rang. He moved to answer it but then hesitated. The phone gave a half ring before going silent—not his phone; their phone. He picked up as quietly as he could, his hand clamped over the mouthpiece. He heard two black voices this time, a younger one and what sounded like Bullet's voice. Finally. The younger man's voice was overlaid with heavy machinery noise that sounded like one of the main-propulsion spaces.

"Hey, man, what you want me to do with this here brine pump? I got less'n fifty ohms to ground, but the first class, he wants me to leave it runnin'."

"Put a heating blower on it," Bullet said. "Dry it out. Megger it again at the end of your watch. If it's still got grounds, you'll have to take it off-line, bring it back here where we can bake it out. Tell the top watch that. If he has a problem with that, have him call me."

"You got it, man. But I think this sucker's gonna die."

"Then get some heated air to it. Now." Bullet hung up, followed a second later by the engine room electrician. Jackson hung up his phone and settled back in his chair.

Well now, that's what I wanted to know. No Rastus talk there. Straight technical orders from a senior electrician. So we have one face for whitey and another for the brothers, do we? He chuckled. For him, Bullet used the shuck and jive: Shows where I stand, he thought. But a college education, a brain, and an attitude problem that gets him lowered marks but no words in his evaluations. Well now, indeed. He grabbed the phone and dialed the goat locker.

"CPO mess, Chief Hallowell."

"Hey, Hally. Jackson here. Martinez in there?"

Petty Officer Second Class Marcowitz sat in the straight-backed chair in Jackson's office in a cold sweat. The Sheriff had just finished explaining to him what was coming: captain's mast, transfer to the brig in Subic to await court-martial, the court-martial itself, probably up at Clark Air Force Base in Manila, and then shipment back to the States and out to Kansas for a minimum ten-year stint at the Leavenworth Federal Penitentiary.

It was 2100; the ship had begun to settle down for the night. Sounds of the crew's movie on the mess decks could be heard outside in the Broadway passageway. Jackson kept his eyes down on his desk and worked some papers, letting the pressure build. He already knew that the guys in the Fire Control Division were beginning to turn on Marcowitz for sitting on his ass in the compartment while they had to double up on watches. And Jackson, on one of his tours through the berthing compartments, had casually asked Marcowitz if he had seen the chief boatswain. That had been a day ago, and Marcowitz had been looking around every corner when Jackson had brought him to his office a little while ago. Just for the hell of it, Jackson had faked a reply to a phone call from the bridge about eight o'clock reports.

"Yeah, Boats. No. I don't know where he is. He's supposed to stay in his berthing compartment except for meals and head calls. Yeah, I will. Thanks." He had then gone back to his paperwork, still not looking at Marcowitz. Finally, when he figured he had the petty officer's full attention, he looked up at him.

"Well, Marcowitz, I sure hope that was some good dope. Because you're going to pay a serious price for it."

Marcowitz looked around the small office, then swallowed but said nothing.

"Of course, there is a way you can maybe mitigate some of this offense. Although I don't know . . . you were drugged on duty, at the missile-radar consoles, in a war zone, where enemy aircraft have made threats against the ship. Those Air Force flyboys up there at Clark, they're not going to be too sympathetic to that kind of shit, you know?"

Marcowitz nodded, his hands twisting in his lap. Jackson laid it on some more.

"I need to verify your next of kin's address—that's your parents, according to the record."

Marcowitz cleared his throat. "My parents?"

"Yeah, your parents. We have to write them and tell them why you've been transferred off the ship. Give 'em time to find out where Leavenworth Penitentiary is. It's kinda remote, out there on the Great Plains somewhere. Big fuckin' walls, like a goddamn castle, steel gates, and a coupla thousand murderers, rapists, embezzlers, child molesters in the cage."

"Cage?"

"Cage. Prison. Figure of speech, Marcowitz. Slammer talk."

"You're gonna tell my parents?"

"Absolutely. We don't just make guys like you disappear. And this Central High, that was your high school, correct?"

"My high school?"

"Yeah, see, we always report back to a guy's school when he gets discharged. See, most of them keep records on how well their graduates did out here in the world. Unfortunately, we'll have to tell them you're in federal prison for ten, maybe twenty years. They want to know this shit. And, of course, the Navy has to do a press release to the hometown news service. It's all in the regs."

Marcowitz was visibly shaken. "You have to tell—"

"Oh yes. Have to. Full public disclosure. Otherwise, all these Communist war protestors will say we're running a secret police state, imprisoning people without a trial or a hearing, making them just disappear, like that gulag thing over there in Russia. No, we have to keep the whole thing pretty public. It's a shame in one sense, but then, who's gonna give a shit about a guy who does dope at his watch station in a war zone, you know?"

Marcowitz put his face in his hands and bent over in his chair. Jackson waited for him to remember where they'd started. Finally, Marcowitz looked up.

"You said . . . you said there was a way I could mig—mata—"

"Mitigate?"

"Yeah. Mitigate. That means like cut me some slack, right? If I do something?"

Jackson appeared to think for a minute. "Probably not, now that I think about it. I mean, what can you do for me that would possibly count against what you've done to us, to the ship?"

Marcowitz studied the deck again, gnawing his lower lip. Jackson watched him, a twenty-five year-old petty officer second class, an E-5 with eighteen months of advanced electronics training and three years' experience in the fleet. He could have gotten out and named his starting wage with those credentials in half a hundred businesses. But right now, he looked like what he was: a badly scared kid. Finally, Marcowitz looked up.

"I can tell you where I got it."

"Hell, son, I *know* where you got it. You talked to a black guy and he got it for you." Marcowitz blinked.

"You don't want to know who he is?" he said.

"What good's that do me? I can't arrest him on just your say-so."

Marcowitz bit his lip, but then a crafty look came into his eyes.

"But what if I made a buy for you? Something you could watch? Then you could bust him."

"You think this same guy's gonna get within thirty feet of you now? After *you've* been busted?"

292

"Awright. Shit. I guess it doesn't matter," Marcowitz said. "I didn't want to say this, but you guys have my ass in a crack. It isn't just one guy or a coupla guys. It's any of them." Marcowitz stared up at Chief Jackson. "Any of the nonrated black guys. Shit, I figured you had to know this—you're black. You wanta score in this boat, man, you just go see a black dude."

Jackson stared back, trying to control his growing anger.

"And who's the main man?"

Marcowitz snorted. "Shit! How would I know that? But I'll bet you one thing."

"What's that?"

"It ain't no fuckin' white guy, is it?"

26

Brian stood out on the darkened bridge with Jack Folsom, who had the 04-08 OOD watch. It was a warm, humid, moonless night, punctuated occasionally by sudden showers. Brian had borrowed the quartermaster's binoculars and was staring off to the starboard beam, trying to make out the nuclear cruiser *Long Beach* in the gloom. She was only two thousand yards distant, a bare sea mile, but totally darkened and thereby invisible except for a busily winking red signal lamp high up on her boxy superstructure.

"Think this'll work, Mr. Holcomb?" asked Folsom.

"It will if some MiGs come up. We've been letting it slip discreetly over clear radio circuits that *Long Beach* will be relieving us in two more days."

"Is there some reason we're expecting MiGs?"

"In our vicinity, no. But they fly all the time around Hanoi and Haiphong. That's the beauty of this little op—they know *we* can't touch anything beyond forty miles, so they feel safe up-country at eighty miles, as long as that cruiser over there isn't around. They know her Talos birds go a hundred miles."

"But if she lights off her radars, won't that give them time to hit the deck?"

"Well, that's the essence of this caper. She came out of Subic radio-silent, so, in theory anyway, the Soviet ocean-tracking systems don't know where she is. We'll light off *our* missile radars and track the distant MiGs; they won't give a shit because they'll recognize a Terrier radar, and they know we can't reach 'em. But we'll be passing precise tracking data over to *Long Beach* via the NTDS link, and when the MiGs are up at altitude and think they're safe, she'll launch her Talos birds on our data. When they're about eighty percent of the way down their flight path, she'll bring up her own illuminators and, yes, the MiGs will have warning, but by then intercept will be about six seconds away. Those Talos birds are ramjets—they just keep accelerating until they hit something."

"I saw a Talos once—they're huge—forty-two feet long, four feet in *diameter*."

"Yeah. They're designed to fly right through their targets at around three thousand miles an hour."

"So the trick is to make sure the bad guys don't know she's here yet."

"You got it."

Folsom scanned the darkness with his own binoculars. "Who thought this little scam up?"

"Believe it or not, someone down on CTF Seventy-seven's staff. They've apparently even spread deception around Subic and Olongapo."

Folsom nodded in the darkness. "They better; those bar girls know more about ships' movements than the Seventh Fleet schedulers."

"So I've heard. Course, there's not much I haven't heard about Olongapo."

Folsom laughed. "It's all true and then some. You want an experience, get the chief boats to take you on the beach."

Brian thought about that for a minute. "I'm not exactly used to going on liberty with the enlisted," he said.

Folsom chuckled. "Yes, sir, that's all that East Coast Navy training you've had. I hear it's a little more formal back there. But I'm serious. He'll show you the sights, and he's big enough that nothing bad will happen to you, which, for a makee-learn, is something to consider. Trick is to know when the firewater has gotten ahold of the Injun; then you cut out and get back to the main gates. You know about the curfew?"

"No. What curfew?"

"When you go over in Subic, you sorta have to decide what your plans are. The base has a curfew, with time limits set by pay grade. Nonrated enlisted have to be back to the main gates by midnight; lieutenant commanders and above back by oh-one-thirty. Everyone else is somewhere in between. They reopen the gates at oh-seven hundred, so you either have to make your gate or else fall in love and stay out in the town overnight."

"That lets me out; I'm already married."

Jack snorted. "Nobody is married in WESTPAC, Mr. Holcomb."

Brian had no answer for that. He'd heard that rule, too. Cross the international dateline and one's marital status became a very private affair.

"What happens if you show up at the gates, say, at oh-two hundred?" he asked finally, to get off the subject of marriage.

"They let you in and write you up."

"Officers, too?"

"Yes, sir, officers especially. Marines love that shit. They got the XO once, but he talked 'em out of it by pointing out that he had three women chasing his ass back to the gate. They were so impressed, they let him off."

Brian grinned again in the darkness. They both moved back out of the bridgewing's doorway as the rain swept in again. Folsom checked the radar to make sure the big cruiser was staying at around two thousand yards on *Hood*'s starboard beam. Brian pulled his red flashlight out and checked his watch. He needed to get back into Combat.

"Guess I'd better get back in the house," he said. "Everybody's busy packing up for turnover. It's like moving day in there."

"Yes, sir, so I understand. That flashing light has been going nonstop since they showed up. All sorts of 'do you have' spare-parts messages coming in for the Chop."

"Yeah. I'll be glad to get the turnover done with my systems intact, although it's the Count who usually has to give up the most stuff."

"Couldn't happen to a nicer guy."

"Now, now, Mr. First Left Nut. Ensigns can't be critical of light commanders."

"If you say so, sir."

Brian laughed. "The bulkheads have ears, as they say. I'll see you later."

Brian put the binoculars back in the holder by the chart table and went back into CIC. Fox Hudson was the SWIC; he was concentrating on the northwest radar sector, looking for MiGs.

"Any business?" asked Brian.

"No, sir. Although we're a little early yet. If they're gonna fly, they usually do a dawn sweep from the bases up the Red River Valley. We've still got an hour or so. Otherwise, nothing going on. *Long Beach* is remaining in radio, link, and radar silence, and we're not talking to her, either."

Brian nodded and looked around Combat. The cave was manned at half station, while the rest of the radarmen packaged their message files and scope templates into aluminum boxes for the morning transfer to their counterparts in *Long Beach*. There was a general sense of excitement as the first line period drew to a close, with the older hands trying to outdo one another with tales of Subic.

"Sounds like a good bit of bullshit going down around Combat," Brian observed.

"Yes, sir. New guys're getting their ears filled."

"I can imagine. The missile systems set up to do business?"

"Yes, sir. We've got the first team on the consoles down in plot. Soon's we get a contact, we'll start painting them with the track beams, get 'em used to seeing their cockpit alarms."

"But not illuminators, right?"

"No, sir. An illuminator means you've got a missile in flight. They're used to our tracking beams—we track 'em even when they're a hundred miles away, even though they know we can't touch 'em."

"They'd recognize the Talos radars, though, wouldn't they?"

"In a heartbeat. You want to see MiGs falling out of the sky, just let them get a whiff of a Talos radar. That's why this ought to work."

Brian looked over at the weapons module. Both FCSC and EC were manned by chiefs. After the Marcowitz incident Brian had insisted on the first team when the message had come in about the *Long Beach* deception operation. He had gotten the impression that the exec would have ordered it if he had not beaten him to it. He also knew that the passive tracking fire mission with *Long Beach* was going to take some precision coordination if a target presented itself. The cruiser would essentially be firing her Talos missiles at a point in space that *Hood*'s computers predicted would have one or more MiGs flying through by the time the Talos got there. To be fooled, *Hood*'s computers would have to be told some elaborate lies.

"CO and XO both want to be called if we get something going, Mr. Holcomb?"

"Yup. Austin, too. And we have to remember to get the BARCAP out of the way if we decide to try an engagement."

"Ain't no problem, there," said the AIC, who had been listening in. "You start talkin' Talos, I'll salvo them sumbitches outta there in a flash. Ain't no CAP ever argues with a salvo order from a G-ship."

"That's good," said Brian. "We won't have a lot of time to screw around once we get into this little deal."

He walked over into surface to make sure the cruiser was not drifting in on them. With her radars silenced, the big cruiser could not keep station on *Hood* in the darkness, so it was *Hood*'s job to keep the two-thousand-yard distance. The cruiser was still on-station. The surface guys were glad to have something to do; other than for the monthly run down to Yankee Station for replenishment, there had not been another ship within fifty miles of *Hood* for weeks.

At 0520, Fox made the call everyone was waiting for.

"Unknown air, three-three-five for one hundred twenty-five miles! Estimate composition two."

Brian peered down at the scope over Fox's shoulder. Fox had assigned the unknown symbols right away. There appeared to be two MiGs, loitering north and west of Hanoi, where there were several military airfields. The video blips were tiny, but they were definitely there.

"The geometry feasible?" he asked.

"Not yet, but they usually drift down to the capital on their way to altitude. After that, anything under one hundred miles is feasible; we should wait till they climb to altitude, though."

"We need to alert *Long Beach*?"

"No, sir. They're in the link, passive. They already know these guys are up. We should probably creep ahead of her, though, so they don't have to fly those things over top of us."

"Good thinking," Brian said. He gave the orders to surface for relay out to the bridge, then began his calls to the CO, XO, and the Ops officer. By the time they arrived in CIC, the two MiGs had climbed out to nearly thirty thousand feet and a small crowd was gathering in D and D. The MiGs continued to circle lazily, coming closer on each orbit to the data point on the screens marking the North Vietnamese capital city. Brian saw that the AIC was practically gnashing his teeth; with two slow-moving MiGs on his screen, he would have loved to dispatch the BARCAP, even though it was against the rules to go after MiGs near Hanoi. But he could not say anything over the uncovered air-control circuits that might alert any listeners ashore.

Although Brian was technically the evaluator, Austin began acting as evaluator as soon as he had absorbed the tactical picture. Brian found himself being eased to the back of the crowd of khaki bunched around the SWIC console. The captain asked Fox Hudson for an update.

"Two bogeys as candidates for *Long Beach,* Captain. Tracks zero-three-two-three and zero-three-two-four, currently in the system as unknowns. Our intentions are to convert them to hostiles and place them under special track."

The captain leaned closer to study the scope. "We got a shot here?" he asked.

"Yes, sir. They seem to be operating in a pattern that brings them between ninety-one and a hundred and five miles from our position, so this'll be a max-range shoot. *Long Beach* will fire on command guidance when we give the word, and we'll continue to track with the Spooks. At mark intercept minus twenty seconds, we'll key *Long Beach* to bring up her own tracking beams and illuminators, and she'll release the missiles to semiactive homing. After that—"

"After that, it's 'Good Morning, Vietnam,' as that DJ says," the exec finished.

"Yes, sir."

"Okay, inform Alfa Whiskey we're going to start the program, and let's do it," said the captain, climbing into his chair.

"Aye, aye, sir." Fox punched some buttons, converted the two tracks to hostiles, and sent the engage order to weapons control. Brian headed for the weapons module when he heard the order. Out of the corner of his eye, he saw Garuda Barry come into Combat. When something goes down up here, the word sure gets around, he thought. The alerts were buzzing at FCSC by the time he stepped into the module. The FCSC made the assignments and the directors swung around overhead to flash the tracking beams onto the two aircraft orbiting over the North Vietnamese capital.

"SWIC, FCSC, System One tracking." A pause. "System Two tracking."

Brian tried to envision the sequence on the cruiser: The link tracking data from *Hood* would be feeding into their Talos missile fire–control computers. Their own EC would give the load command, and the two-story high launcher on the cruiser's fantail would line up with blast doors, lock the track latches, and then the forty-two-foot-long missiles would slide out onto the launcher rails like a brace of Dobermans on a wire. Then the launcher would train out to the firing bearing over the ship's port quarter and elevate to boost position. Within seconds, internal power warm-ups would begin and the missiles would assign their guidance packages to command guidance.

Brian could see that Austin was talking on the secure UHF circuit to the cruiser. He nodded once and hung up the handset.

"*Long Beach* says they're ready, wants us to give the shoot order the next time the MiGs get out to max range of their orbit and turn inbound," he told the captain. There was a hushed silence in D and D as Fox studied the screen, watching the unsuspecting MiGs.

"Ignorance is bliss," muttered the exec.

"But they know we're tracking them, don't they?" Brian asked from the door to weapons.

"Yeah, but they don't care about us. We track those guys all the time. As far as they're concerned, we're forty-five miles out of range."

"But the eight-hundred-pound gorilla next door isn't," offered Garuda.

"Give him a one-minute standby," said Fox softly. Austin passed it over the secure circuit. Sixty seconds passed, then another fifteen.

"Okay," said Fox. "They're turning. Give him shoot."

Austin pressed the key and simply said, "Shoot." Almost at once came the bellow of a Talos solid-rocket booster from somewhere on the *Hood*'s starboard quarter, a huge noise that transitioned into a sustained thundering roar as the Talos howled out into the dawn sky, followed seconds later by its twin. The sound of the two missiles rattled the bulkheads in CIC for a full minute.

"Probably should have alerted the crew," observed the exec. "Some guys are going to be jumping out of their racks with all that racket."

"What's the time of flight, Count?" asked the captain as the thunder of the boosters died away.

Austin turned around and looked at Brian as if to say, That's a Weapons question.

Brian had worked it out with the FCSC. "About a

hundred and ten seconds, Captain. We should bring them on the air in thirty-five more seconds," Brian answered, looking at the countdown clock on FCSC's console.

The Captain nodded. "Okay," he said. "Your call, Brian."

Brian stared at the clock while he recomputed the math in his head. Eighty-five miles, final velocity of three thousand miles an hour, but some seconds required to accelerate up to that speed. Yeah, about that.

"Mr. Austin, stand by, ten seconds to light-off."

Austin keyed his handset. "*Long Beach,* this is *Hood.* Stand by"—he waited until Brian started to mouth the word *ten*—"ten, niner, eight, seven, six"—a pause to avoid using the word *five,* which in Weapons parlance could be confused with the word *fire*—"four, three, two, energize. I say again, energize."

The intercom panel on the evaluator table squawked into life. "Evaluator, EW, *Long Beach* missile-tracking beam is on the air!"

Brian watched the little A-scope on the side of the EC console as the rest of the officers bunched in around SWIC's console. In theory, the warning lights in the MiG cockpits would already be alight because of *Hood's* tracking beams; hopefully, they would not notice the addition of the Talos tracking beams to the radiation being bounced off their aluminum skins.

"Evaluator, EW, Talos continuous wave illumination is on the air."

"Okay, shut down," ordered Brian. FCSC took the Terrier radars off the two MiGs to avoid creating mutual interference. There was a flurry of conversation in D and D as the altitude readings on the MiGs began to unwind in the SPS-48 readouts.

"Lookit them boogers head for the deck!" exclaimed Garuda. "They know what's comin' or what!"

Suddenly, the altitude readings stopped, at 18,500 feet.

"SWIC, Forty-eight Special Tracker: no video. I say again, I've lost video on track numbers zero-three-two-three and zero-three-two-four!"

There was a chorus of cheers in D and D. For the first time, a transmission from *Long Beach* came over the

301

secure-voice radio speaker, now that radio silence was no longer needed.

"*Hood,* this is *Long Beach.* Mark intercept, mark intercept. Video in the gates. Got the bastards. Two for two."

"*Awright!*" exclaimed Garuda, doing a little victory jig behind the SWIC chair. The captain and exec were grinning broadly, and even Count Austin was smiling.

"*Hood,* this is *Long Beach.* We will be ready for turnover ops at first light. Request first helo to me at oh-seven-thirty."

The Captain nodded and Austin acknowledged. Brian walked back out into the D and D area from weapons, and the captain motioned for him to come over to his chair.

"That was a good piece of work, Weps. Tell your people 'Well done.' Your guys can paint one of those MiGs on a barbette. *Long Beach* was the shooter, but we were the scope."

"Thank you, sir. It was kind of neat."

The captain leaned back in his chair, apparently well satisfied with the outcome of the operation. Brian, standing right next to his chair, felt like he ought to say something. He suddenly thought of Marcowitz. He cleared his throat while glancing quickly around D and D to see whether the exec was nearby. The exec was talking to Austin in the doorway to the surface module.

"Uh, captain, I was wondering what's going to happen to Marcowitz."

"Marcowitz?" The captain turned to look at him, a puzzled expression on his face.

"Yes, sir, FTM Two Marcowitz—the guy I caught in missile plot the other night."

"Well, you've caught me somewhat off base, Brian. The exec hasn't briefed me on anything to do with a Marcowitz. Is there some problem I should know about?"

At that moment, Brian saw the exec turn back into D and D and he almost panicked.

"No, sir," he said hastily. "It's routine. I guess my mind just turned to admin matters now that we're going back into port." The exec walked over to the captain's chair.

The captain smiled. "Well, I'm sure there's lots of admin waiting on the pier for all of us." He looked at his watch. "Breakfast time," he said with a yawn and a stretch. "Then we have to do turnover. XO, this was a pretty good morning's shooting."

The captain and the exec then launched into a conversation about the MiG shoot-down while Brian withdrew to the weapons module. *He didn't know! He didn't know a damn thing about the Marcowitz drug bust!* Brian thought hard. The exec had clearly told him that the captain wanted to hold off prosecuting Marcowitz until they got to Subic. And here was the captain completely in the dark on the whole incident. What the hell was going on?

The captain and the exec left Combat a minute later after voicing another round of congratulations to the watch team. The exec did not appear to have any inkling that Brian had asked about Marcowitz. And what would happen if the captain mentioned the name to the exec? Brian did not want to think about that possibility. He walked over to the SWIC console, feeling more than a little uneasy. Hudson looked over his shoulder at him.

"Got the watch back?" he asked.

"I guess now that all the luminaries are leaving, I've become the evaluator again, huh?"

Fox laughed. "Roger that. But you'll get used to it. Anytime we do some big deal, you'll usually find the Count and the CO and XO gravitating to D and D. It used to really piss off the engineering officer when Austin would come in and just start issuing orders. One day, he announced that Mr. Austin had the watch and walked out."

"What happened?"

"Old Man fanged him." Fox looked over his shoulder to see whether the big three were in hearing distance. "See, there're insiders and then there're *insiders,* if you get my drift. Nothing personal, just the way this command operates."

So I'm finding out, Brian thought. "Okay. So what's left of our watch?"

Fox looked at his watch. "We ought to have the Wager

Bird checking in pretty soon; I saw a track coming in from the east before we went MiG hunting. Rest of the Heavenly Host will be along shortly. But the big deal for us today is turnover; we'll start handing over our participating unit symbol in the link right away, then transfer Big Mother, the BARCAP control, the TACAN channel, and finally the call sign. When they start answering up as Red Crown on all the nets, we're gone."

"I'm ready. I think I'll sleep through Subic."

"Bet you don't, sir."

27

With turnover day finally over, Brian Holcomb was relaxing on the bridgewing, shooting the breeze with Jack Folsom, when Chief Jackson found him. The Sheriff hung back, staying on the catwalk that led aft from the bridgewing. He appeared to be enjoying the afterglow of the sunset, but he was obviously waiting to talk to Holcomb. A fine breeze streamed over the bull rail as the ship plowed through the South China Sea on her way to the Philippines, some six hundred miles to the east. Folsom finally noticed the chief master-at-arms.

"Sheriff," he called. "Ready for Subic?"

"Not hardly, Mr. Folsom," said Jackson, moving over to join them on the bridgewing. "Liberty nights in Subic are great for the troops but hell on the Sheriff. You figure: two hundred, three hundred guys discovering each night they like beer all over again."

Folsom laughed. "Sailors belong on ships, and ships belong at sea, right, Chief?"

"Absolutely right, sir."

Folsom rolled his eyes. The boatswain's mate of the watch called Folsom into the pilothouse, leaving Holcomb and Jackson alone. Jackson debriefed Holcomb about the information he had extracted from Marcowitz. Brian was silent for a minute, considering the implications.

"If what he says is true," Jackson continued, "this makes the third witness that has said that the drug ring here is a black operation."

"With a black guy running it."

Jackson was silent for a moment. "I'm embarrassed to say it, but that's what it looks like, yes, sir."

A large figure appeared along the port-side catwalk as Chief Martinez loomed up out of the darkness. He paused when he saw that Jackson and Brian were talking, but Brian waved him over. In the near darkness, the chief's face was a large round shadow. He had a long cigar in his left hand and his coffee mug in the other. His hat sat on the back of his massive head like a doll's cap.

"Boats here know what you just told me?" Brian asked.

Jackson said no, then recounted his session with Marcowitz while the boatswain listened intently. At the end, Martinez shook his head.

"Dead end," he pronounced. Jackson noted that Brian was nodding his head, agreeing with the boatswain.

"Why so?" Jackson asked Brian. Brian looked around the bridgewing area and into the pilothouse before replying. It was nearly full dark. The port running light cast a red penumbra into the mist blowing along the ship's sides.

"Because there's no way we could make an accusation like that without touching off a larger race problem."

"Not if *I* made the accusation," said Jackson defensively.

Brian shook his head. "You say Marcowitz is saying any black guy. That's ridiculous. Any black guy would have to include you, the chiefs, half a dozen E-Sixes, and the Supply officer. You and I both know that every black man aboard this ship is not in the drug business. The real druggies are probably trying to make their customers think so, because that's one way to make it look like there's a pretty big mob out there should a guy, especially a white guy, think about turning snitch. Uh-uh, I don't see anything that you can do with this for now."

"Maybe, maybe not," Jackson mused. "I pulled EM One Wilson's service record the other night. There were some surprises in it. Like he'd been an MAA at one time. And has a college degree."

"Why's that make him a suspect?" Brian asked.

"Because he comes across like some illiterate dummy when he's talking to anyone senior to him. He's sand-bagging."

"You figure Bullet could be the kingpin?" asked Martinez.

"I don't know," said Jackson with a sigh. "There's nothing firm in any of this—just a bunch of scared fish running their mouths. There's gotta be another way in." Jackson sighed again. Holcomb was right. He should have seen it himself. Maybe he was getting too close to this thing. "There's gotta be another way in," he repeated.

"This drug shit," rumbled Martinez. "For the kids, it's cops and robbers, getting high, givin' the finger to the Navy regs. For the dealers, it's money. Find a guy with lots of money, more money than he oughta have, and lean on him. Maybe get lucky."

"I haven't seen anybody on board wearing banker's clothes," Brian said.

"You say banker?" asked Jackson, looking at Martinez.

"Shit, yeah, the banker," Martinez said. "The loan shark."

"Garlic," Jackson and Martinez said together.

"You guys just lost me," Brian said.

"Garlic, the mess decks MAA. Big fat guy. The head cook. He's the ship's loan shark. You know, we get to Subic, a guy runs out of liberty money, he goes to see the loan shark. Garlic loans him five for six: Every five bucks you borrow, you pay back six on the next payday. You borrow two hundred bucks, you owe two forty next payday. Ship's gonna go back out on the line for six weeks, that's three paydays. Plenty of time to pay it back, specially when you ain't got nowhere else to spend it when we're on the line."

"And Garlic has cash. Always has lots of cash," said Jackson.

"At those rates, he ought to have cash," muttered Brian. "I thought this sort of thing was illegal."

"It is," Jackson said. "But most ships let it go on as long as the chiefs keep an eye on it, make sure there's no enforcers getting loose. Somebody's always going to go into business, so the theory is better to know who it is and what he's doing than to have it out of control."

Brian thought of Martinez when Jackson mentioned enforcers; what else was the boatswain but an enforcer for the XO? But what was the connection between the loan shark and the drug business?

"So what we have to do is to tie Bullet to Garlic," Jackson was saying. "If we can show that drug money is somehow tied to Garlic's bank, we might be able to break the whole thing up—if it is."

"Yeah," agreed Martinez. "Take their money, they can't buy no resupply. You could really put the hurt on 'em."

"How would you do it?" asked Brian.

"I get one of my snitches to make a buy with marked money, say a bunch of twenties," Jackson said. "Then I wait a couple of weeks and get Garlic's owe-me list. Like I said, he operates with the chiefs' permission, so to speak. I call his fish in, see if I can find any of the marked bills. I also check with the ship's store operator, see if any of those twenties are back in circulation. If they are, it means the drug guy is investing instead of just stashing."

"How's that get you to the kingpin?"

"Only the main man is going to have enough money to invest it with Garlic's bank. The boats here and I lean on Garlic."

"I've seen Garlic. That would take some leaning."

"I'll lock him up in an off-line boiler. Fat guy like that, he'll talk to me," said Martinez. Brian shuddered at the thought.

"But first we have to get some marked money out. I'm going to have to wait until after we get back out on the line again, because otherwise, it'll just go ashore," Jackson said.

"Shit, that's going to take a while," Brian said.

"It's the only lead we have right now, unless the Marcowitz case comes up with something once we get in. In the meantime, I'm going to put the eye on Bullet Wilson.''

28

San Diego

Maddy turned on the evening news and looked at her sunburned arms in disgust. *This is going to peel tonight and I'm going to look like a damn leper at work tomorrow.* She had spent Saturday with the wives at the North Island Naval Air Station's Navy beach, where Mrs. Huntington had reserved a family cabana for the afternoon and evening. There had been enough children flitting around the beach that all of the women had to assume Mom duty, taking turns overseeing playtime and then generally interfering with one another to cook hamburgers and hot dogs over a charcoal fire that had taken forever to get going.

Tizzy Hudson had even shown up, which was something of a rarity. She had not joined in the surrogate motherhood activities, choosing instead to spread out a large beach towel and soak up some rays. Maddy had enjoyed watching how the male traffic patterns on the beach changed when Tizzy arrayed herself in a careless sprawl, her gold bikini glinting in the afternoon sun. She had wandered over.

"What's that thing made of, Reynolds Wrap?"

Tizzy had grinned beneath her opaque sunglasses. "If I get it wet, it's even more interesting."

"Well, I swear, Tizzy. One would think you're fishing instead of sunbathing."

"Well hell, Maddy, it *is* the beach. I sure as hell don't come down here to swim in this frigid water. How you and Mr. Autrey doing, dear?"

Maddy had looked around quickly to make sure none of the other wives could overhear. She plopped down beside Tizzy; in her Bermuda shorts and knotted jean blouse, she felt like a frump next to long, tall Sally there.

"*If* you can keep that delirious mouth of yours shut, I'll tell you. And the answer is, we are not doing anything. He asked me to go to dinner with him, and I . . . well, I felt I owed him that courtesy, given what he did for me."

"And what exactly does he do for you, Maddy?"

"Did. The operative word is *did*. He's a pretty exotic guy, actually—teaches Marine officers how to take care of themselves when they go behind enemy lines, or so he says. But I went to dinner, and that's that, okay?"

Tizzy had flopped over on her tummy and slowly adjusted the bottom of her bikini, causing two officers walking along the beach to collide.

"If you say so, Maddy," she said. "But you sure are sensitive about all this. I mean, if all you did was go to dinner with this guy, what's the big deal? He didn't ask you out again, did he?"

"Nope. And if he should, I'm not available. Hell, Tizzy, think of the trouble I'd be in if anyone found out—"

"Found out what, for crying out loud? Just for grins, you went to MCRD—with me, I might add, although that might not be held in your favor by this bunch—you got in a little jam, this guy bailed you out, you went out to dinner with him to say thanks. So what? Fox would just laugh."

"Brian would not laugh," Maddy had replied. "Definitely not."

Tizzy propped herself up on one arm. "The presumption being that you've done something wrong?"

"Well, not if he thought it through. But I think it's more a question of bad form—he's stuck out there on that ship and his wife is going out with an unmarried man to the Grant Grill?"

"Oooh, the Grant Grill. I like this guy's style. Next time he calls, you tell him you're married and serious about it, then give him my number."

Maddy had laughed. "And how do I describe you, Tizzy? Married and not serious about it?"

Tizzy had pulled her sunglasses down on her nose to look at Maddy. "Why not, dearie—you don't want him, do you?"

Maddy had spent Sunday morning running household errands and recovering from sunburn, having been deceived once again by the cool beach breezes and the gentle San Diego sunlight into thinking that there was not much sun out. The tanning lotion had not done much to keep the red away and now she smelled like mothballs after lathering on a few pounds of a white sunburn cream.

After an entire day with her 'Navy family,' as Mrs. Huntington was fond of calling them, she felt like she had done her duty for the week. And Saturday *had* been a good day, although everyone there recognized it for what it was—a diversion, a way to have a day out of the house, in company with other women who were all in the same spouseless boat. It was hard to be lonely and depressed when chasing a bunch of kids around the surf, even if none of them was hers. Her mind veered away from the subject of children. In her heart, she really wanted to start a family with Brian, but she could not bring herself to do it when Daddy was going to be away at sea for months on end. She sometimes wondered if that was an excuse, a way to cover up the real reason—her old phobia. Her father had left her; *their* father was not going to leave them, by God.

Amidst the busywork, Maddy had just about managed to squeeze Autrey back into his box. She had mentally arrayed layers of excuses between what she had felt—she had to admit it, what her body had felt—and what she knew to be her true feelings about Brian. And her marriage. But that was the problem, wasn't it? When Brian was gone for seven months, she didn't have a marriage. Okay, so you focus on Brian, on your feelings for him, on your love for him and his for you. There, that's straight, she thought. Her brain had no problem making the distinction, but she was having more trouble than she had anticipated keeping another facet of her personality in its box. Damn the man: The fact was, he could make Brian disappear by just standing there. And damn Tizzy Hudson. She acted as if she and Autrey were in this together just to get Maddy Holcomb into trouble.

The phone rang. She got up to turn down the television and then went to the phone and picked it up.

"Hello?"

"Maddy Holcomb."

She gripped the phone, pressing it tightly to her ear, and tried to think of what to say.

"Got back tonight," he was saying, his tone of voice easy, as if they had been having this conversation for an hour. "I've been up at Warner Springs—in the mountains east of San Diego, where the Navy runs the POW training camp. Man, you should see it. They have an honest to God prison camp: barbed wire, vicious-looking dogs, towers, searchlights, big ugly guards, even these scary interrogation rooms, the whole bit. Any officer going in-country to Nam and all the aviators have to go through this course; they call it SERE: survival, escape, evasion, and resistance. They turn a class of about forty officers loose in a two-hundred-acre high desert area and then hunt them down with dogs and helos and round them up. Then they get to experience what a prison camp is like. Damn fine training. And you are trying to decide what to say to me, right?"

She hesitated, swallowed. "Yes."

"Well, that's a good start. All the Gods smile on a woman who says yes. You don't have to say anything else, because *yes* is the right answer. Wednesday night, there's a dynamite folksinging group going to be playing at Parker's Place, up on College Avenue, in the university district. They're called The Three of Us; they do Peter, Paul, and Mary stuff. They're from Long Beach, and they're outta sight. I'll be there from about nine-thirty. I'll have a table right up front, because I've bribed the manager. Actually, he owed me a big favor and I've called it. Please come, Maddy Holcomb. Wednesday night. Nine-thirty. Dress casual. Parker's Place. See you. Please."

She closed her eyes, lowering the phone to hold it in both hands but not hanging up. Now. Do it. Tell him thank you, but you can't. Give him Tizzy's number. Anything. But this is over. Good night. Good-bye. Then hang up. It's easy. Just do it.

But she didn't. Okay, don't tell him. Just hang up the phone. But she didn't.

311

Neither did he for a moment, but then, before she was ready, just as she was remembering to breathe, she heard the phone click and then the dial tone. She sighed and put the phone down. She hadn't said yes. You hadn't exactly said no, either. But I don't have to go. I can just—I can just stay home, or I can go over to Tizzy's, or I can—. Or you can go to Parker's Place and listen to some folk music. Damn this man. Mr. Cool himself. Every time, he makes the decision mine.

A jazz bar. She had done that scene in Boston many times, usually with some guy she was toying with, tantalizing a little bit. The music . . . well, the music wasn't the point, was it? The music, the bar, the drinks, that was the playing field, and she had always been in charge. Her rules, her game. But Autrey: . . . well, Autrey was acting as if it was his rules, his game. She felt the old familiar challenge. And what the hell, this isn't for score: He's not going to do anything—that's the beauty of it. He doesn't paw, he's not a covert toucher, not one of those clowns who get too close and breathe in your ear. You go in your own car, come home in your own car. Just like last time.

Except the last time—well, that's the damn problem. Yeah, but last time it was all the booze—champagne, red wine, liqueurs. That was the mistake. You can go this time and stick to Coca-Cola, or maybe have one beer. Yuk. Hate beer. Okay, but don't drink. Don't let that other part get out of control. Play it cool, listen to the music, and then go home. Recapture the game and the rules. Just another diversion, no different from going to the beach with the wives: one more day down.

She sat down on the couch and gnawed her lower lip. That last bit was, of course, a bunch of BS. It was not at all like going to the beach with the rest of the WESTPAC widows. How did Brian put it, about the old Navy headquarters rule: the *Washington Post* test? If you would not want to read about it in the *Washington Post*, then don't do it. If she wasn't ready to tell Mrs. Huntington that she was going up to a bar in the university district with a single man, for the second time, to listen to some folk music, then she ought not to do it. Tell Mrs. Huntington? How about telling Brian?

Fine. I just won't do it. I didn't say I would. End of problem. See? That was easy.

On Tuesday, she had received mail from Brian. She had been delighted, almost relieved, to find the letter, until she read it. It was a say-nothing letter, just more about what they were doing, PIRAZ jargon, the weather, the Weapons Department. No more dirt about the drug incident or news on the prospects for his fitness report or how he was getting along with the captain and the exec and the other department heads. He closed with his usual "I love you and miss you." Except for the closing, it was about as personal as a Navy newsletter. She sighed and put it down on the table with the bills. It was good to get mail, but she wished—oh well. During the *Decatur* deployment, he had occasionally written soulful letters, late-at-night letters—okay, love letters. These she had opened when the mail came, read a few lines, recognized them for what they were, and closed them back up at once, to be savored, again and again, just before she went to sleep. She sighed again.

As she had flipped through the rest of the mail—the bills, a promotional flier from the Exchange, notice of a rate increase from San Diego Gas & Electric—she had to admit that her letters to him had not been much different. Her job, activities with the wives, progress with her backhand, a late-arriving allotment check, a mysterious noise in the car, all the mundane events of her life that she seized upon and even magnified to make the days go by. He'd been gone for over two months and she hadn't written any love letters, either. Why was that? she wondered.

Brian's letter said he had little time to do anything but stand his watches and sleep, that he was port and starboard with Austin. Maddy did not know what that meant, and, not up to another verbal sparring match with Tizzy, especially after Autrey's latest call, she phoned Angela Benedetti, a fellow department head's wife. Angela was an abrupt, sensible woman from a large Italian family in New Jersey; she managed a family of four kids with an iron hand. She had been married to Vince Benedetti since he was a fresh-caught ensign right out of Officer

Candidate School. She was normally bright and cheery on the phone, but tonight she seemed to be down. She told Maddy that she had received almost no mail from Vince, which usually meant he was struggling, if not over his head, in his current assignment.

"Vinnie's a trooper, you know? He slugs away at it, whatever they hand him, and he usually gets it done. But he can't handle problems when the command won't admit they're there, like all the druggies he's got down in the holes."

"Brian mentioned in one of his letters that drugs were involved in whatever went wrong with the shooting mission, but he hasn't said any more about it."

"Yeah, see? There's something funny going on in the *Hood* on the drug scene. I think Vinnie knows but feels he's gotta go along with it, and he doesn't like it, you know what I mean? He gets like that, I don't get any mail. So, enough already. How you doin'?"

"Depressed, lonely, horny. Feeling sorry for myself."

"Yeah, right, the usual." Angela laughed.

"But I had a question: What's port and starboard mean? Brian says he's port and starboard with Austin."

"Means Brian is standing watch six hours on, six hours off, alternating with Mr. High and Mighty. That's kind of a bitch, although I've gotta say, the enlisted engineers do it all the time. Practically speaking, it means the guys stand their watches, grab some chow, hit their racks, and get up again in five hours to do it all again, day in, day out. It's okay for the enlisted; that's all they have to do anyway when the ship's out at sea. Really makes the time go by. But for the officers, with all that paperwork and the personnel stuff on top of their watch duties, port and starboard gets old quick. Especially if he's stuck with the mids, which I suspect Prince Austin or whatever they call that jerk has sluffed off onto Brian. Hey, that also might explain why I'm not seeing much mail. It probably means Vinnie's off the CIC watch bill so's he can keep an eye on all those potheads he has running around in the boiler rooms. And knowing Vinnie, he feels bad about putting the other two guys in port and starboard, and so he's spending twenty-six hours a day in the main spaces. I guess I'm glad you called me."

"You are?"

"Yeah. See, I don't get letters, I never know whether he's just not writing, or the Navy's losing them, or I've done or said something wrong and he's mad at me, or what. But from what you've said, now I think I know the score."

"Couldn't you just ask?"

"No way, Maddy. See, you ask a question like that, it's automatically a criticism. Think about it. How do you phrase it: Why aren't you writing me? Have you been writing me? Are my letters getting through? Yours aren't, and I've sent three a week since you've left. And then you wait five, six weeks for an answer. It's almost like asking someone if they've stopped beating their wife. There's just no good answer to questions about mail on a WESTPAC deployment. You can bitch to the other wives, but you can't ask."

"Wow. I write Brian about once a week and I get a letter back about once a week, although, of course, there's all that dead time. For me, it's sort of a monologue. I tell him stuff, he tells me stuff, but we don't actually connect much."

"You connect by dropping it in the mailbox."

"I suppose. But I'm wondering now if I'm sending enough letters. One a week—is that enough?"

"Probably not. You gotta figure they'll lose every fourth or fifth letter. All it takes, one mailbag blows off the carrier's deck and a whole week's worth of letters is gone. That's a disaster. Vinnie's told me a million times, it's not the news; it's the piece of paper, the contact. Getting mail when everyone else gets mail and not being the only guy who *didn't* get mail. So I do three a week and hope for the best. Keep the bad news out and don't bitch and moan too much—they can't do anything about your problems; you can't do anything about theirs. And even knowing about them is pretty frustrating. You got problems—and who doesn't?—you cope, that's all. You handle it."

"No matter what it is?"

"Yeah. Like I said, they can't do anything for you, three weeks later and from a gazillion miles away. I tell

Vinnie about the successes and let the failures sort of age. You'd be amazed how many crises can dry up and blow away six months later when they get back. Hell, he knows he's not seeing the whole picture, but then, I don't think he really wants to. It's not like he doesn't have problems of his own, like all those bozos in his department. This your first deployment?''

''Well, not actually, although my first one was only three months long, when Brian was in the Med. But he could call—Europe, you know, they have phones. And it wasn't wartime.''

''Yeah, well, you want to keep track of when they go back to Subic, then. They can make a phone call back to the States from the base, although there're only ten phones for all those ships. But if you're stepping out, make sure you're home for that week or so they're in port.''

Maddy felt a sudden constriction in her throat. ''Stepping out?'' she said weakly.

''Hey, figure of speech. I was just kidding. You just don't want to miss the one and only phone call you'll get during the cruise, unless they get to Hong Kong. Soon's he tells you when they'll be in port—and it should be coming up pretty soon, a coupla weeks, I'd guess, then give him some dates to shoot for. And remember, they're a day ahead, so they'll call at two or so in the morning here. It's expensive, but it's nice to hear their voices, you know?''

''Yes, I'm ready for that. Thanks, Angela. I'm glad I called you.''

''Call anytime, Maddy. It's good to keep in touch. The problems don't get so big that way.''

Poor woman, she had thought as she hung up. No mail. She would definitely follow up Angela's suggestion about the number of letters. They lose one out of four? How would you ever know which one got lost, with six weeks of turnaround time? She would write him tonight, right after she had dinner. And tell him what—you've got a hot date for tomorrow night? She groaned and shook her head again, then went to change for tennis.

By midday on Wednesday, she was a nervous wreck.

Her supervisor in the accounting department had shaken her head when she had seen Maddy's morning balance sheets, kindly suggesting that she might want to use a machine the next time. Maddy had used a machine, but her mind was only partially present for duty in the Bank of America. The other part, the worried part, was on Parker's Place. She had stolen a few minutes to look up the address and then a few more to scan a map of San Diego they kept tacked to the back of a door in the bookkeeping offices. From the Balboa Park area, it was easy—down Route 163 to Highway 80, east for six miles, and then off on the College Boulevard exit to College Avenue. She had actually looked around the office to see whether anyone was watching her consult the map.

She stacked the morning's balance sheets on her desk, carefully arranging the edges, her mind drawing bright square lines around the next eight hours. Nine-thirty. Maybe she should call Mrs. Huntington, go over there tonight, tell her she needed company. Mrs. Huntington had often said that any of them could call anytime if they needed to. I need to do something, she thought. You need to see him again. You want to see him again. Damn him! He's playing head games with me. Used to be your game, Missy. What she could not decide was whether she wanted to see him because he was that attractive or if she just wanted to win this little game once and for all. And just how, pray tell, will you know you've won? How does one declare victory with an Autrey, Just Autrey?

She squirmed in her chair, her fingers unconsciously tapping the edges of the balance sheets into an ever-neater stack, all the edges just so, straight, sharp, solid, longways there—damn it! She felt a wave of giddiness, as if her mind were perched on the edge of a cliff, watching the struggle below between her fireside and her heartside, and right now her heartside was scrambling to find safety in a cave somewhere. What is it about this man? Okay, he's physically attractive, but so are a lot of men. He has an aura of danger about him, partly because of what he does, what he says he does, and partly because of how other men react to him. That's exciting. He's in control of himself when he's focused on me, which suggests that he might be a very good lover. So it's sex. I'm just horny, and this guy might be a white-hot wire when it comes to the bedroom. He's nice, diffident, occasionally awkward, self-effacing, and, underneath all that, focused on me. He wants me. I'm sure of it. And I want him. There. Okay, so now we know what this is all about. It's got nothing to do with Brian or the fact that I'm married and everything to do with the fact that I'm alone and here's this powerful man who put one fingernail on my belly and lit up half the San Diego skyline.

She leaned back in her chair, her eyes closed, a fine sheen of perspiration on her upper lip. What the hell is wrong with me? I'm Mrs. Brian Holcomb, church-married, ring on my finger, vows taken with no one objecting at the wedding. My husband is overseas, serving his country, even if great parts of it spit on what he does every night on the evening news. He's doing the honorable thing. Why can't I? I love the man. I like the man. He's fun and he's caring and he's loving and he's strong when he loves me. What's this other half, this devil half that's driving me to go to the flame like a moth, wings spread, legs trembling, around and around, back to this man, this Autrey, just because he asks nicely and can light my fires with one look. Is this what I did in college? I know it is. But those poor bastards were fair game. Maybe that's the fascination with Autrey. Maybe *I'm* the game this time.

"Mrs. Holcomb? Maddy? Are you all right? Do you need to go home, dear?"

She had given her supervisor a quick smile and nodded emphatically. Yes, that's exactly what she needed. Practically bolting from the office, she fought it all the way home, thinking up alternative plans: go see a movie, go to the library, go for a drive. But in her belly, she knew. She was going to go home, wash her hair, pick out something provocative to wear, take her time with the war paint, and then go out there tonight to see what this was all about.

At ten o'clock, she found a parking place just off the main drag, parked and locked the car, and sat there for a minute. The university district was so named because of

San Diego State. The university sat up on the edge of a mesa overlooking the valley through which interstate Highway 80 ascended the foothills east of San Diego and headed for Yuma, Arizona. College Avenue contained the usual college town collection of bars, cheap restaurants, bookstores, laundromats, grocery stores, and dry cleaners.

The sidewalks along the street were crowded with young people of every description, costume, and length of hair. Maddy smiled at their ardent efforts to be non-conformists, with most of the boys wearing exactly the same thing: faded jeans, loose shirts, sandals or shabby sneakers, headbands, granny glasses, and various kinds of Indian jewelry, as if there was a de rigueur, up-yours dress code for college students in honor of the Age of Aquarius. Many of the young women looked almost as if they were trying to be unattractive, with lots of Mother Hubbard dresses, baggy shirts, flopping, braless fronts, deliberately unkempt or frizzy hairdos, no makeup, and what looked like downright dirty clothes. From the shadows in the darkened car, Maddy shook her head, brought up as she had been to accentuate whatever attributes the Good Lord had provided.

Attributes. Yes, well, and weren't we dressed for trouble this evening. She wore a tight-fitting cream-colored skirt that came to just above her knees when she was standing, shiny white stockings, medium heels, and a peach-colored short-sleeved knit sweater over a push-up bra that very definitely accentuated the assets. She had fixed her luxurious hair to obscure partially the left edge of her face, then topped it off with a black velvet beret. She glanced over her shoulder. The sign for Parker's Place was about ten doors back up the street. She waited until the crowd on the sidewalk had thinned out a bit before getting out, locking the door, and heading for the club.

She had to keep her eyes lowered as she walked toward the club in order not to laugh out loud at the boys, who tried to stay in character as dedicated hippies while trying not to trip over themselves looking at her. Maddy knew she presented something of a college boy's dream as she walked as fast as the heels would allow to Parker's Place, wreaking havoc among the boys while drawing disdainful stares from all the Mother Hubbards, even the occasionally good-looking ones.

Parker's Place was long and narrow, decorated in a western motif. There was a crowded anteroom up front where a girl dressed up as an Indian princess, right down to braids and buckskins, was trying to sort out tables and reservations. Behind her podium was the entrance to the actual bar area, through which could be seen a long room of closely spaced tables, a sit-down bar along one wall and a tiny stage at the very back, where the group was setting up for the first set. Maddy caught the attention of the first man at the back of the crowd by pressing her front into his back and, when he turned, easing her way through the crowd, murmuring soft "excuse me's" in her best Atlanta drawl as the men drew back to stare while they let her through, their dates rolling their eyes. Once in front of the podium, Maddy waited to get the hostess's attention, then asked for the manager.

"Is there a problem?" The hostess frowned.

"Not at all, but I think he's holding a table for a friend."

The manager solved the problem by appearing from the smoky haze of the bar, taking one look at Maddy, and beckoning her to come around the podium. The manager was a beefy young man with very short hair and a *Semper Fi* tattoo on his right biceps.

"Maddy?" he asked as she stepped around the podium.

"Yes."

"Damnation. I just lost twenty bucks. Bet Autrey that you wouldn't show. After he described you, I thought he was connin' me just to get a good table. C'mon. He's up front, like he promised."

Maddy lowered her lashes, smiled, and followed the manager as they wound their way through the packed tables, creating something of a ripple movement of turning heads and a moving dip in the noise level as she went by. She gazed straight ahead and wondered why people were bothering to wait up front—all the tables were taken. And then she saw Autrey. He was standing there, practically in front of the stage, with a big grin on his face. He was wearing a flowing white long-sleeved silk shirt that draped from his wide shoulders and was open at the throat. The shirt was straight out of a Three Musketeers movie; she almost checked to see whether he was wearing a sword and sash. But instead, he was wearing tight, well-worn jeans, brown loafers, and a belt buckle with some kind of turquoise design worked into a matrix of silver.

He continued to smile as she came to the table. He palmed the twenty from the manager without taking his eyes off Maddy. She smiled demurely and sat down. Autrey jabbed the manager on the shoulder; the manager shook his head and tipped him a one-finger, edge-of-the-eye salute before heading back to the bar area.

The singing group consisted of two men and one very good-looking young woman. There appeared to be more instruments than people, and the whole arrangement was barely able to fit on the stage. The singer was ready, but the other two musicians were making small noises, tuning amps and adjusting dials. The singer smiled and nodded at Maddy, who smiled back. Autrey was speaking.

"Nice *hat*," he said, emphasizing the word *hat,* as if the rest of the package was just okay.

She laughed out loud as a waitress arrived with two glasses of white wine. She looked at the two glasses.

"Pretty sure of me, Mr. Catches Crow?"

"It's Autrey, just Autrey. And these represent high hopes more than anything else."

"And the twenty-dollar bet—what did that represent?"

"Revenge. Buddy said there was no way I could get a woman who looked as beautiful as I described you as to meet me anywhere this side of heaven."

Then it was his turn to laugh as she groped for a way around the compliment. Buddy appeared at the microphone at that moment and announced The Three of Us to enthusiastic applause. The group went right into their first song, and Maddy relaxed as she recognized that they were not only good but very good, the singer comfortable in her range and the musicians adept at making several black boxes sound like a seven-member rock group. Maddy concentrated on watching the singer, taking care not to look directly at Autrey while moving around in her chair just enough to let Mr. Smart Ass there get a good look—at the hat.

As she sipped her wine and absorbed the songs, she tried to think about what they would talk about when the first set ended. She knew that she had lost control the last time she was with him, and that was not the way she liked to conduct relationships with men. That would have never happened when she was in college, unless she wanted it to. So what's the game this time? Tantalize and then go home? Show him who's in charge? What's the point? He's an attractive man; this is the second time you've gone out with him. All the other times you've indulged in cock teasing, there was an objective, something you wanted well over and above sex. So what is it you want from Just Autrey? She conjured up the mélange of images she had of him, standing by the table, his long, lean body, the tight jeans, his fingernail edging across her stomach, the studied way he had of moving, the implied power, grace, and control. As a song hit a quiet spot, he was saying something.

"What?" she whispered.

"I've got something to tell you," he replied, leaning forward, making her look at him. "I guess I'm going to get my chance to go see what it's really like."

"What what's really like?"

"What I've been teaching these guys. I'm going over to Nam."

She sat upright, barely restraining a loud 'No!' He saw it in her eyes and nodded. "They figure I ought to see it firsthand, make me a better instructor, give me more credibility with the new guys and the other instructors."

"But you're a civilian." Because the music was still going, they spoke softly. She was having to lean toward him, faces nearly touching, her breasts on the table a few inches from his hand.

"Yeah. But there are other civilians over there, from different government, uh, agencies, if you know what I mean. They dress you up in jungle gear; everybody looks the same."

"When?" Suddenly it was important. She felt his knee just barely touching hers under the table.

"Two, three weeks. Scheduling's not their strong point. They just told me to get myself ready, shots, passport, and they'd let me know."

The first set ended and they sat back in their chairs. Maddy was suddenly very thirsty; she finished her wine. He signaled the waitress to bring another round, but she changed hers to ginger ale, remembering her plan. After the applause, the level of noise in the room had risen precipitously, so she had to lean closer to him again to hear what he was saying. If he was wearing any cologne, she could not detect it.

"It's actually a pretty good deal," he was saying. "This thing can't go on forever, and I don't know what I'll be doing after Nixon shuts it down. But if I have some actual in-country experience, it will help me keep a job with the military after the war is over."

"How long will you be over there?"

"Nobody can say right now. Probably until I say, I guess. Being a civilian, I can probably wrap it up when I want to."

She ran her finger through the ice cubes in her ginger ale, thinking about Brian, who was stuck on the deployment for seven months. Why was he telling her this? I'm shipping out, baby, so how's about let's get this thing going, a last fling at love before I face the hostile shores?

"I'm very glad you came tonight," he said, staring down at his own drink. "I really did want to see you again."

"Why?" she said, looking up.

He looked at her for a long moment. "These are interesting times. Everybody says you do your own thing, let it all hang out—you know the words. So the answer to your question is, Because you are a very beautiful woman and I'm very much attracted to you."

Well, that was pretty straightforward. She felt all her aspirations to control fraying around the edges a bit. Suddenly, she wanted to tell him, had to tell him. She wanted the truth out on the table, almost as if it would protect her from herself.

"Look," she said. "You're a very attractive man, and I'm . . . I'm at somewhat of a disadvantage here. I'm married." She looked sideways at him, to see if this was news. "Perhaps you knew that."

"Yes, I think I knew that," he said. He steepled his fingers in front of his face, obscuring all but his eyes.

She looked back down at the table, her hands flat in front of her, uncertain of how to proceed. "My being at MCRD was an accident, a sudden whim of a friend whom I went along with. It was a dumb idea. I should never have done that, but I was curious, and bored, and depressed at the thought of my husband's being gone on a ship for seven months. And going to dinner with you . . . well, I thought I owed you something for saving me from . . . well, you know."

He nodded deliberately. "And tonight?" he asked.

"Tonight. Tonight because I wanted to see you again." She lofted his words back to him. "Because you are a very attractive man and I'm attracted to you, too. But, in my heart, in my head, I just can't. I mean—"

"I understand, Maddy Holcomb. And if that's how you feel, that's okay." He touched the back of her right hand with his left; his fingers were warm. "Look," he said. "We've become aware of each other, as a man and a woman. You must know I want you. But put your mind at ease, because I will settle for your company." He withdrew his hand.

She nodded once, felt relieved, and then, perversely, let down. She felt like saying, You give up pretty easy, Just Autrey. He was watching her face, trying to read her thoughts. Afraid that he might see her reaction, she hid her eyes behind her hair and began to stir the ice cubes again.

"You think I have been trying to seduce you, don't you?" he said after a few minutes.

She shook her head but did not answer.

"Even if I knew how, I wouldn't do that. See, I know a secret."

"What secret is that?"

"Men don't seduce women, not beautiful women with brains, women who are aware of themselves. If women

324

are seduced at all—and I often wonder about that—they seduce themselves. The woman chooses. The best we men can do is to put ourselves in the way of love and hope that we get lucky. You tell me that you cannot bring our acquaintance to love. I accept that. You have either chosen not to or you have not made up your mind, but either way, I accept it, because that's how it works. If I try to force something, the result is probably going to be ugly and barren. If you choose, it is passion and love."

She did not know what to say. You wanted to be in charge, in control. Well, there it is, she thought. He's telling you that it's up to you. Just like you wanted, right? Then he was smiling.

"And besides," he said, "there are some things that are exciting not to know."

"Oh?"

"Yes. It is exciting *not* to know whether you've made up your mind or if you are still thinking about it." His eyes were alight with humor, and, despite herself, she found herself smiling back. Devil.

"I thought I made that clear, Autrey. I—"

"Yes, or at least you started to. But now I've told you what I do *not* want to know, so the least you can do is to have a little pity and keep the news to yourself—at least until we've heard the second set. Here comes the group."

She studied her glass, uncertain of what to say or do. They sat somewhat more at ease to listen to the second set, but inside, Maddy experienced a kaleidoscope of emotions: relief, disappointment, gratitude, and even tenderness toward this man who was gently willing to be rebuffed for the privilege of her company. She almost wanted to reach over and take his hand, but she knew, suddenly knew, that there was fire in that direction. Damn it. Here I go again. The man is just . . . there, and he has me spinning. She blanked out her mind and focused on the music.

When the set was over, he escorted her to the front of the bar, where they both said good night to Buddy, the manager, who tried manfully to keep his eyes on her face. She wanted to say her own good-bye right there and flee to the car, but she realized that this might embarrass him in front of his friend, so she asked him to walk her back to her car. The chill of the fall air was in marked contrast to the general fug in the bar, and she tried not to shiver, despite the sweater, which was made for purposes other than warmth. There was almost no traffic on the street, as most of the clubs were still going.

As she unlocked the door, he once again stood patiently by her side, not too close, not pressing her. She managed to unlock the door, open it, and slip into the seat, not trusting herself to get through another counting experience. She pulled the door to but did not close it. Only then did she turn to look up at him. A line from a movie occurred to her.

"Well, Just Autrey," she said. "In another time and place . . ."

He smiled down at her as if he recognized the line. Despite the heavy black brows, the hooked nose, and what looked like small muscles in his face, he was a very handsome man, she thought. From her vantage point, his chest blocked out the whole street. She wanted to reach out and put *him* through the count test. Damn. I may regret this—a lot.

"Yes, Maddy Holcomb," he said. "Stay away from unwholesome places from now on. You never know what kind of people you might meet."

Then he pressed the door shut and stepped back, keeping one eye out for cars. She started the engine, turned to wave at him, and then drove off down the street. She looked in the rearview mirror and could see him standing there, that impossible white shirt remaining visible in the mirror long after she could no longer see the rest of him. Damn. Damn. Damn!

29

Brian was a man with a plan as he walked along the palm-lined waterfront sidewalk on his way to the Subic Officers' Club. He could feel his freshly laundered whites beginning to wilt in the tropical humidity, even though the sun was already sinking behind the hills of Cubi Point. To his left were the oily waters of Subic Bay itself, or what could be glimpsed of it between the nested bows and sterns of assorted Seventh Fleet warships. Ahead was the Subic Officers' Club, a low, flat-roofed building perched on a point of landfill at the end of the bulkhead pier. Brian walked faster to reach the next oasis of air conditioning before he melted completely.

Following the turnover with *Long Beach,* the air side of Combat had virtually shut down and Brian had reverted to his job as the Weapons Department's head. He had spent the first day of the two-day transit back to Subic catching up on the piles of routine paperwork that had been faithfully saved for him by his division officers over the past six weeks. He was blissfully unaware that there would be twice that amount of paperwork waiting on the pier in Subic. He had also experienced the seeming luxury of two full nights of sleep.

To everyone's great relief, *Hood* had arrived for her two-week stay at a time when there was no carrier in port, which meant that the main Exchange would still have things to sell and there would be a chance to get a table in the O Club dining room. As he walked to the club, Brian's mind was barely recovering from the mass confusion of arrival day, when it seemed that everyone had headed off in thirty different directions at once. They had tied up a few minutes after 0800 alongside the main bulkhead pier, pushed sideways into the berth by two tugs accompanied by much hooting of tug horns. Their berth was marked by a crowd of flatbed trucks and pallets and the first of what would turn out to be an all-day parade of the yellow-gear trains coming from the supply center. And despite the fact that there were dry stores, fresh food supplies, new people, fuel, mail, spare parts, and general supplies to be loaded, most of the crew and half the junior officers had seemed hell-bent on getting ashore and into the various clubs for that first ice-cold San Miguel beer, and perhaps a quick shuttle bus out to the exchanges for their first shot at WESTPAC loot. All of the department heads spent the morning trying to cope with the avalanche of things and people coming aboard and saying no to what seemed like a hundred special-request chits for early liberty, special liberty, a day's leave, and several other artful dodges. Just before lunch, Brian had summoned his division officers for some shared thinking on the subject, losing his temper when his senior lieutenant, Fox Hudson, had made light of the first day's madhouse. Reiterating the exec's instructions, Brian explained that ships had been pulled out of Subic on the second day of a port visit for operational or weather emergencies and that the objective of day one was to get everything that was waiting for them on the pier safely on board. Only after that had been accomplished could liberty be considered. He had characterized the division officers' eagerness to get ashore as bordering on negligence and threatened to put every one of them in hack if they didn't get their enlisted people under control.

Walking back to his stateroom from the boat decks, he had realized after his shouting session that he was still desperately tired. The sheer physical fatigue of six weeks of evaluator watches, most of it on a port-and-starboard basis, the tension of learning his way around technically and politically, and the growing realization that he had been checkmated over the drug bust had all stretched his personal mooring lines to the point of breaking. Seeing his stone face at lunch, the exec pulled him aside afterward and recommended that he take a long nap and let his people manage the rest of arrival day on their own.

"Crap out for a few hours—you need it. Tell your chiefs you'll take a tour topside with them at around sixteen hundred, just before liberty call. They'll get it done; you'll see."

He had taken the exec's advice and ended up sleeping right through until 1800. The chiefs had come knocking on his door at 1600, but apparently not too emphatically. He had awakened feeling much better, and now, as he walked toward the O Club, he knew instinctively that any sojourn into the boozy warrens of Olongapo would probably be a disaster. Besides, he had the command duty officer duty starting at 0800 in the morning; there was time enough to see the fabled fleshpots of Olongapo the day after. So the plan was to go to the club, have one of their famous, five-dollar steak dinners and a glass of wine, and then back to the ship for some more rack time. Packed into his back pocket were three letters from Maddy. For reasons he could not identify, he wanted a drink in him before attending to the mail from home.

He stepped through the club's front doors into a wave of icy air conditioning. To the right were the double glass doors of the entrance to the main bar and the slot-machine rooms. Straight ahead was the dining room. He hesitated as other officers streamed by on either side. He knew that the rest of the wardroom would probably be in the bar, crowded around a couple of tables and well on their way toward the third or fourth round of drinks. But after the scene with his JO's earlier in the day, he really did not feel like going in there for some noisy alcoholic male bonding that would precede a night on the town.

He headed for the expansive dining room, where he was met by a diminutive Filipina hostess dressed in a full-length sequined gown. He asked for a table out of view of the dining room's entrance, feeling a little guilty as he followed her to a back corner of the bustling dining room. Real WESTPAC sailors did not spend their first night in port having a quiet dinner and avoiding the rest of the wardroom. Too bad, he thought, with a small flare of irritation. He had felt more than a little isolated since coming on board this ship, a feeling accentuated by all the derogatory talk about Atlantic Fleet sailors and the insider knowledge of the old WESTPAC hands. He realized suddenly that he had been in this ship for nearly five months and still had no real friends, no shipmates to whom he could really talk. Compared with his days in the destroyer force, *Hood* had been a foreign experience so far.

The Filipina cocktail hostess seemed to know he was from *Hood* and that this was his first time in Subic. She recommended a Subic Special and he agreed, wondering how she knew all that. She returned with the drink, and he sipped on the tall concoction and wondered why everyone grinned when they talked about Subic Specials. It tasted like mostly fruit juice, lightly flavored with rum. While he waited for a waitress, the lights at the bandstand came up and a quintet of Asian musicians all dressed like Elvis Presley launched into a Peter, Paul, and Mary song about a magic dragon. The female lead was a curvaceous Filipina with improbably large breasts. Her eyes had been surgically altered to sort of round and then painted with enough mascara to give her a panda bear–ish look. The rest of the group were all razor-thin, young Japanese men, some of whom were barely tall enough to swing their electric guitars. Brian decided that they weren't half bad if one closed one's eyes and didn't listen too hard to the words with *r* in them. As he drained his fruit juice concoction, the cocktail hostess appeared with a refill. He had finished that and started in on a third before the waitress found him in his darkened corner and took his dinner order, which he had to shout over the noise of the amps on the stage. He ordered a half a bottle of wine with his dinner and began nursing the third Subic Special.

By the time his steak arrived, the group was sounding really good and the singer was definitely beginning to turn him on. He found himself wishing he could trade places with the microphone stand, given the liberties it was taking with her ample bosom. He managed to knock over his empty Special glass when dinner arrived, an event the waitress seemed to take in stride. She poured his Paul Masson red wine and then went through the tasting ritual, which Brian found vastly amusing. All these Oriental people trying so hard to act and look like Americans. At about that time, the group took a break and he concentrated on dinner. He was surprised at exactly how much concentration the familiar maneuvers of knife and fork were taking. He thought absently about the three Subic Specials, then dismissed them as he reached for his wine, being very careful to wait for the waves in the glass to subside before picking it up. He spilled only a little bit onto his baked potato; probably improve it. Then he became dimly aware that someone was standing next to his table. He looked up and found the smiling, if slightly out-of-focus, countenance of the exec beaming down at him.

"Mr. Holcomb, I presume?" The beam expanded to a broad smile. "Mind if I join you? They're out of single tables."

"By all means, XO. Please do," Brian said, not sure whether he should or even could stand up. The exec was a full commander, and Brian was, after all, only a lieutenant. A senior lieutenant, but still. The exec was down and settled in while Brian was still grappling with this complex question of etiquette, a fact not entirely lost on the exec, who eyed the empty Special glass.

"I see you've discovered the Subic Special. What'd you think?"

"Well, sir, it's awfully sweet, but, well, I kind of liked it. Them. What's in it—them?"

"Seven jiggers of rum, all different kinds and brands, a jigger of vodka, some pineapple and orange juice, and grenadine for color. Oh, and a cherry."

"Shev-uh . . . seven kinds of rum? I see."

"But not that well, I do suspect. And how many did we have?"

"We had just two. No, three. No problem, really, although this wine is going to my head."

"I'm surprised there's any room. But what the hell, that's what the club is for." He gestured at a passing waitress and ordered a steak with the works. He looked back at Brian, who was trying to decide how to switch his fork from the left to the right hand now that he had managed to cut a piece of steak. What to do with the steak knife was the tough part. The exec tried not to laugh.

"We missed you in the bar," he said finally.

Brian managed to swap his knife and his fork and then focused on what the XO was saying. "I overslept, XO.

By the time I got here, I figured the wardroom would be way ahead of me, so—"

"Yeah, I can understand that. So you're not thinking of going over tonight, I take it."

"No, sir. I'm still pretty tired. Everybody tells me I have to go see it. Olongapo, I mean. But not tonight. And there's another reason. What was it? Oh yeah, I've got duty tomorrow."

"Good thinking. And when you do go over, make sure you go with somebody. Olongapo is interesting but not necessarily safe for officers on their first safari."

"Why's that, sir? Do they pick on officers? If everybody's in civvies, how do they know we're officers?"

"Believe me, Brian, they do. They not only will know you're an officer but they'll know you're from *Hood* and that you've never been to Olongapo before."

Brian thought about this news for a few minutes while he figured out the movements to get another bite of steak. It seemed to take a long time. Then he remembered the chief.

"Chief Martinez offered to show me around," he said. "I wasn't too sure about the, uh, propriety of going on the beach. You know, with one of the enlisted. On the other hand, Mr. Hudson said, uh . . . Damn, I can't remember." The knife problem was back.

The exec managed to keep his face composed as his dinner arrived. "I suspect he said something along the lines that the chief boats was big enough to keep you out of trouble. And don't worry about the propriety. Like you said, you'll be in civvies, and everyone in the ship, including me, would think you were very wise to go ashore the first time with Louie Jesus. Very wise indeed. But here, let me pour you some more wine."

With Brian operating his knife and fork at about half speed, they finished dinner at about the same time. The exec, a man of limited mercies, ordered brandy for both of them. The band had resumed by then, so they both sat and enjoyed the music while Brian tried manfully to stay awake. The waitress had removed the steak knife; now the decision was between finishing his wine and drinking his brandy. He decided to hold the wineglass in one hand

and the brandy snifter in the other, which simplified the decision-making process. After a half hour of the music, the waitress complicated life by bringing him a cup of the club's thick black coffee. He felt the beginnings of a headache gathering around his temples. Realizing that the exec was in civvies, Brian asked if he was going into town.

"Absolutely. There's a bunch of us going over. Normally, I'd insist you come with us, but I think you've got the right idea, especially with the duty tomorrow."

"I feel like I'm letting down the side a little," Brian said. He surprised himself by saying it. The exec studied his brandy snifter for a moment before replying.

"Don't let it bother you. You had the tough watch section, with all those midwatches. Count Austin's got the duty, Rafe Hatcher is already back on board, and Vince is going ashore with us tonight, but only because he has the duty the day after you do and doesn't want a big head on his duty day."

Brian found that the coffee was reviving him somewhat. "Yes, sir," he said. "I guess what I was saying was that I still don't feel like I'm really part of the wardroom yet. Hell, with all these watches, port and starboard, I don't even feel like I'm really part of Weapons Department. I've seen more of Combat and my rack than anything else on the ship."

"I know. Having Vince off the watch bill has been the killer. But everyone understands, believe me. I hope the next line period to have all three of you in rotation."

"You hope, XO?"

"Yeah, well, I think you know what the problem is down there. And I'm not sure it's going to change all that much, especially after a Subic port visit."

"Why's that, XO?"

"Because the little dears get resupplied here. Marijuana, pills, hell, even heroin is available in Olongapo. And whoever the main man is who's supplying our dopers will get a new stash here. We'll probably go through some trying times the first couple of weeks out."

Brian shook his head. The room tilted a little when he did it. But this was important.

"I can't believe we can't get a handle on this problem, XO. I mean, here we are talking about a main man, a druggie kingpin, and it sounds like we just have to live with it." Brian realized he was speaking a little more frankly than he should, but he remembered all too well his discussion with Jackson and Martinez about the drug network. He assumed Jackson had shared his theories with the exec.

The exec was frowning but nodding in reluctant agreement. "We do what we can, Brian. Some of the chiefs and I have some things going that I don't want to talk about, but basically, until the fleet units, the Navy's ships and air squadrons, get the authority to impose mandatory random urinalysis screening on all our people, where everybody has to take a piss test, and I mean the whole ship—officers, chiefs, white hats—we're kind of boxed in by our own legal system."

"Well, yes, sir, but all the COs and XOs in the Navy must know that, which means the admirals have to know it, so why doesn't the Navy just do it?"

"Two reasons, I think. The first is political; the second is practical. Political because the sixties have unhinged everything we military guys took for granted since the Second World War. We've got damn near every kid under twenty-one running around back there in the land of the big PX protesting this war, growing hair down to their asses, doing dope, marching around with no clothes on, listening to this screechy shit they call rock and roll, and generally acting like freaking Martians. I don't know these kids, which means I don't know these sailors anymore. And I think the big guys back in the Pentagon aren't entirely sure where *they* stand, because you only have to watch TV to see that there's more of the longhairs and all the liberals who agree with 'em than there are admirals and generals. So I think they're a little bit afraid to impose mandatory urinalysis, because that would put us too far out in front of the rest of the country, especially in the first year of a new administration."

"And the practical reason?"

"That's a little more clear-cut. You piss-test this whole crew two days after we leave here, we'd have to turn around and come back in and shut her down. Hell, we'd probably get thirty percent of the crew and maybe even some khaki. It's basically the old Washington rule: Don't ask the question if you can't stand all the possible answers."

"But XO, if that's true, then what the hell are we doing out on Red Crown station, controlling aircraft, operating helos, firing missiles, doing shore bombardment? I mean, those aviators depend on us in all sorts of ways. And what happens if the MiGs come all the way the next time?"

The exec stared down into his coffee. "We're doing the best we can, Brian," he said again, softly. "We're not fooling ourselves, if that's what you're asking. We're just getting through the deployment, line period by line period, like everybody else. We'll get through the next one, and the one after that, just like the rest of the ships are doing it, and hope to hell we don't fuck up so bad one night that we fail to bring her home. And Brian? So far, it's basically working. And it requires an all-hands effort, comprende? For better or for 'worser,' we're all in this boat together."

Brian was silent for several minutes. Through his alcoholic haze, he knew full well what the exec was talking about, but the Marcowitz business was very much on his mind. The exec had obviously not been telling the truth when he had said that the captain wanted to wait until Subic. Was it because it had to do with drugs that the captain had been cut out of the loop? That wasn't right. It just wasn't the right way to do it. He decided to misunderstand deliberately, maybe push it a little.

"Well," he said, "at least we got Marcowitz. I assume we'll be processing him for a court-martial pretty quick."

The exec gave him a quick look but did not actually say anything. Brian was about to pursue it when the exec made a show of glancing at his watch and then shoved back in his chair.

"Time to rock and roll, as they say," he said, rising. "I'll see you bright and early at officers' call. Enjoyed dinner."

The exec had grabbed both their checks and was gone

before Brian could even gather his thoughts. With a sinking feeling, he knew he'd made a mistake. The exec had been asking nicely for him just to go along. And instead, he'd brought up the Marcowitz case. The XO had said they'd process Marcowitz when they got into Subic. So why wasn't he willing to confirm that?

He looked around for his own bill and then remembered that the XO had picked it up. His head began to swim again as the coffee wore off. He got up and threaded his way unsteadily through the dining room, accompanied by a blast of noise as the band started lustily into the third set. He could already feel the beginnings of a real hangover.

The walk back to the ship cleared his head a little, but the clearing left more room for the headache, which took immediate advantage. The night air along the piers was steamy, filled with a mélange of scents from tropical flowers, freshly mowed grass, burning charcoal, fuel oil, and an occasional whiff of stack gas from the nested ships. The harsh, hot glare of the sodium-vapor lights contrasted starkly with the soft, shadowy palm trees and the muted glimmering of tiny waves out in the harbor. He tried to figure out how he could have handled his conversation with the XO better, but the Subic Specials, wine, and brandy were still in charge of his think box.

He straightened his back and squared his shoulders as he approached the ship. He was perspiring profusely by the time he reached the gangway and even he could smell the alcohol fuming out of his pores. He wondered whether the people on the quarterdeck would be able to smell all the booze. He climbed the steel stairs up to the quarterdeck, puffing by the time he reached the top of the brow stand, and saluted the OOD, Ensign McCarthy, carefully, taking care not to stumble across the quarterdeck. The ensign returned his salute, taking care himself to take no official notice of the Weapons officer's condition.

"Mr. Holcomb, sir?" he asked as Brian started to walk by him.

"Yep?" Brian turned around, overshooting just a little. He grabbed a lifeline to keep it from getting away.

"Did you hear about Petty Officer Marcowitz?"

Brian suddenly felt a sobering chill run through him. Ensign McCarthy had the collateral duty of being the ship's legal officer. Although not a lawyer, he was responsible for setting up all the paperwork for mast cases and court-martials. Earlier in the day, Brian had signed some of the preliminary legal paperwork on Marcowitz.

"No," Brian replied. "What about Marcowitz? He's on premast restriction, right?"

"Uh, no, sir," McCarthy said. "Marcowitz went over on liberty tonight."

"What!" The headache reprimanded him for speaking loudly.

"Yes, sir. The exec hadn't put him on any premast restraint. At least he wasn't on the list of restricted men. But it doesn't matter now."

"Why?" Brian tried hard to concentrate.

"Because the base front-gate Marines picked him up on a possession charge. They found three Baggies of marijuana in his overnight bag as he was going through the main gate. They have him in the base brig right now. And with three Baggies, they'll go for possession with intent to sell. The real good news is that since he did it on base, *they'll* get to court-martial his ass, instead of us."

Brian nodded slowly, his brain trying to catch up with the suspicion that was starting to bounce around in his head. What had the XO actually said about the Marcowitz case? We'll process him when we get to Subic? Or we'll take care of him when we get to Subic? His mind wouldn't focus. He cursed himself for getting drunk. Just had some fruit juice, XO. . . .

"Thanks," he mumbled, turning to head carefully up the port side toward the security of his stateroom. He clumped up the interior ladders, made the right turn toward his stateroom door, and stepped inside. He closed the door behind him, shucked off his sweaty uniform in the darkness, and dropped it in a heap on his chair. He flung himself down on his rack and breathed deeply of the blessed air conditioning. He once again tried to size up the significance of his talk with the exec, but his mind

337

couldn't get going and the bulkheads were revolving unnaturally every time he cracked open his eyelids. He was asleep in minutes. He didn't hear his uniform trousers slither off the chair onto the deck, Maddy's three letters still unopened in the back pocket.

He was awakened several hours later by the sounds of reveille being announced over the 1MC. He sat up in his rack, gasped, and flopped back down again in an effort to keep his head from toppling onto the deck. Jesus H. Christ. Seven kinds of rum. Seven thousand determined Oriental devils hammering on his brain cells was more like it. Maybe he ought to go ahead and let it topple. He sat up again, slowly this time, and swung his feet over the side of the rack. He took several deep breaths to celebrate this achievement, wondering why it was so dark, and then opened one eye experimentally. The slit of white light coming from under the door looked like the headlight of an oncoming train. He blinked at it several times even as he grappled with the problem of getting off the tracks. Then he decided it might be better to let the train come ahead. He could even hear it, a knocking sound that reverberated in his head, before he realized that some Communist was knocking on his door.

"What!" he croaked.

The door opened and a huge silhouette filled the blaze of light in the doorway. He'd been right the first time. It was a train.

"Mr. Holcomb? You alive in there?"

"No, goddamn it. I died and I wanta be left alone. Jesus Christ, Boats."

"Yeah, well, they tole me you was shorin' up the bulkheads last night when you came back aboard. I was jist comin' to remind you we got the duty today." He peered intently at Brian's face and shook his head. "I'll send up the doc with the first rites. You jist sit right there and don't go nowheres."

The door closed and Brian's eyes stopped hurting in the sudden darkness. Through the bulkheads, he heard the noises of the ship coming to life as the 1MC went about its business of announcing mess gear and breakfast for the crew, sweepers, and mustering of the restricted

338

men. He thought briefly about breakfast, which was a mistake. Full-color images of creamed chipped beef, powdered scrambled eggs swimming in catsup, and greasy bacon and oily sausages paraded through his mind, all of which prompted him to visit his commode at high speed, head or no head. When his tortured stomach had stopped spasming long enough for him to straighten up, he had crawled back to his stateroom and tried to brush his teeth, but the noise of the toothpaste coming out of the tube was too painful. He was sitting in his chair in his Skivvies, his forehead resting on the rim of the steel basin, when the chief hospital corpsman knocked gently and came into the stateroom. He carried a small green steel bottle of oxygen attached to a medical ventilator mask, several small pill envelopes, and a stainless-steel cup that held about a pint of ice water. He switched on a desk light and grimaced when he saw Brian's face.

"Yup, that's a hangover. Morning, Mr. Holcomb. You puked yet?"

Brian nodded his head slowly, mindful of upsetting the devils.

"Yeah, you don't wanta move your head around just yet. Might come off, roll down the passageway, scare the stewards. Here, breathe into this here mask."

Brian accepted the mask and began taking in deep breaths of pure oxygen. He felt better almost at once. The doc took away the mask.

"Now, take all of these here pills."

"What are they?" Brian croaked, his mouth dry from the oxygen. The doc was holding out an entire handful of pills.

"They're part of the cure. Mostly vitamins. These little bitty suckers, they're B-one, B-seven, B-twelve, and a coupla E. These bigger ones here are APCs. Just take 'em all and chug this whole cup of ice water."

Brian complied, gagging initially on the larger pills. When he was finished, the chief corpsman gave him back the oxygen bottle. Brian settled back in his chair and breathed hungrily, feeling his throat dry out and not caring. After five minutes, the doc signaled to remove the mask. Brian felt almost normal, the headache gone, his stomach settled, and a sense of energy filling his body.

"Now," the doc said as he gathered up his kit, "that'll give you a good hour and a half of normal ops. That's time enough to get to quarters, take over CDO from Mr. Austin, and get the working day under way. End of an hour'n a half, the cure wears off, okay? Then you're gonna crash again, so you need to get back to your stateroom, get flat, and keep the lights low. But at least you've got ninety minutes, okay? Wear sunglasses so's people won't see your eyes and piss their trou. And don't forget: You're Cinderella—ninety minutes or so, the port anchor's gonna come outta the hawse pipe up there on the bow and find you and drop on your head, okay? I'll see ya later, Mr. Holcomb. You have a real nice day now."

The chief left. Brian was amazed at the transformation. He went back into the head, took a quick shower, shaved, brushed his teeth, and put on a fresh khaki uniform. As he stuffed the whites into his laundry bag, he found Maddy's crumpled letters. He put them down on his desk with a pang of embarrassment, but with less than ninety minutes on the clock, Maddy would have to wait. He headed out the door to get the day under way while he still could. God bless Louie Jesus and his magnificent friend, the doc.

30

By nightfall, the last remnants of his hangover were almost gone. His head seemed soft, like a submarine that had been depth-charged all day and survived. By comparison with the morning, he was feeling pretty good. By comparison with the morning, just being alive felt pretty good. He stood up on the forecastle as the sun set over Grande Island out in the bay, nursing a cup of coffee and trying to ignore the lumps of heavily preserved Navy ham that crouched in his stomach like escaped criminals. Sailors in civvies streamed along the bulkhead pier and sidewalks leading to the shuttle bus stops. The last of the supply trucks rumbled back toward the supply depot around the corner. Across the street, the Filipino workers shuttered the galvanized-steel warehouse doors for the night with a loud rattle. The messenger of the watch stood by the jackstaff, ready to execute evening colors when the sun officially set.

The ship seemed a bit more relaxed now that she was refueled and all the stores and supplies were safely loaded belowdecks. Tomorrow, the weapons station would deliver two pallets of five-inch ammo and a Terrier missile, which would complete the load-out. Brian was grateful to have made it through the day with his head in one piece. The doc's hangover cure had worked as promised, with the headache, a general feeling of wooziness, and a racing heartbeat returning shortly after he had handled quarters and put out the instructions for the day to his departmental officers and chiefs. The boatswain had been discreetly solicitous when Brian had thanked him after quarters for getting the doc up. The exec had been businesslike at officers' call, though not unfriendly, but he had also seemed interested in getting quickly through the morning's first meetings. Brian wondered whether the doc had been making rounds throughout officers' country this morning, as there seemed to be several officers interested in the passage of time. Brian had spent the morning in his stateroom, alternating an hour of rack time with an hour of catching up on old paperwork and beginning to work on the stack of new paperwork delivered with the mail.

Brian faced aft, stood to attention, and held a salute as a long blast on a police whistle came over the 1MC, announcing evening colors. The sound echoed across the harbor from the 1MC speakers of every ship in port. The messenger of the watch slowly hauled down the Union Jack from the jackstaff at the bow. After several more seconds, three blasts on the police whistle sounded "carry on," indicating that God now had permission to complete sunset. Another Navy day was officially over.

As the messenger walked aft with his prize, Brian heard the handwheel on the forecastle hatch scuttle turning. The leonine head and shoulders of the chief boatswain lifted out of the round hatch like a slow-moving Polaris missile. The chief had a cup of coffee in one hand and two long green Tabacalera Grande cigars in his right fist. He flipped the hatch back into place and spun the wheel with his boot; then walked forward to where Brian was standing in the eyes of the ship. He handed over one of the cigars.

"Evenin', boss," he rumbled. "Got a Grande for ya. Good goddamn cee-gars, and they're even fresh."

Brian dutifully hauled out his knife and whacked one end off the nine-inch-long cigar. The chief did the honors with a Zippo embossed with *Hood*'s crest. They puffed fragrant clouds of blue smoke into the night air and listened with satisfaction as the harbor mosquitoes banked away into the gathering darkness to find other victims.

"Know how they make these?"

"I'm not sure I'm old enough."

"They got these really fat ole women, see, and when the guys've got the cee-gar rolled nice and tight, they hand it over to these sweaty ole women, and they pull up their dress and seal it by—"

"Chief."

"Yes, sir?"

"I had to eat Navy ham for dinner. Let's just enjoy the cigars, shall we?"

"Yes, sir."

They stood in silence for several minutes, watching the orange sunset paint the tips of the mountains to the east. The pastel colors were gradually overcome by the sodium-vapor lights along the pier. Brian found himself actually enjoying the cigar.

"Chief."

"Yes, sir?"

"I'm curious. How was Marcowitz set up?"

"Marcowitz, sir?"

"Yeah. Marcowitz, sir. The guy I busted for doing dope in missile plot. The guy who was picked up with dope in his overnight bag by the Marines at the main gate. I'm just sort of curious, Chief: Why wasn't he on premast restriction, and what kind of a guy takes three Baggies for one night's liberty into Olongapo, Chief?"

The boatswain was silent for a minute. "A dumb-ass doper, maybe?" he said. Then he grinned, nodded, and flicked a long ash over the side. A passing seagull jinked briefly to examine the ash and then flew on.

"Okay. So maybe somebody planted a little somethin' from the XO's evidence locker. You know the OOD inspects overnight bags at the quarterdeck, makes sure guys aren't takin' more'n two packs a cigarettes into town—you know, stuff from the ship's store or the PX. Black-market rules and shit."

"So who had the quarterdeck last night?"

"BTC Franklin; he's the Boilers Division senior chief."

"Okay. So then what happened?"

"So then maybe the BTC calls the base CDO office, talks to a chief he knows over there, tells him what's gotta go down. CDO chief calls the Marines at the main gate. Franklin sends a guy inna ship's truck, he drives out to the main gate, meets the gate gunny, points out our boy, and comes back to the ship. Jarboons make the grab, find the shit right where it's s'posed to be, and our dickhead gets hauled off to the brig."

"And now it's the base legal officer's problem and we're done with it."

"And Marcowitz goes down, don't forget."

Brian nodded slowly. He had figured it would be something like that. He flicked his own ash off over the lifelines into the darkness under the bow. A swarm of seagulls was screeing and squawking over a dumpster on the pier as the mess cooks carried out the evening meal's garbage.

"And I don't suppose that Chief Franklin did all this on his own, did he?"

The boatswain stared out over the row of metal warehouses cooling in the early darkness. Farther down the pier a yard crane rumbled down the tracks, escorted by two shipyard workers, its warning bells making a racket. The crowd of sailors going on liberty parted on either side of the yard crane like a stream around a rock.

"I ain't sure how much I kin say, boss. I mean, you're my department head an' all, but—"

"I think I understand, Boats. There's an inside operation going down and you don't know if I'm on the inside yet. Right?"

"Yeah, well, somethin' like that. I don't wanna—"

"Don't sweat it. The XO and I had a little talk last night in the club. I'm guess I'm still sorting out how I'm going to play it, and I think he's waiting to see how I'm going to come down. My problem is that I still want to see it done regulation Navy. The XO obviously thinks his way, your inside operation, is the only way to go. He explained it a little bit last night."

"We do it regulation, mosta them dopers get off and we end up fuckin' ourselves."

"Yeah, I know those arguments. But by the same token, your way, the *Hood* way, most of the dopers stay on board and someday they may fuck *us* because they'll be on the missile console or in the mount or in the fire room at a critical moment, and they're still just potheads with oatmeal for brains."

"Yes, sir, I hear that," the chief said. He gave Brian a speculative look around his cigar. "You tell the XO that?"

"No. I was too drunk and too tired. But mostly drunk. I've never been much of a boozer."

The chief chuckled. "Me, neither, but it don't stop me none."

Brian smiled and flipped the remains of his cigar into the harbor. "Look, Chief," he said. "I'm not going to screw up the works here, okay? I don't approve, because I think the regulation Navy way is always the best way to go. You know what they say about every Navy regulation being drafted in the blood of someone's mistake at one time or another. If the insiders are worried that I'm going to blow the whistle, forget it. But if *I* find another guy doing dope, like Marcowitz, *I'm* going to write him up—by the book. What happens after that is a command decision, even if it's like what happened to Marcowitz."

"I hear that," the chief said. "Sounds fair enough to me." He looked down at his watch. "I guess I gotta go get ready for eight o'clock reports, boss. I'll see ya on the quarterdeck."

"Okay, Boats."

Brian watched the chief shamble down the sloping steel deck of the forecastle and disappear into the starboard-side breaks. He poured the cold remnants of his coffee over the side and listened to it dribble into the water twenty-five feet below. The night air settled over him like a wet blanket; the temperature had come down only grudgingly into the low nineties out of respect for nightfall. Brian wondered whether he had done the right thing. Whatever he told the chief would probably get back to the exec. That was okay. The exec would probably be relieved he was not going to rock the boat by talking to any outsiders.

On the other hand, Brian desperately wanted to be on the inside himself. Every ship was the same: There was always a small group of officers and chiefs who actually ran things. Sometimes this group coincided with the formal chain of command; sometimes it did not. Here in *Hood,* when it came to the drug problem, the chain seemed to run directly from the exec to some of the chiefs, with the tacit acceptance of at least two department heads, Austin and Benedetti. But right now, he, Brian, was the wild card. So far, he was not included. He figured it was not that he was excluded so much as not yet trusted enough to be let into the real power structure. In a sense, what happened to Marcowitz was probably a test of sorts. They knew he would figure it out, and now they would wait to see what he would do or not do. Well, he had just given his answer.

And, hell, maybe they were right. Marcowitz was a doper, no doubt about that. He would now be court-martialed, but it would be a base court-martial, a base drug incident, not a *Hood* drug incident. And, in a back-handed way, their way achieved his own objective, which was to purge the doper from the ship before he could put the ship in harm's way. Brian was increasingly worried about the prospect of going in harm's way. The old WESTPAC hands had been coming out here to Vietnam and the Gulf for so long that, to most of them, anything that happened was routine. To Brian's uninitiated way of thinking, what the MiGs had been doing was immensely

345

threatening, but the WESTPAC mystique seemed to require that everyone be nonchalant about it. If Soviet MiGs had run a feint like that against Sixth Fleet ships in the Mediterranean, they would have risked starting World War III.

He stared out over the harbor again. The channel buoys were winking and blinking, casting flickers of red and green light on the still black waters of the harbor. Over on Grande Island, the flare of a barbecue fire shone through the palms as one of the ships held a ship's picnic on the Special Services recreation beach. What he could not figure out was where the captain was in all of this. The exec seemed to be firmly in charge of the doper retribution program and every other aspect of discipline. Well, on one level, that was normal: Supervision of good order and discipline was the XO's job.

But the captain seemed to be the man who wasn't there. He was rarely seen out of his cabin, and Brian had had very little contact with him except up in Combat. In his last department head's job in *Decatur,* he had seen as much if not more of the captain than the exec. Maybe it had to do with *Hood*'s being a cruiser-sized "frigate" with some four hundred people aboard. Twenty-six officers in the wardroom, not counting the four helo pilots, instead of the fourteen in *Decatur.* In the destroyer, the captain took his meals with the officers and was all over the ship throughout the day. Here, the captain lived in splendid isolation in his cabin, had his own private mess, and seemed to confine his excursions to Combat and occasionally the bridge. And, come to think of it, Brian had not seen the captain since the ship landed.

Benedetti thought that the CO did not believe that there even was a drug scene aboard the ship. And Brian's brief discussion with the captain about the Marcowitz incident in Combat seemed to prove that the exec was screening the Old Man from even hearing about drug incidents. Or else the captain was a very good actor. And then there was his personal appearance: Was there something physically wrong with him? Brian thought back to the times he had seen him during the first line period. He never did look particularly well, certainly not when compared with the hale and hearty exec. Okay, in comparison with the rest of the officers and crew, Captain Huntington was an old man, but there were a couple of times when the captain had looked . . . well, almost drugged. Brian's eyes widened as he tried to get his mental arms around that notion, but then the 1MC announced eight o'clock reports. He headed aft for the routine evening in-port ritual of eight o'clock reports, held on the quarterdeck, where the Duty Department officers reported to the CDO that their spaces were all secure for the night.

After eight o'clock reports, Brian made a tour of the ship from bow to stern, checking to see that the spaces were indeed secure for the night. He would take another tour around 2300 before securing himself for the night. On his way back to the wardroom, he passed the Sheriff's office. He was surprised to see Jackson, who was wearing reading glasses, working at his desk on a liberty night. He stopped in.

"Sheriff, I'm surprised to see you on board. I thought it was a chief's duty to tear up Olongapo every night."

Jackson smiled. "It's the troops that go tearing up the town every night. We chiefs know how to pace ourselves. You know, the old bull/young bull story."

"I think I gained some direct experience on that score last night."

"Yes, sir, I heard that the doc had to bring the first rites to you this morning."

"The first rites. I love it. He did indeed. I embraced a concoction called a Subic Special last night. Proved once again that I have no real head for booze. So what's happening in the cops-and-robbers department these days? I hear our boy Marcowitz had some, uh, misfortune at the main gate."

Jackson leaned back in his chair, his expression neutral. "Yes, sir. I've got the report right here."

"Seems he was taking coals to Newcastle."

"Sir?"

"An English expression. Like taking ice to Alaska. If I have it right, Olongapo is a place where an American *buys* dope, not sells it." Brian leaned back out of the doorway to check the passageway. "My take is that this was a setup. Somebody planted the stuff in the guy's overnight bag and then fingered him at the main gate."

The Sheriff gave him a speculative look but said nothing.

Brian sat down in one of the two chairs in the office. "Let me tell you a story," he said, then recounted his conversation with the captain up in D and D, where he had found out that the exec had *not* briefed the captain about Marcowitz.

Jackson took his glasses off and rubbed his eyes for a moment, then put them back on. "Well, sir, I guess that's possible," he said. "That the XO didn't tell the Old Man. The impression I have is that Captain Huntington lives in his memory of the old Navy. Maybe he just refuses to accept that his sailors are doing narcotics right here in the ship. Or maybe the exec has given up trying to convince the Old Man that we have a problem and so he's decided to work the problem on his own."

"Who's doing the planting and fingering?"

Jackson seemed to withdraw a little. Brian realized that the Sheriff was probably trying to figure out how much he could or could not say.

"Forget I asked," he said. He thought for a minute. Then he looked up at the Sheriff.

"The exec sort of let me in on it last night in the club. He says the legal system can't do anything for him, so he's doing it his way. Guy gets caught with drugs on the base, it's a base drug incident, not a *Hood* drug incident. And a guy who we know is dirty is taken off the boards. He calls it justice."

"Sounds like justice to me, actually."

"Yes, but—"

Jackson leaned forward. His glasses glinted in the fluorescent light. "Yes, sir, I know about that 'but.' So maybe the XO is running a vigilante operation here."

"The XO is dispensing military justice in the ship, and that's supposed to be the sole prerogative of the captain—who's apparently turning a blind eye to the whole deal."

Jackson sat back and began to play with a pencil on

the desk. They were both silent. Brian was trying to grapple with the professional dilemma he faced. He was becoming increasingly convinced that the XO's system was an illegal perversion of the military justice system that was only driving the drug problem further underground. One fine day, some young pothead would get them all killed. But on the other hand, isolated from the real power structure in the ship, he was worried that his career, which was on the cusp of a promotion and the opportunity for the XO/CO track, might be destroyed if he pushed the drug issue. The exec had gently put him on notice last night. If he chose to, he could put it not so gently. Brian knew full well that the executive officer was a very powerful man in the chain of command: He could put the knife in a department head's career in about twenty different ways, all of them as lethal as they were legal. And then there was Maddy. What chance did he have of keeping Maddy if his career went off the rails? Maybe guys like Austin had the right idea: Go along, watch where you put people, let the XO play his game, get your fitrep, and get on down the road. He looked up, to see Jackson watching him. He shook his head.

"I'm not sure what to do with all this, Sheriff. As somebody else said, it's the captain's boat. If this is how he wants to run it, I guess I don't have a lot to say about it."

Jackson nodded slowly.

"Don't get me wrong," Brian continued. "I think the world of Captain Huntington. He seems to be honestly sincere about caring for his people. And I'm also not implying that there's corruption here. But I think he's deluding himself on this drug thing and that it's going to bite us in the ass one day."

Jackson nodded again. "He has been a damn fine CO, Mr. Holcomb. I'll tell you what—anybody who worked the bomb squad and who personally saved a ship by disarming a bomb is okay in my book. I don't know if he's deluding himself or if this is just the way he wants it done. Personally, I don't reckon the XO could do any of this, the Old Man didn't give him the nod. But that's an issue that's above my pay grade. That's kind of why I'm looking down, not up. I'm trying to find out who's really running the drug operation. But I agree with you on one point—we may be running on borrowed time here."

"You find out anything more about that Bullet guy?"

"Close that door, please? Yes, sir, I did. I talked to some of the other chiefs."

Jackson reminded Brian about what he had found in the record. "The other black chiefs confirm Bullet's got a clique, but they wouldn't go so far's to call it a gang. If he's running drugs, they've seen no sign of it. I did get some marked money into the system, though. If the main man is investing with Garlic, I may or may not find it while we're in port, when the kids start running out of cash."

Brian nodded. "The black chiefs—how do they feel about the fact that you're focusing on another black man?"

Jackson grinned. "Well, it wasn't the most comfortable discussion I've had. But the way I put it, if the drug ring here is black, it's in our interests and a matter of pride for us to clean it up."

"That satisfy them?"

"I guess. For the ones who're secure about the race bit, that rang a bell. For those who're still figuring out where they stand, well . . ."

Brian got up. "I didn't mean to pry," he said. "This whole race issue is such a raw nerve, everyone's afraid even to talk about it, call a spade a spade."

Then Brian realized what he had just said, but Jackson was grinning at him. "So to speak, Mr. Holcomb?"

"Aw, shit, Chief—"

Jackson laughed and waved off Brian's apology. "I know what you're saying—if you weren't color-blind, you wouldn't have used that expression. Sometime we ought to talk about this."

"But it's going to get in the way of your investigation, isn't it, Chief?"

"Yeah, it might. Depends on how much I let it. Wouldn't be the first time I lit a fuse that 'everybody' would rather I hadn't. But in reality, it pisses me off. These guys were given an opportunity they didn't deserve."

It was Brian's turn to laugh. "I may know more about that position than you'd think. I'm going to finish my rounds. Then I'm going to get a good night's sleep, because tomorrow night, I want you to know I'm going on the beach with Godzilla himself."

Jackson grinned. "The bosun? Get *lots* of sleep, Mr. Holcomb."

"I will, but I'm going to make another round about twenty-three-thirty, see what it's like when the liberty party returns."

"I'll be doing the same thing, sir."

"Well good. Why don't you meet me on the quarter-deck at twenty-three-thirty."

31

San Diego

Maddy lay in bed at 2:30 on a Friday morning and tried not to cry. Brian had finally phoned from Subic Bay, and it had just about been a complete disaster.

First, they had been disconnected. She had picked the phone up, awakening from a troubled sleep, and not recognized who it was until the static diminished and the connection suddenly cleared.

"Brian, is that you? Oh, I can't believe it!"

"Hey, Maddy," he had said, using the traditional Georgia salutation.

"Brian, where are you—what time is it—oh, I'm confused. I'm not awake."

"Sorry, babe, I'm lucky even to get a line. I—"

And then the line had gone dead, his voice replaced with a roar of static. She had groaned, sworn, and hung up. He had told her this might happen; now the trick was for him to get his operator back without losing his place in line. She had waited, rubbing her eyes, afraid to leave the phone even to go to the bathroom. He had come through again ten minutes later, and, after an incomprehensible exchange with a Filipino operator that she had finally recognized was a request for a collect call, Brian was back.

He had asked how she was doing and she had said, "Fine, good as can be expected. I miss you. Do you miss me?" He had told her about the big foreign-exchange building and that he was going to get himself a stereo and her a surprise present. She asked how he was doing in *Hood* and he said that he had seen the special fitness report, and that, if they sent it, it looked good for promotion, even though there were some things about the *Hood* that were not . . . well, he'd tell her about it later.

"What do you mean, *if* they send it? Why wouldn't they send it?"

He had demurred at first, but she had pressed, and then he had started talking around the drug problem, trying to disguise what he was talking about because all the phone lines from Subic were monitored by a Navy security group. He had told her of his somewhat anomalous position vis-à-vis the exec and the captain on what happened to people caught with drugs aboard ship, how his future fitness reports would depend on going along with the ship's system, and how he was having trouble coming around to doing it their way.

"Brian, is that smart?" she had asked. "I mean, the whole point of taking this ship, this damned deployment, was to get to lieutenant commander, wasn't it? Maybe you're just going to have to go along, get through it, and get off the ship as soon as your tour is up."

"But Maddy, this isn't right, what's going on here. I mean, it may be politically the right move, and there are guys like Austin who think that is exactly how we should play it, but I hate the thought of some pothead with his fingers on the missile radars. Look, we should probably stop talking about this, okay?"

"Okay, but Brian, don't throw away this whole deployment. I mean, I hate your being gone, and I'm . . . I'm probably not doing a terrific job adjusting to this side of the Navy, but please, don't let it all be for nothing."

"Maddy, you don't understand. As a department head,

I've got a responsibility to the ship, not just to the political interests of the CO and the XO to keep their drug problem under wraps. I'm just not sure how long I can go along with this stuff."

"Brian, think about it, okay? Just think about it. It's only for this one tour of duty. You said that, remember? That we had to go through this to get well and to get you back on track for lieutenant commander? Once you've got that, you have a shot at being an XO yourself; then you can call the shots and run a ship the way you think you should. This is what you told me, remember?"

"Yeah, I know. But there's so much happening out here—things I can't talk about, operational stuff. Everything's a whole lot different from what I expected. And this port-and-starboard business, I'm just barely getting back to normal after almost two days in port."

"Okay, honey, I know. Angela told me what that was all about. Just get some rest there while you're in port. But Brian? Don't be a crusader. I don't think the Navy likes crusaders."

Brian had been silent for a moment. She almost thought the connection was gone again when he spoke.

"Maddy, I'm going to have to play this one by my conscience. If the Navy is going this route with druggies, then maybe I don't want to be a lieutenant commander. But I don't think it's the Navy. The Navy's policy is pretty clear. I think it's this ship, this command. There's something going on with the captain, and I can't figure it out."

None of this had sounded very good at all to Maddy. For the first time during the conversation, she wondered whether he had been drinking. Brian tended to get very serious, almost morose, if he had been drinking. He had almost no capacity for liquor.

"Brian, Brian, just hunker down and do your job."

"That's what I'm talking about, Maddy—doing my duty as an officer and not as some kind of flunky who's desperate to get promoted. I thought you'd support that notion."

"Not if it means we're going through this deployment for nothing, Brian. That doesn't make sense. I know there's a lot I don't understand, but just remember why we're putting up with this . . . this hateful separation."

"Well, I'll try, Maddy. Look, there's a big line here—"

There had been some pain in his voice, and Maddy recognized that she had somehow said the wrong thing. But she hadn't really known what to say. She fell back on something reliable.

"I love you, Brian. Tell me more in your letters so I can understand it better. I didn't mean to sound selfish. It's just that I need you here."

"I know, Maddy, I know. And I love you, too. Things aren't that bad. I may be all wrong about this, but I don't think so. I guess I do need to fill you in some more so you'll understand. I can't really talk on this open line."

"Okay. I'm really glad you called. Just do what they want and hurry home."

"You surviving all this?"

"Fair, Brian. Just fair. Thank God for the job at the bank, or I'd be out of my mind. I know this much, wherever we do go after this tour, I'm going to have to have a job, a career even, if you're going to deploy some more."

"If I go to a ship, I'll deploy. That's kind of what we do."

"I know, and I hate it." That last had popped out without a lot of thought, and she had cringed when she heard his reply.

"Well, Maddy. Maybe I should have drawn a clearer picture when we got married."

"Oh, Brian, let's not fight. You're way over there and I'm here. We can't do anything about it, so let's just grit it out. Which is why I think you ought not to fight the system on whatever it is about the ship that's bugging you."

"Well, like I said, I'm going to have to sort this one out by myself, I guess. I thought you'd—well, never mind. I'm getting some looks, taking up the phone. I love you, and I'll write soon. Bye-bye."

And he had gone, just like that. She had hung up the phone and lain back on the bed, sudden tears stinging her eyes, trying to recall her exact words, wondering how in the hell she had managed to say precisely the wrong thing on what was probably the one and only phone call she would get during the whole cruise. She drummed the mattress with her fists. It was so damned hard, with all their communications compressed into little scraps of paper that were weeks old when you got them, and a five-minute phone call every three months. What the hell kind of marriage was this? And if he does real well, they'll let him do it again. Maybe right away. Wonderful. One of the other wives had even said that *Hood* might have to deploy again next year. Brian was assigned for two years. She really didn't think she could do this again.

But Brian had been trying to tell her something, some-thing going wrong in the ship, some kind of mystery about people using drugs. This was news. His letters had mentioned that there was some kind of drug problem, but there had been no hint that Brian might be getting himself sideways with the captain and the exec. Most of his letters had been entirely routine, the mirror images of her own weekly reports on the home front. The captain's wife had made a big deal about not filling her letters with the "poor me's," as she called it. Maybe the captain or that big commander, the executive officer, had made the same point to the officers—tell the home front every-thing's just fine; that way, we don't get the girls all upset. God. Two sets of people, both desperately wanting to reach out and touch, to communicate, to be with one another, if only in letters and phone calls, and both playing by a set of rules that makes real communication almost impossible.

She turned the bedside light off and stared out the top half of the apartment windows at the late-fall overcast, illuminated by a city full of rose-colored streetlights. She could never get used to the way it looked like rain every morning, only to have that perpetual overcast burn off into a gloriously clear, sunny day. Every day. She was sick of perpetually beautiful weather. She missed the seasons, whether at home in Atlanta or in New England.

It had been such fun with Brian when they were approaching engagement and marriage. But since then, life in the Navy had settled into one long wait. She could understand why some of the other wives had opted early for children, if only to so fill their daily lives that missing Daddy was a pastime that could be confined to the long hours after midnight. Or they found jobs, a career of their own, and maybe somebody else to share them with.

Which brought her to Autrey. Autrey the campaigner. She could now well believe that he was a skilled stalker, patient in the woodscraft ways of a hunter. She didn't feel threatened in any way—it wasn't as if he were menacing her. But she felt like the white men in the Western movies who look around from time to time and see distant figures on the hills around them. Autrey was campaigning, in the sense that he was—how had he put it?—putting himself in the way of love and hoping. Quiet, persistent, projecting a lot of sex appeal without being a macho idiot about it, and making it very clear that he was attracted to her, that he wanted her. Nothing complicated, not marriage, not a love affair, not their life stories. He just wanted her, desired her, a man wanting a woman and being strong enough, unafraid of rejection, to tell her so. She smiled. If men only knew what a powerful force that was, no marriage would ever be safe.

And every time she had broken it off, he had gone along with grace and a smile. And then he had appeared up on those hills again with the same grace and smile, the same focus and direct awareness of her, even when she did something outrageous like wearing the high school cheerleader outfit to Parker's Place. All he had done was look and smile and then up the pressure a few notches by telling her he was shipping out. And then saying, with that insouciant grin, that the news was absolutely a ploy to win her heart. Three months ago, she could never have even speculated about an Autrey, and now she was living in two well-developed spheres of imagination, one in which she loved her husband, yearned for his return, and wondered about their future and a second where she sometimes yearned just to call Autrey on the phone and tell him to get over here. Call him on the phone? She didn't even have his home phone number. She was tempted to turn on the light and look him up in the book. Under what—Crows? Catches Crows? She realized she knew nothing about him, not where he lived, not his phone number, not his domestic habits. Which is one of the reasons he is so attractive—you haven't seen him on a Monday morning.

She was almost shocked to hear rain against the windows. She listened hard. It never rains in Southern California. But how did that song go? It never rains in Southern California. It just pours. Oh yes, sometimes it just goddamn pours.

32

Brian followed Chief Martinez off the gray Navy shuttle bus in front of the main gates. It had been a hot and sweaty ride from the pier area out to the east side of the base. Brian had met the boatswain near the base telephone exchange, after his phone call home to Maddy. He had expected to feel good after calling home, but instead he was . . . well, disappointed. She had missed the whole point about his dilemma in *Hood*, about whether or not he should do the right thing. All she could talk about was how miserable she was, how lonely, and how depressed at the thought of more deployments to come. Of course there would be more deployments—that's what the hell successful officers did, take their ships to sea. But underneath his professional indignance, he feared that his wife was beginning to orbit that question that hung like a dark star in the night sky of every Navy marriage. One day, you may have to choose: a married life with me or a career in the Navy. She hadn't said it in so many words, but, listening to her tonight, she sure as hell was beginning to think it. Thank God I have a job. And I'm going to keep it. I hate the idea of more deployments. And I hate you for bringing them on our heads. No, no, she hadn't said that at all. Bet she thought it, though. But there's been nothing like this in her letters. Of course not, you don't put that in a letter. So when do you talk about it? When you're not deployed, dummy. He sighed, realizing that what he really needed was a sailor's liberty. He had the sudden urge to get drunk and howl at the moon. And from the looks of this crowd, he'd be just one more coyote.

Stepping off the bus, they were enveloped by a noisy crowd of American Navy men, sailors, chiefs, and officers, the officers wearing slacks and sport shirts; the enlisted, jeans and T-shirts, with even an occasional sport coat in view. The main gates at Subic reminded Brian of the starting chutes at a racetrack: There were actually a dozen gates opening through a fifteen-foot-high chain-link fence stretched across one end of a broad bridge. Each gate was guarded by an armed Marine who checked the ID cards of the officers and chiefs, the ID and liberty cards for the other enlisted, and everybody's overnight bag if he had one. It was fully dark at 2030, but the day's heat had not yet broken. Everyone perspired freely in the humid night air, especially the Marines in their fatigue uniforms. Both sides of the liberty gates were illuminated by spotlights mounted on top of the high fence. The spots actually appeared to sputter because of the clouds of insects swarming around the fixtures. The curfew hours, arranged by pay grade, were posted on signboards beside each gate.

The chief carried a small overnight bag, but Brian went empty-handed. He had no intentions of staying over in the town. Warned about thieves and pickpockets, he had left his wallet and rings on the ship, carrying only fifty dollars' worth of pesos and his ID card. As they neared the sweating Marine checking cards and bags at their gate, Brian could see the edges of Olongapo across the bridge. The town was a blaze of colored neon lights that stretched down an unpaved main street teeming with people and wildly decorated vehicles, known locally as jeepneys. The street resembled a frontier town, false fronts emblazoned with neon signs giving way to ramshackle corrugated-iron roofs crouching in the darkness beyond.

Once through the gate, they walked toward the bridge, which spanned stinking mudflats and a canal that appeared to run completely around the town like a moat. As they crossed the bridge, Brian glanced down into the canal to confirm what his nose was already telling him. The chief began his instruction as they crossed over the bridge amid a happy throng of boisterous sailors.

"This here's called the Shit River; yer nose'll tell you why. It's kind of a *benjo* ditch for the whole town. See them kids?"

Only then did Brian notice a collection of naked Filipino urchins perched in the weeds under the bridge. The scrawny boys jumped up and down, yelling in their piping voices, trying to get the sailors' attention. When they succeeded, some of the sailors would toss coins into the malodorous stew and the kids would dive in to retrieve them, creating a brown maelstrom of stagnant water, sewage, and bare legs kicking in the air as the boys probed the muck at the bottom for the coins.

"I can't believe they jump into that," Brian said.

"Yeah, but watch what happens when they git it."

As the chief spoke, one child scrambled back onto the muddy banks, a shiny coin held high in his hand, while the sailors cheered. In the next instant, a teenaged boy stepped forward from the shadows under the bridge, cuffed the smaller boy on the side of the head, and took the coin. The boy complained in a gibber of Tagalog, but the teenager ignored him and melted back into the darkness to wait for the next success.

"Good deal, huh?" said the chief. "The little kids gotta pay the big kids so's they git a spot near the bridge. It's a protection racket."

Brian shook his head as they moved with the crowd across the bridge. The concrete pavement ended at the town side of the bridge, giving way to a hard-packed dirt street. As they stepped off onto the dirt, they were assaulted by a wave of Filipino hustlers, all trying to get them to go to this bar or that *mamasan,* to hire a jeepney for the night, or to meet virginal relatives. The noise was incredible. Brian took a moment to survey the jeepneys. There were dozens of the brightly painted vehicles waiting at the bridge, each completely covered in flashing lights like mobile Christmas trees and playing at least one very loud radio station over external speakers. The jeepneys were further decorated in chromium medallions, hubcaps, flags, banners, religious icons, and festooned with young boys and monkeys hanging from the sides or the roof or even from handles on the hood. Every driver kept one hand pounding on the horn to attract the attention of potential riders. When they had a full boat of sailors, they would roar off into the main street in a cloud of exhaust and cheering Filipinos.

"We're walking'," shouted the boatswain over the noise, pushing his way through the crowd, with Brian in close-column formation to take advantage of the chief's broad wake. Several of the nearby Filipino promoters greeted the chief with shouts of "Hey, Chief!" or "Over here, Bosun Mate!" A couple of them eyed Brian and then shouted out, "Who'sa officer you got there, Bosun Mate? He cherry? First time Olongapo, okay? You come with me for good time, Charlie!"

"These guys know who you are?" shouted Brian over the din.

"Nah. They jist know I'm a CPO and a bosun mate."

"How the hell they know that? How the hell they know I'm an officer?"

"They jist do. These little fuckers know everything. Besides, you look like an officer."

Brian recalled the chief's instructions on the way out to the main gate about officer bars and white-hat bars.

"The Flips," the chief had said, "they know the difference. They can spot an officer a mile away, jist like they can tell when a white hat walks inna officer bar."

"There's separate bars for officers and enlisted?"

"Hell yes. Everythin's organized out there. Officers kin go to officer bars or enlisted bars, but white hats'll git throwed out, they go inna officer bar. Chiefs, they go to either one, seein's they're khaki but usta be white hats. Girl works inna officer bar, she'll turn her nose up at any girl works a white-hat bar. And the *mamasan,* that's the woman who runs the bar, she won't let no white-hat bar girl in her officer bar."

"Sounds complicated. How do I know which bar is which?"

"They'll let ya know, and 'sides, once you been out there a coupla times, you kin tell. Officer bars are quieter, usually, unless there's a carrier in port. Them fuckin' aviators are all crazy bastards. The officer bar girls got better English and are better-lookin'. And cost more, of course."

"Of course. I suppose they figure the officers have more money."

The chief had laughed. "Naw, they know the officers *got* more money, but they also know it's the white hats that'll *spend* it. And what them broads're interested in is the spendin' bit. Best I can tell, the officer-bar deal is jist a way of makin' the officers feel easier 'bout gettin' fucked up without the troops seein' 'em."

"In other words, same fleece job, only a little more genteel."

"Yeah, sorta. But it all beats a midwatch."

After clearing the bridge, the chief pointed toward the left side of the main street, which stretched into the night for about a half mile in front of them. The street was lined on either side with bars, restaurants, hotels, souvenir stores, dance halls, and more bars. The main drag, unpaved, hardpan dirt, was filled with sailors, bar girls, young Filipino men, jeepneys, pushcarts, and the occasional dazed water buffalo. The sidewalks were raised wooden plank walks, with each establishment having a different height of plank walk in front of it. Street kids huddled in small knots at each step up or down in the plank walk, waiting for someone to trip so they could "help" him back up while they picked his pockets. On every corner, there were noisy vendors stoking charcoal braziers mounted on bicycle carts, selling food, Olongapo souvenirs, cold drinks, ice cream, smuggled cigarettes, T-shirts, cheap jewelry, and carved monkeypod plates, mugs, bowls, and animals. The smoking braziers offered aromatic bamboo skewers of meat, which the sailors universally called monkey meat.

Brian found it all rather overwhelming as he followed the boatswain, trying to keep up in the mixed throng of sailors and Filipinos moving down the boardwalks. Everyone seemed to be shouting at once, trying to make themselves heard over the din of jeepney horns, the heavily amplified rock and roll blaring out of the bars, and the incessant din of the Filipino radio stations coming from seemingly everywhere. As they threaded their way through the crowds, Brian twice felt tiny hands slide furtively across his back pockets or along his left wrist as children sized him up as a potential mark for his wallet or his watch. He suddenly found himself face-to-face with a stunningly beautiful Filipina girl who pressed against him in a cloud of sweet perfume and whispered something in his ear before the chief yanked her roughly out of the way and signaled Brian to follow, growling, "Fuckin' Benny boy."

"What's a Benny boy?" Brian asked, still shouting to make himself heard.

"Guy in drag hustlin' blow jobs."

Brian looked back over his shoulder in astonishment. "That was a guy?"

"They're pretty fuckin' good, I gotta admit. There's a coupla bars here specialize in Benny boys. The base cops stake 'em out sometimes, lookin' for Navy queers."

Brian caught up as the crowd thinned out enough for them to walk almost side by side. "So where we bound, Bosun Mate?"

"We're goin' to Josie's place fer starters. It's a nice joint, and the girls are clean if you're inna mind to get laid. We'll have a coupla beers there and then maybe go over to the crocodile bar. After that, we'll see what's shakin'."

"You're staying over tonight?"

"Yes, sir. Always do. I get me a room for the whole port visit. Safer that way. Here's Josie's."

Josie's place turned out to be a dimly lighted single large room that combined the functions of dance hall and bar. Most of the floor was packed with small tables, almost all of which were filled with noisy Americans and Filipina girls of varying sizes, ages, and descriptions. A low ceiling was draped with rattan mats and some vaguely nautical decorations; several fans overhead made a meager attempt to stir the cloud of cigarette smoke in the room. The floor was constructed of wooden planks covered liberally with sawdust. On the right side of the room, another collection of Asian Elvises manfully attacked an American rock-and-roll song at full volume on a raised stage. A stand-up bar ran the whole length of the back side of the dance floor, from which a continuous stream of harried waitresses ferried trays of beer to the thirsty sailors. There were a half dozen couples dancing or otherwise making intimate contact on the open space in front of the band, the Americans towering over their tiny "dates." The chief spied an empty table on the left side of the room, away from the band, and pushed his way through the closely packed tables. Brian followed obediently in his wake and sat down on a spindly wooden chair. A waitress appeared at once, followed by two heavily painted, miniskirted Olongapo debutantes.

"San Magoo. Pitcher," the chief rumbled. He waved off the debutantes, whose hopeful expressions quickly changed to vocal contempt and mutterings about Benny boys. The chief ignored them and a frosty pitcher appeared a minute later, along with two questionably clean glasses. Brian reached for some money, but the chief shook his head and poured.

"They run a tab; they figger you have enough of this stuff, you won't be countin' so good."

Brian grinned and tried the San Miguel beer, for which Subic was famous. It wasn't bad at all, but he was wary after his encounter with Subic Specials.

"This is just beer, right? Not seven kinds of beer with some vodka thrown in for emphasis?" He almost had to shout over the noise from the band.

The chief grinned. "You musta hit some Subic Specials."

"Naw, it was just some fruit juice lightly flavored with rum. I think it was bad juice."

The chief nodded sagely. "Yeah, juice'll do that. This here San Magoo, you get a green one, you'll have the runnin' shits for a week or so."

"How can you tell if it's green?"

"You can't, 'cept'n greenies always come in bottles. That's why you get pitchers."

"That sounds like a story cooked up by the San Miguel people to sell more beer."

The chief nodded. "More beer is better than less beer, I always say."

They nursed their pitcher of beer for a while and watched the action. Almost every table had its allotment of hostesses who sat variously on the laps of their companions or very close alongside. There seemed to be quite a lot of motion below the tablecloths, accompanied by a lot of squealing and giggling. The men drank beer for the most part, while the hostesses sipped on glasses of tea disguised as whiskey and negotiated sexual favors. The chief explained that these ranged from what could be achieved at the table all the way to buying the girl out of the bar for the night.

"Who do they buy them from?" Brian asked.

"From the *mamasan* who runs the place. In this place, it's Josie."

"*Mamasan*. That sounds more like Japanese than Filipino slang."

"Same difference—it's all WESTPAC Navy talk. I ain't never seen a guy runnin' a bar out here in WEST-PAC, whether it's Korea, Taiwan, Japan, or here in Hukapino land. Always a *mamasan*."

"They must be tough old women."

"Not always old. Like Josie here. She's a looker. Wanna meet her?"

Brian did not know what to say. He was curious but totally unsure of how one was supposed to act around the Asian version of a madam. The chief grinned at him, then whispered in the ear of a passing waitress. A few minutes later, the chief nudged Brian; he turned and saw a statuesque Asian woman gliding across the room toward their table. She was taller than the other women in the bar and was dressed in a clinging low-cut floor-length gold lamé gown that revealed the full figure of a mature woman. Her face was round and definitely Asiatic, with arched black eyebrows, dark eyes, and a full mouth. She exuded a sense of class and poise that set her entirely apart from the brown-faced Filipina girls working the tables. The busy waitresses and Olongapo debutantes smiled nervously and made small bows as she walked past. She ignored them and the hot stares of the sailors as the dress parted along the side, revealing a flash of thigh. Brian wondered how old she was, then felt his cheeks redden as he realized that she was looking directly at him, watching him stare at her.

She reached the table before Brian had figured out what to say or do. He wanted to look away but could not, there was so much of her to look at. The chief was making introductions as if he had known Josie for a long time.

"Josie, this is Mr. Holcomb, the new Weapons officer inna *Hood*. Boss, this here is Josie."

Brian started to stand up, but she put her hand on his shoulder, the beginnings of a smile on her lips. "I'm pleased to meet you, Mr. Holcomb. Welcome to my place."

Brian found himself looking up and nodding at her, tongue-tied. He suddenly felt like a bumbling idiot. *Pleased,* she had said, not *preased.* He found himself dying to know *what* she was, whether Chinese, Japanese, or whatever other exotic mixture. He detected a faint scent of expensive perfume that was a far cry from the cheap colognes of the bar girls. Josie was speaking to him again.

"So what do you think of Olongapo? This is your first time here, yes?"

"It's, uh, it's quite something," Brian replied. "And it's my first time here. First time in WESTPAC, for that matter." Her breasts were large and pointed right in his face. She had not removed her hand from his shoulder, and he thought for an instant that her fingers were rubbing the back of his shoulder as she talked to him.

"Is there anything you need? Anything we can get you?"

Before he could stop himself, Brian asked her if she wanted to dance. The chief's mouth began to work as he tried to keep from laughing. Josie smiled down at Brian and shook her head gently.

"No, no, Mr. Holcomb. That is not done. I'm the owner, you see. But it is sweet of you to ask. Please enjoy yourself in my place. I will stop by again later. Louie Jesus, good to see you again."

"You bet, Josie."

Brian watched in awe as Josie moved away toward the back of the bar; he thought there were a hell of a lot of things in motion on just one woman. He then stole a quick look over at the chief.

"I suppose I just fucked up," he said in a low voice, looking down now at the table and studying his glass of beer. The glasses on the table started shifting, and when he looked sideways at the chief, he found him shaking with silent laughter.

"Well, boss, that *is* a hell of a lot of woman right there. At least you didn't come out and ask if you could go down on her right here and now, which's what usually happens first time a horny sailor gets a look at Josie in her running gear. You ast me, I think she kinda liked you."

Brian shook his head. "That was indeed a lot of woman. Do all the *mamasans* look like that?"

"Hell no. Most of 'em are short, fat, ugly, and mean-er'n a sumo wrestler what ain't been fed since the mid-watch. Naw, Josie's kinda special."

"What is she?"

"Whadaya mean, what?"

"I mean is she Japanese, Chinese? She's definitely not Filipino."

The chief snorted. "No 'fense, Mr. Holcomb, but you white guys are alla time too hung up on breeds. *What* she is is a good-lookin' woman who's stacked to the gills and got class besides. I mean, you did notice, am I right? Couldn't talk 'cause your tongue was too hard, right? Shee-it, finish up that beer and let's go over to the crocodile bar."

They left Josie's as Brian gave one last hopeful look over his shoulder as they pushed through the entrance, but Josie was nowhere to be seen. They joined the throngs on the boardwalk, heading deeper into the town. After about a hundred yards of pushing through the noise and the crowds, the chief turned to cross the street. Ahead was a much larger establishment than Josie's. To Brian's astonishment, there seemed to be more noise coming from inside than from out on the street.

"This here's the crocodile bar," shouted the chief. "This here's special, even for Subic. You stay close to me so's we can git up front."

"Why?"

"You'll see. Stick close."

Brian followed the chief into a mob scene inside. This bar was jammed with Americans, all of whom were drinking beer, singing along with yet another Elvis group jamming somewhere over in a smoky corner, or chasing the bar girls. There was no room for tables, and the bar girls were doing the best they could in the press of milling bodies. The room was hot and the atmosphere of cigarette smoke, cheap perfume, human sweat, beer, and something Brian could not identify was nearly overwhelming. There was an anxious crowd packed at the front door, trying to get in, but the chief just started forward through the door and onto the dance floor. Some individuals complained as he started through, but then they subsided and gave way to the laws of gross tonnage when they realized they were bitching at a belt buckle. Brian stayed tucked in close astern, hoping he was invisible.

The real crowd, the source of most of the noise, and the chief's objective, was in the center of the room, where there was a hollow square, twenty feet on a side, formed by a chest-high chain-link fence. Inside the fence was a pool of noxious-looking water, and in the pool were about a dozen crocodiles, ranging in size from three feet to one monster that appeared to Brian to be as long as the pool. Sailors crowded in on all four sides of the fence, yelling encouragement to two of their buddies who stood on a small platform at one end of the square. Each of the men had a canvas bag clutched in his left hand. Whatever was in the bag was alive. Brian watched in fascination as one man reached into the bag and pulled out a baby chicken. The chick was dyed bright pink, as if painted up for Easter. At the sight of the chick, every one of the crocodiles turned its horrendous snout in the direction of the man, who held the chick up and shook it at the crocs. An answering chorus of hisses and grunts rose from the pool and a long cheer of encouragement issued from the onlookers. Then the man lofted the chick into the center of the pool and the crocs jumped, slashed, roared, and splashed while the cheering section roared their own approval at the bloody scrimmage. When the chick had disappeared, the second man stepped up to the fence and brandished a new chick, this one bright blue, and the crocs and the crowd got set again.

"I can't fucking believe this!" Brian shouted over the noise.

"Yeah, well, you had to see it," said the chief. "You kin buy a baga chicks for five hunnert pesos, you want."

"That's okay; I think I'll just watch." There was another great shout as the chick went airborne, to be snapped up in midair this time by the monster. Brian saw some money changing hands and realized the guys were making bets.

He and the chief stayed and watched the proceedings for almost an hour. Martinez snagged four bottles of San Miguel from a passing waitress who had her hands full, then pressed some pesos down her front when she started to object. She shrugged, grinned, and disappeared into the crowd. There was a burst of noise when one of the chicks managed to avoid being eaten, fluttering over the backs of three snapping crocs and into the hands of a sympathetic sailor at the other end of the enclosure. The sailor carried the chick triumphantly out a back door and let it go into the alley, to the mixed jeers and cheers of his buddies. The escape of the chick started a fight in the pool, which ended when the monster dragged one of the smaller crocs, squirming in its massive jaws, under the swirling water to a bloody resolution. Brian saw the First Division side cleaners, Coltrane and Hooper, in the crowd. Hooper was speaking urgently to one of the pit bosses and Coltrane stared at the thrashing reptiles with his usual stupid grin. Hooper gestured to the crocs in the pool and shouted something about money.

After the chief lost four bets in a row, he signaled Brian that they were leaving. As they pushed their way out onto the boardwalk again, Brian asked what time it was. The chief consulted his watch, a stainless-steel job lashed to his massive wrist with a pickpocketproof steel band.

"Twenny-three-fifteen," he announced. "We got time to get some chow, then I gotta get you back ta the gate."

"Chow? You eat stuff out here?"

"Movin' or settin' still, I eat it, damn right. First night out, you gotta try monkey meat." The chief steered Brian toward a nearby street vendor, who started his sales pitch as soon as he saw the chief.

Brian was hanging back. "Uh, I'm not sure—"

"Yeah, hell. C'mon, try it. It's cooked an all, and it beats the shit outta that goddamn green Navy ham. Here, try a stick."

Brian held the foot-long stick on which strands of sizzling aromatic meat were twisted. He tasted some gingerly and found it delicious. He nodded at the chief as he ate the rest of it. The chief grinned and bought two sticks for himself, which he made disappear in about three seconds. As they walked on, Brian asked if it was really monkey meat.

"Naw, it's dog. They catch an old dog, stuff it with rice for about three weeks, and then beat it to death with sticks, make it real tender. Then they soak it in soya sauce and—whatsa matter, you get a greenie back there at the croc pit?"

Brian composed his face while he tried to control his stomach and banish the image of a bloated dog being tenderized in some back alley. They walked back down the boardwalk toward the Shit River and the main gates. Across the street, Brian saw the sign for Josie's bar. The chief saw him looking and they stepped out of the stream of traffic and stopped across from the bar. The crowds on the street were thinner as curfew approached.

"You wanna see Josie again? You go in there, you know, she likes you, yer gonna have to git yerself back to the gates. You only got—what, an hour? Josie don't do no short time, you follow me?"

Brian was acutely embarrassed. He *did* want to see her again. And he might manage just one more beer—with all this heat, the San Miguel had barely affected him. And, by God, she was the most exotic woman he had ever seen. He could not bring himself to admit that sex might be part of it. Might be, hell. But he was married, for Chrissakes. The chief was watching him carefully.

"Well, I'd kind of like just to talk to her, you know. I mean, I'm married and I can't go fooling around with Olongapo whores. But—"

"Yeah, that 'but' is a bitch, ain't it? Tell ya what—you go on in there, git you a table inna corner, outta the way, okay? Should be thinnin' out, anyways. Tell the waitress you wanted to have one drink with the *mamasan*—don't call her Josie in fronta the waitress—before you have to git back to the base. If it's on, she's gonna surprise the shit outta you. If it ain't, have one fer the road and make yer gate. Just jump on a jeepney and say, 'Main gate.' Twenty pesos max, okay? I gotta go see a girl I know, git her bought out, okay?"

"Okay, Chief, and thanks for the grand tour. I'll see you back aboard."

"Maybe, maybe not." The chief grinned as he walked away.

Brian, who was scampering across the dirt street to avoid a stream of passing jeepneys, did not hear him. He went into Josie's place and sought out a corner table. He waved away three debutantes and signaled a waitress, to whom he gave the message. She seemed vastly amused as she headed for the bar, where a giggling session broke out. Nothing happened for fifteen minutes. The bar was about half full now and the Elvises had mercifully shut down for a while. Brian wondered just how big a fool he was making of himself, and also what time it was, when one of the bartenders slipped under a hatch in the bar and came over to his table. The man seemed to get bigger as he got closer, and he, too, did not appear to be Filipino. His face was impassive as he approached Brian's table.

"You come," he ordered, then turned around, assuming that Brian would obey his curt command. Brian took a deep breath, got up, and followed the burly man to the back of the room. They walked past the bar to a door Brian had not noticed earlier. The man knocked once, stuck his head in, said something, bowed once, a sharp, formal movement, and stood aside, nodding with his head for Brian to go inside. Brian stepped through the door and into another world.

He found himself standing in an anteroom of some kind, the walls of which were paneled in a reddish wood. There were Oriental rugs on the floor and side tables with brass lamps. The air was cool and quiet, with no trace of the smoke and the beer stink of the bar beyond. An ornately carved large door beckoned at the other end of the room. A very pretty girl dressed in what looked like white silk pajamas materialized, bowed silently to him, and pointed to his shoes. He realized they were supposed to come off, so he obliged. She passed him a pair of soft slippers and then led him to the other door. She repeated the procedure used by the barman, knocking softly, putting her head in, bowing, and withdrawing with a motion for him to go inside. She bowed as he went past her and he tried awkwardly to bow back, causing the girl to put her hand in front of her mouth.

The inner room was much larger. Its twelve-foot-high ceilings and walls were papered in a heavily embroidered material displaying several shades of red. Three upholstered rosewood armchairs and a couch occupied the foreground; a huge Chinese rug spanned the entire room. There were brass standing lamps with ivory-colored shades, recessed bookshelves along the right-hand wall, and a large intricately carved mahogany desk at the other end of the room. To one side of the desk stood a four-paneled Chinese screen framed in rosewood, with alternating panels of painted silk and translucent parchment. The room had no windows, only a single door at the other end, identical to the one he had come through. Brian took a breath and detected a tendril of incense in the air, mingling with beeswax furniture polish and the rich smell of old leather. Josie was sitting at the desk.

She let him drink in the rich hues and elegant trappings of the room, waiting for the contrast between the beer bar out front and this luxurious inner sanctum to sink in. Then she rose. She had changed; she now wore a different gown, this one green and embroidered with silver dragons. Slit up one side to just above her knee, it had a high-topped collar above her bodice. As before, he could only stare. Her gown and her movements were modest and restrained, but that same gown managed to show off the luxuriance of her body with every step. Compared with this regal beauty, Brian felt severely underdressed in his sweaty sport shirt and chinos dusty from the Olongapo streets. He realized that she was much taller than he had remembered. With a gracious gesture, Josie invited him to sit down in one of the chairs.

"Would you like some champagne?" she asked. He loved her voice, which was husky but beautifully modulated. Her English was precise, unaccented, and bespoke an educated person. As she sat down, he figured that she was probably in her early thirties, although her flawless skin and unwrinkled eyes made it very difficult to tell. If she was wearing makeup, he could not see it, except for the intense red of her lipstick. She sat upright in the chair with her back straight, her legs uncrossed, and her hands in her lap. He noticed that she had tiny hands and feet.

"Yes," he said, clipping off the *ma'am* that had almost popped out. As if she had heard it in his thoughts, she smiled in mild amusement and then clapped her hands once. The girl in the white silk pajamas appeared from behind the screen with a silver tray holding a bottle of Piper-Heidsieck champagne in a silver ice bucket and two crystal champagne flutes. She set the tray down, nudged the cork out of the bottle, poured out the golden wine, passing one glass to Brian and the other to Josie, before withdrawing with a bow.

"To your very good health," Josie said.

"To yours," he replied, and tasted the champagne. It was marvelous, cold, sweet, and astringent all at the same time. The sweaty taste of the Olongapo beer bars was swept away.

"Now, Mr. Holcomb, why have you come to see me?"

"Please call me Brian. If that's okay, I mean."

"Very well. Brian."

"Well, to tell the truth, I, uh, I really wanted to see you again. I've never seen anyone like you before. I guess that's sort of dumb. But, well, there it is." He smiled lamely, running out of words. He really did just want to look at her.

She looked back at him, directly into his eyes, her eyes widened and her lips parted slightly. Brian felt his peripheral vision blur just a bit.

"Do you think that I am beautiful?"

"Oh yes, very much so. I didn't think that . . . out here in Olongapo, I mean, I just didn't expect . . . you . . . all this." He embraced the richly appointed parlor with a sweep of his hand. "Damn. I'm acting like an idiot. Maybe I should just apologize and get out of here. I shouldn't be here. I shouldn't be bothering you."

Josie smiled again; this time it was more friendly than amused. "Please relax, Mr. Holcomb. Brian. You cannot offend a woman by telling her she is beautiful. You are curious about me, and how there can be a room like this in a village with dirt streets, three hundred bars, two hundred brothels, and wooden sidewalks."

Brian smiled back and sipped some champagne to gain a moment in which to compose his thoughts. "Yes. But I didn't know anything about all this, this room, when I saw you. I'm still mostly curious about you."

"Is this about sex, Brian?"

Brian colored. "No, no. I mean, I'm married. I didn't come out here to get—to find a woman. It's my first time in WESTPAC, in Subic. The chief brought me along so I could see the sights of Olongapo. I'm sorry if you—"

She waved her hand as if to dismiss his protests.

"Then I shall tell you about me. My father was Chinese; my mother, the daughter of an American sailor and a Filipina woman. I was raised in Hong Kong. My father was wealthy. He died during a typhoon, when our house was taken by a mud slide. My mother moved back to Manila, where she had family. They did not approve of her because she was of mixed blood. But she also had money, so she decided to come to Olongapo. She bought several of these establishments that service the American Navy. When the war in Vietnam came, she became very rich. I was her only child and business partner, and I now run the many businesses. In Hong Kong, were I a man, I would be *taipan*. To answer your unspoken question, all of that, outside that door, pays for all of this."

Brian nodded his head slowly. "But I thought that in Asia, women would not be permitted to be what we call a boss. How do you get away with it?"

"You are perceptive. The hatreds exist on many levels.

As a woman, I am by tradition usurping my rightful place, which is on my back in the boudoir. As a business-woman who owns more than a third of the bars and establishments in Olongapo, I am resented for my wealth. As a person of mixed race, I am despised by the Filipinos and the Chinese alike. I get away with it because I am very rich and can buy the power to hurt or even destroy my enemies if I choose to.''

Brian smiled. "It's funny. I asked the chief *what* you were, and he didn't understand the question. I meant what racial origins you came from. He said that we white people care too much about race. He said you were a beautiful woman and that nothing else really mattered.'' His brain flirted with the image of Josie on her back in the boudoir.

"Chief Louie is a special man. You and I would never have met if you had not been with him.''

"He's special all right. He's the tall dog in the chief's locker and nobody, but nobody gives him any trouble.''

"He and I are alike in that manner,'' she said. "Have some more champagne.''

They talked for what seemed to Brian like a short time. He could feel rather than hear the thump and twanging of the rock band in the front of the building. There was the niggling thought in his mind that he ought to know what time it was, but he was absorbed by this woman. Even as they talked and she told him how the town had boomed once the war began in earnest in 1965, how it was now awash in money, drugs, and crime, only part of him was listening. He was drinking her in with his eyes—her face, the genteel voice, the way her lips formed the words, and the way her hand would occasionally rub the length of her thigh, absently, as if it needed an occasional touch. A sudden silence in the room brought him back, but something was different. She was looking at him now; her face and hands were still. He felt a rush of blood beginning to fill his head; it became difficult to breathe.

"Do you know the Asian custom of the bath?'' she asked in a low voice.

"I've heard the officers on the ship talk about hotse baths,'' he replied. His throat was dry. It must have been the champagne.

"My servant will assist you. I must withdraw now. When you are finished, I will see you again."

She rose from the chair, smoothed the dress over the front of her body in a sweeping motion with both her hands, barely touching, and then she bowed slightly with just her head and disappeared behind the screen. The servant girl waited for Brian by the door at the end of the room.

Brian took a deep breath. For just a minute there . . . Then he remembered the curfew. But he did not have his watch on. What the hell time was it? And what was he going to do if it was past curfew? Go back to the gate? Get written up like a drunken sailor? The servant girl was saying something.

"What?"

"You come now."

"But I have to—"

"You come now." She tipped her head at the door as if he was being obtuse. What the hell. Might as well go down clean. He walked toward the door, which she opened for him. He walked through and she closed it behind them and then led him down a long, dimly lighted, carpeted hallway. There were doors on either side that gave no hint of where they led. No noises from the street or the dance bar penetrated the hallway. Brian could not figure out exactly where he was in relationship to the street. They seemed to be going back, away from the street, but the building had not looked that big.

At the end of the hall was another ornate wooden door. The girl led him through it into a humid wooden-walled and -floored room that had benches on three sides and a metal locker on the fourth. A bare lightbulb hanging from the ceiling gave the only illumination. There was a set of metal double doors next to the locker, and the metal was sweating.

"Your clothes," she said. "I take." She held out both hands as if to receive an invisible tray. He realized that she wanted him to take his clothes off and give them to her. She stared demurely at the floor. Well, in for a penny, in for a pound. He took off his shirt and pants, then his T-shirt. She waited patiently, still looking at the floor. He shucked his underpants awkwardly, wondering whether or not to hand them to her. Finally, she reached for them and nodded with her head at the double doors. He understood and paraded across the room and through the double doors.

In the next room was a pool of heated greenish water, about fifteen feet on a side, with steps cut into one side. To his left was another set of double metal doors. There was almost no margin to the pool, only a small apron leading to the steps. He stepped down into the pool, gingerly at first, but found that it was not that hot. He went all the way in and then stretched out on one side, surprised to find a stone bench in the pool wall. Sitting on it put his head just barely above the water, which was roiling gently from unseen pumps. He relaxed in the water and let it extract the sweat and beer and the smell of the town. He had a slight buzz on from the champagne, but the moist, warm air fizzing quietly off the top of the water was soothing.

After ten minutes or so, the servant girl appeared again. She gestured for him to come out of the water. For some reason, he was no longer embarrassed by his nakedness. He climbed the steps up out of the water and stood obediently before her. She was tiny, her head coming up only to his chest, and she did not look directly at him. She turned, went through the next set of doors, and he followed her into the room, where there was another pool. The surface of this second pool was roiling more vigorously than the first and there was a good bit of steam in the room.

"Hot," she said, bowing, and then she was gone. There was the same arrangement of steps, but this time it took him a few minutes to get into the water. It was almost uncomfortably hot but increasingly relaxing. He found the submerged bench and sat back, his arms stretched out along the rim of the pool, and soaked up heat. The ceiling of the room was in shadow. The only lights came from what looked like fluorescent fixtures embedded high in the walls. The steam was thick enough to obscure the other side of the pool. "Rich," she had said. Rich indeed. One pool for warm, one for hot. This place must be enormous. He was dozing comfortably in the water when the girl appeared again, beckoning him.

"Follow you anywhere, ma'am," he said cheerfully when he stood once again on the stone floor. "What's next?"

She led him through a third set of doors into yet another pool room. In this one, the water was still and there was no steam. When he touched a toe to sample the temperature, he found it to be cool. There seemed to be more light in this room, and this time the girl stayed. He noticed she was holding a large white towel in her hands. He submerged himself a couple of times to cool off and then, aware that she was waiting, he came out. She stepped behind him and wrapped his midsection in the towel in three deft movements, then headed for the final set of doors.

They turned right, walked down a small carpeted hallway, and into a square room about the same size as the pool rooms. It had wooden walls and was carpeted in some kind of matting. Two overhead fans turned very slowly above a stainless-steel massage table in the middle of the room. There was a small tray table on wheels alongside the main table and there were four smoked-glass bottles on it. The massage table was padded on the top and had a single white towel rolled into a tight log on one end to serve as a pillow. She indicated that he should get on the table, which he started to do, except that he did not know what to do with the towel. She solved the problem for him by taking it off and, once he was lying facedown on the table, draping it demurely over his buttocks.

He lay there for a few minutes, his muscles relaxing even more, his eyes closed, the light downdraft from the fans drying off his skin. He didn't hear the girl return until she was standing behind him and opening the bottles. He had never had a massage in his life and his skin tingled with anticipation. She started on his back, standing by his hips and reaching up to stroke the long muscles of his upper back, then smoothing the skin down along his flanks. Brian wondered what his body looked like. He had done all the compulsory athletics at school and had even fooled with weight lifting for a while, but he had not done much since then. If anything, he was probably a little skinny after the long line period out in the Gulf and those torturous midwatches.

Her fingers were oiled in a fragrant ointment and they probed deeply, maintaining a sinuous rhythm from his neck down to the small of his back. He put his head to one side on the towel, his arms crossed under his chin. He felt drowsy but did not want to miss any of the wonderful sensations. Her hands were competent and strong, much stronger than he would have thought possible from such a tiny thing.

Then she changed position, moving around to the head of the table so that she could reach over his head and down his back. As she reached, he was aware of the warmth of her body inches from his arms and he detected a faint perfume. That perfume, he had smelled it once before. He wondered. Moving very slowly, he tilted his head up slightly and cracked open one eye. A drape of diaphanous white cotton gown filled his vision. Holy shit. Definitely not the servant girl. She was too big, too strong. My God, could it be—

"Relax, Brian. The massage does not work if you are tense." There was a hint of amusement in her voice.

"Josie?" he said, his voice slightly strangled because of the position of his head.

"Straighten your neck, Brian." She took his head in her hands, brought it around so that she was holding him, her fingers against his cheeks. "Yes, that's it. Rest your chin on the tips of your fingers. Just so. That is much better."

Boy was it. As she reached over and down, the top of her mons rose above the edge of the table, the vision of her nakedness swimming into his face and then away, her creamy skin shimmering through the cotton gown. The curve of her hips filled his peripheral vision and he felt himself stirring under the towel. Then she started working the back of his neck, stepping back slightly from the table and giving him a fuller view of her lush body, lovingly enfolded in the gossamer embrace of the gown, tantalizing him as the translucent material gathered and relaxed with her efforts. Then she took his right arm in her left hand, held it straight out, and turned herself around so that she could pull the muscles in his arm, stroking them from the shoulder to his fingertips with her right hand, pressing her buttocks against the edge of the table, letting his forearm barely brush against her right breast. By the time she had repeated the procedure with his left arm, he had to restrain himself from touching her, but he sensed that, whatever was going on here, it was not yet time for touching.

She folded his arm back under his chin and walked around to the tray table, where she replenished the oils on her hands. Then she moved to the opposite end of the table, where she began to massage his feet, left first, then right, gripping and smoothing. He wanted to see her, wanted to turn around, roll over, and look at her, but he knew he couldn't, not yet. And he suddenly realized that rolling over was going to be a protuberant maneuver, a fact that probably was not going to come as a surprise to the lady. She started on his legs, reaching up his calves, rolling her hands on the back of his knees, and then higher, strong fingers searching out the major muscles, holding, weighing, and then pressing down and along the full length of his limbs. Then she was moving again, back to the tray table and then back to the head of the table.

She stood before him once again, took his hands in hers, and indicated that he should roll over. He complied, the towel deserting him. With his hands tightly held in hers, he was not embarrassed. She made an "mmm" of appreciation and then placed his hands flat under his hips. She poured warm oil on his chest and began to stroke the front of his body, leaning over him farther and farther, her breasts heavy beneath the fabric, settling lower and lower to envelop his face and barely brush his chest. His lungs were filled with the scents of her, her perfume, the salty tang of perspiration, and something far more elemental. When he thought he couldn't stand another minute, she stepped back, shed the gown, and then came around to the side of the table and mounted him, taking him inside in one smooth, exquisite movement that brought him immediately to climax. As the breath shuddered out of him, he reached for her, but she put his arms back, pinning them under his hips again. When he was finally still, she began to move her hips, gradually restoring him while lifting her weight from his body until their only contact was where their cores connected, a continuation of the massage by a less familiar but no less effective channel, until he sensed that her control was finally beginning to slip. He opened his eyes and looked at her face, her eyes opened but unseeing, her mouth parted, and her breathing quickening. He recognized the moment, and this time his arms came out and would not be denied. He pulled her face down to his and kissed her lips and her mouth while taking over control of the movement, moving harder and faster now, pulling her down and into him, his lips glued to her mouth. As he felt her going over the edge, he arched his back and doubled the rhythm until she cried out and collapsed on top of him, her breath coming in great heaving sobs as her limbs dissolved and she seemed to melt.

Afterward, they lay entwined on the table for some time, he stroking her back and calming her, both of them trying to regain their breath. For the first time on the cruise, Brian's mind was perfectly clear, the pumice of fatigue gone from those seemingly permanent pockets behind his eyes, all of his apprehensions about career and promotion kicked into a mental corner, where right now they seemed to belong. He searched his heart for the expected strands of guilt over betraying his wife and found none. Maybe later, but not now. Not during this perfect here and now, joined with this exquisite woman who had coiled him up like a spring with just her hands, released him, and then done it again long enough and well enough for him to be able to send her over the mountain when her time came. He had never known what satisfaction could be had from bringing a woman to such pleasure. Maddy in all her days with him had never come like that, and a part of him wondered why that was so. But she was moving again and he closed his eyes and stopped thinking about Maddy.

33

San Diego

The afternoon after the aborted phone call from Subic, she came home from the bank an hour early, just to get out of there. The accounting department was so dreadfully dull, she thought she would scream by 3:00 P.M., so she had just gathered up her purse and left. The supervisor had been in a meeting that was supposed to last until 5:00 P.M.; Maddy hoped that it would—she had been pushing the limits of that nice lady's patience. Once home, she looked through the mail, found a letter from Brian, and, for once, didn't open it at the front door. After talking to him last night, this morning, whenever the hell it was, whatever was in the letter would be very definitely old news. She decided to save it, an unopened treat, for a day when she hadn't had mail for a while.

She went into the bedroom, shucked her clothes, and got out her tennis outfit. It was a one-piece short white skirt and halter top number with a built-in bra, under which she wore cotton underwear and white tennis panties. The skirt was pleated and was probably about two inches shorter than it had looked when she bought it. White tennis shoes and short white socks completed her outfit, along with a bag for her Kramer and a couple of cans of tennis balls and a towel.

She played just about every day at the public courts in the park across the street from the apartment. She could usually rustle up a set with one of the women who showed up every day around five. She deflected the male mashers by pretending that she couldn't keep up with men players and was waiting for a girlfriend. She had one other tennis dress, which Brian had bought her in the Exchange, but the color was a vile lime green. She wore it only if he was joining her on the courts, and there wasn't much chance of that these days, was there?

She glanced at her watch. It was a little early, but then again, the end of daylight saving time was darkening the days about an hour sooner, so a little more daylight wouldn't hurt. There was always the backboard until someone showed for a game. She tied her hair back with a large barrette, grabbed her keys, and started out the door, when the phone rang. She put her stuff down and answered it. It was the exec's wife, Barbara Mains.

"Maddy, I'm putting together a scratch potluck for tonight. We've got most of the wives who can come, or at least those who can get baby-sitters. Honestly, that's a real chore these days—you don't know of a good one, do you? But of course, you don't live near me. What am I thinking. Anyway, my house, sevenish?"

Maddy hesitated. She had no real reason not to go, but all of a sudden she didn't want to. Didn't want to see the rest of the wives, or talk Navy, or listen to the latest kinder crisis from the diaper-and-tricycle set. Maddy thought the exec's wife was a sweet lady, but Barbara was one of those flaky Southern California blondes who often appeared to have misplaced their trail of bread crumbs while tripping through the magic forest.

"Barbara, I've got a tennis match starting at five-thirty, and that usually goes for an hour and a half. Then I'm probably going to take a shower, nuke a TV dinner, drink some wine, and go to bed. But thanks for calling. Another time, okay?"

"Oh, sure, Maddy. It is short notice. No big deal. A bunch of us were just really bored, you know, Friday night and everything? But Mrs. Huntington said to be sure to call you, to be sure to call everyone, actually—didn't want anyone to feel left out, you know?"

"Right, Barbara. Thanks. Say hi to everybody. Bye now."

Maddy trotted across the street in front of the apartment building and into the public park that fronted the renowned Balboa Zoo park on the other side. The park was about six blocks by three in size, with softball diamonds, ten tennis courts, and even a boccie lawn at one end. Grand old eucalyptus trees stood everywhere, above lots of grass and graveled walkways. It was a very pretty oasis among the parched hills of Southern California, and one of the main reasons they had taken the apartment. Maddy crossed the park, threaded her way through some energetic Frisbee teams, ignoring the bold looks and a wolf whistle, and set up shop at one of the two backboards on the south end of the courts. The courts were filling as she arrived, but none of her regular partners had shown up yet. She warmed up and then began working on her serve. She had the form right but not enough power, and for some reason, she had been chunking balls about six inches below the net line for about twenty minutes when a voice interrupted her.

"Look over the net after you hit it, then the balls will go over."

She was bending over to retrieve the returning ball, forgetting about the skirt, and she straightened up quickly and turned, to find Autrey standing by the bench that had her bag on it. He was smiling as usual, and she felt a sudden warmth in her cheeks. He was wearing a gray sweatshirt that had been hacked into a vest, a pair of loose khaki shorts that might have been swim trunks at one time, and some dirty old tennis shoes with no socks. He leaned one arm on the back of the bench, his tanned body loose and lanky, almost insolently posed, and yet poised to move if he had to. She looked at him for a long moment, her racket held in both hands, before walking over from the back of the backboard court.

"You're a tennis expert, too?" she asked.

"No expert. But I'm tall enough to do some damage, especially on the serve. If you can win the serve, you don't have to win the point."

She handed him the racket and the ball, nodding sideways with her head to show her what he was talking about. She was working hard to keep her mind in neutral. He grinned again, took the racket, grunted in approval at the wooden Kramer, walked to the baseline, and bounced the ball a couple of times. Then he set himself, threw the ball impossibly high over his head, put the racket back between his shoulder blades, waited for a fraction of a second, and hit it so hard that she could barely see it go, not focusing on it again until he was scooping it off the court. The ball had hit the board hard enough to attract the attention of the players in the near courts. Then he did it again, once more producing a resounding whack on the board. He scooped up the ball and held on to the racket.

"Height is what does it. Long arms. You've got the form right, but you're not tall enough to do a power serve. You need to be tricky instead. Let me show you?"

He squared his shoulders; the movement seemed to make every muscle in his arms and legs move. At that instant, it wasn't about tennis anymore. She knew if she closed the eight feet between them, let him stand behind her and position her body, and then work her arm through the serve, it wasn't going to stop there. She hesitated, almost forgetting to breathe, and waited for him to shamble and grin, take her off the hook. But this time, he didn't do it. He turned instead to face the backboard again and continued to talk, instructing an invisible person by his side, explaining where the feet went, how to turn and throw it while positioning the racket, how to substitute control for power, while she stood behind him, her hands clenched in front of her, trying not to watch the muscles of his upper back as he set the racket or the way his legs tightened up when he hit the ball. He kept talking, his voice steady, unexcited, mesmerizing her until she found herself stepping forward, getting closer until he sensed she was there, and then letting him put the racket in her hand, adjust the grip, and show her the moves. She could smell the fine mist of perspiration on his face, an intensely male scent, and waited for him to close in from behind. But he didn't do it. He stood just outside of her space, not touching anything but her hand and her elbow, forcing her finally to concentrate on what he was saying and not what she was feeling.

It went on for about forty-five minutes before she began to tire, some newly used muscles in her arm and shoulder complaining. But he had shown her something about serving, and she had been hitting consistently into a difficult backhand corner by the end of the lesson. They sat together on the bench afterward, she sharing the towel with him as she talked about how hard she had to work at tennis. She was perspiring by then and her hair felt like a damp mop on the back and sides of her head. But after fifteen minutes, the sun slipped behind her apartment building and suddenly it was cool again. She wanted to reach for her sweater. She was dying for something to drink.

"So when do you leave for Vietnam?" she asked, draping the small towel over her thighs.

"I think in two more weeks. I finished up with my last class of new guys today, and the training schedule is blank after that. I may go do some weapons training up at Pendleton next week. I don't know yet."

"How do you feel about it? I mean, the news is full of talk that it's going to be over soon, that we're going to pull out."

He shook his head slowly. "I think there's going to be a lot of talking first. The Corps, the military, hasn't forgotten Tet; that was just last year. It was a surprise, but we kicked their asses for it, and the people I work for still think we can win it on the field. I think it's going to be interesting times for a while longer."

She rubbed the top of her thighs with the towel absently.

"I sometimes believe the antiwar people have it right, that this is a hopeless cause that we have no business being involved in—if only because the people we're supporting don't really care."

"They care, the ones who have to live there. The generals, the ones with Swiss bank accounts and French wives, they don't care. But there're people over there, people who will have to stay there if the Communists win. They care. But it's not the politics. It's just me, I guess. The way I am and what I am. Hell, I want to go. It's what I do. I want to see how good I really can do it."

She nodded this time. That was more like it. It was what he did, just like deploying and going to sea was what Brian did. It was simply the way men were. Women were a part of their life's experience but would never be the objective of their life's experience. A breeze swept across the courts. The people playing welcomed it, but Maddy shivered.

"Time for you to go in," he said.

"Yes, I suppose. I'm not up for a game right now; I think my arm would fall off." She turned to face him, her mind made up, the decision solidifying in her brain and in the sexual part of her with astonishing ease. "But I do thank you for the lesson. You've taught me a lot."

He did not reply, just looked into her face. She cocked her head to one side and looked back.

"Want to go get something to drink?" she said softly. "I'm simply dying . . . of thirst."

"Yes."

They walked in silence across the park, he carrying the bag, she with her head down, the racket in her hands, the delicate fabric of her skirt lifting in the breeze, making her feel almost undressed in the cool night air. She was conscious that her hair was a mess and that she needed a shower and that her heart was pounding just a bit. They went through the lobby of the apartment and took the elevator to her floor. She did not look at him while they stood together in the elevator. She unlocked the door and went straight into the kitchen, dropping the racket onto the couch. In the kitchen, she retrieved two glasses from the cupboard and then began rummaging in the refrigerator. There were some diet Cokes, a can of beer, a half bottle of Gallo's finest plonk, and a jug of spring-water.

Autrey came into the kitchen. Out of the corner of her eye, she watched him standing there in the dim light, his long, lean body a study in bronze, his dark face in shadow, eyes shining softly, an expression of gentle interest barely imprinted on his face. He folded his arms across his chest and leaned back slightly, his left hip propped against the kitchen counter but the rest of him posed in tension. She was glad she had not turned on the light.

She brought out the various bottles and put them down on the kitchen table, trying not to look at him, her face down so that her eyes were hidden by her hair. But she could not avoid the image of his shorts against the mahogany skin of his legs, the smooth muscles of his thighs. She felt a wave of warmth in her belly and her thoughts began to tumble. She began to move things around on the table, aware that she ought to turn the light on or do something to break the spell that was growing between them. The tips of her fingers tingled as she touched the smooth glass of the wine bottle, the solid heft of it inducing unbidden images to invade her mind as Autrey, Autrey of the slow moves and languid grace, held himself motionless across the room. Her hands became still. She had to swallow to find her voice.

"Autrey." The strength of her voice surprised her. Then more softly, the emerging edges of desire drawing a flush to her face and arousing the sensations of a tingling web settling on her breasts and a feeling of liquid awareness in her thighs, she said, "Autrey . . . for God's sake."

He moved then, reaching her with soundless steps, standing behind her and pulling her in, his hands on her stomach, his muscular scent all around her, his hands on her hips, pulling the backs of her thighs into demanding contact, kissing her hair while he moved slowly against her body, his movements lifting the tennis skirt and pressing the front of his shorts against her panties until she moaned. He turned her around then, touching only her hips, and lifted her onto the kitchen stool, her knees apart, her hands resting on his chest. He stood between her knees, the outside of his thighs touching the inside of hers, his hands on the edge of the table behind her, and began to kiss her mouth, pressing closer until she put her hands on his back and began to pull. He kissed her mouth and then her throat, moving in a circle as the hard edges of his thighs pressed her knees farther apart in time with the insistent pull of her hands but keeping the rest of his body from touching hers. He reached down to her shoulders and pushed aside the straps of her halter top and then released the hooks at the back. As the halter fell away, he bent forward and touched her breasts with his lips, kissing her front, her throat, her mouth, and back down again. At last, she put her fingers in his hair and then he knelt down between her legs, stripped off the rest of her clothes, and kissed her whole body until she rocked in glorious climax, pinioned on the stool by his insistent mouth. As she regained her breath, he rose, shed his own clothes, and then lifted her legs in the crook of his arms to enter her and begin again, his movements controlled and deep, giving her time to catch the rhythm, her arms flung wide, her hands gripping the edge of the table now, her weight partly on the stool and partly on him as, together now, they climbed the mountain, rocking faster and faster, until he reached down and lifted her fully onto him, holding her full weight in an exquisite penetration, vibrating more than moving, their bellies fusing as they came together with an indescribable sound.

Afterward, he picked her up and carried her easily to the bedroom, where they lay on the bed together in the darkness. Her heart would not slow down and she could feel every single cell of her skin responding to his smooth, strong hands as he stroked her body, front and back, keeping her near the edge. When she finally felt the need to move, she pressed him onto his back and then lay down full length on top of him, applying her mouth to his in small liquid kisses, then moving to the rest of his face and gradually down the smooth muscles of his chest. He reached for her, but she pressed his arms back down on the bed, holding his wrists tightly while she explored his body with her mouth, taking her time, marveling at the contrast between the smooth expanses of his skin and the hard ridges of sinew and bone just beneath, the acrid scent of their lovemaking, and the swell of his revival. She pulled herself up and then lowered herself onto him, bending forward from the hips so that the mass of her hair enfolded and obscured her face while she dragged individual strands across his chest. Every time he started to move, she signaled for him to stop, wanting to control it, wanting to get it just right, rocking back and forth for a long time, her eyes tightly shut as she felt the wave rise and recede, and then he was moving anyway and she couldn't stop him and didn't want to, holding on as he moved harder and harder until she cried out and collapsed along his length, gasping for air as he held her gently until she was asleep.

34

The next ten days in Subic passed without major incident for Brian. He did not return to Olongapo, heeding Josie's advice that perfection should not be improved upon. After the failure of his first phone call home, Brian waited for three hours in line the day following his next duty day to place another call, but she wasn't home. Well shit, he had tried. He then sat down and wrote her a lengthy letter that tried to minimize any political difficulties he was having aboard the ship, especially since he had found out that the special fitness report had indeed gone out. The board was supposedly only another month away, so unless something spectacular happened, he was fairly certain of promotion. He also focused on the possibilities of shore duty following the *Hood* tour, while omitting to mention the distinct probability that he would have to make at least part of another deployment during his Weapons officer tour in *Hood*. He thought of the letter as damage control when he mailed it off the ship.

The boatswain studiously pretended that nothing out of the ordinary had happened in Olongapo, and Brian was careful not to conjure up any images of his night in Olongapo whenever he grappled with the problem of Maddy back in San Diego. The day after, he had constructed an elaborate set of rationalizations to assuage his guilt over going to bed with—what would you call Josie? Certainly not a prostitute, and not technically a madam—her place wasn't a whorehouse, any more than the whole town was a whorehouse. Hell, the whole town *is* a whorehouse, God love it. Hey, dipshit, like the chief said, why are you worried about *what* Josie is? How about just an exotic, beautiful, mature, rich, exciting, voluptuous woman who turned you every way but loose? Yeah, that's the one. Then he rationalized the problem using the white man's excuse: It didn't count; she's just an Oriental woman. Right. Just an Oriental woman. Stooping pretty low, boy. And then: This is WESTPAC; there are no married men west of the international dateline. Everybody goes over into Subic at least once and gets his rocks off. It doesn't count for anything. It's not like going out and having a real affair; it's just a short time in a bar with a hooker. Oh Lord, suppose she gave me something? Who would I go see? I couldn't go to the doc or that pasty-faced staff doctor—they'd have to report the case to the exec and the captain.

For three days after, he urinated gingerly, holding his breath to see if there would be a twinge of pain. But after a while, embarrassed by his almost juvenile fretting, he arrived at the conclusion that Josie had been one of those secret life experiences, a marvelous woman who had responded directly to his own unabashed admiration, desire, and need and who had given him a night to remember. He wondered whether projecting simple desire like that could ever get the attention of an American woman. He doubted it.

The ship had settled into a routine of in-port work, followed by a diminishing level of liberty ops as wallets thinned out. Brian limited his shore-leave excursions to the main Subic O Club, where he stuck to San Miguel and avoided the lethal Subic Specials. The captain surfaced after a few days and hosted a private dinner for the exec and the four department heads, which he had catered in one of the bungalows reserved for senior officers near the club. It was to be the only time Brian actually saw the captain during the port visit. The entire wardroom attended a "lunch" aboard a visiting British frigate, where Brian reacquainted himself with the Royal Navy's tradition of serving everything but food at lunch. Several of the WESTPAC officers had to be helped back to *Hood* after the visit, and Brian, who had remained reasonably sober, had had the pleasure of chiding some of them about LANTFLEET knowledge.

The rest of the time was spent in making repairs to the Engineering Department's main propulsion plant machinery, refurbishing the motor whaleboat, laying new nonskid decking on the helo flight deck, and painting out the sides after their forty-five day siege up in the Gulf. The engineers especially wanted repairs done in Subic, because the level of workmanship was so much better and cheaper than what could be found in the union-infested shipyards of San Diego.

Brian made one three-hour excursion to the big Foreign Merchandise Exchange with Fox Hudson. He was astonished at the scale of the Exchange, which was a giant warehouse over on the Supply Center, filled with the latest in Japanese stereo equipment and televisions, Chinese tailors and suit makers, Philippine woodwork, and shelf after shelf of guns, jewelry, china, and crystal, as well as Oriental rugs, artwork, and furniture, all at one-third their U.S. prices. The Exchange was one of the main objectives of any WESTPAC sailor, outdone only by its Japanese equivalent, building A-33 in Yokosuka, Japan, or a port visit to the fabled city of Hong Kong.

The Exchange was the only way most young Navy married couples could acquire a first-class set of table china or a modern stereo set, and every married man arrived in Subic with his wife's dream list in his pocket. Brian, being new to WESTPAC, had come without a list, but he did buy a set of Noritake china, eight goblets of Waterford crystal, and a Mikimoto pearl necklace for Maddy. He would have to save some money before he could indulge in a stereo set, but the ship was scheduled for a final out-chop visit before heading home, at which time he ought to have enough for the set he wanted. Fox Hudson had stocked up on treasures, knowing that he would never be back.

The day after his Exchange run, Brian once again had the duty. He had secretly come to welcome his duty days, which came every third day, as they gave him an excuse not to go ashore at night with the rest of the wardroom officers. Most of the officers felt that they were duty-bound to go over into the town and howl, since they were, after all, in Subic and that's what Subic was for. He settled into a routine of doing his administrative work in the mornings and then spending the afternoons overseeing the Weapons Department technicians as they groomed the weapons systems, which included a complete refurbishment of missile fire–control System Two, damaged by the electrical transients out on the Red Crown station. If he did not have the duty, he would go to the club for dinner, but he was usually back on board by 2100.

After working some accumulated paperwork for a few hours, Brian in his capacity as command duty officer went topside at midnight to watch the liberty party return to the ship. He took his usual vantage point up on the flight deck, where he could look down on the quarterdeck one level below from above the deck-edge floodlights. The midwatch OOD, petty officer, and messenger of the watch had been relieved at 2345, and at a few minutes after midnight, the first shuttle bus discharged some fairly well oiled cargo up at the head of the pier. Brian watched as the men struggled up the steep angle of the brow to the quarterdeck, there to be met by the OOD, the chief signalman. If they were carrying packages or bags, the petty officer of the watch would have them open each bag for inspection to check for drugs, liquor, or other prohibited items. If a man was excessively drunk, the OOD would have the messenger, a junior enlisted man himself, escort the individual to his compartment. After that, the theory went, he was on his own, and if he made a spectacle of himself or a mess of the compartment, his division mates would sort him out.

After a half hour of watching, Brian became aware of a khaki-clad figure leaning against the rail high up on the signal bridge who also seemed to be watching the returning liberty hounds. A second tier of floodlights was mounted on the 04 level and pointed down at the pier in the vicinity of the quarterdeck, to ensure good lighting for those who were coming back with somewhat impaired vision. Looking into the lights, Brian could not make out who was up there in the gloom above the floodlights, but he thought it must be Chief Jackson. He decided to check it out.

He walked forward along the port side, past the three-inch mount gun tub, across the boat decks, and then began climbing the two ladders needed to get up to the signal bridge. Upon reaching the signal bridge, he indeed found Chief Jackson leaning on the pipe rails, smoking a cigarette and nursing a cup of mess-decks coffee.

"Evening, Sheriff. Watching the sights again?"

"Yes, sir, Mr. Holcomb. Be amazed what you see from up here that they might not catch on the quarterdeck."

Below them, from about amidships all the way forward to the bow, the pier was in shadow, lighted dimly by the streetlights along the frontage road across the pier area, some one hundred yards distant. Only the area around the ship's quarterdeck was brightly lighted. A corridor of darkness stretched between *Hood* and the destroyer berthed ahead, where bright lights again flared around the ship's quarterdeck area. Brian had never noticed the alternating pattern of bright lights and deep shadows before.

"I was back there on the flight deck watching the first batch of liberty hounds come back," Brian said. "Seems pretty tame so far."

"Yes, sir; we're about halfway through our stay, so most of 'em are getting short for money. But this is when the badasses try to bring their shit on board. First week, all the quarterdeck guys are looking hard, but after that, well, we have to start looking."

Brian nodded in the darkness. From the pier, the two of them would have been next to impossible to see. They watched as another bus from the front gates discharged a group of happy-sounding drunks. The liberty hounds ambled down the pier to the quarterdeck area in small groups, tossing cigarettes into the water between the ship and the pier before heading up the brow. By the time the fourth bus showed up, Brian was getting a little bored with it all. Most of the liberty party had staggered on board, and the ship was getting quiet. He was about to call it a night when the Sheriff touched his shoulder and pointed down to the pier.

Coming down the pier well behind the last crowd were two individuals who always bore watching, Coltrane and Hooper. The smaller of the two, Hooper, was having a great deal of difficulty with his walking, while Coltrane struggled with what looked like a large leather golf bag.

Hooper led, ostensibly carrying half the weight of the bag, but to Brian's eye, Coltrane bore most of the weight. Hooper was issuing his usual steady stream of profane orders, which Coltrane manfully tried to obey. When the pair stopped in the shadows abeam of the boat decks, however, Brian began to pay attention.

"Uh-huh," muttered Jackson. "Thought so. We've got us a little something to sneak aboard."

"You think those two are into the dope scene?" Brian asked.

"No, sir, leastwise not Coltrane. The guys gave him a cigarette once and he burned his lips with it. Hooper now, he's a messy drunk ashore; I wouldn't put anything past that little lizard."

They watched with interest as the pair wedged the golf bag between two horns of the midships bitts. Hooper tied a hank of line around the golf bag's handle and threw the other end up into the shadows on the boat decks. In his condition, the tying and the throwing took several minutes. Then Hooper steered Coltrane back down the pier toward the quarterdeck. Jackson looked at his watch.

"You going to nab them on the boat decks?" Brian asked.

"No, sir, I think I'm going to follow 'em and see where they go with it. There may be others involved."

"Mind if I tag along?"

"Not at all, CDO. These two could be up to anything at all."

They quickly went down the two ladders to the boat decks, checked to see that the other end of the line had indeed made it up there, and then hid themselves under the gig davit's foundations. In about five minutes, Hooper and Coltrane showed up, Hooper with his fingers to his lips and making loud shh-sh-sh-ing noises, and Coltrane nodding obediently, echoing some of the same noises himself. The two of them stumbled around in the darkness for a few minutes before finding the line. There followed a lot of heaving and grunting to bring the bag aboard. They picked it up and began dragging it toward the hatch that led down to the wardroom passageway.

Hooper sat down hard once while trying to maneuver the heavy end of the bag in Coltrane's direction.

"Jush pick it up, Coltrane, goddamn it. Pick it the fuck up, and help me out heah, man—it's kinda drunk out, you know what I'm sayin'? Theah ya go, that's right, don't drop it, don't drop it. Theah ya go, yeah, that's it. Now let's drag it over heah to this hatch, and then you goes up—I mean, shit, down the ladder and I'll hand it down to ya, awright? Yeah, that's it, oops! Now look it what ya made me do. For Chrissakes, Coltrane, pay fuckin' attention heah. That's the way. . . ."

From their vantage point beneath the davits, Brian and the chief watched with some amusement.

"I'd have sworn something in that bag was moving," Brian whispered as Hooper and then Coltrane ended up on the deck at the entrance to the hatch.

"We're gonna be calling out the baby doc here in a minute if this keeps up," replied the chief. "I actually think he's gone and got Coltrane tanked, too."

The dynamic duo grunted and heaved the golf bag down the hatch with a great deal of effort and encouragement from each other, Hooper giving orders and Coltrane making incomprehensible sounds in return. Brian had the impression that Hooper could probably even understand Coltrane. When the two had disappeared down the ladder, Brian and the chief hurried over to the top of the hatch. Below them, the bag was already tilting precariously down the second ladder that led to Broadway. Hooper kept up his steady stream of directions and Coltrane gabbled away in alarm as the bag threatened to drop on top of him. When the noise indicated that they had reached the bottom of the ladder, Brian and the chief quickly scampered down the first ladder and peered carefully over the hatch coaming of the second.

At the bottom, Coltrane was seated in the passageway, the bag between his knees, his arms wrapped tightly around it, while Hooper was trying to extricate himself from the operating wheel of a hatch scuttle positioned beneath the ladder. Hooper directed some interesting invective at the operating wheel, which remained unmoved. Coltrane was trying to keep the top of the bag closed. Brian noticed a red cloth of some kind stuffed into the top of the bag. He definitely saw the cloth move, independent of Coltrane's efforts to keep the top closed.

"They've got some kind of animal in that bag," he said to Jackson, still keeping his voice low.

Jackson looked over the edge of the hatch. "Animal? What kind of animal would fit in a golf bag?"

But at that moment, Coltrane heaved himself up onto his feet, grabbed the top of the bag, and began dragging it down the passageway in the direction of the mess decks. Hooper finally got his feet untangled and lurched down the passageway after him. Brian and the chief tiptoed down the ladder, still not wanting to make their move until they found out what was going on. When they reached the bottom, they could see the two sailors, the bag dragging between them now, stepping through the doorway onto the mess decks, which were darkened down to night lights at this hour of the morning. The only white light came from the galley itself, where the night baker, Poppa Steiner, was bashing dough for the next day's bread and rolls.

They crept slowly down the passageway, keeping themselves to the sides and flattening quickly into doorways if they thought either of the two drunks was going to turn around. When they got within ten feet of the mess decks door, they could hear Hooper, stage-whispering now, and, as usual, he was berating Coltrane.

"Awright, man, we've made it this far. We gotta get this sucker to the compahtment, awright? We gotta get it to the compahtment, and then we can put it in the bosun lockah an' tell the guys, an' then, an' then, we can put it down in the chain lockah, see, so's nobody's gonna find it, an' then, an then—*shit*! *Shit*! We went the wrong fuckin' way, Coltrane, goddamn it. You was s'posed to go the othah way, to Foirst Division compahtment—this is the fuckin' mess decks, man. Whoa—who's that? Who's that!"

Brian and the chief were standing with their backs flattened to the bulkhead just outside the mess decks doorway. Brian was sure one of the two drunks had seen them, but then he realized Hooper must have discovered

Poppa Steiner from the noises coming through the shuttered serving line. They listened as Hooper and Coltrane scrambled to hide behind one of the tables, Hooper swearing furiously and Coltrane making little eeping noises as they dragged the bag behind the table. Then came a long silence. The chief looked across the doorway at Brian, who shrugged his shoulders. They heard Hooper again.

"Coltrane, you know what? That's fuckin' old man Steineh in theah. You know fuckin' Steineh? He's that fuckin' guy works all fuckin' night and sleeps all fuckin' day. Yeah. That's who that fuckin' is. We rip off sweet rolls from him on the four-to-eights. Hey, Coltrane, let's fuckin' scare him a little. You wanna fuckin' do that, huh? Yeah, let's fuck around a lil bit heah. C'mon, help me with this fuckin' bag. Heah, help me drag it over theah. Yeah, let's go mess with ole Poppa Steineh."

Through the crack between the mess decks door and the doorjamb, Brian could see them dragging the golf bag over toward the galley door. He signaled the chief that it was clear to look around the corner of the doorway. Coltrane and Hooper had the bag right up against the galley door, and then Hooper had another bright idea.

"Stay right fuckin' heah, Coltrane. Don't let nobody fuck with this heah fuckin' bag. I'm gonna go douse the fuckin' lights, make it real fuckin' dahk out heah, okay? Then we can fuckin' do it. You wait right heah now; don't go nowheahs, awright, man?"

Hooper lurched over to the back bulkhead of the mess decks and opened the lighting panel, something he knew about from his days as a mess cook. After a couple of false starts, he managed to turn off all the lights, including the night lights, on the mess decks. Now the only light was coming through the cracks in the serving line's shutters. The silhouette of the night baker could be seen moving around behind the shutters, accompanied by a thumping noise as he began to knead several large lumps of bread dough. Hooper crossed back over to the door and crouched down by Coltrane, who had gone quiet when the lights went out. Together, they maneuvered the bag right up to the door.

"They got some kind of animal in there, all right," Jackson said, joining Brian on his side of the door. "Bet you it's a goddamn monkey. Steiner's gonna go apeshit, a monkey loose in his galley."

"We gonna let 'em do it?"

"Well, you're the CDO. . . ."

Brian grinned at the prospect of a monkey loose in the galley, then watched as first Hooper and then Coltrane set up howling and wailing noises outside the galley door, apparently trying to sound like a couple of ghosts. Their noises were muted at first, but the two soon warmed to their work. From inside the galley, the noise of Steiner whacking on the mounds of bread dough stopped.

"All rrr-ight, all rrr-ight," came Steiner's voice through the steel shutters. "Who izz dis mezzing around mit me, what? Izz trying to sound like ghost, izz not scaring me, no, izz bunch of drunks, I'm tinking. You go way now. You go to bed, sleep it off. There's a good boy, go on now, before Poppa Steiner has to call the Sheriff."

Hooper tried to keep the ghost sounds going, but he had started laughing and was trying to cover his mouth and make the noises all at the same time. Coltrane looked alarmed but kept on with his version of the ooing and moaning, trying, as always, to do what Hooper said. Steiner kept up his admonitions for the drunks to leave him alone and get along to bed as he began unlocking the galley door.

When they heard the galley door being unlocked, Hooper reached forward and pulled the red cloth out of the top of the bag, pointing the mouth of the bag at the door. The galley door swung open in a blaze of white light, revealing Poppa Steiner's expansive flour-covered paunch standing in the doorway, a huge blob of bread dough in his two hands and an annoyed look on his shiny red face.

"Now I'm tellink you, you—*Gott in Himmel!*"

With an incredibly loud hiss, a four-foot-long crocodile lunged out of the bag and into the doorway. Steiner tried to turn around, run, scramble backward, and simultaneously pick up both feet to get away from the equally terrified reptile, who himself was trying to get away from the bag at a great rate of knots. Steiner did the only sensible thing, which was to pitch the entire ten-pound blob of bread dough at the croc, who, failing to reach the night baker, obligingly tried to bite it. Steiner ended up sitting down abruptly on his considerable posterior while scrambling backward away from the monster in the doorway, knocking over a table of bread pans and sending up a huge cloud of flour in the galley. The croc froze in place, trying hard to hiss but mostly strangling on the bread dough, making noises similar to those being made by Hooper, who was rolling around in tears out on the mess decks. Even Coltrane was grinning.

Brian was laughing so hard, he had to sit down himself, and Chief Jackson, who had been trying to look stern, finally gave it up and roared with laughter. The baby croc staggered around the mess decks with the blob in its mouth, manfully trying to eat it while he looked for a way out of the situation. Sixty million years of evolution told it to head for the nearest hole, which turned out to be the scullery. Slithering rapidly across the waxed tiles of the mess decks, the croc, blob and all, dived into the open door of the scullery. Jackson ran over to the door and slammed it shut, then called the quarterdeck to get some help.

It took him several minutes to convince the petty officer of the watch that it was indeed the chief master-at-arms on the line, and that, yes, he did need some assistance on the mess decks to deal with a stowaway crocodile. His case was not strengthened by occasional fits of laughter on his part. The command duty officer, still sitting on the deck, tears of laughter running down his face, was of no help whatsoever.

It took another hour to assemble a suitable task force to capture the croc, and a half hour after that to convince Steiner to come out of the galley, whose door he had barricaded with every piece of movable equipment in the galley just as soon as the croc had manned up the scullery. The flour-covered croc, who had made considerable progress with the blob by the time the final assault was made on the scullery, was captured by six volunteers using a ten-foot-long divisional laundry bag. Then he was pitched unceremoniously off the fantail into the harbor, a couple of feet of white bread dough hanging from his mouth. Two Filipino welders coming aboard for the second half of the graveyard shift saw the disposition and did an abrupt about-face on the brow to go report to their supervisor that a crocodile had eaten a white man in the *Hood*. When it was all over, the OOD asked Brian what he should put in the deck log.

"Not one word, Chief. Not one goddamn word."

Rockheart sat back in his seat on the shuttle bus headed for the main gate. It was one of the late buses, purposefully chosen to ensure that the bulk of the night's liberty party had already gone through the gates by the time he got there. The sun had long since set and the base was almost pretty in the early evening, with all the carefully trimmed lawns and flowers, the waving palms, and the first signs that the day's heat was breaking. He wanted the gate Marines to be bored and tired of searching bags and looking at ID cards, indifferent to an E-6 strolling through at the back of the crowds.

He shifted again on his seat, the chest pack filled with bills creating a large square patch of perspiration under his T-shirt. He had called his contact, and tonight was the night. This was another sweet deal set up by Rackman and carried on by Rocky. To resupply, all he had to do was make one phone call into town and then check back each afternoon at 1500. When the stuff was ready, he would strap on his money pack, make a liberty run to a certain bar, ask to have a hotse bath, and leave the money pack in his clothes with the bath attendant. When he was finished with the bath, his clothes would have been cleaned, pressed, and relieved of the fifteen thousand dollars in mixed bills. He could then go out and have a beer, maybe catch the animal acts at the crocodile bar, and be back aboard before midnight.

The sweet part was the delivery. His source had a guy, a Filipino civilian, in the base post office. The stuff would be put into two fourth-class mail packages, suitably wrapped against drug dogs, and then the inside guy would put all sorts of customs and post office stamps and inspection stickers on them, label them with a fictitious return address in the States, bash them up a little, put a "Cookies, please do not crush" stencil on them, and then spirit them past the internal customs people and into a mail sack destined for *Hood*. Once aboard, the ship's postal clerk would call Rocky down in his compartment and laughingly tell him to come get his latest batch of home-cooked crumbs, and his biggest problem was being razzed for not sharing his care package with the other guys in OI division. He had even taken to buying bags of cookies in the Subic base commissary so that he did have something to share. As long as they had the inside guy, it was foolproof. For once, he was getting extraordinary service from his friendly post office.

The bus pulled up to the main gates and the small load of sailors got out. Rocky stayed in the middle, Mr. Casual, his MAA badge strapped to the inside of his wallet opposite his ID card to make sure the gate guard would recognize a kindred spirit. He was waved through with a big yawn. When he crossed the Shit River and got to the beginning of the main drag, the crowd of jeepneys and hustlers was much depleted, as the action had already moved uptown. He found the driver almost at once, parked at the head of the jeepney line, and slipped into the back of the small Japanese car. The car made good time, dropping him at the bar in five minutes.

He walked in and headed directly for the back row of tables, where he ordered a San Miguel and watched the band for a few minutes. He told the first hostess that he was here for a bath. She disappeared and he began idly counting the minutes. He smiled when he sensed a new presence behind him, smelled the rich perfume, and felt the soft hand on the back of his neck. He covered the hand with his and pulled it forward, pressing a soft kiss on her wrist.

"Josie," he said without looking up, "it's good to see you."

35

The night after the crocodile incident, Chief Jackson invited Brian to have dinner with him at the Subic Chief Petty Officers' Club. Brian recognized the invitation to be the extension of an offer of friendship on the part of the chief. Under the unwritten rules of naval etiquette, a chief petty officer could invite a commissioned officer to his club, although the converse was rarely done. Jackson probably wanted to expand their official relationship into something more personal, and Brian thought that it was related to *Hood*'s drug problem.

They arrived at the Subic CPO Club at 1830, both of them dressed in civvies. Brian was surprised to find that the CPO Club was bigger than the Officers' Club and slightly more posh. Jackson explained that the chiefs were simply ready to spend more money on the club amenities than the officers, and besides, there were more of them. They took a table in the main dining room, where Brian was surprised again to see chiefs enjoying dinner with women who appeared to be their wives.

"Lots of CPOs stationed here at Subic," Jackson said. "It's an accompanied tour, so the families are here, too. It's actually supposed to be great duty. Everyone has at least one maid, and usually a gardener—the labor's from Olongapo, and it costs next to nothing."

They ordered steak dinners and reminisced about the infamous crocodile. The exec at officers' call the next morning had given a straight-faced lecture about the evils of importing dangerous species aboard ship that had everyone in stitches. The engineer was less amused, as he could not get the Filipino welders from the shipyard to come back on board until their shop stewards had inspected the entire ship for lizards. The Supply officer had had to borrow bread and rolls from another destroyer because Poppa Steiner refused to go back on the mess decks until daylight.

Over dinner, their conversation inevitably moved to the problems of race relations in the Navy. Brian realized that he would have felt just a little conspicuous sitting in the Officers' Club with a black man, but that in the CPO Club, he felt entirely at ease. He hesitated, then mentioned that observation to Jackson.

"That's because the officer corps in the Navy is almost entirely white," Jackson said. "The chiefs are at the top of the chain of the enlisted world, so we got all kinds—white, black, Spanish, Filipino, you name it."

Brian nodded, looking around the dining room, remembering Martinez's remark about white people's hang-ups on race.

"But if we really go after the drug ring here in *Hood*, does that put you in a bind as a black chief petty officer?"

"No—but it will as just a black man. See, how it is: A black man in the Navy has two identities—one as a bosun's mate, or a gunner's mate, or whatever, and a second one as a black man."

"Which identity rules?"

Jackson put some sugar in his coffee and smiled at that one. "Way *I* see it, the one that gets you where you wanna go. I signed up, wanted to move up, get my chief's hat one day. So the black man, he went into the background in what I saw as a white-run Navy, and I got my hat. Problem comes for those guys who don't stand much chance of going up in the ranks, for whatever reason, and then the black man steps out of the shadows, and he's pissed."

"Which is where we get the so-called radicals."

"Yeah, I think so. Some of those guys, they aren't going anywhere because they don't have what it takes, you know? Maybe they came from the ghetto or from the farm, didn't have two sticks to rub together coming up, no schooling, no parents pushing on them. They basically come in with almost no hope of a future in the Navy, where everything's technical and where you have to take exams to get ahead. The Navy makes a big mistake in trying to give these guys an opportunity: They don't have what it takes to make the opportunity go."

Brian nodded. These were the professional deckhands

or laundrymen. He reflected that all the ship's laundry-men were black.

"But even if the drug ring is black, I still can't see them confronting you in some kind of effort to make you lay off," Brian said.

"Right. But I'll be hearing it from some of my brothers in the chiefs' mess, and maybe from other people, too. We start busting chops, and they're black chops, it's only a matter of time before I'm gonna get some heat."

Brian stirred his own coffee. The dining room was thinning out. He looked over at Jackson, choosing his words carefully.

"You've made it to chief. Is this the kind of heat that's going to matter to you?"

It was Jackson's turn to think, to choose his words.

"It matters in the sense that now that I've got my chief's hat, now that I've fulfilled Jackson the Navy man, I feel some responsibility to fulfill Jackson the black man. It's almost a question of honor."

Brian nodded. He wasn't sure he understood where Jackson was coming from, but then he had not had to be a black man in a white Navy. But he understood the idea of it being an issue of honor. "You still want to go ahead, then?"

"It would help to have some top cover, Mr. Holcomb."

"Meaning me."

"Meaning you, yes, sir."

"Well. I've got a problem that's similar to yours, only it's political—career, not racial."

"The command. The XO."

"Yeah. The XO's kind of made it clear to me that it's in my best interest to go along to get along, you know what I mean? They sent in a special fitness report that's going just about to guarantee that I make lieutenant commander. O-Four, that's a big gate; once you get O-Four, you have a shot at selection for an exec's job, and the XO job leads to command, see? Command of my own ship someday, that's my chief's hat. But I'm pretty sure there was a price tag on that fitrep."

"Usually is. Lemme see: Play the game our way. That was the Marcowitz bit."

"Yeah."

"But what the hell, they've sent it in. When's the promotion board?"

"End of this month."

"So you're set."

"Except, the way I see it, I accepted their terms, so to speak, if only tacitly. That puts me in the same boat you're in—I kind of have a duty to go along; it's also kind of a question of honor."

"You mean, the XO, he feels since he did the fitrep and you accepted it, you bought in."

"Right."

Jackson nodded.

"Now, I guess the thing I have to decide is which duty draws more water—my obligation to go along with the system because I took the king's penny or my duty to the ship to clean out the dopers. I mean, shit, I've already said it: I find another guy doing drugs in *my* department, I'm gonna write him up. Once I sign a report chit, that makes it official. They can't just do a Marcowitz. They either have to take the creep to mast or suppress a report chit, falsify the paperwork, and I don't think Commander Mains is the type to falsify an official charge sheet."

"Yeah. I see it. So far, he's seen to it that there aren't any report chits."

"Right, so if I write somebody up, that's a declaration of war of sorts."

"Can they hurt you?"

"Oh, hell yes. Even if I'm promoted, the XO can poison my career about twenty different ways."

"Sounds like we both have some thinking to do, Mr. Holcomb."

Brian sipped his coffee. "Yeah, well," he said. "Yes and no. I've about decided that the ship ought to come before my career, because if she doesn't, I'm not sure I want a career in this outfit. You know, we all play these political games, but when it comes to the ship, the ship's just there. And all it asks is that we all do our duty. Simple. Clear as a bell."

"And one tough motherfucker sometimes."

"Yes," Brian said, then grinned. "But when you take

a ship to sea, the gods have this way of getting even when everybody doesn't do his duty. I think you have the tougher dilemma: We're all going to move on one day, but you're going to be a black man forever."

"Tell me about it, Mr. Holcomb. Tell me about it."

It was Monday noon when the weather warning came in. Brian was CDO and thus was the first to see the message, which was serial 001 on Typhoon Mary, now positioned on the back side of Mindanao. The storm was expected to come northwest, crossing over Luzon Island and into the South China Sea, and then probably continue northwest to smack the upper coasts of Vietnam. Brian took the message up to the chart house and plotted the present position and expected track of the typhoon on a wide-area chart. The projected track of the eye came within sixty miles of Subic. Shit. If that held, they would be chased out of port. No ship wanted to be caught in a harbor if a typhoon came. Safety, such as it was, lay out in deep water. He called the exec, who came up to look at the chart. He shook his head.

"That's too close. We're probably going to have to sortie. Get word to the engineer to start buttoning up his job orders."

He took a set of dividers and measured the distance.

"Yeah," he muttered. "At a forward advance speed of twenty knots, that sucker could be here day after tomorrow. Tell Vince to make preps to light off his ready plant by tomorrow morning. We'll plan to beat feet around eighteen hundred tomorrow."

"Uh, will you inform the captain? I'm not sure where to contact him," Brian said. He had not seen the captain for days, nor had the other department heads.

"Yep." The exec brushed aside the implied question. "But right now, we gotta move. You get the word out to the rest of the department heads. This thing may come on fast. Thank God we got all the stuff on board that first week. Oh, and alert the chief bosun early—he'll need to do a lot of lashing down between now and then."

"You really think we'll have to go?"

"Oh shit, yes. Go get that chart of prior past typhoon

tracks; any of these cyclones that start out there off Mindanao this time of year almost always comes over Luzon, trashes Manila, and then tears up the South China Sea for forty-eight hours before impaling itself on Cochin China. What the hell, we were about done here, anyway."

"Will we still go to Kaohsiung after we do storm evasion? We're not due back in the Gulf for another two weeks."

"Right. But first we gotta do storm evasion. Out there, not in here. You don't have typhoons in LANTFLEET, do you?"

"No, sir, we have hurricanes, but they mostly stay down in the Caribbean. Worst I've seen is the North Atlantic in winter, which can be medium shitty."

The exec smiled. "As the man says, you ain't see nuttin' yet, bwah. Let's get the word out—we're blowing this pop stand."

Word of the ship's unscheduled departure created a whirlwind of activity, most of it business but some of it personal. All the machinery sent off to the Subic ship-repair-facility shops had to be returned, fixed or not. With every ship in the basin having to sortie in the next thirty-six hours, the Base Supply Department dispatched a wagon train of fresh stores down to the piers for all the ships, creating a working-party circus on the piers as the Supply officers fought for their fair share of fresh fruits and vegetables.

Everyone knew that a storm evasion did not automatically mean the ships would get to come back into port when the danger had passed. The fleet schedulers would often take advantage of the fact that the ships were at sea to return them to the gun line or to carrier escort duty. The Exchange procrastinators hustled over to the Foreign Merchandise Building to lay in treasures, creating a small mountain of boxes on the pier the next morning. The chief boatswain had watched it all with a cynical grin from the forecastle, where he, Folsom, and Brian had been taking a tour to check on the lash-down of topside gear.

"We git out there, all that shit's gonna go flyin' around

the berthing compartments. You'll see more broken dishes and busted stereos than Carter's got little liver pills," he predicted.

Brian returned to his own stateroom with a couple of hundred feet of twenty-one-thread manila line to do some lashing down of his own. The chief had warned him that the ship was going to be tossing around like a cork if they were not able to outrun the typhoon, and Brian took him seriously. He also took twenty minutes to compose a quick letter to Maddy, telling her about the crocodile invasion and the reason they were bailing out of Subic. He also told her he had tried to call again but had missed connections with her. He decided to gloss over the discussion he had had with Jackson. If the dopers kept themselves out of sight and out of trouble, there might not be an issue at all. Even as he thought about that, he recognized that this was probably wishful thinking. But she had been quick to see the potential for folly in his stand on the druggies, so he minimized the issue in his letter. He got the letter into the last outgoing mailbag, hoping along with the rest of the crew that the postal clerk would come back with a final bag of incoming mail for the ship, but there was nothing. *Hood* got underway at 1830, the third ship in the line of destroyers abandoning the harbor for the safety of open water.

36

The approaching typhoon made its presence felt as soon as *Hood* came out of the lee of Luzon Island. As the ship pointed due west, she picked up a deep long-period swell from the southeast that heaved her into a slow roll. The swells came in a steady line, deepening as *Hood* left the protection of Luzon. They looked like an endless series of glass foothills that moved under the ship without a sound, lifting her port quarter effortlessly, sending *Hood* first into a deep heel to starboard and then rolling her back to port as they swept by on their march to the China coast. There were no whitecaps, just the unending progression of swells, eighteen feet from trough to crest and probably a quarter mile in breadth.

Brian watched the train of swells from the port bridge-wing, wedging himself between the mahogany bull rail and the port pelorus to keep upright against the ponderous rolls. The quartermasters were plotting the track of the storm on the large-area South China Sea chart. The most recent weather report had the eye just entering the South China Sea as *Hood* ran west toward Vietnam, six hundred miles distant. The typhoon's predicted track was northwest, which would aim it at Mainland China, but no one could tell where these monsters would go.

"Wherever it wants to," the exec had answered when asked the question at an all-officers meeting to plan the sortie. "Our best bet is to get across the South China Sea into the western semicircle of the typhoon before the eye overtakes us. These things rotate counterclockwise. If the thing is headed north and you end up in the eastern half of it, the wind velocity is *added* to the storm's own track velocity. If you can get into the western half, the vectors subtract and you can cut twenty, thirty knots off the wind speed. That can make a *big* difference."

Brian, looking at the chart, had observed that the South China Sea did not seem to offer much maneuvering room, containing only six hundred miles within which to outmaneuver a storm that spanned two hundred miles from edge to edge.

"You've got that right. We're in for a blow, any way you look at it. Some of the ships currently in port are probably going to head due north and then back east behind Luzon. But if this thing recurved, they could be in deep shit. Like I said, best bet for us is to run for the western semicircle. If we can run twenty, twenty-two knots for the next twelve hours, we have a chance of getting across its track before it catches up with us, assuming we can maintain speed. Once these swells get big enough, we'll have to slow down. I hate these god-damn things. They scare my ass to death."

Brian had experienced two winter storms in the North

Atlantic, but the legendary typhoons of the western Pacific were something new. Looking back now across the ship's port quarter, he could see a thin black wedge-shaped line of solid cloud enveloping the entire quadrant of the southeastern horizon. The late-afternoon sunlight had developed a bronze hue and the sea air seemed oppressively dense and humid, as if the atmosphere was being compressed ahead of the storm behind them. Even though the ship was driving along at twenty-two knots, Brian could feel no relative wind coming over the bow, which meant that the true wind was coming from astern at around the ship's own speed. The hull throbbed every time the stern lifted far enough out of the water to expose the propeller tips.

Brian looked into the pilothouse and saw the captain in his chair over on the starboard side. Despite the heat, he wore a foul-weather jacket and slumped into the big chair, a *Hood* ball cap pulled low over his forehead. The captain had returned to the ship the night before their departure, arriving in a Navy sedan, looking pale and wan and not walking too well. On the quarterdeck when he returned, Brian had been almost shocked by his appearance. At first, he thought it was a hangover, but then he decided that this must be something medical. The exec had whisked him off the quarterdeck almost at once, issuing a flurry of orders to all the officers nearby, as if he wanted to distract them. Brian had said something to Vince Benedetti, wondering aloud where the captain had been during the port visit and why he looked the way he did.

"Beats me, man," Vince had replied. "But he looks like he got shot at and missed, shit at and hit."

After coming out of his cabin this afternoon when the ship left port, the captain had been up in his chair on the bridge for the past two hours, staring silently through the green-tinted windows. The exec had conferred with him a few times about the weather and the track, but otherwise he was acting as if nothing was wrong. The rest of the bridge watch officers had been keeping their distance, as had Brian. He remained out on the bridgewing, soaking up some of the thin sunlight, as other officers circulated through the pilothouse to report their preparations for the storm to the exec and to look at the typhoon track chart or to watch the seas build.

Down below on the forecastle, Brian could see the chief boatswain directing First Division in the final lash-down of seamanship gear in anticipation of heavy weather. The mooring lines had been struck below and all the portable damage-control equipment and fenders were being lashed into place with twenty-one-thread manila line. The nylon webbing they called snaking, which was laced through the lifelines to catch a man before he was washed through the lines and over the side, paradoxically had to be rolled up and struck below in the face of really heavy weather, or the waves would tear every bit of it off. The men staggered around the broad forecastle as the ship rolled. With the seas astern, the forecastle was still dry, but when the body of the storm caught up with them, *Hood* inevitably would have to come about and face the seas to keep from being swamped. By then, things could get very interesting, Brian thought, especially as this would probably happen at night. Brian waved to Jack Folsom and the chief boatswain as they checked over the lash-down on the forecastle. They both waved back, and then Brian felt the first hot breath of the typhoon and heard a moaning sound begin in the running rigging of the forward mast.

Brian bumped awake later that night in momentary panic, his ribs wedged against the storm railing on the edge of his bunk, the aluminum rail pushed so tightly into his side that he could almost not breathe. While he was still gathering his wits, he was thrown to the other side of his rack, bouncing off the padded aluminum bulkhead, his head buffeted by his book collection that was slithering all around the top end of his bunk. As he tried to sit up, he was once again heaved over to port, the movement amplified by a stomach-hollowing drop in the bow, fol-lowed seconds later by the thrash of a large sea against the exterior bulkhead. He shook his head in the darkness, awake now, but the ship rolled again, this time way over to starboard, and he was flattened once more against the exterior bulkhead. Gotta get ahold of something, he thought. Gonna get pitched on the deck. He could not hear anything in the stateroom but the roar of the wind outside, a steady, sustained rush, with ghosts of sounds like thunder and crashing waves barely audible over the massive sound of the wind. *Taifun*.

He had met with Jack Folsom and the chief just after sunset on the flight deck, all of them wearing kapok life jackets and staying close to the inboard lifelines that had been rigged out in strategic places around the ship. The Clementine helo was tied down in the hangar. *Hood* had slowed to only ten knots. The horizon was a mass of boiling black clouds for nine-tenths of its circumference, flickering with distant lightning, with only one bloodred wedge of light showing to the west to confirm the sunset. The ship still tried to claw her way west, but the seas were building rapidly, sometimes being engulfed by the giant swells, sometimes riding on top of them and crashing alongside in acres of seething foam, red in the light of the sunset. What was it the chief had said? "God's on the move." He lost his foothold in the bedding and cringed as he was thrown against the exterior bulkhead. Sounds like God's here, he thought, and He's not happy.

He rolled onto his back and jammed himself diagonally in the bunk, wedging his feet on the bottom pan of the upper bunk to stabilize himself. The bow rose sharply, coming impossibly far up, then hung suspended for an instant before dropping into a watery Grand Canyon with a sickening rush, bottoming out finally in a huge wash of water that broke over the forecastle, loud enough to penetrate the shrieking wind for just an instant. Something hit him in the face: his red-lens flashlight. He grabbed for it as it almost rolled over the side of the bunk, lost his upside-down foothold, and was again thrown against the exterior bulkhead. Love my bulkhead.

It took him two roll cycles to stabilize, and he had to clench the flashlight under his chin. At one end of a roll, he switched it on, then had to grab metal again. The bobbing red light showed his room in a shambles, with chairs, uniforms, the wastebasket, and most of his paperwork sliding around on the deck. Only the boxes of

WESTPAC Exchange goodies remained in place, the twenty-one-thread line doing its job. He looked at his watch; 0215. When he'd gone to bed at 2200, the ship had been rolling and pitching, but nothing like this. Well, I guess it caught up with us, he thought, as the bow slammed into another monster wave with enough force to stop the ship in her tracks, quivering from end to end.

Then he heard another sound, but he could not quite place it as the wind rose in volume to a prolonged shriek before being drowned out by the roar of another wave crashing on deck. He figured it out: the telephone. He thought he had heard the telephone ring. The phone was mounted on the bulkhead next to his desk. His heart fell: He would have to get out of his bunk to get it. No problem, he thought. Just let go. Ship'll pitch you right over to the other side of the room, and then when you get flung back, you'll be *on* the telephone. . . .

He jammed the flashlight into the space between mattress and bunk edge to provide some light, rolled over on his side, and grasped the storm rail along the side of his bunk with both hands. On the next roll to port, he half-slid, half-fell out of the bunk and onto the deck, where he hung suspended as the deck sloped thirty degrees down until the ship righted herself and rolled back over to starboard. On the next roll, he got up on his knees, put his right arm through the bunk's storm rail, and reached up and grabbed the phone with his left. But he promptly dropped it when the ship lurched over to port for several seconds before bounding up under him into a corkscrew as the bow caught another greenie. He lost his grip on the rail and was rolled over under the steel sink, where he grabbed the sink supports and splayed his legs again to try to find a purchase. The phone, dangling from it cord, was bouncing against the small of his back, so he grabbed it and shouted his name.

"Mr. Holcomb, this is the OOD," came a voice, barely audible above the howling wind outside. "The gig has broken loose in its skids. I got the chief and First Division comin' up to the boat decks."

"Where's Mr. Folsom?"

"He's got OOD; cap'n said to call you right away."

"Okay," Brian shouted. "I'll try to get aft."

He tried to hang the phone up but gave it up after cartwheeling around the room and banging his shins on an overturned chair. Moving between roll cycles, he crawled around the room to retrieve his uniform, then rolled over on his back on the rug to pull on his shirt and pants. It took him a few minutes to find his boots in all the debris on the deck and another minute to get his hands on the flashlight. That was the easy part. Getting through the ship to the boat decks would be the fun part.

The trek to the boat decks took him fifteen minutes of crawling and crabbing through the passageways, down one ladder and up another one before fetching up in a small vestibule in front of the hatch leading out to the weather decks. During the whole time, he had not encountered a single human being. He imagined that anyone not on watch was hanging on for dear life in his rack or on the deck in the berthing compartments. A lot of the crew's berthing was up forward, where it must be pretty lively. He had managed to retain his flashlight, which was good, because a short circuit had taken out the red night lights in the vestibule. On the other side of the hatch, the wind and the seas were doing their best to batter their way in, even though this particular hatch faced aft. The hatch was dogged full down, but a slick of salt water sloshed the vestibule. The noise here was overwhelming and he had to work hard to find a wedging position that would allow him to remain in one place as the big ship bucked and heaved.

He felt his trouser leg being tugged and he looked down the ladder. Chief Martinez grinned up at him in the light of the flashlight. He had one paw on the ladder railing; the other held the bitter end of a six-inch-circumference nylon mooring line. With a kapok life jacket and climbing harness on, the chief completely filled the ladderway, so he didn't need to wedge in place. A coil of twenty-one-thread manila line was looped over his left shoulder. There were two deck apes behind and below him, wedged together in the bottom of the ladderway, their frightened faces white in the shadows. Brian tried to say something, but conversation was simply not possible in the wind noise. It was like standing next to a fighter with its jet engines running full out, a sustained roar interweaved with higher-frequency shrieks.

The chief pantomimed his intentions: I'm going out there. Brian shook his head. No way. The chief nodded vigorously and drew a picture in the air of the gig up on its davit skids, and then of him wrapping the mooring line around it, and then some men in the passageway below pulling on the huge line and securing the boat back in its skids. Brian knew that the gig weighed twelve tons. It had probably broken its gripes and was swinging free in its davit arms. If it broke all the way loose, it would careen down the starboard side, and, if they were *lucky*, it would be snatched clear of the ship by a passing wave. If they were not, it could be picked up by a wave and thrown through the helo hangar or into the gun mounts aft. They could not just let it go.

The chief watched him work it out, then moved up into the hatchway vestibule, a space that was only four feet by three. The two men at the bottom of the ladder became four and then six as they heaved coils of the mooring line into the passageway below the ladder until there was about 150 feet of heavy nylon line coiled at the base. Brian caught an occasional glimpse of arms and legs flailing around on the deck as the men tried to hang on. The chief motioned for Brian to help him haul the coils up the ladder, recoiling it in front of the hatch, which was visibly vibrating on its coaming. The chief then signaled one of the men, who threw him a climbing harness, which he passed to Brian, indicating that he was to put it on. Brian complied and the chief snapped the stainless-steel clamps onto a fire-extinguisher bracket next to the hatch, leaving Brian about three feet of freedom. Martinez wrapped one coil of the six-inch nylon around his waist, laid the bitter end against the standing part, and secured it with twenty-one-thread line tied in a bowline. He signaled again and one of the men threw him a steel helmet, which he jammed on his head, securing it with a chin strap. He checked that his knife was accessible in his boot holster and pushed Brian back against the inner bulkhead of the vestibule. He lifted the hatch handle.

The thirty-pound hatch whipped open, banging all the way back against the exterior bulkhead, sucked out into the maelstrom by the pressure differential created by 120-knot winds. Then it blew back into their faces, nearly decapitating the chief, before flying back out again, this time catching on its holdback. Brian, stunned by the attack of the hatch, forgot to hold on and was himself sucked partway out onto the boat decks for what seemed like an eternity. While the chief was grabbing the back of his harness and trying to pull him in, Brian got a face-to-face look at a typhoon.

The roaring wind overwhelmed all other sounds, including the incessant thunder and lightning. Although it was fully dark, the lightning was almost continuous, flaring in great sheets across the night sky and stabbing into the mountainous seas, raising blasts of steam that were instantly blown flat. The wind drew sheets of rain horizontally across the boat decks, lashing everything in sight, hitting Brian's face so hard that he had to shield his eyes and curl his fingers against the stinging force of the rain. Every few seconds, a mountain of black water would stride down the side, followed by great sheets of spray as the bow blasted a way through the next wave. All of the guy wires on the davits and replenishment gear crackled with blue-white static discharges. The boat decks looked like a mudflat as the tide comes in, with sheets of water sliding across the metal.

And then he was back inside the vestibule, wedged between the bulk of the chief and the bulkhead. Framed in the open hatch, they could see the port and starboard boat davits, each with two boats stacked one over the other. In the flare of lightning the gig, top boat in the starboard davits, swung out over the side with every roll to starboard and then lurched back, thumping into the skid when the ship went back to port. Although he could not hear it, Brian thought that he could feel the boat hit the skids.

How in the hell was the chief going to get across the open boat decks? He looked up at the chief and framed the question with his eyes, but Martinez just grinned, a flash of white teeth in that simian face. He poised in the hatch, waiting for the ship to finish a roll to port. As she started back, he ran straight out onto the boat decks, pointing aft along the centerline until the wind caught him. He then did a belly flop into the sheeting seawater, sliding almost to the after end of the boat decks. As the ship rolled, he slid with her, suspended on the wet deck by the mooring line, his body describing a great arc across to the starboard lifelines, where he grabbed on. A wave came aboard and buried him under ten feet of roaring water.

Brian grabbed the mooring line and started hauling in to take out the slack, gesturing for some of the men to climb the ladder to help. But the first man up into the vestibule was the exec, suited out in a kapok jacket, his khaki trousers, and a T-shirt. He backed Brian up on the line, peering out the hatch and shaking his head in disbelief at the scene outside. Three men came behind him to take a hand with the heavy mooring line. Looking out, Brian saw to his horror that the mooring line had gone *over* the starboard side, which meant that Martinez, if he was still there, was suspended over the side. Just then the next wave came sliding by and Martinez hove into view above the lifeline, neck-deep in the crest of the wave and grappling along the line until he regained a handhold in the lifelines. Brian and the exec pulled hard on the mooring line, which tightened under the lifeline, enabling Martinez to scrabble back under the lifeline, only to have the next roll start him on another great arc, this time to the port side.

"Slack!" shouted the exec. Brian let go and they paid out twenty feet of line, which had the effect of lengthening Martinez's arc so that he could slide down to the after end of the boat decks. A great sheet of spray lashed down on the deck from above, checked the chief's swing across the flooded deck, and washed him under the starboard davit foundations. As the mooring line tightened, Brian saw static electricity crackling along its entire length and felt all the hair on his arms stand up. But the chief had reached his objective, the starboard boat davit. He appeared again in the lightning flashes, signaling for more slack. They paid out more line, then had to retrieve most of it when a wave came across the deck and almost snaked the whole thing out of their hands. The burn made Brian wish he had gloves.

It took fifteen minutes to pass enough line out to the chief, who was wedged between the starboard boat davit foundation and the ship's superstructure. The thundering wind drowned out even their thoughts, and Brian's heart pounded every time the chief disappeared under the torrents of water that went rushing aft along the boat decks. At one point, a gear locker tore off the forward bulkhead and was swept down the deck, just missing the chief, whose back was turned as he clamped onto the davit foundations. The chief struggled to take up the slack in the line, coiling it under the davits, where he stopped it off with a hank of twenty-one-thread line. Then he formed a bight in the end of the line. Timing his movement between rolls, he came out from under the davit and scrambled up the inboard ladder to the level of the gig skid, the bight attached to his body. This was the really dangerous part, as the twenty-eight-foot-long gig was not stable in its skid but swinging out over the sea, all twelve tons of it, every time the ship rolled to starboard, then pounding back onto the skid when she came back to port.

Brian saw what the chief was attempting. With his legs wrapped around the top of the inboard ladder, he would wait until the gig swung in and then would throw a length of the heavy line over the boat. He would then climb partially down the ladder, wait for the boat to swing out and back in again, and attempt to grab the end of the line. If he could fairlead the end of the line through the davit foundation and secure it, the men inside the ship could pull on the mooring line and gripe the boat back in. But how in the hell could he get the line around the gig in the first place? In this wind, it would just be blown aft.

And then he understood. He grabbed the exec's arm and tried to tell him, tried to say they should stop it, but the XO couldn't hear him against the shrieking wind and couldn't see his face well enough to understand. By then, Martinez was making his move. The chief had climbed back up to the top of the ladder and waited for the gig to roll back into the skid. Then he launched himself onto the boat, the mooring line around his chest, and rode the boat out on the next swing over the depths. When the gig started back in, the chief dropped over the outboard side, hanging now by the mooring line, and swung underneath the boat, grabbing the davit foundations even as the boat took off again out over the seas. He had left himself enough slack to accommodate the gig's swings, but he did not get back under the davits fast enough. A large wave came sheeting along the side and tore his handhold away, flinging him back over the side.

There was nothing the men in the hatch could do, as the line was tangled under the davits. Twice the chief became visible in the glare of lightning, bobbing atop a huge wave as it swept by, jerking back to the ship but helpless to get himself back aboard. Brian stood in shock as they watched, until a brilliant flare of lightning clearly illuminated Martinez's broad face—and he was grinning! Jesus Christ, Brian thought, he thinks he's having a good time. Then the next black mass of water pulled the chief completely under. Brian was ready to snap the climbing harness to the mooring line and go out there when the exec grabbed his shoulder and pointed. Martinez had been swept back aboard, only this time into the starboard side three-inch gun tub, twenty feet aft of the gig davit. The mooring line was still draped over the nose of the gig, although it was threatening to come off with each blast of wind.

Over the next ten minutes, Martinez fought his way back across the deck, bouncing between bulkheads and replenishment stanchions to the gig davit's foundation, where he was able to grab and tie off the end of the mooring line to the foundation supports. He then threaded the standing part of the line around a replenishment sheave in the deck. Waiting for a moment of stability in the ship's gyrations, he shinnied his way back across the deck, pulling himself hand over hand along the mooring line, his knees throwing up bow waves like a water-skier trying to get up. He made it to the hatch as the crew inside heaved around on the line to begin snubbing in the gig.

Brian and the exec snatched him into the vestibule as the ship dipped into a deep roll to port. Brian started to close the hatch, but of course the mooring line, taut with the weight of the boat, was now vibrating in the middle of the hatchway. About fifteen men crowded the passageway now, alternately hanging on to the mooring line against the deep rolls and then pulling on it, their faces wet from the blasts of spray blowing in through the hatch. The chief half-slid, half-tumbled down the ladder and collapsed on the passageway deck among the straining deck apes, a big grin on his face, his steel helmet battered and dented. He lay on his back, gulping deep breaths of air, his arms and legs splayed across the passageway to maintain position, while his men heaved and pulled on the mooring line, gaining a little ground on the swinging boat each time she came into the skid. Brian stared at him from the top of the vestibule and the exec clapped Brian on the back and mouthed out a hearty, if inaudible, "Well done."

37

The ship fought her way through the back half of the typhoon for the next eleven hours before the storm showed the first signs of abatement. By midmorning, they had been able to come about and point east back toward Subic after the most violent sector of the storm had gone by and the rolling was down to an almost pleasant twenty degrees, although the storm still obscured most of the daylight. Except for the watch standers, the entire crew stayed in their racks, the safest place to ride out the pitching and rolling. The winds backed rapidly throughout the morning, but it was not until almost 1500 in the afternoon that visible daylight appeared and normal conversation was possible above decks. Brian and the chief boatswain had made a topside tour of the weather decks, dressed out in helmets and kapok life jackets. Brian was surprised to find the decks littered with dead fish encrusted in caked salt; there was a strong stink of iodine in the air. Topside damage in Weapons Department was limited to the battered gig, three missing gear lockers, one exterior ladder twisted off its moorings, and two dozen downed lifeline stanchions on the fantail.

The story of what the chief had done had been fully circulated and he was either being congratulated as a hero or scorned as a complete idiot, although the latter opinion was not voiced to his face. The remainder of the day produced a confused, sickening chop in the South China Sea as the giant storm drove up into the Tonkin Gulf and began to generate reflected waves off the Asian mainland. During the storm, most of the crew had been too busy hanging on for dear life to be seasick, but now, as the ship corkscrewed her way into evening, the head count on the mess decks and in the wardroom diminished dramatically. Brian found himself affected, not by nausea but by a dull headache from the physical stress of trying to stay upright. He downed two APCs before supper in the wardroom, where he found himself almost alone at the senior table in the company of the exec and the chief engineer. The other two department heads, Raiford Hatcher and Count Austin, had been hard down since they left Subic, and many of the other ship's officers had decided to take a pass on the evening meal. With their usual perfect sense of timing, the galleys had served up a nice beef stew.

There was desultory conversation at supper about the weather and who was or was not seasick, including some sharp jibes about Austin, who had often bragged about being an ocean yacht racer. Supper was a both-hands operation, with one hand holding on to the plate while the other operated the silverware. Condiments and other tabletop accoutrements were placed on their sides in an effort to reduce spillage, and there was a good bit of chasing things around the table when the ship got into a sequence of particularly deep rolls. The exec was telling a story about his last typhoon when a pale-looking radio messenger knocked on the wardroom door and entered, snatching off his blue ball cap as he stepped through the door.

"XO, got an immediate for you sir," the messenger said. His face paled even more when he saw the remains of the beef stew.

"Okay, lemme see it," replied the exec. Eyeing the messenger's face, he asked, "You, uh, want to wait outside, maybe?"

"Uh, yes, sir, if that's okay," gulped the messenger. He practically bolted out of the wardroom. There was a weather decks hatch not too far from the wardroom door.

"That boy's gonna go feed the fishies," observed the engineer.

"And we're going back to the friggin' Gulf," announced the exec, eyeing the message.

"Oh shit." Brian sighed. "What's happened to *Long Beach*? They were supposed to do another two weeks."

"Don't tell me we're gonna miss Kaohsiung?" asked Vince.

"Yup," the exec said, passing the message board over to Brian. "Would you believe, *Long Beach* lost her freakin' TACAN antenna in the storm? Blew clean away. They apparently waited a little too long to get out of the Gulf, so it got pretty bad up there—you know how shallow the Gulf is. So no antenna, no TACAN; no TACAN, no Red Crown. Three guesses whom they've sent for."

"So let's go bust our TACAN antenna, XO," offered Vince. "We've still got some storm left out there. Shit, I'll climb up there and do it. I've got some boiler work to get done, and there's a destroyer tender in Kaohsiung."

"Solly, cholly," the exec said. "They want us back on station ASAP; we've been directed to make best speed up to the Gulf as weather permits."

"I'm not sure what the huge hurry would be," Brian said. "Nobody will be flying off the carriers in this weather."

The exec snagged his coffee cup as a deep roll started it sliding toward Brian's lap, adding to the many stains on the tablecloth. "Well, maybe someone's got something planned for the North Vietnamese," he mused. "You know, as a storm this size plays out over the North, there might be a lot of targets exposed and not much triple-A defense in place until all those creeks and canals go down. Might be an *ichiban* time to go whack some Commies. I better go up and see the Old Man.''

"How's he doing, XO?" Brian asked, trying to keep it casual.

The exec gave Brian a speculative look. "Doing? Well, he's tired—been up on the bridge for nearly twenty-four hours while we rode this bear out. That what you meant?" There was the barest hint of an edge to the exec's voice.

Brian thought fast. That was not at all what he meant, but from the look in the exec's eyes, he had a sense that he was straying into uncharted territory. He cleared his throat nervously.

"Yes, sir. I just hadn't seen him for a while. Guess I have to get out on the bridge more often."

The exec relaxed, apparently satisfied with Brian's answer. "The rack's the only safe place to be when she's wallowing around like this. And since you're not seasick and the Count is, how's about going up to Combat. Get with Garuda. Give him the good news and let's start getting Combat ready to work again. That's assuming you can find a radarman on board who isn't as green as his scope."

"Aye, aye, sir."

The exec left, taking the message board with him topside; the radio messenger apparently was not going to return. Vince was looking at Brian over his coffee cup.

"Touch a nerve, did we?" he said.

Brian rolled his eyes. "It was a semi-innocent question."

"And that was a semiserious warning to keep thine nose out of nooks and crannies where it ain't been invited . . . so to speak."

"You saw him the other night. I mean, I thought he'd been on a nine-day toot, but the more I think about it, the more I don't think that's it. I think there's something wrong, something medically wrong. He actually looked kind of drugged."

"Now there's a thought," said Vince, reaching under the table for the buzzer to summon the steward. They could not leave the dishes on the table with the ship rolling around like this. Then he remembered that the Filipino steward had served supper and then hastily preceded the radio messenger to the weather decks. "I forgot; we have to play steward tonight."

They gathered up the crockery into the middle of the table. The tablecloth had been deliberately wet down to increase friction under the plates, so they put all the plates and cups and saucers into the middle of the table and then balled them up in the tablecloth, tied it in a wet knot, and stuck the bundle on the deck in the wardroom pantry. Brian noticed that there was plenty of stew left.

38

San Diego

Maddy would remember that weekend as two nights and two days of suspended reality, nothing but a marathon of the senses, no phones, no wardroom wives, no bank accounting department, no tennis, just Autrey. Even in their most passionate days of romancing, during the weekends with Brian in New York, she had never stayed so close or affixed herself to a man so hard and for so long. And it wasn't all just sex. They talked a little, dozed, sat in the dark and watched the play of the city's lights on the night clouds, made scrambled eggs in the early hours of the morning, listened to an after-hours jazz station on the radio, and occasionally slept. Maddy found herself entering a state of renewable exhaustion, ignoring the phone when it rang, staying awake sometimes after he had gone to sleep, savoring his presence, the feel of a live, warm man right *there*, anytime she reached out, and she often did reach out, just to make sure.

By Sunday morning, she was hollow-eyed and moving like a zombie, physically worn out, sexually just about burned out, emotionally saturated, but never straying more than six feet away from him. It wasn't love or infatuation: She was simply taking a prolonged drink, deliberately sating herself with this man, who remained as personally remote as he had been for the entire time she had known him, even after they had become so close physically that a simple touch could start it all up again.

Autrey the mystery, Autrey the man. She figured part of it was his Indian heritage, although he did not make a big thing about it. There was none of the sagebrush hocus-pocus, obscure references to spirits, or Hollywood red man dialects she had seen on the television whenever American Indian fads rippled through the young white rebel establishment. There was instead a quiet dignity, born, she surmised, of the combination of his ancestry and his own physical strength and knowledge. Among the young Marine officers he instructed, he was a first among equals, an exemplary specimen of finely honed physical conditioning, mental strength and agility, and the unique sort of self-confidence that is created by a hunting spirit and knowledge of the killing and of the military art. But with Maddy, he behaved as an attentive mentor, watchful to see where her needs were taking her, vigorous in his attention, matching the violence of her passion with his own strength, staying with her when she was in control and dominating when she would start to lose control, all the while taking great care in everything he did with her and to her to be exquisitely gentle, as if understanding that she was capable of overrunning her need and breaking.

She sensed that he had known all along that she was less interested in talking than in just being with him. He took care not to leave her alone and to touch her whenever they were close enough to touch. He made love to her with his hands and his lips as often as he did with his penis, and she learned some things about her own needs that she carefully stored away, delicate scrolls of knowledge, knowledge she would have to impart to her husband one day in such a way as to ensure that he thought of it all by himself. But that was the only thought she had about the future, as she very deliberately narrowed down her time horizon to the next hour of Autrey's face in her hair or her next encounter with his body.

By Sunday night, she was finally exhausted. She was barely able to keep her eyes open, wandering around the apartment in a bathrobe, hugging herself while erasing the inevitable thoughts of guilt as quickly as they appeared on the horizons of her mind. He would follow her as she moved about the room, watching, coming to her whenever she stopped. The only strength left in her was in her right hand, which she locked to his hand when he would join her, wrapping his arms around her from behind, the final expression of the essence of her need. At nightfall, he took her back to the bed and, pulling back the covers, arranged her on her stomach, her arms folded beneath a pillow. He gently turned her face to one side and then pulled the damp mass of her hair to the other side, brushing back the last few reluctant strands off her cheek. He pulled the sheet up over her lower body and then stroked her back until she subsided into a deep sleep.

He showered, dressed, and left a note, saying he would be back in San Diego Wednesday, that he would call her before he came over. He put it down on the night table, stood there for a minute watching her sleep, and then picked the note up and was gone.

39

Two days after getting the message to relieve *Long Beach*, *Hood* completed an abbreviated turnover. The seas in the Gulf were still fractious and liberally sprinkled with the debris of the typhoon's landing ashore in North Vietnam. Great patches of brown water mingled with the gray in the late-afternoon sunset and the surface was littered for miles around with treetops and branches, clumps of thatch from coastal huts, broken boats, and empty oil drums. The storm had taken its toll of animals as well, with bedraggled land birds perching forlornly on bobbing tree branches, which themselves were floating among the puffy carcasses of pigs and water buffalo. The seas were still too rough for safe helo operations, so the PIRAZ boxes came over by light-line transfer, and the briefings were held via sound-powered phones as the two ships steamed along in a side-by-side replenishment formation.

Austin was more or less back in battery but still not looking too well. Brian and Garuda had rounded up the less seasick radar men and posted the Red Crown watch. The same seas that were bouncing the two missile ships around had no effect at all on the 90,000-ton carriers to the south, so the air war had already resumed while the small boys were still picking up the pieces and fire-hosing fish food off their weather decks. Brian had listened in on a sound-powered phone extension while Austin took the debrief from his opposite number in *Long Beach* over the bridge-to-bridge phones. Vince Benedetti was in Main Control, his station anytime the *Hood* went alongside another ship. Brian noticed the captain in his bridge chair; he looked somewhat better than the last time Brian had seen him. He was talking on a separate circuit with the CO of the *Long Beach*. Maybe he had just been seasick, Brian thought. The exec was out on the bridge-wing, coaching one of the junior ensigns as he learned how to conn alongside, with only 110 feet between the two ships. Up on the forecastle, a bedraggled First Division tended the distance-marker line, hunkering down under the frequent fans of salt spray that thumped up over *Hood*'s bow.

The Ops officer in *Long Beach* had finished and was asking whether they had any questions. Austin shook his head, obviously wanting to get below to his bunk. He turned and raised an eyebrow at Brian. Brian nodded and Austin handed him the phone.

"What about MiGs?" he asked. "Been any feet-wet activity?"

"That's a negative," replied the commander on the other end. Brian could just barely see him crouched down out of the wind up on *Long Beach*'s towering boxlike superstructure. "We haven't seen a MiG since you guys helped us prang those two a coupla weeks back. They just don't even come up with a Talos ship around. Maybe you guys'll see more action, but I gotta warn you, the CAP are itching to bag something."

"We saw a report that the eye of the storm passed just about over Vinh military airfield," Brian said. "I suspect we won't see anything in the way of MiGs for some time to come."

"Yeah, well, those little boogers are pretty good at fixing stuff up sooner than we would expect. Keep your eyes peeled. If that's it, we're ready to pass the Crown."

Brian gave him a wait-one and asked the captain whether they had permission to take the station. The captain gave him a small wave of his hand and Brian said the magic words.

"We got it, Commander. Have a good trip."

Brian hung up the phone and went back into Combat, where Fox Hudson and Garuda Barry were studying the message air plans for the two carriers down on Yankee Station. Both men were wedged between consoles and stanchions in order to stay upright. The ship still rolled around enough to warrant the use of seat belts on the console chairs.

"We've got it," Brian announced.

"Red Crown, aye," replied Garuda, slipping down into the SWIC chair. He punched some buttons and verified that *Long Beach* had gone radio-silent in the link. "Yup. We got it."

Over the next six days, the ship settled back into the routine of the Red Crown station, or at least the mavens of Combat did. The weather flattened out and actually began to cool off as the Indochinese winter approached and the northeast monsoon began to form, as if the typhoon had blown away the last vestiges of the hot season. Vince Benedetti was back on the evaluator watch bill, so the evaluator watches rotated and all three evaluators enjoyed a decent proportion of rest to watch standing. For Brian, coming back to the second line period was much less of a strain than the first forty-five days.

He now knew his way around Combat, and the first period was fresh enough in his mind that he knew his way around the Gulf air picture, as well. There had been heavy reconnaissance flights the week after the storm, both to assess damage in country and to evaluate any vulnerabilities that might have been created. Both carriers had been active all week, but there was no word on resuming heavy strikes against the North. On the sixth night after *Long Beach*'s departure, the MiGs reappeared.

Brian had the 1800 to 2400 watch and was plowing through the nightly stack of message traffic at the evaluator's table. They were in the pause between carrier cycles, when one carrier went off-line and the next began her eighteen-hour duty cycle. Garuda sat SWIC, sequencing through the active tracks to see if they all were paired closely with video. The duty AIC was idle, his BARCAP having gone back to the carrier without relief on-station. He would get new CAP on the 2100 launch, which was a half hour away. The AIC was doctoring a mug of evil-looking coffee when the surface tracker, of all people, called over to SWIC on intercom.

"SWIC, Surface Module."

"SWIC."

"SWIC, I got a piece of video on the ten radar that seems to be moving overland. May be a ghost or something, but it just don't look right."

"SWIC, aye, and mark it."

The tracker injected and then transmitted a tiny bright box of light to the SWIC console as Garuda changed down the range scale from 250 miles to 25 on his picture, looked for a minute, and then selected the SPS-10 surface-search-radar presentation. He found the light box at once and stared at it.

"Well, I'll be damned," Garuda muttered. "I think there's skin in there."

"Skin in where?" asked Brian, overhearing the remark but not looking up from the stack of message traffic.

"I think we may have us a bandit creepin' through the weeds near Vinh, say, two-eight-five for forty-four miles. Little bitty piece a video in there. AIC, SWIC!"

"AIC, aye." The controller hurriedly set his mug down and slipped back into his console seat.

"Go special track on the light box you are receiving now. Switch to the ten."

"The ten? The surface search?!"

"Do it. That's where the business is."

"AIC, aye, going special track, on the ten." He switched his range scale down to fifty miles, switched from the SPS-48 air-search radar to the surface-search radar, and then offset the scope picture to center the light box. Used to controlling fighters, he had never even looked at the short-range surface-search-radar presentation. Typically, the maximum range of the surface-search radar was inside the *minimum* range of his air-search radar. When he had the light box with its tiny smears of video centered, he commanded expanded video, which blew up the light box from a quarter-inch-sized box to a display that covered his entire screen. Clearly visible in among all the land clutter was a bit of video, moving from left to right. The AIC inserted an unknown track symbol and commanded the computer to track the symbol and its video in close control.

Insertion of the unknown track prompted a squawk from the track supe, who called SWIC asking what it was. SWIC responded with his customary fanging.

"Why, it's an air unknown moving overland, Supe. You know, the enemy. You mean to tell me you guys in the Cave never saw it? And that a guy in *surface* saw it before you did? Are we asleep back there again? Are we—"

"Okay, Garuda," Brian said, standing behind the SWIC chair. "We got a bandit, no shit?"

"Sure looks like it, Mr. H. But he's low, really low. It's showing up on the SPS-ten but not on either of the air-search radars."

"SWIC, Track Supe, Alfa Whiskey wants to know—"

"SWIC, aye, tell him it's valid and we hold skin."

Brian picked up the bat phone and buzzed while Garuda and the AIC refined the tracking data. It was movie time in the wardroom.

"Captain."

"Cap'n, Evaluator, we have a possible MiG, two-eight-five, about forty-five miles, heading north, very low and visible only on the surface-search radar. We have a track in the system."

"This is near Vinh? I thought they were out of business because of the typhoon."

"Yes, sir, so the Intel people said. I guess nobody told the bad guys."

"He's out of range, right?"

"Of our systems? Yes, sir. And we've no BARCAP just now—we're in the cycle shift."

"Those little bastards keep track, don't they? Okay. Put a missile system on him just so's he knows he's being watched. Let me know if anything changes."

"Aye, sir." Brian hung up and ordered Garuda to assign the unknown to a tracking system. Garuda sent the assignment over the network and one of the Spooks rumbled into life above them. The bat phone buzzed.

"Evaluator, sir."

"XO here. Make sure somebody's still on the forty-eight radar; if all you guys are focused on a twenty-five-mile-range ring on the ten, there could be trouble coming out at seventy-five or a hundred miles, right?"

"Uh, yes, sir. Got it."

Brian hung up again, then told Garuda to go back to the SPS-48 presentation and why. Garuda nodded emphatically.

"He's absolutely right. All three of us here were on the surface-search. Classic mistake."

"Well, we do have the whole Cave purportedly minding the store on the air side."

"Right."

"Yeah, well, it was a thought. What's he doing?"

"System Two is tracking; video intermittent due to ground clutter," reported the FCSC.

"SWIC, aye. He's just toolin' up the coast, like always. Apparently knows the range, too."

"Mr. Holcomb, sir?" It was the FCSC. He was motioning for Brian to come over to the weapons module for a private conversation. Brian glanced at the screen for a moment and then walked over to the weapons module.

"Yeah, Chief?"

The chief spoke in a low voice so that the EC sitting six feet away could not hear. "Uh, sir, I'm not sure about this, but I think we got maybe another little party goin' down in missile plot, you know, like the one you busted in on? You mind calling Jackson and havin' him go take a look-see?"

Brian looked at him, his heart sinking. "Of course, Chief. But I hope to hell you're wrong about this."

"So do I, sir, so do I. But you know, we've just come outta Subic and all the dopers got their stashes right—you know what I'm saying?"

"All too well. I'll get the Sheriff." Brian walked back over into D and D and made a discreet phone call while looking over Garuda's shoulder. The air unknown was still showing on the screen, loitering along the coastal mountains. Jackson said he'd get right on it. Brian hung up.

"What's his range now?"

"Forty-six and a half. And he's not comin' our way. Just the usual shit, now that *Long Beach*'s gone."

"But they waited six days this time, didn't they?"

"You betchum, Red Ryder. That musta been a nasty surprise up there over Hanoi."

"How's your track, Chief?"

FCSC waggled his hand. "Just so-so. He's in the weeds."

The bat phone buzzed. It was the exec again. Brian could hear movie dialogue in the background.

"What's happening with the bandit?"

"He's loitering out at forty-six miles. Making lazy eights along the coast and staying feet-dry. Uh, XO?"

"Yes?" The exec's tone sharpened.

"I may have another deal going on down in missile plot. Like the last time? I've got the Sheriff en route. May be nothing; may be something. You, uh, want to call me back in about, say, fifteen mikes, XO?"

There was a moment's pause. "Yes. That's fine, Weps. Keep us advised, especially if he changes his profile."

Brian hung up. Still keeping secrets. He hoped fervently that FCSC was wrong.

"Evaluator, SWIC. Bogey is slowing, appears to be returning to its base. And AIC reports we have BARCAP inbound to station, ETA fifteen mikes."

"Right, Garuda. Let me know when you lose video on him, and tell the Cave to watch for surprises on the coast. We don't need to get jumped again."

"I roger that. But I think with the BARCAP inbound, we're probably not going to see any more bogeys for a while."

Radarman First Class Rockheart stuck his head into D and D. "Mr. Holcomb, you've got a phone call on the admin line in surface."

"Okay, Rocky." Brian walked over to surface, wondering why someone would call the evaluator in surface and not D and D. And then he knew.

"Weps here."

"Mr. Holcomb." It was Chief Jackson. "We've got a mess down here in missile plot. I've got three E-Fives from Fox division partying down on weed. Got 'em cold. They're so high, they don't even deny it. Offered me a toke, if you can believe it."

"Fuck me," Brian said. "Are you alone, or do you have a witness?"

"I've got Mr. Hudson with me, sir. I picked him up on the way aft."

"Good move. Lemme talk to him, Chief." There was a moment of silence and then Fox came on the line.

"Mr. Hudson speaking, sir."

"Fox, how bad is this?"

"This is a goddamn disaster, Boss. With Marcowitz gone, we bust these guys and we have no more E-Fives in missile-fire control. The next senior guy is a fresh-caught E-Four with one year of experience."

"Any doubts about what you got?"

"Not one, Mr. Holcomb. These suckers are flyin' and proud of it. The watch stander is FTM Three Warren; he's the same guy who was in here with Marcowitz, the black guy, and it's almost the same deal, except these guys went in the back, in the switchboard room, to have their crotch-hair ciggie weeds. The hatch was closed and Warren got antsy when these three wipes got loud. The chief up in Combat picked up on it, and here we are."

"Write the little fucks up," Brian said. He thought that Rockheart appeared to be eavesdropping. "Get 'em piss-tested and then get report chits. I'll sign 'em as accuser."

"Sir, we do that and—"

"You got a hearing problem, Fox? Do it."

"Aye, aye, sir, but—"

"Just do it, Fox," Brian said, a little more gently this time. "I know what you're trying to tell me." Brian hung up and walked back into D and D. Garuda brought him up to speed.

"Bogey is RTB. BARCAP's almost on-station. No more activity on the coast for the moment, but we're watching. I secured System Two when he went on the deck. He wasn't tracking too well, anyway. Is there something—"

"Yeah, there is." Brian picked up the bat phone.

"XO." So the exec was guarding the phone. Good.

"XO, the bogey has returned to base. I'll be doing an intel report to confirm Vinh military airfield is operational again. Oh, and the BARCAP are back on-station."

"Okay. Any other activity?"

"Not outside, sir."

A pause. "Yes?"

"Inside, the Sheriff and Fox Hudson caught three FTMs smoking pot in missile plot's switchboard room. I've directed the Sheriff to piss-test them and Mr. Hudson to write them up."

There was silence on the line. Brian had the feeling that the exec wanted to tell him to wait, to stop the report-chit process until he could get into it, but with the captain right there . . .

"Okay. Keep us advised if any more come up." The phone clunked in his ear. The XO was probably going to sit there for a few minutes and then ease out of the wardroom and head for the Sheriff's office. Brian decided he wanted to get there first. He made one more call.

"Chief master-at-arms office, Baby Doc here, sir."

"Baby Doc, the Sheriff back with those three guys? This is Mr. Holcomb."

"Yes, sir, here he is."

"Jackson speaking, sir."

"Sheriff, Mr. Hudson has some doubts about the wisdom of putting these three guys formally on report. I'd appreciate it if you'd get the paper moving ASAP, before there's, uh, any interference, if you know what I mean. And I'm going to sign them, so get someone to bring the roughs up here to Combat."

"Uh, yes, sir. But there shouldn't be any—"

"Yeah, I know. Just remember that I called you."

"Aye, aye, sir."

The remainder of the 1800 to 2400 watch passed uneventfully.

Chief Jackson had brought the three rough-draft report chits to Brian thirty minutes after his call and Brian had initialed them. He tried to keep his mind on the Red Crown business, but the incident in missile plot sat on his shoulder like one of Goya's nightmares. But when the exec came into Combat at 2330 with Count Austin and Fox Hudson, he knew that he had trouble on his hands.

Brian turned over the watch to Austin and Garuda gave SWIC to Hudson. The exec busied himself with his own message stack at the evaluator's table, obviously waiting for the watch change. When Brian announced that Austin had the watch, the exec got up and signaled for Brian to follow him. The exec headed for the ladder, preceded Brian down to the next level, and walked directly into Brian's stateroom. Brian took a deep breath and followed him in. The exec flopped his big frame down in a chair and indicated that Brian should do the same.

"Well," he began, "this is a fine mess you've got in Fox division."

"Yes, sir," Brian agreed. "That's four E-Fives in less than a month."

"The Sheriff showed me the report chits. That's what I want to talk about."

"Yes, sir, I figured you might."

"I'll get right to it: We have our system for handling this here, Brian."

"Yes, sir, and it's not working. I think these guys ought to go on report and be processed for drug offenses. Go to mast, get their general or whatever discharges, and take their doper asses back to the streets."

"Have you thought through the consequences of doing that?"

Brian sighed. "Yes, sir. It means I have two FTM chiefs, one first class, and the next rated guy on the ladder is FTM Three Warren, fresh-caught and pretty green. We kick those three guys off the ship and we have a ferocious hole in missile-fire control."

"And you still want to do this?"

Brian rubbed his eyes as he gathered his thoughts. The only sound in the stateroom was the rush of air from the vents. Did he really want to do this? Besides gutting Fox division, it might also mean the end to any chances he had for a brilliant regular fitness report in this ship, because pressing on with the report chit would mean that the captain would have to confront the drug offenses at mast. That's what the exec was really asking him: Do you really want to do this?

"XO, I understand what you're saying. And I'm not oblivious to the system you've been running here on the drugs. But I just feel it in my bones that *Hood*'s not doing it right. The Navy's policy and regs on drug use aboard ship are crystal-clear: You kick 'em out for it."

The exec shook his head. "Navy policy, shit. You've got a lot to learn, Brian. The Navy policy is two-faced: You kick 'em out, but then the ship gets a bad reputation for having a drug problem, *and* you decimate your crew, which means your department doesn't perform well. And guess, Mr. Department Head, who suffers for that?"

"I know that, XO. I know. But every time we point one of those missile directors, or launch a helo, or an AIC sits down to direct a fighter, these guys have to be clean. They can't be on the back side of a buzz, or hungover, or fixating on their next dose of whatever shit they're into. For me, that's what's at the heart of this."

The exec shifted in his chair and shuffled his stack of messages, his face grim. Brian had the sense that, while the exec did not disagree with him, he was struggling with other loyalties. Finally, he looked up.

"You realize, of course, that the skipper has very little idea of how bad this drug problem is, don't you? You've figured out that our 'system,' as you call it, is something

I'm running, not him? You press on with those chits and I have to take 'em up the line, to captain's mast. And that's something I really don't want to do."

Brian leaned forward. "But XO," he said, "if the ship had cracks in the hull and you had guys down below patching and plugging every day to keep up with them, you'd be obligated to tell him, whether he wanted to hear it or not, wouldn't you? I mean, he's the captain. He's the owner. He's supposed to know. He's *required* to know, by Navy regs and two hundred years of Navy tradition. And since he can't be everywhere at once, he depends on the wardroom to tell him, even when it's bad news. I can understand a guy his age, with his temperament and his 'take care of your troops' approach, I can understand why—"

The exec put up a hand. "No, you can't. There's more to it. And unfortunately, I can't tell you any more than that. But keep in mind that he did send in a special fitness report on you. He didn't have to do that. *We* didn't have to do that. Not that you haven't earned it—you've done a damn good job. But we did you a big favor. I kind of thought you'd be disposed to do us one. So right now, I guess I'm calling that in. Pull those report chits. For the sake of the ship, and for the sake of Captain Huntington." He paused. "And, if I have to spell it out for you, for the sake of your own career."

He reached into his message stack, pulled out the three report chits, and put them on Brian's desk. "Think about it. I can just about guarantee that these three guys will never touch dope again. But even if I couldn't, I still want you to think about it. Come see me after quarters in the morning. Okay?"

"Aye, aye, sir," Brian said stiffly.

The exec pushed himself out of the chair with a groan. "Getting old myself," he muttered. "Like you will someday."

Brian sat in his chair after the exec left. He listened to the tramp of feet in the passageway outside his door as the men coming off watch headed down below for midrats and their racks. Then it was silent, with only the background noises of the vent fans. Think about it. He read the chits; it was all there in black and white. Violation of Article 92, Uniform Code of Military Justice, Title Ten, United State Code. Drugged on duty. Urinalysis positive for all three. Apprehended and witnessed by a chief and a lieutenant.

He scanned the forms for the background information. Boyle, Lanier, and Corey: all E-Fives, all with nearly four years of service, all missile school and basic-electronics school graduates, smart guys. He turned the forms over and saw the priors. He sat up. Corey and Lanier had been busted before for possession, at missile school. Boyle had been busted for failing a random urinalysis screen at a transient barracks on the way to *Hood*. Shit. These guys were habitual dopers. He put the forms down on the desk. The only way the exec could guarantee that these guys would smoke no more dope was to rip their lips off and pass them around at quarters. And while he thought that some of the chiefs would happily perform the surgery, he did not really believe in his heart that this would end their drug problem.

You will never know, know for sure, when you call for a missile on the rail or you assign a director in a no-shit situation if these three guys will be clean. That's why the regs say to throw 'em out. That old saw again: Navy regs are written in blood; every regulation in the book is derived from some memorable incident whose procedural or operational lesson was first engraved on the hull of a drowned ship or etched in the memory of those who mourned dead sailors. So what it comes down to, bucko, is, what is the honorable thing to do here? You did understand that the special fitness report came with a string. I never explicitly agreed. You never went back and put any boundaries on the deal, either. You pocketed that fitrep. Now they're calling in the favor. Okay, but if I go along, the drug decay festers and we're back on the line with certified dopers on the missile consoles.

There was a soft knocking on his door.

"Yeah, come in."

It was Chief Jackson, who stood in the doorway with his red flashlight. "They told me you left with the XO. I figured it had to do with those chits. I guess I got curious."

"Come in, Sheriff," Brian said, tossing the chits on his desk. "Grab a chair. It's decision time."

Chief Jackson came in, removed his hat, and sat down in the other chair. He tipped his chin toward the report chits lying on Brian's desk.

"Those are rock-solid. You noticed the priors?"

"Yup. I've just about made up my mind."

"Just about, sir?"

Brian smiled. "The XO was in here to tell me the price tag of going forward."

"Ah."

"But I think I know the right answer, Chief. Lemme give you some history first. See, I needed a special fitness report, something to get before the lieutenant commander board, something recent that would help overcome a not-so-good fitness report from my last ship. They sent one in, and it's gonna do the job."

"And for that they expect you to be a go-along guy."

"Right."

"Yes, sir. I copy that."

Brian studied the chief's black face in the dim light of his stateroom. Jackson wasn't challenging him. He was sitting there waiting to see, waiting to take Brian's measure. How many of these little dilemmas had he been through, Brian wondered, trading off his feelings and ambitions as a black man to stay on track for that chief's hat? Brian suddenly had the feeling that he was in sympathetic company.

"And the answer is this, I think: I have a moral obligation to honor the deal with the XO. But I also think I have a larger moral obligation to do my duty to the ship. And that duty tells me to nail these jerks and get 'em off the ship." He sighed. "Maddy—that's my wife— Maddy's always saying I'm an idealist, a crusader, which in America is not a compliment. But there it is, Chief. So here: I've signed them. If they want to tear them up, so be it. But I think now these need to go into the hopper."

The chief took the report chits and looked at them, nodded once, and got up.

"Harder than it looks, isn't it, Mr. Holcomb?"

"Oh yes, Chief. It sure as hell is."

The chief nodded again. "And you're not the only one in the squeeze."

"Oh?"

"Yes, sir. FTM Three Warren, he's getting some heat, too. This is the second time he's been there for a drug bust. He came to see me tonight. Guys in the division have been giving him the cold shoulder."

"I'm sorry to hear that. But he didn't blow the whistle—it was khaki both times."

"Yes, sir, but, well, the bustees have been running their mouths: Isn't it a coincidence Warren's been the guy on watch when both deals went down? 'Wonder why that is' sort of shit. And there's another angle."

"What's that?"

"Warren's black, remember? He kind of waltzed around it, but I think he's frightened of what the sellers might be contemplating."

"He say that? He's been threatened?"

"No, sir, not yet, anyway. Don't get me wrong—Warren's a good kid. But I think he's heard some shit. Probably from the three shitbirds we just nailed. And if the drug ring is black, he's probably gonna get a racial guilt trip laid on him. At a minimum."

"Shit. I never thought of that."

The chief stood up, the report chits bunched in his hand.

"Gets damn complicated, doesn't it?" he said as he opened the stateroom door.

Brian couldn't think of anything to say as the chief left with the report chits. Only a few minutes later, as he hit the rack, did it occur to him that Chief Jackson was going to get that same guilt trip laid on *him*. He thought back to that last letter home; he'd been right—this little issue was not going to go away.

40

This time, Bullet came to find Rocky. He had called the surface module at about 2200 on the admin phone, asked for Rocky, and then suggested to Rocky that he make a head call. They met not ten feet from Rocky's main hashish stash, in the passageway outside the forward crew's head. For once, Bullet was visibly perturbed.

"So Holcomb's actually going to write them up? Go to mast? The whole bit?" Rocky asked.

"Uh-huh. Them dumbasses was havin' a damn party in the missile plot. My man says one of 'em axed ole Jackson, he want a little toke."

"Jesus Christ. If they go on the pad, they'll have to go see the Old Man. He's gonna have to court-martial them. That could mean NIS out here, an investigation."

"Already got one a those goin'."

"Who? What?" Rocky tried not to let panic show in his voice.

"My man Jackson, Mistuh Marshall Dillon. Man's been givin' me the eye. I think my man Marcowitz done sung a song 'fore he went to the front gate, got his ass set up. Him or that Warren kid."

"You ever have anything to do directly with Marcowitz?" asked Rocky.

"Shee-it. I don't deal with no skins. Thass whut I got my 'ssociates for."

"Then how in the hell—"

"Doan know. Whut I do know is, my man Jackson, he been lookin' at me, been hangin' around the shop. Actin' like one a them big damn birds, sits up in a tree all day. Waitin' for meat. I turn around, I keep seein' the man."

Rocky lifted an eyebrow at Bullet as two First Division types turned the corner, heading for their berthing compartment. By the time they were abreast, Rocky and Bullet were talking football. When they had passed, Rocky tried to calm Bullet down.

"Look, you're always telling me we've got a good system here, good security, cutouts, the whole bit. There's no way Jackson can *know* anything; if he did, there'd be NIS all over this boat. I think it's time for you to take the advice you're always giving me: Be cool. Sit tight."

Bullet shook his head. "Doan like things changin'. First Marcowitz—Injun didn't go after him; he gets set up at the front gate, he gone, just like that. Now you tell me: Who's organizin' that shit? Now these three skins, and this new officer's writin' 'em up, 'steada Martinez kickin' they asses. And now Jackson, he bird-doggin' *me*."

"I keep telling you, there's no way in hell that Marcowitz could even know anything about you—or me."

"Then where it comin' from? Who's talkin' to the Sheriff, puttin' him on *my* black ass? You tell me that."

"Who else knows, besides your 'associates'? Knows and might talk?"

They looked at each other. Garlic? Rocky thought about it. If Bullet was right, and the blacks held their silence, as it seemed they would, then maybe old Garlic had dropped a dime. One of them needed to talk to Brother Garlic. Bullet agreed.

"But it cain't be me; Jackson see me up on the mess decks, spendin' time with Garlic, he already sniffin' around my trail—"

"Yeah. Okay. I'll do it. But damn, it's such a sweet deal. Why in the hell would he ever expose it?"

"Doan know, man. You lemme know how it goes down. And you watch yo ass—they's things movin' around out there, things I doan like."

"Yeah, okay. Just be cool. Let me scope it out. I'll call you in the shop. And maybe have your guys lean on that Warren guy. He's one of, uh, yours, right? Way I hear it, he's just been a bystander, but—"

Bullet gave him a strange look. Rocky would have sworn Bullet was laughing at him for a moment. "One of mine. Yeah. I take care of it."

Rocky sensed he had made some kind of mistake, but he couldn't put his finger on exactly what it was. "Yeah, okay. Meantime, we need to cool the action down a little bit.''

"Shee-it. Thass the thang. We didn't sell them three twidgets that shit. They bought they own, man. They bought they own. Now ain't that a trip?''

Rocky had left Bullet standing in the passageway and headed back to Combat. When he got off watch at midnight, he went down for midrats and then to his compartment, where he stretched out on his rack in his dungarees and waited for the compartment to settle down after midrats. An hour later, he rose and headed aft to the mess decks. He had his MAA badge pinned on his shirt in case anyone saw him snooping around this late at night. Midrats was over and the mess cooks had swept down one more time before securing. The only people on the mess decks were those two weirdos, Hooper and Coltrane, playing cards at one of the corner tables. A light was on in the galley and he could hear Poppa Steiner in there pounding dough. Garlic ought to be in his office balancing out the day's breakouts. Arriving at the door, Rocky looked around and then knocked.

"The fuck outta here; galley's closed,'' grumped Garlic from behind the door.

Rocky knocked again, once, hard. He heard the door being unlocked and then he grabbed the handle and pushed it in, catching the big man by surprise.

"Rocky, what the fuck—''

"We gotta talk, Garlic. Lock this fucker again.''

Garlic scowled but locked the door while Rocky found a chair. The galley office was long and narrow, squeezed in between the galley itself and the scullery compartment. There was one overhead light fixture, a desk counter mounted to the bulkhead, some beat-up file cabinets, and two adding machines. The galley crew's GQ helmets and life jackets hung on the opposite bulkhead. The room smelled of cigarette smoke and stale grease.

"Anybody comes in, I'm doing an investigation about a missing wallet you've heard about.''

"Yeah, okay. So what's this all about?''

Rocky filled him in on the developments with the three fire-control technicians. Some of it Garlic had already heard, although the part about mast was news. Rocky explained how a mast case like that might attract attention higher up and result in the Naval Investigative Service being brought in, especially if the admiral's staff was still harboring suspicions about a drug problem in *Hood*. Garlic listened to all this with a bored, sour expression on his face.

"So why do I give a shit?" he asked, stubbing out his cigarette and fishing for another.

Rocky watched him closely. "Because," he said, "Jackson has started to keep an eye on Bullet, and Bullet's getting a little antsy about it."

If Garlic knew anything about this development, he didn't show it. Rocky saw no flick of recognition in Garlic's eyes or any other hint that Garlic knew something about the Sheriff's newfound interest in Bullet.

"Yeah, so?" he said.

"So Bullet and I can't put a connection together between the drug bust in missile plot and Bullet. He never deals, and he didn't even know who Marcowitz was. There's no way Jackson could be making a connection, and yet it looks like he has."

Garlic stared at Rocky for a moment and then a nasty-looking smile began to gather on his face.

"And you two think your ole buddy Garlic is talkin' to the fucking Sheriff? The only other guy in the ship who knows the connection? That what you thinkin', motherfucker?"

Garlic lunged out of his chair before Rocky had a chance to react, grabbed him by the shirt and one arm, whirled him around, and slammed him face down onto the countertop, holding him bent over by his sheer bulk. Rocky, stunned at the speed of the fat man, had the wind knocked right out of him. His ribs creaked with the weight of Garlic pushing against his back as Garlic yelled at him.

"You listen to me, pretty boy," he shouted. "I run the bank on this fuckin' ship, and I'm doing you two assholes a favor, got it? You piss me off, I will drop a dime on both of you so fast, your fuckin' head'll come right off. You an' Bullet both. I ain't afraid of you and no posse

444

a niggers, neither. You hear me, motherfucker? You hear me?''

Before letting him go, he bent Rocky's arm up his back until Rocky yelled with the pain of it. Rocky slid off the counter and sank down to his knees on the deck, trying to get his breath.

"Yeah, that's where you belong, you goddamn pussy, on your fuckin' knees, where you can suck my dick 'fore I'll move any more a yer fuckin' money. Get outta here 'fore I hurt yer sorry ass.''

Rocky pulled himself up to his feet and reached for the door, pulling on it for a moment before realizing it was still locked. He worked the latch in the knob and let himself out onto the mess decks, catching a sharp crack on his heels as Garlic slammed the door shut behind him. He staggered for a few steps, then slumped into a chair at one of the tables. That son of a bitch. Waves of fear and anger swept through him. He looked around: Hooper and Coltrane had vamoosed, probably when the yelling started. He briefly wondered what they might have heard, but their table was all the way across the mess decks. He tried to get his breath back, but every inhalation sent a lance of pain through his ribs. Bastard. Big fat bastard. Big, fat, *strong* bastard. Came at him like a junkyard dog.

After a few minutes, he forced himself to get up. He walked aft, still bent over to ease the pain in his ribcage. He had to do something. For starters, he could not let Bullet know this had happened. And he could not let Garlic walk all over him, or he would be out of business. He thought about it. Get to Bullet. Get to Bullet, fast. Tell him there *was* something going on with Garlic; tell him to keep his distance until they could see what was happening. Get Bullet on his side and isolate Garlic. Because if Garlic got to Bullet first, what would they need Rocky for? He headed for the nearest admin phone.

41

Officers' call the next morning was held in the wardroom because of the noise of helo operations on the flight deck. Brian met with his departmental officers in one corner of the wardroom after the exec had put out the day's orders. Fox Hudson was somewhat bleary-eyed, having had the 00 to 0600 watch at SWIC. He was also down in the dumps over the drug incident in missile plot. Brian briefed all of his officers on what had happened. Jack Folsom had the important question.

"You gonna write 'em up, boss?"

"Yes, I am. I have. I've signed as accuser. I want these shitbirds gone. Taken to mast and shipped back to Clark air base for processing."

"You talked to the XO about that?" asked Fox, stifling another yawn.

"A little bit, late last night. I'm scheduled to see him right after we're done here."

Fox shuffled his shoes on the carpet for a moment. "He's not going to want to do that. You do know that."

"Yes, I do. But I figure it's time. I can't speak for the ship, but in my department, drug use gets you thrown out of the Navy."

"No matter what?" asked Folsom.

Brian sighed, aware that the question was friendly fire.

"Yeah, guys, no matter what. Okay, turn to. And Jack, tell the chief to find me in an hour."

Brian dismissed the Weapons Department officers and waited for the exec to finish chewing on the Supply officer about something. Raiford Hatcher nodded vigorously, and then he and the disbursing officer went to confer. From the expression on the Disbo's face, he understood that the principle of gravity was about to operate. The exec went over to the sideboard, lifted the coffeepot, poured himself a refill, and offered one to

Brian, who accepted. The exec put the pot back in its holder.

"From the look on your face, you've decided to go through with it," he said without preliminaries, his face all business, a commander talking to a lieutenant.

Brian took a deep breath. "Yes, sir. I think—"

"No more time for thinking. Gimme the chits. Have Mr. Hudson do the premast investigation this morning. I'll schedule my XO's hearing for sixteen hundred this afternoon and mast for oh-nine hundred tomorrow morning."

"I gave the chits to the Sheriff, XO. To get them typed up."

The exec stared at him. "Is that so. Very well, sign the smooths and give them to the chief personnelman for processing."

"Aye, aye, sir. XO—"

"That's all, Mr. Holcomb." The exec turned on his heel and left. And so it begins, Brian thought. It's back to Mr. Holcomb and the deep freeze. Standing on principle could be a chilly experience. He went back to his stateroom to drudge through some paperwork. He was rereading Maddy's last letter and imagining the feel of her hair when, after about an hour, his stateroom door rattled around on its hinges.

"Come in, Boats."

The boatswain opened the door and lowered his head as he entered. "You wanted to see me, Boss?"

"Yeah. Let's go find some coffee. I need some advice."

"That I got. Prolly worth what it's gonna cost ya, but advice I got."

They went to the wardroom for the familiar coffee routine, then stepped out onto the weather decks into a blaze of sunshine and cool fresh air. The seas were relatively flat, with only a few whitecaps showing from the beginnings of the northeast monsoon winds. The water was a deep blue, reflecting skies that appeared to have been cleansed by the typhoon. The ship still drove along at twenty knots for helicopter operations. Three men on the leeward side were replacing the snaking in the forecastle lifelines, so they walked over to the windward side and stood by the rails, inhaling fresh sea air.

"You heard about the three guys in missile plot last night, right?" Brian began.

"Oh yes, sir. Whole ship's done heard about it. Word's out there's gonna be a mast case even."

"Yeah. That's my doing. The XO asked me nicely not to write 'em up, but I think it's time to draw the line on this dope stuff."

"Long's you ain't drawin' that line on yer ass, if you don't mind my puttin' it that way. Word is that the XO's pissed off about the report chits."

"Word's pretty well informed. And if that's how it goes, that's how it goes. He's a commander and I'm a lieutenant. But I'm also a department head, and I'm not going to tolerate these people in *my* department, guys who're supposed to be ready to fire missiles or shoot guns or launch torpedoes, being drugged on duty at sea."

"Yes, sir. I hear that."

"But my question is this: What's likely to happen now?"

"Well, standard mast case. XO'll hold his screen hearing, listen to the Sheriff read the report chit, listen to the witnesses to the crime, listen to the bad guys' division officer and their chief as to what kinda guys they are, and then he'll bump it up to captain's mast, seein' it's a serious offense."

"And then?"

"An' then the Old Man will hold mast on all three together, most likely, since they was doin' it together, and he'll—"

"Yeah, that's my question. What will *he* do?"

"Well, this Old Man, he's usually sorta lenient, you know? He's as like to talk to 'em as bust 'em, fine 'em, and restrict their asses."

Brian glanced up at the bridge windows but could see only the reflections of the bow waves shimmering in the green glass. If the captain was there, he was invisible.

"But the Navy's policy on drug use aboard ship is that they get court-martialed and discharged," Brian said.

"Yeah, but the Old Man, he don't *have* to do that, he

don't wanna. Yer talkin' about the max he can give 'em, but he can let 'em go, he wants to. Ain't likely, but he can.''

Brian thought for a minute. It had not occurred to him that the captain might just let them go with an admonishment, but, of course, he could. Punishment at captain's mast was governed in terms of maximum limits on what could be imposed, but there were no minimums. Maybe that was one of the reasons the XO didn't want to go to mast—suppose the captain just chewed their asses and let them go. Everybody in the crew would be reaching for a roach within the hour.

"Course, you ask me," the chief was saying, "I figger they're gonna get their butts flown offa here on the next log helo to one a the bird farms and then sent back to Hukapino land for a court-martial. But, like I said, it's up to the Old Man. It's his mast.''

Brian was coming to hate that refrain. It's his boat. It's his policy. *And it's his fault that we're even talking about this.*

"What I'm wondering, Chief, is whether or not it will make a difference—if these guys get thrown off the ship, will that deter others?''

The chief scratched his head. "I dunno, boss. That's kinda hard to say. There're kids in this here crew that'd like nothin' better than to git a discharge and go back to the world. There's others, got wives, kids, you know, bills to pay. A discharge, some brig time'd be a real no-shitter for 'em.''

The SH-2 helicopter lifted off the flight deck behind them and clattered into the morning sky. Almost at once, the ship began to slow and the word was passed to secure from flight quarters. The fresh breeze across the forecastle began to die down and veer as the ship came about.

"Well, I hope it does. I think I'm pretty much alone on this one, and it'd be nice to think it was doing some good.''

The chief looked sideways at him from under his tattered ball cap. "You doin' this to make some kinda statement or you doin' this because it's the way you gotta do it?''

"This probably sounds like the Boy Scouts, but I just think this is the right thing to do, Chief."

"Well, all right, then. That's all there is to it. That's what officers' s'posed to do: the right thing."

"You make it sound easy, Chief."

"Doin' it *is* easy, boss. It's jist the 'after' that can get noisy sometimes."

Jackson looked up as Lieutenant Holcomb knocked and came through his office door. Jackson had had the ship's office type up the report chits, then called Lieutenant Holcomb down to sign the typed versions. Holcomb sat down and read through them, looking at his watch as he started: 1110. He had to be on watch in thirty minutes.

"It's the priors that decided me," Brian said as he signed each form on the accuser block, all thoughts of his talk with Jackson last night banished from his mind. Jackson was keeping his face neutral. "All three of 'em had priors. These guys aren't going to stop doing dope just because they got caught again. This is the essence of a screw-you crime."

"Yes, sir," Jackson said. "And the whole crew's talking about your taking them to mast."

"Tell me about it. I'm already getting the cold shoulder from the XO. Officers' call was not a pleasant experience this morning. You any closer to the guys who count?"

"We might be. You want to shut that door? Okay. I've been sort of shadowing one EM One Wilson, and I think he's getting a little nervous."

"How do you 'shadow' somebody in a ship?"

Jackson grinned. "Just be there, like the song says. He's an electrician, so he does jobs all over the ship. The chief electrician keeps me informed as to where he's going to be working, and I just, well, come around. Except in the main spaces—too damn hot down there for me. But I come around the electrical shop, and I stand to one side at Engineering Department quarters in the morning, or in the chow line at noon meal, or at the back of the movie in the evening. And I just sort of look at him. He's feeling it, believe me. And we have another development."

"The money."

"Yes, sir, the money. Three of those marked twenties have shown up. And all three of the people who passed them are on Garlic's loan list."

"Did *you* go see Garlic's list?"

"No, the senior chief of the mess did. He does it every month, anyway, to make sure nobody's getting in too deep. Of course, Garlic's the kind of guy to keep two lists, but I don't care now. He loaned marked money—which means it's at least possible that he's the bank for the dopers."

"And you've told the exec all about this?"

"Uh, no, sir. Not just yet. I'm waiting until I develop a little better, uh . . ."

"You don't want the XO telling you to stop it, right?"

Jackson looked at him. "If he did—"

"If he did, it might mean something a whole lot more sinister is going on around here than we thought."

"Yes, sir, it sure as shit could. But I can't feature this XO or this CO being dirty. There's just no way."

"Yeah, I agree with you. Wanting to keep the scope of the problem under wraps to get through the cruise is one thing. That would keep everybody's reputation intact. That, I can feature. But still . . ."

"Yes, sir. Mr. Holcomb, nobody in this ship has ever stood behind me when I wanted to go after the really bad guy, the kingpin—until you came along."

"My standing by you might not be the best thing in the world for you right now, Chief," Brian said with a wry grin. "Right now, I'm old Mr. Farts in Church."

Jackson did not smile. He leaned forward. "We're getting closer, Mr. Holcomb. I know we are. And I haven't told anybody about what we're doing except you, but I want to tell Martinez. This shit could get heavy, and he's just the guy to have along, something goes down. The senior chief knows I wanted some information, but I told him not to ask me any questions. I think the next step is for Martinez and me to do a little visitation on Garlic."

"What's your angle going to be?"

"He gives us the source of those twenties, he doesn't

451

take a fall for drug-money laundering, and he gets to stay in business."

"You probably can't tie him in any legal sense to drug-money laundering. He could have come by those twenties anywhere. Depending on how smart he is, that might blow up in your face."

"Then he becomes a boiler inspector."

Brian shook his head at the thought of Martinez squeezing three hundred pounds' worth of Garlic Wolcezjarski through the burner register of an off-line boiler's firebox. They'd have to take the front fire walls down. Hell, they'd need a crane. It was time for watch.

"Okay, Chief, I've gotta split. Another wonderful six hours in Combat as the main man of Red Crown. I guess I'll see you next at captain's mast tomorrow morning."

"Looking forward to it, Mr. Holcomb."

Brian took over the evaluator watch at 1145 from Vince Benedetti, who had also heard about the report chits and the upcoming mast case. When they had completed the operational briefing, Vince had paused for a moment before heading down for lunch.

"Really gonna do it, huh?"

"Done done it. It's time, Vince. Hell, you should know that."

Vince shrugged. "Good luck, man," was all he said.

Garuda was more enthusiastic.

"Look at that scope, will ya, Mr. H.," he said. "The Heavenly Host is up and runnin', we got helo ops scheduled for most of the afternoon, we got BARCAP on the line, two carriers turnin' and burnin' on Yankee Station, the Wager Bird relayin' for the world up on Green, two recce flights on the boards this afternoon, flat calm friggin' seas, the Air Farce is gonna run a strike package in from Thailand, and we got three dopers on horseback with ropes around their necks. Crown is back in business, regular Navy, just the way I like it."

Brian grinned. Garuda would spend the whole cruise on Red Crown station if he could have his way, with maybe an occasional weekend in Subic for a San Magoo. He had his WETSU ball cap on and was in generally fine fettle, smashing buttons on his console and chewing various asses in the Cave on the intercom. The scope was indeed filled with air tracks, and the PIRAZ controller had his hands full.

"Yeah, well, I've got some things on my scope that aren't on your scope."

"Yes, sir," Garuda said. "I heard about that. We gonna finally do it regulation Navy. Personally, I think it's about time, although I suspect you're not number one on the hit parade right now."

"Depends what you mean by 'hit.' "

Garuda laughed. "I hear that. Mast is always a crapshoot. We haven't had anybody go to mast for drugs since I've been here, and this captain is kinda light even on the regular criminals. But he'll do what he's gonna do. Your biggest problem now is the watch bill. If those three shitbirds fly away tomorrow, who sits the consoles down in plot—the chiefs?"

"The chiefs sit the consoles up here in Combat. I've still got one first class, and since Marcowitz went down in flames, that leaves me FTM Three Warren as the next senior guy, then about a half dozen nonrated guys after him. They're just going to have to learn fast."

Garuda reached for his coffee mug and a cigarette. "Long as the MiGs stay in their box, don't pull any more a that raid shit, won't take much to hold her together. Warren's a good kid; he's just green. Long's you've got a chief and first class up here in Combat, the kid on the console can be walked through it, they have to."

"*If* there's time, and *if* everything works. Actually, if everything is working, the guy on the console down below has nothing to do. Where they become important is when the system faults out or drops track. Then the guy in plot can save your ass, because he's the only one who can actually see the track-radar video."

They were interrupted by a call from CTF 77 on Air Force Green, confirming the impending reconnaissance run. Brian called the captain to report the run and received a curt acknowledgment. He hung up the bat phone, an uneasy feeling in his stomach. Word travels fast.

Garuda came back to the problem of bringing the junior

missile techs up to speed. "What we should do if these three dopers go bye-bye is put one of the chiefs down there in plot for a couple of hours each watch and let him hold school call on the greenies. We can run a bunch of missile-tracking drills from up here in Combat, walk 'em through the gray areas, and hopefully not bust the Spooks in the process."

"That's a great idea, Garuda. But first let's see what happens at mast."

42

Brian stood slightly apart from the mast case's participants at 0900 the following morning. Captain's mast was being convened on the mess decks, where an oak podium had been placed in an open area, the three report chits lying on top. Assembled in a line in front of the podium were the three accused, dressed in clean dress whites, including caps. On the right side of the lineup, in his capacity as MAA, was RD1 Rockheart. Standing behind them were the division officer, Lieutenant Hudson; the fire control division chief, Chief Hallowell; and the divisional leading petty officer. Standing in two ranks to the left were selected petty officers from every division in the ship, brought in to witness the proceedings. Opposite and facing them were the doc, baby doc, and FTM3 Warren, the primary witnesses. The mess decks were hot and humid as usual, with the smells of breakfast lingering in the steamy air. CS1 Wolczejarski and two of the mess cooks were watching from the partially opened door of the galley office.

The 1MC announced that captain's mast was now being held on the mess decks and commanded silence in the area. As if on cue, the chief master-at-arms came through the forward door to the mess decks and yelled, "Attention on deck!" He was followed by the captain and the executive officer, both in working khakis but wearing their dress caps with the brass scrambled eggs to add a note of formality. The three marched up to the podium, where the Sheriff stepped aside and nodded to Rockheart. Rockheart stood to attention, faced the three accused, and barked, "Mast cases, ten-hut! Uncover, two!"

The three petty officers whipped off their caps and faced the podium. Only one, Boyle, looked directly at the captain. The other two stared at the base of the podium. Petty Officer Lanier had an angry expression on his face and stood fractionally apart from the other two. The captain stepped up to the podium and picked up the first report chit. Brian thought that the captain looked fairly well for a change, with color in his cheeks and an alert expression in his eyes. His uniform still draped on him as if he had been fasting and the skin on his face was drawn tight over prominent cheekbones, but otherwise there were few signs of the torpor and fatigue Brian had seen before. The captain studied the first report chit for a full minute, then looked up at Boyle.

"Petty Officer Boyle, you are accused of violation of Article Ninety-two, UCMJ, being drugged on duty on the twenty-eighth of October, in the guided-missile plotting room. You have seen this report chit and signed it?"

"Yes, sir."

"I will warn you now that anything you say during these proceedings may be used in evidence against you in any subsequent trial by court-martial. That means that if you do not want to say anything, you don't have to, but what you do say can be used against you if we choose to. If you choose not to speak, this fact will not be held against you. Do you understand this warning?"

"Yes, sir."

The captain addressed the same words and warnings to the other two accused and received their individual acknowledgments. He put the report chits down and looked at all three.

"Now, gentlemen, you are all charged with the same offense, essentially at the same time and in the same place. Smoking marijuana in missile plot. You've read the report chits. The officers and petty officers who caught you at it are present and ready to testify, and their testimony is summarized in the report chits you have signed, which you have read, correct?"

The three accused nodded silently. Lanier glanced over at Warren with a stony look, but Warren stared straight ahead.

"All right. The results of a medical urinalysis test for each of you is contained in the report chits, and for each of you it was positive. The executive officer has caused these matters to be investigated, and he has recommended that you be brought to mast. Do each of you acknowledge that you have read and understand the charges and supporting evidence in the report chits?"

All three replied with a muted "Yes, sir." The captain leaned on the podium for the first time. Brian detected a faint note of fatigue in his voice. Or was it disappointment?

"Very well, then. I'm going to ask each of you the same question, which is: Are you guilty or not guilty? Remember that you are not required to answer the question. Petty Officer Boyle, are you guilty of the offense charged?"

Boyle shook his head.

"Is that a no, Boyle?"

"I don't want to say anything, Captain."

"All right, Boyle. Corey?"

"I don't wanta say nothin', either, Captain."

"Very well. Lanier?"

"Yes, sir, I did it. Done it before, and I'll do it again, I get the chance. Same as these two chickenshits here."

"Lanier, watch your mouth," growled Chief Jackson.

There was an uncomfortable silence in the small gathering as the captain stared at Lanier, who now would not look at him, a defiant expression on his young face. Brian was suddenly struck by how young all three were. They were E-5s, petty officers two grades away from being chiefs, and yet they were what—twenty-two, twenty-three years old? And headed for a court-martial, he believed, judging from the captain's expression.

"Well, gentlemen, one of you admits the offense, and the evidence is pretty damn clear on all three of you. I am disgusted with what you have done, have obviously been doing, which is getting yourself drugged on the ship. You three, of all people, who man the ship's primary self-defense system, the guided missiles, when we're in a war zone, and in the presence of enemy aircraft based only fifty miles away from our station. The whole crew depends on you people to do your job flawlessly if we ever get attacked, and your response to this responsibility is to indulge in drugs on your watch station. You disgrace yourselves, the ship, and the reputation of the whole crew by your actions. In another place and time, I would have had you lashed and then hanged."

The three sailors' heads snapped up at this last statement. Everybody in the room looked up at the captain, whose face had hardened perceptibly. Out of the corner of his eye, Brian saw Wolcezjarski and his crew back into the galley office and quietly shut the door.

"But since I can't do that, I am awarding each of you a special court-martial, to be convened at Clark Air Force Base in thirty days' time. I am placing each of you on pretrial restraint. You will be flown off the ship on this afternoon's log helo to the carrier and from the carrier to the naval air station at Cubi Point, and from Cubi Point you will be taken to the Air Force stockade at Clark to await trial. That is all. Chief Jackson, take them to their compartment to pack their seabags."

Jackson acknowledged and then nodded at Rockheart.

"Mast cases, ten-hut!"

Everyone in the room stood to attention.

"Mast cases, cover, two!"

When the three accused had put their hats back on, RD1 Rockheart marched them out of the mess decks, leaving the officers and witnesses standing around the podium. The captain straightened up.

"XO, I will see you and the Weapons officer in my cabin now."

"Aye, aye, sir."

Chief Jackson preceded the captain out of the mess decks, announcing, "Gangway," scattering the people who had been watching from Broadway. The exec stepped forward to the podium and gathered up the papers. "That's it, gents," he said. "Mr. Holcomb, let's go topside."

Brian followed the exec forward to the wardroom passageway, up the ladder to the next level, and into the captain's cabin. The captain was standing by the portholes, looking out at the sea. Brian and the exec stood by the table until he turned around and indicated that they should be seated. The captain remained standing.

"Well now," he began, looking back out the portholes, "Mr. Holcomb. Given the seriousness of the crimes charged this morning, I had little choice but to get those men off the ship. The Navy's policy is fairly clear on that matter, as the exec reminded me this morning. But this incident has created something of a hole in the missile fire-control division, has it not?"

"Yes, sir," Brian said, expecting a different question.

"What are your intentions?"

Brian remembered Garuda's suggestion. "I plan to cycle the chiefs who normally stand the FCSC watch in Combat through the console positions down in plot for a few hours each watch. They'll take the three best makee-learns we have under close instruction. I plan to augment that arrangement with a number of tracking drills that we can initiate from Combat with the cooperation of support tracks in the Gulf."

The captain turned around. With his back to the portholes, the glare streaming through the glass had the effect of putting his face in the shadow.

"The missile plot positions are important?"

"Yes, sir, they can be. When SWIC sends a designation to FCSC and he assigns a director to the target, in theory that's all it takes. The target data is fed from the SPS-forty-eight radar to the director's computers, and the director should slew right to it, in range, bearing, and elevation angle. But when the designation is fuzzy or a little off, or there's weather in the target area, the guys in plot enter into it. They can physically see what the director's acquisition radar is seeing, and they can coach the tracking circuits onto the target if required."

"So if everything works perfectly, they're bystanders."

"Yes, sir. And if everything is not working perfectly, they can become vital to getting the director on target. Without that, of course, we can't shoot."

"Well, we could," interjected the exec. "You can always cancel the designation and then redesignate and hope the second time around it's more accurate."

"Yes, sir," replied Brian, "but that can eat up precious seconds. By the time you recycle the designation, the bad guy can be in your face."

"Quite," said the captain. "Now, I suppose you got what you were looking for at mast this morning?"

Brian paused. Here we go. "I want to root out the druggies in my department and get rid of them, so, yes, sir, Captain, in that sense I got what I wanted. Of course, I would rather not decimate my department to do that."

The exec snorted. "You more than decimated it. Decimation was killing ten percent. There are only sixteen people in Fox division. Three people, four, if you include Marcowitz, constitute a loss of twenty-five percent. Who's the senior guy left now, below the chiefs—Warren?"

Brian took a deep breath. The exec's tone of voice implied that he, Brian, was somehow responsible for the fact that twenty-five percent of the division did dope.

"Yes, sir. FTM Three Warren."

The exec shook his head.

"Which one is Warren?" asked the captain.

"He's the young black E-Four, Captain. He was standing next to the docs this morning. Good kid, but pretty green. There's no way around it—Fox division is down twenty-five percent, all of it in experienced petty officers."

Brian decided it was time to speak up. He addressed the captain directly. "Sir, the way I see it, twenty-five percent of the division was dirty. They're gone now. I'm hoping that's all, or if it's not, that the rest of them will stop it, at least while we're at sea."

The captain was silent for a long moment. The exec studied his cap, which he had placed on the table and was now turning slowly in his hands.

"Are you aware, Brian, that CTF Seventy-seven's staff

is of the opinion that we in *Hood* have a fairly significant drug problem? That they have thought all along that the incident on the Sea Dragon operation was caused by drugs? Can you imagine what they're going to think now?"

Brian decided to hold his ground. "Well, Captain, if twenty-five percent of a division is representative, we *do* have a big problem here. And I would think that they would think we're aggressively pursuing illegal drug use in the ship and cleaning house when we find it." And it *was* drugs that caused us to lose the load during the gun shoot, he wanted to add.

"Hmmm. Yes, that's one interpretation, I suppose."

The exec spoke up. "The other, of course, is that we have had the problem for a long time and not done anything about it, and that now it's a big-enough deal, we're losing a quarter of a division at a time when it's exposed."

It was Brian's turn to study the table. He could not state the obvious without bordering on insubordination. The exec pressed on.

"But as you are aware, I think, we *have* been doing something about it, something admittedly a bit unorthodox, but nonetheless, an active program that brought direct consequences to anyone caught using drugs aboard the ship. But consequences for the individuals, not for the ship."

"Yes, sir."

"And the problem with your putting these men on report is that it invoked the UCMJ and the process of captain's mast, which carries some consequences for the ship this time. I have no doubt that at least two of these guys will actually be pleased: They get off the ship, get out of the Navy, and get to go home, with maybe a little brig time thrown in. And second, the consequences to the ship are that we've lost twenty-five percent of the missile fire–control division, and we now have to shore up the watch organization with quick fixes in the middle of a deployment. And three, *Hood* gets a black eye."

Brian remained silent. He wasn't sure his opinion was being solicited here.

"Well, Brian, you see our problem?" the captain asked.

"No, sir."

"*No*, sir?" The exec sounded exasperated.

"May I speak, Captain?"

"Certainly, Mr. Holcomb." No more Brian, he noticed.

"Sir, my concern is for the ship. I'm the Weapons officer and I'm responsible for making sure the ship's missiles, guns, and torpedoes are ready when you need them. If up to a quarter or more of the men who actually operate these systems are possibly going to be doped up when we call on them in an emergency, then I can't deliver."

He turned to the exec, addressing him directly now. "Your way brought direct consequences but did not remove the problem. All three of these guys had priors for drugs. My way gets them off the ship. I think I have a much better chance of answering the fire bell with them gone than I would with them limping around the ship with broken bones. And I figure if we have to peel it down to just the officers and chiefs, then that's what we'll have to do. As I said, my main concern is the ship."

"Don't you think that's my job, Mr. Holcomb?" asked the captain in a reproachful voice.

Yes, and you haven't been doing it, Brian wanted to shout. Instead, he bit his lip and remained silent. The exec looked at the captain and gave a little shrug. The captain nodded.

"Okay, Mr. Holcomb. Carry on," he said. "XO, we need to talk about some things."

Brian rose from the table, grabbed his cap, and left the captain's cabin. Closing the cabin door, he exhaled audibly and then went directly to his stateroom, where he tossed his cap on the top rack and flopped down into the lower rack. It was midmorning, when he was normally coming back up to speed, but he was suddenly very tired. He wanted to crawl into a hole somewhere. The captain and exec had obviously turned against him. Big deal: just a captain and a commander against a lieutenant.

He thought about what he had said and how in retrospect it might have sounded naïve. The captain had almost thirty years' experience in the Navy; the exec, over twenty. Who the hell was *Lieutenant* Brian Holcomb to come aboard this ship and suddenly decide that their way was wrong and that he knew better than they did how to handle a problem that afflicted every ship out here in WESTPAC. Well, *man*, he thought, using that whiny, hip, sixties appellation he had come to hate, you may have really blown it now. Then he remembered he had to go back on watch. Jesus, what would they think if they knew what Jackson and Martinez were up to?

43

Chief Jackson was holding his daily after-supper meeting with all the MAAs in his office when the phone rang. He indicated for one of the MAAs to get it. Rockheart was closest.

"Sheriff's office, RD One Rockheart speaking, sir."

"Yeah, Rocky, this is Chief Martinez. Tell Jackson I said tonight's the night."

"Tonight's the night; got it, Chief." He hung up the phone, and looked over at Jackson. "That was Chief Martinez. He said—"

"Yeah, I heard. Okay, guys, unless somebody's got something else, let's wrap it up. Marsden, you owe me that report on the liberty cards that went missing in Subic. Carter, you keep an eye on that redheaded mess cook, the new guy. I think he's lifting stuff out of the Supply storeroom. That's it, everybody. I got a date on the mess decks."

There was general laughter at the thought of a date with LJM2, and the MAAs cleared out of the office. Rockheart lingered.

"Something heavy going down?" he inquired as casually as he could.

"Nothing I can talk about," replied Jackson, distracted by an in basket he had just overturned. "You the deputy dog for tonight?"

"Yeah. Marsden's supposed to have it, but he's got watch from twenty to twenty-four, so I'm taking it. It's just the movie detail. One of these days, we'll get the day's watch bill for the MAAs and the rest of the ship in synch."

"Nevah hotchee," replied Jackson absently. "Give me a call here when the movie's over." He had recaptured all the papers. Rockheart said he was probably right and left the office.

Five minutes later, Chief Martinez called again.

"I'm gonna go cruise by the electrical shop, see if Bullet's around. Maybe go in there and mess with his head, bend some steel bars or somethin'. Give that boy some food for thought. Then let's meet on the mess decks right after the movie's over."

"Okay. I'll give you a call when the duty MAA has it secured. We'll do it the way we said? Me first, Mr. Nice Guy, and if that doesn't work—"

"Yeah, me second. Mr. Hell on Wheels."

"If the left one don't git ya . . ."

"Yeah, buddy. How 'about those mast cases today, huh? Some good shit, or what? See ya around twenty-two hundred."

Rockheart called Jackson at 2150. The crew's movie had ended at 2130 and the mess decks had been swept down and secured for the night. Jackson thanked him and told him he could secure for the night himself.

The mess decks still smelled of popcorn and cigarettes by the time Martinez and Jackson showed up. Garlic's office was locked as usual, but Jackson had made a wrong-number call twenty minutes ago and found him in. Martinez refilled his coffee cup and went to the back of the mess decks, switched off two lines of fluorescent lights, and took a seat on a life jacket locker—he was too big to fit at a mess table. Jackson banged on the door.

"Garlic, it's Chief Jackson. Open up."

Garlic opened the door seconds later. He was wearing stained white trousers and a sweaty T-shirt that didn't quite make it to his waistband. A bulbous band of fat hung over his belt. As usual, he needed a shave. He held a wet cigarette butt in his let hand.

"Yeah, Sheriff, what's up?"

"We need to have a private talk, Garlic. You and me. Subject is money."

"Yeah, sure," Garlic said, backing into the room to allow Jackson entry. "No prob with the bank, is it? I mean, I just went over everythin' with senior chief. He didn't have no probs."

"Not exactly, but what I'm after is, shall we say, related to your loan operation." Jackson moved a pile of magazines out of an armchair and sat down at Garlic's cluttered desk, which was littered with breakout chits, adding machine tapes, requisition forms, and next week's menu draft. A small fan with a missing blade pinged away in the corner of the overhead, moving some of the cigarette smoke around.

"Related."

"Yes, related. Have a seat."

Garlic grunted himself down into the other office chair. His huge belly billowed over his thighs, lifting the bottom of his T-shirt higher.

"I don't understand."

"Right. Let me walk you through it. You run your loan operation here with the permission of the chiefs' mess. You loan at standard rates, six for five, and you keep a book, a single book, I presume, that you show to the senior chief once a month. Any problems, you bring them to the senior chief, he gets me, we talk to the guy and work something out. Okay so far?"

"Yeah, Chief. That's how it goes," said Garlic, clearly mystified.

"Okay, so where's the money come from to establish your bank? Where do you get the cash to make the loans?"

Garlic frowned and shifted in his chair, still not getting it. "I been doin' this for what—three years now on this boat? Six for five, well hell, that's pretty good return, you know what I mean? It builds up pretty good. I can show—"

"No. I'm not interested in your accumulated profits. I think you have another source for cash, once that's probably not in your book, or at least not in the one you show the senior chief."

Garlic's face changed, his eyes becoming watchful, his expression hardening.

"I don't follow you, Chief."

"Yeah you do. Let me clear it up for you, Garlic. Just before Subic, I had one of my people make a controlled buy of some marijuana. He used some marked money. That marked money has turned up in the hands of three guys you made cash loans to." Jackson leaned forward in his chair. "See, way we figure it, whoever's running the dope in this ship accumulates cash, lots of cash. Now, he can hide it in a void somewhere in the ship, where it's safe, or he can invest some of it, where it can make even more money, and maybe even get washed a couple of times, see what I'm saying? We figure you're accepting money from the top man in the drug organization here and loaning it out. Sharing the profits somehow. You know, a little venture capitalism?"

Garlic's face became an impassive mask as he started to shake his head from side to side. But Jackson noticed fine beads of sweat appearing on Garlic's temples.

"No way, Chief," Garlic protested. "I ain't runnin' no charity here, okay, but I don't know nothin' about no drug money. You say you've traced marked money to me, well hell, that can come from the guys're payin' me back—that's all the cash."

"Not the way we see it, Garlic. Two of the three guys got that money from you, spent it for the first time in the ship's store. I watch the ship store, see? Guy who operates the store is my guy, okay? He spots the mark, calls me. I ask the guys where they got this money; they say they don't know. I take 'em to my office, explain about the bank here, how the chiefs know about it, and then they tell me, yeah, that's where they got it—from you. I ask if they can produce more twenties—it was twenties we marked, by the way—and yes, they can. Guys who were broke last week are now paying guys back and buying cigarettes in the ship's store. Now the third guy, he got it from one of the other two—they owed him money, see—and then showed up at the ship's store. All of it comes back to you and your bank."

Garlic started to protest again, but Jackson put his hand up in the air.

"Lemme finish here. Logic says, if the money came from you, two things are possible. One, *you're* the main man; you're the guy dealin' drugs out here in the ship, and that's how you got the money. Two, you're taking cash off the hands of the guy who *is* selling all the dope, then putting it back to work and laundering it in the process. You see my logic here?"

Garlic was finally silent. His massive forearms were stretched straight out on the arms of his chair, and Jackson could see that his knuckles were faintly white. He wondered for a second whether Garlic would come at him.

"So here's the deal, Garlic. That's what I'm here for, by the way, to make a deal, to solve this little problem in a grown-up way so that no has to get hurt—no one who cooperates, that is. Anyway, you give us the name of the guy who's feeding all this cash to you and testify to that fact when and if the time comes. In return, we'll let you keep playing Mr. Banker here in the ship, and you don't burn for being involved in a money-laundering operation associated with narcotics. How's that sound, Garlic? That sound like a reasonable deal? I mean, it sounds really reasonable to me. What do you say, huh?"

Garlic stared at Jackson for about a half a minute, his fat eyes narrowed. Jackson had to work at staring back: Garlic's mean streak was not only well known but never very far beneath the surface, and it was showing a mile wide right now. Jackson tensed his legs in case Garlic flipped out. He hoped Martinez was where he said he would be once he was inside. Garlic took a deep breath and then shook his head.

"I don't know nothin' about no drug money, and you can't prove nothin' otherwise. All the cash I move here is from the operation. That's all I got to say. You guys wanna shut me down, I'll shut down. I don't give that much of a fuck—I've made my money. But for the rest of all that shit, I got nothin' to give ya."

"That your final say-so on the matter?"

"Yep."

Jackson gave him the benefit of about a thirty-second look and then stood up. Garlic remained in his chair, looking up at him. Jackson went to the door, opened it, and stepped out, leaving the door ajar. Chief Martinez was right outside, holding something in his hand that Jackson could not quite see. Martinez stepped around Jackson, went through the door, and closed it. Jackson stepped clear of the office door and looked both ways into the darkened mess decks; he saw nobody. Inside the office, there was a sharp crack, followed by a cry of pain. Then silence, and then three enormous thumps that shook the bulkheads. The night baker came to the door of the galley, looked out, saw Jackson, who shook his head. Poppa Steiner, being no fool, ducked back into the galley, closing the door firmly. After a minute, the door to the galley office opened and Martinez stuck his head around the corner, jerking it to indicate Jackson should come back in.

Garlic was sitting in the same chair Jackson had left him in, but his face was pale white and he looked as if he was trying to breathe and not breathe all at the same time. One leg stuck out at an odd angle. Garlic had his right hand on his shin, rubbing very gently. Martinez stood over him like an oak tree, an eight-pound stainless-steel dogging wrench in his hand. Jackson went back to Garlic's desk chair, pulled it around, and sat down.

"Like I was saying, Garlic, we're here to deal. We don't want problems. We just need to know a name. Now, you want I should go away again, give you some more time to, uh, think about this? I can do that, you know, leave the bosun here to, uh, stimulate your thoughts, so to speak. That what you want?"

Garlic closed his eyes and gave a weak cough, covering his mouth with his left hand. Jackson could see a trace of bright red blood on his hand when he finished. Then he realized Garlic probably couldn't talk so well.

Martinez leaned forward and tapped Garlic on the shoulder. "You tell him what you told me, asshole."

Garlic moaned, wiped his mouth, and then shook his head weakly. Jackson got his attention.

"Hey, listen up. We think it's Bullet—EM One Wilson. Are we right?"

Garlic nodded, his eyes closed.

"And it is drug money, isn't it?"

Another nod. Garlic's mouth was filling with something. Jackson thought he looked really bad.

"And you're ready to tell this to the XO or to a court-martial, with no second thoughts, right?"

Another nod, smaller this time. Garlic was sitting a little crooked in his chair.

Jackson looked up at Martinez, who nodded. Martinez lifted Garlic's triple chins with the edge of the wrench, gave him a steely look, and then left the office. Jackson, with one last look at Garlic, followed him out and closed the door. He thought he heard a trash can moving across the deck inside.

"Let's go to my office," Jackson said.

"Funny thing," muttered Martinez as they headed toward Broadway.

"What's that?"

"After I got his attention, he gimme Bullet like we figured."

"Yeah, and?"

"Then he had a problem with somethin' in his throat, started mumblin'. I asked him how they worked the money—how he and Bullet moved it around. He said—I think he said—that he just got it from 'em from time to time and then loaned it out."

Jackson stopped in front of his office to unlock his door. "Right. The operation accumulates cash, you get a wad built up, give it to Garlic—"

"No, you ain't seein' it. He said *them,* not him. He got it from them. Like they wuz two of 'em."

"Two kingpins? Naw. These druggies don't work that way. They're like animals with a territory. One boss animal per patch. These assholes aren't into sharing."

As the two chiefs hurried by, Rocky stood motionless in the back shadow of the scullery gripping the stainless-steel counter with both hands and trying not to breathe. Alerted earlier that something was up, he had watched their visitation to Garlic's office through the tray window in the scullery after securing the mess decks. He had seen Jackson go in first and had listened to Chief Martinez settle himself on a locker not two feet away on the other side of the bulkhead. Then Jackson had closed the door. He had frozen in place, not wanting to take the slightest chance of attracting Martinez's attention. When Martinez had crept to the door, where he would be close enough to listen, Rocky had let his breath out in tiny little puffs, a cold feeling spreading in his stomach as he bent over and watched through the tray window.

This was not good at all. Bad enough to have Jackson talking to Garlic after hours, but with Martinez along, it meant Jackson wanted something very specific from Garlic—like maybe some kind of confirmation about Bullet.

Trapped in the scullery until both Jackson and Martinez had gone, he had been considering the possibilities when he had seen Jackson come out, to be replaced by the monster. He heard what happened next. There had been a flare of light from the galley door as old man Steiner had come out to see if the overhead had fallen in. The light had disappeared. Moments later, Garlic's door had opened and Jackson had gone back inside Garlic's office. He would have given anything to have heard what was being said, but he didn't really have to: This had to be about drugs. The sons of bitches had figured out the money angle. Now, the big question: Who was Garlic going to finger—both of them, or just him, or just Bullet? His ribs still hurt from his last encounter with Garlic, so he felt a tiny bit of satisfaction that Garlic was now getting his. But the fact remained that the operation was probably blown all to hell, and the baddest badass in the boat would soon be on somebody's trail. He shivered at the thought.

He had been about to steal out of the scullery and get gone while they were still in there when Garlic's door had opened again and he had heard Jackson say something about his office. He had frozen again as the chiefs went by. Now, what did they know? He could go to the office and try to eavesdrop, but if Garlic had fingered him and Monster Man caught him, he'd be dead meat. On the other hand, Jackson had been bird-dogging Bullet, not him. If Garlic had fingered only Bullet, then he, Rockheart, could show up at the MAA's office on a pretext, listen outside, and, if caught, say he had to see the Sheriff. He had to go for it. He had to know.

He looked both ways out the small tray window and then let himself out of the scullery, locking the door behind him. He walked quickly forward to Broadway and then stopped. He could just see the CMAA office, thirty feet down the passageway. There was light coming out from under the door. It took everything he had to walk to that door, treading on his tiptoes, hoping fervently that nobody else would come waltzing down Broadway just then.

"So now we know, what do we do about it?" Martinez was asking.

Jackson sat in his chair, while Martinez stood with his back against the door. "Sixty-four-thousand-dollar question," he said.

"I can go get him, break his ugly neck, and throw his ass over the side," Martinez said helpfully.

Jackson grinned. "No, I want the satisfaction of busting his ass and shipping him off to pound some government rocks. The problem is, now that we know what we know, how do we nail his ass good enough for a court."

"Buy some dope?"

"I don't think so. The two controlled buys I've made in the past six months have been from pretty junior people. The guy who runs one of these operations never sees the customers and they never see him."

"Those buys from black guys?"

"Yup. Both of 'em, which confirms what Marcowitz told me. Actually, it's a pretty clever system—the chances of a black guy ratting out on another brother are slim to none. Even if it's just a small hard-core bunch doing it, any guy who buys, especially any white guy, has to feel that all of them would come get his ass if he ever talked about it. And the bad guys will stand by one another as a matter of racial pride."

"All that shit's gonna come up, we go after Bullet."

"True. I think the next step is to talk to Holcomb, tell him what we've found out. Maybe he can think of a way to get at Bullet and his gang."

"How 'bout the XO?"

Jackson shook his head. "I don't think so, not yet. If he was dicey about the drug angle, he'll be really dicey about the racial angle. First, I'm gonna talk to Holcomb."

"'You prolly ought not to tell him how we convinced Garlic to talk to us; he's too much a straight arrow for that kinda news."

"Yeah. I'll just say Garlic decided to cooperate rather than lose his little banking business. Holcomb's a good head; he'll probably figure it out, but if we don't tell him—"

"He don't know it for a fact. Yeah, I like the guy. I think he's gettin' his ass inna crack over the mast cases."

"Probably—what the hell was that!"

Rocky's heart was pounding when he finally heard the name Bullet. They were talking about how to get evidence on Bullet, not him. Now he could—

Shit! He nearly jumped right out of skin when a hand touched his shoulder. He whirled around, forgetting where he was or what he had been doing. It was Seaman Coltrane, the side cleaner, the guy who couldn't talk, out on another one of his walks in never-never land.

"Coltrane, what the fuck are you doing out here?" he demanded in a loud voice, just as the CMAA's door swung open and the figure of Martinez filled the doorway.

"What's goin' on out here?" rumbled the boatswain, looking from Rockheart to Coltrane. Jackson was trying to see under Martinez's shoulder.

"I was coming up the passageway and this guy was standing here outside your door, Sheriff, like he was listening or something," replied Rocky, his voice a touch higher than usual. He had a hold on Coltrane's left biceps, as if about to take him into custody. Coltrane looked at all the faces around him, blinking at everybody and making a gargling noise in his throat. Jackson stepped around Martinez and looked down at Coltrane.

"Seaman Coltrane, you come to see me about something?"

If he had, it was now the last thing on Coltrane's mind as he twisted away from Rocky's grip and scuttled up the passageway toward First Division berthing.

"Crazy little fucker," muttered Rocky, trying not to look at Martinez, who was staring at him.

"He's okay," said Martinez, still looking at Rocky. "He works and he don't talk, which is the opposite of what the rest of those dickheads do."

"Why are you still up, Rocky?" Jackson asked.

"Two guys got into it over a seat at the movie; I went back to M Division compartment to make sure they didn't continue it back there. Snipes, what can I tell you. I was on my way to OI berthing. It's all cool back there."

"Yeah, okay. I'll see you in the morning."

"Right, Sheriff," Rocky said as he headed forward.

Rocky hurried forward once he was out of Broadway, his thoughts tumbling over one another. They had Bullet, or at least his name. Garlic had squealed, probably in return for getting to stay in business. What would Bullet do when they went after him? That was the question. Would it do him any good to finger Rocky? Not if the Sheriff still thought that Bullet was the main man; any accusations he made against Rocky would be just accusations. And they wouldn't believe him—unless Garlic corroborated. Then he would be in the shit. So the trick was to silence Garlic. That would leave Bullet swinging and Rocky safe.

Wait a minute. Martinez had done something to Garlic back there in the galley office. Three big thumps, and then Jackson is in and out of there in a few minutes. Suppose . . . suppose Garlic's injuries were worse than Martinez or Jackson knew? Suppose he had some internal injuries, took a while to do their damage? He owed that fat fuck for busting his chops. He stopped dead in the missile magazine's passageway and looked at his watch: 2240—about a half hour to midrats time. Maybe, if he moved real fast. He doubled back, climbed one ladder, and headed back down Broadway. He hesitated when he got near the CMAA office, but there was no light showing under the door, so he walked boldly by, pretending he wasn't afraid. What the hell. He was an MAA; nobody would question what he was doing up, especially when he had taken movie duty in place of Marsden. When he got to the mess decks, it was dark and quiet except for Steiner in the galley. He looked at his watch again. In fifteen minutes, maybe twenty, the midrats mess cooks would show up. Unless one of the other cooks had been rousted, Garlic was supposed to have soup made and something to eat out on the line by 2315.

He looked around the mess decks again to be sure he was alone, then knocked softly on the door of the galley office. Nothing. He knocked again.

"Garlic, it's me, Rocky. Open up, man. I gotta talk to you."

There was a groan from inside and the sound of a chair moving, then silence.

"Garlic, I know what happened. I saw the fuckers who did it. Let me in, man. I'll get you some help. Those chiefs can't do this kind of shit. Unlock the door."

There was another minute of silence and then Rocky heard the door being unlocked. He waited and then pushed it open.

Garlic was half in, half out of an armchair. His face was deathly pale and he held a blood-soaked rag to his mouth. His little pig eyes were pinpoints of pain. The clear plastic bag in the trash can under the desk was filled with blood-soaked rags and paper towels. Garlic looked like a wounded whale, but there wasn't a mark on him. Rocky went over to him and knelt down on one knee.

"Goddamn, man. What'd that bastard do to you?"

Garlic tried to talk, but he could only groan, covering his mouth again as more blood welled up. He was having trouble breathing and he was inches from falling on the deck.

"You want me to get the doc, man? I can get the doc—"

Garlic tried to nod his head, but then he began coughing on his own blood. He tried to get up but finally lost his balance and fell over onto the deck like a 250-pound sack of potatoes. Rocky had to jump to get out of the way. He looked down on the hugely fat man sprawled on the galley deck, doubled over as he fought for breath and spraying bright red blood out of his nose.

This is the only guy who can finger you, Rockheart thought. They're after Bullet as the main man, and only this obscene piece of shit can corroborate anything Bullet might say when they arrest his ass. Yeah, but you don't get the doc in here right fucking now, you're talking murder here, man. Big step up from moving a little dope.

Garlic moaned again from the deck as he slipped in and out of consciousness. But you didn't kill him; that gorilla did. Bullshit. You found him. You don't call for help and he croaks, you own a big piece of it. And if he dies that way, it's no help, man. As long as it's called a murder, this ship will be swarming with cops, NIS, feds, the works. Whole thing's gonna blow up.

He thought fast. Gotta fix it. Gotta make it look like something else. Garlic moaned again, his breathing taking on a rasping sound. Rocky stepped over the mounded heap that was Garlic and reached down to feel his pulse along his neck. He had to feel for a long time to find it, moving his finger around a deep crease in all that fat to find the big artery, and when he did, he pressed down hard with his thumb. Bust up my ribcage, will you? Garlic made a grunting sound but did not really move, and after a couple of minutes, he stopped breathing. Rocky made sure, then straightened up. Fat bastard was finished, anyway; he just speeded it up. Now let them go after Bullet.

He looked at his watch again. One minute before 2300. He looked around the galley office, saw the plastic trash bag full of bloody rags and paper, and the rag Garlic had had in his hand. He grabbed the rag and the plastic bag, secured the bag, and began to scrunch it up as tightly as he could get it. He looked back at Garlic, lying in an inert heap on the deck, a thin trickle of blood coming from his mouth and nose. Heart attack. Stroke. Big fat guy like that. That's what'd they say. And ole Garlic, he'd have nothing to say at all.

He flicked on the other overhead light, turned on the

adding machine, and spread some papers across the desk, knocking a few onto the deck with his hand. He upended Garlic's chair, then reached down and took Garlic's fat right paw and put it up to his neck, as if he had grabbed himself, choking maybe. He headed for the door, taking one last look around. Perfect, fucking perfect.

He cracked the door open and looked out. The mess decks were still dark. The mess cooks would be here in ten, fifteen minutes for midrats. He wiped off both sides of the door handle with the rag, checked again, then reached inside and locked the door before pulling it closed. He went aft this time, heading for the nearest weather-deck door, out by the fantail, the plastic trash bag rolled up under his arm like a slicker. As he hurried through the red-lighted passageways, he considered what he had done: He had saved his ass, that's what. And the beautiful part of it was that Martinez would think *he* had killed Garlic. Rocky's only regret was not knowing where Garlic kept his bank.

44

At 2340, Brian was being relieved by Vince Benedetti when the bridge called in on the bitch box.

"Combat, Bridge, Evaluator?"

Brian still technically had the watch, so he answered up. The OOD, Lieutenant (junior grade) Bendtner, asked him to pick up the bat phone. He obviously wanted to speak privately, but without calling the CO in the process.

"Yeah, Paul. What's up?"

"I've got a report from the mess decks that the head cook, Garlic Wol-something or other, has been found dead in his office."

"Holy shit. Any idea of what happened?"

"They called in the doc, and he says it looks like a heart attack or a stroke. Maybe both. Garlic is, or was, that big fat guy, the mess decks master-at-arms and the senior stew burner. I've notified the XO and the Old Man."

"Yeah, I know who he is. What's the plan?"

"The plan is to get about a dozen guys to carry him to sick bay. I think they're gonna bag him up, put him in one of the reefers overnight, and send him on down to the carrier. The Sheriff's down there, and he says there's no sign of foul play. Just looks like the guy had a seizure of some kind and croaked. His office was locked. They didn't find him until the mess cooks realized there was no chow for midrats."

"Bet that dampened appetites somewhat. Okay. Are there some reports that have to be made?"

"Yes, sir, but XO's gonna take care of it; a personnel casualty report is the first thing that's gotta go out. XO says they'll probably take him to Da Nang, box him up, and ship him home with all the rest of the boxes they send outta there."

"Lovely. Okay. I'm sorry the guy's dead. I'll pass on what's happened to Mr. Benedetti."

Brian hung up and told Vince the story. Vince shook his head. "Not too surprising," he said. "The guy was huge. And he smoked perpetually. Okay, Brian, I got it. This is Mr. Benedetti, I have the evaluator watch."

After a chorus of "Aye, aye, sir", Brian left Combat and went down to the wardroom. The stewards had recycled the evening meal as midrats, so Brian elected to hit the peanut butter and jelly, accompanied by a glass of reconstituted milk. The 2000 to 2400 watch section was relaxing in the wardroom, taking the luxury of their time because they knew they had a full night's sleep coming to them, even though it was just after midnight.

The exec came in as Brian was finishing his sandwich. He went directly to the coffee urn and drew a cup. He sat down at the head of the senior table and began working on a message draft, ignoring the other officers in the wardroom. Everyone had been talking about Garlic's demise, but after looking at the exec's face, no one wanted to interrupt him for more news. At last, they glanced at one another and began to gather up plates and cups. Brian wanted to know, as did everyone, whether there were any more details on why Garlic had expired, but the exec was studiously ignoring everyone. Brian looked around at the other officers, gave them the high sign to leave, and followed them out of the wardroom. He was surprised to find Chief Jackson waiting outside. Jackson told Brian he was waiting for the XO but that he would like to speak to him if he could.

Brian glanced at his watch. "I'm going up to my stateroom; if you can be up there in twenty minutes or so, come ahead. Otherwise, I'll see you in the morning. I'm coming off six hours in Combat."

"I'll be there," Jackson said.

Fifteen minutes later, he was knocking on Brian's door. Brian was sitting in his bathrobe, yawning and sifting through his in basket when the Sheriff came in. Brian indicated a chair.

"What ya got, Sheriff?"

"I've got the name of the guy who runs the drug operation in the ship," Jackson said. "Only problem is, my source and only corroboration kicked the bucket down on the mess decks about an hour ago."

"That guy Garlic?"

"Yup. The ship's loan shark. He'd been accepting cash from our guy and putting it into his loans operation. The feds call it money laundering. It was a way to put a cash hoard to work, especially an illegal cash hoard."

"And the guy is—"

"EM One Wilson—the electrician they call Bullet."

"I vaguely remember him. He's a main-hole snipe, isn't he? Was this guy Garlic aware that he was moving drug money?"

"Had to be. How else could an E-Six be coming up with boxes of cash every month? But I suspect no questions were asked and no answers given."

"Why did Garlic give him up?"

"Because we made it clear to him that we'd shut him down and prosecute his ass for being an accomplice to a narcotics operations if he didn't. If he cooperated, we'd let him stay in business and testify as a government witness."

"We?"

"I took the chief bosun. Garlic is—was—bigger than me."

Brian thought about it. With Garlic to testify and theoretically with some evidence of the money changing hands, they could have nailed this guy Bullet. But without Garlic, all they had was a name. Jackson was watching him work it out.

"Yeah. No Garlic, no witness, no proof. We've got a name, but we kind of had that name, anyway. That's the reason I wanted to come see you, even before Garlic croaked. I'm not sure where to go with this now."

Brian nodded slowly. Neither was he.

"Have you briefed the exec?"

"No, sir. Frankly, I'm almost afraid to." He filled Brian in on their concerns about a large-scale investigation and the racial angle. Brian noted the chief's embarrassment when he brought up the subject of race.

"We're kind of at a brick wall, as I see it. The command is already spooked over these mast cases; we don't have any real proof that Bullet is the man, and between the heat we might get from the task force commander and the possibility of a racial reaction, I think the XO'd step on our necks."

"So maybe the thing to do is to keep plugging, see if you can get enough on Bullet to get him to confess or to take him to jail on the evidence. You go that way, nobody in authority has told you *not* to pursue it. The other way, I think you're right: They may shut you down officially, and then if you kept after it, you're disobeying orders."

"Yes, sir. That's kind of how we see it, too." Jackson was rubbing the black plastic bill of his cap with his thumb while he thought. "But we're not exactly sure what to do next to go get that evidence."

"Well, for one thing, where's Garlic's bank? If there's more of that marked money in it, you have stronger evidence that some of the drug money was getting to him."

Jackson stared at him. "Damn, you're right. I forgot all about the marked twenties. And if Bullet is our man, *he's* going to have a cash stash somewheres, too. Yeah, follow the money."

"And follow Bullet. Watch him. Bug him. Put the pressure on. Hell, sic Chief Louie Jesus on him, put some of that evil spirit medicine on him. If he's not the guy, he'll come forward pretty quick to complain about it. If he is, he'll go armadillo on you. Meantime, find Garlic's bank. Now, I gotta get my tree time."

Jackson stood up. "Right, Mr. Holcomb. We'll keep you cut in. And I appreciate the support."

"Just remember, Sheriff, support from a guy who's already out on a limb isn't something to bet the farm on, if I can mix my metaphors."

"We want this bastard, Mr. Holcomb; we'll take support where ever we can get it. Good night, sir."

45

During the next ten days and nights, the tempo of operations over the Gulf steadily increased. Passage of typhoon winds had produced a rich target list by blowing away many of the elaborate camouflage structures all over North Vietnam. The recce runs were bringing back unheard-of tallies of artillery parks, ammo dumps, and fuel farms, all of which revealed preparations for a major push into the South. While there was no formal U.S. announcement of full-scale bombing operations over the North, the President had authorized a steady escalation in the U.S. air attacks, especially in the southern half of North Vietnam. The SAR helos were seeing plenty of action, and both carriers were flying at least part of the time, which in turn meant that *Hood*'s air controllers were exceedingly busy. The task force developed a routine of increasingly active operations from about 0500 until 2300, after which things subsided for both the Americans and the North Vietnamese until the next morning.

Brian, Vince Benedetti, and Count Austin settled into their watch rotation, each silently glad for the chance to stand one in three instead of the mind-numbing port and starboard. Brian found himself better able to sustain the watches by being able to sleep from midnight to 0530 at least two nights out of three. He was also becoming much better attuned to the sounds and electronic cues of the operations displayed on the scopes, and he no longer had to badger the SWICs every few minutes with "what's that?" questions. He was also able to spend more time managing his weapons department, getting to know the people better, and catching up on the Navy's unending paperwork.

Brian thought he detected a new measure of respect from his own people after the mast cases. The three miscreants had been flown off the ship on the afternoon of the mast proceedings, showing nervous grins as they suited up in cranial helmets and life jackets for their sojourn to the Philippines and trial by court-martial. Some of the more hip enlisted, lined up on top of the helo hangar, had sent them off with surreptitious thumbs-up and peace signs, envious that they were going home, no matter by what route and to what fate. Brian had instituted a crash training program in Fox division, using the FTM chiefs to sit the consoles in plot side by side with the junior enlisted men. His plans to conduct missile-tracking drills with the support tracks over the Gulf were not as successful, as the powerful Spook radars generated real alarms on cockpit instrument panels, and there were enough enemy alarms showing up already with the increased air activity over the North. But after a week, there was visible improvement among the men in plot.

The only discordant note came when the exec had watched a training session one night that did not go perfectly. He had turned to Brian, who had the evaluator watch.

"You better hope nothing happens, Mr. Holcomb, because if it does and your missile system makee-learns fuck it up, I'm going to hold you responsible."

"I think I'm responsible in any event, XO," Brian had replied. The exec had given him a frosty look and left.

Brian noted that the captain continued to hibernate in his cabin. Operating alone in her box, the ship made no maneuvers requiring his presence on the bridge, and the evaluators' main contact with him was through the bat phone. The exec checked in during the day when things got hectic over the beach, but he, too, seemed to be holing up in his cabin and attending to paperwork and people problems, the mainstay of any exec's life aboard ship. Count Austin had made a vaguely displeased reference to "interest" from CTF 77's staff in the drug incident. Austin seemed to think that Brian's action in precipitating the report chits had done some damage to the ship's reputation. Brian had responded that people using drugs aboard the ship did the real damage to the ship's reputation, but Austin had only scoffed at his naïveté. Their relationship cooled, and Brian had the distinct impression that Austin was creating distance between them, as if he anticipated that Brian was going to take some kind of fall for interfering in the *Hood* way of doing things. Vince Benedetti remained on the fence about it, one day talking wishfully about doing the same thing in Engineering to the men he knew were still using, then adamant the next day that he could never afford to knock that many people off the watch bill and still be able to run four main engineering spaces. Brian pointed out that, eventually, if enough guys were smoking dope in the main spaces, the decision would be made for him. It turned out to be a prophetic statement.

On the evening of the eleventh day after turnover, the 1MC burst into life with the chilling announcement of a Class Bravo fire in Number One Fire Room. In Navy parlance, Class Alfa was paper and wood; Class Charlie was an electrical fire. But Class Bravo meant an oil fire, a major disaster potentially in the making down below. Vince Benedetti was standing the evaluator watch in Combat. When the word was called, he had bolted from D and D and was crashing down the ladder as Brian was opening his stateroom door.

"Take the watch!" Vince yelled as he flew down the next ladder. Brian grabbed his flashlight and ran up to Combat as the general quarters alarm began to sound. There he found the Weapons people busily taking their systems off the line in anticipation of power fluctuations.

Garuda Barry had the SWIC watch. He was standing next to the evaluator's desk, his headphones pushed to the back of his head as he transmitted a message to the staff down on Yankee Station via Air Force Green about the fire. The captain and the exec were apparently already out on the bridge. Count Austin strode through the door to Combat, followed by the rest of the CIC GQ team.

Everyone in Combat was tight-faced. A Class Bravo fire in a main engineering space was serious enough to warrant the immediate setting of the tightest damage-control condition, material condition Zebra, throughout the ship. Condition Zebra effectively closed the ship up into hundreds of watertight compartments. An oil fire in a main space usually meant that pressurized oil, either fuel oil or a lubricant, was burning out of control in a confined, hot space, turning the cramped and tangled maze of propulsion machinery, steam pipes, and pressurized water lines into a roaring firebox and creating a fireball that sucked up all the oxygen in seconds and made escape from the space almost impossible. If left uncontrolled, main-space fires could lead to boiler explosions or steam-line ruptures that would release superheated 980°F steam into the affected space and even into adjoining main-propulsion spaces. If the watch standers could not get a Class Bravo under control in the first minute, their only option was to try to shut off the source of the oil and then to get to the escape trunk or dive into the bilges, where they would lie on their backs in the rolling bilgewater, exposing only enough of their faces to get some air, while they watched the cataclysm develop above them and prayed that there would not be a main steam leak.

Austin formally assumed the watch in D and D and Brian manned his GQ station in the weapons module. There was none of the usual chatter and questions from the off-watch people as everyone waited in tense silence for word that the fire was under control. The lights blinked a couple of times when the engineers switched power centers as they isolated the foward fire room. While the officers listened to the damage-control efforts going on over the bitch box between Main Engineering Control and the bridge, Garuda continued to make radio reports to the staff down on the carriers. The other watch standers communicated with their aircraft to explain why Red Crown was coming off the air. Brian checked to see that the missile systems and the SPS-48 radar had been put in standby. The Operations people had secured the TACAN and the secondary radars. In theory, the engineers would shift the electrical load to the after main plant's generators, which should not be affected by a problem in the forward plant. Everyone understood that the operative word was *should*. With a Class Bravo fire going in a boiler room, nothing was certain.

It took thirty minutes before a damage-control team was able to enter the forward fire room, climbing down the escape hatch from the weather decks, lugging heavy fire hoses, and breathing through OBAs. They reported back through sound-powered phone circuits that the fire had burned itself out. It had apparently been centered in the area of a main feed pump, and the probable cause was lube oil spraying out of a lube oil strainer onto the hot steel casing of a steam-driven main feed pump. The fire room's crew had been able to pull fires under the steaming boiler and shut down the feed pump before diving into the bilges, which had allowed the fire to burn itself out. The damage-control team reported that they were ventilating the space, whose atmosphere was almost totally obscured by heavy black smoke. There was no word on injuries among the boiler room's crew of four watch standers. Austin forwarded this information to the staff via Green.

"Damned lucky if that's all we got," observed Garuda, fondling an unlighted cigarette. Smoking was not permitted during general quarters. "I was on a destroyer once; we had six guys killed in a Class Bravo fire. Melted a six-hundred-pound steam line. Stripped all the meat off their bones in about fifteen seconds. All they found were six skeletons, bones clean as a hound's tooth. Bad shit. Real bad shit."

"That'll be enough of that kind of talk," barked Austin as several radarmen started to look sick. "I'm waiting for a 'power stable' report, and then we get Red Crown back on the air."

Brian waited along with the rest of the GQ crew as the situation was sorted out down below. Although Combat was full of people, all the console screens were dark and the radios silent. He had a sinking feeling that the days of three-section evaluator watches had just come to a close. The exec came into Combat a few minutes later and gave Austin a final wrap-up report to be sent to the staff. As Austin wrote down the details, the exec saw Brian watching him from the weapons module. He gave Brian a look that seemed to say, Don't start. . . . Then he focused again on the report.

Brian wondered what they would find when they did the investigation—which one of Vince's stars had been high when he tried to shift lube-oil strainers. He remembered from Destroyer School that an oil leak from a feed pump strainer was almost unheard of, but a mistake in shifting from the pressurized strainer to the alternate strainer was a well-documented cause of oil fires in boiler rooms. The exec went back out to the bridge.

"Main Control reports power stable on Two B generator," announced a GQ phone talker. Austin gave a nod and Garuda ordered the various module supervisors to begin restoring the electronics systems. Garuda brought the operations program back to life with his finger drill on the master key sets. Console alert buzzers began to sound all over Combat. Fifteen minutes later, the bridge passed the word to secure from GQ.

"All stations, SWIC," Garuda bawled over the intercom. "Gimme manned and ready."

Brian walked into D and D and stood next to Austin. "So who takes the watch?" he asked.

Austin glanced up from the message he was writing and then looked at his watch. "Oh, right. Vince. Let's see. I've been off the longest," he said. "I'll finish out Vince's eighteen to twenty-four, and you pick up the mid. After that, we'll have to see what happens."

Brian nodded. "I think I can guess what will happen," he said, his voice already weary. But Austin was studying his incident-report message. Brian went below to grab a few hours of sleep.

46

The exec made it official the next morning after officers'
call. The chief engineer needed to come off the evaluator
watch bill to oversee the repairs in the forward fire room.
Austin would have the 0600 to 1200 and the 1800 to 2400
watches; Brian would take the 1200 to 1800 and the 2400
to 0600 watches. Brian's heart sank at the thought of
another month of the midnight-to-dawn stints as evaluator. Even when he tried to budget time for sleep, his
body resisted the strain of staying awake during his entire
natural rest period. The exec saw the look on his face.

"You said the other day you were ready to take it down
to just the officers and chiefs," he said, closing his
notebook. "Well, this is what happens when the wardroom gets shorthanded."

Austin studied the deck as the exec walked forward,
aware of the rebuke hidden in the exec's words and its
relation to Brian's action against the three missile techs.
Brian said nothing as the other officers gathered into
departmental groups. Austin paused to speak to him
while the Weapons Department people waited.

"It won't be for that long," Austin said. "There was
surprisingly little damage. Nobody really got hurt.
There's some burned lagging and some copper tubing
melted around the feed pump, but they're mostly cleaning up down there, what with smoke soot all over everything. Vince thinks he can get the fire room up and
running in a couple of days."

"What about the feed pump?"

"It's out of commission until they can inspect casing
specs to make sure nothing warped, but he's got two
more in that space."

"And I suppose there's no word on what caused it?"

Austin gave him an arch look. "Officially 'unknown'
for now," he said. "And if I were you, I wouldn't push
that question too far."

"Sounds to me like some people are getting sensitive to the truth."

Austin looked at him. "Sounds to *me,* Mr. Holcomb, that certain lieutenants are starting to live dangerously." He moved away to join the Operations officers for the morning's instructions.

Brian walked over to the Weapons group, where the chiefs waited with the division officers. A strong northeast breeze flowed over the boat decks, causing everyone to hang on to his ball cap.

"Well, guys, I'm back on afternoons and mids," he announced, "which means I'll see you guys at officers' call and at some meals. I guess we go back to the same system as before. You can catch me in Combat unless the Red Crown business happens to be really cooking. Otherwise, if it's routine, handle it."

"How long this time, boss?" asked the chief boatswain.

"Don't know, Boats. Depends on what they find down there, I suppose. Mr. Austin thinks just a couple of days."

"Way I hear it, Mr. Benedetti had the watch standers take a piss test after they pulled 'em outta the bilges."

"Oh my," said Brian.

"And?" asked Fox Hudson.

"That's all I heard," the chief said, shrugging his shoulders.

"Probably all we're going to hear," muttered Jack Folsom.

"Okay, guys, turn to," Brian said. He signed a couple of special-request chits and approved the monthly ammunition summary message draft. The officers headed down to the wardroom for coffee refills, but the chief boatswain lingered. Brian noticed that the boatswain did not have to hang on to his hat.

"Yeah, Boats?"

"I figgered ya might wanta know somethin'," he said, "'bout them piss tests."

"Well, I'm curious, of course. But it wouldn't astonish me if the lid was clamped down on the results."

"Yeah, well, the way I hear it, the doc took the samples

with Jackson watchin', but Jackson didn't get to see what happened when the doc put the chemicals in—you know, if anybody changed color? And the doc, he's doin' the armadillo. He ain't sayin' nothin' to nobody. XO's orders.''

"Which means the XO wants to keep the results to himself.''

"Well, you know, things are kinda up in the air since you took them shitbirds to mast. And Jackson ain't too happy he's bein' cut out. And doc ain't too happy about doin' the cuttin', you follow my drift.''

"I think I'm missing something—''

"Yeah, well, under the old deal, who took care of the bad guys?''

"Oh, I get it now. The chiefs—who are now being cut out of the pattern.''

"'Zactly. He can't keep it a secret, he wants some ass kicked. An if he does keep it a secret—''

"Nobody's ass get's kicked. His system falls apart.''

"'Causa you.''

"Because of me. Right. Terrific. I think I'll go pack my seabag right now. Do a good inventory. Make it easy on my next of kin.''

The boatswain laughed. "You hang in there, boss. We might get this bucket back to regulation Navy yet.''

"Anything more on Bullet?''

"He's startin' to get nervous. I been layin' the heavy vibes on him.'' The chief rolled his eyes to show what he thought of the expression. "But I think we're missin' something. Something Garlic said, night we went to talk to him.''

"What was that?''

"Jackson don't agree with this, but Garlic, one time he said he got the money from him, meanin' Bullet, I guess, and then the second time, he said he got it from *them*.''

"Meaning the drug gang, maybe?''

"Yeah, that's the way Jackson sees it. Them is the drug gang. But me, I think he meant that he was gettin' money from two guys, not just one.''

"Meaning what? Bullet's a deputy dog and there's another guy, the real boss?''

"Yeah, maybe."

Brian thought about that for a moment. But why would there be two guys—why would the operation need two guys? He asked Martinez.

"I dunno," the chief said. "It's just somethin' stickin' in my head."

"If you think that's how it is, maybe you guys ought to go have a session with Bullet like you had with Garlic—if there's a bigger fish to catch here, it might be worth it. Long as you could do it without giving the guy a heart attack," Brian said pointedly.

Martinez shrugged. "Shit happens, Mr. Holcomb. Shit happens."

Brian was on his way forward when he saw Austin talking to the exec by the port-side boat davits. They both gave him a look as he went by but did not resume their conversation until Brian was out of earshot. He was restowing some laundry when his phone rang.

"Lieutenant Holcomb speaking, sir."

It was the exec. "Mr. Holcomb. I'm told you think the command has a problem handling the truth."

Fucking Austin! "I simply meant—"

"You had better take some care with what you say, mister. We'll find out what happened down in that fire room, but I think you have enough problems of your own without sticking your snot nose in other people's business. If you don't, come see me—I've got lots of problems I can share with you. Understand?"

"Yes, sir."

"And where's the report on your preps for the admin inspection? And your next quarter's OpTar budget—got that ready yet?"

"No, sir." Brian sighed.

"Well, make sure I have them both by the close of business today, hotshot. Man of your vast interests and talents ought to be able to handle that, no sweat."

Brian was silent.

"I don't hear you, Mr. Holcomb."

"Aye, aye, sir."

"There you go."

Brian hung up and finished stowing his laundry. He was wondering whether he could still grab a quick pre-watch nap when there was a knock on the door and Chief Jackson stuck his head in.

"Mr. Holcomb, got a minute?"

"Yeah, Chief. Why not."

Jackson came in and closed the door behind him.

"FTM Three Warren came in to see me. It seems he's catching some heat from some of the other junior enlisted. He wouldn't come right out and say it, but the impression I got was that it was the other black junior enlisted."

"What kind of heat?"

"Somebody stenciled his pillowcase with the name Tom Fink. As in Uncle Tom, the white man's boy, and a stool pigeon besides. That was two days ago. Last night, some guys ambushed him in the missile house's passageway, turned off the passageway lights and pushed him around. Guys were wearing their knit caps over their faces. Said he better stay off the weather decks, because they were gonna fix his ass for messing around in some of the brothers' business."

"But none of the guys who went down were black."

"Exactly. Which means the warning is probably coming from Bullet—it's his drug business that Warren is supposedly messing around with."

"Shit. I don't need Warren hassled," Brian said. "Below the first class FTMs, he's the senior petty officer watch stander I've got left."

"Yes, sir. He knows that. He seems like a good kid, but this is starting to get to him. I just thought you ought to know."

"Okay, thanks, Chief. Please tell his division officer, Mr. Hudson. Ask him to counsel Warren. Is there anything you can do?"

"In what sense, Mr. Holcomb?"

"I don't know, exactly. Maybe in the sense that you're one of the more senior black men in the ship."

Jackson looked down at the deck. He had an embarrassed expression on his face.

"As the Sheriff, I've got some power, Mr. Holcomb,

but that's not the same as saying I have any influence on the guys who are probably doing this. When I try to talk to them as a black man, the younger ones look at me as the Uncle Tom of Uncle Toms.''

"Names shouldn't bother us, Chief.''

" 'Us,' Mr. Holcomb?''

"Right. I beg your pardon. Point taken. I guess what I meant was if you and Chief Martinez cornered some of these guys and put the fear of God, or at least of Godzilla, into them, they might leave Warren alone.''

Jackson grinned. "Like that gun-deck justice stuff, now, do we?''

" 'We,' Chief?''

Jackson laughed out loud and then shook his head. "Yes, sir, I hear you. But then they would know we're aware of them as a drug organization. We should probably not confirm that right now.''

"Yeah, that's true. Okay. We'll do what we can for Warren. But here's another thing—Martinez told me he thinks there might be two kingpins, based on something Garlic said.''

"Yeah, he's run that by me, too. The druggies don't operate that way, though. There's one guy—just one guy who runs the show.''

Brian stifled a yawn. "But suppose Garlic was lying. Suppose there is just one guy but that it isn't Bullet. Suppose Bullet works for the one guy and everyone else works for Bullet.''

"Everything we've got so far points at Bullet. There's nothing pointing to a second guy, Mr. Holcomb. I think we gotta concentrate on where the evidence is leading.''

Brian yawned. "Okay, Chief. I have to concentrate on saving my young ass from the XO's ire. You go catch Mr. Bullet Wilson.''

When Jackson returned to his office, he found Radarman First Class Rockheart sitting in one of the chairs, filling out a divisional inspection report.

"Yo, Chief.''

"Yeah, morning, Rocky. What's happening.''

"Not shit, Chief. Just doing some MAA paperwork. You look like you died and just woke up.''

Jackson shook his head wearily and sat down.

"I tell you, this drug shit has me coming and going."

"Yeah, well, we got three—no, I guess it's four in the past month. That has to be some progress."

"Users, Rocky. Users. Not the guys I really want."

"Any ideas on that score, Chief?"

Jackson eyed Rocky for a minute. He hadn't brought any of his MAAs into the investigation up to this point—only Chief Martinez. But maybe it was time. And hell, this was Rockheart.

"Lock that door, RD One. Let me tell you about it."

When he was finished, Rocky was staring at the deck.

"Bullet," he said. "Hell, I know the guy, or thought I did. He seemed to be upstanding people among the first class. Shit."

"Yeah, shit. My problem is, I don't have one shred of real evidence on Bullet, much less on any second guy."

"What would you consider real evidence, Sheriff?"

"Drugs or money, or, hopefully, both. Especially some of that marked money I put in circulation before Subic. Oh, and a witness or three. And a signed confession would be nice—shit, you know."

Rocky grunted but then was silent for a few moments. The Sheriff was locked on Bullet. The trick was to keep him there. Jackson sighed and turned to the paperwork on his desk, and Rocky finished his own report, which he turned over to the chief. He got up to leave.

"That's all close-hold stuff, Rocky," Jackson warned over his shoulder.

"Absolutely, Chief. But I'm glad you told me. Maybe I can come up with something—who knows? Another pair of eyes, right?"

"Evidence, RD One. What I need is evidence."

47

San Diego

Maddy awoke from a dreamless sleep to the sounds of someone ringing the front door bell. She lay on her stomach, trying to focus her mind, to understand what that noise was. The bedroom was fully dark. All of her muscles were stiff with fatigue. The bell rang again. She lifted her head and looked at her watch, struggling to see the radium dial. Eight-thirty. Day or night? The windows were dark. Night. The bell rang again. She felt across the bed for Autrey, but he was gone. Gone. She sat up then, quickly enough to make her head spin for a few seconds. She turned on the bedside light. Gone. No clothes. Just gone. Damn. She took a deep breath, then focused on the insistent bell.

"Just a minute," she called through the bedroom doorway. Her voice was weak. She cleared her throat and said it again, louder. She swung out of bed and shoved her hair from her face. She went into the bathroom, got a nightgown and her bathrobe. Maddy looked at herself in the mirror. Hope to hell this isn't one of the wives, she thought. There wasn't a woman alive who wouldn't be able to recognize the symptoms of what kind of weekend this had been. She washed her face with a cold washcloth and then went through the apartment, turning on some lights and wishing she could just go back to the bathroom and ruminate for a while. She peered through the peep-hole. Oh my God. Mrs. Huntington. She stepped back from the door, ran her hands through her hair once more, gave up, took another deep breath, and unlocked the door. The captain's wife gave her a five-second long, studied look before speaking.

"Well, Maddy. I'm glad to find you're all right. May I come in?"

Maddy wasn't sure what to say. If Mrs. Huntington

could see that she was all right, why did she have to come in? Don't be an idiot, girl. This is the captain's wife. She wants to come in so that she can give you a lecture about your evil ways. She stood aside.

"Yes, of course, although I'm not very presentable. I was asleep."

Mrs. Huntington paused in the doorway. "Are you alone, Maddy?"

Ah, there we are. "Yes, Mrs. Huntington. I am." She looked straight at the other woman. "Now."

Mrs. Huntington smiled, and Maddy was slightly embarrassed to see that it was not a bitchy meow smile. Mrs. Huntington walked past her and went over to the sofa, where she sat down, placing her purse and a jacket on the table. She was wearing slacks, a long-sleeved blouse, with a scarf at her neck, and penny loafers. Maddy stood there in her bathrobe feeling as rumpled as she undoubtedly looked. Mrs. Huntington looked at her.

"Why don't you go freshen up, dear. Freshen up and wake up a little. Tell me, if I go out there in the kitchen, would I find some coffee makings? I could use a cup and so could you, I think. Yes? Good. Go right ahead. Take your time, get yourself together. I know that my visit is probably a little unsettling, but we do need to talk. I'll find what I need out there, so go on now."

Like a chastened teenager, Maddy left the room. When she returned twenty minutes later, she was showered, dressed in slacks and a sweater herself, and fully awake. And a little worried. The captain's wife walking into her little love nest. The only thing worse would have been if Autrey had answered the door.

Mrs. Huntington had two cups of coffee on the living room table, along with a small pitcher of milk and the sugar bowl. There were even napkins and spoons. Maddy gave a tentative smile and sat down, not really knowing how to proceed. Over Mrs. Huntington's shoulder, she suddenly focused on Brian's picture, and the room tilted. She waited for Mrs. Huntington, who smiled and passed her a cup of coffee. She then looked around the room.

"This is a nice apartment, Maddy. And a lovely location, right across from Balboa Park."

"Yes, we like it," Maddy said. "It seems to be secure, and I can play tennis every day, too." How inane, she thought. This visit is sure as hell not about tennis.

Mrs. Huntington sipped some coffee and then put the cup down, sat back, crossed her legs, and smiled again. Damn woman was full of smiles.

"Maddy," she began, "I have sensed that our wardroom wives' organization is more than a little foreign to your experience. I know you and Brian are new to *Hood,* and that you are relatively new to Navy married life. And it's not that I think you don't like us; I suspect it's more a matter of lifestyle. Most of our wives do not have jobs and have a houseful of kids to chase after. You have a full-time job and no children. Most of our wives have college degrees, but the objective for many of them was always the Mrs. degree. You have a professional business education from a first-rate school, and you're on a career track with the Bank of America. As I said, I think it's cultural—our worlds impinge on each other because of your husband's career and his assignment to this ship, whereas otherwise, I don't think you and I would ever cross paths."

It was Maddy's turn to sit back, cross her legs, and wait to see where this was going.

"Yes?" she said, with a coolness she did not feel.

"Over the past few weeks, you've regretted several invitations, some of them spur-of-the-moment, some of them more along the line of our regular wives' functions. I decided to see if we've managed to offend you, or if perhaps you were depressed and just holing up here. Sometimes that happens, especially to women who are new to these awful deployments and who have less of a family focus than our girls with children do. I called several times this weekend, and when you didn't answer, I decided to check it out."

"I see. Well, there's certainly been no offense, Mrs. Huntington. Everyone's been very nice and I've met some lovely people, but you're right: I have a full day in the office, and I have to pursue a vigorous sport daily or my body blows up like a balloon. The deployment . . . well, the deployment is just there, I guess. I hate every minute of it, and most of the time I try just to stay busy enough so that I don't get irretrievably down about it. In a way, being with the wives makes that harder. Maybe it's because I look at them and see the future. But no, I'm not mad at anybody, and I'm no more depressed than I should be, I suppose."

Mrs. Huntington studied her coffee cup for a minute. Maddy waited, really curious now. Mrs. Huntington appeared to make up her mind about something.

"Maddy," she said. "There is, of course, always another possibility why we're not seeing much of you. And that is you've found a way to make up for the fact that your husband is gone for seven months. Taken up with another man, or men, for that matter. Now—" She put up her hand as if to stifle any comment from Maddy.

"Now, on one level, that's none of my business, and none of our business, if you follow me. I know the times have changed a lot from when Warren and I were coming up in the Navy, and perhaps these sorts of arrangements are more—I almost hate to use the word, but more— common."

Maddy almost laughed. This woman should hear herself. Why doesn't she just come right out and say it?

"And the more I think about it, a young woman with your face and figure, two salaries, and thus the money for expensive clothes and your own car, the more I think about it, the more I think this latter possibility is closer to the mark. Yes, I think it is."

Mrs. Huntington looked around the apartment as if to corroborate her conclusion. Maddy wondered what the apartment would tell her. She sighed but held her tongue. Mrs. Huntington was smiling again.

"You've got that 'give her enough rope, she'll soon hang herself' look on your face, dear. Please, relax. I'm not here to brand a scarlet letter on your forehead."

"Then why are you here, Mrs. Huntington?"

"I'm here, I guess, to give you some advice. Let me tell you a little story. I'll give you my advice and then I promise I'll leave and hope we can still be friends. The story goes like this: Warren was the executive officer in a destroyer back about eight years ago, which, of course, made me the XO's wife. As I'm sure you've figured out, the captain's wife and the XO's wife have a fairly traditional division of labor when it comes to the wardroom wives. They share the mentoring duties, and they share being the hostess for when the wives get together, especially during deployment, and they share the duty for taking calls in the night when someone's wife gets into a pickle. They sort of share the same coordinated partnership that the CO and the XO share on the ship, only, because we're wives, there's not the distinction of rank. Wives who wear their husband's rank tend to be kind of ridiculous, anyway, so that's not really important.''

Maddy sat back with her coffee and listened.

"One of the problems we wrestled with in that wardroom was the Supply officer's wife. She was very pretty and very vivacious, and a dedicated party girl. The ship went off to WESTPAC and Shirley went off to town with her red dress on. She was not very discreet, and soon all the wardroom wives had their tongues aflutter. Then Shirley found out that *we* had all found out, and then we indulged in a mutual shunning exercise.

"Halfway through the cruise, the captain's wife got a phone call in the middle of the night—with deployed ships, it's always in the middle of the night—and was told that the ship had been in an ASW screen exercise and had managed to collide with another destroyer, and that there was very serious damage and nine people known dead or injured, but worse, twelve others were missing. Now when you've been around the Navy for a while, you know that missing at sea is almost always the same as dead. Nature of the beast, I guess. Well, she called me, and between us we called the rest of the wives. Naturally, she being the CO's wife, we gathered at her place. Except for Shirley, of course, because we weren't speaking to Shirley, because she was being such a 'shameless hussy.'

"The problem was, of course, that Shirley's husband turned out to be one of the missing, the only officer, in fact, who was missing. We didn't know that when we first made the calls. Around about morning, we were given the list of names by the base chaplain, and suddenly we knew somebody was going to have to start speaking to Shirley again. Well, the captain's wife and I were elected, so to speak, and we went with the chaplain to Shirley's house. We got there about eight in the morning, and, poor Shirley, she had a gentleman caller, as my mother used to say. He actually came to the door. He was Navy, and when he saw two distraught wives and a chaplain, he knew *instantly* what we were there for. But Shirley did not; she had to be told."

Mrs. Huntington paused, her face grim in the memory of that morning.

"And I will *never* forget the look on her face, beyond the shock, beyond the beginnings of grief, the look that echoed the unspoken question on her lips, which asked, And what was I doing when my husband went over the side in the night? I don't think Shirley was ever the same again after that morning. Oh, of course we told her that her husband was missing, that nothing was confirmed yet, and that they were searching, but women who've lost a mate seem to become clairvoyant at times like that and they see right through those charades. She knew. Maybe she knew because we knew and we transmitted that knowledge. I never knew before that day that one could see a soul break right in half, but I did that morning.

"Anyway, that's the story. Now for the advice: First, if you decide to see other men, be discreet. If nothing else, you can do mortal damage to your husband's career if it gets out that you're seeing other men when the ship is gone. I don't know if you're in the same boat with the Hudsons—Tizzy's told me they're going to get out, so maybe the career aspect doesn't matter. But if that's not decided yet, be very discreet. Second, keep in touch with us, in touch with me, actually, so that the kitty cats don't get started and make it hard for us grown-ups to keep in touch with everyone in the fold, lambs, sheep, and wolves. Third, remember that *Hood* is at war, whether the politicians call it a police action or a counterinsurgency, or whatever. Make sure you are strong enough to take a visit like Shirley's one morning after a night like, well, like this past weekend, perhaps. And lastly, I presume that one of the reasons, if you had a reason, that you have been with another man is that your husband is gone. Consider this, Maddy: Where's the other man now? Is he coming back? Will you see him tomorrow? Or is it possible that he's gone, too? I'm not condemning you, Maddy, and I don't expect you to say anything at all. I just think it's my . . . well, my duty, as the woman in the wardroom with the most experience with the stress of deployment, to pay you this call. Now, you will keep in touch with us?''

Maddy took a deep breath. Had she not been breathing? "Certainly," she managed.

"Oh good. I was so afraid you'd get angry and shun *us*. Because that's the other thing I learned—we were terribly wrong to shun her. I don't know if it would have made a difference, but the news might have been a little less destructive if there had been someone besides a one-night stand with her, some friends, perhaps. The wardroom wives are special that way, you see. Most of us may or may not have ever been natural friends, but since there's always the possibility that something's going to happen, most of us feel that there's a modicum of safety in numbers. In truth, as Shirley found out, there's no safety at all, but it makes us feel better just the same. Shirley killed herself a few months later, which is why I still feel bad about all of that.''

She got up, gathering her purse and jacket. "And now I've said enough and I'm going to get out of your hair. This has been what's called friendly fire, Maddy, and I thank you for hearing me out. And I promise, this will remain between you and me. But please, think about it, think about why you've been doing what you've been doing. And call me if you'd like. You can talk to me, Maddy—I don't tell Warren things he doesn't need to know, so you won't hurt your Brian. Okay? Bye, now.''

Maddy could not speak. Mrs. Huntington saw herself to the door. She waved once and was gone, the door pulled firmly behind her. After a minute, Maddy got up in a daze and went over to put the chain in place. She leaned her forehead on the door and thought about what the captain's wife had said. Was she strong enough to take a visit like that? Since Friday night to this very moment, she had squeezed everything, including Brian, especially Brian, right out of her mind. How would she feel about a chaplain standing at her door? Shattered? Would her very soul fracture? After what she had done with Autrey this weekend, to say that her soul would break would be the height of hypocrisy. Sad, yes. Sorry for herself, yes. But she had dishonored her marriage, and you can't break a soul that has no honor. "Think about it," the woman had said. Think about why she had been doing the things she had been doing.

She loved Brian, but she had *needed* Autrey. As she thought about it, Autrey the person was practically anonymous, and yet, at one elemental, almost atavistic level, the level where the *she* had been summoned out of the cave, flattening the *her* en route, Autrey had turned her head and then her body every way but loose. Autrey had come right at her, and something very basic in her had responded. Brian, the nice guy, the idealist, the guy who had simply fallen in love with her—and married her—Brian had never done that. And Brian had elected to go away. But no, that wasn't correct, either. She had married a naval officer. He had been very clear about the going-away part of it. She had even experienced it in the *Decatur* tour. Brian was simply doing his duty by going away. But where the hell do you strike the balance between the dishonorable need and the honorable need, between sex and love, between a man who hunts women and a man who marries one? Mrs. Huntington had been very grown-up about this, and Maddy now thanked God she had not tried to deny everything: Lying would have provoked contempt on top of censure. *Was* she strong enough? In her lust, she had never considered any particular consequences.

And the ironic thing was, Autrey was where? Autrey was gone. Mrs. Huntington had unwittingly put her finger right on it. Maddy had checked the bedroom and the kitchen for a note, a sign that it wasn't over, but there was nothing. Autrey was gone, just like Brian. No, not just like Brian, is it? And now that he was gone, she remembered something she had read once, that the difference between making love and just fucking was that after making love, both people wanted to stay, but after fucking, at least one, if not both, wanted to go.

She sighed again, deciding to take another bath. She wondered how she would face the wardroom wives again, even if Mrs. Huntington did keep her word to tell no one.

Three nights later, Mrs. Huntington called her. The wives were congregating at her house this coming Friday—nothing special, just a potluck supper, something to chase away the Friday night. Maddy had hesitated.

"Mrs. Huntington, I'm not sure I should. I guess I'm still in the 'thinking about it' mode right now."

"I told you I would keep this whole thing to myself, Maddy. And I have. I've told no one, not even Barbara Mains, with whom I normally share everything that's going on in the wardroom. So it's not like anyone will be pointing fingers."

Maddy had nodded, as if Mrs. Huntington could see her.

"Maddy?"

"Yes, sorry, Mrs. Huntington. And I'm deeply grateful for that. I guess it's just that I would know, and you know, and that still makes me uncomfortable. I'm doing what you said—thinking about what I want. I'm just not done yet, if that makes any sense."

"Well, yes, dear, of course it does. But you don't have to do all that by yourself, you know."

"But this *is* something I think I do have to do by myself." Maddy thought for a moment. "It's not . . ." she began, then paused.

"It's not what, Maddy?"

"It's not that there's anything still going on. I mean, that's all over. If that matters to you, I mean."

"It does matter, Maddy. I'm just trying to help, you know."

"Yes, I do know. I'm just not ready yet to talk about it. But I will be. And then I'm probably going to call you, if that's still okay."

"It is, and I'll make your excuses for Friday. But if you change your mind, just come—you don't have to call or anything. Just come, okay?"

"Thanks, Mrs. Huntington. Good-bye."

Maddy put the phone down and turned the TV back on to the evening news. She watched it for a while, not really seeing it. She had told the truth; she had been thinking about it—nonstop, as a matter of fact. During the day, her mind was carefully focused on her job. After work, and especially at night, she ran through the entire gamut of emotions—guilt, anger at Autrey, anger with herself, with the world for interfering, afraid of what might happen, deeply embarrassed at who might know, defiant if they did, afraid that what she had done might eventually mean she would be left alone again, very afraid of opening the door to find uniformed men with hats in hand.

She had begun and then ripped up several letters to Brian, ranging from full confessions to nothing, everything's just fine letters. Each time, she could not get around the basic obstacles: tell him, and destroy him; don't tell him, and deceive him; tell him how very much you love him, and make him wonder what's going on. And all of her anxiety revolved around the basic question Mrs. Huntington had posed: What do you want, Maddy? Do you want to go through life walking on the wild side, playing manipulation games with exciting men? Or do you want a loving, stable marriage, one where it is so good for both of you that what your father did will never even cross Brian's mind? That's easy to describe, but how in the hell do you achieve that in the Navy?

As she thought about it, the mechanics were becoming clear enough: You soldiered on. You accepted that the separations were going to be a fact of life and you made the best of them, just like all those women were doing. Friday-night potluck dinners, for instance. And days at the beach with the kids. With the kids you don't have. Who's to say that you will be able to have kids, anyway. But you made the best of the times together and lived on the memories in between, like a desert flower that blooms and then waits for the next season of rain. You stop whining and complaining and you get on with it. Just like they do. Which means that what they do is not to be despised or ridiculed, that what they do is an honorable

501

endeavor, that the Tizzy Hudsons of the world have it all wrong.

Well, okay, that's how it's done. But could *she,* Maddy Holcomb, manage it? She hadn't managed worth a damn so far, and the deployment was barely three months old. *This* deployment. What about all the rest, the deployments yet to come, the empty piers, the empty mailboxes, the everyday crises that greeted every wife and mother like the sunrise—could *she,* Maddy Holcomb, handle all that? Your mother did, girl. Talk about a deployment—at least you've got a schedule on the refrigerator of when your man's coming back. Maddy gritted her mental teeth every time she thought about her mother, and yet, and yet: Maybe just a smidgin of sympathy was in order there.

She refocused on the TV again and then got up and turned it off. She decided to clean the apartment again, for the third time this week. She decided to put her mind back in neutral again and go to work, substituting activity for thought, tire herself out as she had on the backboard for the past three afternoons, blasting the fuzz off those tennis balls with a fierce determination that had kept the mashers at their distance. She thought again about Friday. Not yet. Eventually, I'm going to have to do that, to rejoin, maybe to find out how this business is done. Because I'm pretty sure that I do know what I want. The weekend with Autrey had been time in the furnace, all heat, all her female nerve ends thrumming at once, glorious, frightening, exalting, thrilling—and pointless. After all the noise, just fucking, not loving. Mrs. Huntington had done her an enormous favor in reminding her that there was a difference. All she needed now was some time to regroup, to step back and look again at what she wanted out of life. Yes, she would think about Friday.

502

48

WESTPAC

Rocky leaned on the temporary lifelines rigged across the back of the helo deck. It was nearly sundown. He and several other men stood around the flight deck, smoking the day's last cigarette after chow or just hanging out. The western horizon was beginning to bloom in all the colors of a fantastic sunset. Down below, on the fantail, he saw Bullet holding court with some of his young disciples. They were gathered on the port side, in the shadow of the five-inch gun mount. Bullet was reading from a book and then explaining what he had just read as the others listened carefully. With the wind astern, Rocky was able to catch bits and pieces of what Bullet was saying, and he was struck by Bullet's language, which was definitely not of the street-talk variety. There was a lot more to this guy than met the eye.

His immediate problem was to place Bullet squarely and irretrievably in the path of Jackson's manhunt, but he hadn't the first idea of how to do it. Bullet knew that he was under suspicion but also knew that, with Garlic out of the picture, the only guy who could finger him could be fingered back. The Mafia called it a lock for a reason. Jackson was already predisposed not to believe the second-man theory, and Rocky had dismissed it, too, during his last session with Jackson, on the basis of the well-known fact that drug organizations were clear-cut about who was in charge. He had fed back to the chief as subtly as he could the idea of Bullet as the kingpin, trying to reinforce the prime suspect in the Sheriff's mind. But the longer Jackson went without substantive evidence on Bullet, the more likely that he'd start branching out and looking for other suspects.

He watched the group of blacks below out of the corner of his eye, trying not to be too overt about looking at them. He was surprised, therefore, when about fifteen minutes later Bullet wrapped it up down there and looked up to the flight deck and gave Rocky the high sign, the signal that he wanted to meet. They met in the laundry, after Bullet had told the two black servicemen working there to get lost for half an hour.

"What's up?" Rocky said after Bullet had closed and locked the door.

"Money, man, thass whut."

"Okay. I'm into bread, although this is probably not the time to go expanding the operation."

"Uh-uh. Talkin' about my man Garlic's money. Talkin' about the bank, man."

Rocky was suddenly very interested. "You know where it is?"

Bullet shrugged. "Thinks I does, man. Somethin' Garlic be sayin' to me, 'while back. 'Fore his unfortunate *accident*."

Rocky snorted. "Accident? Like in train accident? 'Cause that's the way I hear old Garlic met his untimely demise, man. Got hit by a train, a train called Louie Jesus."

Bullet looked down at the deck, his face solemn. "I be hearin' the same thing, man. The baby doc, he be sayin', it was a stroke or heart attack, shouldn'ta been no bleedin' out the mouth. Shoulda been out the nose and ears, but not out no mouth."

"Yeah, well, shit happens. My sources in the MAA shack say that Garlic didn't give up anything, or they would have moved by now."

Bullet gave him a speculative look. "I need some cover gittin' to the bank. You gimme the help, I'm willin' go sixty-forty with you."

"Sixty-forty? Shit, man, when'd we start with that garbage? Look, man, we got a good deal goin' here. Yeah, there's been a couple of setbacks lately, but even with the Sheriff and his buddies lookin' hard, they got jackshit. You got something to do, we go fifty-fifty."

Bullet walked around the laundry area, appearing to think about it. Rocky pretended to be bored: Yeah, he was interested, but he could walk away, he had to. But at the thought of Garlic's cash hoard, he was beginning to get the glimmer of an idea. Bullet finally made up his mind.

"Yeah, okay. Fifty-fifty. I be gittin' back to you, time to do it an' shit."

49

Brian settled resignedly into the routine of port and starboard watches again, adjusting his days to grab a nap in the morning and another one after supper in the evening, expending six hours of energy in the afternoon watches, then fighting his leaden eyelids from midnight to dawn. The afternoon watches became almost frantically busy as the task force stepped up its flight operations over the southern districts of North Vietnam and in the DMZ areas. While there were no more Alpha-Strikes, there were several two- and three-plane attack sorties against specific targets that began around first light and extended into the 2000 to 2400 watch period. Then CTF 77 had tried running precision strikes without the normal covering flights, but a pair of MiGs had slipped down from Hanoi along the Laotian border and nearly bagged a section of A-6s at twilight on Brian's second day of port and starboard watches. The Red Crown BARCAP Phantoms had joined the ensuing mêlée, but the MiGs had managed to vanish into the highlands of western North Vietnam, pursued by much foul language in Combat. After that, the carriers launched the standard strike-protection aircraft for MiGCAP and SAM site suppression.

The flight density going over the beach was not very heavy, but the augmented Heavenly Host kept Red Crown controllers going all day and part of the night. Each afternoon was inevitably complicated by the helo dance, when Big Mother had to lift off in order to land the daily log helo, or to set up either Big Mother or

Clementine on the SAR station. Brian found himself exhausted by the end of the 1200 to 1800 watch.

It took everything he had to stumble up to Combat at midnight again, trying to pretend along with all the other zombies up there that he was awake, alert, and ready for the watch. So it was with great relief each night that the SWIC announced the last recovery aboard the on-line carrier. Once the carriers secured for the night, the level of activity over the Gulf dwindled to just the BARCAP on their patrol line. The Red Crown air controller head count would go from three to one, and the main problem for the midwatch people became one of staying awake. The officers in D and D would execute a set routine: settle in to the tactical picture from relief time to 0100; screen all the night's message traffic from 0100 to 0200, sorting out the action messages for the rest of the ward-room to handle in the morning; from 0200 to 0300, oversee the setting up of the big vertical plotting boards around D and D with the next day's air plan, showing all the scheduled landings and launches from the duty carrier for the next day's operations; from 0300 to 0400, drop and reload the NTDS operational program on all consoles throughout CIC, doing minor maintenance where necessary on consoles, displays, headsets, or other equipments; from 0400 to 0500, do communications checks on the twenty-two voice-radio circuits and the NTDS link transmitters and tune the radars; at 0500, send a radar-man down to the galley to expropriate a tray of freshly baked sweet rolls from the night baker; from 0500 to relief, prepare to turn over the watch to the 0600 to 1200 watch standers.

With the repairs to the fire room taking much more time than originally expected, Brian slogged through this same routine for the next week. He knew that the midwatch routine assumed that nothing happened on either the air or surface side, and for the first five nights, nothing did happen, except that the northeast monsoon built in intensity, whipping up the seas to the point where one of the biggest tactical decisions of the midwatch was picking a course to steer that did not roll everyone out of his chair. It was nothing like the typhoon, but the ship's rolling and pitching in seven- to ten-foot seas added a physical strain to the mental stress of staying awake and effective through the long night hours.

Brian had not seen the captain since the Class Bravo fire in Number One Fire Room, due mostly to his watch rotation. The captain would come into Combat when the action got hot and heavy over the beach in the mornings, but he had not made an appearance after noon except for the MiG incident, which had happened on Austin's watch. The exec kept his finger on the Operations pulse by phone, but since the fire he, too, had not come into Combat when Brian had the watch. Now that he was back on port and starboard watches, Brian saw his departmental officers and chiefs after breakfast at officers' call, in Combat when they stood watch with him, and otherwise not very much.

Brian noticed that Austin was continuing to distance himself. He missed no opportunity to point out any mistakes Brian made in Combat, and he made sure that Brian knew how often he was seeing both the captain and the exec, in contrast to Brian's increasingly infrequent contact. Brian wondered whether he was being deliberately frozen out or if the combination of his watchstanding hours and the fact that Austin was the Operations officer were the real reasons he was not seeing the ship's two most senior officers on a regular basis. He decided just to put his head down and get through it.

After a week of waiting and wondering whether Bullet had decided to try for the bank on his own, Rocky got the call in Combat at 0300. Bullet told him to take a head call and meet him on the mess decks. The surface module was absolutely dead, so Rocky had no problem stepping away from his watch station to meet Bullet. Bullet was leaning against the galley office's door. Rocky wondered whether that's where the bank had been hidden, after all. Shit, he should have come back and looked himself. But now, if Bullet actually could produce the money, he had formulated a plan to nail Bullet once and for all.

"I'm here," Rocky said.

"Yeah," Bullet replied. "So's we."

"We?" Rocky looked around, then saw three of Bullet's larger associates lounging in the shadows at the back of the mess decks. "What's this 'we' shit?" he asked.

"Way it goes, is: What's this 'we' shit, white man?" Bullet smiled. "What it is, they's security. We goin' to mess with some real money. Don't want no surprises."

Rocky stared at the three blacks in the corner. This was a major development: Thus far, Bullet had been careful not to let anyone see him and Rocky meeting on anything other than routine ship's business. Bullet was tightening his lock, and there was nothing Rocky could do about it.

Rocky straightened up. "And why should I go with you, then? Seems to me, I'm the one who might be risking a surprise."

"Uh-uh. These dudes gonna keep the area secure. They ain't gonna be round where we goin' to do it. We cool?"

Rocky looked at the three men again. His plan depended on finding Garlic's stash but not on keeping his half. The damage as to his identity had been done, but the muscle would come up empty if they went for him after he and Bullet uncovered the bank.

"Yeah, okay. Let's do it—I'm supposed to be on watch."

"Okay. We goin' to the Lucky Bag."

"The *Lucky Bag*! You gotta be shitting me."

Bullet grinned at him. "Uh-uh. Ole Garlic, he smart. He want to hide somethin' from the Sheriff, he do it in the Sheriff's own locker. Why I needs you: Only MAAs got keys to the Lucky Bag. You got your keys?"

Rocky nodded and then shook his head in wonder. He followed Bullet back down the main passageway aft of the mess decks to the Lucky Bag. Bullet's hoods split up, one in front, two behind, to make sure no one came down the passageway to cause trouble. When they were safely out of sight, Rocky took out his MAA keys and opened up the Lucky Bag, which was a small locker containing unclaimed laundry, uniforms, or any other lost and found articles. Whenever the Lucky Bag filled up, the CMAA would declare it open and anyone could take whatever was useful to him. A lot of the unclaimed clothes and gear had been tossed around during the typhoon, so the closetlike locker was a mess. Bullet stared in at it for a few seconds, then stepped in, snapped on a flashlight, and started looking around.

"You know where the money actually is?"

"Uh-uh."

"There's an overhead light in there, you want."

"Uh-uh. See better with this. It's gonna be hid, man."

Rocky was following the bouncing beam of light around the darkened locker from the doorway when a low whistle came from the after end of the passageway. Bullet snapped off the light and motioned for Rocky to step into the locker. He pulled the door shut after them and they waited, finally hearing footsteps go by outside, then silence. After a minute, Bullet reopened the door and checked the passageway. All clear.

"See?" he said. "Security. Like I said."

"Yeah, okay. Now where's the fucking money?"

"Doan know. Tryin' to figure where I'd hide it, this had to be my place."

Rocky pulled out his own flashlight and began searching with Bullet. The locker was hot and stuffy. Rocky looked around to see whether the ventilation had been cut off. The diffuser handle was in the open position, but there was no air. While Bullet started rummaging through the pile of used dungarees and shirts on the deck, Rocky ran his light down the vent pipe until he came to an elbow in the four-inch pipe on the back side of the locker. A dented foot-and-a-half-long section of the vent pipe had been temporarily repaired, because there were collars screwed into the pipe at either end of the repaired section.

"Hey," he said. Bullet looked up at where Rocky's light was pointing.

"Oh yeah," he said. "Oh yeah. Thass it." He pulled a Phillips screwdriver out of his electrician's tool kit and began backing out the brass screws holding in the collars.

"How did you find out he hid it in here?" Rocky asked.

"Man said one time. Kept his stash in a lucky place. Didn't mean shit to me till I started thinkin' on it. Lucky place. Lucky Bag. Worth a shot, anyways."

He got the last screw out and backed both collars away from the pipe ends. The eighteen-inch section dropped into his hand. It was stuffed with highly compacted rolls of bills.

"Oh yeah," Bullet said. "Oh yeah."

They set to work counting it. Ever the bean counter, Garlic had segregated the rolls into denominations, which expedited the count. Bullet did the sorting and Rocky did the counting.

"Eighteen thousand and some change," Rocky announced. He had the money in two neat piles.

"Awright." Bullet grinned. "Thass some beer money, anyways."

"Damn straight," Rocky replied. Then he began to roll up his share and stuff the rolls back into the vent pipe.

"Man, what you doin'?" asked Bullet.

"Gonna leave mine here," Rocky said. "It's a safe place, and I've got a key, remember?"

Bullet stared at him suspiciously. Rocky caught the look.

"What do you care?" he said. "You got yours. I just don't like to keep all my money in one stash, that's all. Got several of 'em throughout the ship. That way, somebody gets lucky, I don't go losing my ass. You ought to be doing the same thing."

"Doan you go worrin' 'bout me, man. My shit's plenny secure."

"Well, okay, then. Anyhow, I'm gonna put this pipe back together. Why don't you split now. And take your guys with you—I'll feel safer."

"Shee-it," spat Bullet, gathering up his money. He stuck his head out the door, then stepped out. Rocky looked over at him as he finished putting back the section of vent pipe.

"Easy pickings, man," he said. "Smile. It'll do you good."

After Bullet had gone, Rocky secured the Lucky Bag and, watching his back, returned to Combat to resume his watch. He got off at 0600, had breakfast, and then hit his tree for the morning. Before lunch, he stopped in to see Chief Jackson, who was talking to Martinez in the Sheriff's office.

"Got something for you on Bullet, maybe," he said, closing the door behind him. Chief Martinez gave Jackson an alarmed look.

"I filled him in, Louie," said Jackson. "Figured another brain wouldn't hurt." He looked over at Rocky expectantly. Rocky noticed that Martinez did not seem too happy with having some help. No matter. He would be. Rocky had thought long and hard about how to use that cash stash to nail Bullet.

"I think I have a line on where Bullet keeps his money," Rocky said. "You'll never believe it."

"Try me," Jackson said.

"The fucking Lucky Bag."

"What!"

"Yeah. I heard him in the chow line talking to one of those group fours that hang around with him. Said you want to hide something from the cops, you hide it in the police station. Guy asked if he meant your office. Bullet says, 'Naw, man, someplace that only the MAAs have access to.' I figured out he was talking about the Lucky Bag, so I went and searched it. Found a vent pipe with over nine thousand bucks in it."

"Jesus Christ, no shit!" Jackson exclaimed. "But where the hell would an electrician get a key? Only MAAs have keys."

"From Garlic, I figure," Rocky said. "You said they were partners. Remember, Garlic was mess decks MAA. The Supply Department office keeps all the keys—all he had to do was ask them for one as the mess decks MAA and they would've given him a key to the Lucky Bag. There's nothing valuable in there."

"Yeah," Jackson nodded, working it out. Rocky waited for them to make the next jump. "Hey," Jackson said, looking at Martinez, "you know what this means? We can set the fucker up—catch him with his money, we got his ass."

"How we goin' to do that?" asked Martinez. Jackson paused to think it out. Rocky was ready with a suggestion.

"Bullet does the mids in Main Control. You get the word to Bullet one night when he's on watch that you're going to tag E Division for a working party. He's the E Division LPO, so he's the guy you'd call. You need three hands to clean out the Lucky Bag first thing next morning. After the typhoon, place is a fucking mess; everything needs to be sorted out and restowed. But you also tell him you need everything out of there because you're gonna get a welder in there to repair a jury-rigged vent pipe, to get some air in there. Place stinks, which it does. Going to fix it with a proper weld. That's the main reason we have to get all those clothes out of there—you know, fire hazard for the welder. He hears that—"

"Yeah," said Jackson. "He hears that and he'll know he's only a got a coupla hours to get his money out of there." Martinez was nodding his head slowly.

"Right. You pick the night, Chief. I'll show you where the money is in that vent pipe. He has to go for it or else lose all his profits."

"Fuck, I like it," Jackson said, rubbing his hands. "Catch that bastard with a big chunka change, we got his ass."

"It's even better than that, Sheriff," Rocky said. "Some of that money looks like the shit you marked."

Two nights later, the E-2 saw the ghosts. It happened at 0115, almost an hour after the watch had changed hands in Combat and Brian's watch team was fixing its second mug of coffee and preparing to go into the stay-awake routine. The E-2 was headed back to the carrier, descending from 25,000 feet toward Yankee Station, when its backseaters detected five radar contacts headed out over the southern Gulf from the lower portion of North Vietnam. They immediately slapped unknown air track symbols on them, which flashed around the Gulf to all the NTDS-equipped ships. In Red Crown, Garuda Barry yelled at the Cave.

"Track Supe, what's this shit? There's no video under those symbols. You doin' that or is that the E-two?"

"Track Supe, aye, and that's a negative. Those are E-two tracks."

Brian stared down at the scope. There were five unknown symbols, all grouped together and all headed due

512

east off the coast of North Vietnam toward the Red Chinese territories on Hainan Island. Their projected tracks would take them between the carriers on Yankee Station and the Red Crown station. On that track, they threatened none of the ships unless they made a sudden turn to the north or south. SWIC ordered the duty air controller to execute special tracking, then expanded his own scope to enlarge the area around the tracks. He checked the SPS-48 displays and also the secondary air-search radar, the SPS-40. There was no video visible under the symbols.

"Fuckin' ghosts is what this is," muttered Garuda.

"Ghosts?"

"Yes, sir, radar ghosts. The Gulf is famous for 'em, especially when the northeast monsoon comes along. Commies must be putting some shit in the air or something, but the radars start seeing contacts that aren't there. Sometimes you even get what looks like video."

"I better call the Old Man."

"That's a roger. But tell him we think they're ghosts. The E-two radar is famous for this shit. I'd talk to staff on the Yankee Station, but the Wager Bird's gone home. I'll talk to the guys in the E-two."

While Garuda conferred over secure UHF voice with the E-2, Brian called the captain in his cabin, but he could not get a reply. He called the exec on the internal admin phones.

"XO."

"XO, this is Mr. Holcomb in Combat. I tried to call the captain but couldn't raise him. We've got five unknown air tracks in the system heading from North Vietnam to Hainan Island. They're E-two tracks and Garuda says they're probably ghosts."

"Okay. It's northeast monsoon. But put a Spook Fifty-five on one just to make sure. If there's no video in the gate, just watch 'em," the exec said, yawning.

"Uh, yes, sir, roger that, and do you know where the captain is? I tried the bat phone, but there's no answer."

There was a slight pause at the other end. "I think he may have taken a pill or something. Said he hadn't been sleeping well with all this bouncing around; the doc was going to give him something. Consider the report made unless something breaks."

"Aye, aye, sir," Brian said, and hung up the phone.

"These are ghosts, all right," said Garuda. "Even the E-two guys think so now."

"Anyone have skin?"

"We don't, but the E-two has video, but it's too good, too perfect, all in formation, line abreast like that, all the same speed. The carrier radars don't see 'em either. There's no airfield down there, and they'd never pull a stunt like that with the E-two up and the BARCAP on-station—they know we'd nail their asses."

"SWIC, Track Supe, the E-two has lost video on the air unknowns. Dropping tracks from the system."

"SWIC, aye. Like I said, ghosts."

The hubbub in Combat died down as the word went out that the unknowns were ghosts and not a formation of enemy aircraft. The air controller was explaining to the BARCAP pilots why they could not go roaring down the Gulf in hot pursuit. The E-two continued on its way home to the carrier. Brian refreshed his coffee and brought Garuda a refill.

"Weird stuff," Brian observed.

"Yeah. There's talk that the original Gulf of Tonkin incident, back in '64, was all about ghosts. It was fall and the northeast monsoon was up. There're people who say there never were any PT boats or anything else out there that night."

"I've heard that story. I think *Maddox* and *Turner Joy* had PT boats—I've seen the pictures. But the second one, with *Morton* and *Edwards,* that was at night. They shot off a couple of hundred rounds of five-inch. Said they held good solid video, and their sonars even heard screw beats, but they never found any sign of wreckage, oil, debris—nothing. And nothing was ever sighted visually."

"Yes, sir, but as I remember it, that incident, the second one, was the one they went in and bombed North Vietnam for, like the very next morning."

"Well, they're Commies. They probably deserved it—if not for that, then for something else."

"I hear that," Garuda said with a grin.

A few minutes later, the door to Combat opened and the captain came into D and D. Brian saw him first and did a double take. Speaking of ghosts. The captain's face was haggard and pale, almost white, scored with deep lines and shadows. His hair looked thinner, and even the Navy foul-weather jacket could not disguise the fact that he had lost even more weight since Brian had last seen him. He wore khaki pants and his bedroom slippers. He held on to the back of his captain's chair to steady himself against the ship's slow rolling.

"Captain's in Combat," Brian announced to the world after finding his voice. People turned to look and the noise level began to diminish.

"XO tells me you had some ghosts?" the captain said. Even his voice sounded thinner, Brian thought.

Brian explained the E-two's contacts and the sequence of events. The captain asked whether Brian had put a Spook 55 radar on the tracks. Brian remembered the exec's instruction.

"No, sir, we didn't. The E-two downed the tracks before we could do it and we had no video to designate to. Neither the forty-eight or the forty radars saw anything, nor did the carrier air-search radars."

"Okay. Next time, even if we think they're ghosts, assign them to the missile systems and take a look, anyway. In the northeast monsoon, you never know what the radars are doing. Everything else quiet?"

"Yes, sir. So far. Air ops secured about an hour ago."

"Okay. And if you can't raise me by phone, always send someone down to the cabin."

"Yes, sir. I did call you, and then—"

"You did the correct thing, but next time, send someone down."

"Aye, aye, sir."

The captain looked around Combat for a few seconds and then walked out. When he had gone, Garuda let out a low whistle.

Brian nodded. "Looks like hell, doesn't he?" Brian said. "I wonder what's going on there."

Garuda took a long drag on his cigarette and shook his head. "I don't know, but that man looks sick."

"I haven't actually laid eyes on him since the mast cases with the missile techs."

"Come to think of it, neither have I. What with these midwatches and everything . . ."

"Yeah. Austin says he sees him several times a day for messages and ops briefings. I should ask Vince."

Garuda turned around in his console chairs and sequenced through the remaining tracks in the system. The 48 picture was unnaturally clear as the northeast monsoon streamed clean, cold Manchurian air across the Gulf and down into the humid river deltas of Southeast Asia. Even though they were over one hundred miles down the Gulf, the carriers could be seen as points of video under their link symbols. The ridges of the coastal mountains in North and South Vietnam were also visible as ripples of amber light on the screens. The BARCAP Phantoms stayed at the far southern end of their barrier line, also clearly visible as pinpoints of light under their Combat Air Patrol symbols. Garuda switched presentations to the SPS-10 surface-search radar and brought the display range down to sixty miles. The coast of North Vietnam jumped into view, as did the point of light representing the South SAR station ship, the guided-missile frigate *Preble,* fifty miles to the southeast.

"Even the ten is a perfect picture tonight, double its usual range," Brian said.

Garuda nodded and switched displays again, this time to the SPS-40 radar, the ship's secondary air-search radar. The 40 radar painted air contacts as large fuzzy blips instead of the pinpoints of the digital display 48, but even the 40 was much clearer than usual, showing the BARCAP Phantoms as relatively small video smears moving along the much larger video cloud bank of the North Vietnamese coast. Garuda went back to the 48 radar and the 250-mile-range scale.

"*Ichiban* good radar tonight," he declared. "Now if only we didn't have to rock and roll so much to get it—"

"Yeah, I'm getting tired of this bouncing around. It's not enough to make you seasick, just enough to keep you tense all the time trying to stay steady. We get this for how long?"

"The northeast monsoon runs until March or April, and then it gets hot and still again."

The radio messenger came into Combat with the night's stack of traffic. "Yuk," Brian said. "I guess I'd better go work the paper mountain."

Brian sat down at the evaluator table, wedging his chair between the SWIC console and the support stanchion to keep it in one place and pulling the burn bag close. He sipped some cold coffee, made a face, and started in on the four-inch-high stack of messages, scanning each one and discarding most of them into the burn bag. Occasionally, he would set one aside, scribbling a note on it as action or info to one of the other department heads.

Garuda busied himself at the computer-control key sets, cycling through the system-monitoring panels and checking on the digital health and status of each of three big Univacs one deck below in computer control. HooDoo, the duty AIC, gave an occasional control order to the BARCAP while playing idly with the button controls on his key set and waiting for the first tanker to come up from Yankee Station. Throughout the rest of Combat, people settled into the nightly routine. Over in weapons, Brian could see Chief Hallowell, who was holding down both the FCSC and EC consoles while the first class, FTM1 Barker, was down in missile plot, supposedly holding training with the junior man on watch, FTM3 Warren. Brian made a mental note to go down there later on during the mid and see what was actually going on. Maybe they would do some trial designations with the BARCAP after the first tanker had come and gone. He shook his head, trying to clear out the cobwebs. Goddamn midwatch. The afternoon had been hectic, with several raids going in over the southern provinces and one actual SAR operation that had tied up both helos for over two hours with no results. The messages began to blur as he stared at them, and he wondered whether maybe he could read with one eye while he rested the other, just for a moment.

Over in surface, RD1 Rockheart was having no trouble staying awake. He looked at his watch again. Anytime now, they ought to have his ass. The chiefs had set tonight as the night, after Jackson had gone to see the money for himself. Finding some of the marked bills had made the chief's day. Jackson was supposed to make the call right after 0130. He and Martinez were going to hide themselves in the after officers' head, which was right across from the Lucky Bag. They would let Bullet get into the locker, get the vent open, and then nail his ass.

Rocky originally had counted on Bullet's greed to entice him to go for the hidden cash, but then he had decided that there was a decent chance Bullet would assume Rocky knew about the welder and would have removed the cash himself. So he had added a wrinkle. When Jackson had called him in Combat and told him that the deal was on for anytime after 0130, Rocky had stepped into the chart house forward of Combat and called Bullet in a faked panic. He told him that this time, he needed a favor—a big favor.

"The fucking Sheriff's got a wild hair up his ass. He just told me he's gonna have a working party clean out the Lucky Bag and then he's gonna have a welder fix that vent pipe. I can't get out of Combat—we've got too much shit going on tonight. I need you to go up there and get my money, man. Get it out of there before those fuckers find it. I've left a key in the CO-two extinguisher rack right by the scullery. Will you do it?"

Bullet had laughed softly. "Yeah, man. He already call me. Some of my guys gotta do the cleanin' out. But lass I heard, you wasn't too secure with me and my dudes. How come you trustin' me with nine grand all of a sudden, you tell me that."

"Hey, man, those are scary guys you got hanging around. I don't know those guys. But more to the point, the Sheriff finds that money, there's gonna be hell to pay around here."

"You the one with the key; sounds to me like you'd be payin' it 'fore I did."

Rocky, mousetrapped, had no answer for that, other than his fervent hope that, if nothing else, greed would rule: There would be no way that Rocky could *make* Bullet give the money back. For a long minute, the line had been silent.

"OK, man. I do it. Where that key again?"

Rocky had told him and then thanked him warmly.

"I owe you, man."

"Sixty-forty?" Bullet had asked slyly.

"Yeah. Fuck yeah. It'll be worth it."

Rocky looked at his watch again. Anytime now. Any fucking time now.

50

"That must be a damn interesting message," said Garuda as Brian snapped awake. "You been readin' it for three minutes now." Garuda was grinning and holding out a fresh mug of coffee. Brian shook his head again, put the message down, and reached for the coffee. He looked at his watch: 0230. Christ. Three and a half hours to go. The ebb of human consciousness—0230. Garuda sat back down at his console, keeping one hand on his coffee mug to prevent it from rolling onto the deck plates.

"Tanker inbound to BARCAP," reported the AIC. "I'm gonna hold 'em at the southern end, hook 'em up, and then tank 'em in the northerly direction."

"SWIC, aye."

"Let's do a trial missile designation on the tanker," Brian said.

"SWIC, aye. AIC, call your tanker and tell him we need to shine on him with fire control for a test."

"AIC, aye."

The AIC spoke briefly to both the BARCAP pilots and the tanker driver, then gave a thumbs-up to the SWIC, who fired off an engagement designation to weapons module, following it up with the announcement that this was a drill. The chief, who had heard Brian's order, leaned forward and processed the designation; the directors rumbled into action. They had a lock-on in fifteen seconds with both systems.

"Give 'em CWI."

"CWI shining."

"AIC, get an alert report."

"Tanker has SAM warning lights, and so do the BARCAP."

"Down CWI."

"CWI is down."

"Break track; break engage; centerline your systems. Good track."

"FCSC, aye. Warren says they landed right in the gate. He didn't have to do anything."

"Tell him well done," Brian said. "Guy's been catching some shit lately."

"I heard some of the badasses been picking on him," said Garuda.

"Yeah. That and all this extra training. He's a good kid, but I'll be glad when we get some replacements for the three shitbirds. At least the systems are seeing well tonight."

"Given this atmosphere, I'm not surprised," said Garuda. "I haven't seen it this clear all cruise."

They watched the symbol of the tanker merge with the symbols of the BARCAP Phantoms, and then the AIC reported laconically that he had them hooked up. Brian thought about what that brief report meant: One hundred and twenty miles away, at 42,000 feet in the icy dark, the two Phantom pilots had pulled astern of the tanker aircraft, an A-6 with fuel tanks strapped under the wings, found the twin refueling booms, and driven their fueling probes into the cones, where they would stay mated to the tanker for twenty minutes while refueling. The AIC had effected the rendezvous at the southern end of the BARCAP barrier line and was now bringing the mated trio up the line toward Red Crown.

"Tanker is sweet," reported the AIC, announcing that both Phantoms were able to connect and draw fuel. Sometimes one or the other would not be able to get fuel; in that case, the tanker would be reported as sour.

"The big event for the night," Brian said, sighing.

"That's as big as we want it; anything else that goes down at this hour of the morning is by definition bad, and I'm too old for bad on a midwatch," replied Garuda, reaching for the umpteenth cigarette.

Down in the after officers' head, Martinez and Jackson waited to see what would happen. They had been waiting almost an hour, and Martinez was beginning to have some doubts. Like every head in the ship, this one had inadequate ventilation and stank of running seawater and more noxious things. The chiefs had backed out two screws in the joiner bulkhead between the head and the passageway. The resulting peepholes were tiny but gave a direct view of the locker across the passageway.

"We could be here all goddamn night," Martinez grumped. "Man's got until reveille to get his ass up here."

"Keep it down. And I don't think so," Jackson said. "He'll come before the watch change at 0345; too many people up and walking around after that." He peered through the screw hole in the door again. "Speaking of the devil," he said softly.

The boatswain leaned down to look through his own peephole. Bullet was bent over the door to the Lucky Bag, working the key. He got it opened, looked both ways up and down the passageway, stepped inside, and closed the door. Jackson had been holding his breath and released it now that Bullet was out of earshot.

"Okay," he said. "Now we wait."

"Not too fuckin' long," growled the boatswain.

Brian looked at his watch again: 0245. Wow, fifteen whole minutes had elapsed. Wasn't the time just thundering by. He put his finger in his coffee cup. Time for a reheat. The intercom spoke.

"SWIC, Track Supe."

"SWIC, aye."

"Track Supe, my forty operator reports a clobbered sector on the forty."

"Jamming? You gotta be shitting me."

"That's what he says. I'm lookin' at it, and there's something definitely fucked up with it."

Garuda switched over to the SPS-40 display while Brian watched over his shoulder. In place of the clear display of a half hour ago, there was now what looked like a cloud of snow over the landmass of North Vietnam.

"Supe, that does look like jamming. The forty operator got ECCM fixes in?" asked Garuda.

"Track Supe, and that's a negative. That's a clean screen."

"Fixes?" asked Brian.

"Yes, sir, the forty operator can put antijamming fixes into the system to clear it up. That sure as shit does look like jamming, though. One way to prove it."

"Put the fixes in, you mean."

"Roger that. If it's not jamming, the fixes don't do shit. Supe."

"Track Supe."

"Enter fixes, serial order."

"Supe."

Garuda looked over his shoulder. "You better report this to the Old Man. I'd call Austin, too. Jamming is news. Wish the E-two was still up. I'll get the Cave to encode a jamming report and get it down to the carriers."

Brian went over to the evaluator's desk, grabbed the bat phone, and held the buzzer down. He stared at the 40 radar presentation over Garuda's shoulder and saw what appeared to be differences in the scope presentation as the operator back in the Cave put in one fix at a time to see which one might work. He buzzed the phone again, but there was still no reply. "Send someone down," the captain had said.

"Surface," he yelled across D and D.

"Surface, aye," replied the supervisor, RD1 Rockheart.

"Send a guy down to the captain's cabin, wake the Old Man up, and ask him to call D and D on the bat phone. I can't wake him up."

"Surface, aye."

Brian hung up the bat phone and called Austin's number on the admin phone. Austin answered after three rings; Brian told him what they had. Austin expressed his disbelief but said he would be right up. Brian hung up and saw the 40 radar presentation go suddenly clear.

"Whoa, Supe. That did it," Garuda said.

"Track Supe, affirma-hotchee. That's the antijitter fix. Means some Commie is definitely fuckin' with us."

"And every other forty in the Gulf should have seen it, too," muttered Garuda. "There shoulda been some other reports of this." He switched down to the sixty-mile scale to see if it made any difference.

"There would be if Green was up, but everyone else's in the same boat—they have to encode the report first before going out on clear HF nets. Just like us."

Garuda shook his head wonderingly. "But why the forty? Bad guys gotta know we use the forty-eight as primary, not the fucking forty."

"You're not looking at the forty-eight right now, are you?" observed Brian, a sudden tingling apprehension beginning to intrude at the edge of his mind.

"Oh, fuck me," whispered Garuda, switching back to the forty-eight just as a chorus of late-detect alerts began to sound on the consoles in the Cave. There, at the very edge of the screen, just off the coast of North Vietnam, were four bright pips of light moving in from the edge of the screen—right at them. As Brian stared in growing horror, the first unknown symbols popped up on top of the incoming video.

Garuda didn't hesitate. He smashed some buttons and made all four unknowns hostiles, then sent the first engagement orders over to FCSC.

"This is a no-shitter, everybody," he yelled his voice rising. "Bandits, inbound, taking with birds! We have a *fucking raid*!"

Brian leaned over the evaluator's desk and pushed the bat phone's buzzer down, mashing it down in groups of three, the agreed-upon panic signal. With the other hand, he grabbed the 1MC microphone and shouted into it.

"Captain to D and D. I say again, Captain to D and D! We have an inbound air raid. All hands prepare for multiple-missile launch. Officer of the Deck, come right to three-zero-zero, speed twenty—NOW!"

"SWIC, FCSC. System One is locked on; having a problem with System Two. Range to bogey one is forty-seven miles and closing. Launcher is loading. Request batteries released when ready."

Garuda twisted around in his chair and looked at Brian, who nodded vigorously while repeating his announcement over the 1MC.

"SWIC, Track Supe, Alfa Whiskey is asking in the clear if hostile tracks are—"

"Tell him they better Hong Kong fucking believe it, and we are taking with birds!"

"SWIC, FCSC, range to bogey one is forty miles. Launcher is loaded and assigned. I have video in the gate, taking track two-one-seven-seven with two-bird salvo."

"SWIC, aye, take in sequence. Where the fuck is System Two!"

FCSC's reply was buried in the thunder of a Terrier missile blasting off the forecastle launcher, followed seconds later by a second missile. The ship began vibrating as the engines came up to twenty knots and heeling over to port as she came about to the northwest to give the missile directors a clearer field of tracking vision.

"System Two is back up, taking track two-one-seven-nine with System Two. Range is thirty-five miles. Bogeys inbound and low. Solid video in the gates!"

"SWIC, Track Supe, Alfa Whiskey says to verify that we are not engaging ghosts."

Garuda had to think about that for a second, but then FCSC shouted a mark intercept on track 2177, video merge in the tracking gate, evaluate hit. One down, Brian thought. FCSC then redesignated System One to bogey three and assigned the launcher to System Two. Brian continued to buzz the captain's cabin as sounds of people running up ladders became audible. Then there was the roar of another missile leaving the launcher, followed by its brother as System Two launched against bogey two.

Two engaged, two to go, and the fuckers are already inside thirty miles, Brian thought frantically. Not enough directors! They're too close! The ship's hull was trembling now as the snipes, galvanized by the 1MC announcements and the roar of missile launches, poured on the fuel oil. Two of the AICs came crashing through the front door to Combat, puffing from the ladders.

"SWIC, Track Supe, Alfa Whiskey says they hold no video in our sector, but they do report jamming on their forty radars. Alfa Whiskey wants—"

"Fuck Alfa Whiskey!" shouted Garuda. "I'm fucking busy here!"

"SWIC, FCSC, System Two holding good track on hostile track two-one-seven-nine. Stand by for intercept—mark intercept, track two-one-seven-nine!"

The bitch box sounded off at that moment, reporting explosions visible off the port side on the horizon. Brian thought fast. Where the fuck was the captain? For that matter, where was the XO? Or Austin? Surely they had heard the word. At that moment, the door to Combat banged open again and Austin came through, wearing only khaki trousers, his seaboots, and a T-shirt. For once, he looked disheveled.

"SWIC, FCSC, assigning System Two to bogey four, track number two-one-five-six. This is gonna be a close motherfucker; these bastards are into eighteen miles! Warren, calm down, now stay on it, just stay on it!"

"Get on that fucker!" yelled Garuda, switching down his range scale to stay with the picture. The pile of messages slid off the evaluator's table as the ship bounded onto the new course. The AICs stood helpless at their console, the BARCAP still mated for refueling, which everyone realized now was no accident and the air around the bogeys filled with American SAMS. The CAP were out of the game.

"SWIC, FCSC, mark intercept, System One, evaluate bogey three hit." A pause as the chief pressed his earphones to his head. Then he shook his head, an agonized expression on his face. "SWIC, System Two can't get on, can't get on. Warren's taking it in manual. Range is ten miles! Fuck, he's gonna get in; he's gonna get in! Range is eight miles, System Two can't—System Two is *on!*" The chief assigned the launcher, waited three seconds for the launcher-loaded light, and then mashed the firing key almost through the console and another Terrier left the rails as more people burst through the front door into Combat. The stink of booster smoke came through the air-conditioning vents as the ship turned across the wind.

"We're fucked!" yelled FCSC. "He's inside minimum range. He's—"

Austin, who had been standing next to Brian, gave a cry of fear and bolted out of D and D toward the front door of CIC, knocking down two sailors who had just come through the door. Brian stared down at SWIC's console and watched the final hostile symbol merge with their own. The fourth bogey was inside the minimum range of the missile system and the ship's radars.

There was a single instant of total silence and then came a thundering boom very close off the port side of the ship. The port-side bulkhead of Combat ballooned inward in a blast of torn aluminum plating, dust, and debris. Amid the noise of shrieking metal, a long black object crashed right through the electronic warfare NTDS console, obliterating the operator and a second man in a bloody cloud, and then smashed up against a second console before falling to the deck plates. The impact blew down ventilation ducts all over Combat, deforming the overhead of CIC enough to explode most of the fluorescent bulbs out of their holders, adding a cloud of phosphorus to the blizzard of debris flying around the space. Almost simultaneously, the entire ship shuddered with a cruiser-sized gut punch, the impact of something very big striking the port side, followed by the bellowing roar of an explosion back aft. The few remaining lights in Combat flickered out, on, and then back out, leaving only the battle lanterns to penetrate the clouds of dust hanging in the air. The sound of the ship's GQ alarm sounded through the initial silence, joined by a shocked chorus of groans and cries of injured men.

Everyone in D and D had been thrown on the deck except Garuda, who had snapped on his seat belt when the ship made its turn to unmask the missile directors. Brian pulled himself out from under the evaluator's table and looked around for Austin. He finally saw him lying unconscious by the front door to Combat, his face covered in blood. The FCSC, Chief Hallowell, was standing, bent double over the back of his console chair as if he was trying to throw up. Brian tried to clear his head, but there was too much smoke and noise in Combat as men shouted for help or yelled in pain. He heard the incongruous sound of spraying water, until he remembered that the consoles were water-cooled. Some cooling lines must be severed, he thought, trying to pull himself together. He had a cut on the back of one hand, but otherwise he seemed to be uninjured. He looked over at Garuda, who was spitting shards of glass from a fluorescent bulb out of his mouth while wrestling with his radio headset. Brian heard him trying to get contact with the rest of the intercom stations in Combat. Several men from surface were over on the port side trying to tend to some of the injured. Chief Hallowell straightened up and discovered Austin. He went over to check out the extent of the Ops officer's injuries.

"Combat, Bridge!" The frightened-sounding voice of Jack Folsom came over the bitch box. Brian keyed the box. He felt the ship slowing down, her bows beginning to mush into the seas. There was an ominous roaring noise like a firebox coming from the midships area, then a blast of high pressure steam from the after stack.

"Combat, aye, Jack. What the hell happened out there?"

"Our last missile hit something right off the port side. I think it was a MiG, but we were blind from the booster flash. I think the MiG hit the water and then hit the ship. What happened in Combat?"

"Something came through the bulkhead. Maybe it's part of the MiG. I'll have to go check. We have personnel casualties and no power and the place is full of smoke and dust. I can't see much from D and D."

"Do you need a damage-control team in there?"

Hearing the sound of CO_2 extinguishers going, Brian shook his head. "No, I think we need the docs in here, unless there's bigger problems down below. One of 'em, anyway. I don't see any fires, just smoke. Hey, is the captain out there?"

"That's a negative, and I'll get the baby doc in there. The XO was out here, but he went down somewhere amidships. He thinks we got hit down there, gonna go check it out."

"Rog, lemme go see what we got here. Austin is knocked out, in case anyone's wondering."

"Bridge, aye."

Brian moved over to Garuda's console.

"We got anything left up here?" he asked.

527

"Shit no. Snipes have cut the power, or else the local panels went out. The radars are all down, and guys're all over the place in the Cave. I think I'm outta business here, boss. You need a dressing on that hand."

"Yeah. Okay, make a quick survey of Combat. Tell me what we got in the way of people hurt and stuff broke. Have Radio get me a working voice circuit so we can let the staff know we've been hit up here."

"That was a hell of a bang amidships. What the fuck was it?"

"Bridge thinks our last bird winged bogey four but that he kamikazed us. XO and the damage-control people are working that prob. Go see what we got here."

Garuda grunted, unhitched himself from his chair, fished in his foul-weather jacket for a flashlight, and headed into the gloom of the Cave, picking his way through the jumble of deck plates and sprawled men. Brian joined the chief in trying to revive Austin, but he was out cold. The chief passed Brian a small square bandage, which he taped over his hand. A white-faced young radarman appeared next to them. His uniform was clean and not covered in dust and bits of insulation like those of everyone else in Combat. His eyes were huge and he looked terrified.

"S-sir?"

"Yeah?"

"Sir, I was sent down to get the Old—uh, I mean, to get the captain to call you? Just before we got hit?"

"Oh yes. Did you get him?"

"Sir, the door was locked. I knocked and I waited around, 'cause you sounded like it was real important, and I guess it was, seein'—"

"Yes. Right. Okay, but you never actually talked to him? The cabin door was locked?"

"Yes, sir, it sure was. Sir, are we—"

"I don't know what happens next, sailor. I suggest you get back into surface and help the guys who're hurt."

"Aye, aye, sir." The radarman stepped back into the smoky shadow that was the surface module. Brian saw several people being attended to in the gloom. He felt totally isolated in the darkened Combat. The contrast was incredible—one minute the heart and nerve center of the ship and all the air operations for two hundred miles around, and now just a bunch of dazed guys staggering around and picking themselves up in the murk of smoke and dust. The debris began to shift as the ship's rolling increased. Definitely going DIW, Brian thought. Then Garuda reappeared, his face set in a mask of shock.

"Garuda?" Brian asked.

"You won't fuckin' believe what we got back there. I gotta sit down." He fished for a cigarette, spilling three before he got one lighted and shoved into his mouth. I guess a little more smoke won't hurt anything, Brian thought. Garuda picked up the evaluator's chair and turned it right side up.

"First off, we got two, maybe three guys got fucking pulverized. I mean, they're spread all over the fucking EW module, and nobody can even tell who they are—were. I'm talkin' Waring blender here, okay?" Garuda swallowed hard before continuing. "Then we got about eight other guys got thrown around when the bulkhead caved in, buncha broken bones, cut heads, bleedin' every-goddamn-where. They've got every first-aid kit in Combat opened up back there. Some a those guys need a swab, not a bandage, and we need the fuckin' corpsman up here right fuckin' now, so—"

"Okay, okay, I get the picture. I've already told the bridge that. They're working it, so first aid is the best we can—"

"No, that ain't it. What's got me and everybody back there pissin' our pants is this big black bomb that's sittin' on the deck plates next to the ASW module's door."

Brian felt his vision veer; an icy wave of fear gripped his stomach. He felt the blood leaving his face.

"A *bomb*? Is it live?"

"I didn't go over and ask it, okay, but one a the guys, useta be an aviation bosun, said it's makin' a noise inside and it doesn't have no arming wire hanging on the tail. No wire usually means it's armed. We gotta get everybody the fuck outta here right now. That thing goes off—"

"Yeah, got it. Okay. I don't think anyone in the front

part of CIC knows this, so let's get the wounded moved out, orderly fashion, before there's a panic, and then—''

Garuda got a grip on himself. "Right. Hey, Chief Hallowell. C'mere. We got us a little leadership situation here.''

The chief paled as Garuda explained what they had in the back part of Combat. Garuda instructed the chief to clear the Cave out but to send all the able-bodied men over to the port side through the surface module to help carry out the wounded from EW and ASW modules.

"They may all wanna take a quick hike, but we can't go leavin' the wounded, okay? That's what I meant by leadership. Nobody able-bodied goes outta here without helpin' the disabled. Got it, Chief?''

The chief could not help giving a wishful glance at the front door to Combat, but he nodded and headed into the Cave. Garuda shook his head in disgust, took a single tremendous drag on his cigarette, and heaved himself out of his chair, dropping the butt onto the deck for the first time in his career. "You better tell the bridge what we got here; this kinda changes things.''

"Right. Then I'll come in there to help.''

"Bring your barf bag. You ain't gonna believe what it looks like back there.''

Brian called the bridge on the bitch box and told Folsom to pick up the captain's bat phone.

"Sir?''

"I want privacy, goddamn it. Do it.''

While he was waiting, both the doc and the baby doc came into Combat. Brian pointed to the port side of CIC and the two corpsmen rushed through without a word, bags in hand. There was another roar of high-pressure steam from back aft, a long, sustained exhalation from a 1,200-psi boiler. This time, it didn't quit. A moment later, Brian pressed the handset key. "You there?''

"Yes, sir?''

Brian told him what they had. "Oh Jesus,'' gasped Folsom. "Now what the hell do we do?''

"Get word through the damage-control circuits to the XO. Let him know we got a serious problem up here and that we're clearing people off this level.''

"Jesus Christ," Folsom groaned. "XO's up to his ass, Mr. Holcomb. We got us a major fire amidships—Class Bravo jet fuel it looks like—and we got big-time flooding. That MiG hit us on the waterline, port side, just forward of Mount Thirty-two. XO's directing one of the repair teams; chief engineer has the other one. Two Firehouse has been shut down; Damage Control Central thinks it's flooded to the mark. We've got the forward plant intact, but power distribution is all fucked up 'cause the guy hit us amidships. None of my radios work and I don't know what the fuck to do about this—"

"All right, Jack, calm down. We're getting all the people out of here. You pass the word to evacuate Radio Central and all the spaces beneath Combat, and the signal-bridge people above. Just draw a mental picture of the spaces that surround CIC and get everybody away. Assemble them down on the fo'c'sle. That's probably the best place."

"Should I clear the bridge?"

"Yeah, you probably should. You stay for now—you're the OOD. Keep a phone talker and your JOOD, and tell Main Engineering Control that you're having to clear out. And Jack?"

"Yes, sir?" Folsom sounded thoroughly frightened now.

"Keep it orderly. I don't want a panic. We may need those people for damage control, especially if this thing goes off."

"Aye, aye, sir."

Brian hung up. He tried not to think of the bomb sitting some twenty feet away behind the bulkhead of the EW module and fought off a very strong urge to bolt out of CIC himself. Then Garuda appeared, leading a file of battered sailors through D and D, two able-bodied men on either side of each injured man. Nobody was talking as they concentrated on stepping through all the debris on the deck. It was clear that some of the men were seriously injured. The last three men in the line were being carried between three pairs of the biggest radarmen. Rockheart and Chief Hallowell brought up the rear, along with the two corpsmen, who were starting an IV on a man with a bandaged head as he was being carried through D and D. All of them seemed to be trying to walk without making any noise.

"Take 'em all right on down to the fo'c'sle, Chief," Brian ordered. "Garuda, you stay with me. I need to get some kind of radio on the air and make a report to Yankee Station."

"Right, boss. May have to go get one of the emergency HF jobs out of Radio."

"Shit. I just ordered Radio Central evacuated. I think we gotta get all the people away from that bomb in there first, and then we can try to work the Ops problem. Now look, you want to go below, I'll under—"

"Fuck that noise. Combat's my space. I ain't goin' nowhere."

"Okay, then. See if the chief radioman is still in Central. Have him break out the emergency radios and get one down to the forecastle. Somebody in the link had to see us go off the air, and the BARCAP are probably wondering what the hell's happened to their controller, so we're gonna get help up here, even at this hour of the morning. I'm gonna take a tour, make sure we've got everybody."

51

Down below in the after officers' passageway, the two chiefs had collided with each other as they tried to get out the door when the 1MC let go with its scarifying announcement. They caught a glimpse of Bullet as he hightailed it aft, empty-handed from the look of him. Both chiefs hesitated for about one second, then ran forward to their GQ stations.

Jackson had been on the first step of the ladder going up to the captain's cabin level when the unmistakable roar of a Terrier lifting off from the forecastle had stopped him for a second. Up to that instant, even as he had sprinted through the passageways, his mind had been filled with bitter disappointment over missing Bullet. The bastard had shown up, just like Rockheart thought he would, had been in the Lucky Bag, probably with his hands on the goddamn money when whatever the hell was going down had started. *Shit!*

Then another missile had let go, then another and another. His brain cleared right up. Jesus, this sounded serious. The sounds of other men pounding up the ladders behind him spurred him back into action and he headed for the bridge. Unlike the other chiefs, who were all specialists in Engineering, Weapons, or Operations and who thus had specific GQ stations, the chief master-at-arms did not. For peacetime exercises, he would normally lay up to the bridge with the exec, there to be dispatched to do whatever needed doing. But if the ship had already been hit, his principal duty was to make a sweep of the ship to ensure that wounded or unconscious men were not left behind in damaged or smoke-filled compartments. His secondary duty was to pick up any stragglers and herd them to the nearest damage-control party.

Another Terrier let go, followed by its twin—dual launches. This was a no-shitter, as the snipes would say. He had been rounding the base of the final ladder leading up to the bridge when he had heard another missile launch, followed by a loud booming noise close aboard to port. One second later, he had felt the first impact of the bomb hitting Combat. He was frozen in his tracks when the second, much larger impact had bounced him back off the ladder and up against a bulkhead. He had rolled back out onto the deck of the passageway as the ship heeled first to starboard and then back to port. Stunned by the force of that second impact, he knew immediately that the ship had been hit, and hit hard. A terrified young radarman was shouting to him as the interior lights failed in the captain's cabin passageway.

"What?"

"Chief, I'm supposed to get the Old Man up to Combat. I can't wake him, and his door's locked. What do I do?" The kid was badly frightened.

"Go on back to Combat; tell your chief. Move it!"

The young radarman practically climbed over him in his haste to get up the ladder, and now, as the ship began to slow down and more lighting circuits and the ventilation failed, the GQ alarm finally sounded.

"Right, a fucking day late and a dollar short," Jackson yelled to no one. There was a long blast of high-pressure steam from the after stack; the first tendrils of smoke wrapped around his face as he stood at the base of the ladder. Smoke. Hell, there was no point in going to the bridge now, he had to find the source of that smoke and start to do his GQ job of getting people clear if that shit was inside the ship. He turned around and jumped back down the ladder, heading for Broadway. As he came out into the wardroom passageway, there were no signs of smoke or fire in the immediate area. But that had been a big, deep hit, back aft on the port side. He knew instinctively that there would be fire and smoke, lots of smoke, back there somewhere, so the first order of business was to get to his stash of EEBDs. The EEBDs, emergency-escape breathing devices, were a combination of a clear plastic hood and a steel cylinder the size of a road flare. To wear it, one pulled the bag over his head, tightened the collar string, and then pulled a lanyard on the cylinder, releasing a measured flow of compressed air. They were good for about five to eight minutes of clean air, typically long enough to escape from inside a smoke-filled ship to one of the weather decks.

By the time he had reached his office on Broadway, black oil-fire smoke was beginning to seep up the passageway from the area of the mess decks. The lights were out, but there were several battle lanterns positioned on Broadway and a steady stream of men hustled both forward and aft along Broadway, on their way to GQ stations or their damage-control lockers. Jackson saw Martinez go by, headed aft, an OBA already strapped on. The boatswain appeared to be heading for the after part of the ship. He looked like a khaki-clad battleship steaming down the passageway, throwing up a wake of sailors trying to get out of his way.

Jackson unlocked his office and, by the light of the

single battle lantern, retrieved his canvas bag of EEBDs. He stuffed six of the cylindrical packets into various pockets and carried one in his hand. He grabbed a spare flashlight from the rack of flashlights mounted on a bulkhead and jammed it into his belt. Out of habit, he closed the door and locked it. The other MAAs could get in if they had to: They all had keys. He headed aft with the diminishing crowd of damage-control people, toward the smoke.

52

RD1 Rockheart followed the battered parade of CIC watch standers down the first ladder, making sure he was the last man in the line, behind Chief Hallowell and the two docs. He had to break loose, and he was desperately trying to figure out a way to do it. The baby doc had said the remains of the North Vietnamese jet had crashed amidships, flooding out Two Fire Room and doing a lot of damage to the spaces around the fire room, like the starboard shaft alley. All of his money was in that starboard shaft alley. He figured if he could get down there in the confusion, he could find his rag bag and salvage it before this goddamn boat sank or whatever it was going to do. Nearly twenty thousand dollars was in that bag.

As the surface supe, he had been completely out of the picture when the action broke loose over on the air side, preoccupied as he was with what should have been going down at the Lucky Bag. Holcomb's shouted order to send a man down to wake the captain had been the first indication that it wasn't just another Red Crown air-side flap, and the thunder of multiple missile launches had underscored that impression. He had been reaching for his steel helmet when the bomb had come through the bulkhead. Fortunately, he had been bending over, his head below the level of the DRT, when the bomb's impact shattered the plotting surface, spewing glass all over the surface module. The two plotters had been cut to ribbons, but Rocky, ever the lucky guy, had picked himself up unscathed. He had quickly turned to help bandage the plotters, not looking into the EW module for several minutes until someone reported the bomb. When he finally glanced in there, he had very nearly puked at the blood, the only thing saving him being the sight of that big black *thing* lying there on the deck. The baby doc's news that his hidey-hole might be in danger had galvanized him as the casualties and the damage could not. He had to get his money out of there. But first, he had to get there.

As the group of wounded and their helpers reached the 01 level by the wardroom doors, they encountered the smoke from the fires amidships, which was beginning to fill the interior passageways. Several of the men started coughing and choking. The smoke gave Rocky an idea. He tapped the chief on the shoulder.

"You don't need me to get these guys to the front porch," he said. "The hatch to the weather decks is right there. I'm an MAA. I'm going to go aft, make sure all the stragglers are out of the interior. This smoke is getting pretty thick."

The chief nodded as the first of his charges made it through the open weather decks hatch. "Yeah, do it. Maybe find an OBA first, though. It's only gonna get worse the farther aft you go."

"Right, Chief." Rocky waved them on through the hatch, dogged it down behind them, and then headed down one more ladder and turned toward Broadway. He had to bend almost double to find clear air down near the deck; it was really getting thick down here, complicated by the fact that all the overhead lights were out and the only illumination came from the battle lanterns, themselves shrouded in smoke. No way he could get his hands on one of the big oxygen-breathing apparatus used by the on-scene firefighters, but there were some of the EEBDs that Chief Jackson kept in his office. Rocky figured if he could get four or five of them, they would provide enough breathing time to penetrate *into* the ship to get his stash *out* of the shaft alley. The hoods had the added advantage of being semi-opaque, so his face would be masked.

The smoke was noticeably thicker when Jackson reached the mess decks, although the source of the smoke did not seem to be on the mess decks themselves. The Repair Five damage-control team, which was responsible for covering the midships and the main propulsion spaces, had obviously manned up its locker and already gone to the scene of whatever the problem was, leaving behind a pile of equipment, a phone talker, and the plotter. Jackson went over to the plotter, an auxiliary-gang fireman. The plotter's job was to plot the status of damage-control efforts in the Repair Five area of responsibility on a multicolored diagram of the ship's internal structure that showed every compartment, ladder, trunk, void, and their associated fire-main systems. He bent over the plotting board, where he translated the reports coming from the scene via the phone talker into symbols on the status board. He used a grease pencil to mark down fire and flooding boundaries and the symbols for fire, flooding, and smoke.

Being a chief, Jackson knew the symbols. The board revealed what they had: a fifteen-foot-wide hole in the port side, at the waterline, toward the back end of Number Two Fire Room. A maze of diagonal lines with a large *F* in a circle indicated that Number Two Fire Room was flooding out. There were also indications of flooding aft of the fire room, in a supply storage room on the third deck, and possibly in the starboard shaft alley. Fire and smoke symbols were marked on the main deck above the fire room and up along the port-side boat decks. Since Repair Five did not handle anything above the main deck, the bomb hit in Combat was not shown.

Jackson frowned. If the hit was in Number Two Fire Room, why was there all this smoke infiltrating the mess decks and surrounding areas? He grabbed a sound-powered phone handset, rolled the barrel switch to the bridge position, and cranked the hooter. A frightened-sounding voice responded, "Bridge."

"This is Chief Jackson. I'm on the mess decks at Repair Five and I'm heading aft to look for stragglers. Tell the exec."

"XO ain't here, Chief. Word we got is, he's back aft somewheres, where that fuckin' MiG hit us. They got a big-ass oil fire out on deck."

"MiG?"

"Yeah. Word up here is that one a them MiGs did a kamikaze number on us, put a bomb into Combat."

"Holy shit! Okay—tell the Captain, then."

"He ain't here, either. Chief? They're talkin' about evacuatin' Combat and the bridge area on accounta that bomb in there. OOD says it might go off anytime now."

"Ah. I get it—you've got a ticker sitting in Combat. Okay. I'm still going to do my sweep. Tell the OOD, he needs me, use the One MC. We're getting a hell of a lot of smoke inside the ship."

"Will do her."

Jackson hung up the phone. Things were clearer now, although the atmosphere on the mess decks was going the other way. Repair Five was one of four stations on the circuit: Repair Two forward, Repair Three aft, and Damage Control Central, located on the third deck between the forward engine room and the after fire room, almost beneath the mess decks. He wondered briefly how long the Repair Five plotter and his talker would be able to keep their stations. Or DC Central, for that matter— the smoke was streaming in through the vents, even though they should have been shut off. That didn't make sense either, although the source did: an airplane full of fuel had crashed aboard, like the Japanese used to do during Willy Willy Twice. What is it with these people? he thought. You got a bomb in, what's with all this suicide shit, anyway? Aviation fuel scattered all over the place, lots of fires, lots of holes, and even more smoke. Smoke, that was the killer. His eyes were already stinging. The kid trying to plot was wiping his eyes continuously.

"You guys, you got somewhere else to set up shop? You're gonna get smoked out of here."

"Yeah, Chief," the plotter said. "We're supposed to relocate to the oh-one level, starboard side, by the three-inch fifty. There's a DC phone jack up there."

"You better do it to it; I'd say you've got five minutes

of air left in here, maybe less. Tell Central you're going off the line, and warn them that the space above them is being smoked out. They may want to move, too."

"Aye, Chief. You ain't gotta say it twice."

Jackson moved to the after end of the mess decks, unfolding his EEBD hood. If the fires were topside, why the hell was the smoke coming *into* the ship when all the vents were without power? He reached the hatch to DC Central. It was dogged down tight. If they had closed their vent registers, they would be safe from smoke—unless he opened the hatch. He decided not to open the hatch. He slipped the hood over his head, pulled the neck tapes tight, and then pulled the cylinder lanyard. He headed aft into the gloom of the after officers' passage-way and began checking berthing compartments. He almost hoped he would stumble into his dear friend Bullet.

As Rocky remembered, Chief Jackson kept a dozen or so EEBDs in his office, because it was the chief MAA's duty to go through the ship after battle damage and make sure no one was trapped in damaged spaces. Rocky counted on there being some left, even if Jackson had taken some already. He reached the office, coughing in the smoke, looked up and down the deserted passage-way, and unlocked the door. Inside, he grabbed a spare flashlight from the flashlight box and saw the canvas bag of EEBDs out on Jackson's desk. Good, Jackson had already been here, and apparently for the same reason. He looked in the bag, counting quickly. There were five left. He took them all, lifting the bag itself and slinging it over his shoulder, and headed back out into the passage-way, closing the door behind him. He could not see very far down Broadway, but from the sounds of things, there was obviously a hell of a problem down around the mess decks. He undid one of the EEBDs and pulled the bag over his head. He made sure his silver MAA badge was visible on his pocket, snapped on the light, and set out for the shaft alley.

As he went through the mess decks, he could see the late arrivals in Repair Five getting on their gear and hauling cans of fire-fighting foam toward the emergency escape ladder that went up to the weather decks above. There was a lot of yelling going on and the roaring sound of a big oil fire topside. The insulating tiles in the overhead of the mess decks were curling up from the heat above. He saw some of the MMs from Number Two Engine Room standing on the mess decks, their dungarees soaked, talking to the Repair Five plotter as he noted the damage on his board. With his face almost invisible in the hood, Rocky kept going, through the mess decks, past the galley office, and into the after officers' passageway. He fleetingly remembered the setup operation on Bullet and wondered what had happened. The smoke in the passageway was really bad and he needed his flashlight on white even to see the deck. Several times, he had to read compartment labels to know where he was.

The entrance down to the shaft alley was between Number Two Fire Room's after bulkhead and the Number Two Engine Room's forward bulkhead. There were no berthing compartments below this deck, so anyone who saw him down there would want to know what the hell he was doing, but in this dense smoke, that shouldn't be a problem. He overshot the deck scuttle that led to the shaft alley's vestibule before he realized it, then had to double back to find it again, his flashlight probing the twists and turns in the passageway until he found the step-aside alcove. He kept looking up into the smoky haze to make sure no one was around him as he stopped above the scuttle, surprised to find that the air right above the scuttle was for some reason fairly clear of smoke. The plastic hood began to adhere to his face; for a panicky instant, he thought he was suffocating. Then he remembered. He whipped another EEBD out of the bag and was unfolding the hood when he heard a noise.

He turned around, to find Seaman Coltrane staring at him in the murk, his hand held partially over his face, his eyes streaming from exposure to the smoke. What the hell was *he* doing here? Jesus—with the hood off, Coltrane had recognized him, was trying to say something in that horrible gabble of his. Rocky didn't hesitate. He stepped forward and poleaxed Coltrane in the solar plexus in one smooth punch, and when the young seaman was doubled over and sinking to his knees, Rocky hit him on the side of the head with the EEBD cylinder. Bright blood splashed out onto the deck as Coltrane groaned and went down in the passageway. Rocky straightened out his hood and exchanged the new one for the old one, dropping the expired hood onto the deck. He put a foot against Coltrane's inert form and pushed him to the other side of the passageway, up against a small hose-rack alcove. Stepping back to the scuttle, he could no longer see the unconscious seaman on the deck, not five feet away. Shit's getting thick, he thought.

He grabbed the scuttle handle and spun it counterclockwise until the dogs lifted off and the hatch popped up on its spring-loaded hinges. A sudden rush of semiclear air blew into the passageway, pushing aside the smoke for a moment. Below, he could see one battle lantern still shining right above the hatch leading down to the shaft alley. He climbed over the hatch coaming and went down the trunk ladder, pulling the hatch back down over his head but not dogging it. Reaching the bottom of the ladder, he pointed the light around. The trunk was relatively free of smoke, but by the light of the lone battle lantern, Rocky could see the deck of the trunk bulging ominously up along the port-side edge. The port-side bulkhead was also dished in and tiny trickles of water seeped through wireways and screw holes up and down its length. The steel of the side bulkhead was sweating. Could only mean one thing: Whatever was on the other side was flooded out. Rocky hesitated. If that damn wall gave way while he was down there in the shaft alley, he was a goner. On the other hand, it was steel, not aluminum like the superstructure, and it had held this far. There were no sounds coming from the other side, and all that money not fifteen feet away. He made up his mind.

He dropped down onto the deck of the trunk vestibule and undogged the next hatch, the one that gave entrance to the shaft alley below. This hatch popped right off its dogs, rapping Rocky on his right hand. He swore and shook it while locking back the hatch with his left. Beneath was the shaft alley itself. There were three battle lanterns lighted below; he could see immediately that there was some flooding going on. He scrambled down the second ladder and looked around. The big fire pump was askew on its foundations, and the supply line to its suction side spewed salt water around the coupling, making quite a lot of noise. The starboard propeller shaft was not rolling, but it did not appear to be damaged, either. In one corner, an eductor pump still ran, using fire-main pressure to keep a suction on the space's bilges, which he realized was the only thing keeping *this* space from flooding out. Other than that, there wasn't too much damage, except for a couple of power cables that had been pulled out of the fire pump's controller box. Assuming that they were live, he checked to see that they were not in contact with the water or the deck. The inboard bulkhead down here looked to be deformed somewhat, but, again, not very much. The air was clear, so Rocky stripped off his EEBD, pitching the plastic hood and the blood-smeared cylinder into the bilges.

He wasted no more time sight-seeing. He moved over to the empty locker, picked up an eight-pound dogging wrench from its holder, and bashed the wing nuts off the locker. He was rummaging in the rag bag when he felt a pressure drop in his ears. He jumped sideways to be out of view of the hatch. The pressure drop signified that the hatch up above had opened. Somebody taking a look? Coltrane, maybe? Coming down? He reached for the EEBD, but it was gone—in the bilges. He took a deep breath and craned his neck out to look up the two ladders. Nobody. He saw that the upper hatch was open. He hadn't dogged it well enough, that's all. Damn thing had popped open. He went back to the locker and started to discard the rags not filled with cash, throwing them down into the oily bilges.

53

Brian watched Garuda head out the door after the file of casualties, took out his flashlight, and picked his way back through the surface module. The smoke and sooty dust were thinning out, although there was still a cooling water leak somewhere beneath the mangled deck plates. The battle lanterns gave a spectral view of the destruction on the port side, where a huge hole with jagged edges bulged inward at about chest height. Cold air mixed with oily smoke whistled in from the blackness outside, stirring the smoke and dust in the abandoned space. He thought he could hear shouts and the sounds of portable fire-pump engines filtering in from the weather decks outside.

He stopped at the threshold of the EW module. The EW console itself was gone, completely gone, as was the primary anti–submarine warfare console. The stumps of the console chairs showed where the consoles ought to have been, but the consoles themselves were scattered in metallic flinders all over the aisleway on the port side. Brian swallowed several times when he realized that everything in front of the hole in the outside bulkhead was covered in gore. Dripping blood, shreds of dungaree cloth, and bits of human tissue hung from every projection and edge of metal in the area. Brian felt his stomach heave as he stared at the wreckage. What had Garuda said? That they weren't able to tell who had been killed? He had to grab hold of a stanchion as the ship took a deeper roll than usual. It felt as if *Hood* was stopped or nearly so, and the roll had a heavy feel, as if her belly was filling with water.

He looked around, behind the immediate area of the hole. The back part of Combat seemed untouched, with console chairs in position and even papers still on some of the desks. Paperwork endures, he thought irreverently, his brain grasping for normalcy amid the wreckage. On the inside of the aisleway, the bulkheads that covered the forward stack uptakes were spattered in dark spots; a single shard of metal had been driven into the uptake bulkhead. Below that, there was a large depression in the metal, as if it had been hit by something. Then he saw the bomb.

It was not as big as he had expected. It appeared to be about seven feet long, a foot and half in diameter, sharply pointed at one end and blunt on the other, with four crumpled fins encased in a ring of metal at the blunt end. It was unpainted, the metal a dull black color lined with bright scratches and gouges. There was no writing visible on it as there would have been on American ordnance.

He stood still, suddenly and physically afraid to be in its malevolent presence. The bomb was lying at an angle to the aisleway, its nose down, the tail sticking up on top of the wreckage of a locker. The ship's rolling did not seem to disturb it, for which Brian was suddenly very grateful. He was again seized with the urge to run, visions of a fireball and a titanic blast filling his mind's eye. But with his mouth dry and his knees trembling, he forced himself to step closer to the bomb, looking for signs of life in the deadly black case. What the hell, at this distance you might as well go pat it on the ass; if it goes off, you're gonna be cosmic dust.

He knelt down on one knee and reached out to put his hand on it. He nearly jumped out of his skin when a loud click came from inside the case. He froze, closed his eyes, and took a deep breath, then opened his eyes again. He leaned forward and put his head right up against the casing. He listened carefully, shutting his eyes to concentrate, trying to filter out the sounds around him of the leaking, cooling water, the quiet buzz of the battle lantern relays, and the rush of the outside air blowing through the big hole behind him. Something in there, something—grinding. Like tiny gears.

"Stethoscope is better," said a voice. Brian nearly jumped out of his skin for a second time. He looked up, to find the captain standing behind him, holding on to the side of a console to stay upright. Brian swallowed hard.

In the light of the battle lanterns, the captain's face was a patchwork of shadows and lines. His eyes gleamed with visible pain. He wore full uniform, khaki shirt and trousers, regular uniform shoes, and he looked like a famished prisoner of war. Brian straightened up carefully, not wanting to disturb any mechanisms that might be at work in the bomb.

"Captain. Where—"

"Where've I been?" The captain's voice was dry as parchment. "That what you want to know? When my ship was getting her ass kicked, where was the CO, right?"

"S-sir, I—"

"That's okay, sailor. I guess you've got a right. That was you leaning on the buzzer just before we got hit, right? You on the One MC?" The captain paused, then coughed, a single deliberate contraction of his chest that seemed to squeeze his whole body. "You did all right, son; you sounded more pissed than afraid on the One MC. How many were there?"

"There were four, Captain," Brian said, the words tumbling out. "We just . . . we just ran out of directors and time. And Petty Officer Warren clutched up with System Two on the last bogey, and he was here before the birds could arm in flight."

"How did it start?"

"They jammed the forty, and while we were checking that out, they came feet-wet."

"At two in the morning in the northeast monsoon, complete with radar ghosts, the carriers secured for the night, and the E-two in the barn for the night. And I'll bet the BARCAP were tanking, too."

Brian almost smiled. "Yes, sir, they were."

The captain looked like a ghost himself, staring around at the shattered CIC. His eyes were huge in the gloom and looked unnaturally moist. Brian could not stand the silence.

"I've had CIC evacuated," he continued. "And the compartments above and below, too. I don't think we've made a report out to Yankee Station yet, what with Radio shut down. I've got Garuda setting up an emergency radio on the fo'c'sle. And there's no power to the systems. The XO—"

The captain put his palm up. "The XO has his hands full with a fifteen-foot-long hole at the waterline, a flooded main space, and jet fuel burning in the midships section of the ship," he said. "You guys actually did tag the fourth MiG. Your last Terrier knocked a wing off him, but apparently he and one of his bombs pancaked off the water on our port side and skipped themselves aboard. The exec's down amidships, coordinating the topside damage control; Vince is in DC Central, or Main Control, I'm not sure which, trying to keep a plant on the line."

Brian exhaled. He looked down at the bomb. Somehow, with the captain here, he was less afraid of it. "So what do we do with this thing, sir?"

"I thought I'd try my hand at disarming it," the captain replied, lifting a black plastic toolbox he had been holding in his left hand.

"Sir?"

"Well, when I was enlisted, I was with the EOD. Explosive ordnance disposal people. This is my tool kit. I've always taken it to sea with me."

"Sir, you know how to disarm this thing?"

"I know more than anyone else in the ship, which may or may not be useful. It won't be the first time I've tackled a bomb in CIC."

"Oh. Yes. Garuda told me. You won a Navy Cross for it."

A ghost of a smile passed over the captain's face. "Garuda probably got it wrong. They didn't give me that medal for taking the fuze out. They gave me the medal because I was technically competent to know that it was armed and counting down and yet I *still* grabbed it and threw it overboard." He paused, remembering. "That's something you'll come to learn in the Navy, Brian. You have to do something exceptionally foolish to win the big medals. Now why don't you leave me with this beauty and go below. Regroup all the able-bodied men you can out on the fo'c'sle and hook up with the XO. He's going to need some help with the mess amidships. I understand Mr. Austin's out of commission, and with Vince running DC Central, you're the only evaluator left."

"Aye, aye, sir. Will you need some, uh, assistance?"

The Captain moved around Brian and lowered himself to the deck plates, gently pushing aside some debris so that he could sit right next to the bomb.

"You volunteering?" he asked without looking up.

Brian swallowed hard again, looking around at the devastated CIC, the shattered consoles, the vent ducts hanging from the overhead, and the tangle of cables and light fixtures. The bulkheads on the superstructure creaked as the ship rolled into the trough, and the distant shouts of the fire-fighting teams amidships seemed louder.

"Well, I just—"

"Right. It's good of you to make the offer. But ordinarily, the way this works is that I put on sound-powered phones and somebody a couple of hundred feet away gets on the other end of the circuit and take notes on what I say and do. That way, if I screw it up, they'll know what *not* to do the next time. But this is just a standard Soviet two-hundred-and fifty-kilogram general-purpose bomb. The Russians make crude but resilient weapons. If I can get inside without tripping some kind of booby trap, I can shut it off. So your best move is to clear out and leave me to it."

The captain had opened his tool kit and began to lay out several strange-looking instruments. Brian stood behind him, wanting desperately to get the hell out of there but equally desperate to ask the captain a final question.

"You're still here." The captain took a shiny Allen wrench and began probing the holes in the round access plate at the back end of the bomb.

"Yes, sir. There's something . . . there's something I've got to ask before I go. I mean—"

"You mean before I go, I think. But okay, it's your nickel." He put the Allen wrench down and chose another, continuing to probe the holes. Brian found himself wishing he would stop that.

"The drugs. I don't understand why you let the drug thing go on. Why you let the XO run his gun-deck justice system. I don't understand any of that."

The captain stopped what he was doing, put the tool down, and let his hand fall to his lap. He sat there, his head down, his eyes closed, for almost a minute. The ship took a long roll and hung to port for what seemed like a very long time. Brian realized that she was getting less responsive to the seas outside, a bad sign. The bomb shifted infinitesimally on its pile of debris, startling both of them.

"I suppose . . ." the captain began, picking up yet another Allen wrench. "I suppose you probably think it's some kind of deep, dark conspiracy." He paused, as if to mobilize his thoughts, and then he groaned in pain and slowly doubled over, his forehead ending up resting against the cold steel casing of the Russian bomb.

"Captain?" Brian started to move forward.

But the captain straightened up and took a deep breath. "I'll make you a deal," he whispered. "Go to my cabin. In the head. Bring me my Dopp kit—small brown leather bag. Bring it up here and then I'll tell you what's been going on."

"Yes, sir. I'll get it. Should I call the—"

"They're busy now. Go get it."

Brian backed away and then picked his way as fast as he could through surface and D and D to the front door, which was swinging back and forth on its hinges as the ship rolled. The door to the pilothouse was open. Jack Folsom stood in the darkened doorway as Brian came out of Combat.

"Secure the bridge," Brian ordered. "Go down to the fo'c'sle and set up shop down there. Make sure you take the deck log and some sound-powered phones. Come up on the One JV phone circuit, and put somebody on the JL, the lookout circuit. Move it. Bring the log up to date as soon as you get down there."

Folsom nodded and disappeared back out into the pilothouse as Brian hurried down the ladder to the next level. It was amazing to him how everything one deck below was perfectly normal, battle lanterns shining down on highly polished tile decks, the row of stateroom doors looking like the hallway of a hotel. There was only the strong stink of burning oil coiling up from the next level down to indicate that something might be wrong elsewhere in the ship. He banged through the captain's cabin door and turned right. He found the Dopp kit and headed back for CIC. He slowed down as he approached the area aft of surface, trying not to look at all the gore. He knelt down on one knee and offered the Dopp kit to the captain, who was sitting motionless next to the bomb, his eyes agape in a vacant stare.

"Captain?"

The captain blinked. "Open it," he croaked.

Brian opened the leather bag and was stunned to find four medicinal vials and three syringes. He peered at the labels on the vials. Morphine sulfate. Three unopened bottles and one partially full.

"Give me one bottle and one needle."

Brian passed them to the captain, who with a practiced motion put the syringe case between his teeth, pulled off the protective cap, spit out the cap, and drew back the handle of the syringe, pressing the glinting needle through the membrane of the vial to inject two cc's of air. Then he withdrew an equal amount of the amber fluid, dropped the vial at his feet, and stabbed the needle into the large muscle of his thigh.

Brian winced when he did it, but the effect was almost immediate. After about a minute, the captain exhaled, a long and weary sighing sound, and discarded the syringe. He shuddered once and then looked up at Brian.

"So now you know. The captain is a morphine addict. Sort of, anyway. The difference is that I don't do this for fun, Brian. I have a cancer in my guts, and this stuff controls the pain. Only I'm about at the end of my string." He sat back, resting his left side on the bomb casing.

"At the beginning of the cruise, I needed morphine only twice a day. Not too bad, except for the last couple of hours of each period. But I learned to schedule it, see. Take it at oh-six hundred so I could see people, do my job, especially in the mornings. Then some pills around lunchtime so I could get through the afternoon, when the ops got heavy in CIC. My second shot around eighteen hundred so I could be up to it on the twenty to twenty-four, the night ops stuff.'' He held his breath for ten seconds, coughed once, and then continued.

"The doc was my ally. And the exec, of course. They both owed me. Professional favors. I made a deal with them. If I had gone to the docs ashore, they'd have yanked me off the ship in a heartbeat, stuffed me into a hospital, and taken my plumbing out. If it hadn't already got loose, I'd spend the rest of my life with a bag of shit under my shirt.''

He paused again before tilting his head up to stare directly at Brian.

"See, *John Bell Hood* was my big ship command. This was the battleship I was never going to have, because there weren't any more battleships. I've been in the Navy a long, long time. White hat to four-striper. Done everything. Only in the American Navy is that possible these days. *Hood* was my big ship. No way was I going to trade that for a plastic bag. Miss my wartime WESTPAC cruise. My ship, the crew *I* trained up, the wardroom *I* nurtured. So I made a deal. The doc would keep me in meds for the cruise. When we got back, I would turn myself in.''

Brian nodded. "Only the cancer got ahead of you.'' A battle lantern nearby expired, its relay buzzing for fifteen seconds before the light dimmed out.

"It sure as hell did. These last days, since we left Subic, it's been terrible. They can give me only so much morphine. The body can take only so much, and they couldn't hit the ship's supply so hard that we wouldn't have any for, well, for what we have on our hands tonight. The doc faked some of it—turned in reports saying stuff had expired, had been destroyed, got some more. When we were in Subic, I checked into a private clinic up near Baguio, the resort city.''

"Ah. I saw you when you returned, when we got underway for the storm. You looked—''

"I looked like death warmed over, I suspect. They did an exploratory at the clinic. Closed it right back up. Too far gone. The Filipino doc there said I had maybe a month or so. Said I ought to tell my wife.''

"Mrs. Huntington doesn't know?''

"I haven't told her. That's not the same as saying she doesn't know. Navy wife. They know everything, after a while. You may not necessarily want to know how they learn in every case, either."

Brian nodded, understanding that comment perfectly.

"And the druggies in the crew: Yes, I knew the scope of the problem. At first, the XO told me everything. It was his idea to use the chiefs to keep the dopers in their boxes if we could."

"You couldn't stand to expose the problem because it would expose you."

"Right. Simple as that. When you came aboard and started asking questions, I wondered if it was all going to blow up. The XO suggested we checkmate you with the fitrep. Worked for a while, didn't it?"

"Yes, sir. But dopers on the missile systems—I just couldn't stand that anymore."

The captain fell silent, looking across the wrecked module, looking at each piece of twisted equipment, at the bloodstains and human bits showered across the bulkheads. He shook his head.

"You were right," he whispered finally. "The Navy way, the regulation way—always the best way. Always. I knew that. We thought we could hold it together. We thought the problem here was no better or worse than that in any other ship out here. That's what other skippers were doing—getting by, getting the job done, getting the ship back home in one piece and with our careers intact. Should have known better, I guess."

Brian nodded slowly. "We almost pulled it off, actually."

"What was the problem with System Two? The one that cost you time?"

"I don't know, sir. FTM Three Warren was on the console down below. The chief thinks the kid panicked when it got hot and heavy. Maybe he did, maybe not. One of the first class was with him, but he was probably sitting System One. Maybe if we had had a more senior man on the console . . . I just don't know."

The captain nodded. "You realize that's just what the XO is going to say—you come along, stick your nose in, and decide to clean house, and then when the shit hit the fan, we had novices on the consoles."

"I guess he has a point," Brian said, his voice low.

"No, he doesn't. Look at me. Look at me. You did the right thing. He and I did the wrong thing. Look, there's going to be a serious investigation, probably a court of inquiry, on this incident. Those things have a tendency to stray beyond their immediate objective. The drug thing is going to come out. There might even be a court-martial or two. You just tell the truth, from start to finish. I'll back you up. If I can."

"If you can?"

The Captain gave a twisted smile and tipped his chin at the bomb. "If I don't screw this up. And if I live that long. Now, you get out of here. But first get me a set of phones. If I succeed, I want to be able to tell somebody it's clear in here. Keep everybody out until I call."

Brian scrounged a set of sound-powered phones from the darkened and deserted bridge and took them back to the captain, who was moving his tools on a foul-weather jacket spread across the deck plates. Brian plugged the jack into the JL circuit. He went back out into the passageway and unscrewed two battle lanterns and brought them back, positioning them so the yellow spots of light shined directly on the plate.

"Good," the captain said. "Now shove off."

"Aye, aye, sir. Good luck."

The captain twisted around to look at him. "Good luck to you, young man. One day, you'll have a command of your own. Just make sure you play by the rules."

"Aye, aye, Captain."

54

Thirty minutes later, Jackson headed back up after officers' passageway, navigating the passageway by keeping
one hand out to touch a bulkhead. The visibility in the
smoke-filled area was down to about zero. He stopped
when his foot slipped on something on the deck and he
felt a breath of rising air against his hand. He groped
around in the murk and put his flashlight on the bulkheads, trying to figure out where he was. The passageway
was almost totally obscured by smoke now, but he had
definitely felt moving air, cooler air, from below his
knees. He groped around with his right hand and found a
step-aside alcove. Here, definitely here. He felt the brass
wheel with his fingers, and as he did, the hatch undogged
and bounced up on its springs, once again blowing away
the smoke for an instant. He looked down into the trunk
and saw the hatch to the shaft alley wide open at the
bottom of the ladder leading down from the passageway.
There was a flashlight probing around down there. Somebody there. An investigator from Repair Three? Looked
like there was some flooding down there, water sloshing
around, almost over the deck plates. But would a DC
guy leave hatches open? Suspicious, Jackson latched the
scuttle hatch fully back. He started down the hatch, only
to have his EEBD begin to give out, forcing him to climb
back out to unwrap another EEBD and change the hood.
Then he started down again.

He climbed down the first ladder carefully, having
trouble seeing through the hood as the cooler air fogged
the plastic. He thought about taking it off, but there was
still smoke present, and he didn't want to waste the pure
air in the cylinder, which, once fired, discharged until it
was depleted. He took the spare EEBDs out of his
pockets and laid them out on the deck. He could hear
water spraying in the pump room below, and from the

sound of it, there was a pretty good leak going down there. He tried to wipe the hood clear, but it only smeared. He knelt down on one knee and peered into the shaft alley pump room, twisting the hood to find some clear plastic.

He was stunned to see Rockheart collecting a large pile of money from a bag of what looked like rags. Rockheart? He leaned back, away from the hatch, in case Rockheart happened to look up. With a sinking feeling in his gut, he figured it out. Goddamn Martinez had been right—there had been a second guy. Rockheart in the passageway outside their door the night they had visited Garlic. Rockheart devising the setup on Bullet. Rockheart the MAA, with access to his office and effectively anything in it. Jesus H. Christ. An MAA! Down there with a huge bag of money. Drug money—it had to be. That son of a bitch! Deserting his station in Combat to rescue his drug money. He peeped over the edge again, staring in disbelief at the amount of cash—hundreds, thousands of dollars in cash—that Rocky was stuffing back into the rag bag. And he wasn't wearing a hood.

Enraged at the betrayal, Jackson lost it. He ripped the EEBD hood off his own head, put his feet carefully on the ladder, and then started down, facing forward on the ladder, being careful not to make any noise that could be heard above the spray from the broken pump coupling. When he reached the next to the last rung above the propeller shaft's cage, he collected himself and sprang halfway across the pump room, landing on the metal deck plates with a loud clang and hitting Rocky on the side of his head at the temple with his clenched fist as Rocky started to turn around and look up. The blow knocked Rocky backward, fetching him up against the tilted body of the fire pump, where he slumped into a moaning heap, the rag bag spilling its contents into the bilges.

Jackson straightened up, his right hand stinging. He walked over to where Rocky was lying and kicked him in the stomach. Rocky gasped and doubled up into a tight ball, his eyes shut, his face white with pain. Jackson reached for him, grabbing a handful of shirt.

"You *motherfucker*!" he shouted. "You son of a bitch!

You're a fucking MAA! I trusted you—the whole fucking ship trusted you, and look at you." He slapped Rocky across the face with his left hand. "All this fucking time, we're lookin at Bullet, and it's *you*! Guys dying up there, guys drowned next door in the fire room, ship's on fire, and you're down here getting your fucking drug money! You *bastard*!"

Rocky opened his eyes and tried to speak, but Jackson continued to slap him in the face, screaming at him, incoherent in his rage at the depth of Rockheart's betrayal. He didn't see Rocky's right hand reach for the nest of loose cables at the base of the fire pump's motor, didn't see him rip a 440-volt cable out, felt too late the sudden movement by his knee, and then a giant humming vise grabbed the entire left side of his body and drew him headlong and paralyzed into blackness.

55

Chief Martinez bounced off the bulkhead for the fifteenth time and cursed it roundly for being in his way, his voice muffled by the OBA mask. He was trying to get back up the after officers' passageway to the mess decks to find some more OBA canisters. Martinez normally headed up Repair Two, stationed in the forward part of the ship, but since there was no damage in his area, he had taken his fire-fighting team amidships to help the exec and repair teams Five and Three with the fuel fires there. They had been making progress until some of the aviation fuel, pooled in pockets around the boat decks, had been sucked into an inadvertently energized supply vent fan, spreading an aerosol mixture of fuel and air into some of the officers' staterooms, where it had ignited with an ominous roar beneath their feet. The exec had reorganized the teams and sent Martinez and his repair party into the ship to come up from the fantail and attack the fires from the inside. Martinez had dispatched his four-man OBA team into the thick of it, unsnarled the fire hoses with the rest of the DC team, and then gone to get more breathing canisters.

The smoke in the passageway was now so thick that he could only feel his way forward, relying on his day-to-day memory of the passageway to know where he was. As he went past the after officers' head area, he wished he could be dragging Bullet into the smoke with him. Pissed him off, they came so close. But now they *knew,* thanks to Rockheart. He knew he was nearing the mess decks area, near Two Firehouse, when he could no longer feel the heat from the fires aft. But the smoke from the fuel fires was a solid, toxic, roiling black wall of soot particles, carbon monoxide, and other poisonous gases. The chief wore a red damage-control steel helmet on his head, his entire face contained in the OBA mask, perched above the black canvas breathing bags on his massive chest. His khaki uniform was completely soaked through with fire-fighting water and perspiration, and his hands were covered in heavy asbestos gauntlets. The miner's light strapped to his helmet was totally useless in the smoke; he had long since turned it off.

He swore again as he slipped on something on the deck and nearly lost his balance, his arms freewheeling for a few seconds until he found the bulkhead. He sensed what felt like a current of air rising from the deck, knelt down, awkward in the OBA rig, and took off a glove. He found a hatch open, from which a rising current of air was flowing. Suddenly, he could even see a little bit. He snapped on his helmet light, realizing this was the hatch down to the starboard shaft alley. He remembered catching a couple of his stars sleeping down there when they were supposed to be on a working party.

Why the hell was the hatch open? Then he heard a noise, an unmistakable gargling, gabbling noise a few feet away in the gloom of the smoke. What the fuck! He moved across the passageway, once again encountering something slippery on the deck. He shone the light down and saw blood smears on the deck. He heard the noise again and found Seaman Coltrane, suddenly visible in an alcove. The air rising from the hatch had scoured out a pocket of breathable air in the alcove opposite, and Coltrane was curled up in a ball, holding his bloody head. The chief pushed his mask aside.

"Coltrane, what the fuck? What're you doin' here?" he asked, before remembering whom he was talking to. Like asking a door what day it was. Except that Coltrane had grabbed the chief's sleeve and was trying desperately to tell him something, pointing down and gesturing at the nearly invisible open scuttle across the way, babbling incoherently, pointing to his head, then miming a—what? A punch?

"What? What is it?! Calm down. Spell it out for me."

Coltrane stopped struggling and looked at his chief. Then he reached out and took the grease pencil from Martinez's OBA pocket and bent down on hands and knees. Printing laboriously on the deck tile, he spelled out the name Rockheart on the tile deck. Then he pointed to his head and gestured urgently down at the hatch.

"Jesus Christ, Coltrane. I didn't know you could write. All this fucking time—wait a minute. Rockheart did this? He hit you? And he's down there in the shaft alley? Right now?"

Coltrane nodded vigorously, then winced with pain. Martinez looked over at the opened hatch. What the fuck was going on around here? What would Rockheart be doing down in the shaft alley? He stood up, the light from his helmet again obscured in smoke. With his mask askew, he immediately started coughing. He squatted down again. What was Rocky, a senior radarman, doing in the starboard shaft alley in the middle of a no-shitter crisis, the ship on fire, everything all fucked up, and everybody going crazy? He knelt down on one knee and grabbed Coltrane's chin in one massive paw.

"You stay where you are. You got an air pocket's long as that hatch is open. I'll come back, get you when I'm done down there. But don't try to go nowheres, 'cause it's all smoke in either direction. Keep your head right on the deck. Got it?"

Coltrane nodded again, this time with more care. Martinez stood up and moved over to the hatch. He looked down, surprised that he could see anything, but the engineering spaces had their own independent air-supply systems, and this one was still running. The ladder led down to the next hatch, which was also locked back and fully open. Something definitely going on here, something not right. In the yellow glow of the battle lanterns, he spotted the shadow of somebody moving around down there. He began to strip off the OBA—with his girth, he could never fit through the hatches with an OBA on. He stripped off his mask, laid aside the breathing bags and harness, and started carefully down the ladder. He reached the vestibule below and heard the spray of water from a ruptured line. Being very careful now, he got behind the hatch and looked around its edges into the shaft alley. There he saw the inert form of Chief Jackson sprawled next to the fire pump, his left leg bent under him. And across the pump room was Radarman First Class and Master-at-Arms Rockheart, gathering the last sodden bills out of the water and stuffing them into a rag bag full of money that he was clutching to his chest.

And suddenly Martinez knew. It wasn't Rocky the radarman, was it? It was Rocky the main man, the second man. Them, Garlic had said. Money from them. And it was Rockheart that night who'd been yelling at Coltrane outside Jackson's door. It hadn't been Coltrane listening to them, it had been Rockheart. And somehow, Jackson had caught on, too, and Rocky had taken him out. Rocky, after his goddamned money in the shaft alley, thinking the ship was going to go down, which it might. As he watched, Rocky straightened up, causing Martinez to jerk his head back. He saw Rocky's leg strike out at Jackson's chest and then he saw Rocky's hands reach for the ladder rails beneath him. Okay, fuckhead, you got the cowboy, but you ain't gonna get the Injun.

As Rocky started up the ladder, the chief sat back on his haunches behind the hatch and reached around to release the holdback latch. When Rocky's hands came off the ladder and rested for a fraction of a second on the lip of the hatch, Martinez slammed the hatch down with all his strength, the knife edge of the round scuttle nearly amputating all of Rocky's fingers. Even with the noise of the spraying water below, Martinez heard a very satisfactory scream. He popped the hatch back up and saw Rocky drop all the way to the steel deck plates below, his precious bag tumbling open, spilling money all over the pump room, Rocky landing with a crash on the deck plates. With a growl that would have done a grizzly bear proud, Martinez stood up and dropped straight down through the hatch, crashing onto the deck plates with enough force to catapult Rocky over into the bilges below, where he landed on his back with another shout of pain. As he tried to sit up, Martinez was already there, casually stomping him in the face. When Rocky flopped back into the bilgewater, Martinez stepped down and stood with one foot on Rocky's chest, the other in the calf-deep bilgewater.

"Yo, kingpin, how they hangin'?" Martinez asked as he saw the shock spreading across Rocky's face. "What, you havin' a bad dream, Rocky? Things goin' wrong all of a sudden?"

He pushed hard with his foot and Rocky's chest and head were forced underwater, where Martinez held him for many seconds before relaxing some of the pressure. Rocky's face burst out of the water, his mouth open, his chest heaving, and his eyes blinking rapidly from the oil in the bilge. He tried to raise his mangled hands to wipe his eyes but screamed again with the pain.

"What'd you do to the Sheriff here, huh? You hurt my buddy Jackson, did you, you *fuck?*" He pushed Rocky underwater again, holding him longer this time. When he eased off, Rocky spluttered to the surface, trying to draw breath and talk at the same time, his bloody hands staying underwater this time. It sounded to Martinez as if he was saying the word *deal*.

"Deal? You wanna make a deal with me, scumbag? Not in your lifetime, Mr. Dealer."

"Don't kill me! Please. I'll testify," shouted Rocky, his eyes wild. "I can give you Bullet. You can have the money—I even got more!"

"Oh yeah? You already gave us Bullet, remember? And I don't give a shit about your money, or Bullet's money, or Garlic's fuckin' money. Garlic's fuckin' dead, see? And I ain't sorry he is. And you're next."

"No, please, no! I can't breathe . . . your leg . . . this oil . . . Jesus Christ, my fucking hands! Please. There's thousands here. You can have it all. You can keep it, you want to. I won't tell. I'll do anything you want, man. I'll testify—I can give you the whole thing. But please, please don't kill me, man!"

The chief stared down at him as Rocky's lungs spasmed and he had a choking fit from inhaling oil. When he got his voice back, he said, "Please, man. I don't wanna die. I can tell you about Garlic, too, but you gotta let me outta here. I don't want to drown. Oh, God, my hands. I'll take the fall, I don't care. I'll testify, say anything you want, just don't let me drown in this shit—"

The chief loomed over Rockheart like a gathering storm. "What else you gonna tell me, we don't already know? Bullet? We got the goods on fucking Bullet, got his ass in the box. We don't need your ugly ass."

"But you think you killed Garlic, don't you? You beat him up and then he croaked. They'll find out, they do an autopsy at Da Nang. They'll find out he got the shit kicked out of him before his so-called heart attack. But I can get you off. You didn't kill him, man—I did."

"You?"

"Yeah. I found him, beat to shit, probably bleeding internally. He could finger me; he was the other guy could finger me, besides Bullet. I . . . I pressed his carotid artery until he shut down. He was probably finished anyways, okay? So I just did it. You didn't kill him. I did."

Martinez stood up. "Well shit, I don't think I wanted to hear that. I thought I *had* killed the slimy fuck, and now you're telling me *you* did it? After I counted coup and everything? Son of a *bitch*!" Martinez took his foot off Rocky's chest. As Rocky sat up, he kicked him hard in the face, bouncing his head off the fire pump's foundations and knocking him cold. Rocky's upper body settled down into the bilgewater. Martinez reached down into the water and pulled him up the sloping deck to the base of the fire pump, propping Rocky's head up out of the water. He lifted one of Rocky's eyelids and, satisfied that Rocky was truly out, left him, fighting hard the urge to choke the life out him.

He climbed over the bilge strakes to the pocket of water where Jackson lay. He saw the 440 cable sticking down into the pocket of bilgewater and wondered. Breaker should have popped, but . . . Being careful not to touch the water, he checked for signs of life. Jackson was breathing, but he didn't look right, and he was also out cold. Martinez unholstered his knife and went over to the fire-hose rack next to the eductor pump, looking to make sure Rockheart was still out.

He sawed through the canvas and rubber-lined fire hose and cut out a ten-foot length. He slipped this around Jackson's chest and dragged him upright to the base of the ladder. Then, holding the ends of the hose in one hand, he climbed the ladder one step at a time, lifting Jackson by his improvised sling up through the two hatches to the alcove above, where he placed him on his side. Coltrane stared at them from across the passageway, his eyes streaming from the smoke. Jackson groaned but did not come around.

Martinez checked to make sure the alcove was still relatively free of smoke and that Jackson was still breathing. He climbed back down into the vestibule above the pump room. He looked through the hatch. Rocky lay where he had coldcocked him, sitting slumped, with his lower body in the bilges and his chest and head resting against the fire pump. The pump room was wrecked, the fire pump useless, and the bilges were awash with oily water—and greenbacks. Dirty water, dirty money, dirty guy. Needs a good bath. He had an urge to go over to the eductor suction pump in the corner and shut the isolation valves, let the fucker just drown. Martinez thought about it for a moment, shook his head, slammed down the hatch, and climbed back up to get his OBA so he could take care of Jackson and Coltrane. He also had to tell Repair Five that they had flooding in the shaft alley.

Ten minutes later, Rocky started to come around. He tried to move his head, but the resulting pain brought stars to his eyes and he groaned out loud. His body felt pummeled, as if he had been tenderized, and his hands felt as if they were wearing puffy, stinging gloves. He couldn't quite get his breath as he tried to remember where he was. Then he became aware that someone was with him, someone moving around. He cracked open his eyes but couldn't move his head for the pain. A dark figure in an OBA mask was standing a few feet away, looking down at him. He thought he recognized the guy, but his mind was fuzzed up. *I know that guy.* He tried to speak but could only croak. *God! His head and his hands hurt so bad. Where the fuck am I? What's that guy doing?*

The helmeted figure had gone over to the pipe racks and had begun to pull down lengths of pipe and sections of steel angle iron. *What's he doing? Hey, man,* his mind shouted, but his voice wouldn't work. He tried to move, tried to lift himself using his hands, but the pain lunged back at him, turning his vision red, and his question became another groan. When his eyes cleared again, he saw that the masked figure was pulling sections of angle iron and pipe over to where he lay, dragging them across the room so that they landed on top of Rocky, slowly burying him in a mound of loose steel. *What the fuck's he doing—hey!* He tried to move again, but now there was all this metal shit on top of him. When the figure had piled on all the metal he could find, he stepped to the edge of the pile and just stood there, staring down at Rocky. Rocky tried to move, but the pain slammed him back to the edge of consciousness. Rocky tried to protest, to say something, anything, but his voice still couldn't form any words. Wherever he was, the ambient light seemed to brighten and dim in time with the waves of pain in his head. He tried to swallow, but his mouth was dry.

Who is this guy? Why is he piling metal on me? He tried to move again, but suddenly he realized that he wasn't going anywhere. He watched as the figure stood up and looked around. *Black guy. He's a black guy. Three chevrons on his shirtsleeve, right beneath the OBA straps. Repair Five stenciled on the OBA bag. First class. He's an investigator from Repair Five. He's a first class, just like me.* His fractured mind reached for the name. *Know him, know him sure as shit. It's . . . it's—*He closed his eyes for a few seconds, and when he opened them, the guy had the money bag in his hands and was dumping money into the bilges. Then he sloshed over to the corner, where the eductor pump suction inlet was, and stuffed the plastic bag into the suction line. Rocky heard the sucking sounds of the eductor pump choke off. He closed his eyes again, trying to think. Have to do something. This guy, this isn't right. Guy's dumped my money, all that money, and fucked up the eductor. Rocky tried to concentrate on what that might mean. He knew the eductor was important.

He was distracted by a sound, glass breaking, and he opened his eyes again. The guy was deliberately smashing in the glass faces of the three battle lanterns with a dogging wrench, plunging the compartment into darkness. The only light now was the shaft of yellow-white light streaming down through the hatch. The guy was looking at him again.

"Adios, motherfucker," he said, his voice distorted by the OBA mask. He tossed the wrench into the bilge with a splash. Then he was climbing up the ladder, a long, thin figure, struggling through the hatch with the OBA. A moment later, the hatch slammed down, plunging the compartment into total darkness. Rocky focused on the voice. Know that guy, he thought before drifting off again.

He came to in the humid darkness a few minutes later. His ears were ringing and there was the sound of water spraying nearby. He could smell the iodine stink of seawater and he could feel and taste a warm, salty mist in the air around his face, but he could see nothing. Gathering his wits, he realized that he was on his back, his head jammed up against a heavy metal object—the fire pump. He remembered now: The fire pump had been knocked off its foundations, its fire-main couplings leaking. It felt as if the lower half of his body was partially submerged. The side of his face hurt like hell. He tried to heave himself upright, but there was a heavy weight of metal pinning him against the fire pump. His left arm was stuck under what felt like a pipe, but his right arm was free. He felt around in the dark, but his hands were numb and clumsy. Pipes. Pipes and angle iron, that's what this is. Shipfitter gear. That guy.

He tried to roll over, to get off his back, pushing hard with his right arm, but he could not move. Slowly, he became aware of the ship's motion, a deep, slow roll, as if she was wallowing in the trough of the sea. It sounded like there was a lot of water sloshing around in the compartment. It was not deep, but he could feel it, swirling around his legs, washing up in small waves on his stomach. He could hear the steel plates of the hull creaking around him in the darkness.

As the ship took a longer roll, the weight of metal piled up on his chest shifted. He could distinguish between the individual edges of angle iron and the smoother skin of pipe. He shook his head and immediately winced; his whole face hurt. His mind went fuzzy with the pain, and then, in a sudden wave of clarity, he realized where he was, that he was pinned to the deck in the pump room. I can't fucking move, man. He felt a surge of panic and gave a mighty heave, putting his whole body into it, trying to pull himself out from under the tangle of steel. He felt the pile move slightly, but then the ship rolled back the other way. There was a clatter as the pile shifted back, this time pinning both of his shoulders down against the wet foundations of the fire pump, pressing his cheek right up against an oily hose coupling. Another small wave of seawater sloshed up his body, reaching his chest this time. He began to feel real panic.

He was faintly aware of noises in the compartments above the pump room, or maybe it was in the fire room next door. Somewhere close. It sounded like men up there, shouting in the distance, pulling fire hoses. Right, yeah, that's what it is: fire hoses. A damage-control team. There should be an investigator coming. Guy the team sent out in advance to see where the damage was. They could get him out. Like that guy? Oh God. That guy had done this, piled this shit on him, left him here. Have to get all this shit off my chest, get up that ladder. Damn pump room was taking on water. He could hear the spray more distinctly now; it sounded as if it was no longer hitting metal, but water instead. The water slopping around his hips and legs sounded heavier, deeper. Where the fuck is the eductor pump?

He gave another great heave, pushing up with all his might. I'm a big guy, goddamn it, ought to be able to move this shit just a little, just enough, get my arm out, get two hands free. But then his heels slipped and the pile sagged back onto his chest. The stink of fuel oil became more pronounced, as if he had stirred something up. Face it, man, shit's got you pinned down.

"*HEY!*" he yelled. "*Hey,* get me outta here. Hey, man, need a hand down here! HEY!" He was shouting as loudly as he could, the noise breaking his head. Goddamn, it hurt. But a part of his mind knew that the spray was masking his shouts for help. Nobody came. There was no blaze of light through the hatch in the overhead, no hatch opening up, no guy sticking his head in. Nothing. Just the dark and the water. He yelled again.

As if in answer, the ship lurched in the trough. There was a distinct metallic crack from the other side of the fire pump. The spraying sound of the leak became more substantial, deeper, and louder. Oh shit, damn fire main's busted. I gotta get up, get higher, get my goddamn arms loose or I'm gonna fucking drown in here. He yelled again, then thought he heard a response. Sounded like someone was banging on the overhead, maybe the hatch. Adrenaline pumping now, he began to twist and flail in the oily water, trying desperately to get both arms free, his head held rigidly off the cold steel of the fire pump, using his legs, his hands useless. Pull, man, pull! Move *something,* anything to get out from under this shit. He started to cough and choke on the pungent mix of salt spray, fuel oil, and warm seawater that seemed to be everywhere. It felt as if he was trying to pull a train uphill, all this metal, uphill like in a nightmare, and then he realized, Oh Jesus, the deck's moving, the deck's tilting, the ship's tilting over to one side—and staying there.

He was crying now, his eyes stinging from the oil and his own fear. He wished he had a light, any kind of goddamn light. There should be battle lanterns in here. There *had* been battle lanterns before—before what? He couldn't remember why he was down here. The pile of pipes and angle irons moved then, not much, but just enough so that he could roll to the left. He jumped at it, pushing with his legs, tearing his shirt, getting over on his left side, something sharp digging hard into his ribs, breaking the skin even, the cut stinging when the water came sweeping back across the compartment, washing all the way up to his shoulder. But he could move. He was moving, pushing with his hips and his one good arm, until he could roll all the way over on his stomach, freeing both arms. Yeah, that's it. Now you've got it, man. Now, just hunch up and do a push-up. Oh God, my hands. Heave it up; tighten it up. You can make it, man. You can make— But then the ship rolled back the other way and down he went, the pile of steel banging onto deck plates and the pump foundation, flattening him, one big pipe hitting his head hard enough to dazzle him. He felt his mouth pressed down onto cold steel in an oily kiss.

And then blessedly, the water all drained away, down his back, down past his waist, his thighs, and he could feel air on his legs. Oh thank Christ. He could hear it rushing away. And then it paused, gurgling, gathering, and, to his horror, came rushing back, sweeping all the way over his body and over his face and head, foaming in his ears like a wave on the beach, the oil stinging his eyes even though they were clamped shut like his teeth. For several terrifying seconds, he couldn't breathe, and then, miraculously, he could. Gotta get up. Gotta get up. Move your face before it comes back. You know it's coming back. Move, move anything, strain every muscle, kick, break your bones, you have to, but move before the— And then he heard it all withdrawing again, sloshing away like a live thing, the spray from the cracked fire main really loud now, lots of goddamn water gathering in the darkness there, gathering to come back and— Then it came, a rushing swirl of oil and water, some bits of wet paper, submerging his face and eyes and ears, making his hair stream out, stealing all his air. Grimly, he squeezed his eyes shut and held his breath and waited for the wave to recede. It'll go away, and then you can breathe, and then you'll have to do it again, keep doing it until those guys get down here. They're coming. They're working on it. Yeah right, that's what they always say—they're fucking working on it. But they are. You heard 'em. There, the water's going back down. There, now breathe, once, twice. Don't try to move. Conserve your energy. But breathe deep, get that fucking air, get it all, store it up, and don't worry about the deck.

As the water gathered again across the compartment, he felt the ship move, and then he heard a new sound, something big and really heavy shifting, making a deep creaking groan of wounded metal, the voice of a billion crystals of steel deforming, bending, shearing. Oh Jesus, the fire pump, the fire pump was moving, the four-hundred-pound fire pump. It was moving. Maybe, maybe he could get clear. Which way's it going? Where— And then the water came rushing back for a third time. Used to it now; you know what to do. Let it come. You've got lots of air. Wait it out, wait for it to retreat. What's that, what's that on my arm? My arm! An immense, crushing, amputating steel weight settled down on his arm and he forgot about the water, forgot his face was submerged, forgot there was no air, and opened his mouth and screamed his way into eternity.

This time, the water stayed.

56

Brian left Combat, checking both the damaged and un-damaged modules once more to make sure no one had been left behind. He hurried out to the catwalk on the port side and then headed aft to reach the ladder leading up to the signal bridge. The signal shack was empty and the door locked. The night was clear, with stars visible and a cool wind blowing out of the northeast. The ship rolled slowly, with no way on, but the blowers were still going high up on the forward stack, which meant the snipes still had one boiler on the line in the forward plant. The two Spook directors towered above him in the darkness; they were slewed out on the port beam, one pointing high, the other almost flat. System Two. He walked over to the forward end of the signal bridge area and looked down on the forecastle. There he could see several dozen men congregated, with the uninjured staying separate from the area behind the missile-launcher ramp where the docs had set up. Someone had energized the forward replenishment lights; the entire forecastle was bathed in red light, lending a hellish appearance to the scene. Brian looked around at the horizon, but there was only darkness. The nearest ship was *Preble,* and she was sixty miles out to the southeast. He assumed that she would be on the way by now.

He went back down the ladder, stopping on the last rung to look down two levels to the boat decks. Under the glow of the midships' red replenishment lights, several men were gathered in damage-control gear, some wearing OBAs, others tending portable fire pumps and eductors. A thick cloud of black smoke interlaced with streaks of steam boiled out from somewhere low on the port side and from two exhaust vents at the after end of the boat decks. A diminishing cloud of low-pressure steam vented from the after stack, which meant that Two Firehouse was out of business. There must be a hell of a damage-control battle going on inside, he thought.

Then he realized he was standing just about level with and behind the EW module in CIC. He quickly walked forward along the catwalk on the starboard side to the pilothouse. With the power out on the 03 level, the only energy left on the bridge came from the battery-operated battle lanterns. The radar repeaters and other bridge instruments were lifeless. Brian checked to make sure Folsom had taken the deck log. He thought about the captain back there in the wreck of Combat, probing the brains of a five-hundred-pound high-explosive bomb with morphine sulfate flowing in his veins and a cancer dining on his belly. He shivered and headed for the interior ladders to get down to the forecastle, holding his hand over his face against the rising pall of oil smoke.

He arrived on the forecastle and found Jack Folsom conferring with the medical officer behind the missile launcher. Folsom had the deck log rolled under his arm like a morning newspaper. They stopped talking when he walked up. The medico went back to the triage station. Folsom started right in.

"Mr. Holcomb, I've got the chief radioman rigging an HF portable set up on the bow. The docs have set up a triage station out here and they're treating people in the wardroom."

Brian had a quick vision of the *Berkeley*'s wardroom and shuddered, but Folsom was talking again.

"I guess you're still technically in charge of the watch section. We got Mr. Austin out here in the triage area. He's out of his head, babbling on about how he ran away, how ashamed he is. He's really carrying on."

"I don't know what he's talking about," Brian said. "I never saw him run. But look, we need to get a guy on the One JL circuit right away. And where's the exec?"

"XO's running the damage-control effort amidships, sir. Mr. Benedetti's in DC Central, and the XO's amidships, directing traffic from the sounds of it. They've got all three repair parties working the midships damage, but the rest of the ship seems to be okay. Everybody's at their GQ station except the people who had to evacuate amidships and the injured from Combat and the main spaces, and we've got comms with all the major GQ stations. The after plant is out of commission, with Two Fire Room flooded out and Two Engine Room smoked out. Forward plant is running and we have power everywhere except where there's been damage." Folsom looked around for a second and then asked in a lowered voice, "Sir, what's the story with that unexploded bomb?"

Brian filled him in. Folsom shook his head. "He's gonna try to defuse that thing? They've got EOD guys down on the carriers; they can probably have somebody here in a couple of hours!"

"We may not have a couple of hours. That *thing* is armed and ticking, Jack. He used to be EOD himself, and he thinks it's going to go off. And there's . . . well, there are other factors involved that I can't get into right now. Get a guy on the phones with him, and then I want to get on the circuit myself. Where's Garuda?"

"He's helping the radio pukes set up the emergency radio."

"Get him over here and get him in contact with gun plot. I want them to energize the SPG-fifty-three gunfire-control radar and start sweeping the horizon with it. If the bad guys are listening to us electronically, I want them to see fire control. Even though they lost all their planes, this would not be a good time for a second air raid. And if he can put the SPS-ten or the forty on the air, even better, although I think we'd have to reenter Combat to do that. Then see if Main Control can give us the starboard main engine, and let's head south at ten knots; steer from after steering. Go."

Folsom ran off to get a man on the phones and to talk to Garuda. Brian found the 1JV talker crouched down at the base of the missile launcher, wedged between his phone box and the base of the launcher to stay upright against the slow roll. The paint on the deck crunched under his feet; all the missile launches had burned the deck paint and nonskid to a crisp. The stink of boosters was still very strong. The chief boats would have a fit, he thought idly. He wondered what Martinez was doing right now. Probably standing in front of the fuel fire and pissing on it. The phone talker, a sonarman, was tied into a barrel switch, which gave him access to any sound-powered phone circuit in the ship. He tapped the man on the shoulder.

"If you've got midships, see if you can get the XO on the line, and then give me the phones."

The talker did some talking and then nodded at Brian, handing him the headset.

"XO?"

"Yeah. What are you doing up on the fo'c'sle?"

"Sir, can you get to an admin phone? Or a barrel switch?"

"Admin phones are out. I can get to a barrel switch. What circuit you want?"

"Let's try JX." JX was the communications circuit, and the primary stations, Radio, the signal bridge, the bridge, and Combat had been evacuated; it ought to be private.

The talker switched over to JX for him and Brian waited. When the XO came up, he gave him a quick update, describing the damage to CIC, the unexploded bomb, the orders he had given since arriving on the forecastle, and what the captain was doing. The talker's eyes widened as he listened, but Brian couldn't help that. There was a long moment of silence. Brian could just imagine what was going through the XO's head, but this was an open line to every major GQ station in the ship if anyone had switched to JX when they had.

"Okay," the exec said finally. "You stay with him on the JL phone circuit. We've about got this fire under control here, but some of the burning fuel got inside and we've got a long night ahead of us with the flooding problem. Two Fire Room is open to the sea; there's nothing we can do about that. We're shoring like bastards in Two Engine and in the engineering admin spaces, and the repair guys are trying like hell to get the smoke out of the ship so we can see what we really have inside. Once the smoke got loose, everybody just had to bail out. We're presuming the BTs in Two Firehouse are goners—the guys in Two Engine heard main steam get loose in there. How far away's the nearest ship?"

"*Preble*'s about sixty miles to the south. If the BAR-CAP's on the ball, they'll have sounded the alarm. That's why I'm trying to get the forward plant on the line, so we can start south."

"There's some kind of problem in the starboard shaft alley, although the shaft is apparently able to turn. EM One Wilson—he was the investigator—says the space is flooded to the mark, though. But go ahead with the starboard engine. If the shaft will turn, get her going. May even stop this goddamned rolling. But you stay on the phones with the Old Man. Soon's I feel this shit's under control, I'll come forward and take over. I may even go up there with him."

"He said not to do that, XO. If that thing blows, we lose the CO and the XO."

There was a moment's silence on the line. "You and him have a talk, did you?"

"Yes, sir, we did." Brian hesitated. "I understand a lot more than I did."

"Do you understand that by fucking with our system here you have a lot to answer for tonight?"

Brian paused before answering. The exec was under a lot of stress and was probably exhausted after an hour of leading a fire-fighting effort, not to mention furious about what had happened.

"Well, hotshot?"

"He said that you would say that, XO. And he said that you were wrong. That you were both wrong."

This time it was the exec who went silent. There was going to be one hell of an after-action report to do here.

"All right, Holcomb. I'm not going to talk about this now. Get on the circuit with the captain. I'll be up on the fo'c'sle as soon as I can."

"Aye, aye, sir."

Brian handed back the phones, instructing the talker to go back to 1JV and keep his mouth shut. When he turned around, Garuda was standing there with Jack Folsom.

"Well?"

"Sir, we've got an HF circuit up with Alfa Whiskey, but we've got no codes, and that's a very unsecure net. He's got questions out the ass, but—"

"Tell him we request an immediate—and stress the word *immediate*—rendezvous with *Preble,* at my location—say those very words, *at my location*—and that we need the BARCAP to mark on top. Then tell him this is a no-shitter and go off the air.

"Sir, you want me to say—"

"Yes. Do it. They'll understand. And then send a radioman back into Central to see if you can activate the land-launch UHF circuit, and tie a KY-eight to it so we have a secure circuit. That way, when *Preble* shows up, we can talk secure. But have him check with me before he goes back up there."

Garuda nodded. "I'll go patch it myself," he said. "I know the patches as well as any of the radio pukes."

"Okay, but check with me before you go back inside. Jack, you got me that One JL?"

"Yes, sir, right over there."

Brian walked over to a set of bitts on the port side and sat down on one of them, where a deck seaman handed

572

him a set of phones. He put them on and then called the captain. He was aware that several of the men sitting on the deck nearby were clearly interested.

"Captain, this is Lieutenant Holcomb. Can you hear me, sir?"

There was a long silence, although he thought he could hear someone breathing on the line. Then a voice.

"Yes, Mr. Holcomb. I can hear you just fine. I was looking for the button, but it's taped down. I'm afraid the medicine has got me just a wee bit spacey at the moment. I've had to stop. I thought I heard my wife calling me, you see. Knew that was unlikely, but, well, it was not all unpleasant. But it seems to have passed and now I'm going back to work. You and the XO have everything else under control?"

Brian's mind raced. The morphine had him. Jesus Christ, he was up there fiddling with an unexploded bomb and he was flying on morphine. Answer him. Talk to him. Maybe get him to stop, get him out of there.

"Yes, sir, I just talked to him. They have the fires amidships under control and they're working on the smoke. I've got comms with Alfa Whiskey, and I think *Preble* is on her way."

"Oh, that's very good. XO's very good at what he does. Very good."

"Sir, you want to rest for a while? I can come back up there, bring you something—"

"No, no, no, Mr. Holcomb. I'm actually making progress up here. I've got the S and A section open. That's safing and arming to you, Lieutenant; that's EOD talk. I can see the fuzing circuits. But there's something in here I don't quite recognize, so I'm going slow, really slow, until I sort it all out. You've got everybody out of the area, right?"

"Yes, sir, the bridge, Combat, Radio are all clear. XO said he was going to come up there."

"No. I don't want that. I forbid that. Expressly forbid it. *Expressly*. That's why you keep the CO and the XO physically separated in battle, remember? So you don't lose them both. I forbid it, expressly forbid it."

Brian's heart sank. He was repeating himself. Babbling. This was a disaster. That damned bomb could go off on some kind of timer, or that sick old man might set it off in a haze of morphine sulfate. He couldn't let this go on. But he'd need help. The CO had forbidden the exec from going up there. But not Lieutenant Holcomb. Garuda. Garuda Barry would do it. He saw Folsom watching and he waved him over.

"Captain, I'm going to put Mr. Folsom on the line. He's the OOD. I've got to see about getting propulsion power back. Mr. Folsom will be right here. You need anything, you tell him and we'll jump right on it."

"Jump right on it. Okay. Jump right on it. But no jumping around up here, all right? This is a tricky bomb I've got here. Tricky Dicky bomb. Something not quite right with it. Not quite right."

"Yes, sir. Here's Jack."

Brian stood up and unhitched the phones, handing the set to Jack but putting his palm over the mouthpiece.

"He's on morphine, and he's floating in and out."

"Morphine! And he's fucking around with a—"

"Right. Maintain contact. Don't spook him. Just stay with him. Talk to him. Ask him to describe exactly what he's doing. It's a long story."

"Yes, sir. What are you going to do?" Brian looked at him. Folsom wasn't dumb; his eyes suddenly widened.

"I'm going to try to get him out of there," Brian said. "The XO's coming up here as soon as he can. He was going to go up to Combat, but the Old Man said no, for the obvious reasons. But he didn't say *I* couldn't go up there. I'm going to ask Garuda if he'll come along."

"Jesus Christ. All three of you could get—"

The sound of a Phantom jet cruising overhead at low altitude shattered the night air, making everyone jump. If it had not been such a distinctive noise, the thundering, complaining howl of two J-79 engines operating low and slow, some of the men out on the forecastle looked like they might have gone over the side. Garuda came over, with HooDoo in tow.

"Ain't got a radio, but it sounds like the BARCAP's back on station," Garuda said with a weary grin. He looked like he was painted for the stage in the garish red lights. Brian pulled him aside and briefed him on what was going on up in Combat. He told him everything.

"Son of a bitch. No wonder he stopped coming out. No wonder he looked like he did. Does."

"Garuda, I'm going back in there. I'm going to try to get him out, get him away from that bomb. It hasn't gone off yet, and Jack reminded me they've got real EOD teams down on the carriers." He looked straight at Garuda, who figured it right out.

"And you want some adult supervision, right? Somebody who knows where CIC is?"

Brian took a deep breath. "I sure do. But this is pure volunteer time. I don't want to think or talk about it much longer or I'll chicken out. But I can't leave him up there like that."

Garuda snatched another cigarette out of his pocket and lit up. "He's gonna fight it, you know," he said. "There's more goin' on there than disarming some damn bomb."

"Yeah, I figured that. That's why we'll need two guys. I hate to ask, but—"

"But you done did. Let's rock and roll."

Brian saw Fox Hudson come out of the port-side breaks hatch. He told Folsom to brief Hudson and to put Hudson in charge of coordinating with main Control to get the ship moving again. Then he and Garuda headed for the breaks, ignoring Hudson's questions. Garuda yelled back over his shoulder, "Log it, OOD. That way, we get medals if it goes off." Folsom just stared at him.

They went down the breaks and into the port-side weather decks hatch. Inside, they encountered a thin haze of smoke and the smell of medicinal ointments. Both men snapped on flashlights as they passed the wardroom door, where there were large plastic bags full of bloody dressings scattered around the vestibule. Brian had his foot on the ladder up to the next level when Chief Martinez came clumping up the ladder with Chief Jackson over his shoulder like a sack of potatoes. The chief had to turn sideways to get both Jackson and his OBA up the ladder. Jackson had a plastic bag over his face. Seaman Coltrane climbed the ladder behind them, his face also covered in a pastic bag. Garuda and Brian helped the chief get Jackson into a better carry, stripped off the EEBD hoods, and then helped to take him through the door into the wardroom. They sent Coltrane out to the forecastle, Garuda snatching his hood off before he ran out of air and suffocated himself. Once inside the wardroom, Brian almost did not want to look.

The emergency medical lighting had been rigged in the wardroom overhead and the three docs were scrambling with the wounded. Both tables had been covered in green surgical drapes and there were steel trays of instruments, portable respirators, piles of towels and bandages, and a good bit of blood everywhere. With triage being performed forward, the room was not crowded, although every chair, table, and open space on the carpeted deck held men in various states of injury. The medical officer, who was masked, looked over at the trio as they brought Jackson in.

"He been to triage?"

"No, Doc. Chief here just brought him up from down below. I don't know—"

"He bleeding?" the MO asked impatiently.

"Head wound, Doc," grunted Martinez. "He's breathin' okay. He can wait, I guess."

"Put him in that corner, but if he's not bleeding, I've got—" He gestured around the room and turned back to the table. Garuda and Martinez put Jackson down in a corner of the wardroom. His uniform was wet, but there did not appear to be any serious wounds. Brian could not see the head wound.

"Where'd you—" he began.

"I'll tell ya later, if that's okay, boss. Where you two bound? The ship's full of goddamn smoke."

"Let's get back outside," Brian said. Once out in the passageway, he briefed the boatswain on what they had topside and what they planned to do.

"Beggin' yer pardon, Mr. H., if he's spaced out and fuckin' around with a bomb, what we oughta be doin' is getting the fuck back outside."

"I can't do that, Boats. When I left him, he was fairly alert and operational, and probably the only guy in the

576

ship who could shut that thing down with some hope of success. Now that I know different, I can't just leave him to it. He'll set it off, kill himself, and do some big-time damage to the ship.''

Martinez looked at Garuda as though asking for some support, but Garuda just shrugged, as if to say, He's the lieutenant and yeah, he's crazy, but I'm dutybound to lend a hand.

"From what you're sayin'," the chief said, "Combat's fucked, anyway. And if it was me and I had a cancer in my belly, a bomb would beat what he's lookin' at.''

"I know, Chief. I expect that's part of it. But I couldn't live with myself knowing that I'd left him up there like that.''

"What you're all going to do is get back out on the fo'c'sle," a voice ordered. They turned, to find the exec standing on the top tread of the ladder, an OBA twisted across his chest, the breathing mask dangling over his shoulder by the two black hoses, his uniform soaked and his face caked with sweat and soot except for the white patch where his mask had been. "I'll take care of Captain Huntington.''

Brian stepped forward to face him. "He specifically ordered you not to, XO. If it goes wrong up there, we lose both the CO and the XO.''

"It's too late to play hero, Holcomb," the exec sneered. "It's because of you we're in this mess, and I'm not about to let you redeem yourself with some grandstand play. You're going to pay for this.''

Brian's face turned white in the gloom of the passageway. "Grandstand play?" he whispered, and then his voice rose in fury. "Is that what you call it? If we leave that man up there, his head full of morphine, he's going to set that goddamned thing off. And then we take another hit, a five-hundred-pound bomb that's already *inside* the ship. How about just once you start thinking about the *ship*, XO? Not about your career, your political reputation, or any of that shit. The *ship* is in this mess because you and he fucked it up. The *ship's* been hurt because *you* let dope run wild here to the point where *any* effort to straighten it up takes out half the rated men in a division! That's *your* doing, XO, you and the captain who didn't think straight. But at least he had an excuse— he's a sick old man. *You* damned well knew better! The real reason you want to go up there is you're afraid to face what's coming when this is all over, when the Navy finds out how you've been running things here, right, XO? Well, guess what, XO. If we're gonna get blown away here, *you're* the one's going to answer for this, not the junior officers. I've got two witnesses right here, heard him say it: The captain forbids you to go up there. CO and XO separated, so the *ship* is not left without a senior officer. Just like it says in the regs. So just for once, godammn it, take care of the ship. That old man's as good as dead, so we're saving the *ship*, okay? Just do your fucking job! For once, XO, just do your fucking job!''

Brian turned and sprinted up the ladder, with Garuda and Martinez in hot pursuit, leaving the exec in stunned silence on the ladder. At the top of the second ladder, they stopped. The smoke was thicker up here, a combination of residual oil-fire smoke and pall of smoldering electrical insulation coming from Combat. Brian saw that all the doors were closed. The three men crouched down to get closer to the deck and cleaner air.

"Open the door to the pilothouse; that'll let some of this shit out," Brian ordered. Martinez went through the chart house's passageway and locked back the doors, creating an instant draft from the lower decks. They went to the front door of combat and let themselves in, stepping quietly over the jumble of CIC furniture, dislodged consoles, the forest of light fixtures dangling from the overhead, and the tangle of tipped deck plates. Brian's throat was dry as he climbed through the wreckage in the surface module, his feet crunching on the broken glass from the DRT plotter. The battle lanterns had dimmed to yellow and some of their relays were chattering as the batteries ran out. Brian heard Martinez inhale sharply as they rounded the corner into the EW module with its grisly paint job.

The captain sat trancelike over the bomb, his tool kit spread out in a glinting pattern in front of him. He gave no sign that he was aware of their presence. As Brian stepped closer, he could see that the captain's eyes were closed and that he was rocking back and forth slowly, a trickle of drool coming from the right side of his mouth. The bomb was where it had landed, with two access panels unbolted, each one revealing a nest of wiring. There were no sounds coming from the bomb. Brian could see that two red wires had been pulled out of the rear access hole and clipped. He motioned for Garuda and Martinez to slip around behind the captain. Then on signal, all three bent down and lifted him away from the bomb, the tools tinkling as they scattered on the deck plates. It was like lifting a scarecrow, Brian thought. The man weighed nothing. The captain's head lolled forward and he mumbled something as Martinez took over, cradling the old man in his arms like a child, and carried him out of the space.

Brian looked down at the bomb, its deadly black shape made somehow less threatening with its innards exposed, and resisted the temptation to nudge it with his boot. He got down on his hands and knees and put his ear to the front section and then the back section, remembering what the captain had said about the stethoscope. Nothing, not a sound. By God, the Old Man had done it. He'd put it to sleep. From out of the corner of his eyes, he saw Garuda standing rigid, his fingers in his ears. He couldn't help himself; he started to laugh.

57

By the time Brian and Garuda had made it back down to the wardroom area, Martinez had carried the captain to his cabin and then gone to fetch one of the docs. The chief corpsman had come right up, leaving the medical officer and the baby doc to continue with their surgery. Out on the forecastle, Brian sent Garuda aft to the helo hangar to see whether they had a UHF radio working yet; then he went back up to the captain's cabin. He found the exec, Martinez, Jack Folsom, and the doc in attendance. The captain lay on his back in his bed, his head thrown back, his neck dry as crumpled parchment. The doc had an IV going and was fishing in his black bag for the makings for a second one. The stony-faced exec would not look at Brian. The captain made a sound and the doc bent over him.

"Say again, sir?"

"The log. I want the deck log," the captain whispered.

"I've got it with me, Captain," Jack said. "It's right here."

"Sit down here. Write what I tell you. Everybody else go away. Get back to your GQ stations. I'll call you. Doc, go get me some oxygen." The captain's voice was very weak but clear, the tone of command still present.

The doc left immediately; Brian, the exec, and Chief Martinez followed. The exec began issuing orders as soon as they were clear of the cabin, still not looking at Brian as they went down the ladder.

"Mr. Holcomb, you are still the evaluator. Reman Radio Central long enough to establish communications with the task force commander on a secure net. Patch it back to the helo deck control station. Then clear them out of radio until we get the ship desmoked. Give Alfa Whiskey a battle-damage report and an initial OpRep on the incident. When *Preble* shows up, tell them they're on-scene commander, and then you coordinate transfer of additional medical supplies and their corpsmen over here to help in the wardroom. Set up the bridge watch back on the helo deck and keep the area around CIC clear of people until we can get EOD up here and we *know* that bomb has been safed. I'll go to DC Central and continue the damage-control efforts. Understood?"

"Yes, sir. Understood."

The exec refastened his OBA mask and then dropped down the ladder to Broadway. The doc came back out of the wardroom with a green oxygen bottle in his hands and hurried back up the ladder. Brian fleetingly remembered the first rites. From the looks of the captain, they might need the last rites pretty soon. He stood there and looked up at Martinez.

"What's the story on Jackson?" he asked.

The chief took off his battered hat and wiped his massive brow. "Let's go out front," he said. "It's complicated."

The captain slumped back down onto his pillows. "Did you get it? Did you get it all down?" His voice was paper-thin.

A stunned Jack Folsom nodded. "Yes, sir. It's all in the log. But sir—"

"No, Mr. Folsom. No more talk. I'm out of energy and time. Give it to me and give me a pen. I'm going to sign, and then you're going to sign, as a witness to my signature. After that, find the Disbo and have him lock it up in his disbursing safe. Start another one for the rest of the night. No one is to see this one, not even the exec. No one, until the investigation party comes aboard. Those are my orders. Understood?"

Folsom gulped and nodded, handing over the log and the pen. The captain sat up long enough to sign the log, putting down his signature, rank, and serial number. Then he handed the pen to Folsom, who signed the same way. Folsom fully appreciated why the captain wanted this thing locked up.

"Now," the captain whispered, "let me rest. You've got lots to do when *Preble* shows up. Well done so far, Mr. Folsom."

"Thank you, sir. Shall I—"

"No. Nothing else. Pass me that oxygen bottle. Tell the exec to report back to me in an hour when he has more status. That's all, Mr. Folsom."

"Aye, aye, sir."

Folsom left the cabin, the log held tightly under one arm, and went in search of a messenger. Back in the darkened cabin, the captain lay motionless on the bed for a few minutes, sucking on the oxygen bottle. He then deliberately unwrapped the tape on his arms holding down the IVs and removed each one. He took several more deep breaths on the oxygen bottle and then slowly, painfully rolled off the bed and onto his hands and knees. He stayed that way for a few minutes, his head low, until the dizziness stopped. He took one more hit on the oxygen and then got up, staggered, and, holding on to the backs of chairs and edges of his cabinets, stumbled to the head. He knelt down in front of the stainless-steel sink and opened the cabinet under the sink. He fumbled with a green cardboard box marked SOAP, HAND, DISINFECTANT and withdrew a single, large ampoule and a ten-cc syringe. Bracing himself on his knees, his forehead pressed against the steel sink, he filled the syringe to the top mark, and then dropped the empty ampoule into the toilet. He found the biggest vein he could on his left wrist, and steadily injected the entire contents of the syringe. He pulled it out, snapped off the needle, and dropped the needle and the syringe into the toilet, and flushed everything away.

It took him a full minute to get back up to his feet and stagger back across the room, collapsing in the bed and grabbing for the oxygen bottle. After several deep breaths, he pushed the bottle away and began trying to reset the IV needles. His vision was blurring now, the edges of the bedroom growing dark, the darkness lined with tiny crackling flashes of light. His mind began to wander once more, back up to Combat, back to the bomb, finding the right wires, good damn job, that, and then his early days in *Hood,* the better days, the thrill of the big ship command and the loving look in his wife's eyes after the change-of-command ceremony. He had finally made it to his big ship, the WESTPAC deployment right ahead, the deep sense of pride and fulfillment, and the wondering curiosity as to how the darkness in this room could suddenly contain so very much light.

58

San Diego

Maddy sat on the couch by the phone, staring at it as if to draw from the silent instrument the courage to make the call to the captain's wife. She was pretty sure that she was ready to go over there for that talk, but she was having trouble forming the pretext.

She had made some basic decisions. First, Autrey was an episode in her life that she was going to keep secret from Brian. She had tossed and turned about it but finally decided that the damage that would be done was not worth it, especially in view of what else she had decided. Somehow she was going to make a go of this Navy life. If the rest of the wives could manage it, then so could she. She would focus on the mechanics and then wait and see if her own emotions would be as capable of enduring. In making this decision, she had also realized how much depended on Brian, but there was no chance at all if she ever told him about Autrey. So it had to be a secret.

She had been watching the married men in her Bank of America offices, men who went home every night, who seemed content with their life and prospects, and who did not seem to be inferior to those men like Brian who went to sea. Oh, less exciting perhaps, and their lunchtime stories were painfully mundane compared with say, Brian's descriptions of the typhoon and the incredible feats of the chief boatswain. One big difference was this: She could not tell Brian's stories, as their wives probably could tell all of their stories. Brian had his life at sea and a marriage. For the civilians, married life was half their day. And that was at the core of it: She needed the constant sharing that she pictured marriage to be. She needed more than the occasional excitement of a sailor's homecoming. But maybe that's what the wives had found out: You share with your husband when he's there, and with the rest of the wives when he's not.

Now she felt she was ready to talk to Mrs. Huntington, to try to express some of these feelings, not in justification or defense of what she had done so much as in an effort to see if, in the older woman's experience, there was room for her, after all.

She picked up the phone. It was 8:30 at night. She dialed the number. The phone rang four times. She was about to hang up when Mrs. Huntington picked up.

"Hello?"

"Mrs. Huntington, this is Maddy Holcomb."

"Yes, dear. It's good to hear your voice."

"Mrs. Huntington, I, um, I think I'm ready to talk to you. Privately. Actually, I've been getting up the nerve to call you for a couple of days. I'd like to come over. Tonight, if I may."

"Maddy, are you all right? You're not in any trouble are you? Is someone . . . bothering you?"

"No, it's nothing like that. I've made some decisions about my future, and I wanted to talk to someone who, well, who has experience with this Navy wife business."

"I see. I'd be delighted to have you come over. I'll put the coffee on and we can sit up and talk all night if you'd like to; heaven knows, I've done that before. You come right ahead. And bring your things—the ferry stops running a little after midnight. You can use the guest room and go to work tomorrow right from here. It's not a problem at all, okay? You come right ahead."

"Thank you, Mrs. Huntington. I'll be there in a bit."

An hour later, overnight bag in hand, Maddy was walking through the Huntingtons' front hall to the living room. Mrs. Huntington was dressed in slacks and a sweater, with slippers on her feet. She had greeted Maddy with a smile and an uncharacteristic hug, taken her coat, and then led her to the captain's study to talk. Maddy had never been in the study. It was a large square room with bookcases on two sides. On a third wall were ship's plaques, two ship's bells, a barometer, a couple of flags folded into triangular cases, and a dozen pictures of the captain in various naval settings during his career. The fourth wall held a set of French windows that looked out into the Huntingtons' walled backyard. A brilliant

Oriental rug covered almost the entire floor; a small gas fireplace hissed in one corner. Two large leather chairs and a desk completed the room.

"This is the 'I love me' room," Mrs. Huntington said with a smile. "Every naval captain has one."

Maddy laughed as she remembered Brian's efforts to turn one corner of their apartment into a similar shrine. Mrs. Huntington had set up coffee and cookies on a small table between the two leather chairs, along with a silver tray with liqueurs and two snifters. Maddy chose coffee and sat down in one of the chairs, away from the fire. She was wearing wool slacks and a light blue sweater over a silk blouse in deference to the cool autumn temperatures. Mrs. Huntington took a cup of coffee as well, then sat back.

"Well, dear, I think the expression is, It's your nickel," she said.

Maddy took a deep breath. She had been having second thoughts ever since she had seen the pictures and the plaques. Was this a smart thing to do? Was she somehow imperiling Brian's career by coming over here to reveal some pretty private thoughts to the captain's wife? But then she told herself, Consider what she already knows.

"Right," she began, then cleared her throat. "Well, I think this deployment has brought me to kind of a cross-roads in my marriage to Brian. The last thing I ever envisioned happening was what did happen—I got involved with another man."

She told Mrs. Huntington the story of Autrey, starting with the night at MCRD and ending with the fact that Autrey was now gone, probably overseas to Vietnam. Mrs. Huntington's only reaction during the entire recitation was a small frown at the mention of Tizzy Hudson's name, but Maddy pressed on.

"We—I mean Brian and I—did not part gracefully when the ship left. I've come to see now that that was mostly my fault and that I was behaving selfishly. And since then, what with the letters being as much as six weeks out of phase, a not very good phone call from Subic, and some of the things going on in the ship . . . well, Brian's not having the best time of his life, either.

585

Now, what you said the other day really made me think about what I want out of life. I'm pretty sure I can bury the fact that I got involved with Autrey, especially since I think—no, I know—I want to try this Navy marriage business again."

She went on to tell the captain's wife what she had decided, then asked her what she thought. Mrs. Huntington sipped her coffee thoughtfully for a few minutes, staring into the fire for so long that Maddy was beginning to wonder whether she had been listening.

"Well," she said finally, putting down her cup, "that's a big decision indeed. Let me ask you something. In light of what's just happened, do you feel that you can be faithful to Brian from here on out? I mean, what's to keep this all from happening again?"

Maddy uncrossed her legs and sat forward in the chair. "In a nutshell, I think it has to do with my knowing what I want out of marriage. With Autrey, I satisfied my fear of being alone, but it didn't really work, did it? Autrey got what he wanted, and then he, too, was gone. As you pointed out."

"But your own needs had to have had a part in all that, Maddy. Can you reasonably expect Brian to meet those needs, assuming that he's going to stay in the Navy and go on with his career?"

Maddy frowned. "I thought you would approve this decision, Mrs. Huntington."

"I'm all for it, Maddy, as long as you know what you're deciding. Because, believe me, it would be better for you *and* for Brian if you told him what's happened and go ahead and take the consequences than to fool yourself into thinking that all you have to do is join the wives' club to solve your problem. You're a beautiful woman, Maddy. This problem is probably going to come up again."

Maddy shook her head. "My attraction to Autrey was always, to put it bluntly, entirely physical. It surprised me that I hadn't . . . I don't know, outgrown that part of me after college. I was always in control in college. Autrey ambushed me; he was just better at it than I was, I guess. But what I recognized now is that I was all

586

wrapped up in myself, my problems, my loneliness, my needs, instead of focusing on our marriage."

"I guess the key question then, Maddy, is whether or not Brian can fulfill your expectations on a full-time basis, whether he's there or not. Because if you truly need *many* men in your life, then it doesn't matter whether Brian stays home or not, in which case you'd be better off to let him go now and not destroy his naval career."

Maddy shook her head. "Deep down inside, it's not many men I need. I just need a full-time man. Brian and I usually get along famously. It's only when these damned deployments, or shipyard trips, or refresher training, or fleet exercises come along that I have trouble. I've always understood what's expected. What's expected is that I put up with the separation and knuckle down and be a good little Navy wife. I'm sorry—that was patronizing. But what I meant was that there is a clearly defined role. I'm just now understanding that this role can be a means to an end, which is a stable marriage based on all the usual things—love, shared expectations, plans for the future, children. The part of me that fell for Autrey just has to go back in its box until I can figure out a way to make it useful to my marriage. Hell, I don't know if I can succeed at this. What's changed is that I'm willing to try. That's the essence of it, and that's why I'm here imposing on you."

Mrs. Huntington leaned forward and poured herself some more coffee. "You're not imposing, Maddy, and I'm not questioning your sincerity. This must be very difficult to talk about. I know it would be for me. I think a lot of this has to do with the fact that you are a generation younger than I am and that your generation has come along in these . . . Well, disturbed times. Let me tell you a little bit about my marriage so you can see where I'm coming from, as they say nowadays, and then perhaps I can give you some more advice. Mercy, as soon as I think of what to say."

Maddy smiled and sat back to listen. Mrs. Huntington told her the story of her marriage to Warren Huntington, from the early days as ensign through almost three decades of steady advancement in the Navy.

"He's gone from seaman recruit to Captain, USN, Maddy, and the Navy has a special place in its heart for men who accomplish this. They are held up as examples to young recruits everywhere as symbols of what an opportunity a service career presents. And when he got the Navy Cross for throwing that bomb fuze over the side, his future was just about guaranteed. As was mine, you see. I won't say that I was never tempted to stray during all those years, but, for me, it was much easier to play it straight. The direct consequences of being unfaithful became much greater as time went on and both he and I had more to lose as he went up the ladder. I'm not saying it's perfection; far from it. But you learn, over time, what to say and what not to say, when to fight and when to give, how to disagree—you know, the rules, and these are rules you apply only to this one person. And, of course, we had three children, which makes an enormous difference. I think another secret has been that we both used the separations to refresh and strengthen the emotional ties. You tend to say things in letters that you forget to say around the house, and while you may both be a little embarrassed by those thoughts later on, they're still there. And if it works, you tend to become very close indeed. That closeness is amplified by every instance of what you see happening around you in other marriages, where perhaps it's not so good."

"Like mine."

"Well, yes, like yours. And I don't mean that to criticize you or hurt your feelings. But it makes a large difference when marriage is the only or main thing you have at your life's center, marriage, children, a family, even if it's a family operating under special circumstances. Now, of course it makes you more vulnerable, too, because if that all blows up and sinks, you're left with nothing and you have to start over. That's the risk. But the risk is what generates the value, I think, and when you value something, you don't stray. Maybe that's a bit too simplistic, but—"

Maddy shook her head. "No, I understand it perfectly. I do have at least a start on a career in finance, and the fact that we don't have children at least implies that other avenues are still open, I guess. I've never consciously looked at it that way, but I suppose it's true. And maybe having all these alternatives blinded me to what I really wanted out of marriage, and life, for that matter." She paused. "You spoke of risk; for me, the risk is that I'll screw it up."

"Well, and then there's Brian. He'll have something to say about all this, won't he?"

Maddy shook her head slowly. "No, I don't think so, Mrs. Huntington," she said. "This is something else I've come to understand, I think. It's our call, isn't it, as to whether this marriage business works, whether it's in the Navy or in the civilian world? I don't think Brian has all these problems; he's pretty much a straight-ahead kind of guy. He showed me what and who he was, showed me that he loved me, and asked me to marry him. I fell in love, said yes, and then made promises I didn't keep. If this is going to work, it'll be because *I* make it work."

Mrs. Huntington just looked at her for a moment. Then she smiled. "Well, Maddy, if you've grasped that truth, you'll have no problems whatsoever. Being a Navy wife is child's play compared with learning that lesson. Shall we switch to cognac?"

Maddy relaxed with the compliment and they talked after that, comparing their upbringing, their families, and their college and Navy experiences. Inevitably, the conversation came around to the ship.

"You mentioned things going on in the ship that were making Brian's life difficult. I must admit, this cruise in *Hood* has been somewhat different for us. Warren's told me very little about what's going on. His letters have been . . . well, lighter, more superficial than in past cruises. I'm actually kind of worried about him. He is sixty, you know."

Maddy bit her lip. Brian had not wanted to talk too much about this either, at least in part because he was apparently going against the wishes of the captain.

"It has to do with drugs," she said finally. "There's apparently a lot of drug use in the ship and it's caused some big problems."

"Ah. Drugs. Warren feels that's the greatest betrayal

he's faced in his entire career, when the men use drugs in the ship. I think that's one of the reasons he's done things a little differently in this ship."

"Differently?"

"Well, Warren has always been Mr. Straight Arrow when it comes to matters of discipline in his ships. This is his third command, you know. But in *Hood*, I've detected sort of a . . . well, 'let's all just get through this' attitude, especially since the cruise began. I almost think the drug problem is proving to be just too hard to deal with. Some of his letters—oh, there's the phone. My goodness, what time is it?"

"It's almost eleven-thirty."

Mrs. Huntington got up and headed for the kitchen. "Eleven-thirty. If this is the Navy calling, it's not good news, whatever it is."

Maddy helped herself to a small measure of cognac while Mrs. Huntington went to take the call. She felt somewhat better for her talk with the older woman. There had been no blinding light of revelation, but more of a confirmation that she was on the right track. Like the captain's wife, she realized she had a good man. Mrs. Huntington had let the possible consequences be her guideline for how she conducted herself in a Navy marriage. Maddy was going to have to work harder than that, but she was increasingly confident that she had come up with the right answer. Mrs. Huntington returned.

"Well," she said, sitting down abruptly in the leather chair, "my instincts were correct. The ship's been in some kind of incident. That was Capt. Tom Farwell, the local headquarters chief of staff. And that's all they know. He'll call back."

Maddy felt an icy finger touch a nerve somewhere in her stomach. "That's all they know?" she asked, her voice unnaturally loud. "They call you in the middle of the goddamned night and say something's happened and we'll get back to you?"

"Now, Maddy, don't get all excited. Tom said that this was literally all the information they had at headquarters. That's the Navy system—when something happens, the ship is supposed to get a message out immediately, even if it only says something's happened. That alerts the rest of the Navy and gets things moving—you know, other ships, helicopters, whatever. This is standard procedure."

"Standard procedure. My God. So what do we do now?"

Mrs. Huntington smiled sympathetically. "We wait for the next call. When I actually know something and can answer the same kinds of questions you're asking, then you and I will make some phone calls to the other wives. If it's serious, I suspect those who can will gather over here in the morning until we find out the extent of it."

"But did he say it was a collision, or a—"

"They don't know, Maddy. They've received an initial report that *Hood* has been involved in some kind of incident, with amplifying information to follow. That's literally all they have."

Maddy sat back, suddenly ashamed of herself—and afraid. Ten minutes ago, she had been confidently calculating how she was going to put her marriage back on track. With one phone call, she had become, once again, a chip in the maelstrom, at the mercy of whatever news might be winging its way back across the dark Pacific. Mrs. Huntington was speaking.

"It might be hours before they call again, Maddy. Let me show you to the guest room. You can try to get some sleep. I know you have to work in the morning."

"Well, all right, but I don't think I'll be able to sleep. I mean, this is almost cruel, calling the wives like that and then leaving us all hanging."

"Better that we hear it from the Navy than see it on the TV in the morning. The Navy tries very hard to protect its dependents. Come, the room's right down here. Yes, bring that."

Maddy took her snifter of cognac along with her to the guest room. Mrs. Huntington showed her where the bathroom was and then suggested she just turn out the lights and nap until the next phone call. "It literally might be tomorrow morning," she said.

Maddy stood in the bedroom doorway. "Thanks for hearing me out tonight," she said. "I really needed to talk to a friendly face. I think I already knew what I was going to do, but it helps to be able to check it out."

"Of course, dear. Now try to get some sleep. This will probably take a while."

But it didn't. The next phone call came in two hours, after Maddy had finally managed to drift off to sleep for about thirty minutes. Her senses must have been listening, because she sat bolt upright on the bed, still dressed. She waited in the darkened bedroom and then heard Mrs. Huntington coming toward the back of the house. She got up and went to the door; her left foot was asleep. Mrs. Huntington was silhouetted at the end of the hallway.

"What did they say this time?" Maddy asked.

Mrs. Huntington spoke slowly, as if the words hurt. "They said that the ship had been attacked by North Vietnamese aircraft and that there has apparently been some serious damage. There's no word on personnel casualties, and it'll be another hour or so before the nearest ship can get to her. All this came from one of the carrier aircraft when it was still dark out there. Tom says the initial reports are pretty—fragmentary, that was the word."

Mrs. Huntington turned on the hall light. She suddenly looked much older, her normally bright face sagging just a bit around the edges in the harsh light. Maddy's heart went out to her. So close, she thought, so close to capping off a thirty-year career with a big ship command, and now this, this unknown "incident." She took two steps and reached out to touch the older woman's arm.

"It'll be all right," she said, projecting a confidence she did not feel. "*Hood*'s a big ship, and Brian says the Gulf of Tonkin is full of Navy ships and aircraft. Hadn't we better call some of the other wives now? And will the Navy have more information for us pretty soon?"

"Yes, we probably should, and no, I don't think there'll be anything more until the first ship gets there. Apparently *Hood*'s not communicating. And actually, let's not call anyone right now. It's one-thirty in the morning, and we'd just frighten everyone we called for no good reason at this time of the night. The ferries don't even start running until five-thirty. Go back to bed. I'll call you at six and we can let the others know then."

They got back up at six. Mrs. Huntington made the first call to Barbara Mains, the exec's wife, which would bring her to the Huntington's house at eight. Maddy reheated some coffee and tried to sort out her thoughts as Mrs. Huntington delivered the grim news. The rest of the wives straggled over throughout the morning, after dispatching kids to school. Some with infants or preschoolers checked in by phone. Maddy remembered to call the bank, then helped to organize coffee when Mrs. Mains showed up. If the exec's wife wondered why Maddy was already there, she did not ask and Maddy did not volunteer. By midmorning, there were a dozen worried women at the Huntingtons', not including two next-door neighbors who had come over when they had seen all the cars. Both were retired Navy wives and had recognized the symptoms of a crisis. Tizzy Hudson had arrived last, coming from work. She had expressed to Maddy her total impatience with the lack of information.

"Damn Navy, all they do is play these games. Everything's always hush-hush, big deal, big secret. I am so sick of this crap!"

The chief of staff called again at nine with no further news. He called again at eleven o'clock. Maddy answered the phone and handed it over to Mrs. Huntington. The captain's wife listened in silence for a few minutes while the rest of the wives sat around the living room in chairs or on the floor and tried not to stare at her. Mrs. Huntington said thank you in a soft voice and then hung up. When she turned to face the women, her face was gray.

"Well," she announced, "that was Capt. Tom Farwell, the chief of staff. They've confirmed that the ship was attacked by several North Vietnamese jets in the middle of the night, sometime yesterday. Or perhaps it's tomorrow—the time zones confuse me. Anyway, they apparently managed to shoot down all of them except one, which crashed aboard the ship. There's been a serious fire and one of the boiler rooms is flooded. The ship has been taken under tow by USS *Preble* to get her out of range of enemy aircraft. They're going to go back to Subic. He said they had more details on the damage but that they felt we didn't need to know them right now. They have to figure out what they're going to tell the press. And he warned me that the press might try to get information from us. He asked us to be discreet."

"And what about . . . injuries?" asked Mrs. Grafton, not wanting to use the dreaded word *casualties*. Mrs. Huntington bowed her head. She spoke in a small voice.

"Everyone in the boiler room—and I think he said there were four enlisted men there—was killed when a steam line ruptured. There may have been two or three other enlisted killed in the CIC when a part of the jet came through the superstructure; they're still not sure how many."

"So all the casualties were enlisted?" asked Mrs. Mains, posing the question that was on everyone's mind.

Mrs. Huntington stared at the floor. "No," she said finally. "There was one officer who died. The headquarters chaplain is on his way over here right now."

There was a general intake of breath in the room. "You mean he wouldn't tell you who?" Tizzy cried, an edge of hysteria showing in her voice. Mrs. Huntington gave her a severe look.

"They never do that over the phone, Tizzy. They're on their way right now. I think . . . I think we all just have to be patient and quiet, and not get all hysterical. I know . . . I *know* this is very hard, for you, for me, for all of us. It's rather like waiting for a jury, isn't it? I think I'll just go make some more coffee," she said as she turned away from the ring of stunned faces in her living room.

Maddy sat down hard on a cushion on the floor and hugged her knees. She could not bear to look at any of the other women's faces, afraid that she would start crying as two of them already had done. She saw Tizzy staring at the floor and biting her nails. A storm of thoughts whirled through her own mind. It was as if an executioner was coming, an executioner who would pull into the driveway in a half hour in a black sedan, who would get out, knock on the door, and then ask, a piece of paper in his hand, which one of them was Mrs.—who? Everyone in the room was silent, allowing the sounds of a fall morning on Coronado to intrude: birds in the garden singing, the occasional car going by out front, the muted thunder of jets over on the air station heading out for the day's training sessions, the *blat* of the ferry's horn and an answering whistle from a destroyer standing down the channel. Another great Navy day, as Brian would sometimes quip as he headed out to the base in the morning. Jesus Christ, could it be him? She searched her intuition and found nothing. No anticipatory dread, no unbidden certain knowledge, no fatal hunches. Brian was alive. Brian had survived. How could she know that? Was she just indulging in blind optimism, whistling past the graveyard, her subconscious lying to her to protect her from such a calamity? Wives always know when something's happened. Faithful, loving wives always know, that is. Unfaithful, selfish, "it's me or the Navy" wives, they may not know. For the first time, the import of what might be coming and the possible connection, the consequence of her infidelity, began to loom over her like an approaching thundercloud. She hugged herself tighter, her mind squeezing out the images even as her eyes squeezed back the tears.

The sounds of the official car's arrival outside in the street penetrated the silence in the living room like a glass breaking. They could hear every sound—the brakes, the idling engine shutting down, the chunk of doors. Maddy couldn't stand it. She got up and headed for the front door. Mrs. Huntington had come back into the living room and was standing in the middle of the room, her hands worrying a dish towel. Maddy saw her face out of the corner of her eye, saw her expression, and then the cold flash of intuition came. She knew just from looking at the older woman's face. *She* knew. She whipped her face around to look through the window in the door, and when she saw the tall four-striper coming up the walk with the young chaplain, his face grim, the piece of paper in his hands, she remembered what Brian had said about these things. If a lieutenant commander dies, they send a lieutenant commander to make the notification. They had sent a captain.

Her mouth dry, her eyes stinging, she opened the

door. The two officers stopped outside, out of Mrs. Huntington's line of vision. Maddy stared at them until she realized she was blocking the doorway. She stepped back, unconsciously trying to put distance between herself and them. The captain stepped through the doorway and looked across the room directly at Mrs. Huntington. She looked back into his eyes for a few seconds and then visibly wilted, dropping the towel and putting both hands to her mouth and making a small sound of despair. While the rest of the wives looked on uncomprehendingly at first, Maddy moved quickly across the room to hold her, to put her arms around her and to pull her in, and, to her sudden surprise, to hold her upright. Out of the corner of her eye, Maddy saw a gray-faced Tizzy Hudson put her hand over her mouth as if she was going to be sick. Mrs. Huntington had been taller than Maddy, but now she seemed to have shrunk with the blow. There was a chorus of "Oh no," "My God," all uttered from the heart and propelled by a marrow-deep sense of relief among them that the blow had fallen on someone else.

Captain Farwell and the chaplain helped Maddy to shepherd Mrs. Huntington into the study, where she collapsed into one of the leather chairs. Maddy stepped back as Mrs. Mains led the rest of the wives into the study. She joined in the chorus of condolences, torn as they all were between the emotions of sympathy and grief for the captain and his wife and her secret urge to shout with joy that it was not her husband, followed in turn by a small wave of guilt for being selfish at a time like this. Maddy edged out of the room when she could, suddenly needing to be alone, away from this storm of raw emotions and away from the one person in the house who had been touched by death. Besides, she was not one of them; her good intentions had come a little late. She slipped out the door to the garden.

It was a typically bright and beautiful San Diego day outside. She suddenly hated this city with its postcard setting by the sea, its idyllic weather, its perpetually blue skies and balmy temperatures that seemed to be indifferent to the fate of ordinary mortals. She could visualize a massive earthquake, the "big one," as they called it out here, with the city in ruins and thousands perished in the rubble, and the skies would still be blue and the temperature lovely, despite the calamity on the ground. A Navy jet arced slowly over the neighborhood, turning on final for North Island. San Diego had been a Navy town for a long time. She wondered how many times over the decades this scene had been replayed, somber men in uniforms coming in black cars to tell yet another terrified woman that her world had ended on the sea.

Standing in the garden, listening to the sounds of grief, consolation, and anxiety within, she found all of her resolve and resolution dissolving. in the past week, she had learned that Brian and her marriage meant much more to her than she had ever imagined. She realized now that to "do your own thing" with human relationships was a snare and a delusion: It implicitly meant that you were going to go through life forever alone. But now this. Good God, was this how it would end? Last night, she had been ready to muster all of her strength, her powers of manipulation, and her determination to go forward with their Navy career. But now she was afraid again, afraid and very much alone.

Time had slowed down for the rest of the day. Terrified of going back to her empty apartment and too upset to go to work, she had simply stayed there, in the background, trying to be inconspicuous but unwilling to leave. At the end of the day, she had been sitting out in the garden, dozing and drained after the sleepless night before and the trauma of the morning, when Mrs. Huntington had come out onto the patio with the exec's wife, whose protestations had awakened Maddy. Mrs. Huntington was being firm.

"Barbara, go home. Maddy's here. You all have families to attend to. I'll be all right. She'll stay with me. Tom's making all the arrangements, so you guys go home now, please."

"Are you sure? I can get—"

"Please, I've kind of had it with crowds right now. Maddy's here. Please—"

The exec's wife withdrew then, taking along the three other wives still at the house. Mrs. Huntington walked slowly out into the garden and sat down in the chair next to Maddy. For almost a half an hour, she simply sat there, saying nothing at all. Maddy had taken her hand after awhile but kept her own silence. The evening shadows deepened until it was almost full dark, the familiar San Diego evening chill descending on the garden like an invisible mantle. Finally, the captain's wife spoke.

"Well, Maddy. All those brave words."

"Yes."

"They still hold true, you know."

Maddy bit her lip and shook her head.

"Yes, they do. Warren and I had twenty-seven years, only three less than the Navy had him. Death can come anytime, in a car crash, a fall in the bathtub, in sickness, anytime. And usually it's so mundane, so . . . awkward. We don't know what happened out there, but I do know in my bones that Warren would rather have died out there, doing what he had spent his life doing, than in all the hundreds of ways sixty-year-old men die here at home. I am very sad, and I think I'm going to cry a lot before sunrise, but if it has to be, this was a fitting death."

Maddy shook her head again. Her voice was small, as if she was talking to herself. "I'm just not sure. I don't think I'm strong enough to do this. To go through this, what you . . . Because it *is* what they do—they go in harm's way every time they go to sea. Brian told me that once and I teased him for being melodramatic, but it's true. Dear God, it's true! And I'm so scared." Despite herself, her eyes were filling with tears.

The captain's wife's voice was disembodied in the darkness of the garden. "I told you a Navy marriage was about risk, Maddy. Risk is what gives marriage value. The career, children if you have them, a love affair with one person that matures into the best kind of human bonding, these are life's treasures, and now, especially now, I'm counting on their being sustaining treasures. But if they're not at risk, whether because either of you might falter or because the career is inherently dangerous, or because you have alternative lives to fall back on, there's not half the value."

She paused to put her hand on Maddy's. "And now that you know this, what choice do you really have, Maddy Holcomb?"

59

Subic Bay, the Philippines

Lt. Comdr. Brian Holcomb stood on the hot concrete apron in front of the ops building at Cubi Point Naval Air Station. He wore pressed khakis with ribbons and his fore-and-aft cap. His uniform shirt had a black cloth band pinned to the left sleeve. Parked in front of the ops building was an Army Caribou, a short-haul, drop-ramp transport plane that was used to ferry cargo from Cubi Point Naval Air Station up to the big Clark Air Force Base outside Manila. The Caribou was painted out in camouflage, which made it look smaller than it actually was. The back ramp was open and an honor guard of perspiring *Hood* sailors stood in their whites at the back at parade rest, heavy M-1 rifles at their sides. Chief Jackson stood behind them. The crew of the Caribou hung around the flight deck doors, dressed in their olive drab flight suits. It was ten o'clock in the morning and they were waiting for the casket to come down from the hospital. The remains of the other six men killed in the attack were already onboard.

Across the bay, Brian could see the ship, her stern pointing into the opening of the floating dry dock, a clutch of tugs milling around her. They were pushing her back into the dry dock, where they would close the hole in the port side before she went back to the States. Vince Benedetti had estimated it would take ten days to position and weld the patch. Her flags could be seen at half-mast, even from here.

Brian felt as if he was AWOL, standing here on the tarmac while the ship was making the move to the dry dock. The board of inquiry had been going on for three days, and he was emotionally exhausted after being grilled for hours by the panel of captains and commanders, on both the air attack and the drug problem in the ship. And there was more to come when he returned to the ship. He had not yet been designated a party to the investigation, but one of the Navy lawyers on the board had advised him to request counsel. When he had asked whether he was being or going to be accused of something, the lawyer, a commander, had simply shrugged.

"You're going to be a pivotal witness, Mr. Holcomb. Frankly, the board's informal consensus is that you did very well, but I still think you ought to have counsel. If and when indictments are made, important witnesses can become targets, if you follow me."

Brian didn't really follow him, but he had submitted the request, anyway. His duffel bag was already on board the Caribou. The exec had appointed him as the official escort officer for Captain Huntington's remains. He would make the long flight back across the Pacific to Travis Air Force Base with Captain Huntington's body. He would then accompany the casket to Washington, D.C., where the captain would be buried at Arlington. In Washington, a full captain would assume the duties of escort at the national cemetery, but a lieutenant commander would suffice for the flight.

Since the casket would first land at Travis Air Force Base, located north of San Francisco, Mrs. Huntington would be allowed to accompany her husband's remains to Andrews Air Force Base in Washington. Strangely, at least to Brian, she had asked for Maddy to accompany her on the trip to Washington. In their short phone conversation the night before, Maddy had not explained it very well, other than to say that after the word had come in about the attack, they had all gathered and spent most of a day at the Huntingtons' waiting for further word from the Pacific. She said they had been relieved by the first reports that no officers had been casualties in the attack, then stunned when they were finally told that the captain had died following the incident. For some reason, Mrs. Huntington wanted Maddy to be the one who went with her.

Brian had not told her what he knew about it, because the board of inquiry was still going on and everyone had been ordered to keep silent. Austin had recovered consciousness a day out from Subic, but he was concussed and almost useless as a witness. His ravings up on the forecastle the night of the attack had made the rounds of the wardroom, and, while no one could figure out exactly what had happened, many were eager to assume the worst. Vince Benedetti had been fully involved in the damage-control efforts, so he could testify only about what happened after the attack. The South SAR station ship, USS *Preble,* had driven out of the morning twilight with fresh damage-control teams and medical supplies and people. The first helo to come up from Yankee Station brought an investigation team on board, headed by the same captain who had looked into the Sea Dragon incident. As the evaluator on watch, Brian had been debriefed extensively, as had Garuda and the surviving supervisors in Combat. The focus had been exclusively on the attack and the aftermath, until a grim-faced lieutenant commander had come into the wardroom with the ship's disbursing officer, carrying a deck log.

The mysterious log. There were all sorts of rumors flying around about what was in that log. Brian remembered the captain keeping Jack Folsom with him on the morning of the attack, and asking for the deck log. Folsom wasn't talking, but it would make a world of difference to Brian if the captain had come clean about the drug problem. Especially with the exec reportedly claiming that the MiGs got in because the weapons officer had an inexperienced FTM3 on the missile consoles when the attack came. Amidst all the rumors, Brian had resolved to follow the captain's advice: Just tell the truth. He sighed. There were going to be a lot more questions to answer when he returned to the ship again. You could say one thing about the Navy—they might not always want to ask the question, but once a mess was exposed, they would scrape the paint right down to the keel to find out what had happened.

As if in counterpoint to the whole incident, the lieutenant commander's promotion list had come in by an AlNav message the night after the incident, and Brian's name had been on it. Mission accomplished. The exec had signed temporary promotion papers so that it would look better having a lieutenant commander as the escort rather than a lieutenant. Brian remembered reading the temporary promotion language, with its codicil about accepting permanent appointment in the new rank. He wondered now whether he would.

He would have to talk to Maddy at some length about all of this, about going on in the Navy and committing to a thirty-year career. He had encountered levels and degrees of responsibility far beyond anything they had talked about at the Academy, and he had also learned that in a ship, *every* action or inaction has its consequences. And he had to make a final decision about what to reveal to her, if anything, about his experience in Olongapo with Josie. He had talked to Chief Martinez about it during a coffee and cigar session the night before they arrived in Subic, but the chief had just laughed.

"Hell, boss. This is WESTPAC. Ain't no married guys in WESTPAC. Be like tellin' yer wife you went out and got drunk—who gives a shit? Besides, what the hell do wives wanta know about foolin' around, right?"

Brian thought that it would be best to keep the whole thing a secret, something to bury in his past, as the course that would do the least damage. Everyone was entitled to a secret or two in a lifetime, he thought, and he was sick of damage. But the matter would not entirely go away.

Martinez had told him what had happened down in the pump room between Rocky and Jackson and about how they had all missed on Rocky in the first place. Up to that point, Brian knew only that Rockheart had been found drowned in the wreckage of the shaft alley pump room two days after the incident and that there had been a large quantity of cash drowned with him. Rumor had it that both Chief Jackson and Martinez were down in the pump room the night of the attack and that Rockheart had been at the top of the drug ring in the ship.

"Well, Chief, you said you'd off the kingpin if you ever caught him," Brian had said.

Martinez had shaken his head. "I didn't do Rockheart. I wanted to, believe me. And I kicked his ass for what he did to Jackson. But when I left him down there, he was still breathin'. Best the snipes can tell, the eductor pump got clogged up with all that paper money floatin' around in the bilges and the space just flooded out."

"Jesus. His own drug money drowned him."

"Yeah. I love that part."

"So what happens to Bullet?"

The chief had snorted in disgust. "Who's the one guy was home free if Garlic *and* Rocky were outta business, hanh? We still ain't got one fuckin' bit of evidence on Bullet. It was all based on what we got out of Garlic, or was gonna get outta that deal set up by Rocky. An' you wanna know the weird part? Bullet was the Repair Five investigator who found the shaft alley flooded. He said all's he could do was dog down the hatch, that he didn't even know fuckin' Rocky was down there. Talk about doin' yerself a favor. So. Bullet? Look's to me like the fucker's gonna walk."

"How about the money?"

"Bullet didn't get the money in the Lucky Bag, and Jackson says they recovered thousands of bucks from the pump room; said they had a hell of a time drying all that shit out."

"What will happen to it?"

"XO says the stuff in the pump room gets turned in to the Navy. XO don't know about the stuff we got out of the Lucky Bag, so the chiefs are gonna divvy it out to the families of the guys who got killed. It ain't much, but it's somethin'."

There was a bustle of activity out on the ramp as the chief called the honor guard to attention. A gray ambulance swooped down the perimeter road and pulled to a stop behind the Caribou. The aircraft crew gathered up their logs and navigation folders and climbed up into the flight deck inside. Brian drew himself up to attention and watched while the ambulance crew rolled the casket out of the back. The chief ordered the honor guard to present arms, and the two ambulance attendants, trying for a little dignity in their disheveled medical whites, rolled the aluminum casket away from the ambulance and up the back ramp of the plane. Brian saluted and held the salute until the casket had disappeared inside. Then he dropped it and walked down to the apron.

As the honor guard filed gratefully back to their van, Brian walked over to say good-bye to Chief Jackson, wishing him well with the board of inquiry.

"Yes, sir, it's gonna be a bitch, I think."

"And I'm sorry about Bullet. After all this—"

"Yeah. Well, Bullet might walk away from this investigation, but he isn't going to walk away from all the black people I'm gonna tell this story to. We'll run his ass right out of the Navy."

Brian looked in the direction of the ship across the harbor. "This was a hell of a way to get some justice done, Chief. Me and my big crusade—look where it's brought us."

"It's what we were crusading against did this, Mr. Holcomb, not you or any of us. They gonna treat you right?"

"We'll have to see, Chief. There're folks on both sides of that equation right now."

"Remember what you told me, Mr. Holcomb. About what the Old Man said. And hopefully what he wrote down in that log. You were doing your duty. The Navy will never punish an officer for doing his duty."

Brian looked up into the back of the Caribou at the collection of aluminum caskets. "I sure hope so, Chief, but look what happened. And I think FTM Three Warren feels worse than I do about it."

Jackson shook his head. "Warren did the best he could. If he did fuck up, it was because he was rattled and tired from those assholes leaning on him. Martinez and I are gonna do something about that, too. Either way, you can blame the North Vietnamese, the CO's cancer, or the druggies, but like I said, you were doing your duty, Mr. Holcomb. That's all the Navy ever asks, you know?"

"Yeah, Chief," Brian said, looking across the harbor again. "But sometimes that's a hell of a lot to ask."

The Caribou started one of its engines in a cloud of blue exhaust smoke. A crewman standing by the ramp was looking pointedly at Brian. Unable to talk anymore because of the engine noise, Brian and Jackson shook hands, looked at each other for a few seconds, and then Brian walked up the back ramp and into the cargo bay to begin his six-thousand-mile vigil across the Pacific.

60

Washington, D.C.

Brian could hear the approaching cortège before he could see it. It was late afternoon, and the winter gloom was gathering on the hillside below the Lee mansion. The thump of a bass drum, the *clip-clop* of the horses pulling the caisson, the sonorous tones of the funeral march, and the muted tramp of the ceremonial platoon echoed through the drizzle of a dying December day as the official party approached the grave site. Brian stood apart from the crowd of friends and professional acquaintances, his role as escort officer taken over by a senior captain. As the only member of the ship's wardroom attending the funeral, he felt very much alone. Him of all people. He felt as if he should be back with the ship.

Winter had come early to Washington this year. He shifted his feet uncomfortably in the wet grass, conscious of the cold seeping up from the partially frozen ground. He could see that the others waiting on the hillside were just as uncomfortable as he was, huddled into their overcoats, their breath daubing puffs of vapor into the deepening twilight.

Waiting for the captain, that inexplicable man. For an instant, his eyes betrayed him; he forced himself to stare at the black rectangle in the ground, surrounded by incongruously green Astro Turf and the draped chairs, until he regained control. The captain's wife, whom he remembered as the soul of cheer and competent, bright optimism, seemed shrunken now in her black coat, her hair a silver cap in the twilight, standing with her face hidden from view. She was propped up on either side by her two grown sons as they waited for the sad procession to halt in the narrow lane behind them. Maddy stood right behind her, one hand held loosely on her right shoulder. To Brian's surprise, there were four of the wardroom wives in the crowd, as well.

Brian stood patiently for the unloading of the casket, listening to the muted clinks of metal as the troops assembled into ranks and the soft shuffling of the mourners closing in around the grave site as the casket was borne to the chrome-plated rails above the grave. Above, on a low ridge, the ceremonial firing squad stood in front of a grove of bare oak trees, positioned in an exaggerated pose of parade rest, eyes fixed on the ground, their white gloves gleaming along the tips of sloping rifle barrels. Behind them, the bugler, also staring at the ground, cradled his instrument against the cold.

Brian raised his head and forced himself to look at the bronze-coated casket as the chaplain began the reading, but his eyes refused to focus. From across the cemetery, a car's headlights created a sudden golden gleam along the side of the casket, and the image of the first time he had seen the mountains of Luzon rising up out of the South China Sea's eastern horizon filled his vision. That glowing memory drowned out the chaplain's quiet words, the tenebrous cold, and the soft, stamping footfalls in the crowd, bringing back that first day. It seemed like only yesterday.

He contrasted the picture of *Hood* standing into Subic Bay, freshly painted, big, clean, new, full of energy, ready to take the Red Crown station, with what he had seen out the airplane's window, of the ship being pushed backward into the floating dry dock, her port side blackened from the bridge back to the helo deck, an oily suppuration from that gaping hole in her port side, and the two missile directors pointed out to port, one high, one low, as if still looking for the enemy who had done this thing. And as far as most of the wardroom is concerned, that enemy includes you, thanks to the exec. And thanks to your own hubris, for deciding to take those guys to mast, thereby leaving a brand-new FTM3 on the console when the moment of crisis came.

For the thousandth time, he went over it. He knew in his heart that what the exec was saying was just plain wrong. Just as he had told him in the passageway that night. And just as the captain had told him. He had taken the time to tell Brian. He had thought it was important to tell him—bent over a counting bomb in the wreckage of CIC, his guts on fire, his nerves awash with morphine, and yet he'd made a point of it: *You* did the right thing. *We* did the wrong thing. But, Christ, at what cost? The consequences of doing the right thing were supposed to be good! But maybe, just maybe, the consequences, that man in the aluminum box up there, the others in theirs, going into the ground today instead of back on watch, back into Two Firehouse, back into Combat and the Cave, and the broken families, the broken ship—just maybe these are consequences of the goddamned drugs and the command's decision to hide the problem under a blanket of gun-deck justice, like Chief Jackson had said. Just maybe, these were the consequences of doing nothing. He seized on that idea and held it, knowing that it would be his only defense against the hauntings to come.

And Maddy. They had found only one chance to talk, what with his escort duty requiring him to stay with the casket until it had been delivered to the mortuary at Andrews and Maddy's responsibility to stay with Mrs. Huntington until members of her family had arrived in town. Last night, in the BOQ at Andrews, after the exhausting flights—he all the way from the Philippines in a cargo plane; she from San Diego to San Francisco to Washington—they had agreed simply to hold each other in the tiny room with its single bed.

For a while, they had both slept. And then he had awakened and, finding her awake, had told her the whole story, about the impact of the drugs aboard the ship, the command's live-with-it solution, how he had come to upset the apple cart, the rumors about what really had happened to the captain, and what he faced when he went back to the ship. She had asked almost no questions, strangely silent through it all, almost as if she was considering what to do about all of it. It had taken him almost three hours to tell it, and when he had finished, he had fallen asleep, leaving her to stare up at the ceiling until daylight. Not too different from deployment day, now that he thought about it.

And now he wasn't sure what to think. On the one hand, he harbored grave doubts about going on with a Navy career. He was afraid of the consequences of wrong decisions and his own idealistic notions of right and wrong. The bloody, bloody consequences, from the horrors of the *Berkeley*'s wardroom, to the oily black well that was *Hood*'s drowned fire room, to the atomized remains of the men in the EW module. But on the other hand, he was not so sure he had done the wrong thing. If nothing else, he *had* done his duty, and now he must return to the ship and face what was coming, to exonerate himself and his honor, and, most important, give it another try.

But how was he going to tell that to Maddy? How could he admit that he had gone to sea and faced its elemental power, gone to war and faced death, blood, and destruction, assumed the mantle of command as the evaluator in Combat, launched missiles that destroyed airplanes and killed other men, and yet now was *afraid*? While at the same time trying to claim that he was still a man, that he still loved her and wanted her as his wife and mate? And despite everything that had happened, despite the emotional travail she had been through during the deployment, despite the fact that at least some of the wardroom held him partially responsible for the disaster, despite the fact that his career was now facing a gauntlet called a board of inquiry—how to explain to her that he wanted to go on with it, that he felt it his *duty* to go on with it?

He looked across all the backs and heads standing between him and his wife. He wanted desperately to go over there, to stand beside her, to put his hands on her shoulders even as she was supporting Mrs. Huntington. But he had this awful sense that everyone knew what was going on in his mind and what had happened out there in the Gulf of Tonkin, that this assembly of hard-faced naval officers and their wives, being made of stronger stuff, would bar his way.

The burial detail presented the flag, distant headlights brushed once more across the casket, and then it was being lowered into the ground, as if hurried on its way by three volleys from the hillside. How on earth could he ask her to stay the course with him? He waited for it to be over. He waited for Maddy.

61

Maddy stood rigidly in the cold, almost holding her breath lest she begin crying or make some other emotional spectacle of herself. She focused all of her attention on the woman in front of her, leaving her hand on her shoulder, an occasional squeezing pressure to let her know she was there. She heard none of the words the chaplain was saying, although others did, others whose faces were pulled into strange expressions as they tried for control. She wished Brian was up here with her instead of somewhere back in the crowd. But he had insisted. "You go with the family. I can't go up there with you, not now."

There was so much to talk about. Last night, she had known the first peaceful sleep in many months in his arms, if only for a few hours. When she had felt him stirring, she had awakened, and he had begun to tell her what had happened out there. Dear God, in all of the days and weeks leading up to the deployment, in all of her complaining, nothing of this scale and consequence had crossed either of their minds. And now he was trying to make the biggest decision of his life. She wanted this funeral to be over, because there was a lot she had to say to him.

How am I going to do this? she wondered as she

absorbed the elegant ceremony, the stony faces of these men, the stoic strength of these women, the glinting rifles on the hill, the granitelike stillness of the ceremonial detail, and the elegiac grace of the chaplain. How am I going to sustain him in the face of all this strength? How am I going to convince him that he must go on with it, that being a naval officer is what he is, that the Navy would give him a fair shot because the Navy would see that he had been doing the right thing, despite the outcome? And that if it didn't, this time she would be there for him, to help him fight for his honor.

She would never tell him about Autrey; Autrey had been about sex, about the games she used to play, about the girl she had been, before she found out what marriage can really mean. As Mrs. Huntington had said: Where was Autrey now?

How will I tell him that, yes, I am afraid, afraid to be left alone again? Afraid that I don't deserve to succeed, after the things I have done and the betrayal I committed and the secrets I now must keep? It's about risk, Mrs. Huntington had said. The value of marriage is always proportional to the risks.

She felt everyone holding their breath along with her as the bugler played taps and then the three volleys crashed out, burying the final haunting notes of the bugle even as the pallbearers lowered the casket into the ground after presenting the flag. When the Huntington family drew into a close knot and the other wives moved toward them, she stepped back, feeling that her job was done for now.

She had been stunned to see the other wives here. She had flown for free, but these women had come at their own expense to stand up for one of their own. She realized that she desperately wanted to be a part of that now, and if that meant deployments and separations, well, so be it. The physical things she had felt for and with Autrey had been very real, but they paled to insignificance in the light of what had happened to the Huntingtons, the ship, and her husband. She looked around and saw Brian standing at the back of the crowd. She took a deep breath and hesitated for a second, but it was all clear in her mind. She would probably have some hard selling to do, but she was determined. She only hoped that Brian needed her as much as she now needed to sustain him. She turned around and went to find her husband in the gathering darkness.

Author's Note

Naval history buffs are generally familiar with the two 1964 Gulf of Tonkin incidents that are credited with sparking a dramatic escalation of American involvement in Vietnam. It is not generally known that the North Vietnamese attacked U.S. Navy fleet units operating in the Gulf of Tonkin again in the late days of the Vietnam War. The attack on USS *John Bell Hood* depicted in this novel is based on an actual incident that happened in the spring of 1972. The guided-missile frigate (since redesignated a guided-missile cruiser) USS *Sterett* was patrolling the Red Crown station in the northern Gulf of Tonkin, escorted by USS *Higbee*, an all-gun, World War II–vintage destroyer. The North Vietnamese launched a coordinated night attack against the Red Crown station, using electronic warfare jamming, antiship-missile-firing PT-boats, and MiGs configured to carry iron bombs. *Sterett*, which by no means was a drug-infested or incompetent ship, distinguished herself in the ensuing mêlée, driving off the gunboats with her single five-inch mount, downing an antiship missile and two MiGs with her Terrier missiles, and damaging a third MiG. But that third MiG penetrated inside *Sterett*'s minimum missile range and dropped a bomb into *Higbee*'s after five-inch gun mount, doing considerable damage and prompting *Higbee*'s commanding officer to deliberately flood her after powder magazines in order to save the ship. As a result of this daring raid, the U.S. Navy redesigned its entire combat systems training architecture to deal with what then became known as the multithreat environment. Today's advanced Aegis guided-missile cruisers are specifically designed to deal with multiple threats in the air, on the surface, and even submerged. But it was this incident that provided the wake-up call.

The drug infestation in USS *John Bell Hood* is also based on actual conditions in the late sixties aboard too many fleet units. Many writers have described or commented on drug use in Vietnam by Army and, to a lesser extent, Marine units. But the Navy also had a serious drug problem, with as many as thirty to forty percent of a crew indulging at least occasionally in marijuana or hashish at sea or in port. Unlike *John Bell Hood*, most ships had a vigorous antidrug program going, with harsh punishments and discharges meted out to habitual offenders. But while official Navy policy was crystal clear with regard to drug use, it was also true that there were political risks associated with being too successful in the execution of a ship's drug program. There were serious shortages of enlisted personnel in all the critical ratings aboard ship (such as boiler-tenders, fire control and electronics technicians, and radarmen), and the decision to discharge a man for using drugs often meant that the ship might not see a replacement for up to half a year. Captains were evaluated, among other things, on the success of their reenlistment programs, and a drug discharge counted against the ship's retention program statistically. A pattern of drug discharges could often provoke not-so-subtle inquiries through the chain of command as to the general competence of the captain and his command to hold things together in the face of Navy-wide personnel shortages.

The Navy finally came to grips with its drug problem after a serious accident aboard an aircraft carrier in the seventies, when several men were cut to pieces on the flight deck by a snapped arresting wire and an on-deck crash. Post-incident autopsies revealed that a startling percentage of the bodies contained traces of tetra-hydra-cannabinol (THC), the narcotic element of marijuana and hashish. The Chief of Naval Operations (CNO), disheartened with these findings, took the extraordinary and politically courageous decision to impose mandatory urinalysis on the entire Navy, with everyone, from himself on down to the most junior recruit, eligible for random, surprise selection by his or her command to proceed to the head to provide a urine sample. No one was exempt, and I can remember, as a commanding officer and later as a commodore of destroyers, getting the knock on the door, there to find the corpsman with the sample bottle, test kit, and appropriate paperwork. Whatever slight damage was done to the dignity of senior officers, the imposition of mandatory, random, surprise urinalysis screening broke the back of the Navy's drug problem in one year. Today the incidence of drug use in the Navy at large is minuscule, thanks primarily to the random-urinalysis drug-screening program, which is still very much in place, and which, this author fervently hopes, never goes away.

Glossary

1MC	A ship's general announcing system.
A-6	A carrier-based Navy all-weather bomber.
AIC	The air intercept controller—the senior enlisted air controller; directed Navy fighters.
ASW	Anti-submarine warfare.
B division	The boilers division.
Backseater	The radar intercept officer in an F-4 fighter; also the RIO; sits behind the pilot.
BARCAP	Barrier combat air patrol fighters.
Basketball	Marine Corps aerial refueling aircraft.
Bat phone	A sound-powered intercom circuit.
Benjo ditch	An urban open-sewage ditch.
Big Mother	The voice radio call sign of the SH-3 SAR helicopter.
Bingo	An aircraft with enough fuel to get home.
Bitch box	An electrical intercom circuit.
Bulkhead	A wall; partition between compartments.
Buster	Air control slang for "go very fast."
Callsign	Voice radio spoken address.
CAPT	A captain; an O-6.
Cave, the	The detection and tracking module (room) in Combat.
CDR	A commander; an O-5.
Chop, the	The supply officer
Chop	(verb) to initial or agree.
CIC	The combat information center, called Combat.
CINCPACFLEET	The Commander in chief, U.S. Pacific fleet.
CO	The captain of the ship.
CTF77	Commander attack carrier task force 77.
CWI	Continuous-wave illumination (missile-guidance beam).
DC Central	The Damage Control central control station.

617

D&D	The display and decision module in Combat.
DD	A destroyer, armed with guns.
DDG	A destroyer, armed with guns and guided missiles.
Deep six	To throw over the side.
Director One	The gun's fire control radar station.
Disbo, the	The disbursing officer.
DLG	A large destroyer, armed with guided missiles and guns.
DMZ	The demilitarized zone between North and South Vietnam.
E-2	A carrier-based airborne early-warning aircraft.
EASTPAC	The eastern Pacific, home waters off California.
EC	The engagement controller, a position/ console in the weapons control module of CIC.
EM1	Electrician's Mate First Class; E-6 petty officer.
ENS	An ensign; an O-1.
EW	The electronic warfare module in CIC.
F-4	A carrier-based Navy fighter bomber.
F-8	A carrier-based Navy fighter.
FCSC	The fire control systems coordinator, a position/console in the weapons control module of CIC.
Feet-dry	Aircraft over land.
Feet-wet	Aircraft over water.
Firehouse	Slang for boiler room, as in One Firehouse.
Fire room	Boiler room.
First Division	The deck/seamanship division.
First Class	The enlisted rank of E-6, as in Petty Officer First Class.
Fling Wing	A helicopter.
Fo'c'sle	The forecastle (front) of a ship.
Fox division	The fire control division.
Forward	In the front part of the ship.
FTG	Fire Control Technician (Guns).
FTM	Fire Control Technician (Missiles).
FTM1	An E-6 (first class) Fire Control Technician.

FTM2	An E-5 (second class) Fire Control Technician.
FTM3	An E-4 (third class) Fire Control Technician.
Goat Locker	The chief petty officers' mess.
Godown	(pidgin) a warehouse.
GQ	General quarters (battle stations).
Gulf, the	The Gulf of Tonkin.
Gun Plot	The gun's fire control computer room.
Gundeck	(verb) to falsify.
Hard core	(adjective) very serious about it.
Hawse pipe	The aperture from which the anchor drops.
Heavenly Host	All support aircraft flying over the Gulf.
Helo	A helicopter.
Ichiban	(pidgin/Japanese) very good.
ID	Identification.
In battery	Ready to work, as in "back in battery."
In-country	Ashore, actually in Vietnam, as distinct from afloat.
Incoming	Incoming fire or any harassment.
Iron Hand	Carrier aircraft hunting missile sites.
Jaygee	A lieutenant (junior grade).
JOOD	The junior officer of the deck.
LCDR	A lieutenant commander.
Log	The official record book, as in the deck log.
Log helo	The daily supply (logistics) helicopter; flew a circuit from the carrier to the ships in the Gulf.
LSO	The flight deck landing signal officer.
LT	A lieutenant.
LTJG	A lieutenant (junior grade).
Main Control	The main engineering central control station.
Mamasan	(pidgin) proprietor of a bar or whorehouse.
Mess cook	The Navy's version of KP; mess hall/mess decks worker.
MiG	A Soviet fighter-bomber jet, exported globally.
MiGCAP	A Navy fighter hunting MiGs.
Mikes	Minutes, as in five mikes.
Missile Plot	The missile system fire–control computer room.
Nevah hotchee	(pidgin) never happen.

619

NGFS	Naval gunfire support; shore bombardment.
NIS	The Naval Investigative Service.
North, the	North Vietnam.
NTDS	Naval Tactical Data System.
NVA	The North Vietnamese Army.
OBA	An oxygen-breathing apparatus for firefighters.
OI division	The radarman division.
Old Man	The captain.
OOD	The officer of the deck.
Ops boss	The operations officer; a department head.
Overhead	The ceiling.
PACFLEET	The U.S. Pacific Fleet.
PIRAZ	Positive Identification Radar Advisory Zone.
Pump room	The engineering space, belowdecks, containing one or more of the ship's firepumps.
Radargirls	Engineering department slang for radarmen.
Radiopuke	Engineering department slang for radioman.
RD1	Radarman First Class; E-6 petty officer.
Red Crown	Voice radio call sign of the PIRAZ station.
RM1	Radioman First Class; E-6 petty officer.
Salvo	An air control term meaning "get out of there now."
SAM	A surface-to-air missile.
SAR	Search and rescue.
Second Div.	The gunnery division.
Seventh Fleet	One of two fleets in the U.S. Pacific Fleet.
SH-2	A Navy medium-sized SAR helicopter.
SH-3	A Navy large SAR helicopter.
Sheriff	A nickname for the Chief Master-at-Arms.
Sick Bay	The ship's infirmary.
Skosh	A little bit; most skosh: quickly.
Snipes	The engineers.
Snipe, the	The Chief Engineer.
South, the	South Vietnam.
SPG-53	Gunfire control radar.
SPQ-55	Missile fire–control radar; or the Spook-55.
SPS-40	Two-dimensional (range and bearing) air-search radar.
SPS-10	Two-dimensional surface-search radar.

SPS-48	Three-dimensional (range, bearing, and height) air-search radar.
Surface	The surface operations module in Combat.
SWIC	A ship's weapons coordinator; position/console in the display and decision module of CIC.
System one	Guided-missile fire–control system No. 1.
System two	Guided-missile fire–control system No. 2.
TACAN	Tactical Air Control and Navigation beacon.
Talos	A Navy surface-to-air missile with 100-mile range.
Terrier	A Navy surface-to-air missile with 40-mile range.
Twidget	Engineering department slang for everyone else.
Wager Bird	Air Force 707 communications relay aircraft.
Watch bill	At sea or in-port duty roster.
Way	Motion; a ship under way is moving.
Weapons	Weapons control module in Combat.
Weps	The weapons officer; a department head.
WESTPAC	The Western Pacific; Asian waters.
White hat	An enlisted man.
Wild Weasel	Carrier aircraft hunting SAM site radars.
XO	The executive officer of the ship; the exec.

LOOK FOR *OFFICIAL PRIVILEGE*–
THE EXCITING NEW NOVEL
FROM P.T. DEUTERMANN.
AN EXCERPT FOLLOWS:

I'm not gonna let those bastards scare me, Benny thought. I know what those dumb guineas are up to, a couple of 'em probably waiting down here in the dark for me, gonna jump outa one of those hatches and try to scare my ass. He stopped and squinted through the scratched faceplate of the mask at the hull diagram, trying to shine his hardhat helmet light down on the diagram and still keep an eye out in the darkened second-deck passageway. Sonsabitches, screwing off up there at the airlock, while I go nitrogen diving down here, doing *their* damn job.

Benny was nineteen, a high school graduate, and trying like hell to convert a summer intern job in Production into a full-time job in the Philadelphia Naval Shipyard. Which was probably why the ship's supe had told him to go to the battleship and do a no-shit sounding and security tour. Those goof-offs over in Shop 72 were reporting everything secure, but he had seen them up on the main deck, sitting around when they were supposed to be inside, going space by space through the engineering department. You go do it, Benny. I know it's a little spooky in there, no lights and everything, but they'll set you up with the breathing rigs, and you go through the main holes in the *Wisconsin* and do the security tour right.

Benny was doing it right, but it was more than just a little spooky down here. Cold, black steel, some of it five, six inches thick, creating total darkness once you went through the airlock on the main deck. There had been a temporary lighting string hung in the overhead of the main deck athwartships passageway, but once you went down to the second deck, it was like total darkness, man. He had a single air tank rig on with a full face mask, because, below the main deck, the mothballed battlewagon had been backfilled with nitrogen gas to displace all the oxygen. No oxygen, no oxidation—nothing rusted. And no oxygen meant nobody else should be down here, either. Except maybe a couple of wise asses from Shop 72, waiting to scare the new kid.

* * *

Benny shined the light straight down into the fireroom and saw only darkness, except—there. Something white. Like flour, some kind of white powder in the bilges twenty feet below the platform he was standing on, over near the centerline, under 2B boiler. Shit, now what? Definitely not water, but definitely abnormal. Should he log it? He looked at his watch again. Ten minutes. Screw it, go down there, see what this shit is, log it and get out of here.

Taking one last quick look out into the passageway to make sure nobody was creeping up on him, he climbed down the ladder to the gratings of the upper level of the fireroom, where he looked again, down through the deck gratings. Now he could see a white bag. Shiny white powder all around it down in the bilges. Damn mask, couldn't really see shit. His breathing sounded extra loud and raspy in the mask; slow it down, man. Using too much air. He looked at his watch again. Nine minutes. Looked just like a big bag of flour had been dropped into the bilges under 2B boiler, where it had broken open. But no water. Okay. He pointed the helmet light around until he found the ladder to the lower level at the other end of the boiler-front aisleway, and went down one more level. He tramped across the steel deckplates to the front of 2B boiler, and got down on his hands and knees, and pointed the helmet light at the remains of the bag. Even with all the scratches on the mask, he could read the printing on the bag now: *Powder, Desiccant, NSTM 242-55-9010, Milspec 9710-la. For use in watersides of marine propulsion boilers during dry layups only.* There was some smaller print that began with the word *Warning*, but he couldn't make it out through the mask. He sat back on his haunches, and shivered. It was cold down here, really cold. He felt like he was in one of the burial chambers in the Great Pyramids.

What the hell was a bag of desiccant doing in the bilges? He knew what desiccant was—he'd originally been assigned in the boiler shop before landing the intern position in Production. Desiccant was hygroscopic. It soaked up moisture, kept metal structures like the steam drums in a boiler bone dry. He knew that desiccant powder bags belonged up in the steam drum. He looked up, but there wasn't enough light to make out the upper levels of the boilerfront. Watch your time. Eight minutes. He went back up the ladder and walked over to 2B's boiler front. He examined the steam drum manhole, which was visible because the big asbestos pad had been removed. He frowned. Dry layup—the steam drum should be open; each of the boilers in the other spaces had been open. He turned around, and saw that 2A's steam drum was open, the manhole cover laid out on the gratings with the two-inch-diameter bolts collected inside, the big pad hanging on a hook. He looked back at 2B's manhole cover, and saw that the eight bolts were on. He felt one, and found it was only hand tight. Seriously weird. Why was this thing bolted up? He checked his watch again, seven minutes; what the hell, I've got a fifteen-minute reserve on top of the normal stay time.

He took off his glove and began backing off all eight of the bolts. Once he had the bolts off, he pried the manhole cover, an elliptically shaped, one-inch-thick steel cover about thirty inches across and twenty-four inches high, back on its hinges. He dipped his head to shine the helmet light inside, and felt his stomach grab in shock.

"Oh, Jesus. Oh, sweet Jesus," he moaned into the mask, which promptly fogged up from his sudden exhalation. He stumbled back away from the boiler, back away from those staring, wide eyes and the blackened, peeling features, one clawlike hand reaching for the manhole, and ran for the hatch, trying not to piss his pants. He took the ladder up to the entrance grating platform two steps at a time and jumped over the knee knocker, and then nearly out of his skin when there was a blaze of light and a shout as two figures waved their arms and made ghost noises at him through their masks. He knocked one of them flat on his ass and ran right for the hatch up to the second deck. Up the steel ladder, through a second armored hatch, turn right, right again, down the passageway, up the ladder where the light was showing, through the athwartships passageway. He could hear the timer on his breathing rig ringing over his sobs as his pounding lungs fought for breath. He burst through the airlock and back into the blazing sunlight in a clatter.

He ripped his mask off and heard the laughter over his heaving sobs, all the old hand riggers standing around, yukking it up at the new kid getting the shit scared out of him by the foreman and his segundo, who were stepping through the airlock even now. He tried to tell them, but they were still roaring and carrying on. A fat, grinning face stuck itself right in front of him.

"Hey, kid, how ya like the grand tour now, hunh? Shit, look at him, he's—shit, lookit his face, Joey, you fuck, you went an' scared this kid shitless!"

"Dead guy," Benny gasped. It was all he could get out. "Dead guy."

The rest of the guys roared anew as Joe and his helper stripped off their masks, but then the fat man saw the look in Benny's eyes and put up his hand. "Wait a minute, wait a fucking minute, here—hey, guys, hold it, *hold it, awright?*" he yelled. "Benny, what's this shit about a dead guy—hey, Benny, calm down. What is it, what is it, hey? Hey, Joey, the kid's hyperventilatin', c'mere, c'mere."

The gang stopped laughing and crowded around Benny as he sank down on his knees, his lungs scraping for breath, his mask dangling across his thighs. Then he threw up over the edge of the teak quarterdeck, and there was a sudden, stunned silence as the men backed away from the mess.

"Hey, kid, what the fuck," asked Joey, covering his own nose and mouth. "It was just a little joke, okay? Shit, you knew it was us, right?"

But Benny was shaking his head, trying to wipe his chin, his face ashen, miserable at the way his guts had betrayed him.

"Dead guy. In the boiler. Steam drum of 2B boiler," he gasped. "I swear. Jesus Christ, I saw his face. A dead guy. A friggin' mummy..."

OFFICIAL PRIVILEGE BY
P. T. DEUTERMANN—
NOW IN HARDCOVER FROM
ST. MARTIN'S PRESS!